PUTNAM

G. P. PUTNAM'S SONS
Publishers Since 1838
An imprint of Penguin Random House LLC
375 Hudson Street
New York, New York 10014

Copyright © 2018 by Stuart Woods
Library of Congress Cataloging-in-Publication Data

Names: Woods, Stuart, author.
Title: Desperate measures / Stuart Woods.
Description: New York : G. P. Putnam's Sons, 2018. | Series: A Stone
    Barrington novel
Identifiers: LCCN 2018022152 (print) | LCCN 2018022724 (ebook) | ISBN
    9780735219229 (Hardcover) | ISBN 9780735219243 (ePub) | ISBN
Subjects: | GSAFD: Mystery fiction. | Suspense fiction.
Classification: LCC PS3573.O642 (ebook) | LCC PS3573.O642 D47 2018 (print) |
    DDC 813/.54—dc23
LC record available at https://lccn.loc.gov/2018022152
p.   cm.

Printed in the United States of America
10 9 8 7 6 5 4 3 2 1

BOOK DESIGN BY KATY RIEGEL

DESPERATE MEASURES

STUART WOODS

G. P. Putnam's Sons | *New York*

DESPERATE MEASURES

DESPERATE MEASURES

1

THE EARLY-MORNING CONVERSATION had taken place in bed in London, after drinking brandy with guests until the wee hours. So if Stone had once remembered what was said, he had now forgotten it.

He struggled to put it together in his mind during their flight from his house, Windward Hall, in England, back to Teterboro, but he had failed. There wasn't much conversation on the airplane, but he put that down to Kelly's hangover, which must have been as monumental as his, since she had matched him drink for drink. Once they were back at his house in New York, they had dinner and went to bed early.

He woke at seven the following morning, a preordered breakfast on a tray resting on his belly. There were empty dishes on her side of the bed and sounds of packing from her dressing room. His eggs were cold, but he ate them anyway, to settle his stomach.

Kelly came out of the dressing room naked, with predictable results. When they were spent, she stood up.

"I told you yesterday that I'd gotten a chopper ride back to Langley today, didn't I?"

Of course she had, he could remember that much. "Surely, not at this hour," he said.

"I'm to be there at nine-forty-five sharp for a ten o'clock departure, and I can't miss it. Fred can drive me to the heliport."

"No," he said, getting up. "I'll drive you myself."

"Thank you," she said, then went back into the dressing room.

HE SURVEYED HIS FACE in the bathroom mirror and was surprised to find that he didn't look like a man with a hangover. What was more, he didn't *feel* like a man with a hangover. He felt perfectly normal, except that he still couldn't remember their conversation in London. He shaved, showered, dressed, and called down to Fred, his factotum. "I won't need you this morning," he said. "I'll drive myself."

"As you wish, Mr. Barrington," Fred replied.

IN THE CAR KELLY SAID, "Fred is going to collect my other luggage at the hotel and send it to me." She had a suite in a residential hotel not far from his house.

"Plenty of room at my house," Stone replied.

"Stone," she said, "do you remember our conversation in London?"

"Of course," Stone lied.

"Because you're not behaving like a man who's being abandoned."

That rocked him. "'Abandoned'?"

"Do you remember my telling you that I'm returning to the Agency—and that they want me to live down there in a place they've found for me?"

"Yes," he lied again, "and I'm very sad about it." That last part wasn't a lie; he suddenly felt overwhelmingly sad.

"It's sweet of you to say so, but I think you'll have forgotten me before long."

Stone knew a cue when he heard one. "I'll never forget you," he said.

"Oh, shut up!" Kelly cried, beginning to weep. "Did you expect me to pass up a promotion and give up a career I've put fourteen years into?"

"I'm not sure what I expected," he said. And that wasn't a lie, either.

He drove to the East Side Heliport, was admitted to the ramp, and stopped beside the experimental Sikorsky X-2 helicopter the Central Intelligence Agency was testing for the builder. The pilot stowed Kelly's luggage, assisted her to a rear seat, and handed her a headset.

"Well," she said to Stone. "I could never say it wasn't fun."

"Neither could I," Stone said. He kissed her, then closed and locked the door. The rotors began to turn, and he backed away as the machine lifted off and pointed itself to the south.

He was still backing up when he bumped into someone, hard. He turned to find a miniature airline pilot standing behind him. "I'm so sorry," he said.

"You shouldn't walk backward at a heliport," she replied. She was, in fact, not a miniature at all, but a small woman in an airline captain's uniform.

"What can I do to make it up to you?" he asked, for she was quite beautiful, too.

"If you have a car, you can give me a lift," she replied.

"I do, and I'd be delighted. Where to: Westchester? New Jersey? Los Angeles?"

"Lexington Avenue will do," she said.

He took her single bag and walked her to the Bentley.

"I hope this is not a joke car," she said.

"It's a perfectly serious car," he replied, stowing her bag in the trunk and opening the front passenger door for her.

"Are you a chauffeur?" she asked.

"Only for you," he replied, getting into the driver's seat. He held out a hand. "I'm Stone Barrington."

She took the hand. "I'm Faith Barnacle," she said.

"Faith?"

"It's better than Hope or Charity, isn't it? I'm the victim of a pious Catholic mother."

"It's certainly the best of the three. I'm trying to think of a barnacle joke, but I can't remember one."

"That's all right, I would have heard it in high school, anyway."

Stone got the car started and moving. "Where on Lex?"

"East Forty-seventh Street," she replied. "It's one of those seedy hostelries where they store airline employees when they're not being used."

"For whom do you fly?"

"Pan American Airlines," she said.

"Didn't they go out of business a couple of decades ago?"

"I just wanted to see if you were paying attention. I fly for Trans-Continent, a charter airline. We've only got three airplanes, and I fly them all."

"How many pilots do they employ?"

"Somewhere between a dozen and a dozen and a half, depending on the season and the day of the week."

Stone pulled up in front of the hotel and popped the trunk, so the doorman could take her bag.

"How does the week ahead look?" he asked.

"I'm here for three nights."

"Will you have dinner with me tonight?"

"Thank you, yes. It's either you or *Jeopardy!*, and I hate *Jeopardy!*"

He gave her his card. "I'm just a few blocks downtown. Come for a drink at my house, and we'll go out from there."

"At what hour?"

"Six-thirty?"

"Fine. How shall I dress?"

"Nicely."

"What are you wearing?"

"A necktie."

"This is going to be interesting," she said, getting out and waving goodbye.

Driving back to his house, Stone suddenly recalled, in great detail, his conversation with Kelly in London. It made him sad again.

2

STONE PULLED THE CAR into the garage and went into his office. Bob, his Labrador retriever, and Joan Robertson, his secretary, greeted him with equal enthusiasm.

"I perceive that you are alone," Joan said.

"You are very perceptive. Bob doesn't seem to mind." Bob was offering him his favorite toy, a red dragon. "Nobody wants that dreadful toy," Stone said, scratching his ears.

"He wasn't going to give it to you," Joan said. "He just wants you to know he has it."

"Do I have anything to do?" Stone asked.

"No, I've done it all," she replied.

"Then I'll find something else to do," he said, slipping into his chair. He picked up the phone and dialed.

"Bacchetti."

"How do?" Stone asked.

"I do pretty good," Dino replied. They had been partners

many years before on the NYPD; now Dino was the police commissioner for New York City.

"Come for a drink at six-thirty, then let's have dinner."

"I take it you're back on the right side of the Atlantic."

"If I'm not, I will be by cocktail time."

"Are you bringing what's-her-name?"

"No. What's-her-name has taken flight from my existence; Lance Cabot has lured her back to her nest." Lance was the director of the Central Intelligence Agency.

"Smart girl," Dino said. "I'll check with Viv. If I don't call you back, we'll see you at six-thirty."

"Done," Stone said, then hung up and buzzed Joan.

"Yes, boss?"

"You must have something for me to do," he said.

"Do you do windows?" she asked.

"I do not."

"Then there's no hope for you. Go watch those political programs you love so much."

Stone hung up, yawned, and turned on the TV.

FAITH WAS PUNCTUAL. He met her at the door and walked her through the living room to his study. "Another couple is joining us shortly," he said. "Let's get a head start on them. What would you like?"

"A bourbon on the rocks," she said. "Knob Creek, if you have it."

"I have it in abundance," Stone said, pouring them each one. They sat down before the fire.

"This is a very nice room," she said.

"Thank you."

"And the living room was very nice, too, as is the house and the neighborhood."

"On behalf of the neighbors, I thank you."

"How do you live so well?"

"Well, I got the house cheap: I inherited it from a great-aunt. My father, who was a cabinetmaker and furniture designer, made all the paneling, shelves, and did the woodwork."

"I see," she said, "sort of. Did you get the Bentley cheap?"

"I got a pretty good deal on it."

"What do you do?"

"I'm a partner in a law firm, Woodman & Weld."

"Never heard of it."

"There's no reason you should have, unless you're suing or being sued or want an estate managed or a will written."

"None of the above," she said.

"How long have you been flying?" Stone asked.

"Since I was sixteen," she said. "I went to high school in the town where I was born—Delano, Georgia—then graduated from the aviation university, Embry Riddle, in Florida, with a diploma and an ATP license. I flew packages and freight, was first officer on a Lear, then got in a lot of single-pilot jet time in Citations. I flew for an airline, right seat for eight or nine years, then I joined Trans-Continent and made captain as soon as they needed one."

"Total time?"

"A little over fifteen thousand hours. You sound like a pilot."

"I am. I fly a CJ3-Plus."

"Nice. I flew one for a charter service for two years. Total time?"

"About four thousand hours, half of it in Citations. Lately, I've been flying a borrowed Citation Latitude."

"That's a great airplane. My charter service ordered three of them and sent me to Flight Safety for a type rating. Then, the day I got my rating, the charter service went bust. They reneged on their order for the three Latitudes, and I had to buy my own ticket home."

"That's a sad story, but at least you got the type rating."

The doorbell rang, but Stone kept his seat. "They'll let themselves in," he said. "Their names are Dino and Viv Bacchetti." He spelled the name for her.

The Bacchettis spilled into the room and demanded liquor. Stone introduced them to Faith, then did the pouring of Dino's scotch and Viv's martini.

"So, how did you two meet?" Viv asked.

"She body-blocked me at the heliport today," Stone said.

"He was walking backward and nearly knocked me down," Faith explained.

"Why were you both at the heliport?" Dino asked.

"Stone was seeing a friend off, and I had hitched a ride into the city from JFK on a chopper," Faith said. "The pilot's a friend."

"Sounds like fate at work," Viv said.

THEY FINISHED THEIR DRINKS, then left the house and got into Dino's car. "Patroon," he said.

"What's Patroon?" Faith asked.

"A very good restaurant," Stone replied.

"Dino," she asked, "why does your car have a blue light on top?"

"It's a police car," Dino replied.

"In a manner of speaking," Stone said. "Not every police officer has this ride, but Dino, for reasons I've never understood, is the police commissioner for the City of New York."

"I've never felt so safe," Faith said.

THEY ARRIVED AT THE RESTAURANT, were greeted and seated by the owner, Ken Aretsky, and ordered drinks. When they had been delivered, Dino took a deep breath. "Faith, this is not a good time to feel safe."

"What are you talking about, Dino?" Stone asked.

"While you were swanning around London, we had two homicides on the Upper East Side."

"Only two?" Stone asked. "Why is that remarkable?"

"Because both were small, blond, and beautiful," Dino said. "Like you, Faith."

3

STONE AND DINO had worked homicide together, so Stone thought about this the way a cop would. "Anything else in common?"

"The manner of their deaths," Dino said.

"Which was?"

"I don't want to talk about it."

Stone frowned. Dino never didn't want to talk about anything at all. Stone took a breath to ask another question, but Dino gave him the slightest shake of his head, and he didn't ask it.

"Come on, Dino." This was Faith talking, and she looked as though she was going to get an answer.

"I haven't had enough to drink to tell you about that," Dino replied.

Faith was going to persist, but Stone said, "Drop it. He's serious."

"Well, I have a license to carry," Faith said, "so I will."

"A New York City license?" Dino asked.

"New York, Florida, and California," Faith replied. "It's an option for airline pilots. I have to shoot twice a month, requalify once a month, and pay for my own gun and ammunition, but it makes me feel better. I fly charters, and sometimes the groups get rowdy. I've had them banging on the cockpit door."

"Have you ever had to draw your weapon?" Dino asked.

"Only once. I didn't point it at anybody, and there wasn't one in the chamber. Still, its presence had a calming effect on the two-hundred-and-fifty-pound guy who wanted to fly the airplane."

"Good for you," Dino said. "That shows judgment and restraint. Would you like to be a police officer? I'll give you a good assignment right out of the Academy."

"Do you have an assignment available that involves flying an airplane?"

"How about a helicopter?"

Faith shook her head. "They scare me shitless."

"Me, too," Dino said, "and that's just riding in them."

"Well, this is a first," Stone said. "Dino has never offered my date a job."

"I'm serious," Dino said.

"I know," Stone replied.

"Thanks, Dino," Faith said. "I'm flattered, but I like wings on my aircraft, and I enjoy travel."

"You should hire her, Stone," Viv said. "You've been flying the Latitude with pro pilots."

"Only because it's illegal for me to fly it alone. Anyway, it's not my airplane; it belongs to your boss." Viv worked for Mike Freeman, at Strategic Services, the world's second-largest security company. Viv was also a retired NYPD detective. Stone had recently swapped airplanes with Mike—on a temporary basis—when he had wanted to fly to London, and he would have to give back the Latitude soon.

Dinner came, and they enjoyed it.

DINO'S CAR DROPPED them off after dinner. "Nightcap?" Stone asked Faith.

"Sure."

They went into the study.

"You haven't seen the master suite, have you?"

"No," she replied, "but I have the distinct feeling I'm about to."

He poured them each a drink. "Right this way," he said.

They took the elevator to the top floor, and Stone showed Faith into the master suite. Shortly after that, he gave her a tour of the bed.

"Well," she said afterward, toying with the bed's remote control until it sat her up. "When my day started in Miami this morning I didn't expect to finish it in your bed."

"I'm glad to be of service," Stone said.

"You serve well," she replied. "There's something I have to explain to you, though."

"You don't have to explain anything to me, unless you have an angry husband tucked away somewhere."

"I have an angry *ex*-husband," she said, "but he's well out of the picture, in Chicago, and I hardly ever fly there. But he's not the problem."

"All right, what do you need to explain?"

"I'm a three-time girl," she said.

Stone shook his head. "I'm not following."

"I'm not interested in getting married," she said, "not even interested in having a regular boyfriend."

"Okay," Stone said.

"Maybe not," she replied. "The way I keep either of those things from happening is, I never fuck any man more than three times." She sighed. "Not that I don't *love* sex."

"How did you happen to select the number three?" Stone asked.

"Three times is a turning point: either I'm sick of a man by then or I want to continue to fuck him. The way I keep from continuing is by stopping at three times."

"We'll see," Stone replied.

"I'm not kidding," she said.

"It's too early to make that decision," Stone pointed out.

"You're right, of course; we've got two more times to go."

Stone reached for her. "Let's use number two now," he said.

"Good idea," she replied. "We can save ourselves for number three."

He pulled her on top of him and slipped inside of her.

She smiled. "No lubrication required," she said.

They moved together. "This is awfully good," Stone said. "Seems like a shame to limit it to three times, when we're just learning about each other."

"Oh, don't worry," she said, moving faster, "by the time we've done it three times, we'll know all there is to know about each other."

He rolled over on top of her without losing his place. "I think you're the smallest woman I've ever made love to," he said.

"Do you like that about me?"

"There isn't anything I don't like about you, except the three-strikes-and-you're-out thing."

"This isn't a strike," she said, "but it's a ball."

"Well put," Stone said, sensing that she was about to come and moving faster.

Faith began to make the right noises, and in a moment, they came together.

WHEN THEY RECOVERED THEMSELVES, Faith produced an iPhone from the purse at her bedside and began to tap it.

"Checking your e-mail?" Stone asked.

"That and the *New York Times* online," she said. "Oh, Jesus."

"What's wrong?"

"I just found out why Dino didn't want to tell me how those two girls died."

4

———

S TONE GOT READY to go down to his office while Faith was still in bed, reading the print edition of the *Times*.

"Are you going to tell me how those girls died?" he asked.

"No."

"Why not?"

"Because, like Dino, I don't care to discuss it."

"I can read the paper, too, you know."

"Then read it, but that subject is not going to pass my lips."

"As you wish," Stone said. "I've got to go downstairs and at least pretend to work. Can you amuse yourself?"

She smiled. "That won't be necessary," she said, "you've already amused me."

"You've got two more nights in town, right?"

"And you know how to count!"

"I do. What would you like to do with them?"

"Well, I think it's best if I go back to my hotel room and watch *Jeopardy!* tonight, but we can have dinner tomorrow night."

"Why not both nights?"

"Because we have only one fuck left, and I'd rather it be departure sex, so I'll have something to think about on my Saturday flight."

"You're determined to stick to that rule, then?"

"Unalterably."

"As you wish," Stone replied and headed for the door.

"Stone," she called, stopping him in his tracks. "I absolutely *love* fucking you. Doesn't that count for something?"

"Sure, but it would count more if you weren't counting."

"When I've finished the *Times* I'll shower and let myself out," she said.

"Do you do the crossword?"

"No."

Stone separated the Arts section from the paper and gave her the rest. "Six-thirty here, tomorrow evening? I'll have Fred drive you to the airport Saturday morning."

"I don't have to be there until noon," she said.

"See you tomorrow evening." He ran down the stairs for exercise and went to his desk.

Joan came in with the mail. "Have you read the *Times*, yet?"

"Sort of, Faith commandeered it."

"Terrible what's happening to those girls on the East Side, isn't it?"

"That's what I hear, but neither Dino nor Faith would tell me about it. Will you?"

"It's just as well you don't know," Joan replied. "You'd toss your breakfast."

"I've got a strong stomach," Stone said. "I don't know why nobody believes that."

"It's not as strong as you think," Joan said, then went back to her office.

STONE HAD JUST FINISHED the *Times* crossword when Joan buzzed him. "Mike Freeman on one," she said.

Stone picked up the phone. "Mike?"

"Good morning and welcome back."

"Thank you, good to be back."

"Did you enjoy the Citation Latitude?"

"I did. It's a lovely airplane, and I enjoyed all the space. I actually got some sleep on the transatlantic."

"How would you like to make our swap deal permanent?" Mike asked.

"Are you serious?"

"Well, not permanent without some money changing hands."

"Why would you want to swap?"

"Because I've discovered that we're using your CJ3-Plus a lot more than we were using the Latitude. It has just the right range and capacity to meet more than ninety percent of our needs. On the other hand, you have lots of longer flights: Key West, Santa Fe, L.A. We've put only about two hundred hours on the Latitude, not counting your transatlantic, and we've got the Gulfstreams for longer flights."

"How much money are we talking about?"

Mike mentioned a number.

Stone mentioned a smaller number.

"Let's split the difference," Mike said. "Remember, you get to expense one hundred percent of the depreciation; that almost pays for the difference in price. And you'll continue to enjoy the privileges of our hangar space. If you want to keep your tail number, our shop can do that for you."

Stone thought about that. "All right, done."

"I'll send you a sales contract before the day's out," Mike said.

"I'll look forward to receiving it." Stone hung up and thought for another minute, then he picked up the phone and buzzed the master suite.

"Yes?" Faith said. "You looking for me?"

"I am," Stone said. "How would you like to fly a Citation Latitude today?"

"Goody, yes!"

"Get dressed and get down here." He hung up and buzzed Joan. "Please call the Strategic Services hangar and ask them to refuel the Latitude and have it on the ramp in an hour, and ask Fred to drive me to Teterboro and wait for me for a couple of hours."

"Will do."

STONE AND FAITH did the preflight together. "You've never flown the actual airplane, have you? Just the simulator."

"Right."

"Then you're flying left seat today," he said.

"Where are we going?"

"Nowhere special."

FAITH SEEMED RIGHT at home setting up the avionics and completing the checklist. "Have you filed an instrument flight plan?" she asked.

"No, we'll go VFR," Stone replied. "Ask departure for direct Carmel." He explained the autothrottles to her.

She called ground for permission to taxi. Five minutes later they were headed north toward the CMK VOR beacon. They leveled at fifteen thousand feet, and Stone asked her to do some turns and stalls, then he pretty much ran her through the checklist for a checkride. She handled everything perfectly.

"Okay," he said, "let's go back. Ask for the ILS 6." She contacted New York Approach, asked for the instrument approach, and got it.

Back at the hangar she shut down the engines. "That felt like a checkride," she said.

"It wasn't a checkride," Stone replied. "It was an audition."

5

THE FOLLOWING EVENING Faith arrived on time, and they had a drink in Stone's study.

"How much money did you make last year?" Stone asked her.

"A hundred and six thousand dollars," she said. "Probably about the same this year."

"I've bought the Latitude," Stone said. "Signed the contract today."

"Really?"

"Really."

"Does this have something to do with the offer I can't refuse?"

"It does. I'll pay you a hundred and fifty thousand dollars a year to be my full-time pilot."

"Are you . . ." she began.

He cut her off. "Wait, you haven't heard the whole deal. You'll get free medical insurance; when we're traveling you'll get five hundred dollars a day, per diem, to cover a hotel, meals, and transportation. If we're where I have a house, you can use a guest room and keep the money. You won't just be my chief pilot; you'll be my flight department. You'll keep the maintenance logs up to date, make sure we don't miss any inspections, and order any necessary repairs and approve the work. Whatever is to do with the airplane is your job. Got it?"

"Got it."

"Also, you'll maintain a list of another few pilots who are qualified, should you fall ill or be otherwise unavailable. I expect you know about Pat Frank's service?"

"I do."

"She'll be a good source for pilots. Anytime we fly transatlantic I'll want two pilots aboard, so I can get some sleep. You'll also be in charge of arranging catering, when we need it, and of hiring a flight attendant for some flights."

He opened a leather folder on the coffee table and handed her a sheaf of papers. "Here's your contract. Read it carefully and tell me if you have any questions."

It took her only a few minutes to read it. "What's this about annual training?" she asked.

"Are you a certified flight instructor?"

"Yes."

"Then you'll be in charge of training me. I insure myself, so I don't have to go to flight school, though I do have to take a checkride every year, just like you, and keep my medical current. In fact, you can conduct the training while we're flying, and once in a while we'll do turns and stalls. You'll do a three-day refresher at Flight Safety every year, and so will your backup pilot."

"I can do that." She signed the document and handed it back to him. He signed a copy and gave it to her. "Welcome aboard," he said. "Do you have a New York apartment?"

"No, I'll have to find a place."

He handed her a key and pointed to a door off the living room. "Go through there, then through another door, and take the elevator to the fifth floor. I own the building next door, and my staff lives there. Fred and Helene moved in together, so there's an empty on the top floor. Go look at it; I'll wait."

She took the key and disappeared. Fifteen minutes later she returned. "It's perfect," she said.

"There's a Mercedes station wagon in the garage; Fred uses it for shopping. It's yours whenever you need it; just check with Fred first."

"Do you want me to be in uniform when we fly?"

"Yes, but you won't need the jacket and cap; just bars on your shoulders to let people know you're crew; same with any backup pilot: that helps when dealing with ground personnel at strange airports and, especially, overseas."

"Oh, by the way," she said, "I'm qualified for London City Airport."

"Good, but you won't need that often. I have a seven-thousand-foot runway on my property in the south of England."

"I'm qualified for Aspen, too."

"Okay. I've never flown in there, but you never can tell. Any other questions?"

"Nope."

"Then let's go up to P. J. Clarke's and have some dinner."

THEIR TABLE WASN'T READY, so they sat down at the bar to wait. A bartender Stone didn't know came over; he was staring at Faith.

"Patty?" he said, as in disbelief. "Patty Jorgensen?"

Faith shook her head. "No, that's not my name."

He took their drink order and went to fill it.

"What was that about?" Stone asked.

"You heard him. He thought I was Patty Jorgensen."

"Who's Patty Jorgensen?"

"She's the latest murder victim. Her picture was in yesterday's *New York Times*. I was struck by the resemblance, too. We could have been sisters."

"I'm glad we're getting you out of that hotel," Stone said.

"Me, too. I'll move into my new apartment tomorrow."

Stone still didn't know how those girls died and nobody would tell him. He made a mental note to find out.

"Why don't you move into your new apartment tonight?" Stone asked.

"Okay. I have another small bag to pack back at the hotel.

FRED DROVE THEM BACK to her hotel, and they waited for her to pack the rest of her things. Fifteen minutes passed, and Stone began to worry. He got out of the car and walked into the hotel lobby, which was deserted; not even a night clerk. A mop bucket on wheels stood in the middle of the floor, unmanned, the mop standing up in the bucket. A few wet swipes on the floor were drying. The guy must have gone to the john, he thought.

He went behind the desk and looked up her room number, then dialed it on the house phone: no answer. The elevator was the old-fashioned kind: no operator. Stone got on and tried the control lever: no joy. He pressed buttons, but nothing happened.

Suddenly, a man in a greasy uniform appeared. "Help you, mister?"

"Yes, tenth floor, get moving."

"Right," the man said. He took a key from his pocket, inserted it into a slot, and turned it, then pressed the control lever. The elevator began to move, but it was a slow one. Stone stood, tapping his foot.

"Tenth floor," the man said, opening the doors.

"Wait here," Stone said.

"Can't do that, mister."

Stone reached out, turned the key and put it in his pocket. "Wait here," he said and strode down the hallway. Her door stood ajar, a key in the lock; an eerie glow came from the room, some sort of night-light. He opened the door with a detective's caution and walked into the room, ready for anything, staying close to the walls. The bathroom door was closed; he hammered on it twice, then flung it open. Nothing. Nothing behind the shower curtain or in a utility closet. He went back into the room and looked around. No luggage, no forgotten cosmetics, nothing.

He ran back to the elevator and tossed the operator his key. "The lobby," he said. The trip down seemed little faster. He gave the man a twenty and strode across the lobby. A desk clerk was on duty, and a man was, once more, swabbing the floor.

On the street he looked carefully up and down and saw no one who looked out of place. He opened the car's rear door—a search was better done on wheels.

"Where have *you* been?" Faith asked.

"Looking for you," he replied. "I went upstairs. How'd you get down here?"

"I used the back elevator that opens onto the side street. Larry, the elevator operator, wasn't answering, which isn't unusual."

"The lobby was completely empty," Stone said.

"There's a game. They would all have been watching in the assistant manager's office."

"Home, Fred," Stone said, taking a deep breath.

"You look funny," Faith said.

"I feel funny," he replied. "And I'm glad to get you out of this neighborhood."

BACK AT THE HOUSE, Fred collected her luggage, and Stone gave her a kiss. "Good night."

"Don't you want that last roll in the hay?" she asked. "It's always the best one."

"Let's bank it," Stone said, then went upstairs, undressed, and fell into bed, still shaking a little.

6

STONE WAS AT HIS DESK as usual when Joan came in. "Do you remember that you have a Centurion board meeting in Los Angeles the day after tomorrow?" she asked.

"I remembered the moment you mentioned it," Stone replied. Centurion Studios was the Hollywood film company where Stone's son, Peter, and Dino's son, Ben, were based. Ben was, in addition to being Peter's partner, head of production at the studio, and Stone served on its board of directors.

"They want to know if you're attending."

"Tell them yes, then call Peter for me and ask if he and Ben and their wives would like to join me at the Arrington Hotel for dinner tomorrow evening."

"Certainly."

"Then tell Faith about the trip and ask her to get everything ready with the airplane. She's my new pilot."

"So I heard on the household grapevine," Joan said. "It's not like you were going to tell me."

"Her contract is somewhere on your crowded desktop," Stone said. "Put her on the payroll and the health insurance policy. She's also the new head of my flight department, so you will be relieved of all those tasks. You might bring her up-to-date."

"Anything else?"

"Anything you can think of," Stone said. He called Dino.

"Bacchetti."

"I heard a rumor you're batching it," Stone said.

"Yeah, Viv is in L.A."

"Dinner tonight at Rotisserie Georgette? Seven?"

"Why not? Are you bringing Faith?"

"No, I bought the Latitude from Mike Freeman, and Faith is now an employee—my chief pilot and the head of my flight department. I don't screw around with employees."

"I didn't know you had a flight department."

"Joan was it, until now."

"See you tonight." They both hung up.

STONE MET DINO AT GEORGETTE, one of their favorite restaurants. They ordered drinks and a roast chicken, specialty of the house.

"So," Dino said, "you got tired of Faith, so you hired her so you wouldn't have to sleep with her?"

"Nope. Faith has a three-fuck policy."

"What is a 'three-fuck policy'?"

"She doesn't want a husband or a regular boyfriend, so she limits sex to three times, then dumps them. She figures the fourth time is when she starts to get into trouble."

"Well, that's a new wrinkle," Dino said. "I sort of admire her logic."

"If she doesn't want what she doesn't want, then her policy is a sane one, I guess."

"So, you used up your three times at bat?"

"Only two. I discovered that I resented the limitation, so I decided to limit it myself instead."

"So the two of you won't be joining the mile-high club on your new airplane? Does the FAA have a regulation barring sex at altitude?"

"There's not a specific no-screw regulation that I'm aware of, but they have lots of loosely worded rules that could cover a multitude of sins."

"Conduct unbecoming a licensed pilot?" Dino asked.

"Something like that. Also, there's a regulation about being in control of the airplane at all times, so I guess if the pilots are screwing there could be control issues."

"Especially on takeoff and landing?"

Stone laughed. "Especially."

"I was going to join Viv for a couple of days in L.A.," Dino said. "Mind if I tag along?"

"Be glad to have your company. Be at Teterboro at nine AM. You and Viv stay with me at the Arrington." Stone had led a group who had begun building new hotels, the first on land in Bel-Air that had belonged to Arrington's first husband, the film actor Vance Calder, and the original contract entitled him to build a house on the property.

"Thank you. We'll take you up on that."

"I've invited Peter and Ben and their wives to dinner tomorrow night."

"Good, saves me the trouble."

"Dino," Stone said, "I want details on the murders of those girls on the East Side."

"Yeah, I knew you'd insist, but you won't like it."

"I don't expect to like it. I just want to know what's going on. I had a scare last night with Faith at that seedy hotel on Lexington, where the charter airlines put their crews."

"Yeah, that place is on the downtown edge of the area where the murders are happening."

"Come on, cough it up."

"Okay, here's what the medical examiner is telling us: the girls are rendered unconscious, maybe chemically, then taken somewhere and stripped by the perpetrators."

"More than one perp?"

"So they say. They're then awakened, beaten, and sexually assaulted. The corpses are covered in bruises and welts."

"Any DNA traces?"

"None. The girls are strangled or suffocated, then bathed to clean away incriminating DNA, then they're redressed, taped into garbage bags, and left in public wastebaskets on the street in the middle of the night."

"That's meticulous," Stone said.

"It gets more meticulous: they're made up and given manicures and pedicures, too, so that there are no traces of another person if they scratch or kick them, and their hair is washed and styled and their clothes are washed before they're redressed and put out for collection. We've notified every trash crew working the East Side to be on the alert for bodies."

"Why the makeup and the hairdressing?" Stone asked.

"The ME says it's a guilt thing on the part of the perps.

They want them to look nice when they're found. They use the girls' own makeup, so they're not buying cosmetics in the neighborhood."

"These people are going to be very hard to catch," Stone said.

"You're right, pal. They're going to have to be caught in the act—the act of murder or the act of disposal—and waiting for that to happen could take years."

"They've got to have a base," Stone said. "An apartment or a room where they take their victims; someplace they won't be seen or overheard."

"We're on that," Dino said. "We're on all of it. I've tripled patrols on the East Side."

"I wish I could think of something to suggest," Stone said.

"I wish you could, too, pal."

7

STONE SAT IN THE RIGHT seat and watched closely as Faith ran through her checklist, then got a clearance from ATC, and taxied to the runway. She began her takeoff run, then rotated; Stone handled the gear lever and the flaps for her, and the airplane climbed to its preset altitude of 1,500 feet. They had a departure procedure to fly, and Stone was surprised that Faith hand-flew it instead of just switching on the autopilot, as he would have done in her place. Stone regarded the autopilot as a better operator than he, as many pilots did.

"Do you hand-fly a lot?" he asked Faith as she got an altitude change and a vector to the west from ATC.

"No, I just wanted you to know I could do it. I don't want you to be wondering if I can handle the airplane."

"I'm impressed," Stone said. They were cleared to flight level 045, or 45,000 feet, and when they had leveled off, Stone unbuckled. "I'm going to sit with Dino," he said. "There's nothing here you can't handle, but let me know if you need somebody in the right seat."

He grabbed the *New York Times* from the cabinet top behind him and walked aft, standing almost erect in the six-foot headroom of the cabin. He settled into the seat opposite Dino and put on a headset, in case Faith needed anything. She came on almost immediately.

"Dino has had a text message to call his office," she said.

Stone passed the message on to Dino and pointed out where the satphone was. "Call home base," he said.

Dino picked up the phone, dialed the number, and spoke to someone for a couple of minutes, then returned the phone to its snap-in cradle.

"Anything urgent?" Stone asked, taking off his headset.

"Urgent, but everything is being done," he said. "A garbage truck from the East Side took its cargo back to the dump, and found a dead girl among the trash. They missed it when loading. According to the ME, she was killed while you and I were dining on roast chicken last night."

"I didn't need to know that," Stone said.

"Listen, you always want to know everything, so I'm not going to edit the news for you."

"Was everything in line with the previous killings?"

"Everything," Dino said. "She even had a purse, with the strap over her arm. The killers thoughtfully supplied her wallet and driver's license, so we didn't have to go to the trouble of identifying her."

"They're getting pretty confident, aren't they?"

"Smug, I'd say. In every other respect, this killing matches the others. Everything is being done that has to be done, and my office is making the announcement over my signature, so I'm not needed back there."

"There are times, aren't there, when it's great not to be needed?"

Dino snorted. "I think my chief of staff enjoys rubbing it in."

Stone handed Dino the first section of the *Times*. "Here, distract yourself."

Dino took the paper but folded it in his lap and stared out the window.

Since the anti-airport fanatics on the Santa Monica city council had made a deal with the FAA to shorten SMO's single runway to 3,500 feet, in order to keep out jet traffic, they landed at Burbank, where a Bentley from the Arrington met them and transported them to the hotel. It was a longer drive than from SMO.

THE BUTLER SITUATED STONE and Dino in their respective rooms and took Faith to the guesthouse. Stone had given Faith an invitation to join them for dinner.

Stone and Dino got into bathing suits and robes and headed for the pool, where the thoughtful butler brought drinks and snacks on floating trays. Viv arrived shortly after and joined them in the pool.

"Dino told me about Faith's three-fuck policy," she said to Stone, amused. "Are you finding that hard to live with?"

"No, that's a choice she gets to make for herself, and I'm not going to try to hustle her into changing it."

"Good policy. That will keep your name out of the papers."

"Sex is fun only when it's freely given," Stone said.

"Good point," Viv said, "though I've known men who preferred to try to take it more roughly."

"How'd that work out for them?" Stone asked.

"On one occasion, a broken wrist," Viv replied, "on another, a fat ear; and on yet another, a rearranged nose, requiring bandaging for several days and steak on both eyes."

"Did they know you were a cop?" Stone asked.

"Not at first, but later. One of them swore he'd bring charges against me, but fortunately for him, he thought it over."

THE BOYS AND THEIR WIVES arrived in time for cocktails, and Stone had a moment to sit down alone with Peter and Ben.

"There's something on the board meeting agenda I should warn you about," Ben said. "There's a move afoot among some of the shareholders—the more recent ones—to sell off our back lot and turn it into condo heaven."

"Do they have anything like the support they need?" Stone asked.

"It's closer than we would like," Peter said. "I think Ben is going to have to make a do-or-die speech to the shareholders to hang on to it. God, I love the back lot; we can do so much with the standing sets to make them into anything at all, from ancient Rome to 1920s New York."

"Not to mention the money we save by not needing to go on location so much," Ben said. "I've come up with a number on our costs over the past five years that should impress the board."

"Who are these stockholders who want to develop the land?" Stone asked.

"Newer directors and production companies who somehow think that, if we sell it off, they'll get a chunk of cash."

"Will they?" Stone asked.

"My plan is to fix things so they won't, and when that incentive disappears, they'll come around, and then they'll go to dinner parties and tell their friends how they saved the back lot."

"What is it," Stone asked, "forty acres?"

"Closer to sixty," Ben replied. "Of course, there are parts we don't use much anymore, like the Mississippi riverboat. I've arranged for the board to have lunch aboard the boat, which is in beautiful condition, and I think they'll want to keep it."

"Good idea," Stone said. "We'll have our shares to vote, and Ed Eagle will be on our side with his shares. Have you heard if he's coming?"

"He's already here," Ben said. "He's bought an apartment that overlooks the back lot, and I don't think he'll want to spoil his view."

8

STONE LOOKED OUT ACROSS the Mississippi River, toward downtown Los Angeles, and listened to a Dixieland band while saloon girls served the board and stockholders drinks and lunch, and a riverboat gambler and a man in a black suit fought a gunfight on the stern of the riverboat.

When everyone was suitably oiled, and the agenda had been ticked off, Ben Bacchetti rose. "What do you think of Old Man River?" he asked, getting a rousing round of applause. He had some sheets of paper passed out to those present and took them through the income and the production savings made from the rental and use of the back lot, and while the iron was hot, he got a vote that saved the property.

As the sun began to wane, the riverboat docked at Natchez and dumped the happy group onto the dock and into horse-drawn carriages that took them back to the parking lot. Stone took his party—which included Ed Eagle and Dino, as well as Viv and Faith, who were there as guests—up to the top deck, where they had a bottle of champagne and watched the sun go down on a fairly smog-free city.

"A good day's work," Stone said to Ben.

"I'm proud of you," Dino said to his son.

"We'll have to fight them again next year, but I have plans to make it harder for them. It always amazes me that a group of stockholders would want to fuck up a well-oiled company so they can make a few extra bucks. It's not as though they need the money: the studio police counted a dozen Bentleys, two dozen Mercedes, and a large assortment of Ferraris, Aston Martins, and Lamborghinis in the guest parking lot. Oh, there was one Prius, for the green-minded, I guess."

They were quiet for a moment, then Viv shaded her eyes from the setting sun and pointed aft, where a pink blob floated in the river. "What's that?" she asked.

Everybody gazed lazily aft, then Dino got to his feet and shaded his eyes. "Get me some binoculars," he said to a crewman. The man vanished and came back with the instrument. Dino focused. "It's one of two things," he said. "It's either a life-size doll or a dead body. I think we should find out which."

Two crew members ran down to the dock, got an outboard motor started, and puttered out to where the pink lump floated. The commander of the studio police came out onto the deck and joined them, radio in hand. The instrument squawked, and there was an exchange of information. "It's the body of a woman," he said.

Dino spoke up. "Then you'd better call somebody you know on the LAPD and ask for homicide detectives, the ME, a crime scene team, and an ambulance."

The man made the call, and the two crewmen began ferrying the body back to the dock.

"I think we'd better have a look at this," Dino said.

Stone followed him ashore and down to the dock. "Leave her in the boat," Dino said to them. He and Stone got in and had a close look at the body.

"Was she serving drinks?" Dino asked.

"I honestly don't know," Stone said. He turned to the captain, who had followed them down. "Do you know her?"

"No," the man said.

"I think you'd better conduct a roll call and see who's missing," Stone said. "That'll give the police a head start when they get here."

The captain left and returned with a clipboard. "I've checked the whole list," he said, "and nobody's missing."

Ben stepped up. "I've given instructions for every department to count heads and report anyone who's missing from their offices."

The LAPD arrived and were greeted by the commander of the studio police, who brought them to the dock.

An older detective said, "My God, is that Dino Bacchetti?"

The two pumped hands and Dino introduced everybody. "This is Lieutenant Molder Carson, known to one and all as 'Moldy.'"

"What've we got here?" Carson asked, walking over to boat.

"What you specialize in?" Dino said.

"Has anybody fucked with the body?"

"Only to get her out of the water and into the boat," Dino said. "I watched them, and they did it well."

The medical examiner arrived with the ambulance and made a quick examination of the body. "She's badly bruised pretty much all over, but I can't find a fatal wound. I need to get her back to the morgue, and on a table, before I can tell you more."

The corpse was placed in a body bag and driven away.

Stone and Dino walked slowly to their waiting carriage, followed by the others.

"Notice anything familiar about her?" Dino asked.

"No, I don't know her."

"Well, she's not much more than five feet tall, a hundred pounds, and blond."

Faith, who was walking beside Stone, stopped, then turned aside and vomited.

9

THEY ALL HAD dinner at the table by the pool. While the others chatted, Stone and Dino managed a more private conversation.

"It's a coincidence," Stone said.

"You think everything is a coincidence," Dino replied. "You say so all the time."

"No, I don't. What I say all the time is that our lives are made up of strings of coincidences, that if you take any important, life-changing event in your history and trace it back far enough, you'll find that some slim coincidence changed everything. And if you string enough of those coincidences together, what you get is fate."

"That's just so much horseshit," Dino said evenly. "I don't believe in coincidences, especially where homicides are concerned."

"Oh, come on, Dino."

"You think it's any kind of coincidence at all that a body

turns up in L.A., where you and I are, and the crime closely matches three, four others in New York?"

"Well . . ."

"These homicides are not only connected," Dino said, "they're perpetrated by the same person or persons."

"Well," Stone said, "if the ME's estimate of time of death is correct, then that couldn't be the case because this murder and the last one in New York were committed at roughly the same time, two days ago—while we were dining on roast chicken at Rotisserie Georgette—so it can't be the same guy."

"There's a connection, believe me," Dino said. "And on top of it all, they're fucking with you and me, just for fun."

"They're not fucking with me," Stone said. "You're the cop. If they're fucking with anybody, it's you. Don't you feel fucked with?"

"Of course, I do," Dino said, "but the connection in all this is Faith."

"Let me get this straight," Stone said. "You think they're picking victims who look like Faith, just to drive me crazy?"

"Aren't they driving you crazy?' Dino asked.

"Well, a little, I guess."

"Then whatever they're doing is working."

"They're driving you crazy, too," Stone pointed out.

"Thank God the victims don't look like Viv, or I would already be crazy."

"Do you think Faith is safe out here?" Stone asked. Faith was tucked up in bed in the guesthouse with a cup of broth to settle her stomach.

"How the hell should I know?" Dino asked. "She was within

fifty yards of our floater half a dozen times this afternoon. The perps could have snatched her, if they'd felt like it."

The butler approached. "The medical examiner is on the phone for Commissioner Bacchetti," he said. He led Dino to a lounge chair a few feet away and handed him a phone.

Dino put his feet up and chatted for a couple of minutes, then he put down the phone and returned to the table. "Okay," he said, "the ME confirms his first estimate of time of death. The girl had a tiny purse tucked into her vagina, just big enough to hold her driver's license, a credit card, and a few bucks. Her name is Elizabeth Sweeney."

"Where does she live?"

"Santa Monica."

Viv came over and sat with them.

"We're going to stop talking about this now. We're going to all behave as if we've had a pleasant day in the California sunshine, riding down the L.A. branch of the Mississippi River," Dino said.

"All that is true," Viv said.

"And we're enjoying a good dinner under the stars, and the ME didn't call."

"The ME called?" Viv asked. "What did he say?"

"You see why I'm going crazy here?" he asked Stone.

"She died in L.A. while Dino and I were having dinner in New York," Stone said. "Her name is Elizabeth Sweeney, and she lives in Santa Monica."

"And Dino thinks the killings are related."

"It was his idea," Dino replied, pointing at Stone.

"Don't point that thing at me," Stone said. "You had the same idea at the same time."

"This is why I'm going crazy," Dino said. "I've already ruled out the killings as a subject of dinner table conversation, so that we can enjoy our dinner and the evening, but you people just won't leave it alone."

Viv kissed him on the forehead. "I'm sorry, darling, of course we'll stop talking about it, won't we, Stone?"

"Absolutely," Stone replied.

"How did they identify her?" Viv asked.

Dino picked up his dinner plate and carried it to the other end of the pool, where he collapsed on a chaise longue and tried to eat.

"Oops," Viv said.

10

THE FOLLOWING MORNING after breakfast Dino con-
vened a meeting around Stone's dining room table.
Present were himself, Stone, and Viv, plus the two LAPD detectives assigned to the case and their captain.

Dino picked up a phone and dialed a number. "Get them
on the speaker phone," he said.

"We're here, Commish," a man's voice said.

"Okay," Dino said, "what we've got present here is a bi-
coastal team to investigate a series of homicides apparently
occurring on both coasts, fairly simultaneously. I've already
assigned a team to the East Coast killings, and present is the
West Coast team. I propose that we have a daily conference
call to share what each group has. We also have the relevant
ME at each end. Everybody on board?"

There was a positive chorus of noises from both coasts.

"Also, I've asked two other people with homicide experience to join us. Both are retired NYPD detectives, both

outstanding ones: Stone Barrington, who is an attorney in New York, a former detective, and my NYPD partner for many years; and my wife, Vivian Bacchetti—who likes to be called Viv—who is very experienced in these things as she also was an NYPD detective, and is now chief operating officer of Strategic Services, a worldwide security company. Anybody object to them helping out?"

There was a positive rumble at both ends.

"There's a stenographer in New York who is transcribing our conversation and will issue notes on our discussions from time to time, so we won't forget anything. Since the killings started in New York, I'll ask Lieutenant Greg Martin to give us a summary of what has been learned there, then we'll hear from the LAPD team. Greg?"

"Thanks, Commissioner," Greg said. "We've had four homicides on the Upper East Side of New York, all fitting a pattern: the victims were all young women of small stature and slim build, with blond hair, all very pretty. They appear to have been taken from their neighborhoods to what the killers believe is a secure location, stripped, beaten severely, and raped. They were then killed by suffocation or strangulation, and their bodies were bathed, their bodily cavities irrigated, and their personal makeup applied to their faces. Their clothing was laundered. Then they were dressed again, placed in a large plastic garbage bag, and dumped in municipal trash bins. All were discovered on garbage trucks, except for one, who was found when her body was dumped at a municipal facility. In some cases, identification was found on the bodies, in others they were identified by fingerprints, DNA testing, or photo ID means. No evidence of any kind relating to their killers was found on them. That's all we've got."

"Thanks, Greg," Dino said. "Moldy? Give us your rundown."

Moldy read from notes. "The subject was found on the back lot of a movie studio, where Commissioner Bacchetti, Mr. Barrington, and Mrs. Bacchetti were attending a social event in connection with a board and stockholder meeting of Centurion Studios. She had been dumped in a lake that's shaped to resemble a river, a lake on studio property, where two other bodies have been found in the past five years. There's fairly easy access from a road. Her appearance was similar to the New York victims: small, pretty, and slight of build, with blond hair. And her corpse had been treated in much the same way as the New York victims. No DNA, traces of fibers, or other evidence of the killers were found on her body. She was identified from her driver's license, found in a small purse, tucked into her vagina. She had a Third Street address, in Santa Monica, and she was killed on the same night as the fourth victim in New York. That's it."

"All right," Dino said. "I believe we can say without contradiction that there is more than one killer involved, on more than one coast, and that they are working in league with each other. Their motives are unknown, unless we believe it possible that the killers may have a motive to embarrass Stone Barrington or me, or both, which seems unlikely in the extreme. Am I missing anything?"

Moldy spoke up, directing his voice toward the phone. "Greg, what have you learned about the employment of your victims?"

"One was a copilot for a charter airline, new to the job, two were secretaries or office workers, the last was an actress, working mostly in TV commercials. There appears to be no employment connection among them. How about yours?"

"She is an actress who may have visited Centurion Studios in pursuit of her career, but we have not been able to ascertain who, if anyone, she saw here. She had no appointments at the studio."

"Greg," Dino said, "what steps are you proposing?"

"Commissioner," Greg replied, "we have identified two NYPD officers, one a detective, who resemble the victims in a general way in size and hair color, both very pretty. We are considering making one of them a presence on the Upper East Side over a period of days, under the strictest surveillance at all times, to see if she attracts the attention of the killers. In addition to surveillance, she will be equipped with an electronic means of signaling distress, to help keep her safe. Our detective is also extremely skilled in personal protection techniques. This plan will require a large commitment of personnel and equipment and will require your personal approval before beginning. Our supervisor and the chief of detectives have already approved the plan."

"Then you may consider the plan approved," Dino said. "Be very careful, but don't waste any time. Moldy?"

"Commissioner, we continue to investigate by every means at our disposal."

"All right," Dino said. "Does anyone have anything else to contribute?"

"Commissioner," Greg said, "we do not place any credence in your theory that the killers' motive is to embarrass you.

Mr. Barrington, maybe. If he's being watched, we might identify the watcher, and if we did, that would constitute a major break in the case."

"Stone," Dino said. "Do you mind being surveilled in connection with this case?"

"Yes, I do, most emphatically," Stone replied, "and I doubt very much if it would produce any leads."

"Greg, you and your team are authorized to surveil Mr. Barrington, whether he likes it or not, starting when he lands at Teterboro on his return to New York."

"Yes, Commissioner, when will that be?"

"Stone?" Dino asked.

"Six o'clock tomorrow evening at Jet Aviation, Teterboro," Stone said, "but I think it's a waste of time and manpower."

"Objection noted," Dino said, "and ignored."

11

S TONE FLEW HIS NEW airplane home, with Faith in the right seat. He had never flown an airplane coast-to-coast, nonstop, because he had never owned one with that much range. He landed with plenty of fuel still aboard.

As he shut down the engines at Teterboro, Fred pulled the Bentley up to the door and supervised the unloading and re-loading of Stone's and Faith's luggage, while Dino's people loaded his and Viv's luggage aboard his police vehicle. They were the first to drive away, but another black SUV lurked on the sidelines.

"Mr. Barrington," Fred said, "the policemen in that car have told me that they have orders to never let you out of their sight, except when you're at home. What shall I tell them?"

"I'd like you to tell them to go fuck themselves," Stone said, "but that wouldn't help. I'm not in any danger, but Faith may very well be." He called Faith over. "I want both of you to understand this," he said. "You two are not to be out of sight of each other except when in your living quarters. Fred, at all other times, I want you armed and ready to intervene should anyone—and I mean *anyone*—approach Faith."

"Yes, sir," Fred replied.

"Faith?" Stone said. "Are you on board?"

"I can take care of myself," she said. "I'll go armed."

"Not good enough," Stone replied. "We have five young women who look like you, all dead, because they thought they could take care of themselves. Your only other choice is to quit your job and go on the run, and that might very well not work."

"Oh, all right," she said, exasperated. "How long do I have to put up with this?"

"Until these crimes are solved and the perpetrators jailed. And I don't think you'll find Fred hard to put up with. He's an ex–Royal Marine commando with many skills, and also a crack shot. If there's any shooting to be done, try to let him do it."

"I'm sorry, Fred," she said to him, "I didn't intend to disparage your help. I'm grateful for it."

"Thank you, miss," Fred said. "Shall we depart for the city?"

They all got into the Bentley and were soon headed for the tunnel into the city. "I should tell you, Faith," Stone said, "this car is armored and will repel gunfire and most bombs. Forget about the Mercedes; if you want to go anywhere, go in this."

"Right," she said.

At the house, Fred pulled all the way into the garage before closing the door behind them, then he asked them to wait a moment while he had a look around the garage. He produced a small but powerful flashlight and illuminated every dark corner and anteroom in the basement, then Stone and Faith disembarked. "If I get scared," Faith asked, "can I come and sleep with you?"

"If you get scared," Stone said, "call Fred. You'll be much safer with him than with me." He went upstairs to the master suite, and she went to her own apartment.

THE FOLLOWING MORNING Stone was at his desk when Faith came in carrying a nylon carryall. "I'd like to get the logbooks in order and schedule some maintenance," she said to Stone. "Is there someplace I can work?"

Stone buzzed Joan, and she came in. "Please put Faith in the little office next to yours, and let her make it her own. It is now the Flight Department. Direct any and all calls about the aircraft to her."

"Yes, sir," Joan said.

"And Joan, you should know that Faith is under the protection of the NYPD, and they are surveilling me, as well. Faith, Joan is armed and so am I, and I assume you are, too."

She nodded.

"I think the most important thing we can all do to get through this, if trouble comes, is try not to shoot each other."

"I'll give that my best efforts," Joan said. Faith nodded.

Shortly afterward, both women were settled and at work in their offices.

Stone called Dino.

"Bacchetti."

"Good morning, sleep well?"

"As well as I can sleep while worrying," Dino said

"Please don't worry about us. We're battened down here, and everybody is armed."

"You think you and your ménage are all I have to worry about?" Dino demanded. "We had two homicides in the city last night."

"Any of them connected to the East Side?"

"No, both of the victims were men—a gay couple in Chelsea."

"I'm glad it wasn't one of ours."

"Every garbage truck in the city is on the lookout for fresh corpses," Dino said. "If there's another one out there, they'll find it."

"Is Viv continuing on to London today?"

"She is."

"Then why don't you come over here this evening and have dinner with Faith and me. I don't think we should be swanning around restaurants, in these circumstances."

"Neither do I. I've got a late meeting—I'll try to be there by seven-thirty."

"We'll save you some scotch," Stone said, then hung up.

AROUND SEVEN, Faith called down from her apartment. "I don't really feel well enough for a jolly dinner with you and Dino," she said. "Helene will bring me something on a tray."

"Now, don't go and get all depressed on me," Stone said. "We'll get through this."

"There's nothing to do but watch TV," she said.

"My library is at your disposal," Stone said, "and you can go anywhere you like, as long as you and Fred are joined at the hip."

"I'd rather be joined with you," she said. "Did you get tired of fucking me?"

"Listen, sweetheart, I'm playing by *your* rules, remember? I have nothing but the most pleasant memories of sex with you, but I'd rather fast than be rationed."

"Oh, all right, then. I'll come down to dinner. What time?"

"Seven-thirty is good," he said.

"How are we dressing?"

"In street clothing—no nightgowns or pajamas, you might get Dino all riled."

"Now there's a thought," she said, then hung up.

12

DINO ARRIVED, and they all sat down before the fire in Stone's study.

"I don't think I've ever seen you look so tired," Stone said to Dino.

"I don't think I've ever *been* so tired," Dino replied, taking a gulp of his drink. "I'm taking the Scottish remedy for fatigue. It'll start to work soon."

"Any news at all?"

"Not a whiff," Dino said. "It's like these people were going full steam ahead, then slammed on the brakes."

"Are you disappointed?" Faith asked.

"No, I'm relieved, but I know more is coming. I just don't know when."

"Dino," Stone said, "I know you've probably investigated it, but I think you should have another close look at the Keystone Hotel, on Lex."

"You're right. We've already looked at it. What makes you think it needs further attention?"

"A few nights ago, I dropped Faith off there to pick up her belongings, and she took so long, I got worried and went looking for her. The lobby was completely deserted, and that's odd for a hotel."

"Who should have been there?" Dino asked.

"A janitor mopping the floor—only his bucket and mop were there—the elevator operator, and the desk clerk. I tried to take myself up in the elevator, but it was locked. The operator finally showed up and took me upstairs, but Faith wasn't there. When I came downstairs again, the janitor and the desk clerk had reemerged, and everything seemed normal."

"Where was Faith?"

"In the car, waiting," she said. "When the elevator operator didn't answer my ring, I took the automatic elevator in the rear of the building and walked around the corner to where Fred was waiting in the car. I told Stone there was a ball game on TV, and they were probably watching it in the assistant manager's office."

"How long do you think the lobby was empty?" Dino asked.

"There's no way to tell," Stone replied.

"All three of them were there when I went into the building," Faith said. "Between then and when Stone came back to the car again, maybe ten, fifteen minutes. I had some packing to do."

"Is the lobby often deserted?" Dino asked.

"Yes. The only guests these days are airline people, who are on a contract. I think they've stopped taking other reservations."

"Why is that?"

"I've heard that the hotel is scheduled for gutting and a complete renovation as a high-end hotel/condo combination. That's what the desk clerk told me."

"I don't know what to make of that story," Dino said.

"Neither do I," Stone replied. "The whole business just struck me as creepy. Can you think of an excuse to have a look around the place, especially the lower levels?"

"Of course I can," Dino replied, "and if I can't, I've got a few hundred detectives who could come up with probable cause for a search warrant on the fly. I just don't think I can spare the manpower while we're in the middle of this murder spree to look again into something so ordinary and plausible."

"Have you had the FBI in on this?" Stone asked.

"Why would I want those fuckers involved?" Dino asked. "I avoid them like the plague, unless I really need them for something, which isn't often."

"You don't have any profilers on the force, do you? The FBI specializes in profiling prospective murder perps."

"Yeah, and half the time it's a lot of horseshit."

"And what about the other half of the time?" Stone asked. "I think I'd use anything that had a fifty percent probability of producing some real leads."

"Do I look that desperate?" Dino asked.

"You certainly do," Stone replied.

Dino tossed down the rest of his drink and handed Stone his glass. "You still tending bar?"

"Sure." Stone got up and poured the drink.

"All right," Dino said.

"All right, what?"

"All right, I'll call somebody over at Fedville tomorrow morning and get one of their readers of tea leaves sent over."

"Good idea," Stone said. "I wish I'd thought of it."

"Mark my words," Dino said. "They're going to send me some little jerk fresh out of Quantico, who'll gaze at the ceiling and spout a lot of crap."

"Well, if he has only one good idea, it might be worth it."

"Why don't you have profilers in the NYPD?" Faith asked.

"We sent some people down to Quantico to do a course with those people, and they kept dozing off in the classes. When they got back, they were worse cops and more of a pain in the ass than before we sent them down there."

"That sounds like a lot of grouch to me," Faith said.

"Dino is mostly grouch," Stone put in.

"I'm good at grouch," Dino said. "Grouch has always worked very well for me. It keeps people on their toes."

"I never knew *grouch* was a motivator," Faith said.

"It also keeps their ideas on point and their sentences short," Dino said. "You wouldn't believe how much time grouch saves me."

"Right," Stone said. "Nobody wants to argue with somebody they know will bite their head off, if they say the wrong thing or don't say it fast enough."

"That's what I want to avoid," Dino said. "Them saying the wrong thing. I only give them time to say the right thing."

"This is beginning to sound like one of those business management things," Faith said. "'Grouch your way to the top.' That sort of thing."

"Dino," Stone said, "you could make a fortune giving classes to business leaders on grouch and its uses."

"You mean, like Trump University?"

"Well, you'd need less content and more fraud for that," Stone said. "Maybe you should just write the book. Faith has already given you the title. Start taking notes."

"I could just leave a tape recorder running in my office," Dino said, getting into the swing of things, "and have my secretary transcribe the good stuff at the end of the day."

"Good idea," Faith said. "Maybe you should attach one of those GoPro cameras to your head, so you can pick up the reactions of your victims."

"'Victims'?" Dino asked. "What victims?"

"Sorry, colleagues and staffers. Their reactions would be good to use in the television commercials."

"Television commercials?"

"For the book. You'll need a hot-and-heavy ad campaign to move sales."

Fred came into the room with a sizzling porterhouse steak on a platter.

"Saved by the beef," Stone said.

13

THE FOLLOWING LATE AFTERNOON, Stone opened his briefcase, and one end of the handle came off in his hand. Upon examination, it was found to be missing a tiny screw, the sort of part that is available only at expensive luggage stores.

He checked on Joan and Faith, who were both working away like beavers, then emptied his briefcase, tucked it under his arm, and left the house, headed uptown, walking. He finished up at a fancy luggage shop at Park and Fifty-sixth Street, went inside, and had a brief conversation with their repair artist, who eventually admitted he could supply and fit the screw. Stone sat down and picked up a magazine from a table to while away the time. Shortly, a woman fell into his lap.

This was more than a metaphor. She was missing a shoe, the shoe was missing a heel, and when he stood her upright, she rested all her weight on the other foot.

"I'm so terribly sorry," she said.

Stone was not so sorry. She was tall, slim, had auburn hair, was beautifully dressed in an Armani suit, and she had managed the fall without getting so much as a hair out of place. He sat her down in the chair and retrieved the shoe and the heel.

"I'm afraid you're not walking anywhere on this," he said, then looked at her foot, which was beginning to swell. "Nor on that," he said, pointing at her ankle.

"Oh, swell," she said.

A salesman appeared belatedly and made all the right noises, for which Stone was grateful.

"You sold me three cases, a matched set, last summer," she said. "I need one more case, like that." She pointed at a grouping on a high shelf. "The smaller one, second from the right."

While the salesman looked for a ladder, Stone made haste. "May I ask where you're headed?" he said.

"To the Carlyle Hotel," she said.

"While you conclude your purchase, I'll arrange some transport for you."

"That would be very kind," she said.

Stone got Fred on the phone and instructed him, then returned to her side. She was signing a credit card receipt, and the salesman took the case away to have it wrapped. "I'm afraid your ankle is taking on cantaloupe proportions," he said. "Does it hurt?"

She thought about that. "Yes," she said, "but not as much as it's going to hurt when I try to walk on it. I think I'd better go to an emergency room."

"That's not going to be as much fun as it sounds," Stone

said. "You'll be there until midnight waiting for everybody with chest pains to be looked at. Ankles are not high on the emergency list of a New York hospital."

"What do you suggest?" she said.

Stone, from the corner of his eye, saw the Bentley glide to a halt outside. "Put this in your purse," he said, handing her the broken shoe and heel. She tucked it into her Birkin bag, a commodious purse more expensive that many luxury cars. "Let's get you back to the Carlyle. I know a doctor who makes house calls, and we'll get him to look at that. My car is outside."

He got her standing on her good foot, while she rested a hand on his shoulder and tried hopping. It didn't work very well. "There's always the fireman's carry," Stone said. "I learned that as a Boy Scout."

"Not on Park Avenue," she said. "Why don't we try the old over-the-threshold carry, beloved of so many newlyweds. I won't tell anybody we're not married, if you won't."

"Good idea," Stone said. He scooped her up into his arms and strode out of the shop and across the sidewalk, while the salesman tried to keep up with her package.

Fred saw them coming, got a rear door open, and assisted Stone with tucking her into the backseat, while the salesman put her case on the front passenger seat and handed Stone his briefcase. "No charge, Mr. Barrington," he said.

Stone thanked him, then got into the other rear seat and handed Fred the briefcase. "The Carlyle, Fred."

"'Barrington'?" she asked. "Is that your name?"

"It is, first name is Stone."

"I'm Cilla Scott," she replied. "Priscilla, really, but I dropped the *Pris* at puberty."

"One moment," Stone said, whipping out his cell phone, calling the Carlyle, and asking for the concierge. "Good afternoon, George, this is Stone Barrington. Fine, thanks. I'm bringing you a wounded guest, and we need a wheelchair at the East Seventy-sixth Street entrance in five minutes. Thank you."

"Good thinking," she said.

"As dainty as you are, I don't think I could carry you all the way to your room. Excuse me, one more call to make." He pressed the button. "Kevin, Stone Barrington. I have a patient requiring a house call, and bring that portable X-ray thing of yours. Carlyle Hotel . . ." He looked at her, and she gave him the room number. "Twenty-eighth floor. Name of Ms. Scott. Possible broken ankle. Bring painkillers." He thanked the man and hung up. "Half an hour," he said.

"Well," Cilla said. "You are blindingly efficient. I don't think you've forgotten a thing."

They arrived at the side door to the Carlyle and were greeted by a doorman with a wheelchair. "Mr. Barrington? I'm Eddie. We're all ready for Ms. Scott." They got her into the wheelchair. Moments later, they were shooting skyward. She handed Stone her key—the Carlyle still used actual keys—and Stone let them into a large, south-facing suite with a spectacular skyline view. Stone gave Eddie a fifty and thanked him.

"There's a bar over there," she said. "Would you fix me some sort of whiskey on the rocks and make something for yourself?"

"That skill lies within my repertoire," Stone said. He found half a bottle of Knob Creek and poured them each a drink. "Try that," he said, handing it to her.

She took a swig. "Perfect," she said, "what is it?"

"Knob Creek bourbon. Knob Creek is in Kentucky, where Abraham Lincoln once lived. You can't get any more patriotic than that."

"You're making that up," she said.

"I am reciting American history. Google it."

She took another swig. "It seems to be finding its way to all the right places."

"It will do that," Stone replied. He looked at his watch. "Dr. Kevin should be here shortly, and we'll soon know if he has to amputate."

"Sit down," she said, patting the chair beside her.

He dragged over an ottoman, placed her wounded foot on it, and then sat down.

"Tell me about yourself," she said.

"I don't give recitations, but I do answer questions," Stone replied. So she began to question him.

14

THE DOCTOR ARRIVED and was shown his patient. "This is Dr. Kevin O'Connor," Stone said. "Kevin, Ms. Scott." The doctor dragged up a chair and examined her ankle, pressing here and there, while she winced.

"I don't think it's broken," he said, "but we'll get a picture." He set up a contraption on the footstool and looked at the resulting X-ray on his laptop. "It's not broken," he said, "just badly sprained, and not for the first time. There's quite a lot of scarring."

"I've been spraining it since I was twelve," Cilla replied. "On horseback, on tennis courts, on boats, and on golf courses."

"You're going to have to stay off of it for a few days," he said, "and I mean off. Some of my patients believe that means on tippy-toe. It doesn't. If I apply a trusty elastic bandage, will you promise me to stay off it for four days?"

"*Four* days?"

"If you won't promise, I'll put a cast on it."

She sighed. "Oh, all right, I promise."

He taped the ankle, then gave her some folding crutches and two pill bottles. "One is a nonsteroid anti-inflammatory, the other is a painkiller, one that you can't combine with alcohol, unless you want to fall asleep and not wake up."

"You keep the painkillers," she said, "and I'll continue with my medication of choice."

The doctor packed up and Stone walked him to the door. "Send me the bill," he said.

"What's your connection with this ankle?" Dr. Kevin asked.

"It fell into my lap." Stone closed the door and made Cilla another drink. "How are you feeling?" he asked.

"Like a person who's had a couple of drinks," she replied. "I don't know how the ankle feels. It's not speaking to me."

"Just as well. I'd invite you out for dinner, but you aren't going anywhere tonight."

"Then I'll invite you to stay here for dinner," she said. "This hotel still follows the quaint practice of serving food in its suites."

"I accept," he said.

"Back to your interrogation," she said. "What do you do?"

"I'm a lawyer with a firm called Woodman & Weld."

"What is your specialty?"

"Practicing as little law as possible."

"Admirable. Where do you live?"

"I have a house in Turtle Bay."

"I know it well. I had an aunt who lived there until her death a few years ago. As a little girl I used to play in the gardens."

"It's hard to believe you were ever a little girl," he said.

"I still am."

"My turn: Where do you live?"

"In Greenwich, Connecticut, in a house I shared until recently with a husband."

"What brings you to New York?"

"I came to look for an apartment and to consult with my late father's investment advisors. He died last month, and I'm trying to get a grip on his estate."

"Do you have a Realtor?"

"No, I was going to ask you to recommend one."

Stone looked through his wallet until he found a card. "Margot Goodale," he said. "She's excellent."

"Thank you," she said, tucking the card into her bra. "Can you recommend a good divorce attorney?"

"I can," he said, taking a business card from the wallet and writing a name on it. "Herbert Fisher. Is your divorce likely to be contentious?"

"Aren't they all?"

"Is this your first?"

"Yes. I want to present the man with enough legal firepower to let him know I won't be a pushover."

"Herb is your man. He's our firm's lead attorney in that field. Your husband's attorney will know who he is and treat you respectfully."

She bra-ed the card with the other one. "Shall we look at a menu?"

Stone went to the desk and found one. "The dover sole looks good," he said.

"Same here, and the lobster bisque to start and some wine."

Stone made the call and ordered for them, then walked back and sat down. "Do you work?"

"Look at my manicure," she said, displaying her nails. "Does it look like I work?"

Stone laughed. "I wasn't thinking of something in the mines."

"I run two houses and this apartment," she said, "and supervise everything else except my husband's shopping."

"What is his name?"

"Donald Trask. I kept my maiden name, thank God. He operates a hedge fund that was built on referrals from my father and me."

"When did he start the firm?"

"Right after we were married."

"Good, then he won't be able to exclude the business from marital property."

"If I so much as whisper to a friend or two that I'm pulling my father's investment, he won't have a business by this time tomorrow."

"That sounds vindictive."

"It's not. Pulling the investment is why I'm meeting with the advisors. It's done less well than the market."

"Don't whisper to your friends," Stone said. "You might give him grounds for a defamation suit. Who owns the real estate?"

"We both own the Greenwich house and this apartment," she said, waving a hand. "The Maine house was my father's."

"So you'll sell both and divide the proceeds?"

"I believe that's how it goes. I'd keep this place, but you wouldn't believe the monthly maintenance charges."

"Are you angry with your husband?"

"No, just disgusted. He's the angry one because I caught him screwing around, and he's afraid I'll tell our friends."

"Once again, don't talk to your friends, until it's all over and the divorce is final."

"Good advice. I don't want to talk about it anyway."

Dinner came, and they washed it down with a good bottle of chardonnay.

"I'M SO GLAD I fell into your lap this afternoon," she said. "If I hadn't, I'd be languishing in some ER right now, waiting to be seen." She yawned.

"I expect you could use some rest," Stone said. "If you'd like to blindfold me I'll undress you and put you to bed."

"Thank you, but I remember how to undress. If you'll help me into the bedroom, I'll do the rest."

He did so, kissed her good night, and left her to it.

15

STONE WAS WORKING as lunchtime approached, when Joan rang. "Herbie Fisher on one."

"Good morning, Herb."

"And to you, and thanks so much for the referral."

"What referral?"

"Cilla Scott."

"Oh, she's called you already?"

"She's seen me. She just left."

"You're taking her on, then?"

"I certainly am. She's the ideal client—organized, prepared, and, most important, dispassionate. She wheeled in years of tax returns, financial statements, and annual reports for his hedge fund, along with her prenup. She's given me enough to put her husband into a homeless shelter, but she's instructed me to bend over backward to be fair to him. If I were being divorced, I'd love to have an ex-wife like that. How'd you come across her?"

"She fell into my lap. Who's representing her husband?"

"Terry Barnes, at Barnes & Wood. I'm expecting his call. He and Donald Trask are old fraternity brothers from Cornell. I'm guessing Trask will listen to him."

"That could be good or bad."

"No, Barnes will just want to be shed of all this, and he'll know how to give it to Trask straight and make him take it."

"Sounds like the ideal opponent."

"Just an honest one, which is what Trask needs to get him through this with some of his ego intact. The guy's been sucking at her family teat for the past eight years, and he should understand that it's over."

"Well, if anybody can explain it to him, Herb, it's you."

"Yeah, I'm putting on my Dutch uncle mask as we speak. Hang on."

Stone was put on hold for about a minute, then Herb came back.

"Terry Barnes is on the way over here. Things are moving fast and smooth."

"Do I have to remind you that where divorce is concerned, 'fast and smooth' are an illusion?"

"Hope springs eternal. I gotta go make some notes for this meeting."

"Keep me posted."

"Cilla has given me permission to do that; she seems to trust you implicitly."

"I'm flattered." He hung up as Joan buzzed again.

"A Ms. Scott on two."

Stone picked up. "Good morning. I hope you're staying off that foot."

"You and Dr. Kevin would be proud of me," she said. "I've

got myself a little cart to rest my knee on, and I scoot around like that. The concierge has furnished me with a minion to carry my purse and drag my wheelie around with all my documents. I left them all with your Herb Fisher."

"I heard. What do you think of him?"

"I think he's ideal."

"He said pretty much the same about you."

"I'm seeing my father's financial advisors, then having a quick lunch with your friend Margot, to hear about the real estate market, and then we're going apartment hunting."

"You move at the speed of light."

"Every step I take is one away from the marriage, and that's what I want most right now. Here's Margot, gotta run." She hung up.

Joan buzzed again. "A Mr. Trask to see you. He doesn't have an appointment."

"Who Trask?"

"Donald."

"Well, shit, send him in, I guess." Stone stood up to greet a very large man in a well-cut suit. Six-four and two-twenty, Stone guessed. Works out daily.

"Mr. Trask?" He extended a hand.

Trask shook it perfunctorily and accepted an offered chair.

"What can I do for you?" Stone asked, not very invitingly.

"You can stay away from my wife for a start," Trask said truculently. "I know you're behind all of this."

"All of what?"

"This divorce thing. You two have been planning it, haven't you?"

"Mr. Trask, please listen carefully, and remember what

I'm saying because I don't want to repeat myself. I met your wife less than twenty-four hours ago, entirely by accident, when she sprained an ankle in a shop I was visiting. I got her back to her hotel and arranged for a doctor to come and see her. When I told her I practiced law, she asked me to recommend a divorce attorney. I did so and, I might add, without regret. That is the sum total of her relationship with me. Do you understand?"

Trask glared at him, tapping a foot. Stone thought it probable that the man was accustomed to ending talks like this with his fists.

"Is that the truth?"

Stone nodded slowly. "Now, if there's nothing else, please excuse me. I have work to do." That last part was a lie, but Stone thought it sounded good.

"I expect you'll hear from me," Trask said, getting to his feet.

"We won't be speaking again," Stone said. "Your wife is represented by Herbert Fisher of Woodman & Weld. Your attorney can put you in touch with him, should you have any further questions." He stood and watched the man leave, then sat back down just as Joan came in.

"You all right?"

"I haven't been beaten to a pulp, if that's what you mean."

"I had a bad feeling," she said. That's when he realized she was holding her .45 behind her back.

"I don't think he'll be back," Stone said. "In any case, there shouldn't be any occasion for drawing weapons."

"What do you mean? Everybody in this house is carrying, including you."

"Well, yes, but that's another matter entirely. Mr. Trask is not a suspect in the case."

"Who is he?"

"An ex-husband-to-be."

"Oh, shit," she said. "The worst kind."

"He was operating on incomplete information," Stone said. "I augmented his education on the subject, so please decline any further calls or requests for meetings from him, and don't hesitate to call the police if he becomes persistent."

"I can't just shoot him?" Joan asked, half joking.

"Maybe later," Stone said, and she went back to her desk.

Stone took some deep breaths and went back to what he hadn't been doing.

16

STONE, on a hunch, called Dino.

"Bacchetti."

"Hi, will you run a name for me?"

"I'm sorry, you seem to have misdialed the number and been connected to our 'Services Not Available to Civilians Department.'"

"His name is Donald Trask of Greenwich, Connecticut. He also keeps a residence at the Carlyle. He runs a hedge fund."

Stone could hear the tapping of keys.

"I don't have time to read or explain this to you, so I'll e-mail it," Dino said, then hung up.

Stone waited a couple of minutes, found the e-mail, and printed it.

Donald Tyrone Trask had a record of scrapes, some of them violent, going back to college. He had done ten days in the local jail for beating up another student at a fraternity party, and he had had altercations with denizens of Greenwich, all of whom seemed to be service providers or blue-collar workers. Apparently, Donald Trask dirtied his hands only with those he thought to be his social inferiors, who might be less likely to sue or spread gossip among his peers. There was also a juvenile record, which was sealed, and Stone presumed it contained more of the same.

Stone called Cilla Scott's cell phone.

"Hey, there."

"Got a second?"

"Sure."

"Forgive me for prying, but I have a good reason."

"Pry away."

"During your marriage did Donald ever strike or otherwise physically abuse you?"

"You've met Donald, haven't you?" she asked after a pause.

"He called on me this morning. I made assumptions."

She was silent again. "On a couple of occasions he slapped me around. Once he sent me to the ER."

"What, if anything, did you do about it."

"I took a full swing at his jaw with a fireplace poker," she said. "It never happened again. He didn't like having his jaw wired shut."

That's my girl, Stone thought. "Did you mention this to Herb Fisher?"

"No, because I don't want him to use it, if this should go to trial."

"It's important that you tell him about it. You can discuss later how or if the information should be used."

"All right, I'll do that. Or, better yet, it would save me some pain if you told him."

"All right, and I'm sorry to cause you pain. Tell me, is your knee scooter restaurant-certified?"

"It is a fully certified knee scooter."

"Then have dinner with me this evening."

"I have a drinks date, but I'll meet you after that. Where and when?"

"Patroon, one-sixty East Forty-sixth Street, seven-thirty?"

"Poltroon?"

"No, *Patroon*. It's a Dutch title for a landowner. A *poltroon* is a spineless coward."

"I'll try to remember the difference. See you then."

Stone called Herb.

"Yeah?"

"Cilla Scott asked me to convey to you that Donald Trask has a history of beating her up, sending her to the ER on one occasion. It ended when she broke his jaw with a poker."

"Good to know," Herb replied.

"She will want that information used only in extremis, and with her expressed permission."

"Gotcha."

"I also caught a glimpse of Donald Trask's criminal record."

"Tell me."

"History of fighting, going back to college, maybe further; his juvie record was sealed."

"Did he win his fights?"

"I expect so. He chose people he thought were his inferiors, who were not likely to fight back."

"Good to know."

"See ya." Stone hung up.

———

HERB FISHER HUNG UP; his secretary buzzed him. "Terry Barnes to see you."

"Send him in," Herb said, arranging Cilla's documents in neat piles before him.

Barnes bustled in and tried to inject some bonhomie into the occasion. "Morning, Fisher," he said. "Good to see you again. How's the wife?"

Herb rose and shook his hand. "We've never met, Mr. Barnes, and I'm unmarried."

"Oh, ah, my fault. Mistaken identity." He took a seat. "I'm here in the matter of Trask v. Trask," he said.

"Actually, it's Scott v. Trask since Ms. Scott retained her maiden name at marriage."

"As you say. Only met the lady a few times."

"Tell me," Herb said, "are we going to settle this like gentlemen or go to trial?"

"Oh?" Barnes chuckled. "Have you met my client?"

"No."

"Well, if you had met him you'd know that he's a rather combative sort, more inclined to fight than to argue."

"And I understand he has a criminal record to support that position."

"Oh, that thing back at Cornell, you mean?"

"Before, during, and since," Herb said. "Your client and old friend is a nasty piece of work. I'd love nothing more than to depose him for a couple of hours, then examine him in court. He could go directly from the courthouse to the Y, where he would be living, subsequent to the ruling in my client's favor."

"You sound very confident, Herbert."

"That's only because I am confident. Your client, since his marriage to Ms. Scott, has not earned a dime that is not directly attributable to her father, her friends, or his wife's personal funds. His hedge fund is still in business only because of the record upturn in the market the past few months. He would fare poorly in the matter of New York State law requiring equitable division on property."

"What are you proposing?" Barnes asked.

Herb slid a single typed sheet of paper across the desk. "I think that, on reflection, you will find this offer to be much more generous than necessary," he said, "and it will not improve. Your problem is going to be to lead your client to face the reality of his situation. If he does, he can leave the marriage with some money, enough to maintain him in some sort of style. That's if he closes his hedge fund, of course."

"Why should he close it? It's profitable."

"When the investors learn of the divorce they will depart in droves," Herb said. "He would save face by just shutting it down."

Barnes reread the list to gain time. "I'll speak to him," he said.

"Remember, there will be no improvement in the offer, nor will there be in his reputation should we go to trial."

"I'll speak to him." Barnes got up and left without shaking hands.

17

S TONE WAS ABOUT TO WRAP up his day, a little late, when his phone rang. Joan had already left her desk.

"Hello?"

"Is this Barrington?"

"It is."

"This is Donald Trask."

"I've no wish to speak to you," Stone said.

"You can speak to me, or I'll come over there," Trask said. "You wrote this document, didn't you?"

"Document?"

"My wife's demands."

"I do not represent your wife; I have not written or seen any document prepared for her; call Herbert Fisher at Woodman & Weld."

"Tell you what," Trask said, "you know the New York Athletic Club on Central Park South?"

"I do."

"Are you a member there?"

"I am not."

"Well, I am, and that's good enough for both of us."

"Mr. Trask, what are you talking about?"

"I'm suggesting that you and I meet there in an hour."

"I've no wish to drink or dine with you."

"They have a very nice boxing ring upstairs. I suggest we meet and settle the matter of the divorce terms mano a mano in the ring."

"Mr. Trask, I can suggest one of two options," Stone said. "First, seek professional help, which you are clearly in need of. Second, go to the New York Athletic Club gym, find a heavy bag, and punch it until you can't stand up anymore. Either of those options will keep you out of jail. Now, don't bother me again." Stone hung up. He thought a moment, then called Herb Fisher.

"Herb Fisher."

"It's Stone."

"Why do you sound exasperated?"

"Because I am exasperated."

"All right, tell me. Cry your heart out."

"I've just heard from Donald Trask, who persists in believing that I, not you, represent his wife in her divorce action."

"Hey, that's okay with me," Herb said. "I don't want him on my back."

"Well, that's where he's going to be, if I have to hit him over the head and deliver him to you personally."

"How kind you are!"

"I'm just letting you know that I think the man is unhinged and, as we know, prone to violence. He's been set off by a document containing his wife's demands that you apparently handed to his attorney, and eventually, after he's been told a few more times, he's going to finally get the idea that he should be dealing with you and not me."

"I suppose he will, after Terry Barnes explains it all to him."

"Have you met Donald Trask?"

"I have not."

"Well, physically, he makes one and a half of you, and you don't want to let him back you into a corner."

"Thank you. I will avoid corners until further notice."

"Have you heard back from Terry Barnes?"

"I have not."

"Well, I don't think you're going to—not today, anyway. I suspect that Mr. Barnes is in a dark bar somewhere, nursing loosened teeth, broken ribs, and a triple scotch."

"What do you advise?" Herb asked.

"Armed guards," Stone said, then hung up. He rang Fred on the house intercom.

"Yes, sir?"

"Fred, we have an imminent threat somewhere, possibly circling the neighborhood."

"Of what nature, sir?"

"Name of Donald Trask: tall, heavyset, in excellent condition for a man of his age, enjoys inflicting pain on those who annoy him."

"Have you annoyed him, sir?"

"Without even trying."

"Then I'll take a turn around the block, sir, and see if I can spot him."

"Be careful, Fred. Don't let him get a punch in."

"He'll be expecting you, not me, sir."

"A good point. Be careful."

Stone hung up and called Dino.

"And what service may the NYPD render to you this fine day?" Dino asked.

"I believe you employ people who are schooled in the art of removing dangerous characters from the street and housing them elsewhere."

"We've been known to do that."

"Well, there's one around my house somewhere: to wit, one Donald Trask, six-four, two-twenty, good shape, mean."

"Has he threatened you?"

"He has formed the opinion that I am representing his wife in a divorce action against him."

"Are you?"

"I am not. Herbie Fisher is, but I have not learned enough of the man's language to convince him of that. He invited me into the ring at the New York Athletic Club to settle the matter of his divorce."

Dino laughed heartily. "I'd pay for a ringside seat to that! Are you taking him up on it?"

"Are you insane?"

"Well, I don't think an invitation to a boxing match at a gentlemen's club constitutes a threat of actual violence, so I can't yank him off the street. You're lawyer enough to know that. Call me from the ER after he's found you, and I'll see what we can do."

"With friends like you, who needs assassins?"

"All right, all right, I'll get a couple of guys to brace him and tell him he'd be happier in a bar somewhere, getting unconscious."

"I think he may have already spent considerable time in that effort, and you should tell your guys to be careful with him, he's dangerous. Tell them to keep their Tasers at the ready."

"Yeah, I'll do that." Dino hung up.

FRED LEFT THE HOUSE by the front door, pausing to select a golf umbrella with a thick, heavy briar handle from the stand in the hallway. As he descended the front stairs he unbuttoned his jacket and transferred the umbrella to his left hand, leaving his right free for other action. He walked down the street to the corner of Second Avenue, stopped, and looked around. On the corner opposite him, looking thoughtful, was a man answering the description Stone had provided. Fred crossed the street.

The man looked up, saw Fred coming, and clearly dismissed him as a threat.

"Mr. Trask?" Fred asked. "Mr. Donald Trask?"

Trask looked down at him and shifted his weight, as if to be ready. "Yeah, what?"

Fred took hold of the golf umbrella with both hands and swung it at the load-bearing knee.

Trask made a loud noise and collapsed in a heap.

"Have a nice day," Fred said, "but do it in another neighborhood." He walked away, back toward the house.

STONE'S DIRECT LINE RANG. "Stone Barrington."

"It's Dino. My guys located your guy on the corner of Second Avenue, lying in a heap, clutching a knee."

"What happened to him?"

"He said he was attacked by a midget with an umbrella."

Not far wrong, Stone thought, given the disparity between Fred's size and Trask's.

"They got him into a cab and sent him home," Dino said. "Happy?"

"Happy," Stone replied.

"Dinner?"

"Sorry, otherwise engaged." They both hung up.

18

STONE GOT TO HIS FEET at Patroon, but Ken Aretsky, the owner, was already assisting Cilla Scott down a step or two and restoring her knee scooter to its proper place. He waved to give her a target.

She made it with a few deft pushes of her other foot.

"You look as though you were born on that thing," Stone said, helping her to be seated.

"It feels like that long," she replied. "I'm going to try tippy-toe tomorrow."

"Don't rush it," Stone advised, "you could screw up things and make them worse."

"Do they sell alcoholic beverages in this restaurant?" she asked.

"My apologies. What would you like?"

"A very dry Belvedere vodka martini, olives."

The beverage was rushed to her.

"Two-legged days," she said, raising her glass.

"I'll drink to that, but you're supposed to wait four days before you try."

"Oh, all right, I'll wait until day after tomorrow."

"I had occasion to be introduced to your husband today," he said.

She looked surprised. "Where?"

"In my office."

"He doesn't even know your name," she said. "At least, not from me."

"Then he has a spy in your camp."

"What ensued?"

"I explained to him that Herb Fisher, not I, represents you. He seemed unable to make that leap. Perhaps you could tell him that?"

"I already have. Herb had his first meeting with Donald's attorney today. I'm told it went well."

"Then nobody told Donald. He's very upset about the deal offered him."

"Herb says my offer is more than a court would give him. I hope Terry Barnes can make him understand that."

"His judgment was probably impaired by alcohol. He called later in the day and offered to arrange a boxing match at the Athletic Club, in which he and I would duke out a settlement."

She placed her face in her hands. "That is so embarrassing," she said. "Please accept my apology."

"You've nothing for which to apologize. He was hanging out near my house, so Fred went out and had a word with him."

"Your Fred? That darling little man?"

"That darling little man reduced Donald to a quivering heap with a single blow from an umbrella," Stone said. "Two passing police officers got him into a cab and sent him home, wherever that is."

"The Athletic Club," she said. "He's taken a room there. I hope he'll take the opportunity to sober up."

"Is he an alcoholic?"

"Borderline, maybe. I'm not sure. He drinks to excess when angry or unhappy."

"That must be most of the time these days," Stone observed. "Still, I suppose he must have his charms or you wouldn't have married him."

"He used to, really he did. Strangely enough, the success of his fund in a rising market seemed to depress him. I suppose he realized that it was Daddy's money, and mine, he was riding on."

"The realization of one's inadequacies can be a trigger for depression, I suppose."

"Are you speaking from experience?" she asked.

"Inadequacies? Me? I assure you, I am a perfectly adequate person, if imperfect. On rare occasions, I can even rise above adequacy."

"Good to know," she said, taking a gulp of her martini. "God, that's good."

"Tell me," Stone said, "what's your game plan?"

"For how far ahead?"

"The next few months, say."

"One: get divorced. Two: get housed. Three: decorate housing. I haven't gotten much further than that."

"Those seem reasonable short-term goals."

"I've never really had long-term goals; I pretty much just wait for long-term to happen, then deal with it."

"Okay, let's see if you can look further ahead. Describe what you would like your circumstances to be a year from now."

"My circumstances? Still rich—richer, in fact, when I combine Daddy's estate with Mother's, which has been my only money, so far, exceeding any real need, except supporting Donald. Daddy liked it that way, because he could hang on to every dime of his own until the end. In fact, it wouldn't surprise me to learn that he'd found a way to wire-transfer it all ahead."

Stone laughed. "So he didn't coddle you?"

"Oh, he did, from time to time, but I've always been very good at coddling myself without the help of others. Are you rich?"

Stone managed not to choke on his bourbon. "Yes, fairly."

"The reason I ask is: If I'm going to end up supporting you, I'd rather know about it now than wait to find out. All I know about you is that you drive a Bentley—rented? borrowed?—that you are acquainted with a doctor, a divorce attorney, and a Realtor, and that you are known to the management of this restaurant. The rest is a blank slate."

"I own the Bentley, and please don't concern yourself: There are no conceivable circumstances under which you might ever have to support me."

"You understand my concern?"

"Yes, but what does your intuition tell you?"

"My intuition lies to me all the time. Who are you?"

"I believe it's the custom in this country to get to know people by talking to them, not by inquisition. If that's not sufficient, you can hire a private detective and have me investigated, which is probably what your father would have done in the circumstances. For the moment, however, all you need to know is what's on the menu."

She looked at the menu. "Caesar salad, strip steak medium rare." She put it down. "Where do you live?"

"A ten-minute walk from here, Turtle Bay."

"Ah, yes, you did mention that."

"I did."

"In which house?"

"I own two houses there, one for staff."

"Are those the only houses you own?"

"No, I also own houses in Los Angeles, Paris, London, Key West, and the South of England, with appropriate furnishings in each. I also own a jet airplane, a small yacht, and a partnership in a larger one. I don't think you'll ever be called upon to give me anything more boisterous than a necktie at Christmas, which I will return and exchange for one I like."

She threw up her hands in surrender. "Forgive me, that was a shitty thing to say to you. I suppose my wounds haven't healed yet from my last and only experience with a long-term relationship."

"How long have you been married?"

"Nearly eight years."

"It sounds like long enough."

"More than long enough," she replied. "I should have dumped him halfway through. Are you now or have you ever been married?"

"I was married."

"Ended in divorce?"

"Ended in death, hers."

"Again, it's my turn to apologize."

"It was a perfectly straightforward question."

"Why do you have so many houses?"

"Because I can. Anyway, I've always loved houses, and there came a time when I figured out that if I saw one I liked, I could buy it, just write a check. I'm trying to stop, but I can't make any promises."

"Promise me nothing," she said, "and I'll never be disappointed."

19

THEY WERE HALFWAY through their steaks.

"Do you have any children?" she asked.

"One, a son, Peter. He's a film director in L.A."

"Peter Barrington?"

"That's right."

"I have actually seen his work, and it's good."

"I'll tell him you said so."

"I'd like to tell him myself," she said.

"Well, if you someday decide that I meet your standards for male company, that might happen."

"I haven't told you what my standards are."

"I was guessing. All right, what are they?"

"Self-supporting, usually sober, intelligent, kind, and good company."

"Those sound like all the qualities not possessed by your current husband."

"A coincidence, but it's a start. What are your standards?"

"Pretty much the same as yours," he replied. "Oh, and two working legs. I insist on that."

She laughed. "All right, I know enough about you not to be paranoid anymore."

"Is paranoia your usual condition?"

"Only in dealing with men, and as I said, I'm over that now."

"What a relief. There's a Key lime pie in the fridge at home. Would you like to have a nightcap at my house?"

"I'd love that," she said.

Stone paid the bill, and they got into the Bentley. "Home, Fred," he said, "and pull into the garage, so we can take the elevator."

Fred did so, and Stone and Cilla got out at the living room level and made their way across it to Stone's study. He poured them each a cognac, found the pie in the fridge, and sliced it.

"Heavenly," Cilla said, taking a big bite. "This is a lovely house."

"Thank you. I inherited it from a great-aunt, my grand-mother's sister, who thought I'd never amount to anything, so I should at least have a roof over my head. All the wood-work and much of the furniture was built by my father, who was a designer and cabinetmaker."

"A house with a heritage," she said. "I like that."

"I like it, too, and the staff lives next door."

"Why do you have a staff house?"

"The house next door came up for sale, and it's hard for working people to find affordable housing in this city, so I just moved them all in. Also, the purchase doubled the size of the garage."

"I saw another car under a tarp down there."

"That's a French sports car, a Blaise, designed by a friend of mine. I don't drive it very often; it's more convenient to have Fred drive the Bentley."

"Don't be surprised if you get a rock through a front window. That will be Donald's next move."

"The glass is armored, so it won't be a problem. Tell me, does Donald own a gun?"

"Several."

"I was afraid you'd say that. When he sobers up, is he going to come to his senses?"

"I wouldn't count on it," she said. "Are you unaccustomed to women with baggage?"

"Most people have baggage of one sort or another, and with women, it usually seems to be a disagreeable and unmanageable male former companion."

"*Unmanageable* is a good word to describe Donald," she said. "God knows, I tried hard enough, and the most it got me was a sock in the kisser."

"If you have any concerns at all about your safety, I can arrange for someone to watch over you."

"Like the Gershwin song?"

"Not quite. He'll be about Donald's size with a bulge under his arm."

"I think I'm all right for the moment; I'm sure his attorney has instructed him on behaving during trial."

"Do you think he'll go to trial?"

"Maybe, he's very competitive."

"If I may ask, what sort of deal did you and Herb offer him on the real estate?"

"Sell it and divide the proceeds."

"It might help you to avoid trial if you use some of your newfound wealth to just buy his half of the house and the Carlyle apartment. That would put some cash in his pocket almost immediately, which I'm sure he'd like. And there'd be less to argue about in court."

"I'm sure he'd like that, too," she said. "It's a damned good idea. How do we reach agreement on the value of the two properties?"

"Each of you hires your own appraiser, and the two of them pick a third. You take the average of the three appraisals."

"Brilliant!"

"Herb would have thought of it in the second round of negotiations. Wait and see if he doesn't bring it up."

"All right."

"How did you and Margot get on?"

"Blazingly! I forgot to tell you, she showed me three apartments, and I loved two of them. I'm leaning toward the one on Fifth Avenue in the Sixties."

"You can't go wrong there. Put down a deposit, but don't close until after the divorce is final. Another property in the mix might muddy the waters and slow things down."

"Where were you when I was making all the big decisions in my life, like whether to marry Donald?"

"Probably about that time I was a police officer."

"You? A cop?"

"A detective, thank you very much. I was invalided out—a bullet in the knee."

"Then how did you get to be a lawyer?"

"I had already graduated from NYU Law School when I

joined the force, so I just needed to pass the bar exam. I took a two-week cram course and passed, and an old classmate brought me into Woodman & Weld."

"My goodness."

"See how much you learn when you just talk to people?"

"You're absolutely right," she admitted. "And anyway, you're fun to talk to."

"Thank you."

"I'm sorry about my baggage," she said.

"Don't worry about it."

"I hope he doesn't make a further nuisance of himself."

"I hope so, too," Stone said.

HE PUT HER in the Bentley and Fred drove her back to the Carlyle.

20

S TONE WAS SEEING CILLA off when he saw Faith walking past and up the front steps next door. He walked
through the door to the next house.

"Oh!" she said, stepping back. "You frightened me."

"Apparently nothing else does," Stone said. "Forgive me
for sounding like a father, but where have you been?"

"I left a few things at the hotel, and since it was such a nice
evening, I walked over there to retrieve them." She held up a
shopping bag as if it explained everything.

"Come with me," he said, holding the door for her. "Let's
have a drink."

He settled her in the study with a cognac and took a seat.
"Have you forgotten that we're in the middle of a wave of
murders with victims who look just like you and who live in,
roughly, the same neighborhood as that hotel?"

"Well, it seems to me that we're not in the middle of this
wave, but at the end. Nobody's been killed for a week."

"And you took that as a reason to take a stroll in a dangerous place?"

"Pretty much, I guess."

"Faith, you can't just do that."

"I'm a grown woman, I can do whatever I like."

"Not if you want to continue working for me."

"Are you threatening to fire me if I don't do as you say?"

"I'm threatening to fire you if you continue to risk your life by doing foolish things. I've no wish to have to ship your body back to your people in Georgia in a box, and I won't be a party to your murder. Do you understand me?"

She pouted, but said nothing.

"All right, tomorrow morning start looking for another place to live. I'll give you two weeks to move out, and your salary will continue until then."

Faith produced the ultimate feminine weapon, for which males have no defense: she began to cry.

"Oh, come on! You said you're an adult, start behaving like one. This isn't junior high."

"I don't want to lose my job," she said.

"You'll lose it instantly if you're dead. Has anyone told you what these killers do to the women?"

"I read the newspapers," she said.

"Well, sometimes there are things the police don't tell the press. Would you like for me to describe, in detail, what they're leaving out?"

"No!" she said. "Spare me."

Stone knocked off the rest of his cognac and set down his glass. "Come see me tomorrow morning and tell me what you want to do," he said. "Now, if you'll excuse me, I'm going to bed. Finish your drink here, if you like." He went upstairs, undressed, brushed his teeth, and got into bed. He was still angry with her, and it took him a while to get to sleep.

THE FOLLOWING MORNING, Stone made a call to Mike Freeman at Strategic Services and placed an order. The order arrived about an hour later and took a seat outside Joan's office.

Faith knocked and entered his office. "I've thought it over," she said, "and you're right. It was foolish of me to do that last night, and I don't want to lose my job, so I'll follow your orders on this until they catch these people."

"That's good," Stone said. "Now, I have a gift for you." He buzzed Joan. "Send in the gift."

A large man in a dark suit with a bulge under his arm walked into the office.

"Faith, this is Jimbo. He is going to be your constant companion whenever you leave the house, unless we're out of town, and until the killers are caught."

Faith was speechless. "You got me a minder?"

"That's a good way to describe Jimbo," Stone said. "He's your minder during the day. A woman named Sylvia will be on the night shift."

"That's outrageous."

"You're not required to continue to work here, but if you decide you want to, then Jimbo is part of the deal. I've known him a few years, and he's a nice guy. You'll get used to him. You might even begin to appreciate him. Jimbo, will you please see Faith to her office?"

"Certainly, Mr. Barrington," Jimbo replied. "Faith, right this way, please."

She stalked out of the room, followed by the faithful Jimbo.

Joan buzzed him. "Dino, on one."

Stone pressed the button. "Good morning."

"If you say so," Dino said grumpily.

"What's up today?"

"I thought you'd like to know. Yesterday, after my two guys put what's-his-name—?"

"Donald Trask?"

"Yeah, after they put him into a cab, they followed him to see if he went home. He didn't. He went down to the Lower East Side, where there's a gun shop used by a lot of cops, and tried to buy a gun."

"I know the place. He can't buy a gun in Manhattan without a New York City carry permit."

"He bought a gun."

"He has a carry permit?"

"He does, and before you ask, he hasn't done anything that would make it possible for me to have it canceled."

"He got drunk and tried to lure me into a fight."

"He got drunk, maybe, but I keep telling you, all he did was invite you to participate in a sporting event, which is not even a misdemeanor, let alone a felony."

"What did he buy?"

"A Beretta nine millimeter, the small one, and an over-the-belt holster—oh, and couple of spare magazines and a box of ammo."

"What kind of ammo?"

"Federal Personal Defense, the hollow points."

"So he's serious, you think?"

"I don't know," Dino said, "but if I were you, I'd behave as if he were serious."

"Where did he go from there?"

"To the New York Athletic Club."

"That's where he's staying."

"I wonder what their rules are about firearms on the premises?" Dino said.

"I don't know," Stone said, "but we could find out if one of your guys would call the club secretary and tell them there's an armed member in one of their rooms."

"I think you should perform that task yourself," Dino said.

"I would," Stone replied, "but I want to be able to deny having done it."

"Figures," Dino said.

21

STONE THOUGHT ABOUT the dangers of having an armed Donald Trask loose in the city and what should be done about it. He put aside thoughts of his own safety and called Cilla Scott.

"Hello?"

"It's Stone, where are you?"

"In the rear seat of a black town car I've hired for the day, on the way to see Herb Fisher."

"Good. Do you have a will?"

"Yes."

"Who are the beneficiaries?"

"My father, a couple of charities, and Donald. Why do you ask?"

"When you arrive at Herb's office I want you to ask him to draw up a new will for you."

"Why?"

"Your father is dead, and I presume you don't want your

personal fortune to fall into Donald's hands in the event of your death."

"A good point."

"Don't leave Herb's office until the will is properly witnessed and signed."

"What's the rush?"

"Your position will be precarious until you have a new will."

She was silent for a moment. "You don't mean . . ."

"I mean that yesterday, after his encounter with Fred, Donald went to a gun shop downtown and bought a pistol, a holster, and ammunition."

"And you think . . ."

"At this moment Donald is the only person who stands to benefit from your demise."

"Oh, my God," she breathed.

"If you'll do as I ask, I'll give you dinner here this evening."

"How can I resist that. I promise I'll sign a new will."

"Keep your car and have it deliver you here. Call, and I'll open the garage door. Also, bring an overnight bag with a few things. I think it would be best if you stay here for a few nights."

"Well, that's subtle," she said.

"You may have your choice of six guest bedrooms, each with a lock on the door."

"And why do you think this is a good idea?"

"Does Donald have a key to the Carlyle apartment?"

"Oh. I'd be happy to accept your hospitality."

"One other thing. Ask Herb to let Donald's attorney know that you've signed a new will excluding him."

"I will. What time tonight?"

"Six?"

"See you then." She hung up.

HERB FISHER RECEIVED CILLA SCOTT and noted the absence of the knee scooter and the presence of a cane. He got her to a chair. "Are you sure you're ready for hobbling?"

"I spoke with my doctor and got his permission. The Carlyle supplied the cane."

Herb sat down. "I've heard from Donald's attorney. Donald is okay with the deal, but he wants ten million dollars."

"Ha!" Cilla replied.

"It's pretty much what I expected. I have a counteroffer in mind."

"And what is that?"

"You are cash-rich at the moment, are you not, what with your inheritance from your father?"

"I am."

"Offer to buy his share of both properties from him, in cash, immediately."

"That's clever," she said. "What should I pay him?"

"What do you think the properties are worth?"

"The Greenwich estate would probably go for ten million in today's market—there's a lot of land. The Carlyle apartment would probably go for four million. Those valuations are from my Realtor."

"So, we'll offer him seven million dollars for both properties?"

"That's good for me. I'll keep the Greenwich house and sell the apartment. I've already started looking for one."

"All right. Shall I call Terry now?"

"First, there's another matter," she said.

"Shoot."

"My will is among the documents I gave you at our first meeting."

"I saw it, but I haven't read it."

"The beneficiaries are a couple of charities, my father—who's now dead—and Donald. I don't want my death to be an advantage to Donald, and I want him to know I've changed the will."

Herb produced a legal pad. "Who would you like the beneficiaries to be?"

"For the moment, just the two charities, and I'd like to sign it before I leave here today."

Herb pressed a button on his phone. "Come in here, please."

Herb found the will and, momentarily, a young man appeared. "This is Devon, one of our associates; Devon, Ms. Scott." He handed him the will. "Ms. Scott needs a new will immediately, with the charities shown in the current will as beneficiaries. Eliminate the two other parties, print out a new will on our boilerplate, and bring it to me soonest."

"Ten minutes," Devon said, disappearing with the will.

"What sort of apartment are you looking at?" Herb asked.

"Three bedrooms en suite, living room, dining room, large kitchen, library, office, two maids' rooms, on Fifth Avenue, twelfth floor, terrace, park views, parking, twelve millionish."

"Sounds nice. Have you made an offer?"

"Probably today."

"Give them a six-million-dollar deposit, but insist that the closing must be after the divorce is final, so it won't get into the mix."

"All right."

"Are we ready to call Terry?"

"I am."

"If he doesn't bite immediately, can I sweeten the pot by another million dollars?"

"I'd do that to be rid of him immediately."

Herb made the call.

"Good morning, Herb."

"Good morning, Terry. I have a revised offer for you."

"Ready to copy."

"The offer is the same, but Ms. Scott will buy his share of both properties for seven million dollars cash, payable on final decree."

"That's interesting. Can you hold?"

"Sure." Herb turned to Cilla. "I think Donald is in his office now."

Terry came back. "Ten million dollars and we have a deal."

"Eight million, and that's our absolute, final offer—or we go to trial. Tell him for me, he's not going to enjoy it."

"Hold on." Terry was gone for a good three minutes before he came back. "You have a deal."

"I'll send the documents over to you within the hour," Herb said, "and I'll expect them to be returned, signed, today."

"And a down payment?"

"All of it at final decree. Lean on one of your judges, Terry, and we can wrap this up quickly. Oh, and let Mr. Trask know that Ms. Scott has signed a new will that excludes him."

"I'll tell him, and I'll see what I can do about a judge." Both men hung up.

"Okay," Herb said, "now we see if Donald signs."

"Do you think there's a chance he won't?"

"I doubt it, but I want to see ink on paper before I'm satisfied."

Devon knocked on the door and came in with the new will and three secretaries as witnesses. Cilla signed, and they were done.

Herb dictated the terms of the property settlement and sent Devon to print it.

"Are we done?" Cilla asked.

"Wait until we have a copy of the settlement for you to sign."

She waited, the copy came, and she signed it. "If you'll excuse me," she said, "I'm going to go take another look at that apartment."

"Margot will have the documents you'll need to sign. You should let your bank know you'll be writing a big check."

"Will do." Cilla hobbled out of Herb's office.

Herb handed the settlement agreement to Devon. "Hand deliver this to Terry Barnes's office, wait for it to be signed, and bring it back. Here's a copy with Ms. Scott's signature. When you're sure that Trask has properly executed his copy, hand him this one."

"I'm on it," Devon said, departing at a trot.

CILLA WAS PACKING A BAG at the Carlyle when the phone rang. "Yes?"

"It's Herb Fisher. I wanted you to know that we've received the property settlement with Donald's signature on it, and we've given his attorney the copy with yours. All is now in order."

"Oh, Herb," she breathed. "Thank you so much."

"Terry is looking for a family court judge who will give us a quick final decree, so this could be over soon."

She hung up and headed for Stone's house with a light heart.

22

STONE GOT THE CALL from Cilla and told her to take the elevator to the top floor, then he pressed the button on his iPhone that opened the garage door. It would close automatically when her car left.

He was standing next to the elevator when the door opened and took her bag.

"Where would you like to sleep?" he asked, kissing her.

"Wherever you're sleeping," she replied.

He walked her down the hall and put her bag in the second dressing room. "Unpack, freshen up, then come down to the study for drinks. Dinner is at seven."

STONE WENT DOWN to the study and called Fred on the house phone.

"Yes, sir?"

"Fred, I'd like you to have a look around the neighborhood again for our previous visitor."

"Yes, sir."

"If you find him, don't approach. He knows what you look like now, and he will be armed. Just come back here, and we'll let the police deal with him."

"Yes, sir."

Stone called Jimbo on his cell phone.

"Yes, sir?"

"Where are you, Jimbo?"

"In her sitting room, watching TV."

"Is she down for the night?"

"Hard to say. She's impulsive."

"Tell me about it."

"Sylvia comes on at ten. I'll be right here until then."

"If she doesn't want to go out, call Helene in the kitchen, and she'll bring dinner to you."

"Thank you, Mr. Barrington."

STONE LOOKED UP TO FIND Cilla standing in the doorway.

"Knock, knock," she said.

"Come in and have a seat. Martini?"

"Oh, please, yes."

He mixed the drink, handed it to her, and poured himself a Knob Creek.

"Did you have a good day?" he asked.

"I can't remember a better one in about two years. Herb reached a settlement with Donald's attorney, and we've both signed, and I've signed a new will and let him know it. I feel off the hook."

"That's because you are."

"Also, I've found an apartment. Margot is delivering an offer and a very large check as we speak."

"Closing date later?"

"After the final decree, but Herb is optimistic we can get that soon. I'm going to keep the Greenwich house for the time being, and Margot is going to sell the Carlyle apartment for me."

"Well, then, Margot's having a good day, too, isn't she?"

"She is. I can't thank you enough for all your help. A few days ago I couldn't walk; had an out-of-control, estranged husband; and was scared to death. And now . . ."

"I'm glad it's all better."

"Something occurred to me," she said.

"What's that?"

"I've signed a new will, so Donald has no reason to want me dead, but . . ."

"But what?"

"That doesn't mean that Donald feels any better about you. It troubles me that he went out and bought a gun, when he has half a dozen in the safe in Greenwich."

"Sounds rather like he had an immediate reason to do so, doesn't it?"

"It does, so please, please, watch your ass."

Stone laughed. "That's Fred's job," he said, "and he's good at it."

"How did you ever find that dear little man?"

"I didn't. He was sent to me by my French friend Marcel duBois, the same one who designed the Blaise. He gave me a year of Fred's time as a gift. I hired him after a month, then to seal the deal, he and Helene fell madly in love and moved in together."

"How convenient for you."

"Very much so."

A veal roast arrived. Fred served them and poured the wine Stone had chosen.

"So," Stone said, "what are your plans while you're here?"

"If my offer is accepted, I'm going to take a decorator over there and start measuring things, then start placing orders."

"Orders for what?"

"Orders for everything: furniture, beds, kitchenware, china, silverware, everything I need to get established. I have all that in Greenwich, of course, but since I'm keeping the house, I'll need to start afresh." Her cell phone rang. "It's Margot, please excuse me. Hello? Yes, Margot? That's wonderful! Can we gain immediate access? I want to take a decorator over there tomorrow. Let me know, and thank you!" She hung up. "They've accepted my offer, closing date and all."

"Congratulations." Stone's phone rang, and he looked at the caller ID. "It's Herb Fisher," he said, "excuse me. Herb?"

"Stone, can you get a message to Cilla for me?"

"I believe I can do that."

"Write this down."

Stone produced a pen and paper. "Okay."

"Cilla is to be in the chambers of Judge Mabel Watney tomorrow morning at eleven o'clock." He gave Stone the address.

"Okay, what for?"

"The judge is Terry Barnes's sister. She's agreed to issue a final decree, but both Cilla and Trask have to be there to swear that they both accept the property settlement."

"I promise, she'll be there." Stone hung up. "You are a very lucky woman," he said. "Donald's attorney has a sister who is a family court judge. She's going to sign your decree tomorrow morning at eleven, and you have to be there."

"Is that even possible?"

"It's unheard of, but a judge can do what she wants to do."

"I'm stunned. This means I can close immediately on the apartment."

"Let Herb know, and he'll do the legal work. It'll take a few days."

"Can you put up with me for that long?"

"I'll force myself," Stone replied.

23

THEY WERE ON COGNAC when the doorbell rang. Stone picked up the phone. "Yes?"

"It's Dino."

Stone buzzed him in. "You're about to meet my closest friend, Dino Bacchetti."

"Oh, good. Where have I heard that name?"

"He's the police commissioner of New York City. We were detectives together a long time ago."

Dino came into the room. "I didn't know you had a guest," he said.

Stone introduced him to Cilla.

"I don't suppose I can force a drink on you," Stone said.

Dino grabbed a chair. "Just try," he said, accepting a glass of Johnnie Walker Black Label. "Better days," he said.

"Cilla was just saying that they don't get much better than right now. She's getting divorced tomorrow, from Donald Trask."

"Ah, yes," Dino said. "The subject of my visit. And let me be the first to congratulate you, Cilla."

"You are that," Cilla replied, "and thank you. What has Donald done this time?"

"It's good news," Dino said. "When the New York Athletic Club heard about his weapon, they disarmed him and put the gun in their safe."

"He has no access to it?" Stone asked.

"Apparently not unless he moves out."

"Well, that is good news. Fred had a look around the neighborhood but didn't spot him."

"I don't want to throw cold water on good news," Cilla said, "but I should tell you that Donald is a very persistent person. Once he gets the bit between his teeth, he doesn't give up until he has what he wants."

"And is that Stone?" Dino asked.

"He may have been distracted by the news that he's going to get a very large check tomorrow, when he is divorced from me."

"That would divert a fellow's attention," Dino said. "Might it also cool his ardor?"

"Perhaps. His ardor is always cooled when he thinks he has won, and he probably thinks that about the settlement. What he doesn't know is, I was prepared to pay double what I'm paying him, just to be shed of him. So, if I ever want to get his goat, I'll just throw that into the argument."

"Please don't do that," Stone said.

"Don't worry, I'll resist the temptation."

"The City of New York would be grateful for that," Dino

said. "I was afraid we were going to have to arrest him tonight."

"What for?" Cilla asked.

"That's the problem. He has a carry license for the gun, so . . ."

"Hey, wait a minute," Stone said. "As I recall, a carry license lists the authorized weapons and their serial numbers, does it not?"

Dino brightened. "You're right, it does, so unless he had the presence of mind to add his new gun to the list, we've got grounds for canceling his license." Dino picked up his phone and made a call. "It's Bacchetti; I want you to run the carry license for one Donald Trask and tell me if he's added a new weapon, a Beretta, to his authorized list in the past few days. I'll hold." Dino covered the phone. "He's checking. What? No Beretta? Thank you." He hung up. "He hasn't registered it."

"Problem is," Stone said, "he's not carrying it. It's in the safe at the Athletic Club."

"Hoisted on my own petard," Dino said.

"Well, he won't carry it into the courthouse tomorrow morning, but after that, he could check out at any time."

"Jesus, but you're a lot of trouble," Dino said.

"Me? What'd I do?"

"Now I'm going to have to put a man on him, so, if he has a bulge under his coat when he leaves the club, we can bust him."

"How long does he have to register the new weapon?" Stone asked.

"I'm not sure. Three days, maybe."

"I think I can get him to check out of the Athletic Club," Cilla said.

"How are you going to do that?" Stone asked.

"I'll see him in court tomorrow morning, and as soon as we get the decree, I'll tell him I want him out of the Greenwich house by the weekend. He'll have to go up there and pack up his stuff, so he'll check out of the club and sleep in Greenwich, until he leaves the house."

"So," Stone said. "He'll probably check out of the club tomorrow after his court appearance, so Dino's guys can roust him when he's on the way to catch his train."

"That works for me," Dino said, tossing off his drink. "Okay, I'm going home. We'll pick up Mr. Trask's tail when he leaves the courthouse. Which court?"

"Family court, chambers of Judge Watney," Cilla replied.

"Then we'll follow him to the Athletic Club and let nature take its course."

"Cilla," Stone said, "where is he likely to stay after he leaves the Greenwich house?"

"Normally to the Carlyle, but after our hearing he won't have access to that anymore. Margot will be getting it ready to show it."

"So, back to the Athletic Club?"

"Maybe, but there he'll have the inconvenience of checking his gun. Maybe the Yale Club; he's a member there."

"Is there anyone at the Greenwich house you could have call you when he leaves?"

"Yes, the housekeeper, who will be glad to see the back of him."

"Good. Tell her to ask him for a forwarding address and number when he leaves, then call you."

"I can do that," she said. "I'll be speaking to her in due course."

Dino said good night and left.

Cilla finished her cognac, then stretched and yawned. "You can take that as a hint," she said to Stone.

Stone turned out the lights and escorted her upstairs.

He got undressed and into bed, and she went into her dressing room and was there for a half hour. When she came out she was wearing a long negligee.

"Why is it," he said, "that it takes so long for a woman to take her clothes *off*?"

She stood by the bed, slipped the straps off her shoulders, and allowed the negligee to fall to the floor. "I guess I'm just going to have to make that up to you," she said, climbing into bed.

And she did.

24

AT TEN O'CLOCK the following morning, Cilla got into Stone's Bentley, and Fred drove her downtown to the courthouse. They were a few minutes early, so Fred parked near the front steps with the engine idling.

"Fred?"

"Yes, ma'am?"

"Stone told me how you handled my, ah, former husband the other day, and I want to thank you."

"It was my pleasure, ma'am. Please let me know if it needs doing again."

AT TEN MINUTES before the hour, Fred pulled up to the broad front steps and opened the door for her. As she got out, he handed her a card. "I'll be nearby, Ms. Scott," he said. "Please call me when you're on the way downstairs, and I'll pull up right here."

"Thank you, Fred." She walked up the front steps and

found Herb Fisher waiting there, briefcase in hand. They shook hands.

"Donald and his attorney are on their way upstairs to the courtroom," he said. "We'll wait there, until the judge calls us into her chambers."

They went through security, and she drew some comfort from the metal detector. Surely, Donald would not have tried to carry a gun through that. They rode up in the elevator. In the courtroom, Donald and his attorney were sitting in the front row. Herb directed her to a seat a few rows behind them. They sat quietly until a clerk came into the courtroom.

"Scott v. Trask," he called out.

They all stood and were directed into the judge's chambers. She was a small woman, wearing her robe. They were not offered seats but stood before her.

"Your Honor," Terry Barnes said, "these are Ms. Scott and Mr. Trask, and Herbert Fisher for the co-plaintiff." He placed a sheaf of documents on the desk before her. "Both parties have had counsel review the property settlement, and they have both signed. I believe everything is in order. I've printed out a decree, which both counsels have reviewed."

The judge scanned the property settlement and nodded.

Cilla found herself breathing more rapidly. Donald was going to somehow torpedo this, she thought. Perhaps he would produce a weapon and kill them all.

"Are both parties satisfied with the agreement? Ms. Scott?"

"Yes, Your Honor."

"Mr. Trask?"

"Yes, Your Honor."

"Ms. Scott, do you have a financial instrument that will effect settlement?"

"Right here, Your Honor," Herb said. "A cashier's check in the amount of eight million dollars for Mr. Trask, and transfer documents to be signed by him. They already bear Ms. Scott's signature."

Trask signed the transfer documents, and the judge handed him the check, then she signed two copies of the decree and handed them to the lawyers. "If you have nothing else before the court, this matter is adjourned," she said, and everyone filed out of the room.

The attorneys shook hands.

"Donald?" Cilla said.

"Yes?" He seemed surprised to be addressed.

"I have guests coming to Greenwich for the weekend, and I'd be grateful if you would remove your personal effects by five PM on Friday."

"I've already arranged a mover for Friday," Donald replied.

"Then goodbye."

"Goodbye."

They left the courtroom together but took separate elevators down. Cilla called Fred to let him know she was coming.

"Herb, can I give you a lift uptown?" she asked.

"Thanks, but I have a car and driver."

"Oh, by the way, my offer for the apartment was accepted last night, so I'll need you to arrange a closing as soon as possible."

"Have the seller's attorney call me, and I'll get right on it."

"How long should it take?"

"Assuming a clean title, say next Monday, at ten AM?"

"Fine."

"I'll need a cashier's check for the balance on the apartment."

"Here you are," she said, handing it to him. "I'll see you next Monday at ten."

They air-kissed and Cilla got into the Bentley.

"I'm a free woman, Fred," she said.

"My congratulations, miss. Where would you like to go now?"

She gave him the address. "I have a one o'clock appointment there."

THEY MADE IT WITH TIME to spare, and Margot was waiting out front for her. "Here's my check for six million," Cilla said.

"Great. I'll give it to her Realtor. The seller is away for the weekend, so the place is ours." She handed Cilla a set of keys.

"The seller has tagged some pieces of furniture that are for sale; she's downsizing, so she won't need to take a lot of things."

When they were let into the apartment, Cilla's decorator was already there. Margot received the signed contract document and handed the deposit check to the Realtor. "We'll be ready to close next Monday morning at ten AM at my attorney's office." Cilla handed her a card. "Please have your closing attorney call him."

"The place is all yours," the Realtor said. "I'll stay for a few minutes to record which pieces of furniture you wish to purchase."

Cilla went straight to the grand piano at one end of the living room. It was a Steinway Model B, in walnut. She sat down and played for a minute, then checked the tag. "I'll take this," she said to the Realtor. She continued around the apartment with the Realtor and her decorator, taking some things, leaving others. "I'll want the two sofas reupholstered," she said. "And I like the style of the living room and dining room curtains, but I'll want new fabrics."

"I'll get some samples together."

In the kitchen, she was introduced to the middle-aged couple who cared for the place and, after a brief chat about their duties, hired them on the spot, then she continued her tour. When she was done the Realtor added up the prices of the pieces she had chosen, and Cilla wrote a check for them.

IT WAS AFTER FIVE before Fred returned her to Stone's house; she found him in his study and flopped down on the sofa. "What a day! We close next Monday morning, and I've bought enough furniture from the seller to allow me to move in immediately!"

Stone fixed them drinks and sat down beside her. "I haven't heard from Dino yet. His guys are camped out at the Athletic Club."

"I don't care about that anymore," she said. "I'm free of him—signed, sealed, and delivered!"

Stone hoped he would be free of the man, too, and soon.

25

THE TWO DETECTIVES, Sharkey and Paulson, made themselves at home in the commodious lobby of the New York Athletic Club and flashed a badge when a retainer asked their business.

"This is quite a place," Sharkey said.

"You wouldn't believe," Paulson replied. "I used to work out here with a friend who was a member—until he couldn't pay his dues anymore, and they kicked him out. There's twenty-six floors here, a couple of restaurants and bars, gyms, steam rooms, a pool, a running track, everything you could imagine in the way of indoor sports."

"And rooms for the members?"

"A couple of floors of them—for guys whose wives have kicked them out, or guys between apartments, or out-of-towners."

"So, I guess Donald Trask is a regular member."

"I guess so. The commish says he's a member of the Yale

Club, too, and might move over there because of the gun thing. But he's supposed to be going to Connecticut from here, so we can bust him at Grand Central Station."

"Twelve-thirty," Sharkey replied. "And there he is."

Donald Trask entered the lobby from Central Park South, stopped at the front desk for a brief conversation, then got onto an elevator. The detectives walked over and noted the floor number of his stop, then took their seats again.

"Maybe he's packing up to move," Paulson said.

"We'll see."

Shortly after one o'clock, Trask got off the elevator in the lobby, towing a large suitcase and carrying a smaller one. They followed him to the door he had entered. Outside, a black town car was waiting for him. Sharkey trotted around the corner to get their car. The driver stowed the luggage and drove away, making a U-turn toward Columbus Circle, with the detectives following half a block back.

"We'll brace him at Grand Central and take his gun and license," Paulson said.

"Then where the fuck is he going?" The town car had turned uptown on Broadway.

"Beats me."

The town car turned west on West 72nd Street and drove all the way to the West Side Highway, where it turned onto the ramp and headed north.

"Maybe he's staying with friends on the Upper West Side," Paulson said, but near the George Washington Bridge exit, the town car turned east.

"How long do we follow?" Paulson asked.

"I don't know—to the city limits, maybe?"

The town car turned north, and still the two cops followed.

"Suppose he's headed for Boston?" Paulson asked.

"I'm good as far as the Connecticut state line," Sharkey replied, but when they reached that point, he kept going.

"We're out of state now," Paulson pointed out.

"Yeah, but now I'm curious."

Twenty minutes later they were in Greenwich, following the shoreline, and the town car turned through large stone and wrought-iron gates and went up the drive to a large, Georgian-style house, where, from the street, Donald Trask could be seen taking his luggage through the front door.

"All right," Sharkey said, getting out his cell phone and pressing a button. "Detective Sharkey for the commissioner."

"Bacchetti," Dino said.

"Commissioner, Donald Trask didn't go to the Yale Club, and we never had a chance to brace him. We followed him to a big house in Greenwich."

"Connecticut?"

"Yes, sir."

"You know we don't operate up there, unless we're serving a warrant."

"Yes, sir. It looks like he lives up here."

"Not for long," Dino said. "He got divorced this morning, and he's got to clear that house by Friday afternoon at five. Pick him up then, follow him to the city, and do what you've got to do."

"Yes, sir."

"Now get your asses back to New York, where you belong."

Sharkey hung up and reported the conversation to his partner. "I think we should take his suggestion."

"Doesn't sound like a suggestion," Paulson said.

The two drove back to the city.

A WEEK LATER, on Monday morning, a meeting attended by Cilla Scott, the two Realtors, and the seller's attorney, took place in Herb Fisher's office. Cilla signed many documents—the seller had already signed—and handed over a check.

"Congratulations," the seller's attorney said. "The apartment is yours." He handed over four sets of keys and a bill of sale for the furniture she had bought, then departed.

Cilla thanked Herb for everything, then she and Margot left.

"I have an offer on the Carlyle apartment," Margot said.

"Already?"

"I think we priced it right."

"What's the offer?"

"He offered $3,500,000; I countered with four and a half, and he came up to $4,250,000."

"Accept it," Cilla said. "He can close anytime. I'm moving this afternoon."

"May I help?" Margot asked.

Back at the Carlyle, Cilla packed, while Margot phoned and accepted the offer, then they put Cilla's things into a hired town car and ferried it over to Fifth Avenue.

The apartment was neat and spotless, and there were fresh linens on the beds. Cilla hung her things in the dressing room. "Now I have to go buy a car," she said. She found Paul, the male half of her newly hired couple. "Paul, do you drive?"

"I drove your predecessor everywhere."

"Then come with me."

Downstairs, Margot excused herself to deliver the signed offer of the apartment to the buyer's Realtor.

Cilla thanked her profusely. "Margot, do you know where the Bentley dealership is?"

"It's called Manhattan Motorcars, and it's on Ninth Avenue, below Forty-second Street."

Cilla and Paul got into a cab, she googled the dealership for the correct address, and they were there in twenty minutes.

Cilla walked into the showroom, followed by Paul, and a salesman approached.

"May I show you something?" he asked.

"You can show me that," Cilla said, pointing at a silver Flying Spur.

He did so, and she examined the window sticker carefully. "How much of a discount can you offer me?" she asked.

"None, I'm afraid. Everything here is sold at list price. I can offer you your first detailing free, though."

"Write it up," she said, digging in her bag for her checkbook.

A half hour later as they were driving uptown, she caressed the beautiful leather of the seats. "This is going to be your second home, Paul," she said.

"Yes, ma'am," Paul replied. "And a fine home it is."

26

CILLA CALLED STONE.

"Hello?"

"I feel in a celebratory mood," she said. "Can I take you to dinner?"

"Sure. What time should I pick you up?"

"I'll pick you up," she said. "Be downstairs at seven o'clock."

"As you wish."

THE SILVER FLYING SPUR glided to a halt in front of Stone's house, and the driver held the door for him.

"This is beautiful," he said, climbing in.

"It's not as big as your Mulsanne," she said, "but it had the virtue of being on the showroom floor, ready to drive away. I was in no mood to wait three or four months for delivery."

"Where are we headed?"

"Brooklyn," she said.

"I'm in your hands." They crossed the Brooklyn Bridge,

took a right or two, and drove up to the River Café. "Ah, one of my favorites," Stone said.

"They know me here, so I was able to get a table on short notice."

They were seated, ordered drinks, and perused the menu. When they had ordered, Cilla spoke up. "Do you know why I'm so happy?"

"Because you're divorced?"

"That was last week. Now I'm happy because I moved into my new apartment today."

"What are you doing for furniture?"

"The previous owner was a recent widow who was downsizing, so I bought enough of her furniture to live with. Oh, I'll re-cover some things, and buy many others, but I'm comfortable."

"Anything else?"

"Donald is out of the Greenwich house. I expected him to take his clothes and personal things, but according to my housekeeper he took everything—furniture, books, art, TVs, rugs—and he took an early Picasso that was my mother's. I'll probably have to sue him to get it back. Herb is on it."

"What is it worth?"

"Millions, I expect."

"Where did Donald move to?"

"He's rented an apartment on the Upper East Side, in a nice building, far enough from me."

"Good," Stone said. "Just think of the stuff he took as a challenge to your decorating skills."

"I'll do that."

"He took the safe in the study, too. That's where he kept his guns."

"So, he's armed again? Dino's guys never caught him with a gun; they didn't know about his new apartment."

"Herb is going over there as we speak, to get the Picasso back."

"Does he know that Donald is armed?"

"He's taking backup, don't worry."

HERB FISHER, accompanied by two uniformed NYPD officers hired for the occasion, rang the doorbell of Donald Trask's new apartment. Trask opened it, wearing a new-looking silk dressing gown. "Hi, remember me?" Herb asked.

"All too well," Trask replied. "What the fuck do you want?"

"The Picasso," Herb said.

"What Picasso?"

"The one you stole from Ms. Scott's Greenwich home."

"I didn't steal it. It was hanging in my study."

"You also stole the furnishings of the study. There was no such right given to you in the separation agreement. May we come in, or do these two gentlemen have to arrest you first for grand larceny?"

"I want to call my lawyer," Trask said.

"Call whoever you like," Herb replied, brushing past Trask with the cops close behind. He walked quickly around the apartment, which was filled with unpacked boxes, until he found the Picasso on the mantelpiece in a small study.

"That one," Herb said to the cops, taking it down. He

found a sheet of Bubble Wrap in a pile of trash and wrapped the picture in it. "That's it," he said to the cops. "Let's go."

"I'm going to get that picture back," Trask said.

"No, you're not. It wasn't marital property—Ms. Scott inherited it from her mother. If you try, you'll end up in jail. Good evening."

The three men left, slamming the door behind them.

CILLA'S PHONE RANG, and she answered it and listened. "Thank you so much," she said, then hung up. "That was Herb. Picasso recovered and on its way to its new home on Fifth Avenue."

"I expect Herb short-circuited the process," Stone said.

"As long as the picture is mine again," she replied.

UPTOWN, IN TURTLE BAY, Faith went downstairs and looked around for Jimbo. It was past ten, so his relief was due. Impatiently, she left the house and began the walk to Lexington Avenue. "I'm not a baby," she said aloud to herself.

Jimbo came out of the downstairs powder room as his relief rang the doorbell, and he let her in.

"Evening, Jimbo," she said.

"Evening, Sylvia."

"Is she ready for the hand over?"

"Let's go upstairs." They took the elevator to the top floor and let themselves into Faith's apartment. "Faith?" Jimbo called out. No reply.

Jimbo and Sylvia quickly searched the apartment. "She's gone out, and without me," he said.

"Why would she do that? She had the riot act read to her by Barrington."

"She's impulsive," Jimbo said, "and impatient." He dialed her cell number, which went immediately to voice mail.

"Faith," he said, "this is Jimbo, please call me immediately."

Faith had the bell turned off and didn't hear the cell phone. She continued her trip uptown, where she wanted to visit the Caswell-Massey pharmacy on Lex. All she needed was some soap; she'd go straight back to the house after she'd bought it.

She spent a half hour in the drugstore, sniffing things, then bought her soaps and left. She vanished into the night.

27

JIMBO AND SYLVIA walked around the block, each in opposite directions, looking for Faith. She was nowhere in sight. Jimbo called Stone Barrington.

Stone and Cilla were finishing up dessert at the River Café when his phone rang. He glanced at the caller ID. "Please excuse me." He pressed the recall button.

"Stone?"

"Yes, Jimbo, what is it?"

"Faith has disappeared. At change of shift, I was in the downstairs powder room, thinking she was upstairs. Then, when Sylvia arrived, we went up to her apartment and found her gone. We made a quick search around the block, but no joy."

"Go up to that hotel on Lex where she used to stay and start a new search there," Stone said.

"Right."

Stone hung up and called Dino.

"Bacchetti."

"Are you at home?"

"With my feet up," Dino replied.

"I just got a call: Faith has disappeared."

"How'd that happen with her security on the job?"

"She left the house at the change of shift, while one of them was in the john. They've had a look around the block, but no luck. I've sent them up to that hotel where Faith used to stay."

"I'll call it in," Dino said. "We'll saturate the neighborhood." He hung up.

Cilla was signing the check. "I heard, we'll use my car," she said.

JIMBO CALLED STRATEGIC Services for a patrol car, and they went immediately to the hotel. Once there, he and Sylvia walked into the lobby and encountered only a janitor mopping the floor. They went to the front desk.

Jimbo showed his private badge to the desk clerk. "Do you remember Faith Barnacle?" he asked. "She used to stay here."

"The little blonde? Sure, I remember her. I heard she got a job flying private."

"Has she been in here in the past hour?"

"Nope. Hey, Sid!"

The mopper paused in his work. "Yeah?"

"You seen the little blonde, Faith, in here tonight?"

"Nah, not for two or three weeks."

"You're sure she didn't come in during the past hour?"

"I've been mopping for longer than that; she didn't come in."

The clerk turned back to Jimbo. "Sorry, sir, we haven't seen Faith tonight, and not for some time."

"Thanks," Jimbo said, then rejoined Sylvia. "Okay," he said, "you take this side of Lex, I'll take the other; we'll walk uptown and check every side street."

"Right," Sylvia said, then watched Jimbo cross to the other side. They started walking uptown.

Jimbo heard a police car in the distance, then another. He could see the flashing lights way up Lex, coming his way. He flagged down one of them. "You guys looking for Faith Barnacle?"

"Yeah," the cop replied.

"So are we. Any sign of her?"

"Nothing, and there aren't that many people on the street, except around Bloomie's.

Jimbo showed his ID. "I'm from Strategic Services—mind if my partner and I ride with you?"

"Hop in."

Jimbo whistled up Sylvia, and she joined them. They drove up Third Avenue, vainly seeking Faith.

"We haven't had a call on this thing for a week or more," said the cop who was driving. "I had hoped it was over."

"I don't think it's over," Jimbo replied.

STONE AND CILLA got onto Lexington at 86th Street and cruised slowly downtown. Stone's phone rang. "Yes, Jimbo?"

"We're in a patrol car, going up Third, then down Lex."

"Good. We're doing much the same thing. Keep in touch if something happens."

———

FAITH CAME TO SLOWLY, but she couldn't see anything. A soft cloth bag was over her head, there were some holes around her mouth that enabled her to breathe. She could hear the muffled sound of classical music. Her hands were bound to a wooden chair that should have had a wicker seat, but didn't. "Hello?" she said. Then she heard the sound of a heavy door closing and being locked. "Hello!" No response. She squirmed, trying to loosen her bonds, but they were too tight.

Then she realized that she was naked.

28

I T WAS NEARLY TWO AM when Cilla dropped Stone off at his house. "Let me know if you hear anything," she said.

"I will."

He was getting into bed when Dino called.

"Did I wake you?"

"You would have in another ten minutes," Stone said.

"We've got nothing, not a trace. She went into the Caswell-Massey store on Lex and bought some soap, but after that, nobody saw her on the street."

"This is bad," Stone said wearily.

"The search is still on," Dino said. "Not to be pessimistic, but nobody will be able to dump a body in that neighborhood without being seen."

"I don't think it will happen tonight," Stone said. "The kinds of injuries the ME described won't happen fast. He'll want to enjoy himself."

"Until he gets tired of her," Dino added. "Talk to you in the morning."

Dino hung up, and Stone fell into bed, exhausted by his worry and his inability to do anything to help Faith.

FAITH KNEW THE MAN would be coming back for her. She managed to get the cloth between her chin and her shoulder and move it until, with her head pitched back, she could see out through one of the small breathing holes if she tilted the chair back a bit. She nearly went too far and fell on her back, but caught herself in time.

She could see a stool on the floor in front of her, next to the wall, and there was a window above it. The window appeared to be fixed, with four large panes. There was no sign of a lock. Then she heard a noise: the sound of an elevator running. She had an idea, but she would have only one shot at it before the elevator reached wherever she was.

She stood on her feet, bent over because her hands were tied to the chair. For an instant she wondered what floor she was on, but she pushed that thought out of her mind. If she was going to die, then better to do it now.

She backed up against the wall behind her and judged the distance to the stool, then, leaning into it, she began to run as fast as she could under the circumstances. She knew she needed momentum, and her thoughts went back to the high school track team, when she would lean forward into the tape at the finish line for that last bit of speed.

She leapt and got a foot on top of the stool and pushed off, as high and as fast as she possibly could, and dove headfirst into the window. There was the crash of breaking glass, then she was falling in cold air, falling and falling.

IT WAS NEARLY FIVE AM as two uniformed cops sat in their patrol car at the corner of Lexington Avenue, facing downtown. One of them reached for the radio's microphone and called in their position. "We've made two dozen sweeps uptown and downtown and found nothing. Are we getting a shift change soon?"

"Come on in to the precinct," the operator said.

"Let's go, Max," the cop said to the driver, who put the car in gear. Then there was a very loud noise heard from the direction of the driver's window. He stopped the car and reversed a few feet. "What the fuck was that?" he asked.

"I don't know, but I heard it, too."

They both stared east, at the empty street. Nothing was moving or making more noise.

"It sounded almost like a car crash," the driver said.

"I don't see anything," his partner said.

"Let's take a stroll," Max said.

They got out of the car and began to walk east.

"You take the other side of the street," Max said. Halfway down the block he encountered some broken glass on the sidewalk, but he could find no broken windows.

The two cops continued to Third Avenue, then turned and walked back toward Lexington. Halfway up the block, in line with the broken glass, he passed a dumpster and thought he heard a small sound from its direction. He looked up and could see that both of the steel lids were propped open. They should get a ticket for that, he thought.

"Max, where are you?" his partner called from across the street.

Max walked to the east end of the dumpster, stepped up on the bumper of a car parked next to it, and got out his flashlight. He played it over the contents: broken drywall, short pieces of lumber, broken glass—the detritus of demolition. He saw a wooden chair, broken, and fixed on that for a moment. He was about to get down from the bumper when he saw something else that transfixed him.

There was a hand—a woman's hand from the size of it—tied with rope to the chair.

He reached for his radio and called in his location. "I've found something: requesting an ambulance *right now!*"

"Harvey!" he yelled at his partner. "I got something here. Get to the car and turn on the flashers, so an ambulance will see it."

"What have you got, Max?"

"At least part of a woman!" Max yelled back, wading into the dumpster.

STONE'S PHONE RANG, causing him to sit straight up in bed; he was unaccustomed to calls at this hour. "Hello?"

"It's Dino. I thought I'd call you because I'm awake, and I'm not going back to sleep."

"That was thoughtful of you."

"My people found Faith. At least, we think it could be Faith. She's about the right size."

Stone's heart sank. "Is it so bad that she can't be identified?"

"Not yet, not for sure. They're taking her to Bellevue."

Stone woke up a little more. "Why not the morgue?"

"Because she's still alive," Dino said. "At least, she's not dead yet."

"Thank God."

"Don't thank Him too soon," Dino said. "This is really bad."

"Where are you?"

"About to leave home. Shall I pick you up on the way?"

"Please. See you shortly."

Ten minutes later, Stone stood at the curb, watching the black SUV turn the corner. He got into the backseat with Dino. "Anything new?"

"Nope, and no news is good news," Dino replied.

29

THE CAR ROLLED to a stop at the ER entrance to the huge hospital. Stone and Dino jumped out and ran down the hall to a nurse's station.

Dino flashed his badge at a nurse. "Where is Faith Barnacle?"

The nurse consulted a list. "We've got no Faith Barnacle, but there's a Jane Doe in exam room two, Commissioner," she said, jerking a thumb down the hallway.

They ran another fifty feet and nearly collided with a nurse coming from behind the curtain, bearing a pan filled with blood-stained gauze and other horrible things.

"Get back," she ordered the two men. "There're two very busy doctors working in there, and you don't want to screw with them. Siddown!" She jerked her chin in the direction of a row of chairs, and they meekly followed her orders.

"Hey, how is she?" Dino shouted at the nurse's back as she walked away.

"Stick around!" she shouted without turning.

———

THE BETTER PART of an hour passed before a young physician in bloody scrubs came out of the curtained room and was replaced by another.

"Doctor!" Dino shouted.

The man walked wearily over to where they were getting to their feet. "What?"

"How is she?"

"Awful," he said. "I've rarely seen such a mess. I had to bring a fresh doctor down here just to suture her wounds."

"Is she going to make it?"

"She's taken about as much abuse as a human being can stand and still live, but she's stable. She's got some broken ribs and a thousand cuts, but she's been conscious off and on, and that's a good sign."

"How were all these cuts inflicted?" Stone asked.

"Not with a knife or razor," the doctor said. "As I hear it, she fell from three or four stories into a dumpster filled with chunks of old drywall and glass. There must have been enough air in there to offer some kind of cushion. Oh, and her hands were tied to what remained of a chair. That's all I can tell you."

Dino thanked him and got on his phone. "Listen, you've got to figure out which window she fell from," he said. "We've gotta get an arrest out of this." He listened for a couple of minutes. "Keep me posted," he said and hung up.

"They found the room, twelve stories up. It looks like, while tied to the chair, she made a head-on run at the window and crashed through it. Two cops were sitting in their patrol car on the corner and heard the noise when she hit the dumpster. One of them found her and called it in. He thought she was dead."

Stone collapsed into his chair. "Christ, she's got guts, you have to give her that."

"She must have had some idea of what was coming," Dino said. "I hope I'd have done the same thing in the circumstances."

Another doctor came out of the exam room, and Dino braced him. "Can we see her?"

"She's out like a light on morphine," he said. "She may be talking tomorrow, but I'm not promising you anything."

"But she'll live?" Stone asked.

"She's a tough one," the doctor said. "The ribs will be painful, but she doesn't have any internal organ damage, and that's remarkable. She'll be recovering for quite a while."

Stone and Dino made a move toward the exam room.

"Forget it," the doctor said. "There's a doctor and a nurse at work in there suturing, and believe me, you don't want to see her in her current state. She was naked when she went into the dumpster, except she had a hood over her head, so the cuts to her face are less bad. Go home and call here tomorrow before you come over. She needs rest, not questions."

They thanked the man and reluctantly left the hospital. By the time Stone got home, Joan was at her desk. He told her what had happened.

"That poor girl," Joan said, brushing away a tear.

"Where are Jimbo and Sylvia?"

"At home. They're both crushed, but there was nothing more they could do. I'll call them."

"Tell them to put a guard on her room at Bellevue," Stone said. "When word gets out that she's alive, somebody could come after her."

"Will do," Joan said, picking up her phone.

"Send a whole lot of flowers and a cell phone to her room, with a note from me saying that when she feels like talking to call me, but not to rush it."

"All right."

Stone went back upstairs to try to get a couple more hours of sleep. Dino called as he was getting into bed.

"I got a look at the room," he said. "It's in one of two buildings built into the hotel. Apparently, when it was built, the property owners wouldn't sell, so the hotel was built around them. Down a hallway was a door leading to an attic, and through there you could get to the hotel."

"There are those three night guys there," Stone said, "night clerk, elevator operator, and janitor."

"They're at the precinct being separately sweated as we speak," Dino said. "So far, nobody knows nothing."

"Okay, I'm going to sleep. I told Strategic Services to put a guard on her room."

"Already done," Dino replied.

"And I sent her some flowers and a cell phone so she can call when she feels like it."

"Good idea. Let me know if you hear from her."

"Okay, now I'm going back to bed."

"Lucky sonofabitch, I wish I could do that."

"Don't call me before noon, unless something breaks."

"Sure." Dino hung up.

Stone pulled the blinds and lay on the bed in the dark,

wondering what he could have done different that would have avoided this. Finally, he decided that there was nothing he could have done, unless Faith cooperated, and she was clearly not the cooperative sort.

He fell asleep finally and dreamed of falling twelve stories into a dumpster.

HE WAS AWAKENED by the phone at the stroke of noon. "Yes?"

"We're not getting a whole lot out of the three," Dino said, "but everybody's money is on the janitor."

"It's got to be all three of them," Stone said. "He couldn't have done it unless the other three were in on it—or, at the very least, covering for him."

"I won't argue with that," Dino said. "Now, I'm going to lock myself in my office and take a nap on the sofa." He hung up.

30

STONE WAS GETTING HUNGRY for lunch when Joan buzzed. "You had a message," she said.

"Why didn't you put the call through?"

"It wasn't a call, it was a message from Mikeford Whitehorn."

Mikeford Whitehorn had served in three cabinet positions and, in between, had expanded his family's legendary fortune in investment banking. Stone had met him once, three or four years before, at a dinner party. "What's the message?"

"He would be grateful if you would call on him at his home at three o'clock this afternoon. He's at 740 Park Avenue."

"Any idea what he wants?"

"That was the entire message. He didn't ask that you call and confirm, either."

"That was pretty confident," Stone said.

"I guess he's not accustomed to people saying no."

"I guess not." As Stone hung up, his cell phone started vibrating. "Hello?"

The voice was a hoarse whisper. "It's Faith. I'm so sorry."

"Listen, you need rest. You don't have to talk now, not even to the police."

"I'm going to be all right. I'll call tomorrow. I just wanted you to know I'm sorry I didn't listen to you." She hung up.

740 PARK AVENUE was the grandest and, legend had it, the most expensive apartment building in New York. It was built at the dawn of the Great Depression by Jacqueline Kennedy's grandfather and was made up almost entirely of large duplexes and triplexes, one of which was occupied by John D. Rockefeller, Jr., from the mid-1930s. Some of the apartments had been described as "country houses in the city." Stone knew a couple of people who lived there, but he had never visited Mikeford Whitehorn's apartment.

He was admitted by a uniformed butler, seated in a large, paneled library stocked with leather-bound volumes on two levels that were joined by a spiral staircase, and asked if he would like a drink.

"No, thank you," Stone said and was left alone.

A moment later Mikeford Whitehorn entered the room as a bull might enter the ring in Madrid. He was six feet, six inches tall and weighed, probably, two-fifty pounds—his slim weight. He had been an all-American football player at Harvard, back when that school had still produced all-Americans, and was known to intimates—but no one else—as "Swifty."

Whitehorn enveloped Stone's hand in a brief handshake, then he took a chair and ordered a large Laphroaig, a single-malt scotch whisky, neat. Stone reconsidered and ordered a Knob Creek.

"I remember our conversation at that dinner party a while back," Whitehorn said.

That surprised Stone because it had hardly been a conversation: he had just listened while Whitehorn rattled on about whatever crossed his mind. "I remember it, too, Mr. Secretary," Stone replied, "but I don't remember talking much."

Whitehorn laughed. "Maybe not, but you asked the right questions."

"I was surprised to hear from you, Mr. Secretary. Is there something I can do for you?"

"I need some advice from a person of your background," Whitehorn said. "The police thing, you know."

"I used to be a police detective," Stone said.

"Exactly. I don't want to ask my grandson's lawyer about this."

Stone had not known that Whitehorn had a grandson. "I see," he said.

"My grandson is named Michael Adams," he said. "My daughter's boy. He has never amounted to much of anything. He has what I consider to be a menial job, and he is supported by a trust fund I set up for him at his birth."

"Is he in some sort of trouble?"

"He has been arrested, and it looks as though he may be charged as an accomplice in an attempted murder."

"What are the circumstances?"

"He is a night clerk at a fairly seedy hotel on Lexington Avenue in the Forties, and it appears that at least one of his colleagues, the janitor there, is a suspect in half a dozen murders."

"Let me stop you there for a moment, Mr. Secretary, while I declare a conflict."

"A confict?"

"A young woman I employ as an aircraft pilot is a victim in this case, although she did not die."

"How is that a conflict?"

"I can't represent your grandson and advise the young lady simultaneously."

"I'm not asking you to represent my grandson. He already has a competent attorney. I'm asking you to advise me, not him."

"Well, as long as it's only informal advice, not actual representation, I suppose we can talk about it."

"Good. Now, my grandson's attorney is urging him to accept a plea deal, guilty, in exchange for a five-year sentence, but Mike maintains his innocence and doesn't want to do it."

"I know that there are three suspects," Stone said, "and that the police feel the chief among them is the janitor. However, they don't believe he could have pulled off these murders without help, and that leaves the elevator operator and your grandson in a bind, I'm afraid."

"What do you think the boy should do?"

"I think that if he continues to maintain his innocence, he should instruct his attorney to ask for immunity from prosecution, in exchange for Mike testifying to everything—absolutely everything—he knows about the attack on my employee and a number of previous murders, which seem to have been perpetrated by the same person or persons. I should warn you that this is not going to work unless he actually has information that would help convict the janitor and maybe the elevator operator, too, and that once he agrees to help, he must withhold nothing from the police, nothing at all."

"Is that his only option?"

"No, he can refuse to answer any questions, which I'm sure his attorney has already instructed him to do, and go to trial. Whether he does that would, of course, depend on the strength of the prosecution's case, as determined by his attorneys. If he should go to trial, he will need the best criminal defense attorney available, who may not necessarily be his current attorney."

"Can you recommend someone?"

"One of my law partners, at Woodman & Weld, Herbert Fisher, is an excellent trial attorney, and I recommend him unreservedly. However, I must ask you not to use my name as a referer, if you call him, or mention me to anyone else, for the reason of the possible conflict, which I have already expressed."

"I understand," Whitehorn said. "You may rely on my discretion."

Stone nodded. "Thank you, sir."

Whitehorn tossed back his scotch and stood up.

Stone stood as well, leaving half of his bourbon in the glass.

"Can you come to dinner here on Saturday evening?" Whitehorn asked unexpectedly. "I usually entertain on Saturdays, which often causes my invitees to have to choose between my table and others, which sort of tells me who my friends are."

"Thank you, I'd be delighted."

"It's black tie, six-thirty for seven-thirty, and—are you married or have a regular woman in your life?"

"No on both counts."

"Then come alone. I need an extra man."

They shook hands.

"Thank you for your advice. May I call you Stone?"

"Of course, Mr. Secretary."

"Good. Call me Swifty, all my friends do."

"As you wish."

The butler appeared as if by magic and escorted Stone to the door.

Stone checked his watch: he had been there no more than fifteen minutes. Swifty was nothing if not efficient with his time.

31

S TONE WAS HALFWAY home when his cell went off. "Hello?"

"It's Faith." She sounded stronger and spoke more confidently.

"It sounds as though you're getting better fast," Stone said. "How are you feeling?"

"Better, fast. This morning I hurt all over, but they've given me morphine for that, so I can relax. I'm going to take a nap shortly, and I thought maybe you could tell Dino something for me, so his cops won't have to come and question me. I'm not up for that."

"Of course. What would you like me to tell him?"

"Tell him I remember going into Caswell-Massey and buying some soap and walking out the door to Lexington, but absolutely nothing else until I woke up in that room. I had a bag over my head, but I could see out a little through a hole, and I saw the stool and window across the room. I heard the elevator coming, and I decided I'd rather die quickly than slowly, so I used the stool as a running step and went head-first through the window. I remember cold air, then nothing, until I woke up in the hospital. That's it, that's everything."

"Do you remember ever being in the room with someone else?"

"No, but since I was naked and tied to a chair, I knew someone had been there. I feared he was coming back."

"All right, I'll pass that on and see if we can keep the investigators off your back for another day."

"I'd really appreciate that."

"Can I come and see you?"

"Maybe tomorrow. The morphine is putting me to sleep right now. Oh, the flowers are beautiful, and thanks for the phone." She hung up.

Stone called Dino.

"Bacchetti."

"Our victim woke up and called me."

"I'll get somebody over there right now."

"No, she doesn't want that until tomorrow."

"This isn't about what she wants."

"She told me what happened, and I'll tell you."

Dino sighed. "All right, what?"

Stone related Faith's account of her evening.

"That's it?"

"That's it, every word of it, and I believe her. I told her your guys would be there tomorrow. Right now, she's asleep on morphine."

"Well, if she's all doped up I guess that's the best we can do."

"I guess so. Oh, there's something else I have to tell you. How about dinner tonight?"

"P. J. Clarke's at seven?"

"See you then." He made it back to his desk before the phone rang again. "Hello?"

"Hi, it's Cilla. How about I cook you some dinner tonight?"

"I'd love that, but I'm dining with Dino, and we have some business to discuss."

"Saturday?"

"I'm sorry, I have a previous invitation to a dinner party, and I was asked to come alone. I expect I'll be seated next to some highly perfumed, heavily bejeweled deaf dowager."

"If you can't be with me, then I wish that for you. I'm afraid I'm tied up on Sunday, but I cook to order on Mondays."

"Perfect."

"Come at six-thirty, and I'll have a bottle of Knob Creek and a straw waiting." She gave him the address and apartment number.

Stone entered his plans into his iPhone calendar.

DINO WAS HALF A DRINK ahead of him when he arrived at Clarke's, and Stone started catching up. Shortly, they were seated at a table in the back room, ordering dinner.

"Tell me," Stone said, "how is the interrogation of your three suspects going?"

"They've lawyered up, and they're holding their water."

"I can make a suggestion that might help."

"Any help at all would be appreciated."

"One of the suspects, Mike Adams, has been offered a

deal: he testifies and gets five years. However, he stoutly maintains his innocence."

"And how would you know that?"

"You can't ask me, and I can't tell you, but here's what I think might work: ask the DA to give Mr. Adams immunity, and he'll tell everything he knows about the other two."

"Yeah, but what does he know?"

"Listen, he works with the other two guys every day of his life, and the three of them are very frequently alone in that hotel lobby. Even if he didn't watch them kill those girls, he'll know something about their whereabouts on the relevant evenings."

"And what if he was a cheerful participant in the rapes and murders?"

"It's the old choice," Stone said. "One, perhaps two birds in the hand and one out the window."

"You think the desk clerk will crack, huh? I'd sure like to know how you know that."

"I don't know it, but I have every reason to believe that he'll take the deal."

Dino heaved a deep, sorrowful Italian sigh. "All right, I'll suggest it to the DA."

"There's one other piece of information you might drop while you're suggesting it."

"What's that?"

"Young Mike Adams is the grandson of Mikeford Whitehorn."

"You're shittin' me! That little creep is of Swifty Whitehorn's blood?"

"I shit you not. Mike is his daughter's son."

"Then what's he doing working in that fleabag hotel?"

"Mike appears to be the black sheep in the family. I think they're grateful that he has a job, even that one, although he has a trust fund."

"You're just a fountain of fucking information, aren't you. I didn't even know you knew Swifty Whitehorn."

"You still don't," Stone pointed out, "although I'll tell you we were at the same dinner table a few years ago, and I spent the evening listening to him talk about himself."

"And that's where you got all this information?"

"I didn't say that. In fact, that dinner is not the source of my information."

"But . . ."

Stone held up a hand. "Don't ask," he said, smiling a little.

"I'll call the DA."

32

HERB FISHER was at his desk the following morning, dictating a memo, when his phone rang. He answered. "Herb Fisher."

"Herb, this is Ted Faber, over at Littlejohn & Brown. How are you?"

"Real good, thanks. Have we met?"

"At a Bar Association cocktail party a long time ago, but that's not why I'm calling. I may have a client for you."

"Who referred you to me?"

"I can't say, but why don't I buy you a good lunch, and we can talk about it."

"As long as it's a *really* good lunch."

"How about The Grill, formerly the Four Seasons Grill?"

"That'll do."

"Twelve-thirty?"

"Good."

———

HERB WALKED UP THE STAIRS and past the busy bar, and a young man stepped forward and offered his hand. "Herb, I'm Ted Faber."

They shook hands and were seated.

Herb looked around. "Thank God for the Historical Commission," he said.

"Beg pardon?"

"They kept the new building owner from ripping out the interior and starting over. It's exactly as Philip Johnson designed it."

"Right."

They ordered drinks and lunch.

"So," Herb said, "what kind of case have you got?"

"A high-profile criminal one. You know the murders of the small blondes on the East Side?"

"Who doesn't?"

"Well, our client is a suspect."

"It doesn't get any more high profile than that," Herb responded. "Who represents the other two?"

"Two other attorneys from two other firms. They've clammed up their clients."

"Good. How's your client going to plead?"

"Not guilty. He's adamant that he had nothing to do with it, says he'll go to trial."

"What if the other two implicate him?"

"We'd like to head off that possibility at the pass."

"How are you planning to proceed, then, and why do you want me?"

"We've had some very specific instructions about that from a relative of our client, the one who's paying the bills."

"What instructions?"

"First, he's instructed us to hire you. He won't say why."

"And, I take it, he won't let you say who he is?"

"Later," Ted said. "Second, he's instructed us, or you, rather, to make a proffer to the DA: immunity on all charges in return for his testimony against the two other suspects."

"And who are these three?"

"Our client is Mike Adams, the night clerk at a hotel on Lexington Avenue; the other two are the janitor and the elevator operator. We have it on good authority that the cops and the DA favor the janitor as the perp, but they figure he needed help, so they're charging all three."

"That's odd. Hasn't the DA made an offer?"

"Five years."

"And Adams won't take it?"

"He will not, and he is adamant."

"But he's agreed to testify?"

"We believe he will, with full immunity."

"I don't get it. Why do you need me?"

"Two reasons. First, as I said earlier, the relative of our client has specified you. Second, the ADA on the case is Cheray Gardner."

"Ah," Herb said. He and Cheray had had a torrid, albeit brief, affair the year before.

"Did you part on good terms?"

"She still winks at me in the courthouse elevator."

"I'll take that as on good terms."

"So will I," Herb said. "Okay, who's the relative?"

Ted sucked his teeth.

"I need to know that. I don't want to be blindsided later."

"First, let's discuss your fees—with or without trial."

Ted's reluctance to reveal the name more than doubled what Herb had intended to ask. "Twenty-five grand, if I get him immunity. If it goes to trial, a hundred grand against a million-dollar fee, calculated at a thousand dollars an hour."

"I can do that," Ted said.

This indicated to Herb that Ted had already gotten an approval for the fees. "Then all I need is the name."

"Mikeford Whitehorn."

"He's a relative?"

"A grandfather. Adams is his daughter's son."

"What's the kid doing working at a fleabag hotel?"

"Let's just say that Mike is something of a disappointment to his family. He's not starving, though; he has a trust fund from grandpappy."

"Okay, I'll go for the deal, but I want permission to use Whitehorn's name in my dealings with the ADA, and I want to talk to Whitehorn. Phone is okay."

"I don't know about that," Ted replied.

"Tell old Swifty this: if it goes to trial, he's going to be all over the papers and TV, guaranteed. The media will find out; they always do. However, if I can whisper his name into Cheray's shell-like ear, it might carry some weight. It certainly will if she needs an approval from the DA himself to make the deal."

"All right, but I don't think you need to talk to grandpappy."

"All right, but find a way to intimate to him that if he

doesn't know the DA, which he certainly does, but it would be gauche for him to make a call himself, then he might find a mutual acquaintance who can whisper to the DA that he should smile on immunity."

"I can do that," Ted said, "and I'm sure Swifty can, too."

"Before I call Cheray."

"Right after lunch."

"When do I meet my client?"

"How about in an hour at Riker's Island?"

"I can make that. Has anybody grilled young Mike about what he can give the DA?"

"I have. He says he's worked with the janitor and the elevator operator for a year and a half, and he knows they did it, and he can shred any alibi they might have. And he keeps a diary."

Herb looked at his watch.

"Give me a couple of minutes, and I'll give you an answer," Ted said.

Herb went to the men's room, and when he came out, Ted was waiting in the entry hall.

"You can whisper, but not shout, grandpappy's name," he said.

"I'll call you later this afternoon," Herb said. "Thanks for the lunch."

"My car and driver are outside. Take it to Riker's and he'll take you back to your office."

They shook hands, and Herb went outside to the car.

33

HERB WAS LET into a room containing two steel chairs and a table, all bolted to the floor. He sat down and tried to check his phone for messages, but there was no signal.

Five minutes later a guard opened the door, and a tall, slim young man with thinning dark hair and glasses entered the room. His handcuffs were removed and he shook Herb's hand firmly. "I'm Michael Adams," he said, then sat down.

"I'm Herb Fisher. Your grandfather has retained me to represent you."

"He spoke to you directly?" Adams asked, sounding surprised.

"No, through your previous attorney, Ted Faber."

"I'm glad he found you. Faber didn't impress me."

Herb was surprised at how calm and confident Adams seemed. In these circumstances, his clients were usually shaken and worried. "I've been told by Ted Faber that you're willing to answer all the DA's questions, in exchange for immunity from all charges."

"Who wouldn't?" Adams asked.

Herb smiled. "Of course, but I'm going to need to hear your story before I attempt to make that deal."

"Okay, ask me whatever the DA will. This can be a rehearsal."

"Let's avoid that term and just call it a client interview."

"Sure."

"All right, Mike, give me your sixty-second biography, right up to this minute."

"Born New York City twenty-nine years ago, educated at Buckley, had a shot at Yale, but didn't make it there. Got my degree at Fordham."

"Is your grandfather Catholic?"

"You guessed it."

"And after Fordham?"

"I got into law school but left after a year."

"What did you do for work?"

"My father got me a job at his commercial real estate firm, but it didn't suit me. Neither did a couple of other things, but old Dad got me the night clerk gig at the hotel, which his firm owns. It suits me well. I can read and watch a lot of TV and, sometimes, work on my novel."

"When did you begin?"

"A year and a half ago."

"Any problems at work? You get along with your boss?"

"No problems. Everybody there works for my father's firm, and my boss works days, so we don't see each other that often."

"When did you meet your two coworkers?"

"Sid Francis, the janitor, and Larry Cleary, the elevator operator?"

"Right." Herb made a note of the names.

"They were already working there when I arrived. Nominally, I'm their boss; they're night workers, too."

"And who do you report to?"

"The assistant manager, Harmon Wheeler, Jr., who reports to the manager, Harmon Wheeler, Sr., who reports to my father's firm."

"And what were your first impressions of Sid, the janitor, and Larry, the elevator operator?"

"Slackers. They worked slowly, and they paid a lot of attention to the airline girls who stayed with us."

"Flight attendants?"

"And pilots. They worked for a couple of charter airlines that had a deal with the hotel. Until recently."

"What happened recently?"

"My dad's firm decided to gut the hotel and remake it as something that would appeal more to business travelers, so the airline people looked for beds elsewhere."

"How recently?"

"A few weeks ago. There's very little business now because as their contracts expire, they aren't renewed."

"So Sid and Larry liked the girls."

"They did and do. Their problem was the girls didn't like them much. Their approaches tended to get rebuffed, so I guess they looked elsewhere."

"With what result?"

"I noticed that Sid and Larry tended to disappear for an

hour or two late at night—rarely together—one at a time. Sid would cover the elevator when Larry was gone."

"Did you know where they went?"

"I assumed they were taking naps or watching porn in one of the vacant bedrooms. I found some videos in a room on the second floor once, when I was making my rounds."

"How often did you make rounds?"

"When I felt like it, which was not often, but I got curious about where Sid and Larry were going, and I couldn't catch them actually in a room. Then, last week, I noticed the door."

"What door?"

"On the top floor. It's a pull-down door to what I assumed was the attic."

"Did you have a look up there?"

"Once. I found that you could get into the attic in the building next door from there."

"Did you explore that further?"

"I intended to, but then, suddenly, the lobby was full of cops, and there were a lot of sirens outside. This was the night they found the girl in the dumpster."

"How did you hear about that?"

"They arrested me, and the subject came up."

"Did you withhold any information?"

"No. I told them about the attic door, and according to my attorney, that led them to the room the girl jumped from."

"Did you refuse to answer any questions?"

"Not until I got the feeling they thought I was implicated, then I shut up and demanded an attorney. A firm, Littlejohn & Brown, that represents some of my grandfather's interests, sent me Ted Faber. The only advice he gave me was to shut up, which I was already doing. Then he brought me an offer, five years, if I'd testify against Sid and Larry. I told him I wanted to walk on all charges, and then I'd talk to the DA."

"Well, you sound like an ideal client, Mike. I understand you're saying you're innocent of all charges, is that right?"

"That's right. I had absolutely nothing to do with harming those girls. I'm not put together that way."

"All right, tell me what you're going to tell the DA that will want her to make the deal."

"I keep a journal, every day. I have lots of time every night."

"And where is this journal?"

"In a safe place."

"How long would it take for you to produce it?"

"As long as it takes for you to go get it from the safe place."

"And how does the journal relate to the murders?"

"I noted the times when Sid and Larry disappeared. I expect that if you compare them to the dates the girls were murdered, you'll get some matches."

"That's good, but I think we need a little more than that. Are you aware that a murder almost identical to the ones in New York occurred in Los Angeles almost simultaneously?"

"I was not aware of that, but Sid was in Los Angeles for a few days during that time. He took some vacation time to visit his mother, he said."

"The name of the girl who jumped from the building is Faith Barnacle. Did you know her?"

"Sure, she was a pilot with a charter airline; she stayed there at least a dozen times, maybe more."

"Did Sid or Larry pay any attention to her?"

"Yeah, it's the old story: Sid tried to chat her up, but what girl wants to be chatted up by a guy who's mopping the floor?"

"And you saw this happen?"

"I did, and Sid was plenty pissed off about it. I heard him call her a 'fucking bitch,' after she walked out of earshot."

"How about Larry?"

"He was always pretty quiet. Sid did the talking to the girls."

"Anything else, Mike?"

"Have you spoken to my grandfather?"

"No, he preferred to deal through Ted Faber."

Adams snorted. "Yeah, he would. He'd want to keep his hands clean."

"Mike," Herb said, "let me give you some advice. Be grateful to your grandfather. He's the one who's ultimately going to get you this deal."

"Okay, I understand. When will I get out?"

"Not for a while, but I think we can improve your circumstances. If they go for the deal, they'll move you to a hotel, and you'll probably be there until you testify."

"Why?"

"Maybe Sid and Larry have other friends, who might take exception to you testifying."

"Oh, I hadn't thought of that."

"One more thing, Mike. Where's the diary?"

"It's in my office, behind the front desk, in a small safe under the floorboards."

"Haven't the police already searched it?"

"Maybe, but they can be pretty perfunctory."

"What's the combination to the safe?"

Adams gave it to him.

"How do I locate the floorboards?"

"They're under the document shredder."

Herb gave Adams his card. "Call me if you need anything."

"How soon will we know about the deal?"

"Soon," Herb said. He shook Adams's hand, then banged on the door and was let out.

34

ERB GOT BACK into Ted Faber's car and asked to be taken to the hotel on Lex. He walked into the lobby and found it deserted. "Hello?" he called, but got only an echo for a response.

He flipped up the part of the desktop that admitted him to the front desk, then found the door to the small office behind. He dragged the document shredder to one side, found the safe under the floorboards, and entered the combination. The journal was on top of some other items; Herb put the journal into his briefcase and looked through the safe. He found a .380-caliber semiautomatic pistol, some ammo, and a spare magazine. There was also a thick manuscript entitled "Night Job in Hell." Pretty florid for a front desk, he thought. He closed the safe and left the hotel, checking his watch. It was a little past five. He wanted to see Cheray Gardner, and he knew where he was likely to find her. He told the driver to take him back to the courthouse. On the way, he googled the murders and noted the dates of each, then he compared the dates to the notations in Mike Adams's diary. They all matched, even the one in L.A. He marked the entries with his business cards and put the diary back into his briefcase.

Once at the courthouse, he directed the driver to a bar a couple of blocks away. "Wait for me," he said, taking his briefcase inside with him.

The place was going full blast, filled with lawyers, detectives, and court employees. Herb checked his watch and took a seat at one end of the bar. He didn't have long to wait. Cheray Gardner entered the bar and immediately spotted him in her usual corner. She came over and permitted herself to be air-kissed.

"Well, Herb, you're out of your neighborhood, aren't you? Or are you actually trying a case?"

"Certainly not. When all your clients are innocent, why bother with trying cases?"

She laughed heartily. "Yes," she said, "you can buy me a drink."

"Bartender," he said, "a very dry Belvedere martini with four olives, straight up."

"You remembered," she said. "How sweet of you."

"What are you working on these days?" he asked.

"Oh, the usual," she replied. "Why do you ask?"

"Just making conversation."

"How about you?" she asked. "What're you working on?"

"Oh, a very nice divorce case and some real estate work attendant to that."

"Funny," Cheray said, looking at him questioningly. "I thought you might be working on one of my cases."

"What case is that?"

"Oh, just a team of serial rapists and killers who've been terrorizing the Upper East Side."

"I've read about that one, of course, and this afternoon I was asked to represent one of them."

"Which one?"

"The innocent one," Herb replied.

"Oh, ho, ho! Am I supposed to ask which one?"

"You already know which one," Herb answered. "So do the cops."

"Oh, really?"

"Yes, really, Cheray. You're just waiting for one of the three to break and rat out the other two, and you don't really care which one."

"That's not a bad guess," she said.

"Maybe I can help you out," Herb said. "Suppose I can get the innocent one to flip and give you enough to convict the others?"

"Then I'll buy you a very good dinner," she said.

"Tell you what, I'll settle for a steak here. Shall I find us a booth?"

"Sure. We can figure out who's buying over dessert."

"I'm just accepting your offer." Herb went to find the head-waiter and slipped him a fifty. He beckoned to Cheray, and she came over.

"Oh, and the nicest, quietest booth, too."

"Nothing but the best for us." They sat down, and Herb ordered them another drink. Cheray always drank her first martini quickly. They ordered steaks.

"Why don't we get business out of the way?" Cheray proposed. "I don't want it to get in the way of . . . my steak."

"Sure. All Mike Adams needs is immunity on every count of the case and protection from the other two until the trial."

"I've already offered him five years," she said. "Why should I improve on that?"

"Why would an innocent man plead guilty to something he didn't do and serve five years for it?"

"So, he gets himself a smart lawyer, and . . ."

"He didn't hire me, his grandfather did. Old Swifty must have heard about me somewhere."

"'Swifty'? His grandfather is Mikeford Whitehorn?"

"Oh, shit," Herb said, slapping his forehead. "I did not say that, you hear me? The name never passed my lips."

"Well, it passed my ears."

"Cheray, promise me you won't mention that name to anybody, and I mean anybody, in connection with this case."

"Why, is he getting publicity shy?"

"Promise me, or you'll be eating two steaks."

"Oh, all right, I promise. Not that I couldn't eat two steaks. Tell me, how did your relationship with this . . . anonymous person come about?"

Herb shrugged. "I've never met the man. Apparently, my reputation precedes me. So, you want to do this deal and make yourself famous overnight, without all the bother of a trial?"

"First, I want to know what your client has got on the other two that will get them to plead and take a life sentence."

"He worked in that hotel as the night clerk with them for a year and a half. He noticed that one or the other would disappear for an hour or two—never together."

"I'll need more than that," she replied.

"Suppose my client kept a journal of his evenings and noted the dates and times when one or the other was out of sight, and suppose one of them was in L.A. at the time of the copycat murder? Would that be enough to sway you to do the right thing?"

"I'd have to see the journal," she said.

Herb unsnapped his briefcase. "What a coincidence!" he said. "I just happen to have it right here." He handed it over. "Save time and go where the markers are."

Cheray went through the diary, between sips of her martini. "Well, shit," she said. "A chimpanzee could get a conviction with this."

"Not just a conviction, a couple of confessions," Herb said. "Save the DA the time and costs of a trial." He extended his hand across the table. "And all that anxiety, waiting for the jury to come back with a verdict."

Cheray thought about it for a moment, then took Herb's hand. "Counselor, you've got your client a deal," she said. "Subject to the old man's approval, of course."

"Oh, I don't think you'll have any problem getting that," Herb said. He tucked the journal back into his briefcase. "You'll get this in exchange for the written offer."

After dinner, they went back to her place, dismissed the driver, and sealed the deal with an enthusiastic roll in the hay. Herb got back to his own apartment in time to shower and change for the office.

35

As Stone was finishing up his day, Joan came in. "Mr. Mikeford Whitehorn's assistant called and asked if you'd turn up at his dinner party tonight a few minutes early. I accepted for you."

"Thanks for saving me the trouble," he said, glancing at his watch. He could make it. "And please tell Fred we're leaving early."

She returned to her office, and Stone went upstairs to shower and dress. He found a tuxedo that had recently been pressed, buttoned on the suspenders, and got into it. He chose a black tie and neatly knotted it in one smooth motion, something he had once seen Cary Grant do in a movie. He had practiced for days until he got it right, and he regretted that there was no witness to compliment him. He slipped into the waistcoat and got his gold Patek Philippe pocket watch and chain from the safe, wound the watch, attached the bar to its little buttonhole, and slipped the watch into its right pocket. The counterweight, a small gold folding knife, went into the left. He put on the jacket and selected a white silk pocket square and tucked it into the breast pocket. He put his iPhone and pen into their proper pockets and examined the result: presentable. His dowager dinner partner would be knocked out.

Fred was waiting downstairs and drove him uptown to 740 Park. The elevator opened onto a private foyer, where the butler was waiting to show him into the library. There was a Knob Creek on the rocks waiting for him on a small table between two wing chairs facing the fireplace, where a cheerful blaze burned.

Mikeford "Swifty" Whitehorn appeared almost immediately, right after his own glass of scotch. "Good evening, Stone," he said.

Stone stood and took his hand. "Good evening, Swifty," he replied. They sat down, raised their glasses, and sipped.

"Thank you for coming early," Whitehorn said. "I thought, perhaps, I'd give you the news, if you haven't heard."

"I haven't seen or heard any news since the *Times* this morning," Stone replied.

"Well, in tomorrow morning's *Times* you will learn that the district attorney has given my grandson immunity in return for his testimony, and the DA has used that news to persuade the two perpetrators to accept life terms with the possibility of parole."

"Which they are unlikely ever to receive, because of the number and savagery of their crimes," Stone said.

"Your Herbert Fisher wrapped up the whole thing in an afternoon, apparently sealing the bargain in the assistant district attorney's bed, if my driver's judgment is any good. I loaned Mr. Faber my car for the day, and he passed it on to Mr. Fisher."

"I'm delighted to hear it went well," Stone said. "If you're pleased with the outcome, perhaps you might sometime direct some business Herb's way. He's very versatile and can handle just about anything."

"I have already done so," Whitehorn replied.

"On Herb's behalf and that of Woodman & Weld, I thank you."

"And now I'd like to do something for you," Whitehorn said.

"That's not necessary," Stone replied.

"Such things are always necessary," Whitehorn replied, "or Earth would not turn on its axis. Your dinner partner this evening will be an old friend of mine, Edith Beresford. Edie is a widow and a divorcée, the two events occurring almost simultaneously—fortunately before her ex-husband had time to change his will. So, instead of getting half his estate, she got everything, there being no children to squander it all."

"She's to be complimented on her timing," Stone said.

"Edie needs a bit of help in setting her affairs in order," Whitehorn said. "She tends to be impulsive about such things and is sometimes inclined toward people whose motives are, shall we say, questionable."

"I suppose that's always a danger for wealthy widows," Stone said.

"I ran a Dun & Bradstreet on you and poked around in other places, and I'm satisfied that you don't need her money."

Stone didn't think thanks were in order for Swifty's prying, so he said nothing.

"I hope that doesn't offend you," Whitehorn said after a pause, "and if it does, well, tough."

Stone laughed into his bourbon. "I'm not offended, Swifty. You're not the first to have a look under the stones of my life." He was already wondering who he could palm off Edith Beresford on—not Herbie Fisher—perhaps Bill Eggers, who liked old ladies with piles of money for clients.

"There's another matter I'd like to discuss with you, Stone," Whitehorn said, staring into his scotch.

"Certainly," Stone replied.

"It's my grandson, Mike Adams, who this afternoon received his freedom."

"How can I help?"

"I realize you haven't met the boy, but I've always felt he had more to offer than we've seen from him. His father, Howard Adams, is not very well, and I fear we'll lose him in a year or two. Then Mike will be awash in money, which may not be the best thing for him. Howard owns the commercial real estate company that owns the hotel where Mike was given the night clerk's job. They're going to close the hotel immediately; it was scheduled for a gutting and renovation anyway, but its new infamy would kill any existing business. They want to turn it into more of a businessman's destination."

"Do you think that Mike, if given major responsibility, might rise to it?"

"That is in line with my assessment of him. However, he has disappointed his father so often that I think he is unlikely to be given such responsibilities."

"Do you have any influence with the boy's father?"

"I daresay I do. I put him in business and invested heavily with him."

"Has your investment paid off?"

"It certainly has, and beyond my expectations."

"Then, perhaps, his father might be susceptible to a suggestion from you that he put Mike in charge of the revitalization of this hotel. The boy should know something about it, having worked there for a year or two."

Whitehorn looked thoughtful. "And, if Mike looks like he is screwing it up, the brakes could be applied."

"He could start by reconceptualizing the hotel, perhaps as something better than a businessman's destination. There are a lot of hotels in the city that cater to a younger crowd, who seem to have a lot of money to spend, but they're mostly downtown; none in that neighborhood."

"By God, that's a fine idea!" Swifty said. "I'll have lunch with Howard tomorrow and put it to him."

The butler entered the room. "Mr. Whitehorn, Mrs. Edith Beresford," he said, "and there are others arriving, too."

The butler was followed into the library by a tall, slim woman in her thirties, wearing a clinging sheath of a dress that featured a lot of gold thread and accented her full breasts.

"Edith," Swifty said, "may I present Mr. Stone Barrington? Stone, this is Edith Beresford."

36

S TONE SHOOK EDITH'S HAND. "How do you do?"

"Very well, thank you."

Her voice reminded Stone of that of Ava Gardner, smooth and a little Southern.

"Tell me," he said, "were you, by any chance, born in a small Georgia town called Delano?"

"No," she replied, "I was born in a slightly larger Georgia town called Atlanta."

"Ah," he replied. "I seem to meet so many people from Delano."

"I'm afraid I don't have an answer for that," she said. "I believe you must be the attorney Swifty says can put all my affairs into order."

"He did mention something about that," Stone replied, "but frankly, you don't look like a woman who needs her affairs put into order. The impression you give is one of confidence."

She smiled. "Thank you. That sounds like a very good excuse for you to avoid the job."

"I have a better excuse than that," Stone said.

"And what would that be?"

"I would prefer a personal relationship to a business one, and the two are often incompatible. However, I can recommend an excellent person for the job."

"And who might that be?"

"Bill Eggers, who is the managing partner of my firm, Woodman & Weld."

"I've heard good things about the firm," she said, "but why Mr. Eggers? Surely someone a bit further down the ladder—but not too far—might be more interested in my situation."

"Well, Bill has something of a specialty in dowager widows and divorcées, you see." He held up a hand. "I know, but if I tell him you're a dowager, he will have a more immediate reason to see you. Then you can surprise him at your first meeting."

"As I surprised you, Mr. Barrington?"

"I confess you did," Stone replied. "Please call me Stone."

"And I'm Edie," she replied. "What sort of 'personal relationship' did you have in mind?"

"Why don't we start with dinner and see where that leads us?"

"But we're having dinner this evening," she said.

"Of course, but this evening I'll have to share you with whoever is seated on your other side, and while I'm not the jealous type, well, my personal motto is *Si non nunc quando.*"

She laughed. "'If not now, when.'"

"Your Latin is very good."

"It comes from having been a classical scholar. How's yours?"

"I have just exhausted my entire Latin vocabulary," he said.

"All right, we can have half a dinner tonight and a whole one tomorrow evening?"

"What more could I ask?" Stone said.

"I'm sure you'll think of something."

They were called in to dinner. It was a table for twelve; Stone was on Edie's right, and another gentleman, whose place card read "Dr. Johnny Hon," was on her left.

Edie and Dr. Hon exhibited an immediate affinity for each other, and Stone was having difficulty getting a word in edgewise. Between courses, Dr. Hon excused himself for a moment.

"Whew!" Stone said. "I'm glad to see the back of him."

"Why?" Edie asked. "He's perfectly charming."

"I expect that's why I'm mostly seeing the back of you."

She laughed. "And you struck me as a competitive sort. Was I wrong?"

"Well, I could arm-wrestle him for the privilege of your attention, I suppose."

"Think of it as football," she said. "What you need is a turnover."

Dr. Hon returned, and Stone lost the ball again. After dinner, when Dr. Hon's attention was diverted, he took the opportunity to whisk Edie into the library, where they were alone.

"Turnover accomplished!" Edie said.

"Now I have to score?"

She laughed again; he liked it when she laughed. "You'll have to run up a lot of yardage rushing," she replied. "The forward pass doesn't work every time."

The butler appeared with a tray of after-dinner drinks, and they both chose cognac.

"Let me ask you a question," she said, "the answer to which I have always found to be revealing."

"Then I'll be sure to give you a straight answer."

"Where is your second home?"

Stone burst out laughing. "That's a more difficult question than I anticipated," he said.

"Why?"

"Because I have more than one second home. But for purposes of this discussion, and because it's the closest, my reply will be Dark Harbor, Maine."

She looked surprised. "Nothing in the Hamptons?"

"I'm afraid not. I don't think I'd fit in very well out there."

"Very good," she said. "I despise the Hamptons. Now, since you have more than one second home, where is your favorite one?"

Stone thought about it for a moment before replying. "South Hampshire, England," he said. "On the Beaulieu River."

"And why is it your favorite?"

"I like the climate."

That made her laugh again. "Oh, really?"

"There's nothing like curling up with a good book and listening to the rain beat against the window."

"I perceive that you are a contrarian. Everyone else is looking for heat and sunshine."

"Heat is overrated," Stone replied. "I enjoy a cool day."

"And sunshine?"

"Is most appreciated when rare. Now it's your turn. Where is your second home?"

"In the Hamptons," she said, "in Sag Harbor."

"But you despise the Hamptons!"

"Yes, but I despise Sag Harbor somewhat less than the other towns. Besides, I didn't choose it; my husband already owned the house when we married. And anyway, it's on the market. In fact, I was hoping to sell it to you."

"Don't point that thing at me," Stone said. "My real estate portfolio is threatening to explode as it is."

And then, before they could continue, Dr. Johnny Hon appeared and pulled up a chair.

"May I pick you up at seven tomorrow evening?" Stone asked, before the man could get started.

"I have something a little earlier; may we meet somewhere?"

"Do you know Patroon?"

"I do, but not well."

He gave her the address, then ceded her company to Dr. Hon.

37

EDITH BERESFORD WAS TWENTY minutes late for dinner. Stone was about to order his second bourbon when she turned up, all apologies. Her hair was down, and it fell below her shoulders.

"I am so sorry," she said. "I'd give you my excuse, but it wouldn't be good enough. It would get our evening off to a poor start, and I wouldn't want that."

"Then I forgive you all your sins, so we won't have to work through them. What would you like to drink?"

"What are you having?"

"Knob Creek bourbon."

"Never heard of it. I'll have some of that."

He ordered two, and they arrived quickly. They clinked glasses and drank.

"I feel so clean," she said.

"How's that?"

"I haven't had all my sins forgiven since I was in high

school, during my last confession. I stopped going after that."

"What was your sin?" he asked.

"It would be too embarrassing to tell you."

"Then what was your penance?"

"Ten Hail Marys and swearing never to put my hand in a boy's pants again."

"Did you keep your oath?"

"Why do you think I stopped going to confession? I couldn't face that priest again!"

Stone laughed.

"Are you Catholic?" she asked.

"I'm not a joiner, generally speaking. I think I agree with my late friend Frank Muir, who described himself as a lapsed agnostic."

She laughed. "Good choice. If you were Catholic and I were your confessor, what would you confess?"

"Impure thoughts."

"Oh, good. And what penance would you think appropriate?"

"Forty lashes with your hair."

She looked appreciative. "I should get it cut, shouldn't I?"

"No, at least not until I've done my penance."

Then Stone realized someone was standing at their table.

"Oh," Edie said, "Dr. Hon!"

"You've been following us, haven't you?" Stone asked.

"Of course not, but may I join you?"

"Not unless you have the ecclesiastical authority to do so," Stone replied.

"I fear my degrees are in science, not divinity."

"Then we will not require your services," Stone said. "Now, if you will excuse us." He made a shooing motion with the back of his hand.

Dr. Hon looked sheepish. "Well, it was worth a try."

"Good evening," Stone said with finality.

"That was rude," Edie said when he had gone.

"It was, wasn't it? I'd like to have been ruder, but it was the best I could do without taking a swing at him."

"I thought you did very well. After all, he kept us apart for one evening already. He's nothing if not persistent; I hope he doesn't come back."

"Don't worry, I'm armed."

She looked at him in mock alarm. "With what?"

"A little Colt .380 semiautomatic." He patted his chest under his arm.

"And for what reason?"

"A jealous husband."

"I can't say that surprises me."

"That is a slur on my character. I do not dally with married women. She came to me as a client, sort of, and her husband misunderstood."

"What does 'sort of' a client mean?"

"Well, I met her in a luggage store, when she broke a heel and fell into my lap. I offered her a lift home, got her to her apartment in a wheelchair, and arranged a house call from a doctor. While we were waiting for him to show up, she learned that I was an attorney, and she asked me to suggest someone to represent her in a divorce. She also asked me to recommend a Realtor, as she was looking to buy an apartment and to sell her old one."

"And what was the upshot of all that?"

"Her ankle is better, she is divorced, and she has just moved into a new apartment. And sold her old one."

"My, you do give good advice, don't you?"

"I endeavor to—it doesn't always work that quickly."

"I'm beginning to think I should have opted for the professional relationship with you."

"Oh, no, it would have ended badly."

"Why?"

"Because I would still have wanted the personal relationship. If you had taken advice from me under those circumstances my judgment would have been clouded, and you'd have dismissed me and ended up married to a man who was interested only in your money and, because of that, broke."

"You've been listening to Swifty Whitehorn, haven't you?"

"If I had not, we wouldn't be sitting here about to order the chateaubriand and an excellent cabernet."

"Is that what we're having?"

"Unless you are not a carnivore."

"I am, order it."

THEY HAD FINISHED their dinner and were on coffee.

"Are you really armed?" she asked.

"Really."

"Do you always go armed?"

"Only when there's a jealous husband about."

"Does that happen often?"

"I try to avoid the circumstance."

"Doesn't it feel unnatural to have a weapon concealed on your person?"

"It does not. I was once a police officer and, thus, always armed. One becomes accustomed to it."

"*You* were a police officer?"

"A homicide detective, for most of my career."

"How long did your career last?"

"Fourteen years, then they asked for their badge and gun back."

"Why?"

"They attributed my exit to a knee wound, suffered in the line of duty, but that was just an excuse. The truth is: I was a pain in the ass, and they were sick of me."

"Then it is their loss," she said, leaning over and kissing him. "Enough of this chitchat," she said. "Why don't you show me where you live? I'm still looking for clues to your character."

Stone waved at a passing waiter. "Check!"

38

EDIE BERESFORD STOOD in the middle of Stone's living room and turned 360 degrees, slowly. "I like the pictures," she said, "they show good judgment."

"I'm afraid they say nothing at all about my judgment," Stone replied. "They were painted by my mother, so all they demonstrate is maternal loyalty. However, I like them, too."

"Who was your mother?"

"Matilda Stone."

"I remember that name. She has some work in the American Collection at the Met, doesn't she?"

"She does."

"Is the piano in tune, or is it there just as an objet d'art?"

"Both," Stone replied.

"Then play me something."

Stone sat down, opened the keyboard, and played some Gershwin.

"Very nice. Tell me about the rest of the house."

"My study is over there. Would you like a brandy?"

"Yes, please."

He took her into the room, seated her, lit the fire, and poured them both a Rémy Martin. "This room is very much you," she said, looking around. "Who was your decorator?"

"I was."

"Tell me about the rest of the house."

"There are six bedrooms upstairs, on three floors, and seven baths."

"Why more baths than bedrooms?"

"There are two in the master suite."

"Very wise."

"Downstairs are my offices—in what used to be a dentist's office—a small gym, and a kitchen that opens onto the common gardens out back. There's also a garage."

"How did you find the house?"

"It found me. It belonged to my great-aunt, my grand-mother's sister, and she left it to me. I did the renovation, except for the plumbing and electrical work."

"You mean you did the actual work?"

"I couldn't afford to hire a builder on a cop's salary."

"How did you become a lawer?"

"By studying at NYU Law, before I was a cop. When I wasn't a cop anymore, Bill Eggers offered me a job at Wood-man & Weld, if I could pass the bar. After a two-week cram course, I did."

"And the rest is history?"

"History in the making. It occurs to me that you have me at a disadvantage. You know nearly everything about me, and I know nearly nothing about you."

"Pretty straightforward: born and raised in an antebellum

house in northwest Atlanta; Daddy a judge; Mother a college professor; educated at Agnes Scott College, in Atlanta; came to New York looking for adventure, found it, married young—big mistake; married a second time—another big mistake, but he had the grace to die and leave me his fortune. Met a nice man at a dinner party, and that brings us up-to-date."

"I'm sure a lot fell through the cracks in that account," Stone said.

"Then you can explore the cracks for the rest."

Stone's phone rang and he checked the ID. "Please excuse me, I have to take this." He walked across the room. "Hello?"

"It's Faith."

"How are you feeling?"

"More and more human. I'm receiving visitors tomorrow morning."

"I'll be there."

"Night, night." She hung up, and Stone returned to the couch and his brandy.

"Not bad news, I hope," Edie said.

"Good news. An employee of mine is in the hospital with extensive injuries; but she's getting better, and I can see her tomorrow."

"How was she injured?"

"She was attacked, but her attackers are in jail, awaiting sentencing."

"What does she do for you?"

"She's my chief pilot—sorry, my only pilot. I bought a new airplane, and it requires two pilots; I'm the other one."

"Will she come back to work when she recovers?"

"I certainly hope so. She's a very good pilot."

Edie glanced at her watch. "Goodness, is it that late?"

"I suppose it is."

"Then I have to go home; I have an early day tomorrow."

"Fred will drive you," Stone said. "Dinner next week?"

"Of course, call me."

He walked her downstairs, kissed her, and put her in the car.

As he reached his bedroom his cell rang. "Hello?"

"It's Dino. You alone?"

"I just put her into the car."

"Who?"

"You don't know this one. Her name is Edith Beresford."

"You're right. Sounds old."

"It only sounds that way. I have *good* news. Your guys can question Faith tomorrow."

"I'm afraid she's old news," Dino said. "Her assailants have already pled out."

"I heard that."

"Still, we ought to have her on the record, so I'll send somebody around."

"You do that."

"Dinner tomorrow night?"

"I've got plans: Cilla is cooking for me."

"Later, then."

They hung up, and Stone went to bed.

THE FOLLOWING MORNING, TV news caught up to events and reported the guilty plea from the two perpetrators at the hotel. They also reported that Mike Adams had been released.

Stone had just finished breakfast when his phone rang. "Hello?"

"It's Swifty," a deep voice said.

"Good morning. I must thank you for introducing me to Edith Beresford. We had a very pleasant dinner last evening."

"Are you going to represent her?"

"She's far too beautiful for a business relationship. I'm going to turn her over to Bill Eggers."

"That should be fine," Swifty said. "I want to thank you, too."

"For what?"

"My son-in-law, my grandson, and I had lunch together yesterday, and it went well. We went back to Howard's office and went over the plans for the renovation of the hotel, and young Mike had some good suggestions to make. He's now the project manager on the hotel for Adams & Adams, his father's firm."

"That's very good news, Swifty."

"Not as good as the news that he's a free man."

"For that you can thank Herb Fisher."

"I have, and I will be in touch with him about more work."

"I don't think you need to worry about Edie. She has a good head on her shoulders."

"I always knew that, I was just playing matchmaker."

"Nice job," Stone said, and they said goodbye.

39

Stone's cell phone buzzed while he was being driven to Bellevue by Fred. "Hello?"

"It's Cilla, good morning."

"Good morning."

"Are we still on for tonight?"

"We are."

"Good. My intercom is broken. When you arrive, the desk man will have your name and send you straight up to the twelfth floor. I'll leave the door cracked, so just let yourself in. The bar is in the living room so you can make yourself a bourbon and me a vodka on the rocks, then find the kitchen, where I'll be up to my elbows in osso buco."

"My favorite. See you at seven." They hung up.

STONE ARRIVED OUTSIDE Faith's hospital room and looked in to find two men in suits seated at her bedside, so he leaned against the jamb and listened.

"Is there anything else you can remember, Ms. Barnacle?" one of the men asked. "Anything at all?"

"No. I'm sorry to be of so little help."

"If you remember anything else, please call me. I'll leave my card on your bedside table. Good day."

Stone heard the scraping of chairs on the floor, then Faith said, "Wait, I remember something."

The two men sat down again. "What do you remember?"

"Music."

"What kind of music?"

"Classical. On a radio, I think. There was a voice introducing the next piece."

"Could you see the radio?"

"No, I just heard it. After that, I found my way to the window."

The two men thanked her again, then left.

Stone went into the room and found Faith halfway sitting up in her bed, with the sheets pulled up to her neck. He kissed her on the forehead and pulled up a chair. "Feeling any better?"

"I am. The cuts still hurt, but the morphine is taking care of that. I pulled the sheets up because I don't want anybody to see the cuts, which are unbandaged. I was told I have something like one hundred and fifty stitches."

"Then just try to relax. Is there anything I can bring you? Books? Magazines?"

"The morphine makes it hard to concentrate on reading," she said, "but the TV remote is taped to my hand, and I can watch."

"What are your doctors telling you?"

"As soon as my cuts are less painful, I can get out of here; I hope I'm not addicted to morphine by then. The middle of the week, maybe. I won't have to come back to get the stitches out; they'll dissolve by themselves. The cuts are covered by green, transparent tape, which looks like bruising."

"The airplane is waiting for you, when you're ready."

"Thank you, Stone. I'm going to have to take a nap now, so will you excuse me?"

"Sure." He kissed her on the forehead again and left.

THAT EVENING, Stone chose a good bottle of red from his cellar, and on the way to Cilla's apartment he stopped at a bodega and picked up a bouquet of flowers. "Take the rest of the evening off, Fred," he said as he got out in front of Cilla's building. "I'll get a cab home."

"Yes, sir," Fred replied and drove away to his own dinner.

Stone was inspected by the doorman and admitted to the lobby, where he found an empty front desk. Oh, well, he thought, desk men have to go to the john like everyone else. There was a log of visitors on the desk, and he signed in at seven o'clock, then he took the elevator to the twelfth floor and got out. The upstairs foyer smelled deliciously of Italian cooking, and he could hear jazz playing through the door, which was ajar.

He went into the apartment, found the bar, located a vase, put water into it, and fluffed up the flowers, then he poured himself a drink from a new, sealed bottle of Knob Creek and did the same with a bottle of Belvedere vodka. The music was coming from a built-in system and traveled with him as he walked toward the kitchen.

The dining room held a handsome table for twelve, but the walls there, as in the living room, were missing pictures, which were, no doubt, on Cilla's shopping list. "Hello!" he called out as he entered the kitchen.

There were pots simmering on the stove, but no Cilla in sight. "Cilla?" Powder room, he figured. He set the two drinks on the kitchen island, where there were barstools, took one and settled in, glancing at his watch. Five past seven. He sipped his drink, waiting patiently, then it was seven-fifteen. He got up and looked for a powder room. As he turned back, he saw a pair of legs protruding from behind the kitchen island. One ankle was bandaged and the shoe was missing.

He ran to her and found her lying on her back, a large chef's knife protruding from her chest. He knelt beside her, avoiding a pool of blood, and felt for an artery in her neck. Nothing, and her body was cool. He stood up, walked back to his barstool, sat down, and took a big swig of his drink. Then he got out his cell phone and called Dino.

"Bacchetti."

"It's Stone," he said.

Dino must have caught something in his voice because he immediately asked, "What's wrong?"

"I've just arrived at Cilla's apartment for dinner and found her dead in the kitchen, with a knife in her chest."

"Oh, Christ," Dino said. "Are you all right?"

"I am. Will you send your people over here, please?"

"No. You call nine-one-one, like everybody else, and they'll send the people. It's better if I don't get entangled in this since I know both the victim and the prime suspect."

"'Prime suspect'? Are you kidding?"

"I kid you not. That's how the detectives are going to treat you when they arrive, and rightly so. You know as well as I do that the person finding the victim is always a prime suspect. I hope I don't have to tell you not to touch anything and to be completely honest with the detectives."

"No, you don't have to tell me that, so stop telling me that, please."

"Let me know how it goes, pal," Dino said, "but not until you're cleared." He hung up.

"Thanks so much," Stone said to the dead telephone. Then it occurred to him that he might not be alone in the apartment. He set down his drink, pulled his weapon from its shoulder holster, and slipped out of his shoes. Room by room, he searched the place, checking every closet and hiding place, then he went back to the kitchen and did the same there. Nothing. He switched off the burners on the stove.

His mind more at ease, he picked up a wall phone in the kitchen, called 911, and went through their drill. Then he hung up the phone, recovered his drink, went back into the living room, placed his gun and badge on the bar, and sat down to wait for the law to arrive.

40

FIRST STONE HEARD the siren coming down Fifth Avenue, then it stopped outside. Another couple of minutes and he heard the elevator door open.

"In here," he called out. "The door is open."

The door opened the rest of the way, and a young man in a dark suit peered around it.

"I'm alone and unarmed," Stone said. "Come in."

The cop came in, gun out in front of him, followed by his partner.

"I've cleared the place," Stone said. "There's no one else here."

"Are you a cop?" the detective asked.

"Retired. My gun and badge are on the bar, next to the flowers and the bottle of wine."

The cop was still pointing his gun. "Stand up," he said.

Stone stood, holding his arms away from his body.

"Hands on top of your head, fingers interlocked."

Stone followed instructions and allowed himself to be

handcuffed and thoroughly searched. The cop kept his wallet.

"A gun and a badge are over here," the other cop said from the bar. "Detective First Grade."

"Clear the place," the first cop said.

"Will you uncuff me now?" Stone asked.

"You just stand right there. I'll decide when to uncuff you."

The other detective came back. "There's a woman in the kitchen with a knife in her chest," he said. "I called for the ME and a team. Otherwise, all clear."

"Okay," the younger man said, "you can sit down now."

"Uncuff me first," Stone said.

"I'm not concerned with your comfort, I just want answers."

"Well, you're not getting any until you've uncuffed me," Stone said.

The older cop uncuffed him. "Have a seat, Mr. . . . ."

"Barrington," Stone said, sitting down and picking up his drink from the side table. "And you?"

"He's Detective Calabrese. I'm Muldoon."

"I didn't know there was a Muldoon left on the NYPD," Stone said.

"We're a rare breed," Muldoon said.

Calabrese went to take a look at the corpse for himself, then came back. "Did you touch anything?"

"The phone on the wall. And I turned off two burners on the stove. Dinner was cooking."

"Do you always walk around barefoot?"

"I took off my shoes when I was clearing the apartment. They're in the kitchen."

"I'll get them for you," Calabrese said.

"Why are you here?" Muldoon asked. Calabrese came back and tossed Stone's shoes on the floor, and he put them on.

"I was invited to dinner," Stone said. "I arrived at seven. She told me the intercom was broken, and she'd leave the door open for me. The desk man was absent, so I came upstairs. I put the flowers in some water and poured us both a drink, as she had asked me to. Then I went into the kitchen, and didn't see her. I sat on a stool for a while, then I went to look for her and saw her legs sticking out."

"One of them has an Ace bandage on the ankle," Calabrese said.

"A sprain." Stone told them how he and Cilla had met.

"You got a guess on a suspect?" Muldoon asked.

"The ex-husband, one Donald Trask. They've been divorced for two weeks. She gave him a lot of money to get out of the marriage, but maybe not as much as he would have liked."

"You look pretty calm for somebody who's found a corpse with a knife in it," Calabrese said.

"I've seen more corpses than you have," Stone replied.

"Maybe," Calabrese said.

"Certainly," Muldoon offered. "You got an address for this Trask?"

Stone checked his phone and gave him the address. "He moved in there a week ago Friday. He owns several guns, but his carry license may have been revoked. He failed to list a new purchase."

"Was there any animosity between them?"

"Plenty, all on his part. He beat her up a couple of times,

put her in the hospital once. You might want to talk to the attorney who represented her: Herbert Fisher, at this number." He gave Muldoon his own card. "He's my law partner."

"If Trask has guns, why would he knife her?" Calabrese asked.

"No ballistics on a knife," Stone said, rolling his eyes. "And you might check with the desk man to see if Trask announced himself. He may have come in while the man was away from his post, as I did, then left down the stairs to the garage."

"You've got this all figured out, have you?" Calabrese asked.

"I had time to think about it while I was waiting for you to show up," Stone replied.

"What time did you say you arrived?"

"Seven o'clock. You can check the log downstairs; I signed in."

"Trask is a good lead," Muldoon said. "We'll follow it all the way."

"If it doesn't pan out," Stone said, "then I haven't got a clue. She never mentioned anybody else to me. They didn't have any kids, and he wasn't the sort to make fast friendships."

"Do you know him personally?"

"He showed up at my office once, thinking I was her lawyer. I straightened him out, and he left. He called on another occasion; he was very angry. He was hanging around my block, but a friend of mine discouraged him, and I don't think he came back. He did behave himself at the divorce hearing, I'm told. He'll have a gun safe in his apartment."

Then a parade of technicians began to enter the apartment and were directed to the kitchen. The detectives' lieutenant arrived and listened to Stone's story all over again, then told the detectives to go detain Trask. As they were leaving, the ME came out of the kitchen.

"The knife wasn't the cause of death," he said.

"I would have thought that would do it," Muldoon said.

"She was shot first," he said, "then stabbed, probably to cover up the gunshot wound."

"Did you dig out a bullet?"

"We'll do that in the lab. I'll let you know. Oh, I'd put time of death at between six-thirty and seven PM." The ME went back to the kitchen.

Muldoon shook Stone's hand and left with Calabrese in tow. Stone recovered his gun and badge, tied his shoes, and followed them.

Downstairs, the desk man was back at his post.

"I logged in while you were away," Stone said, turning the logbook around. "Did a man named Trask arrive to see Ms. Scott?"

"Nobody arrived," the desk man said. "I saw your name in the log. She had said she was expecting you."

"Tell it all to the cops when they get around to you," Stone said, "and don't leave anything out."

He went outside, where it had begun to drizzle. The door-man managed to get him a cab.

"You a friend of Ms. Scott?" he asked as he opened the door for Stone.

"Yes," Stone replied.

"We hardly got to know her," the man said, then closed the cab door.

Stone rode home depressed. He needed another drink.

41

STONE WENT TO HIS STUDY, poured himself a drink, and called Dino.

"Bacchetti."

"Okay, I'm clear, no thanks to you."

"Who did they send?"

"An old pro named Muldoon and a kid called Calabrese."

"Yeah, I know them both. How'd they do?"

"Muldoon did just fine. The kid could barely keep up and was, in general, a pain in the ass."

"It figures. You weren't such a hotshot, either, when you were a green detective."

"Neither were you," Stone said.

"I got a report on the interview with Faith Barnacle," Dino said. "That's new about the music. She may come up with more later."

"Let's hope so," Stone said.

"What are you worried about? The killers have pled out."

"Yeah, you're right. I'll stop worrying."

"Have you eaten anything?" Dino asked.

"No, but I'll see what's in the fridge."

"Later."

"Sure." Stone hung up and went down to the kitchen. He found half a roast chicken and some peas in the fridge and nuked them, then opened half a bottle of a cabernet and sat down in the kitchen booth, eating slowly and watching the rain run down the windows. The Turtle Bay gardens looked bleak.

He rinsed his dishes and put them in the dishwasher, then went upstairs, undressed, and got into bed. He tried NY1, the local news channel. Cilla's murder had already filled the Breaking News slot; there was no mention of Donald Trask.

SEAN MULDOON AND DANTE CALABRESE got out of their car and went into Donald Trask's building.

"I can't wait to talk to this guy," Calabrese said.

"You shut up, and I'll do the talking this time. You'll learn more by listening." Muldoon flashed his badge at the man on the front desk. "Is Donald Trask at home?"

"Yes, he is." The man reached for his phone, but Muldoon stopped him. "What time did he come in?"

"I came on at six. I guess he walked in closer to six-thirty."

"How much closer? It's important."

"Okay, between six-twenty-five and six-thirty-five. That do?"

"We'll see; what's his apartment number?"

"Seven D, to your left out of the elevator."

"Don't announce us," Muldoon said.

"I'm supposed . . ."

"Do you want to be arrested for interfering with a police investigation?"

"No, sir."

"Then stay off the phone. We'll surprise Mr. Trask."

"All right, sir."

The two detectives got onto the elevator and pressed the button. "Remember," Muldoon said, "I'll take the lead. We're going to be real polite, put the fella at ease, you understand?"

"Whatever you say, Sean."

"That's good. I like that. Remember it."

"I did okay with Barrington, didn't I?"

"No, you didn't. You were up against a man with more experience than you. You'd have gotten along better if you'd treated him as a senior colleague, instead of a perp."

The door opened, and they rang the bell for D. Muldoon saw some light appear in the peephole, then the door opened but was secured by a chain. Muldoon showed him a badge. "NYPD," he said. "Are you Mr. Trask?"

"Yes. What about it?"

"Please open the door, we'd like to talk to you."

"About what?"

"Mr. Trask, would you rather talk to a SWAT team?"

"Oh, all right." The door closed, the chain rattled, and Trask stood there in his pajamas, a book in his hand—*Oliver Twist*. Muldoon thought that Donald Trask didn't look like the type for Dickens. "Let's go sit down, shall we?" he asked.

Trask stood aside and let them walk down a hall to the living room. The place wasn't in perfect order; there were cardboard boxes stacked in the living room. "Sorry about the mess, I just moved in."

"Not at all." Muldoon tossed a pile of books from a chair onto the floor and sat down.

"What's this about?" Trask asked again.

"First, I'm obliged to tell you that you're not under arrest, and you don't have to talk with us. You can have an attorney present, if you like."

Trask thought about that. "I guess I don't need a lawyer. Ask whatever you like."

"Mr. Trask, what did you do this evening?"

"I had a burger and a beer at P. J. Clarke's."

"What time did you arrive at Clarke's?"

"Around five, I guess. I went straight from my office, about a block from there."

"Did you see anyone you knew at Clarke's?"

"No, I don't think so."

"Do the bartenders know you?"

"I've been there before. But there's no reason for them to know my name."

"Had the waiter served you before?"

"I don't recall that he has."

"What time did you leave Clarke's?"

"After six, I guess. It was raining, and I couldn't find a cab, so I walked home."

"And what time did you arrive?"

"Six-thirtyish. The network news was just coming on when I got upstairs."

"What was the lead story on the news?"

"I wasn't listening all that closely. The flu epidemic, I think. I was making myself a drink."

"Did you have a drink before your burger at Clarke's?"

"No, I was hungry. I ordered a beer and drank that with my burger."

"Did you make any detours on the way home? Anything at all?"

"No, I told you, it was raining. I was getting wet, so I hurried."

"Do you mind if I take a picture of you?" Muldoon asked, producing his iPhone. He snapped one before Trask could reply.

"Okay, before we go any further, I want to know what this is about," Trask said.

"It's about your wife."

"I don't have a wife."

"All right, your ex-wife, Priscilla Scott. When was the last time you saw her?"

"At our divorce hearing. There were plenty of witnesses."

"To your knowledge, did Ms. Scott have a will, and are you mentioned in it?"

"Yes and yes. We both did new wills a couple of years ago. Why are we talking about wills? Has something happened to her?"

"Yes, she's deceased, I'm afraid."

Trask's eyebrows went up; it was the first emotion he'd shown. "Jesus, was she in an accident?"

"No, she was murdered."

"You're kidding me!"

"I am not, sir. She was found by a dinner guest with a knife in her chest."

Trask gulped. "Was her dinner guest named Barrington?"

"Why do you ask?"

"Because if he was there, he's the one who killed her."

"Mr. Trask, do you own any guns?"

"Yes."

"Where are they?"

"In my safe."

"May I see them, please?"

Trask walked over to a bookcase and moved some books aside, revealing a safe. He punched in a code, opened it, and stood back. "There you go."

Muldoon walked over to the safe, removed each weapon, sniffed its barrel, and then set it on the bookshelf. "Mr. Trask, do you have a New York City gun license?"

"I do."

"May I see it, please?"

Trask found his wallet and handed him the license.

Muldoon handed it back. "This Beretta has been fired recently," he said.

"I went to the range at lunchtime today."

Muldoon nodded at Calabrese, meaning, *Note that.*

"Do you mind if I take the Beretta with me?" he asked.

"What for?"

"Just to have it looked at. Don't worry, we'll return it to you in good order."

"Okay, sure, why not?"

Muldoon pocketed the pistol and turned to go. There was a coatrack in the hall with a raincoat hanging from it. He made a point of running his hand over it as they passed. "Thank you and good night, Mr. Trask."

"Don't mention it."

The door closed firmly behind them, and the chain rattled.

"Why didn't you pull his license?" Calabrese asked.

"Because the Beretta has been registered, so we have no excuse. I've got the gun, though. If he's our guy, then he thinks we won't find the bullet. And by the way, his raincoat is a little damp, but not as wet as it would get walking here from Clarke's. Let's run over there and see if anybody recognizes him from his photograph."

They did so, and nobody did.

42

MULDOON AND CALABRESE went downtown to the morgue and found the ME working on Priscilla Scott's cadaver.

"Anything?" he asked.

"I found a bullet," the ME replied. "It's a nine-millimeter round, Federal Personal Defense, Hydra-Shok—a hollow point."

"I'd like to run it over to ballistics," Muldoon said.

The ME handed him a small, zippered plastic bag containing the slug. "Good luck. Hollow points expand, and the tip of the knife blade hit it, too. In short, it's a mess. Don't count on it to seal a conviction."

"You're such a pessimist, Doc," Muldoon said, pocketing the round.

"Sign the chain-of-custody log," the ME said, then went back to his work.

"I'm going over to ballistics," Muldoon said to Calabrese. "I want you to go back to your desk, start googling and making calls to find out if Trask used a car service around six o'clock, and if so, where did it pick him up and drop him off. If the name doesn't register, try his description and if he paid in cash."

"Jesus, there must be two hundred car services," Calabrese moaned.

"That's why you're doing it instead of me," Muldoon replied. "Now get on it."

MULDOON FOUND A WOMAN still working in the ballistics lab and showed her the squashed bullet. "It's a Federal Hydra-Shok," he said, and explained the circumstances of the shooting.

"I can fire one into the tank, purely for comparison, but it's not going to come out looking anything like that. I'd have to fire it into a side of beef with the same floor material under it, and even then, it would just be hoping for the best. I'll put your slug under my scope, though, and see what we come up with."

Muldoon handed her Trask's 9mm. "Try firing it from this. I'll wait."

MULDOON WAS NEARLY finished with the *Post* when the tech came back and handed him the two slugs, each tagged, and the Beretta. "The best I can tell you is that your weapon could have fired the murder slug, but any identifying marks have been obliterated by the slug's expansion. The knife point didn't help, either. Sorry about that."

"You can only do what you can do," Muldoon said, sighing. He went back to the precinct and found Calabrese asleep with his head on his desk. Muldoon drew a cup of cold water from the cooler, drank half of it, then poured the rest into Calabrese's ear.

"What the fuck?" Calabrese yelled, raising a laugh or two in the squad room.

"I trust you have succeeded in your task," Muldoon said.

"As a matter of fact, I have, sort of," Calabrese said, sticking a tissue into his ear.

"Really? Let's hear it."

"Well, Trask has an account with Carey Limousine, but he didn't use them. He went halfway down the list and found a service, then ordered a pickup in front of Bloomingdale's, half a dozen blocks from Clarke's. He was dropped off at the Château Madison hotel on Madison Avenue and went inside. The car waited there for twenty minutes before he came back, then dropped him two blocks from his apartment. The driver says he never got a good enough look at his fare to describe him."

"Right," Muldoon said. "Of course, the Château has a side-street entrance on Sixty-eighth, so he could have walked straight from the front door and out of there, walked the two and a half blocks to Scott's apartment building, committed the murder, then walked back to the Château and out the front door, then to the drop-off."

Calabrese beamed at him. "We got him, right?"

"We got him, wrong!" Muldoon said. "That's too thin for a prosecutor to get a conviction."

"How about the ballistics?"

"All they could tell me is that the bullet could have come from Trask's Beretta. The round was a hollow point, which spreads out on contact, so there were no identifying marks good enough."

"Which leaves us where?"

"Outside, in the cold," Muldoon said. "All our evidence is circumstantial. If you could call it evidence. Trask coulda hired the car, he coulda taken the route we think he did, he coulda shot the woman, then knifed her. Coulda doesn't cut it."

"You explain it to the lieutenant," Calabrese said.

"I figured."

STONE AND DINO had dinner at P. J. Clarke's.

"So?" Stone asked.

"So, what?"

"So where is the investigation into Cilla's murder?"

"In a warm, sunny spot called 'nowhere.'"

"Explain, please."

Dino took him through Muldoon's report to his lieutenant.

"None of that is exculpatory," Stone pointed out.

"None of it is incriminating, either," Dino replied. "In fact, young Detective Calabrese thinks you're a better suspect than Trask."

"Swell."

"And he's right."

"So, Donald Trask is going to walk?"

"I didn't say that."

"You may as well have."

"You never know what will turn up. I mean, the guy doesn't have a working alibi. We just need more evidence."

"Didn't your crime scene team come up with anything?"

"Sure they did: your fingerprints on the kitchen counter, the telephone, and, of course, the bar."

"Horseshit," Stone said.

"Listen, if you were investigating this murder, you would be your chief suspect."

"Is this why you didn't want anybody to know I'd called you, instead of nine-one-one?"

"You might say I could see this coming. I didn't want my word to be the only thing clearing you."

"But I'm cleared, anyway."

"Don't count on it. Muldoon and Calabrese are still investigating, and they might come up with more evidence."

"Against me or Donald Trask?"

"Take your pick. You should relax in your personal certainty of your innocence."

"That's not going to carry any weight with Muldoon and, especially, Calabrese, who would love to hang this on me."

"Remember when you were ambitious?" Dino asked. "It's like that. Don't worry, you'll talk your way out of this eventually."

43

MULDOON WOKE UP CALABRESE. "Come on," he said. "Where are we going?"

"To arrest Donald Trask for the murder of Priscilla Scott."

"Have we got some new evidence I don't know about?"

"Nope." They got to the car. "You drive." Muldoon gave him a new address.

"What is that place?"

"Trask's office."

"He actually works? How much did he get from his wife?"

"Eight or nine million, I hear."

"He said she had a will leaving everything to him."

"He may believe that, but it ain't so."

"And you know this, how?"

"I spoke to her attorney in the divorce; he drew a new will for her immediately after she hired him, and he let Trask's attorney know it."

"Then that removes the will as a motive for her murder," Calabrese pointed out.

"Only if he didn't know about the new will. By the way, his attorney's office is in the same building with Trask's. We'll have a word with him."

THEY SHOWED THEIR BADGES at the front desk, and after a phone call, they were escorted to a conference room where a man in his shirtsleeves was working at a table filled with stacks of documents.

"Terry Barnes?" Muldoon asked.

"One and the same. What can I do for you, and make it fast."

"You represented Donald Trask in his divorce?"

"Yes."

"Do you remember Herbert Fisher mentioning to you on a phone call that he was drawing up a new will for Priscilla Scott?"

Barnes screwed up his forehead. "Jesus, I don't know. I've got four hot cases running—just look at this stuff." He waved an arm at the tabletop.

"Try and remember," Muldoon said.

"Oh, yeah, I think he did mention it."

"And did you mention it to your client?"

Barnes thought and took a breath to answer, then stopped himself. "That's privileged information—attorney-client communication, you know?"

"It's a real easy question."

"It's still privileged."

"You know about Priscilla Scott's murder?"

"I own a TV."

"Are you representing Donald Trask in that matter?"

"No, just the divorce and a later real estate transaction."

"Well, the question pertains to the murder, not the divorce, so the communication between you wouldn't be privileged, right?" Muldoon held his breath. He could see Barnes's mind working.

"Nice try," Barnes said finally. "I mean, really nice. A lot of guys would have fallen for that. *I* might have fallen for it, if I had a cold or a hangover. Now, beat it."

They beat it. They got back into the elevator and rode up a couple of floors and found the Trask Fund. They had to back up at the door to let a couple of moving men get a desk into the hallway. The reception desk looked as though it had been pushed to one side, out of the center of the room. Muldoon went through the drill. They were shown into Trask's office, where he was packing files in moving boxes. There were no extra chairs in the room, so Muldoon leaned against the wall.

"What is it?" Trask asked. "As you can see, I'm busy."

"Moving offices?"

"Shutting it down."

"Ah, that's right, with your newfound wealth from your ex-wife's will, you've no need to work anymore, have you?"

Trask shrugged. "So what? If I want to be a gentleman of leisure, that's my business."

"Just out of curiosity, what did her estate amount to? I mean, with the death of her wealthy mother, followed a year later by the death of her wealthy father, her inheritances must have been considerable."

"I guess you could say that."

"How much is her estate worth?"

"Beats me. I haven't seen any paperwork yet. Probate takes time."

"A lot more than you got in the divorce settlement, right? Want to take a stab?"

"No, I don't. I have no idea."

"Fifty million? A hundred million?"

"Could be, who knows?"

"You must have a pretty good idea, or you wouldn't be retiring, would you? I mean, eight or nine million gets knocked down by the purchase of your new apartment; that must be two, three million, and I expect you've got some debt, right? And you have to give your clients their money back from the fund—and the market's way up."

"I'll manage," Trask said smugly.

"Look we can call down to the probate court and get a number; why put us to that bother? Are you trying to annoy us?"

"Nope. I don't give a shit whether you're annoyed or not."

"It looks like you're going to be in a bind pretty soon, doesn't it?"

Trask managed a small smile. "Not much chance of that."

Muldoon stood up straighter. "Then you haven't heard about the will?"

Trask stopped packing files and looked straight at him, something he hadn't done before. "What are you talking about?"

"The new will that Cilla made before the divorce."

Donald Trask's face went slack, but his eyes were still fixed on Muldoon. "What?"

Before Muldoon could respond, the phone on Trask's desk rang and he picked it up. "What? Hey, Terry, what's up? Funny you should mention that, they're here now." Trask listened intently for a minute. "Thanks, Terry," he said. Then he hung up and turned back to Muldoon. "You were saying?"

Muldoon's heart sank. "I was asking if you knew about the new will," he said.

"Oh, sure, I knew about that before the divorce. Her lawyer told my lawyer. Anything else?"

"I got a question," Calabrese said. "Why'd you lie to us?"

"When was that?" Trask asked.

"When you gave us an account of your actions on the night of Cilla's murder. You said you walked home from P. J. Clarke's in the rain, but your coat wasn't very wet. The reason for that is, you hired a car service to pick you up at Bloomingdale's, then you went to Château Madison, and from there you walked over to Cilla's place and shot her, then you knifed her."

"Not me, pal," Trask said. "You can call my car service, Carey, and ask them."

"No," Calabrese said, "you didn't use them. You called Phoenix Limos and paid cash. Your driver recognized your description."

Trask shook his head. "Not me. A case of mistaken identity."

"And no one at Clarke's could put you there for a burger and a beer," Muldoon added. "Not a single person. Imagine that."

"All of which means nothing," Trask said. "Now, I'm all through with this. If you want to speak to me again, call my attorney. Goodbye." He went back to packing his files.

BACK IN THE CAR, Muldoon let loose on Calabrese. "Listen, numbnuts, you just blew everything in about a minute. Now Trask knows everything we've got!"

"Did you see his face when you told him about the will? He had no idea. His world just fell apart."

"Yeah, but the look on his face is not admissible evidence that could help us. Now we're back where we started! And that was Terry Barnes on the phone, telling him he forgot to tell him about the will being changed. So we won't get another shot at him on that!"

Calabrese's face was red, and he turned his attention back to his driving. "I like Barrington for it, anyway," he said.

"I'm caring less and less about what you like," Muldoon said. "Until you get a fresh idea, keep it to yourself, and if you get one, tell only me."

"Yes, boss," Calabrese replied acidly.

"You're goddamned right!" Muldoon said.

44

MIDWEEK, Stone and Fred went to Bellevue to bring Faith home. A nurse brought a wheelchair, and Faith got herself out of bed, walked the few steps to it, and sat down.

"Not too bad," she said. "They've had me walking for two days."

They wheeled her downstairs and got her into the rear seat of the car with Stone. "Have you . . ." he began.

"No, I haven't—not a thing. Well, one thing: I think the music I heard was high-quality sound, good bass and nice midtones. It wasn't tinny, like from a portable."

"But you didn't see the radio."

"No, I didn't."

"The new information might be helpful," Stone said. "I'll pass it on."

"I'd appreciate that. I got tired of talking to cops very early on."

Back in the garage they got her into the elevator and

upstairs and unlocked her front door. She walked in and looked around. "Wow," she said, "this beats a hospital room every time."

"Make yourself at home," Stone said. "Helene will bring you some lunch. Any requests?"

"Something very unlike hospital food," she replied.

Stone went to his office and asked Joan to pass that on. He called Dino.

"Bacchetti."

"It's Stone. We got Faith home from the hospital; she seems to be doing real well."

"Swell."

"She remembered something else," Stone said.

"What's that?"

"It's not much, but the music she heard was high quality, good bass, very clear midrange. It sounds like one of those small, high-fidelity FM radios you see advertised in the *Times*."

"You're right, it's not much," Dino replied, "but I'll mention it. How does Faith look?"

"Much better. The bruising on her face is pretty much gone, or can be covered with makeup. Her cuts will take a while to heal, but they don't seem to be slowing her down."

"I'm happy for her. Can I go now?"

"Make yourself happy."

Dino hung up.

Stone dealt with his correspondence and phone messages, then Joan buzzed. "Edith Beresford, on one."

Stone picked it up. "Hello, there," he said, with as much cheer as he could manage.

"You don't sound so good," she said. "Is something wrong?"

"It hasn't been a good week so far."

"Don't tell me the jealous ex-husband is still around. Has he hurt you?"

"He murdered his wife," Stone said.

"What? Is he in jail?"

"The police don't have enough to put him away. In fact, there's an opinion in the NYPD that I'm a better candidate."

"Nonsense! You wouldn't hurt a fly!"

"I've hurt many flies in my day and a few criminals, too, but you're right. It's just that I arrived at her apartment for dinner and discovered her body. Homicide detectives tend to consider whoever discovers the body a suspect, and now that they haven't been able to nail the obvious killer, the ex-husband, they're looking at me askance."

"Well, you tell them I said to stop it! I won't have it!"

"I'll be sure to pass that along during my next third degree, right after they employ the rubber hose."

"What you need is to go out to dinner with me. I'll cheer you up."

"I may not be cheerable for a few more days."

"Come to me. I'll cook you dinner."

"I'm sorry, I don't think I could handle that twice in one week."

"Oh, God, I can't believe I said that."

"Let me get through the funeral, which should be later this week. I'll call, I promise."

"If you don't, I'll just come and get you." She hung up.

Stone called Herb Fisher.

"Hey. How you doing?" Herb asked.

"So-so. Who's planning the funeral?"

"A cousin of Cilla's. It'll be Saturday at a little church in Greenwich, you should get a note about it."

"I won't count on that, but if I do, I'll accept."

"Yeah, I heard the cops are looking at you a little too closely."

"I guess they've got to do something with their time," Stone said.

"At least Trask won't get a penny out of her death. I drew her a new will, as you suggested, and I told his attorney."

"I know."

"Let me know if you need a good lawyer."

"You know somebody?" Stone asked.

"Just call. I gotta run."

Joan came in with an envelope. "This was just delivered." He opened it.

Dear Mr. Barrington,

I know that you and Cilla were good friends, and I hope you can join us for her service this weekend. The information and RSVP number are below.

Yours,
Mary Scott Dunham

Stone handed it to Joan. "Please tell them I'll be there."

"Are you sure you want to go?" she asked.

"Yes, I'm sure." He wasn't all that sure, but he was just going to have to tough it out.

———

THE CHURCH WASN'T VERY LARGE, and it was packed. Stone sat a couple of rows behind the family seats and paid close attention to everything that was said.

The service ended, and a woman caught up with him. "Mr. Barrington," she said, "I'm Mary, Cilla's cousin."

Stone shook her hand. "She was a lovely person. I'm very sorry for your loss."

She took his arm and walked out with him. "Did you see Donald?"

"No," Stone said. "He had the nerve to come?"

"He did, though I certainly didn't invite him. He sat in the back row and got out as quickly as he could."

On the front steps, Stone looked around the parking lot.

"That's his car," she said, nodding toward a black Mercedes SUV driving away.

"I'll remember it," Stone said.

45

STONE SAID HIS GOODBYES and got into his car. "Let's go home, Fred," he said, "and keep an eye out for a black Mercedes SUV."

"Anybody we know?" Fred asked.

"Somebody I'd rather not know, who's probably still limping from the last time he met you."

"Ah, that gentleman. I'd love to meet him again."

"If you do, he'll be armed. Remember that."

THE FOLLOWING DAY Stone called Edie Beresford.

"Hello, you. How did the funeral go?"

"Beautifully, except that the murderer turned up and sat in the back row."

"What chutzpah!"

"That's the word for it. Are you free for dinner this evening?"

"I am."

"Then I'll pick you up at seven. Do you mind if some friends join us?"

"Not in the least. Who are they?"

"Dino and Vivian Bacchetti."

"Is he the police commissioner?"

"He is. We were partners back during my cop days."

"Where are we going?"

"Caravaggio, in the Seventies."

"It's around the corner from me; I'll meet you there."

"As you wish." He hung up and invited the Bacchettis.

STONE WAITED OUTSIDE the restaurant, and twice, a black Mercedes SUV circled the block and drove past slowly. The windows were too dark to see the driver, but Stone got the Connecticut plate number.

Dino and Viv showed up a moment later, and Stone told him about the car.

"Black windows? That's against the law." Dino made a call. "It's Bacchetti. I want to report a Mercedes SUV with black windows." He gave them the plate number. "Pick up the driver and be warned, he's probably armed. Take him to the precinct, write him a ticket, and relieve him of his weapon and carry license. Reason? He's a suspect in a murder." He hung up. "Now we can eat."

They were in the middle of their main course when Dino got a call. He listened, said, "Thank you," and hung up. "Donald Trask is in custody, disarmed, and Muldoon and Calabrese will be interrogating him as soon as his attorney arrives."

"Well, at least they're inconveniencing him," Stone replied.

"And making him madder," Dino responded.

EDIE INVITED THEM ALL BACK to her place for a cognac. She had an apartment on Fifth Avenue that reminded Stone all too much of Cilla's in its size, shape, and elevation.

"Tell me," Edie said to Dino, "is Stone still a suspect?"

"That's for the investigating detectives to decide," Dino said. "I can't tell them not to suspect him."

"But surely, you don't share their views?"

"Not really. I just can't get in the way of procedure for a friend. He'll sweat it out okay, don't worry."

Dino got another call and listened, then hung up. "Trask, on advice of his attorney, has declined to answer questions," he said. "Muldoon will make sure somebody at the papers gets the story. That'll turn up the pressure a bit. Also, he has to get a new lawyer. Muldoon heard Terry Barnes tell him not to call him again, and he gave him another lawyer's card."

"Want to guess who he'll call?"

"What's your guess?" Dino asked.

"Alfred Goddard," Stone said.

"Isn't he a mob lawyer?" Edie asked.

"You're very well informed," Dino said. "He used to be a mob attorney, but there's not much of a mob anymore, so he now specializes in representing people who are guilty of major crimes, having had a lot of experience at that. My guy, Muldoon, caught a glimpse of his card."

"That's the last word we'll hear from Donald Trask," Stone said, "until the trial."

"Are you kidding?" Dino replied. "What trial?"

"There isn't going to be a trial?" Edie asked.

"Not until my guys have come up with a lot more evidence than they have now."

"Dino," Stone said, "may I make a suggestion?"

"Sure, as long as you don't expect me to take it seriously."

"Get Muldoon to send another crime scene team to Cilla's apartment and lift every print anywhere in the kitchen."

"That's grasping at straws," Dino said. "Do you know if Trask has ever visited Cilla's apartment?"

"He wouldn't have done so," Stone said. "There was too much anger in the divorce to get him an invitation. If they can find a single print of his, he was there for only one reason."

"All right," Dino said, "I'll make the suggestion to Muldoon."

DINO AND VIV excused themselves and left, but a hand on his arm kept Stone from leaving.

"Stay," Edie breathed into his ear. "Stay the night."

"I've already given Fred the rest of the night off," he replied.

They kissed, and she undid one of his shirt buttons, slipped her hand inside and fondled a nipple.

"Sold," Stone said, and they took the walk to her bedroom, shedding clothes along the way.

They turned back the bed's covers and got into it.

"I'm going to make this good for your morale," she said, reaching for other parts.

"I believe you," Stone said, then gave himself to the moment and the rest of the night.

THE FOLLOWING MORNING at the precinct, Muldoon put down the phone. "The commissioner wants the crime scene guys to make another visit to the Scott apartment and go over the kitchen again for prints."

"As long as they're taking another look," Calabrese said, "they might as well get all the prints off Trask's gun. It's in the evidence room."

"Dante," Muldoon said, using his partner's first name for the first time, "I believe you've switched your brain on."

"Yeah, well, we should have printed him last night," Calabrese said.

"Don't worry," Muldoon repled, "he was printed when he applied for his carry license." Muldoon made the calls.

46

STONE, his morale refreshed, slipped out of bed at daybreak, got into his clothes, kissed Edie lightly on the ear, and let himself out of her apartment. Downstairs, he walked briskly through the lobby, nodded at the desk man, and allowed the doorman to get him a cab.

A half hour later he was in his own bed, eating his usual breakfast, when his cell phone rang. "Hello?"

"You sneaked out on me," Edie said, petulantly.

"I didn't know how long you might want to sleep," he replied.

"I was looking forward to waking you," she said.

"My apologies. When next we meet I'll find a way to make it up to you."

"I'll accept that promise," she said, then hung up.

THAT AFTERNOON, Donald Trask sat across the desk from his new attorney, Alfred Goddard.

"Call me Alfie," the lawyer said. "You like to be called Don?"

"I prefer Donald."

"Okay, let me tell you how this is going to go, Don: first of all, you're through talking to the cops." He plucked a few cards from a tray on his desk and shoved them across. "Anybody asks you anything, like, 'Isn't it a nice day?' you give him my card and tell him to call me. Do you clearly understand that?"

"I do."

"If you should find yourself temporarily in a jail cell, especially don't talk to anybody there. The DA is notorious for producing cellmate witnesses who swear the defendant made a full and complete confession, and the prisons are full of people who talked to cellmates."

"I understand," Trask replied.

"I want you to understand something else," Goddard said. "If you went to trial tomorrow, I'd get you off scot-free, based on what they've got now for evidence."

"That's encouraging."

"The thing is not to give them another shred of evidence for free."

"Do you want to know whether I did it?"

"No, and I'll tell you why. If you told me you did it, then I couldn't put you on the stand and allow you to deny it. That would put me in deep shit, as well as you."

"I understand."

"Anything else you say to me is privileged—attorney-client relationship—so, apart from copping to the crime, feel free to talk."

"All right, why couldn't they convict me now with the evidence they have? Can't a jury do anything they like?"

"It's my job to see that they want for you what I want for you, and I'm good at it. I have one client who never confessed to me, but I believe had personally committed at least a dozen murders. He's never served a day in prison."

"Good work," Trask replied.

"Another thing to remember, Don. The cops are not legally required to tell you the truth. They can tell you they've got movies of you killing your wife, if they feel like it. And if you fall for such a lie, you're done. All the more reason not to talk to them, or even listen to them."

"I'll remember," Trask said.

"Donald, have you got a temper?"

Trask shrugged. "Sometimes."

"Not anymore. You can't afford it. If somebody at a cocktail party accuses you of murdering your wife, politely deny it and find somebody else to talk to."

"All right."

"If somebody in a bar takes a swing at you because you were looking at his girlfriend's tits, get up, apologize, pay his bar tab, and get out of there."

"All right."

"From now on, Don, you're going to have to work at being the nicest guy in the world—even to the fucking media. If somebody points a camera at you and sticks a mic in your face, give him a little smile and say, 'I'm sorry, but I'm sure you know that I can't talk about that right now.' Remember, in the unlikely event that this should ever go to trial, there will be future members of your jury watching this on TV."

"All right."

"Help old ladies across the street, and if somebody's dog

bites you, laugh it off, pat him on the head, and get a rabies shot."

Goddard got up and walked him to the door. "Just relax, Don. Keep your mouth shut and everything will be all right."

Trask decided to believe that.

As he walked out of the office building Trask was surprised to see the two detectives, Muldoon and Calabrese, sitting in their car watching him. Muldoon even took a cell phone photo of him. Trask smiled, gave them a little wave, and crossed the street to get a cab.

"He looks awful happy," Calabrese said.

"Don't worry about it," Muldoon said. "He's just had the pep talk from Alfie Goddard, that's all. He's still scared shitless."

47

STONE AND DINO met at their club, known to its members as the Club, and to hardly anyone else. The Club occupied a double-width townhouse in the East Sixties, and also had a garage, which allowed its members to enter the building discreetly.

They had a drink at the bar first and subtly gawked at their fellow members—senators, moguls, athletes, and the occasional movie star, in town to do publicity on his or her new film.

"I've got news," Dino said, taking care not to be overheard.

"I hope it's good news," Stone said.

"It's sorta good news," Dino replied.

"How sorta?"

"About seventy-one percent."

"Seventy-one percent of what?"

"Seventy-one-percent chance of being a hit."

"A hit record?"

"A hit print. The crime scene people went back to Cilla's apartment, which is still an official crime scene, and went over the kitchen with an extremely fine-tooth comb. They came up with a partial print on the wall phone."

"That's fantastic!" Stone enthused.

"Not yet."

"What do you mean?"

"I mean, we don't know yet when he touched it, but the computer that compares prints with our arrest database says the partial has a seventy-one-percent chance of belonging to Donald Trask."

"Couldn't it be encouraged to change that to ninety-nine percent?" Stone asked.

"You don't encourage computers, and they don't have a sense of humor, either."

"Well, seventy-one percent is a lot better than it might be."

"Yeah? Alfie Goddard is going to tell the jury that there's a twenty-nine percent chance that the print belongs to one of the other millions in the national crime database, and that constitutes reasonable doubt."

"Then put an expert on the stand who'll testify that a score of seventy-one percent is a near-certainty, and there's no room for reasonable doubt."

"Then Alfie will put his expert on," Dino said, "and when he gets through, the jury will be so screwed up that their own confusion will constitute reasonable doubt."

"Well, at least it's a hundred-percent certainty that it's not *my* fingerprint," Stone said with some satisfaction.

"Well . . . no, sorta," Dino replied.

"What do you mean?"

"I mean they also found a print on the phone that the computer says is one hundred percent yours."

"But . . ."

Dino raised a hand to stop him. "But you used that phone to call nine-one-one, didn't you?"

Stone slapped his forehead. "I should have used my cell phone."

"No, you did the right thing. Now they have a recording of the call with a time stamp on it, which, along with your fingerprint, backs up your story."

"Well, I suppose that should be a relief," Stone replied.

"Not really," Dino said.

"Why is it not a relief?"

"Because Alfie is going to tell the jury that, while the partial has only a seventy-one-percent chance of belonging to his client, the police have a full print on the phone that has a hundred-percent chance of being yours. How do you think the jury is going to react?"

"They're not going to convict me," Stone said.

"Maybe not, but every defense attorney in a homicide case is looking for an alternative suspect to his client, and even if they won't convict you, they won't convict Donald Trask, either." Dino put down his glass. "Let's get some lunch, you're looking a little pale."

"I am not pale," Stone protested, following Dino to a table where waiters held chairs for both of them.

"Just be glad you're not on the stand testifying right now," Dino said, sitting down and snapping open his heavy linen napkin and then addressing the waiting maître d'. "I'll have the seared foie gras and the strip steak, medium rare." He indicated Stone. "He looks as though he'd like just the clear broth."

"I'll have the bruschetta and the spaghetti carbonara," Stone said quickly.

"If you're sure you can keep it down," Dino responded.

"You know," Stone said, "if you had two detectives on this who were as smart as Muldoon, instead of just one, they would already have cleared this case."

"Well, Calabrese is young, but he's not stupid," Dino said.

"I'll tell you what they need to do," Stone said. "They need to drag Donald Trask downtown and put him in a lineup so the Phoenix driver can point him out."

"That's a big risk because the driver has already said he probably couldn't identify his passenger. If he fails to pick out Trask, then Alfie Goddard will have another point for the jury to consider. Why don't you come up with an idea that helps us instead of Alfie?"

"Okay, how about getting the two bartenders at P. J. Clarke's who were on duty that night at the lineup, too. They'll fail to pick Trask because he wasn't there that night."

"Trask's story is that he sat at a table, not the bar, and ordered his beer from there," Dino said. "And not picking somebody out of a lineup is not incriminating."

"How many waiters were working that night?"

"Twelve, and they were run off their feet that night."

"They could have picked out you or me, if we had been there," Stone said.

"That's because we're in there twice a week and we tip well," Dino pointed out. "Trask says he's there, maybe once a month. You know how many people go in and out of that joint in a month?"

"No, how many?"

"I've no idea," Dino replied, "but Alfie Goddard will find out, and he'll use it against us at trial."

Their first course arrived, and Stone ate only half of his bruschetta.

"What's the matter?" Dino asked, pointing at the other half of the bruschetta.

"I'm on a diet," Stone replied.

Dino speared the remaining piece with his fork and ate it in two bites.

"You're a pig," Stone said.

"Yeah, and I'm a hungry pig," Dino replied.

"You know, Dino, you sound like you're more on Trask's side than mine."

"I'm on the side of the firm of Muldoon and Calabrese," Dino replied, "and every time your name comes up, they look hungrier and hungrier."

48

IT WAS RAINING AGAIN, but Stone didn't have to look for a cab because Dino's official SUV was standing by in the garage. They got into the backseat, the driver opened the garage door with his remote, and they drove into the street. They had driven halfway home, down Second Avenue, when the driver pulled over and stopped.

"Drop Barrington off at his house," Dino said to the driver.

"Sure, Commissioner," the driver said, putting a finger to his ear to listen to the radio. He turned around. "Commissioner, you're wanted at Gracie Mansion ASAP."

As he spoke, Dino's phone buzzed. He answered it. "Yes, sir," he said, then hung up and spoke to his driver. "Okay," he said, "let's get to Gracie Mansion. Hop out, Stone."

"Can't I come?" Stone asked, looking outside at the pouring rain.

"You're not invited," Dino said, reaching across Stone and opening the door on his side. A passing car nearly took off the door. "Beat it, pal."

"Into traffic?" Stone asked. He crawled across Dino and let himself out on that side, stepping into ankle-deep water in the gutter.

"Is that better?" Dino asked.

"Oh, shut up," Stone yelled, but the door had already slammed shut. The SUV was speeding away, its lights on. He ran across the sidewalk and found an awning to stand under while he waited for a cab. He saw one coming, but the shop door behind him burst open, and a woman ran across the sidewalk and threw herself in front of the taxi.

"Hey!" he yelled at the woman as she got in.

"Bye!" she yelled back and slammed the door. The cab's overhead light turned off, and it drove away.

Stone thought about calling Fred, but he knew as soon as he did a cab would arrive. He stood there for another ten minutes before a cruising black town car pulled to the curb, and the window slid down. "Where you headed?" the driver yelled.

"Turtle Bay!" Stone yelled back. "Ten bucks!"

"Thirty!" the driver yelled.

"Twenty!"

"Thirty!" the driver yelled.

Stone ran across the sidewalk and dove into the town car.

"Up front," the driver said, rubbing his fingers together.

Stone dug out his cash. "I've only got a fifty," he said. "You got change?"

"Nope. I just started work. What's it gonna be, pal?"

Stone gave him the fifty. "I'll get change when we get there."

AFTER FIFTEEN MINUTES of dangerous driving, the car pulled up to Stone's house. "Hang on," he said, "I'll get some change."

He got out and ran for the office door, then rang the bell. The town car drove away. "Hey!" Stone yelled at him.

Joan opened the door. "Hey, yourself," she said, then pushed a finger into his lapel. "You're soaking wet."

Stone went inside and shook like a dog. Bob, his Labrador retriever, came over, sniffed at him, and backed away. "We went in Dino's car," he said, "so I didn't take a coat or an umbrella, then Dino got a call and abandoned me."

"Hang on," Joan said, "the phone's ringing."

Stone shrugged off his sodden jacket and hung it on a hat rack; his trousers followed.

"It's Dino," Joan said, "on one."

"Tell him to go fuck himself," Stone said.

"I can't tell the police commissioner that. He might have me arrested."

"Okay," Stone said, dumping out his shoes and squishing across the carpet in his stocking feet, "I'll tell him myself." He picked up the phone. "Go fuck yourself," he said.

"I beg your pardon," a woman's voice said.

"Who are you?"

"I'm Deputy Mayor Whitehorn," she said.

"I'm so sorry. I thought you were Dino Bacchetti."

"Do I look like Dino Bacchetti?"

"I can't see you."

Dino came on the line. "Did you really tell Caroline to go fuck herself?"

"I thought it was you, but as long as you're on the line, go fuck yourself."

"The mayor has asked that you join us for a task force meeting on the Scott homicide."

"When?"

"Ten minutes ago."

"First, I'll need to throw away all of my clothes, which have been ruined in the rain."

"Why didn't you take a cab?"

"Don't start. I'll be there in half an hour. If that's not soon enough, you can tell the mayor to go—"

"Yeah, I know," Dino interrupted. "Shake your ass." He hung up.

"Joan!" Stone yelled. "Tell Fred to get the car out, while I change clothes."

"Fred's out."

"Find him fast and get him here!" Stone went up to his bedroom, hung everything up in his bathroom to dry, and toweled off. He got into fresh clothes and went down to his office, where he pulled on a trench coat, jammed a hat on his head, and grabbed an umbrella.

"Fred's waiting at the curb," Joan said. "When will you be back?"

"Who the hell knows?" Stone said. He hit the outside door at a run, opening the umbrella, then he stopped. He was standing in bright sunshine. The only water around was dripping from the trees on the block. He got into the car.

"Where to, sir?" Fred asked.

"Gracie Mansion."

"I'm sorry, sir, I've never been there. What is it?"

"The mayor's residence: Eighty-eighth and East End Avenue, approximately. Go there, and we'll find it together."

Fred headed uptown, splashing through huge puddles left by the rainstorm. They found the mayoral mansion, more or less where Stone had said it would be, and a guard admitted them to the grounds. Stone got out of his coat and left it with his hat and umbrella on the backseat. "I don't know how long I'll be, Fred. Don't get lost."

Someone opened the car door for him, and someone inside the house opened the front door. The inside door opener turned out to be a leggy blonde in a business suit.

"Hi," she said, sticking out a hand. "I'm Caroline Whitehorn. I've recently gone and fucked myself. Right this way."

49

STONE FOLLOWED CAROLINE Whitehorn down a hallway, appreciating the view from the rear, until she
opened a door, which turned out to be the mayor's office.

"Have a seat," she said, "they'll be here in a moment."

"Keep me company," Stone said.

"All right," she replied, taking a facing chair. "What are
you doing here?"

"I haven't the vaguest idea."

"The task force?"

"That must be it."

"You're not a cop."

"Retired, a long time ago."

"How come you're dry, when everybody else in the group
is soaking wet?"

"It's a long and sad story."

"I'll bet."

Another door opened, and the mayor walked in, followed

by Dino, Muldoon, Calabrese, and a uniformed assistant chief Stone didn't know.

The mayor was Dino's predecessor in the commissioner's job and had engineered Dino's rise in the department. He offered his hand. "Thanks for coming all the way uptown, Stone," he said. "How come you're not soaking wet like everybody else?"

"I lead a pure life, Mr. Mayor. God is good to me."

The mayor chuckled and sat down behind his desk. The others were in various states of dampness. Dino looked him up and down, amazed.

"Don't ask," Stone said before he could.

"All right," the mayor said. "What the hell is going on? Don't you even have a suspect?"

"We have two, sir," Muldoon said.

"And who might they be?"

"The ex-husband and Mr. Barrington."

The mayor laughed out loud.

"Mr. Barrington was on the scene and armed," Muldoon said.

"Don't mention Mr. Barrington and the word *suspect* to me again in the same sentence," the mayor said. "Who's the ex-husband?"

"One Donald Trask, former hedge fund operator."

"I know a Donald Trask from the Athletic Club," the mayor said.

"That's the one," Muldoon replied.

"I can see him as the perpetrator," the mayor said. "The man's a bully and an ass."

"That's the one," Stone said.

"So why isn't he vacationing at Riker's?"

"Sir," Dino said, "we've got circumstantial and inconclusive evidence, but nothing that will convict him." He related Trask's story and what they believed to be the truth. "And," Dino added, "Alfred Goddard just came on the case."

"Ah," the mayor said. "If Trask would just shoot Goddard, we could remove two thorns from our flesh."

"I don't think we're going to get that lucky," Dino said.

"So you want me to declare this little group a task force so it will get your detectives off other cases and make more resources available?"

"In short, yes, sir," Dino replied.

"All right," the mayor said, waving his hands like a magician. "*Pfffft!* You're a task force." He looked around at the silent men. "Come on, one of you must know that joke."

Stone raised a hand. "Guy goes into a soda shop and says to the soda jerk, 'Make me a malted.' The soda jerk says, 'Okay, *pfffft!* You're a malted!'"

The mayor roared as if he had never before heard it. Everybody else pretended to laugh.

"Okay, I said you're a task force. Now get out of here and clear this case." He pointed at Muldoon. "And get Barrington out of your thick head!" He shooed them out of his office.

Stone and Dino walked out of the building and stood on the front porch. Rain was pouring again, and a flash of lightning and a clap of thunder greeted them. Caroline Whitehorn was standing on the porch, clutching a folding umbrella. "I don't think this is going to do it," she said, holding up the tiny umbrella, "and the motor pool doesn't have a car available."

"Can I give you a lift?" Stone said.

She looked at him sharply. "Where?"

"Where are you going?"

"The River Café, Brooklyn."

"Of course. You can drop me at my house on the way," Stone said. He looked through the gloom for his car but couldn't see it. He got out his phone and called Fred.

"Yes, sir?"

"Where are you?"

"They made me wait outside the gate, sir."

Stone looked at the gate that was about two hundred feet away.

"I've got this," Caroline said. She took a remote control from her pocket and pressed a button. Down the driveway, the gate rolled open.

"Okay, Fred, gate's open," Stone said, then hung up.

A moment later, the Bentley emerged from the gloom and stopped. Stone got the door for Caroline.

"How about me?" Dino asked.

"I believe the City of New York provides you with transportation," Stone said. He got in and closed the door, while Dino got out his cell phone and started calling his car.

"That was mean," Caroline said, but couldn't suppress a laugh.

"It's an unhappy story," Stone said. "It will save us both a lot of time if you will just accept that he richly deserves it."

"I'll try."

"Fred, please drop me off at the house, so I can get a ham and cheese sandwich on stale bread, then take Ms. White-horn to the glorious River Café, under the Brooklyn Bridge, where she's having a sumptuous dinner."

Fred got the car back on the streets. "Sir, shall I wait while you eat your stale sandwich?"

"No, I'll have it alone in the kitchen and watch the rain roll down the windows."

"Oh, all right!" Caroline said. "Would you like to join me?"

"That depends on who you're joining," Stone said. "He might not fully appreciate my company."

"It's not a he, it's a she."

"In that case, I'd love to join you. Fred, never mind the stale sandwich. We'll both go to the River Café." He turned to Caroline. "Dinner will be on me."

"Are you sure you can afford three meals at the River Café?"

"Fred can sell the Bentley while we're dining."

"Yes, sir!" Fred said. "I'm sure I can get top dollar in Brooklyn!"

50

STONE AND CAROLINE Whitehorn walked into the River Café and were immediately shown to a table, where a brunette version of Caroline sat waiting.

"Stone Barrington, my older sister, Charlotte Whitehorn," Caroline said.

"I'm not that much older," Charlotte said, offering Stone her hand.

"Ages older," Caroline said.

"A year and a half," Charlotte responded.

"Twenty months," Caroline replied.

"Now, now, ladies," Stone said. "Let sleeping dogs lie."

"Are you calling me a sleeping dog?" Charlotte asked.

"No, I'm simply employing a cliché, to no effect whatsoever. I suppose this argument has been going on your whole lives?"

"Ever since Caroline learned to count," Charlotte replied. "How did you two meet?"

"Stone told me to go fuck myself," Caroline replied.

"That always works with Caroline," her sister said.

"Then he weaseled his way into this dinner by giving me a lift and threatening me with a stale sandwich."

"I'm afraid I don't understand."

"Caroline means that I rescued her from a downpour and ferried her all the way from Gracie Mansion to here, and she only invited me to dinner when I said I'd pay for it."

"That's my little sister," Charlotte said.

"She calls me that because she knows it makes me crazy," Caroline said, "and you didn't offer to pay until after I had invited you to join us."

"Tell me," Stone said, "are your parents still living, or are they reposing in an insane asylum somewhere?"

That got a laugh from both of them.

"I suppose we descrved that," Caroline said.

"You must be related to Mikeford Whitehorn?"

"His granddaughters," Charlotte said. "Our dad was Mikeford, Jr."

Stone was jostled when someone passed his chair. He looked up, annoyed, to see the back of Donald Trask being seated two tables away with a much younger woman.

"Wasn't that Donald Trask?" Charlotte asked.

"It was."

"I read about him in the papers this morning. Isn't he one of two suspects in his wife's murder?"

"He is the *only* suspect," Stone said firmly. "The police finally came to their senses about the other, entirely innocent, fellow."

"Stone was the other suspect, until the mayor cleared him today," Caroline said.

"You weren't at that meeting," Stone said.

"I was, sort of," she replied.

"You were eavesdropping?"

"The mayor often asks me to do so. He sometimes likes to have a witness."

"She's just nosy," Charlotte said. "If Donald Trask is the only suspect in his wife's murder, what's he doing dining at the River Café with someone a third of his age?"

"The police didn't have enough evidence to cancel his reservation," Stone replied.

"And women that young are the only ones stupid enough to be seen with him," Caroline added.

"Are we certain about Stone's innocence?" Charlotte asked, archly.

"Sort of certain," Caroline replied.

"If I'm ever on trial for murder," Stone said, "I hope you two are not on the jury."

"Never mind," Charlotte said, picking up a menu. "What are we having?"

A waiter came and took their order, and Stone ordered a bottle of the Far Niente chardonnay.

"Very nice," Caroline said, sipping the wine.

"I ordered it because it has the most beautiful label of any wine," Stone replied.

"So, apart from the aesthetics, you are ignorant of wines?"

"I didn't say that. I'm also fond of the wine."

"I think you're right about the label," Charlotte said, examining it, "and about the wine, too."

"It's good to have my judgment affirmed," Stone said.

They had finished two courses and had ordered dessert when Stone rose. "Will you excuse me? Nature calls."

They nodded. Stone left the table and headed back toward the entrance, where the restrooms were. When the thick door closed behind him, noise from the restaurant ceased. He attended to nature, and as he was zipping his fly, he heard restaurant noise again, then silence, then a voice.

"Turn around," it said, and it was thoroughly unpleasant, as voices go.

Stone turned to find Donald Trask standing, leaning against the door, holding a small semiautomatic pistol in his outstretched hand.

"You're under arrest," Stone said, because he couldn't think of anything else to say.

"Yeah? For what?"

"For carrying a firearm in New York City without a license."

"I have a license," Trask replied.

"Revoked," Stone said.

"Oh, what does it matter?" Trask said, then he fired the pistol.

Stone had already begun to turn away from him and to sweep an arm toward the gun, when he felt a sharp pain in his head and collapsed onto the floor, striking his head on the sink on the way down. He passed out just as he heard the door slam.

STONE CAME TO ON A GURNEY in the entrance hall of the restaurant with an EMT holding a bandage pressed to his head. His neck was wet and sticky where the blood had flowed down. A small crowd had gathered, including the Whitehorn sisters. "Are you all right, Stone?" Caroline asked.

"I'm not sure," he replied. He tried to touch his head but ran into the EMT's hand.

"Did you do this just to get out of buying dinner?" she asked.

The headwaiter was standing next to her.

"Put dinner on my account," Stone said to him, then passed out again.

WHEN STONE WOKE again he appeared to be in someone's beautifully furnished living room, except he was lying in a hospital bed, surrounded by a bank of monitors, and he had a terrific headache. He groped for a call button but hesitated: Who would show up? God or Satan? This had to be the waiting room of one place or the other. He pressed the button. The door opened and a half dozen people entered the room led by a nurse.

She found a switch and sat him up in bed. "How are you feeling?"

"I have a terrible headache," he said. "May I have some aspirin?"

A doctor stepped up beside her. "How about some morphine instead?"

"That will do," Stone replied. Something was injected into a tube in his arm, and a moment later he felt warm, and the pain receded.

"You've been shot in the head," the doctor said, "but not in a serious way. You'll have a scar on the corner of your skull, but a plastic surgeon closed the wound, and it will be invisible under your hair."

"That's very thoughtful of you," Stone said. "I'm hungry."

"I'm told you had a good meal, but you vomited it up in the ambulance. Between the scalp wound, which bled profusely, and the blow to the head, I'm afraid your suit may be a total loss. However, we've sent it to Madame Paulette to see what they can do with it."

"What kind of a place is this," Stone asked, "that it's furnished like the Waldorf and sends bloody clothes to Madame Paulette's?"

"You are in a suite at New York Hospital," the doctor said.

The nurse handed him a menu. "What would you like?"

There was seared foie gras, a rack of lamb, and a soufflé on the menu. "A bacon cheeseburger, medium, and onion rings," Stone replied. "How much does this room cost?"

"You're not to worry about that," the nurse said. "The Whitehorns are paying for it."

"A policeman would like to speak with you," the doctor said. "He has an Italian last name, but I can't remember it."

51

DINO CAME INTO THE ROOM, walked up to the bed and peered closely at him. "Can't you even go to dinner at a nice restaurant without getting into trouble?"

"What happened to me?" Stone asked, feeling his head. "The last thing I remember, I was peeing in the men's room."

"Yeah? That's it?"

"Is this something to do with Donald Trask?" Stone asked. "He was in the restaurant, too."

Dino shook his head. "The maître d' says Trask left the restaurant with a woman ten minutes before somebody found you in the men's room. Who else hates you?"

"Beats me."

Dino looked around. "Did you bring your own decorator?"

"I'm told this is a suite of some sort."

"Listen, a bed in a shared room in this hospital is something like five hundred clams a day. I can only imagine what *this* is costing." He waved an arm for emphasis.

"I didn't book it, believe me."

"What I don't understand," Dino said, "is how somebody could fire a gun at you in a small men's room and miss. Can you shed any light on that?"

"Jesus, I told you I don't remember. Maybe the guy's just a lousy shot."

"He must have had the shakes, too. I mean, it was what, four feet?"

"I remember a voice," Stone said. "Not so much what was said, just the voice."

"What kind of voice?"

"Male. Unpleasant."

"Hey, that's a big help; I'll put out an APB for males with unpleasant voices."

"I remember getting up from the table, and Trask's table was empty. I guess I didn't see him leave."

"Well, you were having dinner with two beautiful women: Who can blame you? It's nice of you to confirm Trask's alibi, though." Dino touched Stone's forehead. "You've got a bump there, and it's going to turn into a bruise. How'd that happen?"

"Are you trying to trick me into remembering?" Stone asked.

There was a knock at the door and a waiter entered, pushing a room service cart.

"What's this?" Dino asked.

"Food," Stone replied, handing him the menu. "You want something?"

"Thanks, I ate."

The waiter whipped off the silver cover and presented the burger. "Would you like it on your table, sir?"

Stone nodded.

The man pushed the table to Stone's bed and positioned it, then served the burger and a glass of water.

"What, no wine?" Dino asked. "And didn't you already eat at the restaurant?"

"The doctor told me I threw up in the ambulance. They've sent my suit to Madame Paulette's." Stone took a bite of the burger. "Perfect," he said, "and so are the onion rings. Listen, I don't know where my cell phone is. Will you call Joan and ask her to bring me a complete change of clothes?"

"Yeah, okay," Dino said.

"Who are you assigning to my case?"

"Muldoon and Calabrese, who else?"

"Who else?" Stone echoed.

"They're probably still at the restaurant."

"Having a good meal, no doubt."

"They'll get around to you, don't worry."

"Have you posted a guard on my door?"

"For what?"

"To protect me. Somebody just tried to shoot me in the head, you know."

"He'd never get to you in this joint. I had to flash my badge three times to make it to the room. Sorry, suite."

The nurse ushered in Muldoon and Calabrese. They pulled up chairs and watched Stone eat his cheeseburger.

"Something I can do for you?" Stone asked between swallows.

"Yeah," Muldoon said, "give us your account of how you got shot."

"I'm sorry, I don't remember being shot."

"He's also had a blow to his forehead," the nurse said, helpfully. "It's no surprise that he can't remember."

"He remembers a voice," Dino said, "male and unpleasant."

Muldoon made a note. "What . . ."

"He doesn't remember what the voice said."

"Sorry about that, fellas," Stone said. "Does that make me the chief suspect in my shooting?"

"Very amusing," Muldoon said with a straight face. "We checked your weapon, it hadn't been fired. Did you know that Donald Trask was also in the restaurant?"

"Yes, but his table was empty when I got up to go to the men's room."

"That's what the headwaiter said, too."

Another knock at the door, and the Whitehorn sisters entered the room. "Are we disturbing you?" Caroline asked.

"No, ma'am," Muldoon said. "We were just leaving." They left.

"You've met Dino Bacchetti, haven't you, Charlotte?"

"I haven't," Charlotte said, and Stone introduced them.

Stone pushed his tray table away. "Thank you for coming to see me."

"It's the least we could do," Caroline said. "I mean, if you hadn't been having dinner with us, this wouldn't have happened. Did they catch him?"

"Catch who?" Dino asked.

"Donald Trask. He did this, didn't he?"

"If he did, nobody saw him doing it. Everybody says he left the restaurant ten minutes before this happened."

"Oh." Caroline looked at her watch. "Well, if you'll excuse me, I'd better get back to Gracie Mansion and find out if I still have a job."

"Blame everything on Stone," Dino said. "The mayor will believe you."

The women left.

"You seem to know a lot of Whitehorns," Dino said.

"Only three."

"Four. You're forgetting the grandson."

"Oh, yeah. What's his name?"

"Adams."

"Right."

"They've started ripping out the interior of that hotel already," Dino said.

"It must have been scheduled for a while."

"How's Faith?"

"Recovering very quickly, considering what she's been through."

The nurse came back with the waiter and had him take Stone's dishes away.

"When are they kicking you out of here?"

"I can't leave without a suit," Stone replied.

"We're keeping you overnight," the nurse said. "That's standard with head injuries, and you've had two."

"Now he'll have an excuse to stay," Dino said.

52

WHEN STONE WOKE the following morning, a suit was hanging on the back of his door, along with a white paper bag. The suit was the one he had worn the day before, with a Madame Paulette ticket attached, and the white bag held his freshly laundered shirt, underwear, and socks. His shoes, newly polished, were on the floor, stuffed with tissue paper.

Breakfast arrived, having been ordered from a doorknob menu card, as in a hotel. The waiter swept away the lid to reveal soft scrambled eggs, breakfast sausages, a toasted Wolferman's English muffin, fresh-squeezed orange juice, and a thermos jug of coffee, with Hermesetas sweetener in a dispenser, and a *New York Times* next to the tray. It was all exactly what he would have had at home.

He consumed his breakfast greedily, poured himself a cup of coffee, sweetened and stirred it, then picked up the *Times*. He had not made the front page, for which he was grateful, but he was annoyed not to find a report on the inside pages, either. This was the newpaper of record? He scanned it, then went straight to the crossword puzzle.

The nurse entered. "How's your headache?" she asked.

"What headache?"

"I'm glad to hear it. When you finish the crossword, you can go home."

"It's a Saturday; do I have to finish it?"

"Take it with you. The paper is complimentary."

"I'll bet that's all that's complimentary," he said.

"Your bill has been paid."

The doctor came in and confirmed the nurse's instructions. "Take it easy this weekend," he said. "No strenuous physical activity—and that includes sex."

Stone was instantly horny. The nurse, a plump woman of about sixty, was starting to look good. "When will I be healed?" he asked the doctor.

"If you aren't dead or back in here by Monday morning, you may resume all normal activity, including . . ."

"I know, I know."

Stone shaved with a provided razor, showered, then inspected his suit. "Remarkable," he said aloud to himself. "No blood, no vomit."

His cell phone began ringing, and he finally found it in an envelope, fully charged, inside the laundry bag, along with the contents of his pockets. His shoulder holster was there, but no gun. He answered the phone just before it would have gone to voice mail. "Hello?"

"I forgot to tell Joan to send you clothes," Dino said.

"Yeah, I noticed that. Fortunately, Madame Paulette worked

her wonders and delivered this morning, so I won't have to leave in a hospital gown."

"How'd she do?"

"Wonderfully well. I'm not throwing away the suit."

"How's the headache?"

"What headache? You were right about my forehead, though. I have a bruise."

"I'm sure it's very attractive. What are you doing for the weekend?"

"Nothing, if my doctor has anything to say about it, and that includes no women."

"For a whole weekend? You'll explode."

"Why don't you and Viv come over to my house for dinner?"

"Sold. Seven?"

"See you then."

Stone thanked the nurse and anyone else he could see and left the hospital wing by its private entrance, where a uniformed doorman found him a cab in seconds.

HIS HOUSE WAS EMPTY and disturbingly quiet. Stone sat down in his study, picked up the phone, then hung up. He had been thinking about the Whitehorn sisters, but they constituted a problem. They had both texted him their numbers, but by calling either one of them, he would insult the other. And anyway, how to choose? He decided to play for time: maybe something would happen to direct him to one or the other. He called Caroline.

"Good morning," she said. "When do you get out?"

"Half an hour ago," he replied. "I'd like to invite you and Charlotte to dinner at my house this evening."

"On a Saturday night? You're calling a girl on Saturday morning for a Saturday-night date?"

"Two girls," he said. If one of them was busy, that could be his break.

"Hang on." She covered the receiver for a moment, then returned. "We accept," she said.

"You live together?"

"We can't afford to live apart, at least not in the style to which we've become accustomed."

He gave her the address.

"I know," she said. "I stole your card from your wallet while you were still unconscious."

"I forgive you. Seven o'clock?"

"How are we dressing?"

"Up to you. I'm wearing a suit and a tie, both of which have been restored to me by Madame Paulette, in perfect condition."

"It was a mess the last time I saw it."

"It apologizes. Seven o'clock."

"We'll be there. You couldn't decide, huh?"

He started to reply, but she had already hung up. He called Helene and asked if she and Fred had dinner plans; they did not. He gave her a menu. "Dinner at eight, please, and ask Fred to pick us two bottles of good claret." Fred was as good a judge as he.

DINO GOT THERE FIRST. "Viv's coming from the office. Some sort of flap, so she'll be a little late. Did you manage to get a date?"

"Two," Stone replied.

"Two dates?"

"The Whitehorn sisters."

"You couldn't decide, huh?"

Stone shook his head. "Dangerous to decide."

"So you're hoping one will decide for you?"

"I'm leaving this one in the hands of Providence."

"Maybe one of them will fart during dinner, or something."

"Or something," Stone replied. "I have a terrible feeling it's not going to be as easy as that."

"I hope not," Dino said. "If it were, it wouldn't be any fun to watch."

53

FRED MANNED THE FRONT DOOR, taking coats and directing the Whitehorn sisters to Stone's study. Stone had just poured his and Dino's drinks when the women walked in, wearing equally elegant but distinctly different outfits. Everybody kissed the air. Fred served canapés, then went to help Helene.

The four of them sat down, Dino taking a love seat to leave room for Viv.

"You have a bruise on your forehead," Charlotte said.

"I know, and I can't remember how I got it."

"But your hair covers the bullet wound," Caroline echoed.

"I'm pleased to hear it," Stone replied.

"Have you killed that awful Trask man yet?" Charlotte asked.

"I can't answer that question in the presence of the police commissioner," Stone said.

"Well, you are going to kill him, aren't you?"

"Ahhh . . ."

Dino interrupted, "What else can you do? The man's been gunning for you for, what, a month? Desperate measures are required."

"So, you're suggesting I kill him before he can kill me?"

"It's less work for my people and the court system if you do. Who could blame you?"

"A court of law," Stone said. "I think a plea of self-defense requires a little more immediacy than finding him and shooting him."

"You never drew your gun while he was shooting you," Dino pointed out.

"You were carrying a gun at the restaurant?" Caroline asked.

"Caroline," Dino said. "In your line of work you're constantly surrounded by people carrying guns."

"But Stone is a civilian."

"Semi-civilian," Dino said. "He's carrying a badge your boss gave him."

"All right," she said. "Why didn't you return fire, Stone? Were you just standing there with your dick in your hand?"

"You've seen *The Godfather* too many times," Stone said. "I can't remember what happened, but like Dino, I wish I'd killed him."

"You're not even sure who shot you," Charlotte said.

"Who else but Trask?" Dino replied.

Viv joined them, having let herself in with her own key. Dino introduced her to the Whitehorns and fixed her a drink. "Okay," she said, "somebody bring me up-to-date."

Dino gave her a graphic rehash of the conversation so far.

"Yes, Stone, you should hunt him down and kill him."

"Then you could hire Alfie Goddard to represent you," Dino said.

"God," Stone replied, "I hope I'm never in *that* much trouble."

A voice came from the doorway. "Excuse me, Stone?"

Stone looked up to find Faith Barnacle standing there, wearing a coat, her bag over her shoulder.

"Faith, this is Caroline Whitehorn and her sister, Charlotte," Stone said, rising.

"How do you do?" Faith said.

"Would you like to join us for dinner?"

"Thank you, Stone, but I've already eaten. I just wanted to let you know that I'm going out for a walk. I no longer need a guard, do I?"

"No, you don't. Have a nightcap with us when you get back."

"Thank you, I may do that." Faith left.

"She's very attractive," Charlotte said. "Who is she?"

"She's my pilot," Stone replied. "She's also the woman who survived an attack by the East Side Murderers."

"Oh, yes, they worked in Mike's hotel," Caroline said. "Grandfather says you were instrumental in clearing him."

"All I did was recommend an attorney, who did the rest."

Fred came in and called them to dinner.

The leaves of the dining table had been removed, and it was now round, seating the five of them comfortably. Fred had decanted two bottles of Chateau Palmer '78, and the table was set with Stone's mother's china and silver. Stone seated himself between the two sisters.

They finished their first course, and Charlotte said, "So,

Stone, do you have some sort of fantasy about sleeping with sisters?"

"Oh, no," Stone said immediately, "not sisters: twins."

Everyone laughed.

"Then I guess we're safe," Caroline said.

"Not necessarily," Stone replied. "I'm not inflexible."

"Neither are we," Charlotte replied.

More laughter.

"I can't wait to see how you get out of this," Dino said.

"I suppose my next move should be to just take them both upstairs," Stone replied.

"We're not indiscriminate, either," Caroline said, "but we've never been able to share anything."

"Then I guess you'll have to take them upstairs one at a time, Stone," Viv said.

"And therein lies the quandary," Stone replied.

"Who first?"

"Exactly. They're both too beautiful," he said.

"That's a graceful answer, Stone," Charlotte said, "but not a solution to the problem."

"Then there can be only one solution," Stone said.

Everybody got quiet.

"What does Stone mean, Caroline?" Charlotte asked her sister.

"I think he means you and I have to decide," Caroline replied. "And we both know what that means, don't we?"

"Yes, we do."

"Come on, ladies," Dino said, "you're leaving us on tenter-hooks."

"What my sister means," Charlotte said, "is that we never agree on important decisions."

Stone took a deep breath and heaved a loud sigh. "I'm glad to be off *that* hook," he said.

Fortunately, Fred chose that moment to serve the main course and top off everybody's glass. Somebody, to Stone's eternal gratitude, chose that moment to change the subject.

THEY HAD JUST FINISHED DESSERT and were on to cognac when Stone glanced up to see Faith enter the room. She looked very shaken.

"Faith?" he said. "Is something wrong?"

"I've just shot somebody," she replied.

54

STONE TOOK FAITH'S COAT, sat her down, and got her a cognac. She sipped it gratefully.

"Did you call the police?" Dino asked.

"I left my cell phone," she said. "It's in my apartment."

"Did you tell the nearest cop?"

"Dino," she said, "you're the nearest cop."

"Then tell me what happened."

"Wait a minute," Stone said. "Faith, this may not be the best time to speak to the police. You've reported the shooting, and now you need to be represented by an attorney before you speak to them again."

"Stone, you're the nearest attorney," Faith said. "I'd like you to represent me."

"All right," Stone said.

Dino spoke up. "Caroline, Charlotte, Viv, will you leave us, please? Have a seat in the living room, and close the door behind you."

"You mean we don't get to find out what happened?" Caroline asked.

"Not just yet," Stone said, herding them toward the living room and closing the door. He sat down again. "All right, Dino, do you want to go off the record here?"

"I don't see how I can do that," Dino said.

"Then please go and join Caroline, Charlotte, and Viv in the living room, while I speak to my client."

Dino shot him a dirty look. "Lives may be at stake here," he said, closing the door behind him.

"All right, Faith," Stone said. "Tell me what happened."

Faith took a deep breath. "I walked up Park Avenue for a while," she said, "then I started home. I was walking down Lexington Avenue, and I passed the hotel where I used to overnight in New York. Somebody opened a door and walked away, and as the door slowly closed itself I heard something familiar."

"And what was that?"

"Classical music," she said.

"What kind of classical music?"

"Like chamber music. I'm not sure if it was exactly the music I heard after I was kidnapped, but it was a lot like that. I got to the door before it closed and stepped inside. The lobby has been gutted, but it was clear of debris and appeared to have been swept. There was one work light standing in the middle of the room; the front desk was gone, but I could see a light coming from where the manager's office was. The music was full and rich, like before, and it was pretty loud."

"What did you do then?"

"I started walking slowly toward the manager's doorway. I wanted to see who was in there. My gun was in my bag, and I took it out and worked the action as quietly as I could, then I put the safety on."

"Is the gun still in your bag?" Stone asked.

"Yes."

"Please take it out, pop the magazine, and eject the round in the chamber, then put them on the coffee table."

She followed his instructions.

"Now show me how you were holding the gun."

"Like this," she said, holding out the weapon in her right hand and cradling it in her left.

"Your finger is outside the trigger guard," Stone said. "Was it like that when you were approaching the manager's office?"

"Yes. It's how I was trained. You never touch the trigger, unless you intend to fire."

"All right, now set the gun on the coffee table."

She did so.

"Continue, please."

"I could see part of the office, and it seemed to be intact—I mean I could see a corner of the desk and a lamp. I halfway tripped over something, and as I regained my balance, my heel struck the floor, which is marble, and it made a noise. Immediately, the music was turned off."

"Completely off? Not just turned down?"

"Off or down so low I couldn't hear it anymore. I was right outside the door by then, and I heard something move inside the office. I stuck my head inside, and there was a man standing behind the desk."

"Did you recognize him?"

"No, he was wearing black coveralls, like a jumpsuit, and he had a hood over his head, with holes cut out for the eyes."

"Was he armed?"

"He had his right hand inside the coveralls at his chest, so I assumed he was about to draw a weapon. I stepped forward into the office and yelled 'Freeze!' the way I was taught during training."

"Where was your trigger finger at this time?"

"I moved it from the trigger guard to the trigger. Then it was like slow motion. His hand started to come out of his coveralls, and I fired once, at his chest, then the lights went off, and I felt him brush past me, knocking me off balance. I reached for something to steady myself, but I fell to one knee, which hurt, because I still have stitches in that leg."

"Which leg?"

"My left. I reached out ahead of me and felt the desk, and I used that to support myself while I got my leg under me again, then I ran to the door and looked into the lobby."

"Did you see the man?"

"No. The work light had gone off, and the only light in the room came from the lights on Lexington, coming through the glass front doors. I ran out into the street and looked both ways. Some cars passed, but I didn't see anyone on foot."

"Where was your gun then?"

"Still in my hand but pointed down at the ground. I kept it in my hand but turned the safety on and put the weapon in my coat pocket."

"Did you go back inside to look for the man?"

"No, I was afraid to. I looked in my bag for my cell phone, then remembered that I had left it charging in my apartment.

There were no pedestrians in sight and I didn't see a police car. I started to walk downtown, half running, really, but that hurt, so I slowed down and walked as fast as I could without causing pain. Next thing I knew, I was back here."

"All right," Stone said, "I'm going to ask Dino to come back, and I want you to tell him everything you've just told me."

"All right."

Stone went to the door and opened it. "Dino," he said, "Faith would like to speak to you now."

Dino came into the room, sat down, and saw the gun on the coffee table. "Is that the gun you used to shoot the man?" he asked.

"She doesn't know if she shot him," Stone said. "She only knows that she fired, once."

"Okay, let's hear it all from Faith," Dino said.

Faith began again, and when she had finished, Dino started asking her questions.

55

SEAN MULDOON'S CELL PHONE rang, and he answered it.

"Sean, this is Bacchetti."

"Good evening, sir."

"Where are you?"

"Just finishing dinner at P. J. Clarke's," Muldoon replied. He asked for the bill.

"Good. I know this isn't task force work, but I want you and your partner to go over to the Lexington hotel and check out a report of gunshots fired."

"Has a patrol car checked it out?"

"I want this checked out by detectives, and report to me."

"Yes, sir."

Dino told him Faith's story. "I want you to get into the building, go into that office, and see if anybody's there, and if there is, see if he has any bullet holes in him."

"Yes, sir, we're on our way." Muldoon put some cash on

the table, took the receipt, and stood up. "Let's go," he said to Calabrese. "I'll brief you on the way."

CALABRESE PARKED THE CAR outside the hotel and pulled down the driver's sun visor, to show the police ID on the back. They went to the front doors of the hotel and tried each one; the last one was unlocked, and they went inside, weapons drawn. A single work light cast its glow over the gutted room.

They moved toward the light coming from another room, presumably the manager's office.

"Hello?" a voice called out.

"Hello, yourself. This is the police. Come to the door and keep your hands in sight."

A man appeared in the doorway, his hands up. "Don't shoot," he said.

"Who are you?"

"My name is Michael Adams. I'm the project manager on the remodel of this hotel."

They frisked him, found nothing. "All right, relax," Muldoon said. "What are you doing in here on a Saturday night?"

"I worked this morning. I left my wallet in my desk, and I came to get it." He reached into an inside pocket and withdrew a wallet, then put it back into the pocket.

"How long have you been here?"

"Less than ten minutes," Adams replied. "I was going out to dinner and realized my wallet wasn't in my pocket."

"Have a seat," Muldoon said. "We need to look around your office, do you mind?"

"Not at all," Adams replied. "Something I can help you with?"

"We're looking for bullet holes," Muldoon said.

Adams laughed. "In here?"

The two detectives searched the room for signs of gunfire and found nothing. "Smell anything?" Muldoon asked his partner.

"Demo," he replied.

"Are there any bullet holes in you?" Muldoon asked Adams.

Adams laughed again. "I think I would have noticed," he said, pulling back his jacket to reveal a shirt, unblemished by gunfire.

Muldoon pointed at a radio at one end of the desk. "Have you been playing music?"

"It's always on when I'm working."

"What station is it tuned to?"

"WNYC, public radio."

"Mr. Adams, do you own a set of black coveralls?"

"I do not," Adams replied. "I have a set of white coveralls in the closet over there that I used when demo was under way to keep my suit clean."

Calabrese checked the closet. "They're here," he said, "and they're white. No black ones. Some other stuff—a raincoat and some dry cleaning, still in the bags."

"Mr. Adams," Muldoon said, "to your knowledge, is there anyone else in the hotel right now?"

"No, there is not."

"Have you heard any movement, any footsteps?"

"No, I have not."

"How did you get into the building?"

"I have a master key," Adams replied.

"When you arrived, was there an unlocked door?"

"I opened the one on the uptown side of the front. I didn't try any of the other doors, as I locked them on Friday evening when I closed up."

"How long ago did you unlock it?"

"Ten minutes, I guess."

"Where did you have dinner?"

"I haven't had dinner yet. I thought I'd go to an Italian place around the corner and eat at the bar."

Muldoon looked at Calabrese. "I think we're done here. Sorry to disturb you, Mr. Adams."

"Not at all. I'll walk you out."

The three men left by the unlocked door, and Adams locked it. "Good night," he said. He walked to the corner, turned it, and disappeared.

The detectives got back into the car, and Muldoon called the commissioner.

"Bacchetti."

Muldoon gave him a complete report. "That's it," he said finally.

"What was your impression of Michael Adams?"

"Straightforward, not nervous, truthful."

DINO THANKED THE DETECTIVES and hung up. "Well, you heard it. What do you think?"

Stone shrugged. "I think there are two possibilities," he said. "One: there was a third killer and he's still at large. Two: the third killer was Mike Adams."

"Kind of a coincidence that he was there, isn't it?" Dino asked. "But is there a third killer?"

"There sort of has to be, doesn't there?" Stone asked.

"I guess."

"Why else would a man be at or near the murder scene, wearing black coveralls and a mask?"

Dino picked up Faith's gun from the table, pulled back the slide, and sniffed it. "It's been fired," he said.

Faith spoke for the first time in a while. "I didn't fire it at a ghost or a mirror."

"I think you need to put Mike Adams under surveillance," Stone said. "The building, too."

"We've disbanded that task force," Dino replied. "I'm short on manpower."

"Do you have an alternative?" Stone asked.

"No," Dino replied.

56

STONE REASSEMBLED THE DINNER party in his study, just in time for it to break up. The Whitehorn sisters had been waiting for nearly an hour, consoled only by the cognac bottle.

"I'm going to send you home with my driver," Stone said to the sisters. He saw them to the garage and attempted to kiss them both on the cheek, but Caroline, at the last moment, turned her head and kissed him on the lips.

"No fair!" her sister said, then they got into the Bentley, arguing.

Chalk up a point for Caroline, Stone thought.

Dino and Viv were still in the study with Faith. Dino was finishing his brandy. "I think you'd better reinstate Faith's security," he said.

"Oh, no," Faith said wearily.

"There's still a killer, or at the very least a conspirator, on the loose," Dino said, "and he's seen you and knows you're armed. And we don't have any evidence to support arresting Mike Adams."

"What about the radio?"

"There are thousands of radios like that in this city," Dino said. "Possessing one is not a crime, and neither is listening to public radio."

"Dino's right," Stone said. "Viv, will you take care of the security?"

Viv picked up her cell phone. "I'll call the duty officer." She spoke briefly, then hung up. "They'll be here at eight AM tomorrow," she said.

"Here we go again," Faith said.

"Tell you what," Stone said. "Why don't you call Pat Frank in the morning and ask her for a copilot, then go fly for a while? That'll get you off the streets, and you need some left-seat time after your hospital stay."

Faith brightened. "That sounds good." She stood up. "I'm turning in." She reassembled her gun and slipped it into her coat pocket, then left the room.

"That kid has been through a lot," Dino said.

Nobody disagreed with him.

AS DINO LEFT STONE'S HOUSE he looked across the street and saw a street-sweeping machine coming down the block, which was empty of cars due to the alternate-side parking rules. Then, right behind the sweeper, a black SUV turned onto the block and stopped at the curb, several houses up from Stone's.

Dino got into the front passenger seat of his official car and picked up the radio.

"Yes, sir?"

Dino gave them the address. "There's a black SUV parked on the opposite side of the street. I want a patrol car to block the street above it and another to block the street at the corner of Second Avenue."

"Yes, sir."

"Wait here a minute," Dino said to his driver, then he called Stone.

"Forget something?"

"You might want to come out and get into the rear seat of my car, and come armed. There's what looks like a black Mercedes SUV parked across your street and up a little."

"Be right down," Stone said. He ran downstairs, opened his safe, and retrieved a Terry Tussey custom .45, then grabbed two magazines, hurried out the front door, and got into Dino's car.

"Okay," Stone said, shoving in a magazine, slapping it home, and racking the slide.

Dino picked up the radio. "Is everyone in place?"

"Affirmative, sir."

"All right, Tim," Dino said, "drive down the block and stop sideways. Leave no clearance for a car to get past, and turn off your lights."

Tim put the car in gear and pulled out, watching his rearview mirror. "He's still there," he said. "No, he's pulling out, no lights."

"Good," Dino said. "Okay, everybody, the driver of that car

should be considered armed and dangerous. Go ahead and light up everything."

Stone saw flashing lights coming on at the corner of Second Avenue, then looked back and saw the car at Third light up. Tim drove up onto the downtown sidewalk, turned left, and stopped in the middle of the street.

Dino grabbed the front-seat shotgun. "Stone, you stay inside for backup; I don't want you in a firefight unless we need you."

"Shit," Stone said, disappointed. He looked back and saw the black SUV suddenly drive onto the sidewalk, stop, see his way blocked, then execute a U-turn and accelerate toward Third Avenue. Flashing lights were in his way. He pulled onto the sidewalk to avoid the patrol car, but the cop did the same, blocking his way.

"Here we go," Dino said into the radio, then opened his door and jumped out, shotgun at the ready.

Stone saw Donald Trask get out of his car, his hands up. He was immediately overwhelmed by cops from both ends of the street.

Five minutes later, the block was restored to normalcy.

"I'll call you in the morning," Dino said, then he and Viv drove away.

Stone went upstairs and to bed.

HE WAS AWAKENED by the phone just after six AM.

"Bad news," Dino said.

"Give it to me."

"Trask was unarmed. The most we could charge him with was an illegal U-turn and driving the wrong way on a one-way street."

"Thanks, Dino, that was a great way to start the day."

He hung up.

STONE WAS AT HIS DESK LATER when Faith walked in. "I just wanted you to know, I'm going to Bloomingdale's. I've alerted my forces, and Fred is out front."

"I'll go with you," Stone said. "The elastic on my boxer shorts is giving out, and I need some new ones."

"Suit yourself," she said. "Oh, and I'm flying this afternoon."

Stone got up and joined her.

Fred pulled up at the Third Avenue Bloomie's entrance, and Stone and Faith got out. "How long will you be?" Stone asked her.

"I don't know, hours maybe."

"I'll get a cab home. See you." Stone went inside the store, to the ground-floor haberdashery department, found the boxer shorts, picked out a dozen, paid for them, and got them stuffed into a shopping bag.

He was just leaving the store when someone shouted his name.

57

STONE DIDN'T KNOW where the voice was coming from and looked around.

"Mr. Barrington!" came the call again.

Stone finally realized that it was coming from the uniformed doorman, who walked over with his hand out.

"It's Eddie," the man said. "Remember me?"

"The face is familiar, but you're in the wrong uniform," Stone replied.

"Ah, yes, it should be the Carlyle uniform. I helped you get Ms. Scott up to her apartment in a wheelchair, remember?"

"Of course, Eddie, the uniform confused me."

"I moonlight over here a couple days a week." Eddie looked sad. "I want to offer my sympathy over the loss of your friend," he said. "Ms. Scott was a very nice lady, always good to me."

"Yes, she was," Stone replied, "and thank you, Eddie."

"Her husband, though, he was a different kettle of fish, an asshole, if you'll excuse my Irish."

"I can't disagree," Stone said.

"You know, when I read about Ms. Scott in the papers, the first thing I thought of was that Trask."

"Funny, I had the same idea. So did the police, for that matter, after they stopped thinking I was their chief suspect."

"I saw him that very night," Eddie said.

"Which very night?" Stone asked.

"The night she died."

"Where did you see Donald Trask that night?"

"Well, right here," Eddie replied, pointing at the ground.

"I saw him walk up here from the downtown side. I was about to ask him if he needed a cab, when I saw his face, it just stopped me dead. I needn't have worried; he got into a town car and drove off."

"You said a town car?"

"One of them from the Phoenix service," Eddie replied. "They run a shabbier fleet than some others, but they're cheaper."

"How do you know it was a Phoenix car?"

"Because they have a tag on the trunk lids of all their cars," Eddie replied. "I know my car service cars. It was Phoenix car thirty-one. They number their vehicles."

Stone gulped. "What time was it, Eddie?"

"About six-fifteen," Eddie replied. "I had just come on duty."

"Eddie," Stone said. "If we weren't right out in the open here, I'd kiss you!"

"Well, now, Mr. Barrington, I'm not that way inclined," Eddie replied, taking a step back.

"Listen, don't go anywhere," Stone said. "I've got to make a call." He got out his cell phone and called Dino's cell number. Busy. He called the detective squad at the 19th Precinct and asked for Muldoon.

"Off duty," a detective said.

"Give me his cell number," Stone replied.

"Sorry, we don't give that out."

"Then call him and tell him to call Stone Barrington right back. I'll give you the number."

"Barrington? Did you used to be stationed here?"

"Before you were born," Stone said.

"Oh, hell, I'll get the number for you. Hang on." He came back a minute later and read Stone the number.

"Thanks very much," Stone said.

"Don't mention it. I heard you was always a pain in the ass, and I like that." The detective hung up.

Stone called Muldoon, and it went straight to voice mail.

"Sean," Stone said, "it's Stone Barrington. Call me, if you want to break the Donald Trask case. We've got a witness—Eddie, the doorman—who can put Trask at Bloomingdale's, getting into a Phoenix town car, number thirty-one, at six-fifteen on the night Cilla was murdered." He hung up and called Dino again. Still busy. Eddie had left his side, and Stone looked around for him.

Eddie was standing in the middle of the street, blowing his whistle for a cab, while a woman with a lot of shopping bags waited.

"Eddie!" Stone shouted. Eddie looked toward him, and at that moment a passing car struck him and sent him flying into the woman with the shopping bags.

Stone ran toward the heap. The woman was sitting up and

looking around, but Eddie was out cold, and there was blood coming from where his head had struck the pavement.

Stone's phone rang. "Hello?"

"It's Dino. You called three times?"

"I'll call you back," Stone said. He hung up and rushed to Eddie's side. "Are you all right?" Stone asked the woman.

"I think so," she replied.

Stone felt for a pulse in Eddie's neck and thought it was weak and thready. He called 911 and demanded an ambulance.

"You help him," the woman said. "I'll get my own cab." She began gathering up shopping bags.

The ambulance took only a couple of minutes. An EMT took Eddie's vitals, and got out a stretcher.

"How is he?" Stone asked.

"Not dead yet," the EMT replied, locking the stretcher in place, "but he's trying. He's got a serious head injury."

"I'm coming with you," Stone said, flashing his badge at the EMT and crowding to the rear. "Which ER?"

"Lenox Hill," the man replied.

Stone called Dino.

"Bacchetti."

"It's Stone."

"What the fuck is the matter? Why did you call me three times?"

"Because you were blabbing on your phone for all that time."

"That's what it's for," Dino explained. "What are you all hot about?"

"We've got Donald Trask cold."

"You mean he's dead?"

"No, I mean he's on ice, or will be when Eddie wakes up."

"Eddie who?"

"Eddie, the doorman at the Carlyle. He's got a head injury."

"As I recall, you've had a couple of head injuries lately, too, and that could be the problem."

"What problem?"

"The problem that you're not making any sense."

"All right, shut up and listen."

"I'm listening."

"Eddie, the doorman at the Carlyle, moonlights at Bloomingdale's."

"I thought you were going to start making sense."

"Shut up. On the night that Cilla Scott was murdered, Eddie was working Bloomingdale's and saw Donald Trask getting into a Phoenix town car. Number thirty-one."

"You mean this guy Eddie can put Donald Trask at Bloomingdale's?"

"Now you're starting to listen."

"At what time?"

"Six-fifteen."

"Holy shit. Yeah. You get this Eddie to the Nineteenth right away, and let Muldoon know you're coming."

"Muldoon's phone goes to voice mail, and Eddie is in an ambulance headed for the Lenox Hill ER. I'm with him."

"What's the matter with Eddie?"

"He was hit by a car outside Bloomingdale's while getting a customer a cab."

"How bad?"

"Not good. He struck his head on the pavement. I saw it bounce."

"I'll meet you at Lenox Hill," Dino said and hung up.

Stone hung up, too. He had a look at Eddie, who was now plugged into an IV and sucking oxygen. He didn't look good.

Stone looked around for his shopping bag and couldn't find it. "Well," he said aloud, "I hope the lady's husband or boyfriend wears size thirty-four boxers."

"What?" the EMT shouted, unplugging an ear from his stethoscope.

"Size thirty-four!" Stone shouted back.

58

DINO CALLED MULDOON, and the detective answered.
"It's Bacchetti."

"I got Barrington's message," Muldoon said. "I called Calabrese, where should we meet you?"

"Lenox Hill, the ER entrance," Dino said and then hung up.

DONALD TRASK TOOK the call on his cell. "Yes?"

"You know who this is?"

"Yes."

"There's a guy named Eddie, a doorman, who's in the ER at Lenox Hill Hospital."

"From the Carlyle?"

"From Bloomingdale's. He can put you there on the night. I thought you'd like to know."

"I'll leave something for you at the drop," Trask said. Then he got into his coat and took a gun from his safe. A minute later, he was on his way to Lenox Hill, which wasn't far from his apartment.

THE AMBULANCE had some traffic problems—a wreck on Third Avenue—and took longer to get to the ER than Stone had hoped. Eddie seemed to be getting sicker. Finally, the rear door of the ambulance burst open and the EMT was handing over the truck's gurney, while he held the IV bag over his patient.

Stone clipped his badge to his coat pocket and walked rapidly along behind the gurney. Eddie was wheeled into an area marked EXAM 4, and a nurse pulled the curtain closed in Stone's face. "Take a seat!" she yelled. "You can't help here."

Stone took a seat. Muldoon was the next arrival and sat down next to him. "Tell me," he said.

Stone ran down the story for him, and by the time he had finished, Dino had arrived, followed shortly by Calabrese, wearing a new suit. Stone noticed, because he had just seen one like it on a dummy at Bloomingdale's: it was made by Ermenegildo Zegna, an Italian company, and it cost more than three thousand dollars.

Dino noticed it, too. "What's with the suit?" he asked Muldoon quietly.

"He dresses better off duty, I guess," replied the detective, who was wearing a tracksuit and sneakers. "I think he must have a rich girlfriend."

A doctor came out of the exam room and looked at the

group. "Is the guy on my table a cop? He was wearing a doorman's uniform. Was he undercover?"

"He's a doorman," Stone said.

"One we need to speak to," Dino added.

"He's not conscious and is obviously concussed. We're sending him downstairs for scans to make sure there's no brain injury."

"When can we talk to him?" Muldoon asked.

"When he wakes up," the doctor replied, "and I can't guess when that will be. I'll know more when I see his scans."

"Okay," Dino said to his group, "there's no point in all of us hanging around here. Calabrese, you're low man on the totem pole, so you do the hanging and call me the moment he seems to be coming to."

"Yes, boss," Calabrese replied.

"Let's go get some coffee," Dino said to Stone and Muldoon. They found the doctors' lounge, made themselves at home, and took advantage of the free coffee and donuts.

A moment later, a woman who looked familiar to Stone entered the room and looked around. "Ah, there you are," she said, walking over to Stone and handing him a Bloomie's shopping bag. "You dropped these. I had my cab follow the ambulance."

"Thank you," Stone said.

"I'd have kept them, but my husband is a size forty-four," she said, then walked out.

"What was that?" Dino asked.

"Boxer shorts," Stone replied.

"You have them delivered wherever you are?"

"I dropped them when Eddie got hit by the car while try-ing to get her a cab, and they got mixed up with her packages."

"A likely story."

DONALD TRASK ENTERED the hospital by the main entrance, walked through a door marked STAFF ONLY, and found him-self in a locker room. He grabbed a green coat with an ID pinned to it and put it on over his jacket, then he started look-ing for the ER. His cell phone rang. "Yes?"

"He's downstairs from the ER where they do the MRIs and CT scans. I'm there, and it's very quiet."

"Then you take care of him," Trask said. "There's twenty-five thousand, cash, in it for you."

"Nope, I'm not that greedy." He hung up.

Trask walked back into the hallway and checked the signs, then he took an elevator down two floors and got off. The quiet was broken only by occasional hums. He walked from door to door looking through the windows, until he found a room where a man on a stretcher was being buckled in and readied for entering a large machine. Outside the door a cart held an ornate uniform coat. He had found Eddie.

Trask waited for a moment while the medical personnel cleared the room, then walked in, drawing his weapon. A voice behind him shouted, "Freeze! Turn around" He raised his hands, still holding the gun, and turned around.

Calabrese fired two shots: One caught Trask in the neck and the other hit above an eye. He collapsed in a heap. "One case cleared," Calabrese muttered to himself. He walked over to Trask, still pointing his gun, and checked him for signs of life. The man was dead. Then the detective heard another voice.

"That's not how we clear cases," Dino said. "Drop your weapon or join your pal."

Calabrese turned to find the commissioner and Muldoon facing him with drawn weapons, while Barrington looked on. Calabrese dropped his weapon.

STONE, DINO, and Muldoon walked into Eddie's hospital room an hour later to find him sitting up in bed drinking soup through a glass straw.

"Hi, Mr. Barrington," he said, "who are your friends?"

Stone introduced Dino and Muldoon. "They'd like to hear your story, Eddie," he said, "if you're feeling up to it."

"My story?" Eddie asked. "What story?"

"The one you told me a couple of hours ago at Bloomingdale's."

"I wasn't working Bloomie's today," Eddie said. "I was at the Carlyle." He furrowed his brow. "I think. What am I doing here? Nobody will tell me anything."

"You were hit by a car," Stone said, "and you have a concussion."

The doctor entered the room. "I've seen your scans," he said, "and you have no serious brain injury. We'll keep you overnight, which is policy in these cases, and you'll be back at work in a day or two."

Eddie looked at Stone. "Does this make any sense to you?"

"Eddie," Dino said, "I think we'll wait a day or two, then talk again." The three men wished him well, then left.

"That's the second guy in a week I've talked to who had no memory," Dino said.

"I guess we're not going to need Eddie, anyway," Muldoon observed.

"Can I give you a lift?" Dino asked Stone.

"Sure," Stone replied.

59

THEY GOT INTO DINO's car and headed downtown on Lexington Avenue. Stone looked at his watch. "You want some leftovers for dinner at my house?"

"Sure," Dino replied.

"It's weird, but I have a strange feeling of letdown."

"Yeah, I get that sometimes," Dino replied, "when a case is cleared."

"Are you having any luck from your surveillance of Mike Adams?"

Dino shrugged. "Well, we were a little slow off the mark on that one," he said. "But now that we've got Donald Trask off our hands, we can make some manpower available."

"What's going to happen to Calabrese?"

"That's up to the DA, but if he's charged with murder, he'll probably get off."

"You think?"

"The union will weigh in and get him a hotshot attorney.

He'll claim he was making an arrest of an armed suspect, who drew a weapon. Which is true, except that Muldoon and I saw how he handled it."

"I, as well."

"You don't count."

"Thanks a lot."

"Calabrese will be off the force soon, though. You can count on that. Muldoon found an envelope in his partner's pocket with Trask's old Greenwich address on it, containing eighteen hundred dollars and change. He's been tipping Trask along the way. That's why Donald-boy was so hard to nail."

"So Calabrese nailed him for you."

"As a way of covering his ass. Should I be grateful?"

"Well, you cleared a case, and you'll have a bad cop off the force. That's not a bad day."

"I guess not," Dino said, brightening.

Suddenly Stone said, "Driver, pull over!"

"What for?" Dino asked.

"We just passed the hotel," Stone said, "and there was a light on at the back of the lobby. Why don't we check it out?"

"Oh, what the hell," Dino said. "Back it up, Tim."

Tim reversed and set them down in front of the hotel.

"No work light in the lobby," Dino said, peering through a door.

"Looks like it's coming from the manager's office," Stone said.

Dino started trying doors and found one unlocked. He opened it and stood back. "After you," he said, drawing his weapon.

Stone drew his own. "With your permission, Commissioner."

"Granted," Dino said.

They moved quietly into the lobby and toward the rear, from which chamber music was coming. They stopped on either side of the manager's office door, and Dino pointed to himself.

Stone nodded and made an ushering motion with his free hand.

Dino peered around the doorjamb, then looked back at Stone and grinned.

Stone made the ushering motion again.

Dino stepped inside the office, weapon pointed, and said, "Freeze!"

Stone stepped inside behind Dino and peered over his shoulder at the figure behind the desk: black coveralls and a hood with holes for the eyes.

"How nice to see you," Stone said to the figure.

"In fact," Dino said, "let's see some more of you. Take off the hood."

The figure didn't move.

"Stone," Dino said, "you do the honors while I cover you."

"I'd be delighted," Stone said.

"I hope he twitches," Dino said, "because I'd rather shoot him than arrest him."

"I know the feeling," Stone replied. He walked clear of Dino and stayed near the wall, out of reach of the black figure, until he was behind the man. Stone frisked him thoroughly and found a small 9mm pistol tucked into a holster at the small of his back. He also found a flat, plastic box in the man's right hip pocket and he laid it on the desk, then stuck his gun in a pocket. He took hold of a wrist and brought it up between the man's shoulder blades and bent him over the desk. Finally, he reached up and placed a palm on top of the hooded head, grabbed a handful of fabric, and yanked.

"Well," Dino said, "look who we have here." He handed Stone his handcuffs and Stone applied them, the first time in years he had cuffed somebody. He stood the man up and looked at his face. "Good evening, Mike," he said.

Mike remained quiet.

Stone opened the plastic box he had removed and found a syringe and a vial of clear fluid inside, set into a foam rubber bed. "What's this, Mike?"

Mike still said nothing.

"Dino," Stone said, "I think the perp is choosing to remain silent, as is his constitutional right."

Dino read him his rights anyway, then he made the call for a patrol car.

Stone had a look around the office and opened the closet door. Behind a few hanging garments he could see an exposed corner of a sheet of drywall. He gave it a tug, and it came free. "Dino," he said, "closet behind a closet. That's where the costume was."

"Oh, good," Dino said.

A siren could be heard approaching, and a minute later a voice from the lobby yelled, "Commissioner?"

"Back here," Dino yelled back, and two uniforms appeared in the doorway. "Take him in and book him on one count of first-degree murder."

"Only one count?" Stone asked.

"We'll let the DA sort that out."

The cops escorted Mike out of the office and the building.

"Well," Stone said, "I think that somewhere in this building is probably a forgotten room that Mike has equipped for his purposes."

"So, we'll charge him with bad interior decorating?"

"It's better than finding a corpse in a garbage bag on Lexington Avenue," Stone said.

"I'll grant you that," Dino said, taking out his phone. "We'd better get a search started." He started issuing orders.

A few minutes later they were back in Dino's car. "I'll drop you at home," Dino said, "but I won't stay for the leftovers. I'm tired."

Stone realized that he was tired, too.

60

S TONE WOKE the following morning and checked the news shows for something on the arrest of Mike Adams, but there was nothing. He was able to hold his curiosity until after lunch, then he called Dino.

"Bacchetti."

"It's Stone. Why is there nothing on the news about Mike Adams?"

"You want the whole story?"

"Please."

"Okay," Dino said, "young Mike called Herbie Fisher at the first opportunity, and Herbie arrived as if he'd been shot out of a cannon, clutching a copy of the DA's offer of immunity on all charges, in return for Mike's testifying against the other two. You'll recall that, faced with Mike's testimony and his logbook of their movements, they both bought a deal of life in prison without the possibility of parole. So, the DA declined to prosecute, and Mike walked."

"Shit."

"No, really. We have no evidence that Mike has committed a crime, unless you consider dressing up like a killer a crime. His gun was licensed, and the chemical in the hypo kit was insulin. Herbie produced a note from his doctor confirming that he's a diabetic. Also, I had twenty men searching that hotel and the adjacent building, and they found absolutely nothing to indicate that Mike planned to commit a crime there. Finally, no corpses have turned up in trash cans."

"There's nothing you can do, then?" Stone asked. "That black costume, combined with the fact that he didn't report being shot at by Faith, indicates he's not quite as innocent as we all thought."

"For all practical purposes, yes, there's nothing more we can do. What we *think* doesn't matter."

"I'm still surprised his recent arrest wasn't on the news."

"Herbie managed to get a gag order for that, pointing out that if the news story ran, large numbers of people would believe that Mike is guilty, when there is no evidence to support that contention. Mike's life would probably be ruined. It wouldn't surprise me to learn that a member of the older generation may have made a phone call or two, as well. Also, if the story ran we'd get our asses sued for false arrest and defamation, and that includes you, too."

"It makes a neat package, doesn't it."

"Look at it this way," Dino said. "The fucking case is cleared."

Joan stuck her head in Stone's door. "Caroline Whitehorn is on line two."

"I gotta run," Stone said.

Dino hung up.

Stone steeled himself for the blast from Caroline about having Mike arrested. "Hello?"

"Hi, it's Caroline."

"How are you?"

"Very well, thanks. I called to thank you."

Stone was mystified. "For what?"

"Oh, I know you're being shy and all that, but your man Herb Fisher saved our cousin Mike from a fate worse than death."

"I did hear about that."

"Would you like to have dinner with Charlotte and me this week?"

"Caroline," Stone said, "I regret that I don't have the emotional capacity or the moral fiber to deal with the two of you, and if I made a choice, it would probably be the wrong one, so I'm just going to have to take a pass."

"I understand," Caroline said. "We can be a little hard to take."

"Thank you for your understanding." He said goodbye and hung up.

Joan buzzed him again. "Edith Beresford on one," she said.

Stone picked up the phone. "Edie?"

"That's me."

"I can't tell you how glad I am to hear from you. Let's have dinner."

"Sold," she said.

AUTHOR'S NOTE

I AM HAPPY to hear from readers, but you should know that if you write to me in care of my publisher, three to six months will pass before I receive your letter, and when it finally arrives it will be one among many, and I will not be able to reply.

However, if you have access to the Internet, you may visit my website at www.stuartwoods.com, where there is a button for sending me e-mail. So far, I have been able to reply to all of my e-mail, and I will continue to try to do so.

If you send me an e-mail and do not receive a reply, it is probably because you are among an alarming number of people who have entered their e-mail address incorrectly in their mail software. I have many of my replies returned as undeliverable.

Remember: e-mail, reply; snail mail, no reply.

When you e-mail, please do not send attachments, as I *never* open these. They can take twenty minutes to download, and they often contain viruses.

Please do not place me on your mailing lists for funny stories, prayers, political causes, charitable fund-raising, petitions, or sentimental claptrap. I get enough of that from people I already know. Generally speaking, when I get e-mail addressed to a large number of people, I immediately delete it without reading it.

Please do not send me your ideas for a book, as I have a policy of writing only what I myself invent. If you send me story ideas, I will immediately delete them without reading them. If you have a good idea for a book, write it yourself, but I will not be able to advise you on how to get it published. Buy a copy of *Writer's Market* at any bookstore; that will tell you how.

Anyone with a request concerning events or appearances may e-mail it to me or send it to: Publicity Department, Penguin Random House LLC, 375 Hudson Street, New York, New York 10014.

Those ambitious folk who wish to buy film, dramatic, or television rights to my books should contact Matthew Snyder, Creative Artists Agency, 9830 Wilshire Boulevard, Beverly Hills, California 98212-1825.

Those who wish to make offers for rights of a literary nature should contact Anne Sibbald, Janklow & Nesbit, 445 Park Avenue, New York, New York 10022. (Note: This is not an invitation for you to send her your manuscript or to solicit her to be your agent.)

If you want to know if I will be signing books in your city, please visit my website, www.stuartwoods.com, where the tour schedule will be published a month or so in advance. If you wish me to do a book signing in your locality, ask your

favorite bookseller to contact his Penguin representative or the Penguin publicity department with the request.

If you find typographical or editorial errors in my book and feel an irresistible urge to tell someone, please write to Sara Minnich at Penguin's address above. Do not e-mail your discoveries to me, as I will already have learned about them from others.

A list of my published works appears in the front of this book and on my website. All the novels are still in print in paperback and can be found at or ordered from any bookstore. If you wish to obtain hardcover copies of earlier novels or of the two nonfiction books, a good used-book store or one of the online bookstores can help you find them. Otherwise, you will have to go to a great many garage sales.

Solzhenitsyn and the Modern World

Solzhenitsyn and the Modern World

Edward E. Ericson, Jr.

REGNERY GATEWAY
Washington, D.C.

Due to space limitations, permissions appear on page 422.

Library of Congress Cataloging-in-Publication Data

Ericson, Edward E.
    Solzhenitsyn and the modern world / Edward E. Ericson, Jr.
        p.   cm.
    Includes bibliographical references and index.
    ISBN 0-89526-501-X (alk. paper)
    1. Solzhenitsyn, Aleksandr Isaevich, 1918-   —Criticism and
interpretation. I. Title.
PG3488.04Z645 1993
891.73′44—dc20   92-39375
                                                            CIP

Published in the United States by
Regnery Gateway
1130 17th Street, NW
Washington, DC 20036

Distributed to the trade by
National Book Network
4720-A Boston Way
Lanham, MD 20706

Printed on recycled, acid-free paper.

Manufactured in the United States of America.

10   9   8   7   6   5   4   3   2   1

In beloved memory of Edward Einar Ericson, Sr.
and Ethel Marie Hall Ericson

Acknowledgments

I HAVE READ AND PONDERED the works of Aleksandr Solzhenitsyn for a quarter of a century. I have now taken a year out of my life to write down my thoughts about his work, in hopes that some other readers will find them useful. As any author knows, a book is never finished. This one is what I could accomplish in the year's time available to me.

During the labor of composition, I have been cheered on my way by the advice and assistance of many. My first and largest debt of gratitude is owed to Calvin College, which has provided me a safe haven for independent, even unfashionable, thinking. A word spoken in due season by my former Academic Dean, Rodger Rice, prompted me—more than he could have imagined—to take on this task. I have also been the beneficiary of a sabbatical leave and a generous Calvin Research Fellowship, giving me an uncluttered year for this work. It is a joy to be part of a college which actually puts teaching first but also seriously promotes writing for publication.

The secretarial staff of Calvin's English Department, headed by our gracious and reliable administrative assistant, Sherry Koll Smith, has helped me almost daily for a year. Student assistants on this project were Heidi Arkema of Colorado, Gabrielle DeFord of Connecticut, Elisa Spoelhof of Texas, Rebecca Warren of New York, and Kimberly Wedeven of Idaho. They all humored "the right-now kid." Also, Jane Haney, secretary for Calvin's History Department, helped with word-processing.

I have received very valuable advice from friends who have read the manuscript-in-progress: Yuri Maltsev (economics, Carthage College); Charles Strikwerda (political science, Calvin College); Edward Cole (history, Grand Valley State University); Matthew Davis (student of Russian, Crawfordsville, Indiana); and former student David Downing (English, Westmont College). My chief adviser has been John Wilson of Pasadena, California, another former student of more than twenty years ago and now easily my peer. A teacher's life brings great rewards. I am deeply grateful, also, to my friend and editor, Michael Smith. Alfred Regnery, of Regnery Gateway, Inc., has been a thoroughly accommodating and supportive publisher. Production Editor Jennifer Reist and Managing Editor Megan Butler have been unfailingly diligent, competent, patient, and even cheery in their work on this book. Wife Jan, ever tolerant, has let me take over our living room with piles of materials and has given rhythm to my work by regularly hauling me off to the golf course.

I only wish that I could blame someone mentioned above for the shortcomings of the book. They are mine alone.

Edward E. Ericson, Jr.
Calvin College
Grand Rapids, Michigan

Contents

Solzhenitsyn and the Modern World

1

Introduction
A Call for Reassessment

THE IDEAS OF ALEKSANDR SOLZHENITSYN are highly significant and powerfully relevant for the modern world. That is the thesis of this book. The prevailing Western view of Solzhenitsyn is very inaccurate and needs to be revised and corrected. That is the burden of this book. Current events in Russia make this a particularly propitious time to reassess Solzhenitsyn. That is the premise of this book.

The fast-moving events in Communist countries during the late 1980's and early 1990's have been exceedingly dramatic and almost totally unexpected. Virtually no one predicted them. Yet we recognize clearly that they are events of world-historical importance. The face of the globe has changed right before our eyes. One of the two great superpowers is gone, irretrievably gone, its flag lowered for the last time. We wait and watch to see what will take its place, and we wonder how many years, decades, we will have to wait and watch before we know.

These colossal events are unfolding at a time of widespread uncertainty about the meaning of our period of history and even what name we put on it. Academics in various disciplines talk about our having moved beyond the modern era into a postmodernism which lacks any consensual definition. If in past ages people seemed to know who they

3

were, we are not so sure about ourselves. Cultural consensus is long gone, and we greet the future with strange minglings of fear and hope. There is a widespread sense that humanity has lost its way and is adrift without a moral compass. What are we to believe? How are we to live? Will our world threaten us or shelter us? The demise of the Soviet Union seems to change everything. We know that it brings us a new world, but we do not know what order it brings us. Everything now stands in need of reassessment.

I write this book in the conviction that about our deepest yearnings Aleksandr Solzhenitsyn has something very valuable to say. In the cacophony of our time, we should attentively tune him in. If we can block out the static just long enough to hear him out, we will learn something important about this critical juncture of history and serve ourselves well. Solzhenitsyn writes out of vintage twentieth-century experience. Literally a posthumous son of the time of the Bolshevik Revolution, which is arguably the most important and defining event in the twentieth century, he has devoted his life to trying to understand the century in which he and we live.

In whatever else this century excels, it has outdone all others in dealing out unspeakable dehumanizing horrors. As it comes to its end, we must come to terms with its evil and the meaning of that evil. Solzhenitsyn's ideas were formed in the crucible of great personal and national suffering. He has arrived at his analysis of the twentieth century not by abstract philosophizing but by examining the concrete condition of the modern world, the full weight of which he has experienced personally. As we seek to make sense of our time and our lives, he is well-positioned to instruct those of us whose personal experience has been, by comparison to his, pale, tepid, sheltered.

In the early 1960's, when Solzhenitsyn first came to world fame, there arose a saying, "Tell me what you think about Solzhenitsyn, and I'll tell you who you are."[1] In the Soviet Union this saying retained its currency for a long time, and it has potential relevance for us all even today. For if we knew, really knew, what he has to say, his vision of life in our time could serve as a useful touchstone by which we could gauge our own understandings of it.

Unfortunately, those who rely upon the Western media for their estimate of Solzhenitsyn have received a badly garbled transmission of his message. The prevailing view of Solzhenitsyn includes the following propositions. He is anti-Western. He is anti-democratic. He is ungrateful toward the United States, which gave him refuge in his exile. He is a reactionary, chauvinistic, messianic Russian nationalist. His preferred form of government is authoritarian—even monarchist. He has a utopian vision of a good old Holy Russia governed theocratically, to which he would like to see his nation return. He is a romantic primitivist who rejects modern technology. He may be tinged by anti-Semitism. In short, he is an eccentric extremist.

This view of his thinking is false at every point. Yet it prevails. The Western misinterpretation of Solzhenitsyn is a long story, which I shall be telling. However, some of Solzhenitsyn's own words are applicable here: "One thing is absolutely definite: not everything that enters our ears penetrates our consciousness. Anything too far out of tune with our attitude is lost, either in the ears themselves or somewhere beyond, but it is lost."[2]

Here is a writer who has been translated into as many languages as Shakespeare and whose works have sold in the many millions of copies. And now, within his lifetime, he has fallen into general neglect. Sales of some of his books were, of course, generated by the sensational character of his life story; and, because sensationalism is ephemeral, it is natural that some interest in him has waned. But misinterpretation is the larger cause for the neglect. Certainly, the cause cannot be obsolescence or parochialism of his themes, for they are perennial and universal.

Any reassessment of Solzhenitsyn must eventually return the focus of our attention to his literary works. They are the most significant things to know about him, not his biography or his non-fiction essays. The primary intended audience of his literature is future generations of Russians, and with them his literary reputation ultimately will rest. However, it was not literary criticism of his art which caused Western commentators to stumble in trying to come to terms with him. It was the reactions to his essays which generated the fog of misperception. So the first step in getting Solzhenitsyn right is to lift this fog. Once this is achieved, readers can turn, or return, to his literature, unhindered.

About his essays Solzhenitsyn has said, "I am a publicist really involuntarily, against my own will. If I could broadcast to my people I would read them my books, my novels, because in my interviews, my articles, I can't give even one hundredth of that which I have put into my novels."[3] Indeed, most of his publicistic (from the Russian *publi-*

tsisticheskii) work was done, one might say, upon demand, more at the invitation of others than by his own initiative. Yet these are the writings which have caused many Westerners to find him an alien spirit.

Solzhenitsyn has closely linked his personal fate with the fate of Russia. It is especially in his essays, however, that he has explicitly broadened the scope of his analysis to take into account the modern world as a whole. In his view, the twentieth century is "one of the most shameful centuries of human history"; it is "the cave man's century."[4] Toward this modern world Solzhenitsyn takes a *contra mundum* stance. He offers analysis of it and prescriptions for remedying its gravest ills. This is a book about Solzhenitsyn and the modern world. It does not offer an independent analysis of the modern world or an independent definition of modernity. Rather, it looks at the modern world through Solzhenitsyn's eyes, as it were, endeavoring to see what he sees in it, allowing the emphases to fall where his emphases fall. If this book, by focusing on the non-literary writings, is not about the most important thing in Solzhenitsyn, it is about the first thing to be reconsidered for a proper understanding of him by his contemporaries. This first thing is his relationship to the world in which he lives.

What makes this a particularly suitable moment to reassess Solzhenitsyn is that it is his part of the world which is undergoing the greatest upheavals and is itself in need of the greatest re-evaluation. Not only so, but he has presented publicly his suggestions for the shape of things to come in Russia. The earthshaking events which have erased the Union of Soviet Socialist Republics from the face of the map make reinterpretation of the whole of the Soviet experience mandatory. In this process it is also both fitting and necessary that a thinker and writer of such high profile as Solzhenitsyn be reinterpreted.

ALREADY THE PROCESS OF REINTERPRETING Soviet history has begun. As difficult as it is to admit that one has been wrong, already some such confessions are appearing. A particularly striking admission of error comes from the prominent economist Robert Heilbroner:

> . . . what spokesman of the present generation has anticipated the demise of socialism or the "triumph of capitalism"? *Not a single writer in the Marxian tradition!* Are there any in the left centrist group? None that I

can think of, including myself. As for the center itself—the Samuelsons, Solows, Glazers, Lipsets, Bells, and so on—I believe that many have expected capitalism to experience serious and mounting, if not fatal, problems and have anticipated some form of socialism to be the organizing force of the twenty-first century.

That leaves the right. Here is a part hard to swallow. It has been the Friedmans, Hayeks, von Miseses, *e tutti quanti* who have maintained that capitalism would flourish and that socialism would develop incurable ailments.[5]

Mikhail Bulgakov once wrote that "a fact is the most obdurate thing in the world."[6] As Heilbroner honestly faces the facts of current history, he reluctantly concedes that they do not conform to his hypotheses: "From this admittedly impressionistic and incomplete sampling I draw the following discomfiting generalization: *the further to the right one looks, the more prescient has been the validity of historical foresight; the further to the left, the less so.*"[7] The point here is not that Heilbroner is necessarily correct in his assessment, nor that his use of the stations along the economic spectrum is a serviceable approach. Indeed, Irving Howe wrote a reply in which he found Heilbroner "quite mistaken . . . in his attribution of political prescience to the right."[8] The point here is that the kind of reappraisal exemplified by Heilbroner is an ineluctable concomitant of the fact of the demise of the Soviet Union.

Philosopher Richard Rorty follows the point, and he finds his own conclusions "depressing." As he remarks, "Visitors from postrevolutionary Eastern and Central Europe are going to stare at us incredulously if we continue to use the word *socialism* when we describe our political goals." He predicts that it will "take a long period of terminological and psychological readjustment for us Western leftist intellectuals to comprehend that not only *socialism* but all other words that drew their force from the idea that an alternative to capitalism was available have been drained of that force." Rorty speaks not "as a triumphant Reaganite but rather as someone who kept hoping that some country would figure out a way to keep socialism after getting rid of the *nomenklatura*." Despite the concessions which recent events have wrung from him, he cannot bring himself to abandon his Leftism. He is, for example, "unwilling to grant that Hayek was right in saying that you cannot have democracy without capitalism. All I will concede is that you need capitalism to ensure a reliable supply of goods and services and to ensure that there will be enough taxable surplus left over to finance social welfare." Thus shorn of its radical character, the Leftism remaining to Rorty is a severely truncated and intellectually suspect version: "I hope we can stop thinking that, even if Marx got things wrong, we must keep trying to do the *sort* of thing Marx tried to do. I hope we can admit that we have practically nothing in the way of a 'theoretical basis' for political action and that we may not need one." And it is easy enough to guess what his imagined visitors from the east would think of this bit of nostalgia: "For better or worse, *socialism* was a word that lifted the hearts of the best people who lived in our century. A lot of very brave men and women died for that word. . . . They were the most decent, the most devoted, the most admirable people of their times."[9]

History has not been unkind to Solzhenitsyn as it has to Heilbroner and Rorty. I would not have written this book if I thought that the events of our day demonstrated major errors in Solzhenitsyn's thinking about the modern world. I believe that—both generally and in considerable detail—events show how right he has been, even how prescient. Indeed, some of his pronouncements which at the time struck Westerners as the most outlandish now seem the most prophetic.

A case in point: as soon as he was expelled from the Soviet Union in February of 1974, this fifty-five-year-old man announced that he fully expected to return home in person, during his lifetime. All along he has reiterated this confident expectation. He said so despite the fact that he had been stripped of his Soviet citizenship and had been placed under a charge of treason. Furthermore, he declared that his works would have to precede him, that is, that the Soviet leaders would have to permit his literary works, starting with *The Gulag Archipelago*, to be openly, legally printed and circulated before he would come home.

All of this happened just as he insisted that it must. In early 1989, the Moscow journal *Twentieth Century and Peace*, published by the official Soviet Peace Committee, broke the longstanding taboo and published a piece by Solzhenitsyn. Its choice was the brief, thousand-word essay "Live Not by Lies," Solzhenitsyn's parting word to his countrymen as he was being expelled from his homeland and until then published only in the West.[10] Then that most respected of Soviet literary periodicals, *Novy Mir*, which had originally published Solzhenitsyn back in 1962, published large portions of *The Gulag Archipelago*. In August of 1990, his citizenship was restored. In the autumn of 1990, his essay *Rebuilding Russia* saw its first light of day not in the West but in the mass-circulation newspaper of the Communist youth organization, *Komsomolskaya Pravda*, and the next day it was carried by *Literaturnaya Gazeta*, a journal which in earlier times had published slanders against him. Prior to this surge, nothing of Solzhenitsyn's had been legally published in his homeland since 1963. Finally, on September 17, 1991, the charge of treason was dropped. With the falling of this last barrier, he promptly announced that he would return to Russia. He would delay only until he finished the work he was in the midst of writing at that moment, writing for which he still needed access to materials in American libraries.

Through the seventies and eighties, it seemed quite absurd to imagine Solzhenitsyn's returning home. Solzhenitsyn had for decades been the government's most militant and famous critic. In late 1988, Vadim Medvedev, then chief ideologist for the Gorbachev regime, said that Solzhenitsyn could not be published, because "to publish Solzhenitsyn's work is to undermine the foundation on which our present life rests."[11] Exactly so. Solzhenitsyn knew that the country which would allow him to return would have to be something other than the old Soviet Union. It would be churlish, at the least, to say that in all this Solzhenitsyn has just been lucky.

Solzhenitsyn's hostility to the Soviet system cannot be overstated. Here is just one sample of the many available in his writings:

> . . . nowhere on the planet, nowhere in history, was there a regime more vicious, more bloodthirsty, and at the same time more cunning than the Bolshevik, the self-styled Soviet regime. . . . [N]o other regime on earth could compare with it either in the number of those it had done to death, in hardiness, in the range of its ambitions, in its thoroughgoing and unmitigated totalitarianism—no, not even the regime of its pupil Hitler, which at that time blinded Western eyes to all else.[12]

This unremitting antagonism and condemnation has held considerable appeal for the general population in the West. Western scholars, however, have been, for the most part, cool toward it, considering it too simplistic, unnuanced. Yet one lesson of the past few years is how much resonance with Solzhenitsyn's view there is among those who lived under Soviet rule. For them, Communism is as Communism does. And what Communism does is what Solzhenitsyn has described that it does.

Solzhenitsyn saw no way to a healthy future for his people other than the total abandonment of Communism. This route is the one now being pursued. It is true that, on a few occasions, he wavered a bit about when the end would come, but he never doubted that it would occur. Someday the final punctuation mark would be put on the Soviet parenthesis in Russian history (and the history of the other captive nations, as well). For instance, in a 1983 interview, he said, "I have now come to the very pessimistic conclusion that communism still has quite a chance of spreading over the whole world." Yet in the next breath he asserted, "But I am absolutely convinced that Communism will go like the eclipse that I spoke of. . . . I personally am convinced that in my lifetime I will return to my country."[13] About his own *Gulag Archipelago*, he once mused, ". . . the most important and boldest books are never read by contemporaries, never exercise an influence on popular thought in good time. . . . I do not at all believe that it will explain the truth of history in time for anything to be corrected."[14] Still, he was quite confident that "*Gulag* was destined to affect the course of history."[15]

In these tergiversations of mood, optimism always won out over pessimism. Contrary to the widespread image of him as a Jeremiah-like prophet of doom, Solzhenitsyn describes himself as "an unshakable optimist." When his friend Andrei Sakharov expressed a feeling of hopelessness about the future of their country, Solzhenitsyn described his own mood as the opposite: ". . . against all reason I had never in my life experienced this hopelessness, but on the contrary had always had a sort of stupid faith in victory." In his memoirs, *The Oak and the Calf*, he reflects upon his dark day of February 12, 1974, when he was arrested and prepared for shipment into exile the next day. He thinks of the scene back at his apartment: "However you look at it, this spate of sympathizers fearlessly visiting the apartment of a man under arrest shows how times have changed! You Bolsheviks are finished—there are no two ways about it." As he sat in prison that night, his own thoughts were, "The calf butted the oak: a futile enterprise, you might think. The oak has not fallen—but isn't it beginning to give just a little?"[16]

If Solzhenitsyn sometimes grew impatient about the pace of the deliverance of his people from Soviet captivity, he never doubted the outcome. And, in most of his moods, he thought that it would occur sooner rather than later—sooner, certainly, than any Western experts anticipated. One has only to read the books of 1990 about Mikhail Gorbachev and the Soviet Union to recall how far away the events of 1991 seemed to be. On the veritable eve of the vanishing of the Soviet Union into the abyss of history, few could bring themselves to imagine it. We had to get within months of the final lowering of the red flag with the hammer and sickle before we would read such sentences as, "So Soviet history is at last over, with a clear beginning, a middle and an end."[17] But now we read words such as these by Senator Daniel Patrick Moynihan: "Well, the Soviet Union has broken up. No one anticipated it more than Aleksandr Solzhenitsyn."[18]

Not only was Solzhenitsyn a prophet of the demise of the Soviet Union, but he was a major protagonist. Those who wish to understand the underlying causes of the collapse of Soviet Communism could do no better than to dust off their copies of *The Gulag Archipelago* and read it. Of some of the early reviews of this monumental work, Solzhenitsyn declared, ". . . I am astonished to see how clearly its significance was realized"; and he cites, among others, this one from the *Frankfurter Allgemeine*: "The time may come when we date the beginning of the collapse of the Soviet system from the appearance of *Gulag*. . . ."[19] Similar sentiments have reverberated through the years, down to the present. For instance, George Bailey said of *Gulag*, "The work is the greatest single blow ever dealt to the corpus of Communist theory."[20] An editorial of late 1990 said of Solzhenitsyn, "The fact that 'the clock of communism has run out of time' is to a large extent due to him."[21]

It took the witness of many to lodge securely in the modern consciousness the word *Holocaust* as a shorthand term signifying modern man's inhumanity to man. From a single witness has now come another such shorthand term: Gulag. In Bailey's words, Solzhenitsyn's indictment has "branded the letters GULAG on the body politic of the Soviet Union."[22] It is a quite supportable thesis that Solzhenitsyn deserves considerable credit for undermining Soviet legitimacy in the eyes of Soviet citizens. Of course, from another angle of vision, one could say that no one deserves as much credit as the Soviet leaders themselves, whose transgressions Solzhenitsyn was merely bringing to public attention. But someone had to be the little boy who said that the emperor has no clothes. As it turns out, in his revulsion toward Communism Solzhenitsyn was not alone. Martin Malia's analysis of what he calls "the August Revolution" of 1991 concludes by calling attention to what he perceives as a connection between Solzhenitsyn's ideas and the failed coup:

> For the starkest fact of the Russian Revolution of 1991 is that virtually nothing remained of the old Leninist system. No basic Communist institutions have proved salvageable for a "normal" society. In the August Revolution much of the population, as if by a sudden joint decision, refused "to live according to the lie," in Aleksandr Solzhenitsyn's famous summons, and the entire once-intimidating structure dissolved in days. So out of a total system came total collapse.[23]

Solzhenitsyn probably deserves some credit, also, for undermining Soviet legitimacy in the eyes of the rest of the world. Already James Pontuso has offered this intriguing speculation:

> It would be premature to credit Solzhenitsyn with having caused the decline of Soviet power. Yet it is significant to note that after the various parts of The Gulag Archipelago began to be published, public opinion in the West hardened against the Soviet Union and nearly all of the nations in the Western alliance chose governments hostile to Soviet aggression. The United States, in particular, elected the most conservative and fervently anti-Communist president of the postwar era.

Pontuso sides with those who believe that the Reagan administration's military buildup put significant pressure on Soviet officialdom. His speculation continues, "In what must have been a moment of self-doubt, the Soviet leaders turned to a new leader who could both make a deal with the West and bring life to the economy. In other words, the Soviets yielded." This linkage, as Pontuso knows, could be considered just a matter of coincidence. He could be charged with the logical fallacy of *post hoc ergo propter hoc*. Still, his line of speculation

> is given credence by one undeniable fact. While the leader who was the least sympathetic to the Soviet regime was president, the Communists selected the leader who has been, thus far, the most willing to make

domestic reforms and to transform Soviet foreign policy. To state the proposition plainly, if Solzhenitsyn's writings stiffened Western resolve and that firmness helped bring about a change in leadership in the Soviet Union, then Solzhenitsyn had an important hand in bringing Gorbachev, with all his reforms, to power.[24]

One is put in mind here of a pronouncement by one of the characters in *The First Circle*: ". . . a great writer is, so to speak, a second government. That's why no regime anywhere has ever loved its great writers, only its minor ones."[25]

SOME OF THE PRECEDING citations suggest that we are already seeing the first glimmerings of a reassessment of Solzhenitsyn. It will ineluctably proceed apace, I believe, with a reconsideration of some of the arguments in which he has embroiled himself. Two issues, in particular, come to mind. One is the relationship between Lenin and Stalin. The other is whether the horrors of the Soviet period are to be blamed primarily on the ideology of Marxism-Leninism or on some historical defect in the Russian character. On both issues Solzhenitsyn's position has met with strong resistance from Western scholars.

Solzhenitsyn holds that there is much more continuity than discontinuity from Lenin to Stalin, that the machinery of oppression which Stalin used so mercilessly was set in place by Lenin, that the distinction between Stalin and Lenin in brutalizing their subjects was one of degree rather than one of kind. Also, Solzhenitsyn believes that the main culprit accountable for dehumanization in the Soviet period is Marxist-Leninist ideology. The Russians need not be vindicated as somehow pristine and faultless, but there is simply no moral equivalence between the deprivations endured under authoritarian tsardom and the brutalities suffered under totalitarian Communism. Moreover, Solzhenitsyn believes, the Russians were the very ones whose agonies were the greatest under the Soviets.

On both counts Solzhenitsyn's positions appear more credible and tenable today than most Western scholars formerly found them. It is noteworthy how few citizens of the former Soviet Union are rallying in defense of the good name of Lenin. The name of Leningrad reverted to St. Petersburg with unseemly speed. Statues, busts, portraits of the founding father of the Soviet Union have come down. As Malia recently put it, ". . . only party dinosaurs still insist on an essential distinction between [Lenin and Stalin]." With the arguments among Western Sovietologists in mind, Malia adds, "Perhaps the greatest error of revisionism has been to obscure the possibility of such an outcome."[26] Geoffrey Hosking's analysis is consonant with Malia's. By the time of "the complete rehabilitation of Solzhenitsyn" in 1990, says Hosking,

> It was as if the reading public already took for granted the negative evaluation of Lenin. . . . By this time, it had become not only possible, but almost de rigueur for self-respecting intellectuals to trace the current deficiencies of the Soviet system directly back to Communist intransigence and brutality from 1917 onwards.[27]

In the West, as well, the collapse of the Soviet Union is inaugurating a reappraisal of Lenin. Lionel Abel provides an early instance of a downward revaluation, and he explicitly indicates that he now finds Solzhenitsyn's position more acceptable than he once did. Abel notes that Solzhenitsyn labeled Lenin "a criminal," and he asks, "Now is it proper to call him that?" Taking into account instances of "the criminal thinking of the Bolshevik leader from which followed the particular illegalities and cruelties catalogued by Solzhenitsyn," Abel reluctantly answers his own question in the affirmative. That his change of mind is grudging he makes clear: "But I do not want to terminate these reflections without expressing regret for the judgment I have been forced to make of Lenin, whom before this, like others of my generation, I greatly admired." Still, Abel is unambiguous about his new estimate:

> I believe that Lenin's corpse will be removed from his present tomb and be given private burial. But this will not take place in an atmosphere of respect for the Bolshevik leader, rather in one of unrelenting polemic against his ideas and his deeds. He will not be forgiven for all of those deeds. . . .[28]

Rorty, too, concedes that "we can no longer be Leninists." Today, "the image of Lenin at the Finland Station . . . cannot be retouched and revived . . . . In the minds of our grandchildren, that image will form a triptych along with that of Hitler at a Nuremberg rally and of Mussolini on the balcony of the Palazzo Venezia."[29] It is likely that, as the official Soviet archives continue to be opened, scholars will gain much new information for their revaluation of the Lenin-Stalin nexus. The early signs suggest the strong probability that the judgment of historians will more and more be harmonious with the position that Solzhenitsyn formed years ago.

Similarly, the early signs suggest that Solzhenitsyn might well be confirmed in his laying of the blame for the horrors of the Soviet period on Marxist-Leninist ideology, rather than on some defect in the character of the Russian people. The unbridled wrath toward Communism emanating from the great majority of those who lived under Soviet rule is obviously the main datum here. Pontuso offers additional evidence from the sphere of geopolitics: "Further, Solzhenitsyn's judgment that a commitment to Marxist ideology, not Russian . . . nationalism, has been the source of the antagonism between East and West has also been borne out. As the major Communist powers have moved away from Marxism, they have moderated their international stances."[30] As we watch events unfold, it will be easy enough to track whether the death of the Soviet Union makes international relations more friendly or more hostile, better or worse. So far so good.

There is one more reason why the general reassessment of the Soviet experience should include a specific reassessment of Solzhenitsyn. It is that his ideas are popular among Russians. This point can be highlighted by recourse to the now-familiar taxonomy of dissent in the last couple of decades of the Soviet Union's existence. This taxonomy traces three main lines of dissent, represented respectively by three spokesmen: Roy Medvedev, Andrei Sakharov, and Solzhenitsyn. H. Stuart Hughes, for instance, places Medvedev on the left, Sakharov in the center, and Solzhenitsyn on the right.[31] In briefest terms, Medvedev stands for unreconstructed Leninists who blame Stalin for leading the Soviet experiment astray from its healthy Leninist origins. Sakharov stands for a convergence between the socialism of the East and the democracy of the West—in short, democratic socialism. Solzhenitsyn stands for a Russian patriotism which may allow some borrowings from the West but mainly hopes that Russia, with its millennium-long history as a religious people, will find its own organic path to a new national future. Of the three, only Solzhenitsyn's position carries within it the necessary logic of a breakup of the Soviet Union.

About this serviceable taxonomy of dissent, John B. Dunlop, a leading American authority on Russian nationalism and also on Solzhenitsyn, asserts flatly, "It is simply a fact that far more Soviet citizens think like Solzhenitsyn than like Andrei Sakharov or Roy Medvedev."[32] Even Hughes, a man of the Left whose unilluminating use of the label *right* for Solzhenitsyn seems intended to express opprobrium, concedes that Medvedev's position has "long figured as the most quixotic."[33] George Feifer, who became unsparingly hostile toward Solzhenitsyn, says that Sakharov "attracts little following even in Moscow. It is Solzhenitsyn who stirs Russian souls, as it is he who would be acclaimed as the new leader if let loose upon the hungry land."[34] In the words of Czeslaw Milosz, "Solzhenitsyn's is the case of a peculiar rebel who shares the proclaimed values of the majority of people in his country. . . ."[35] It is oddly jarring today to read the characterization of Solzhenitsyn offered by the prominent revisionist Sovietologist Stephen Cohen, who places him among the "extreme anti-Communist dissidents," those who "believe that the entire Soviet system is corrupt beyond salvation."[36] The former denizens of Soviet society are, it seems, all anti-Communists now. And so we read that Russian President Boris Yeltsin is "an avowed admirer of the works of the anticommunist Nobel laureate Aleksandr Solzhenitsyn."[37] Solzhenitsyn expressed his own view of the matter in 1983: "And through my work I know, I can sense, there are many people who think as I do. I do represent people in Russia. If I didn't represent anyone, the authorities wouldn't fear me."[38]

Dunlop documents Solzhenitsyn's "extraordinary popularity among the Soviet intelligentsia" and their "virtually unanimous support for Solzhenitsyn's rehabilitation." He cites a Soviet historian who predicted that in the not-too-distant future "our country will have streets, squares, factories, and libraries named after Solzhenitsyn."[39] These "pro-Solzhenitsyn stirrings" come, Dunlop says, from both the left and the right politically, with only the neo-Leninists holding out. Meanwhile, from the old Soviet establishment have come warnings against "the emergence of a Solzhenitsyn cult." The battle by members of the Gorbachev regime to keep Solzhenitsyn blacklisted has been lost, and by now more works of his have appeared in his homeland than are yet available in English translation. It is no wonder that Solzhenitsyn said, "The country in which my books are printed will not be the country that exiled me. And to that country I will certainly return."[40] In short, Michael Confino is correct to note that "currents of ideas considered yesterday as marginal have moved to centre stage. Aleksandr Solzhenitsyn's views belong to this category."[41]

THIS BOOK IS WRITTEN for Western readers. It seeks to mediate Solzhenitsyn to them. It is written on the assumption that many persons in the West have sensed something noble about Solzhenitsyn but at the same time are wary about him. In short, they are interested enough to welcome some guidance in trying to come to terms with him. Such imagined readers follow world events and recognize that the death of the Soviet Union is an event of epochal import which cries out for analysis of all its facets, not excluding the significance of Solzhenitsyn.

The plan of the book is as follows. The next chapter traces the contours of Solzhenitsyn's overall world view. Although this book is weighted disproportionately toward an examination of Solzhenitsyn's political ideas, he has always considered political issues to be of a secondary level of significance. The most important issues are the moral and spiritual ones. His moral vision of human life frames all of his thinking, including his political thinking. One can make no headway in comprehending any aspect of Solzhenitsyn's thought without first understanding his view of the moral universe.

Chapter Two should suffice to give readers the bearings they need to approach the three subsequent chapters, which are devoted to a chronological account of what the Western critics of Solzhenitsyn said about him and about his works as they appeared. This is not a happy story, for misunderstandings have predominated. Chapters Three through Five lay out the historical record of Solzhenitsyn criticism, with a minimum of commentary. Not everything laid out in that record is wrong, but most of it is.

Chapters Six through Eight take up, in turn, the three topics about which there has been the greatest confusion regarding Solzhenitsyn's positions. They are his views on the West, on democracy, and on nationalism. These are not intrinsically the three most important topics in Solzhenitsyn's works. Rather, they are the three which, because of misunderstandings, have become the major stumbling blocks to a proper appreciation and appropriation of Solzhenitsyn by Western readers. Until these impediments are removed, Western readers may be disinclined to view him as a source of wisdom on any topic whatever.

Chapters Nine through Twelve take up Solzhenitsyn's two essays of practical advice about the future of Russia, the *Letter to the Soviet Leaders* of 1973 and *Rebuilding Russia* of 1990. Solzhenitsyn has often been called a prophet, and one of the connotations of this attribution is that he does not write about down-to-earth, pragmatic matters. Some complain that he tells us what is wrong but not what to do about it. And it is true that, of his millions of words, only these two essays lay out the political steps which he would like to see his nation take. Future generations of Russian readers may well find greater spiritual sustenance in his literary works. At present, however, it is particularly important to understand these two essays. If even here his main audience is Russian, anyone who cares about the plight of our common world must care about what is transpiring in Russia, with its sixth of the land mass of the earth and its many millions of inhabitants, not to mention its nuclear weaponry.

The final chapter of this book is devoted to a sketch of Solzhenitsyn's influence. For all the abundant misimpressions about Solzhenitsyn, it remains true that he has had a very substantial impact upon many of his contemporaries around the world. To do justice to the topic of this chapter would demand a book-length study. What is offered herein is merely a sketch, a selected sample. The brevity of the treatment suffices only to demonstrate a variety of ways in which sympathetic readers have appropriated Solzhenitsyn to their self-proclaimed benefit.

The arrangement of these chapters is driven by my desire to promote a reappraisal of Solzhenitsyn. This is not an exhaustive study of all of Solzhenitsyn's ideas. Rather, it features those themes and essays which must first be understood if the whole corpus of the author is to be approached afresh. Also, I have indulged in some repetition to allow chapters to be read as more or less self-contained essays. To get Solzhenitsyn right means first of all to read his own words. It is startling how many of his detractors quote him very little or not at all; therefore, I have cited him generously. I want readers to hear Solzhenitsyn's own voice.

In the ordering of these chapters, there is also a rough progression from past to future. We shall never get Solzhenitsyn right if, in the spirit of letting bygones be bygones, we ignore the past controversies that swirled about him. At the same time, he has much to say about the future—of both Russia and the world. It is emphatically not the case that the obsolescence of the Soviet Union has made him obsolete. His significance extends far beyond his anti-Communist posture. In addition to predicting and contributing to the demise of Soviet Communism, he offers guidance about what might lie ahead. Indeed, I would venture to guess that someday his greatest achievement will be seen to lie not in his astute analysis of the twentieth century but in his vision of how we can transcend its worst features.

Only time will tell just how deep and wide Solzhenitsyn's influence has been and will be. His beloved Russia is sick nigh unto death. He seeks to aid in its restoration to health. But he knows that there will be considerable hell to endure as a result of three-quarters of a century of Soviet depredations. Once he speculated that the process of healing Russia "could take as long as 150 or two hundred years."[42] Much of Russia's best human capital was liquidated during the days of the Gulag, and the morals of the survivors have been greatly corrupted and deformed by a lawless state. Nevertheless, as breathing and consciousness return to Russia, we shall see free human beings trying to resuscitate their nation and to make of it a normal society living peaceably among the family of nations. However difficult the path to national regeneration may prove to be, there is great cause for hope. And Solzhenitsyn's final note, in work after work, is exactly that: the note of hope.

The world as a whole is not very well either. Modern humanity does not know how to define and interpret itself, and it stumbles from one crisis to another. In Solzhenitsyn's words, it "has not been able to create a stable spiritual system."[43] After the exhaustion of so many schemes and hopes for the saving of the world, perhaps our time is ripe for a new articulation of spirituality of the kind which marks Solzhenitsyn's vision. For the scope of this Russian writer's vision is not limited to the national scene; it is also universal. This fact befits his Christian faith, and indeed grows directly out of it.

How important is Solzhenitsyn? In a world of billions, how important can any one person be? Here is what historian John Lukacs thinks:

Yet history, which means the history of the human mind, still remains unpredictable. For example, something happened in 1945, in a most unlikely place: in the pine forests of East Prussia, forsaken by God, surrounded by the debris of war, under the cap of a Soviet captain. . . . Something had crystallized in his head. A cold and crystalline thought which, through the mysterious alchemy of the human mind, was produced by the passionate heat of intensity. It eventually led this man far, far enough to reject the entire mental system of the world in which he was born and in which he lived, to the point where the very rulers of that enormous empire began to worry about him and to fear him, while to millions of other people he became that new thing, a Light from the East. Truly a single event in a single mind may change the world. It may even bring about—and not merely hasten—the collapse of the Communist system, which is inevitable, though only in the long run. If so, the most important event in 1945 may not have been the division of Europe, and not the dawn of the Atomic Age, but the sudden opening and the sudden dawning of something in the mind of a ragged Soviet officer, Alexander Solzhenitsyn. . . .[44]

Did the dawning come then and there? Did it come a bit later, in the Gulag? Did it come gradually? What is sure is that it came. A man changed his mind. And we stand to be the beneficiaries.

2

The Moral Universe

IF ANY RECENT FIGURE COULD BE CONSIDERED the world's foremost anti-Communist, Solzhenitsyn is the one. Therefore, it may be surprising that he has expressed deep distaste for the term *anti-Communist*. He belittles it as "a poor, tasteless locution . . . put together by people who do not understand etymology." His antipathy toward Communism is so profound that he refuses to dignify it with the status of a social theory worthy of refutation. To use the term *anti-Communism* is implicitly to grant Communism positive status, which makes opposition to it essentially a negative reaction. Rather, he explains, Communism is inherently a negation. The first step in understanding Solzhenitsyn's world view is to be clear about the proper order of things:

> The primary, the eternal concept is humanity, and Communism is anti-humanity. Whoever says "anti-Communism" is saying, in effect, anti-anti-humanity. A poor construction. So we should say: That which is against Communism is for humanity. Not to accept, but to reject this inhuman Communist ideology is simply to be a human being. Such a rejection is more than a political act. It is a protest of our souls against those who would have us forget the concepts of good and evil.[1]

Solzhenitsyn stakes out for himself the position of pro-humanity. Human beings, souls, good and evil—these are essential terms in the moral vocabulary which predominates in his world of discourse.

21

Solzhenitsyn's critique of Communism never starts with its economic theory or its political power. He does not ignore these elements, but they come later, not at the beginning. Rather, he starts with moral terms. He calls Communists "the enemies of the human race."[2] He boldly analyzes the issues with language seldom employed in the scholarship of the social sciences: "Communism has never concealed the fact that it rejects all absolute concepts of morality. It scoffs at any consideration of 'good' and 'evil' as indisputable categories. Communism considers morality to be relative, to be a class matter."[3] Moreover, the moral categories he uses do not have their genesis from within human experience. They come to us from the hand of God. He made a moral universe, one defined in terms of good and evil, one in which freedom and justice are to be pursued, one in which actions have consequences, for better and for worse. And he made humans free moral agents responsible for their deeds. This is simply the way the universe is. Communism gets things wrong at the very beginning. "Atheism," he asserts, "is the core of the whole Communist system."[4] Far from being merely one alternative social theory featuring an arguable ideology concerning politics and economics, Communism is an oppositional metaphysical perspective alien to humanity itself. So from the start we see that something more than mere anti-Communism is at work here.

This chapter sets forth Solzhenitsyn's most fundamental beliefs. All of his thinking grows out of them. We shall start with basic Christian teaching, which not everyone knows anymore. We shall see how Solzhenitsyn's belief in God provides the context for interpreting human life in the moral universe. In his moral vision the individual person has primacy. Individuals, however, live in community, and Solzhenitsyn does not neglect the social dimension of our lives. He writes explicitly about politics, but always within a moral framework and never as if politics were our primary concern. The moral principles which apply to individuals apply also to nations and to the whole world. Finally, we shall see what the concept of the moral universe means for Solzhenitsyn's view of himself as a writer. This chapter is about matters of world view—first of all what the Germans call *Weltanschauung*, but also global consciousness.

*   *   *

SOLZHENITSYN'S WORLD VIEW is the antithesis of that of the Communists. To put the matter in its simplest and most direct terms, his is the Christian world view. I say *the*, instead of *a*, advisedly. For, although his ecclesiastical allegiance is to Russian Orthodoxy, nothing fundamental to his world view is sectarian or idiosyncratically individual. Rather, Solzhenitsyn believes what Christians of all times and places have agreed are Christianity's essential teachings.

In the beginning God created the world and all that is in it. He made humanity to be pinnacle of that created order. Man, and only man (male and female), was created in God's own image and bears within himself the divine spark. God pronounced all that he made, good. Then man fell into sin. He did not thereby forfeit entirely the divine image, but it was now deeply flawed and damaged—distorted, but not erased. And so evil entered into the good creation, and good and evil have been at war with one another ever since, and still. This sin brought real guilt, not merely guilt feelings. It introduced the possibility of bondage where once pure freedom had been. It opened the door to injustice where once pure justice had been. In the moral drama between good and evil now set into motion, lies, crime, violence, war became possibilities—and, soon enough, realities. The more man allowed such evil activities to flourish, the more he suffered the consequence of the further eclipsing (though never the eliminating) of the image of God within him.

At the root of this fall into sin—still in accord with basic Christian teaching—was human pride. And the ultimate in human pride was the exaltation of the self to the imagined status of deity. If and when man imagined himself not subservient to his Maker—indeed, imagined that God did not even exist—he would achieve the height of idolatry, self-worship. However, what was conceived to be a great upward movement to self-sufficiency would be in fact the greatest possible downward movement, a movement further and further away from the God above him, who alone gave meaning to human life, and toward the beasts below him. And so, since the grandeur of man was resident within that divine spark placed in him by God, instead of opening grand vistas of human progress and even perfectibility, sinful pride so much diminished the status of humans that any and all dehumanizing acts of terror and brutality could be justified. In a perverse irony, the grand prospect that self-sufficient man could perfect himself and establish a perfect world led to the perpetrating of the most unspeakable horrors. It is hard enough for those who recognize God to try to follow the laws which he has revealed to his fallen image-bearers through his Word. But, if there is no God, then everything is permitted, for with God go God's laws, the laws which govern the moral universe which he has created and which his creatures inhabit.

With the fall into sin comes utter brokenness, within individual human beings and also among human beings within society and its structures. Human beings are utterly incapable of repairing the ruins that sin has caused within them and among them. But God is ever-merciful. Into this broken world God himself came, taking on human flesh to pay the penalty for the sins of his human creatures. He entered the space-time continuum which he had established as the setting for all earthly life. Thereby, he provided, as a gift for all who would accept it, redemption from their sins. Many did accept it. Many did not. The division between believers and disbelievers in God remains a condition of human life even today.

Nevertheless, the result is not that there are some good people and some bad people. For all people, whether believers or not, remain a mixture of good and bad. All remain image-bearers of God, even though they may deny his very existence. All remain sinners, even though they may have accepted the gift of redemption from God in Christ. The moral universe remains in effect, whether its reality is acknowledged or not. In the Christian understanding, it is a matter of fact, not of viewpoint or opinion. It is a fact even for those whose opinion is that it is not a fact.

The goodness of the ever-merciful God does not end with the provision of redemption by Christ. It continues in the present through God's providential care for his creatures and their history. Its consummation remains lodged in the future, toward which cosmic history ineluctably drives. Someday good will triumph over evil. The Christian version of the human drama always has as its final note the note of hope. And this hope is not a speculative or chancy thing; it is a steadfast assurance that the story which had a good beginning will have a good ending, because it is directed by God himself.

This, in brief, is the Christian world view. To understand it is to begin to understand Solzhenitsyn's view of the modern world. Not to understand it is to get his ideas wrong at the very start. Solzhenitsyn is not a theologian. He is an interpreter of human experience, and one can benefit from his writing without accepting his assumptions. But it is always within this context of the Christian view of the human drama that he does his interpreting.

IN HIS 1983 SPEECH accepting the Templeton Prize for Progress in Religion, Solzhenitsyn opens by asking what is the chief defining characteristic of the twentieth century. He recalls that, as a child, he heard older people explain "the great disasters that had befallen Russia" in these simple terms: "Men have forgotten God; that's why all this has happened." If asked to state succinctly "the main cause of the ruinous Revolution that swallowed up some sixty million of our people," he could do no better, he says, than to repeat the judgment of his elders. "And if I were called upon to identify briefly the principal trait of the *entire* twentieth century, here too I would be unable to find anything more precise and pithy than to repeat once again: 'men have forgotten God.' " Every calamity of the modern world stems from "the flaw of a consciousness lacking all divine dimension."[5]

Nowhere are the effects of this deficiency to be seen more starkly than in his homeland. "In its past, Russia did know a time when the social ideal was not fame, or riches, or material success, but a pious way of life. Russia was then steeped in an Orthodox Christianity that remained true to the Church of the first centuries."[6] But there has been an about-face with the advent of Communist power, for "the main content of Bolshevism is unbridled militant atheism and class hatred."[7] The chief reason why Solzhenitsyn always had hope and faith that this power would someday pass is that it is simply wrong about human nature. The central contest is set not in terms of a struggle between Communism and democracy but in terms of the total opposition between *homo Sovieticus* and *homo religiosus*.

Solzhenitsyn illustrates this clash of world views in *The First Circle*, when Lev Rubin, a loyal Marxist even though in a Soviet prison, tries to set out some sort of secular replacement for the church occasions marking the passages of our lives: christenings, weddings, funerals. Though Rubin thinks of them as belonging to "civic temples," these turn out to be only "Christian temples without Christ."[8] Solzhenitsyn considers them no adequate substitute for the real thing. Communism is an ersatz religion. Rubin the Communist remains *homo religiosus*.

Nor is Solzhenitsyn alone or original in setting the conflict in such terms. In his *Letter to the Soviet Leaders*, he specifically cites the theologian Sergius Bulgakov, who "showed in *Karl Marx as a Religious Type* (1906) that atheism is the chief inspirational and emotional hub of Marxism and that all the rest of the doctrine has simply been tacked on. Ferocious hostility to religion is Marxism's most persistent feature."[9] In his book Bulgakov focuses upon the "inner bond between atheism and socialism in Marx." His exposition of the concept that I have called *homo religiosus* fits Solzhenitsyn's viewpoint exactly:

> . . . the determining power in the spiritual life of a man is his religion— not only in the narrow sense of the word, but in a wider sense as well, i.e., the highest and ultimate values which one admits as being *beyond* him and *higher* than himself and also his practical relation to these values. To determine the real religious center in a person, to discover his genuine spiritual core, is to find out the most intimate and important things about him, and then everything external and derivative will be comprehensible. . . . In this sense there can be no religiously neutral persons. . . .[10]

Sergius Bulgakov was one of several Russian thinkers in the early part of the twentieth century who turned away from Marxism and back to Christianity. Seeing among their fellow intellectuals the attraction of atheistic socialism, in 1909 they collaborated on a collection of essays, entitled *Vekhi* (*Landmarks*, or *Signposts*), to warn their nation away from Marxism's siren song. Though they failed in their main purpose, their joint manifesto provided the model to Solzhenitsyn and compatriots of his for the collection of 1974 entitled *From Under the Rubble*. As the *Vekhi* group had warned the Russian people against entering the abyss of Communist power, so this latter-day group sought to point out to the Russian people the way up and out from under its rubble. In both cases, Christianity provides the motive force for the manifestoes. In both cases, the conflict between rejection of God and acceptance of God is the central issue. Both are rooted in the concept of *homo religiosus*.

This concept is more difficult for the secular modern West to comprehend than is the atheism of the Bolsheviks. For the idea of *homo religiosus* entails seeing religious faith as the mainspring for all human action in all spheres of life. The secularist is comfortable with freedom of religion as long as religion is seen as a strictly private matter which in no way impinges on public policy and practice. It is true that some religionists, as well, nowadays accede to this segmenting off of religion into the domain of the private as a necessity in a pluralistic society. However, for those who believe that humankind is innately religious and is fundamentally defined in religious terms, such a sealing off of religion as a luxury for persons who wish to indulge in it privately is altogether unacceptable. Just this conflict is what Richard John Neuhaus so lucidly describes in his book *The Naked Public Square*.[11]

If the acceptance of God is the bedrock belief forming Solzhenitsyn's world view, the very next piece of it is the accepting of man as God's creature. Solzhenitsyn has demonstrated his understanding of human nature frequently and in a variety of contexts. For example, in 1969, as he was fighting for his literary life, he addressed an open letter to the Secretariat of the R.S.F.S.R. Writers' Union in which he paused to make this observation: "It is high time to remember that we belong first and foremost to humanity. And that man has separated himself from the animal world by *thought* and *speech*. These, naturally, should be *free*. If they are put in chains, we shall return to the state of animals." This distinction between humans and animals is familiar to students of the Great Tradition of the West through the image of the Great Chain of Being. As this quotation indicates, being pro-humanity means being a proponent of human freedom. Solzhenitsyn's passionate commitment to freedom of thought and freedom of speech leads him, in the very next sentence of this open letter, to declare, "*Openness*, honest and complete *openness*—that is the first condition of health in all societies, including our own."[12] Here he uses the word *glasnost* more than a decade and a half before Mikhail Gorbachev gave it global currency.

Human nature is not only free but also fixed, stable; it is not malleable. "Human nature, if it changes at all, changes not much faster than the geological face of the earth."[13] Solzhenitsyn is concerned with "the timeless essence of humanity," with such concepts as those "fixed universal concepts called good and justice."[14] This continuity through history is part and parcel of our being the bearers of the divine image.

Solzhenitsyn sets this view in sharp contrast to that of Communists: "Engels discovered that the human being had arisen not through the perception of a moral idea and not through the process of thought, but out of happenstance and meaningless work (an ape picked up a stone— and with this everything began)." [15]

In a 1967 letter to three students, Solzhenitsyn wrote about justice, another of his staple themes, along with freedom; and he did so in terms which demonstrate his conviction that humans inhabit a fixed moral universe.

> Justice has been the common patrimony of humanity throughout the ages. It does not cease to exist for the majority even when it is twisted by some ("exclusive") circles. Obviously it is a concept which is inherent in man, since it cannot be traced to any other source. Justice exists even if there are only a few individuals who recognize it as such. . . .
>
> There is nothing relative about justice, as there *is* nothing relative about conscience. Indeed, justice is conscience, not a personal conscience but the conscience of the whole of humanity. [16]

The truth of the moral universe, including the principles of human freedom and absolute justice, is what it is, independent of whether human beings perceive it. Conscience is that divinely implanted agency which allows us to perceive it. Conscience is another word for the divine spark.

That Solzhenitsyn's main quarrel with the Communists has to do with the conflict of world views, not with political theory or practice, is a point that has eluded most of his Western critics. One who did understand this point was Sidney Hook. He found in Solzhenitsyn much to praise, but he also recognized that, on the basic issue of the world views out of which their compatible critiques of modern times emanated, they were at odds. Writing for *The Humanist* on Solzhenitsyn's Harvard address, Hook found it sufficient that he and Solzhenitsyn shared a commitment to human rights; they did not need "to agree on a common justification of these rights." In fact, Hook considered it Solzhenitsyn's "profoundest error of all" to insist that "human freedom and moral responsibility derive from belief in a Supreme Being, and that the erosion of religious faith spells the end of moral decency." According to Hook, ". . . men created gods in their own moral image. Morality is logically independent of religion. . . ." It follows that, for Hook, "religion [is] a private matter."[17] We learn two lessons from Hook here. One is that issues of world view are at stake; he got the terms of the argument right. The other is that it is possible to appropriate substantial aspects of Solzhenitsyn's moral vision without accepting its religious context.

Hook wrote after Solzhenitsyn's self-revelations of 1972, which are described in the next chapter and which made clear to all his Christian commitment. However, even before 1972, for those who had the eyes to see, the contours of Solzhenitsyn's Christian world view were perceptible. Alexander Schmemann, a Russian-American theologian in the Russian Orthodox tradition, saw them. In a 1970 essay which remains as useful an article as any ever published on Solzhenitsyn, Schmemann asserted flatly that the author is "a Christian writer." He carefully delineates, based on the limited biographical information then available, what he does not mean: ". . . I do not have in mind whether Solzhenitsyn is a 'believer' or a 'non-believer'—whether he accepts or rejects Christian dogma, ecclesiastical ritual, or the Church herself—nor do I mean specific 'religious problematics,' which I do not consider central to Solzhenitsyn." Then, in a crucial passage, he explains what he does mean:

When I speak of a "Christian writer" and of Solzhenitsyn in particular, I have in mind a deep and all-embracing, although possibly unconscious perception of the world, man, and life, which, historically, was born and grew from Biblical and Christian revelation, and only from it. Human culture as a whole may have had other sources, but only Christianity, only the revelation of the Old and New Testaments contains that perception of the world which, incorporated into human culture, revealed in it the potential, and indeed the reality of a Christian culture. I shall call this perception, for lack of a better term, the *triune intuition of creation, fall, and redemption*. I am convinced that it is precisely this intuition that lies at the bottom of Solzhenitsyn's art, and that renders his art Christian.[18]

This understanding of Solzhenitsyn points in the direction of tying him to the Great Tradition of the West, in which Christianity has historically played the central formative role. As we shall see, a few critics, but not many, took notice of this vital link. In broadest terms, of course, the Western tradition is formed by a merging of those two great ancient sources of culture, the Judaeo-Christian on the one hand and the

Graeco-Roman, or classical, on the other: Hebraism and Hellenism, as Matthew Arnold labeled them. Solzhenitsyn is heir to the tradition as a whole, to both sources of it. So we observe in his writings, for instance, classical allusions and borrowings on occasion. It is, however, to that immense Christian development of the Judaeo-Christian source of culture that he, as a Christian himself, is particularly indebted, though never in a parochial way that would invalidate other aspects of the wisdom of Western antiquity.

It is worth remembering here that Christianity ties Russia historically to the Occident, not the Orient, that Dostoevsky and Tolstoy and the rest are writers in the broad Western literary tradition. So when, these days, we draw a distinction between Russia and the West, we may be speaking of political East and political West, but in larger cultural and historical terms we are distinguishing between one part of the West and another part of the West. Solzhenitsyn's formulations of his ideas may often be distinctly Russian, but his basic beliefs are not uniquely Russian.

In the concluding section of his 1970 essay, Schmemann provides a clear and accurate indication of the main problem which interferes with a proper appropriation of Solzhenitsyn's literary art. "Ours is a time of the obvious collapse of Christian culture. This collapse is related, first of all, to the decomposition of that *triune intuition* from which that culture grew and in which it lived." He goes on to speak of "an apostate culture" with "an irrational hatred for the Christian roots of culture." Schmemann concludes his article with an eloquent peroration, which demonstrates the importance for the modern world that he attaches to the phenomenon of Solzhenitsyn:

> But then, in this dark night, in a country which more than half a century ago officially renounced its Christian name and calling, there arises a lone man who through his art reveals the lie and the sin of that dilemma and liberates us from it. A writer. A Russian writer. A Christian writer. For this liberation, for this witness, and for its coming from Russia, making Russia herself again and again ours; for preserving "unspoiled, undisturbed and undistorted the image of eternity with which each person is born," our joyful gratitude to Aleksandr Solzhenitsyn.[19]

To get the full impact of Schmemann's quoting of Solzhenitsyn's words here, we must restore their original context. A wise old doctor in

Cancer Ward, meditative after an intense conversation with a younger female doctor who may have herself contracted cancer through excessive irradiation during her treatment of patients, is reflecting:

> At such moments an image of the whole meaning of existence—his own during the long past and the short future ahead, that of his late wife, of his young granddaughter and of everyone in the world—came to his mind. The image he saw did not seem to be embedded in the work or activity which occupied them, which they believed was central to their lives, and by which they were known to others. The meaning of existence was to preserve unspoiled, undisturbed and undistorted the image of eternity with which each person is born.
> Like a silver moon in a calm, still pond.[20]

Schmemann's article certainly has not framed the ongoing discussion of Solzhenitsyn and generally has received little attention. It did garner one important reader. Solzhenitsyn said that it was "very valuable to me. It explained me to myself. . . . It also formulated important traits of Christianity which I could not have formulated myself. . . ."[21]

It is supremely important to understand that Solzhenitsyn was a Christian before he wrote any of the works which we now have available to read. Everything that we now have from him grows out of his Christian world view. Schmemann's effect on him was not to teach him, to his own surprise, that he was a Christian after all. Rather, he was confessing his inability to arrive at Schmemann's theological formulations on his own. His move from Marx to Jesus occurred during his years of incarceration, and he has presented this story in bits and pieces scattered through *The Gulag Archipelago*, with other references to it as well. This story is by now reasonably well known to his readers. He was influenced in this "conversion" by many: Dr. Boris Kornfeld, Boris Gammerov, various devout Baptists, numerous others. In a 1989 interview with David Aikman, he clarified this story yet further. He explains that he "was raised by my elders in the spirit of Christianity, and almost through my school years, up to 17 or 18, I was in opposition to Soviet education." Then he submitted to the suasions of Marxism-Leninism, until, in prison, "I saw that my convictions did not have a solid basis, could not stand up in dispute, and I had to renounce them." As he describes it retrospectively, "Other believers influenced me, but basically it was a return to what I had thought before."[22] (Incidentally, this Christian rearing helps explain the frequency and occasional obscurity of his biblical allusions and other Christian references.)

Of all the many ways Solzhenitsyn describes the moral universe, the one to which he reverts most insistently is the conflict between good and evil. Much of the misconstrual of Solzhenitsyn could be avoided if his use of these categories were clearly understood. "The line dividing good and evil cuts through. . . ." How one would choose to finish this sentence tells much about that person's world view. Certainly, not everyone would finish it as Solzhenitsyn does. In a crucial passage early in *The Gulag Archipelago*, he is at pains to make his view clear:

> If only there were evil people somewhere insidiously committing evil deeds, and it were necessary only to separate them from the rest of us and destroy them. But the line dividing good and evil cuts through the heart of every human being. . . .
>
> During the life of any heart this line keeps changing place; sometimes it is squeezed one way by exuberant evil and sometimes it shifts to allow enough space for good to flourish. One and the same human being is, at various ages, under various circumstances, a totally different human being. At times he is close to being a devil, at times to sainthood. But his name doesn't change, and to that name we ascribe the whole lot, good and evil.[23]

Though this passage was not available to Schmemann in 1970, it is a perfect example of his notion of the intuition of creation and fall. For these two seminal Christian doctrines explain how it is that a human being carries both grandeur and misery at the same time. Solzhenitsyn does not draw the line, as would a Manichaean, between two great cosmic forces ever at war over human beings, one good and one bad. Nor does he draw it between one nation and another or even between saints and sinners. Solzhenitsyn embraces this Christian understanding of the duality of human nature in much the same way that most writers in the Western literary tradition do. It is the same view that informs Dante's *Divine Comedy*, Shakespeare's *Hamlet*, Milton's *Paradise Lost*, Pope's *Essay on Man*, Dostoevsky's *The Brothers Karamazov*.

It is highly revealing to observe the context for the above-cited passage. The immediately preceding paragraph says, "So let the reader who expects this book to be a political exposé slam its covers shut right now."[24] Is Solzhenitsyn primarily a political writer? *The Gulag Archipelago* is a perfect test case. It spends eighteen hundred pages flaying the offenses of a political entity, the Soviet government. Yet he energetically denies that the book's primary focus is political. Of course, it has political ramifications; the moral lives of individual human beings are not lived in a political and social vacuum. But it is those individual lives in which he is first of all and most of all (though not also last of all, or only) interested. Even the characters of Stalin and Lenin, as Solzhenitsyn depicts them in *Gulag* and elsewhere, are to be analyzed in the primary moral terms of the line dividing good and evil that cuts through their hearts. So also, in *Gulag*, are the camp bosses, the guards, the trusties, the Communists in prison, the religious believers in prison, the family members still in freedom, everyone brought into the work—and every reader, too, for that matter. Of both zeks and trusties in the camps, oppressed and oppressor alike, he says that each person among them "was a man, that he carried the divine spark within him, that he was capable of higher things."[25] Schmemann, in a later essay, is right about this big book, too: "The *Gulag* is indeed a *spiritual* book."[26]

The primacy of the person underlies the very structure of Solzhenitsyn's novels. Stephen Carter, who recognizes that "Solzhenitsyn is concerned above all with *individual* men and women," notes also how the belief that "all individuals have an ultimate value in themselves" leads naturally to novels which are " 'polyphonic,' that is, where each character steps to the front of the stage in turn as the action centers on him or her."[27] And Vladislav Krasnov, whose book *Solzhenitsyn and Dostoevsky* is subtitled *A Study in the Polyphonic Novel*, observes that Christian doctrine is what validates this narrative technique in both novelists. To this end Krasnov draws upon Mikhail Bakhtin, the chief theorist of literary polyphony, who "considers Dostoevsky's polyphonic technique a function of his 'form-determining ideology,' " which "ideology" Bakhtin defines "as an essentially Christian world view."[28]

Although Solzhenitsyn's articulation of the religious view of life is specifically and unambiguously Christian, it matters to him that all world religions, not only Christianity, teach the primacy of human personhood. He has, he says, "come to understand the truth of all the religions of the world: They struggle with the evil *inside a human being* (inside every human being). It is impossible to expel evil from the world in its entirety, but it is possible to constrict it within each person." He proceeds to recite the famous dictum of Socrates, "Know thyself!"[29] This is the first step toward true human wisdom.

FROM THE FOREGOING DISCUSSION of Solzhenitsyn's view of human nature, we can draw several generalizations. First, Solzhenitsyn's focus is always firmly fixed on the common human condition. Dostoevsky's Raskolnikov is wrong: there are no extraordinary men, only ordinary ones. We may call this attitude Christian universalism. Though this term is sometimes used to indicate universal salvation, that is not the sense of the term here. Rather, what humans have in common is sinfulness. But not sinfulness alone; also the worth which is carried by the divine image in them. The common human condition always entails the mixture of good and evil, even in the redeemed. Solzhenitsyn strenuously resists any reductionism that would eliminate one of the two terms necessary to characterize human nature in its duality.

Second, the presence of evil in man rules out any possibility of utopianism. There could be a perfect society only if there could be perfect individuals. Human beings, however, are by nature not perfectible. Thus, Solzhenitsyn has developed an immunity to the blandishments of ideology and is its sworn foe. Kenneth Minogue defines ideology as "the propensity to construct structural explanations of the human world." He uses the word *ideology* "to denote any doctrine which presents the hidden and saving truth about the evils of the world in the form of social analysis."[30] But the fundamental human reality is not social but personal; the person comes first, then society. Thus, when Solzhenitsyn turned from Marx to Jesus, he did not exchange one ideology for another. On the contrary, he turned his back on ideology altogether, and he is always unremittingly critical of it.

Third, the presence of good in man provides the grounds for hope. For Solzhenitsyn, the world is far from the absurd world with which we are familiar in much of the modern literature of the West. Rather, the moral universe which God has ordered is imbued with purpose. There is objective meaning in the universe because God exists. We find meaning in our lives by attaching ourselves to that objective meaning, not by trying to create our own values. The human task is the one familiar from the old Western tradition of seeking to know the will of God and to make it prevail. One can seek to tell the truth because there is a real, ultimate Truth. One can seek to do good because there is a real, ultimate Good. One can even find a saving grace by pursuing beauty—to which effect he cites Dostoevsky in the *Nobel Lecture*[31]—because there is a real, ultimate Beauty.

Fourth, the presence of good in man legitimates and even requires action on behalf of the moral uplifting of human beings. And this activity can be effectual. Individuals can change history; they are not pawns swept along by huge historical forces outside their control. Persons can make a difference. They are both free to do so and responsible to do so. Thus, Solzhenitsyn's philosophy of history is diametrically opposed to Tolstoy's (among others'), and in *August 1914* he consciously argues against this literary master.[32]

Fifth, Solzhenitsyn's Christian universalism eliminates any possibility of his viewing one group of people as inherently superior to another. To be specific, it eliminates any possibility of his falling prey to Great Russian chauvinism—or, for that matter, to the anti-Semitism which it has sometimes spawned. He may feel especially sorry for Russia. He may devote his career to listening to the sad music of Russia and singing of it. But he cannot adopt the old myth of the superiority of the Russian soul. The Russians may be a deeply religious people throughout their thousand-year-long history. But they are not a holy people, not in any such sense a chosen people. Solzhenitsyn does not claim as his own the concept of Holy Russia.

Sixth, Solzhenitsyn's Christian universalism is precisely what motivates him to speak to the West. In his view, the Russians have experienced suffering beyond what any other peoples have known in the modern world. But it is not a self-contained story, relevant only to Russians. Others can profit morally from knowing it. He often touches upon this theme, as when he writes in the Foreword to the abridgment of *The Gulag Archipelago*, "Alas, all the evil of the twentieth century is possible everywhere on earth. Yet I have not given up all hope that human beings and nations may be able, in spite of all, to learn from the experience of other people without having to live through it personally."[33]

Indeed, however much Solzhenitsyn concentrates upon the individual human heart as the primary battleground in the struggle between good and evil, in no wise is he to be considered a proponent of individualism. This ism, along with Communism, can be considered, from a Christian viewpoint, a heresy, a departure from a true account of the way the moral universe is. In fact, it is useful to consider individualism, as well as Communism, a specifically "Christian" heresy, inasmuch as it arose within the Western intellectual tradition to which Christianity has contributed formative shape. No man is an island, as the Christian poet John Donne said. Social responsibility looms large in Solzhenitsyn's thinking.

The proper relationship of the individual to the group can be seen in the case of Gleb Nerzhin, the author's *alter ego* in *The First Circle*. As he searches for meaning in his life, he considers, as the chapter title has it, "Going to the People." It is a hoary tradition in Russian literature to look at the peasants as vessels of virtue and wisdom, and Solzhenitsyn does feel great affection for them. However, as Nerzhin discovers, "It turned out that the People had no homespun superiority to him." They do not necessarily endure tribulations better than others or more clearly perceive treachery and villainy where they are manifested. In Nerzhin's judgment, "What was lacking in most of them was that personal *point of view* which becomes more precious than life itself." The first step, he concludes, must be inner liberation, self-development. "Everyone forges his inner self year after year. One must try to temper, to cut, to polish one's soul so as to become *a human being*." Solzhenitsyn could have stopped right there, with his usual emphasis on the individual soul. But there is one more point to be made before the chapter can end: "And thereby become a tiny particle of one's own People."[34] Persons are also social beings, and selfhood is not completed until it issues in a sense of solidarity with other selves.

As Solzhenitsyn always starts with the individual and then moves out to the group, so even the magisterial *Gulag Archipelago* follows this pattern. It begins with the arrest of the individual, and then the lens widens to convey the panoramic picture. So at the outset we read, "The Universe has as many different centers as there are living beings in it. Each of us is a center of the Universe, and that Universe is shattered when they hiss at you: '*You are under arrest*.'" To describe each person as a center of the universe comports perfectly with this chapter's conception of the moral universe. But later we read a passage about "the joyous word 'we.'" The use to which this pronoun is put tells much about one's world view.

Yes, that word which you may have despised out in freedom, when they used it as a substitute for your own individuality ("All of us, like one man!" Or: "We are deeply angered!" Or: "We demand!" Or: "We swear!"), is now revealed to you as something sweet: you are not alone in the world! Wise, spiritual beings—*human beings*—still exist.[35]

The difference in usage of this pronoun is the difference between a collectivist world view and a communitarian world view. The pronoun *we* must be brought out from under the rubble of collectivist ideology, reclaimed, refurbished, and cherished.

One part of our social being is politics. It does not diminish the point that Solzhenitsyn is *primarily* a spiritual writer to add that he is *also* a political writer. Spiritual matters, after all, refer not only to the inner life but also to the outer life. It is precisely the fact that individuals live in community which validates his writing about politics. Solzhenitsyn carefully articulates the relationship between the spiritual and the political. In his view, ". . . the state structure is of secondary significance. That this is so, Christ himself teaches us. 'Render unto Caesar what is Caesar's'—not because every Caesar deserves it, but because Caesar's concern is not with the most important thing in our lives." Spiritual matters are the ones of primary significance, and for Soviet citizens "the absolutely essential task is not political liberation, but the liberation of our souls from participation in the lie forced upon us." Nevertheless, spirituality cannot be divorced from politics. "When Caesar, having exacted what is Caesar's, demands still more insistently that we render unto him what is God's—that is a sacrifice we dare not make!"[36] Thus, the Soviet context requires that Solzhenitsyn write about politics.

It is a fundamental principle of Solzhenitsyn's political outlook that the moral categories and criteria which apply to individuals also and equally apply to nations. His term for this mental operation is "the transference of values." To demonstrate the moral analogy between individuals and nations is the burden of his essay "Repentance and Self-Limitation in the Life of Nations." After excoriating the modern social sciences, for which "the evaluation of political life by ethical yardsticks is considered totally provincial," he explains his own evaluative approach:

The transference of values is entirely natural to the religious cast of mind: human society cannot be exempted from the laws and demands which constitute the aim and meaning of individual human lives. But even without a religious foundation, this sort of transference is readily and naturally made. It is very human to apply even to the biggest social events or human organizations, including whole states and the United Nations, our spiritual values: noble, base, courageous, cowardly, hypocritical, false, cruel, magnanimous, just, unjust, and so on. Indeed, everybody writes this way, even the most extreme economic materialists, since they remain after all human beings. And clearly, whatever feelings predominate in the members of a given society at a given moment in time, they will serve to color the whole of that society and determine its moral character. [37]

It is not only easy and natural but also logical for the religious mind to engage in ethical and moral analysis of any and all aspects of human behavior, however small or large are the agents. For the moral universe is imbued with objective meaning which gives real status to the categories of good and evil. Thus, the religious mind readily invokes the evaluative adjectives listed in the quotation above. What is not so logical is that the irreligious mind, particularly the one which posits human autonomy rather than submission to the will of God, would import into one's world view those value-laden adjectives which historically come to us as the heritage of the preceding Christian centuries. It violates all logic to cut off the root but to try to keep the fruit. Yet those who deny the spiritual reality of the moral universe do just that. To put the matter another way, they live off the accrued moral capital of the heritage which they reject. Then again, how could they do otherwise? For they are as they are, not as they think they are. They continue to bear the divine image even as they deny the God who is their source of being. They remain inhabitants of the moral universe. They remain, after all, human beings.

Furthermore, since the moral tone of a society is the composite of the moral quality of its individual citizens, it matters very much what all those individuals believe about the nature of the universe and the nature of man. If, for instance, atheists predominate, human beings will be treated according to that prevailing understanding of human nature. If human beings are perceived to be merely advanced primates, with no vertical relationship to a transcendent sphere of reality, the treatment of them need not be qualitatively different from that accorded to animals, whatever that may be, kind or cruel. Atheists may or may not draw from the accrued moral capital of the Christian centuries in their treatment of other human beings. It is possible, of course, that atheists will find grounds to treat their fellows with dignity and respect other than those inherited from and inherent within the Christian view of the universe and human nature. The Soviet experiment demonstrates conclusively that atheists need not do so; it demonstrates that their view of the universe and human nature has no sure stay against the dehumanization which Solzhenitsyn so fully documents in his writings.

Solzhenitsyn features two moral categories, repentance and self-limitation, by which to evaluate national life. These are meaningful categories to him as a Christian. Christians are taught that the correct path to self-fulfillment is through self-denial. They are taught that true freedom comes within the form of obedience to God. These paradoxes make perfect sense to Christians. To many others they are not mere paradoxes but flat contradictions. Solzhenitsyn is well aware of the problem confronting him in trying to demonstrate the relevance of these categories to persons who consider them unsuitable.

> Whether the transference of individual human qualities to society is easy or difficult in a general way, it is immensely difficult when the desired moral quality has been almost completely rejected by individual human beings themselves. This is the case with repentance. The gift of repentance, which perhaps more than anything else distinguishes man from the animal world, is particularly difficult for modern man to recover.[38]

Among God's creatures only human beings, as free moral agents, can do evil, and thus only human beings can repent of their evil deeds.

One concept which Solzhenitsyn's transference of values from individuals to nation brings into sharp focus is that actions have consequences. Or, to give a biblical rendering of the principle, the sins of the fathers are visited upon the children to the third and the fourth generation (Exodus 20:5, Numbers 14:18). As individuals are bound together in community, what one does affects others. Solzhenitsyn's discussion of Russia past and present is predicated upon this principle.

"For the sins of the fathers"—the saying is thousands of years old. How, you may ask, can we repent on their behalf—we weren't even alive at the time! . . . But the saying is not an idle one, and we have only too often seen and still see children *paying* for the fathers.

The nation is mystically welded together in a community of guilt, and its inescapable destiny is common repentance.[39]

What one generation does affects future generations, whether the community be small or large, a family or a nation. Actions have consequences, and these consequences can reverberate far through space and time. Everyone belongs to one common web of human experience. In the moral universe everything is related to everything, and all are related to all. Every human action is to be judged according to how well it comports with the objective meaning which permeates the moral universe, and it is judged according to the absolute categories of good and evil. Because it comes from the hand of God as our arena of life, the whole space-time continuum bespeaks cosmos, not chaos; order, not chance; purpose, not caprice. Since there is a God, not everything is permitted. Some things are forbidden. They are not value-neutral choices; they are sins. Nor are they self-contained actions; they affect others. Sinful actions violate the created order, which as the Book of Genesis tells us, is good, and pleasing to God. All of human history is governed by the immutable laws of the moral universe.

That national sins have consequences far into the future should not be a difficult concept for Americans to comprehend. Their forebears long ago established the institution of human slavery, and today Americans live with severe racial tensions as a result. Actions have consequences through time. Whenever people today make judgments of others simply because of their race, they do damage to the social fabric. Actions have consequences through space.

There is a character in *August 1914*, Varsonofiev, who speaks at one point virtually as the author's mouthpiece. Some young students seek out this old intellectual for his wisdom. In the conversation he uses two images to illuminate the universality of human community: "History grows like a living tree. . . . Or, if you prefer, history is a river. . . . The bonds between generations, institutions, traditions, customs, are what keep the stream flowing uninterruptedly."[40] About Varsonofiev's evolutionary (as opposed to revolutionary) outlook, Stephen Carter comments,

> This view of history is (surely) remarkably similar to that of Edmund Burke, who rejects the notion of "social contract" as outlined by such writers as Jean-Jacques Rousseau, arguing that the bonds of custom and tradition tend to weld national life in some organic way which links one's ancestors with the living and those as yet unborn.[41]

Varsonofiev locates an absolute reference point by which to judge social actions in history. Because the universe is marked not by arbitrariness but by the purposeful form of objective meaning, "The laws for constructing the best social order must be inherent in the structure of the world as a whole. In the design behind the universe and in man's destiny."[42] When one of the students proposes, "Surely justice is an adequate principle for the construction of a good society," Varsonofiev replies, "Yes, indeed! . . . But not the justice we devise for ourselves, to create a comfortable earthly paradise. Another kind of justice, which existed before us, and for its own sake."[43]

The transference of values which extends from individuals to nations extends also to the whole world. Here again we see Christian universalism of Solzhenitsyn. We have responsibility for ourselves, and also for our nation—and also for our whole world. This theme is expressed most clearly in the *Nobel Lecture*, the occasion for which required that he speak to the world as a whole. Living in the global village of the late twentieth century demands that all of us develop "our own WORLD-WIDE VIEW." Through the international press and radio, "Mankind has become one. . . ." We now experience existentially the ancient Christian principle of the universality of our common lot. If we do not develop a global consciousness, we remain provincials who "confidently judge the whole world according to our own domestic values." The better way is to accept that "[m]ankind's salvation lies exclusively in everyone's making everything his business."[44] Solzhenitsyn's world view is not tribally provincial or nationally particularistic.

THE WORLD VIEW DESCRIBED in this chapter informs all of Solzhenitsyn's writing and gives it its impetus and purpose. The literary artist, too, inhabits the moral universe. Solzhenitsyn has many times explained his central authorial motivation. He avers that "the task of literature is to tell people the real truth. . . ." And the real truth is that all the events and actions of human life take place in the divinely ordered moral universe. In 1967, as his implacable foes were trying to drum him out of the writers' union on charges that he was a political writer of an incorrect persuasion, he himself, rather than arguing on the political grounds that they set out as the terms of the debate, referred to the moral categories explicated in this chapter to explain why he writes as he does. After the above-cited clause about the task of literature, he continues,

> Moreover, it is not the task of the writer to defend or criticize one or another mode of distributing the social product, or to defend or criticize one or another form of government organization. The task of the writer is to select more universal and eternal questions, the secrets of the human heart and conscience, the confrontation of life with death, the triumph over spiritual sorrow, the laws of the history of mankind that were born in the depths of time immemorial and that will cease to exist only when the sun ceases to shine.[45]

That is to say, the writer's mission is not to pay primary attention to either economic or political concerns. It is, rather, to attend to the moral and spiritual issues which are perennial and universal.

As the moral universe extends to all space and time, so the writer is beholden to the entire space-time continuum in his analysis of the human condition. Many of Solzhenitsyn's works—*The Gulag Archipelago* and the novels of contemporary setting—by restricting themselves to the narrow time-frame of current social realities, feature the author's responsibility to the dimension of space. Thus, Solzhenitsyn writes, "Literature that is not the breath of contemporary society, that dares not transmit the pains and fears of that society, that does not warn in time against threatening moral and social dangers—such literature does not deserve the name of literature; it is only a facade."[46] Here he distinguishes his literary art from the ideologically driven art of socialist realism, with its vapid and bogus optimism. Such so-called art does not tell the truth about its times, but only the Party line. He, on the other hand, senses a duty to his contemporaries, especially those ranged across the vast spaces of his homeland.

At the same time, Solzhenitsyn's sense of duty goes further than that of contemporary social responsibility and encompasses the past as well. And so he writes *August 1914* and the sequels to it, which together comprise *The Red Wheel*. Russian literature, beyond perhaps all other national literatures, has been the chief vehicle for carrying on the conversation about the fate of the nation. Solzhenitsyn places himself in that illustrious line. He feels a responsibility to the dimension of time, in the space-time continuum of the moral universe, because the past shapes the present. We cannot know who we are until we understand how we came to be who we are. And so he must write to remember the always relevant, always usable past. It is this kind of duty to the dimension of time that he has in mind when he writes, ". . . I entered into the inheritance of every modern Russian writer intent on the truth: I must write simply to ensure that it was not all forgotten."[47] And that is why, since in later years he has gained the luxury of being a full-time writer, Solzhenitsyn has devoted many, if not maybe most, of his waking hours to historical research. He must bend every effort to get the record right. This duty is particularly incumbent on the writer whose country has long suffered efforts by officialdom to distort and even to erase the truth of history. History is social memory. When it is our turn to keep the memory alive accurately, we must not fail generations on either side of us.

Although Solzhenitsyn specifies his inheritance as a Russian writer, he does not see literature, including his own, as limited to the nation. The space-time continuum encompasses all nations (space) and all ages (time). The writer is beholden to the whole lot of it, for there is "the indivisibility of truth."[48] The global responsibility of literature is the primary concern of the *Nobel Lecture*.

The opening section of the lecture describes two kinds of literary artists. One kind "imagines himself the creator of an independent spiritual world." This kind of artist functions autonomously, without reference to any conception of a moral universe with objective meaning, "retreating . . . into the vast spaces of subjective fancies." The second kind of artist "acknowledges a higher power above him and joyfully works as a common apprentice under God's heaven." This kind of artist, Solzhenitsyn's kind, is self-consciously a derivative creator; he derives his creative power from God the Creator, whose image he bears. The literary universe which he creates and populates with characters of his own devising is governed by the same laws that govern the moral universe in which the author and his readers and all other people live and move and have their being. About this kind of artist Solzhenitsyn writes, "The task of the artist is to sense more keenly than others the harmony of the world, the beauty and the outrage of what man has done to it, and poignantly to let people know."[49] The beauty and the outrage: creation and fall. This kind of artist acknowledges the goodness of divine creation, observes both the good things and the bad things that fallen humanity has done to this creation, and has a passion to communicate to others the truth about it all.

This second kind of literary artist recognizes the duty of literature to convey a truthful interpretation of the human condition from one part of the world to another and from one age to another. Given the indivisibility of truth and the unity of mankind, the modern world needs one single "scale of values" by which to make its moral judgments. It is intolerable that a dehumanization which is disallowed in one part of our world be allowed in another. For Solzhenitsyn, "It is art, and it is literature" which can "coordinate these scales of values" and "give mankind one single system for reading its instruments." Through literature the peoples of the modern world

> have the marvelous capacity of transmitting from one nation to another—despite differences in language, customs, and social structure—practical experience, the harsh national experiences of many decades never tasted by the other nation. Sometimes this may save a whole nation from what is a dangerous or mistaken or plainly disastrous path, thus lessening the twists and turns of human history.[50]

Since human nature is not in flux but is fixed and perennial, literature can highlight the unity of mankind through the ages, also. "Literature transmits condensed and irrefutable human experience in still another priceless way: from generation to generation." For a given people, it can thus serve as "the living memory of the nation." Beyond national boundaries it reinforces our awareness of the commonalty of the human condition throughout all space and time. Art, with all its inventiveness and power, is not merely a human invention; it is a gift from God: "Even before the dawn of civilization we had received this gift from Hands we were not quick enough to discern." Thus, Solzhenitsyn can express himself "encouraged by a keen sense of world literature as the one great heart that beats for the cares and misfortunes of our world. . . ."[51]

The note of hope which is the usual concluding theme of Solzhenitsyn's works concludes his *Nobel Lecture*, as well. Reverting to a general admonition which we have already remarked, he says, "The simple act of an ordinary courageous man is not to take part, not to support lies!" But then he continues, "Writers and artists can do more: they can VANQUISH LIES! In the struggle against lies, art has always won and always will. . . . Lies can stand up against much in the world, but not against art." He concludes the lecture by citing a Russian proverb and giving his comment on it:

ONE WORD OF TRUTH OUTWEIGHS THE WORLD.
On such a seemingly fantastic violation of the law of the conservation of mass and energy are based both my own activities and my appeal to the writers of the whole world.[52]

The moral universe of Solzhenitsyn rests ultimately upon the power of the word. The Word of the Creator established this universe. The word of the writer seeks to be faithful to it. The writer's little stories reflect the Great Story and explore its ever-unfolding details. By such means the human word upholds and even drives the universe bestowed by the original Word.

This chapter has traced the main lineaments of Solzhenitsyn's world view. As it turns out, most of his Western critics did not have the eyes to see or ears to hear it. That story is the subject of the next three chapters.

3

Western Critics (I)
To 1973

FROM GREAT BRITAIN, in 1974: "Solzhenitsyn, I am afraid, is not one of us. That is to say he is not a liberal. I don't know what exactly he is, but whatever it is it is most peculiar."[1] From West Germany, in 1975: "He is no liberal. Let us make no mistake about that."[2] From the United States, in 1974: ". . . he is not the 'liberal' we would like him to be."[3]

It was not always so. It was an exaggeration to say, referring to the date of Solzhenitsyn's forced exile from his homeland, "Until February 13, 1974, Western opinion was united on Solzhenitsyn as on few subjects in living memory."[4] With a slight revision of the date, however, this generalization was not far off the mark. Solzhenitsyn's reputation in the West has experienced a wild swing of the pendulum. Once lionized as a freedom-fighter and anti-totalitarian dissident, he later came in for a barrage of withering criticisms. Eventually, he fell into general neglect. What motivated this wild swing of authoritative opinion? What went wrong between Solzhenitsyn and his Western critics? This chapter and the next two tell that story.

Solzhenitsyn is not above criticism. He has sometimes been prickly and unyielding in his dealings with others. His distinctive style of writing does not please all readers. However, personal and literary factors do not suffice to explain the animosity toward him that one encounters in many of his critics. Something else precipitates this conflict. And that something, in a word, is politics. In this area, too, Solzhenitsyn sometimes errs. He makes unnuanced pontifications and faulty predictions. The dissonance between him and his detractors, however, has much less to do with such occasional lapses on his part than with a clash of world views as they manifest themselves in political positions.

These three chapters set forth the record of Western criticism of Solzhenitsyn. The Soviet scene is brought into play only as it illuminates this exposition. The selections from critics are intended to be a representative sampling. Though I do not at every point try to disguise my judgment of these criticisms, the main purpose of these chapters is to give an account of what was said. Therefore, direct quotation predominates. Ineluctably, this record says as much about the state of Western culture as it does about Solzhenitsyn. It is one thing for a critic to be wrong; it is another thing for many critics to be wrong in the same way. And such a consensus of error reveals much about the ideology of a segment of cultural authorities in Europe and North America.

THE STORY OF ALEKSANDR SOLZHENITSYN is one of the truly dramatic ones in the annals of world literature. A Soviet artillery captain in World War II, he had been arrested for writing private letters critical of Joseph Stalin, and he spent eight years, 1945-1953, in the Soviet concentration-camp system. It was during these years of incarceration that he rejected decisively the Marxism-Leninism which he had learned in school and embraced the Christian faith in which he had received his early rearing. Although from his teens he had planned to become a writer, everything that we have from his pen postdates his imprisonment. Even as his experience of prison set him unalterably in opposition to the whole Soviet system, so it also provided him a rich mine of human experience, that of himself and that of others, to work into literary form.

It was Nikita Khrushchev's effort to find his own niche in history through his de-Stalinization campaign which gave hope to Solzhenitsyn that at least some of his works could see the light of day. The so-called thaw during the Khrushchev years was an on-again-off-again affair. If his works could be perceived as anti-Stalin (which they were), rather than anti-Soviet (which they also were), maybe they would be deemed acceptable. Despite the grave risks involved, he made his move. In late 1961, he got a manuscript into the hands of Aleksandr Tvardovsky, editor of *Novy Mir*, the most prestigious and open-spirited of the Soviet literary journals. Tvardovsky tells of his first reading of a work by this totally unknown author: "I realized at once that here was something important, and that in some way I must celebrate the event. I got out of bed, got fully dressed again in every particular, and sat down at my desk. That night I read a new classic of Russian literature."[5] He was reading what we now know (by the title which Tvardovsky gave it) as *One Day in the Life of Ivan Denisovich*.

Tvardovsky, ever the literary diplomat, got the manuscript into the hands of Nikita Khrushchev, like him of peasant stock and a personal friend, and encouraged him to secure Communist Party approval for publishing the novel. *One Day* was published in late 1962 in upwards of a million copies, and it quickly passed from hand to hand. Overnight, a small-town high-school teacher of physics and mathematics became a literary sensation, all this due to Khrushchev's direct intervention.

Khrushchev's words in reference to the publication of *One Day*, however self-serving, make for intriguing reading. With this novel in mind, he said,

> The party gives its backing to artistic creations which are really truthful, whatever negative aspects of life they may deal with, so long as they help the people in their effort to build a new society, and so long as they strengthen and weld together the people's forces.[6]

Years later, while preparing his memoirs, Khrushchev said that he had read the novel, finding it "very heavy but well written," and adding, "It made the reader react with revulsion to the conditions in which Ivan Denisovich and his friends lived while they served their terms." Overriding the advice from chief ideological watchdog Mikhail Suslov, Khrushchev explained,

In deciding not to interfere with Solzhenitsyn's book, I proceeded from the premise that the evil inflicted on the Communist Party and on the Soviet people had to be condemned; we had to lance the boil, to brand what had happened with shame so that it would never happen again. We had to brand the truth firmly into literature.

Readers really devoured Solzhenitsyn's book. They were trying to find how an honest man could end up in such conditions in our socialist time and our socialist state.

Stalin was to blame. He was the criminal in this respect. . . .[7]

It is apparent that Khrushchev's decision was altogether politically motivated. He saw the book as a tool useful in his de-Stalinization campaign, but not as a threat to Soviet power or the Communist Party. It would soon enough become clear that Khrushchev had let out of the bottle a genie that there was no getting back in. We may call this attempted political appropriation of a work of art the Khrushchev School of Literary Criticism. Politics is not the proper prism through which to look for the essence of *One Day*, but it was the only one available to the premier. Solzhenitsyn had in mind not damage done *to* the Party and the people by Stalin but damage done *by* the Party (including Stalin) to human beings. He wrote in opposition not only to Stalin and to the Soviet system but also to dehumanization *per se*.

The earliest Soviet responses to Solzhenitsyn took two different and ultimately incompatible forms. Predictably, the establishment publications echoed Khrushchev in declaring *One Day* within the pale of political correctness. In *Izvestia*, Konstantin Simonov wrote, "The Party has called writers its helpers. I believe that Alexander Solzhenitsyn, in his story, has shown himself a true helper of the Party in a sacred and vital cause—the struggle against the cult of personality and its consequences." In *Pravda*, Vladimir Ermilov wrote, "On reading this tragic tale . . . the reader feels also that a truth has been told, and that the possibility of telling this truth has been affirmed by the Party and the people, by the whole course of our country's life during recent years."[8] Solzhenitsyn had garnered the official seal of approval.

In stark contrast to the party-liners, there were respondents who did not follow the Khrushchev example of giving primacy to politics. Chief among these was Tvardovsky himself. In his preface to *One Day*, he said that the depiction of Ivan Denisovich "unfolds as a picture of exceptional vividness and truthfulness about the nature of man. It is this above all that gives the work its unique impact. . . . [The characters] are the same sort of people [as readers], but they have been exposed by fate to a cruel ordeal—not only physical but moral."[9] Zhores Medvedev, too, would later avoid political rhetoric in his praise for the novel:

> Ten years ago the author of *Ivan Denisovich* made his sudden, triumphant début, and it was the triumph of truth. The enthusiasm with which the new writer was first greeted was not just an expression of delight at contact with genuine art. It was a delight above all that the time had come when the *whole* truth could be told.[10]

By and large, Western critics eventually followed the Khrushchev line, not the Tvardovsky line. They gave more attention to political considerations than to literary ones. The bane of Solzhenitsyn's reception in the West is that he has usually been viewed through the prism of politics. He has been mediated to Western readers largely through persons for whom politics is the primary grid through which ideas, experience, and human values are forced. For instance, to determine whether or not he is a Western-style liberal has been deemed a significant question. The more time passed and the more we learned of Solzhenitsyn's ideas, the more politicized became the commentary on him. The politicizing of Solzhenitsyn criticism has resulted in a severely distorted view of the man and his literary works, and this distorted view has now achieved the status of received opinion.

Indeed, it is a very odd thing to observe that the early comments about Solzhenitsyn, those dated 1971 and earlier, are generally closer to the truth than are most of the later comments. What was generally missing in the early comments was a recognition of the religious context which framed Solzhenitsyn's moral vision. But what was more or less properly perceived was an awareness of the moral vision *per se*. Then again, this phenomenon may not be altogether puzzling. For before 1972 almost all the written evidence on which to interpret Solzhenitsyn was the body of his literary works theretofore published, mainly *One Day*, *The First Circle*, and *Cancer Ward*.

Thus, in his 1971 book, Abraham Rothberg writes that Solzhenitsyn views Soviet life with "an old-fashioned and refreshingly scrupulous moral scrutiny which refuses to accept ideological cant and hypocrisy. . . ."[11] Giovanni Grazzini remarks that Solzhenitsyn "was the first to recapture all the color and strength of the Russian language, and no other writer made an impact on the civil and moral conscience of the Soviet reader comparable with that made by this novel [*One Day*]. . . ."[12] Donald Fanger points out "the constant attention in Solzhenitsyn's writing to the nature of literature, good and bad; to the duties of the writer, the needs of the reader, to language itself," noting also that "what interests him is the achievement of authentic, moral selfhood."[13] The early criticism commonly focused upon Solzhenitsyn's union of literary form and moral content.

Dan Jacobson was on target when he observed, "Solzhenitsyn takes for granted an absolutely direct and open connection between literature and morality, art and life. He believes our responsibilities in the one to be inseparable from our responsibilities in the other; indeed, to be all but identical with one another." When, however, he added, "In the West today such an assumption about the relationship between art and morality is distinctly unfashionable,"[14] he partially anticipated the problems lying ahead in Solzhenitsyn criticism. When the intellectual culture is ideologically charged, there is a good chance that a moral writer will be misconstrued. This situation accounts, more than anything else, for the "freakishly wide range of response to Solzhenitsyn in American criticism," which Victor Erlich observed as early as 1973[15] and which became even more pronounced later. Writing shortly after the storm of controversy over Solzhenitsyn broke in the mid-seventies, Kathryn Feuer could still speak of the

> remarkable agreement as to the essential features of Solzhenitsyn's art. That Solzhenitsyn's work has already evoked so many studies of high quality is eloquent testimony to his artistic power, and eloquent refutation—should such be needed—of the view that his reputation rests more on his political fate than on his talent.[16]

Actually, though, the agreement of which she spoke was well along in the process of breaking up even as she wrote.

THE INITIAL WESTERN RESPONSE to *One Day in the Life of Ivan Denisovich* was enthusiastic. Franklin D. Reeve, who hailed it as "one of the most powerful prose works of the twentieth century," captures this mood well. The novel is political, he said, only in the sense that it "was approved for publication by the chief political officer of its author's state." Reeve presciently notes how a political approach to the novel could garble its message: "People will gravely say that it's a great book because it exposes the true nature of totalitarian communism—or something as foolish as that. . . . I wish people would stop it. . . . [T]he book is not so much about history or politics as it is about men." This novel, he continues, "jabs us with the question mark: What is a man worth?" It answers that "man has the power to will his own dignity. . . ." Reeve finds in Solzhenitsyn "all the literary skill, acumen, power, and vision to write the *Crime and Punishment* of our time." Also, he fixes upon the relationship between literature and life which Jacobson had described as characteristic of the Russian literary tradition:

> The great achievement of this book, which makes me cry out delight to the political and literary persons responsible for its publication, is that it returns literature to life, that once again in Russia all life is the artist's. Once more his job is to make real the sweet inefficiency of our soul, to put the world into words and make them sing.[17]

Leopold Labedz summarizes accurately the general enthusiasm for *One Day in the Life of Ivan Denisovich*: "The literary talent of Solzhenitsyn was recognized at once: he became a classic overnight." Quickly anthologies of literature designed for undergraduate use canonized him. From the beginning he was compared to the greatest of the many great Russian authors. Again, Labedz is representative: "He is the first great Russian writer to emerge after the Revolution whose humanity can be compared to that of Tolstoy, his awareness of suffering to that of Dostoyevsky, his lack of sentimentality to that of Chekhov."[18]

Of course, from the start there was something less than unanimity about Solzhenitsyn's literary quality. Kathryn Feuer admits,

> I was not among those who recognized Solzhenitsyn's potential greatness in *Ivan Denisovich*. The work's honesty and restraint and remarkable language made it notable, but to me it seemed chiefly a documentary achievement. (I don't think I'd have guessed *Crime and Punishment* from *Notes from the House of the Dead*, either.) For the astute readers however (and there were many) the essential clues were there.[19]

This kind of honest interaction with aesthetic issues, though, was the dominant note.

The same point applies to Irving Howe's review of *One Day*. He opens, "Though a remarkable book *One Day in the Life of Ivan Denisovich* is not the masterpiece certain reviewers have taken it to be." There is, however, an oblique hint of the politicized state of things to come in Solzhenitsyn criticism when Howe emphasizes the political reason why the novel was allowed to be published. "But had Khrushchev not given the signal, would not many 'progressive' intellectuals in the West still be denying the terror of Stalinism and denouncing this novel as a reactionary slander?"[20] In a sequel article, Howe declares, "Solzhenitsyn never calls into question the Communist monopoly of power. . . ."[21] However strange such a sentence sounds today, it does remind us how benign was the atmosphere surrounding the initial Western reception of Solzhenitsyn. This was before all recognized his vehement anti-Communism, also before all knew how far he was from being a man of the Left.

Howe himself was later to turn strongly against Solzhenitsyn, and the case of Howe serves as a microcosm for the history of Solzhenitsyn's Western reception as a whole. In 1971 Howe still saw Solzhenitsyn, like Pasternak before him, as engaged in "a struggle for human renewal, for the reaffirmation of the image of a free man as that image can excite our minds beyond all ideological decrees."[22] In 1980, however, having just read the memoirs entitled *The Oak and the Calf*, he wrote an open letter to Solzhenitsyn, "that splendid writer—the author of *The First Circle* and the series on the Gulag—whom I have strongly admired," in which he complained bitterly about Solzhenitsyn's apparent disdain for the anti-Communist Left to which Howe belongs. Lamenting "that abundance of scorn that is one of your gifts as a writer but flaws as a man," Howe suggests, "Something of the brutality of the commissars has rubbed off on you, I'm afraid." He adds, "It did not seem so in *The First Circle* or *Cancer Ward*. What has happened to you?"[23]

Howe's 1989 review of the expanded *August 1914* opens ominously with the same question: "What has happened to Aleksandr Solzhenitsyn?" Speaking of "the political outlook Mr. Solzhenitsyn has adopted in recent years," Howe charges, "By now Mr. Solzhenitsyn has become too impatient, too irritable for the novelist's job, and one readily surmises the reason: for a writer pulsing with prophetic urgency, mere literature dwindles in importance." So he answers his opening question thus: "The answer is that his zealotry has brought about a hardening of spirit, a loss in those humane feelings and imaginative outreachings that make us value a work of literature, regardless of the writer's political position." And he concludes, "It is all very sad, this self-immolation of a once major writer. . . ."[24]

Well, maybe. But, first, it is prudent to be quite cautious in imputing motives to others. In addition, there is no evidence that Solzhenitsyn has experienced any great change of heart since his religious conversion back in the camps. There has been, rather, a gradual unfolding of views long held—views which, before they were fully known, did not prevent Western readers from appreciating Solzhenitsyn as a literary artist. Nothing in the early novels conflicts with what we later learned of his world view. Furthermore, Howe's question would have greater force if it had not come after years of critical fusillades against Solzhenitsyn for his holding of ostensibly retrograde political views. In the commerce between Solzhenitsyn and his Western critics, the main change has not been in his thinking but in their awareness of it and response to it.

We cannot dwell long on the events of Solzhenitsyn's life during the 1960's. Following his quick admission into the Soviet Writers' Union, they constitute a story of the deterioration in the relationship between the author and the Soviet governmental and literary authorities. Zhores Medvedev has given a close-up account in *Ten Years After Ivan Denisovich*, Leopold Labedz has provided pertinent documents, and Solzhenitsyn has given his own version in *The Oak and the Calf*. Despite the enormous and overwhelmingly favorable response of Soviet readers to *One Day*, only a few of Solzhenitsyn's short pieces were published in the several months following the novel's appearance, and then nothing of his was legally published in the Soviet Union until 1989.

But the novel had made its impression on the minds and memories of its Soviet readers. In a 1967 poll asking, "Who is your favorite Soviet writer?", Solzhenitsyn came in in first place.[25] In 1964 Vladimir Lakshin, deputy editor of *Novy Mir* and author of the 1964 essay "Ivan Denisovich, His Friends and Foes," told visiting Yugoslavian author Mihajlo Mihajlov of the widely circulating saying, "Tell me what you think of *One Day*, and I will tell you who you are."[26] The official effort to suppress Solzhenitsyn began only a few months after *One Day* was published, but it took a few years for the Soviet animus to harden into action against him. Zhores Medvedev reports, "From the beginning of 1966 the name of Solzhenitsyn was no longer mentioned in articles of literary criticism, and references to *Ivan Denisovich* ceased completely in Soviet journals."[27]

It was after this taboo had settled into place that two meetings of Soviet writers in late 1966 and 1967 sealed Solzhenitsyn's fate as an outcast. The main subject at both was whether to publish *Cancer Ward*, perceived by Tvardovsky and his allies as the long work of Solzhenitsyn's least likely to give offense. The tone of the first meeting was generally friendly and supportive. Members of the prose section of the Moscow writers' organization suggested how the author could improve the novel before it was published. Solzhenitsyn responded warmly, "The main feeling which I have experienced today is one of gratitude." While defending his novel at certain points, Solzhenitsyn granted the legitimacy of criticisms at other points. The meeting ended with a resolution to promote the publication of *Cancer Ward*.[28]

On other fronts, however, events were taking a foreboding turn. Members of the KGB were leaking from Solzhenitsyn's confiscated files excerpts intended to blacken his reputation. Scheduled meetings between the author and his readers were canceled without explanation. "Someone at the top had evidently decided that he must be silenced."[29] It was against this background that in May 1967 Solzhenitsyn, feeling endangered, sent an open letter to the Fourth All-Union Writers' Congress, to which he had not been invited. In it he proposed that the Congress "adopt a resolution which would demand and ensure the abolition of all censorship, open or hidden, of all fictional writing. . . ." As for himself, his letter concluded, "I am of course confident that I will fulfil my duty as a writer in all circumstances—from the grave even more successfully and more irrefutably than in my lifetime. No one can bar the road to truth, and to advance its cause I am prepared to accept even death." Labedz characterized this letter as "the most eloquent plea for the freedom of literature that ever appeared in the Soviet Union."[30]

In September of 1967, Solzhenitsyn was hailed before the Secretariat of the Union of Soviet Writers; this was his second meeting with members of the literary establishment. From the start it went very poorly. The chairman of the session demanded, "You must protest above all against the dirty use of your name by our enemies in the West." In the same highly ideologized vein, another speaker asserted,

". . . you must speak out publicly and strike out against Western propaganda. Do battle against the foes of our nation! Do you realize that thermonuclear weapons exist in the world and that, despite all our peaceful efforts, the United States may employ them? How then can we, Soviet writers, not be soldiers?" A third speaker spoke against publishing *Cancer Ward* thus: "No, your story approaches fundamental problems not in philosophical terms but in political terms." He added, revealingly, ". . . the works of Solzhenitsyn are more dangerous to us than those of Pasternak: Pasternak was a man divorced from life, while Solzhenitsyn, with his animated, militant, ideological temperament, is a man of principle." The vitriol continued on, unrelieved, to the very last statement by one of the assembled writers: "You should state whether you renounce your role of leader of the political opposition in our country—the role they ascribe to you in the West."[31]

Solzhenitsyn's rebuttals fell on deaf ears. One would not think, from reading the transcript of the session, that he and his accusers were speaking about the same literary work. He explained that the task of the writer was not to defend or criticize economic or political positions but to deal with those "more universal and eternal questions" which pertain to our moral beings.[32] Solzhenitsyn's language and that of his accusers belong to two different worlds of discourse. Even as they charged him with a political message, it was not he but they who were according primacy to politics—or, in short, following the path of the Khrushchev School of Literary Criticism. Official disapproval was sealed in a speech by M. V. Zimyanin, editor-in-chief of *Pravda*: "Obviously we cannot publish his works. Solzhenitsyn's demand that we do so cannot be met. If he writes stories which correspond to the interests of our society, then his works will be published. He will not be deprived of his bread and butter. Solzhenitsyn is a teacher of physics; let him teach."[33]

The campaign of disinformation and vilification against Solzhenitsyn culminated, in 1969, in his being expelled from the Soviet Writers' Union. One who played a role in this campaign was Victor Louis, a shadowy and duplicitous character whom the KGB used for sending manuscripts to the West when it suited their purposes.[34] He presented to a Western periodical an essay of his on Solzhenitsyn, which he prefaced with the statement, "I admire him as a writer but was disappointed to discover that I disliked him as a person." Within his essay Louis said, "Russians love a martyr and Solzhenitsyn relishes the role."[35] One need not subscribe to any conspiracy theory to observe simply that sentiments similar to Louis's were later to appear in the Western press. The parallel extends only this far: that, first in the Soviet establishment and later in the Western establishment, Solzhenitsyn was found to be politically uncongenial, though not always for the same reasons.

The task of expelling Solzhenitsyn was handed down to the low-profile local branch of the writers' organization at Ryazan, Solzhenitsyn's city of residence. Western protests poured in, most notably from writers. One open letter, saying in part, "We sign our names as men of peace declaring our solidarity with Alexander Solzhenitsyn's defence of those fundamental rights of the human spirit which unite civilized people everywhere," was signed by such luminaries as Arthur Miller, John Updike, John Cheever, Truman Capote, Richard Wilbur, Jean-Paul Sartre, and Kurt Vonnegut. Another open letter, published in the *London Times* and referring to Solzhenitsyn as "the one writer in Russia who, in the words of Arthur Miller, 'is unanimously regarded as a classic,' " was signed by W. H. Auden, Gunter Grass, Graham Greene, Alfred Kazin, Mary McCarthy, Muriel Spark, and a host of other well-established names.[36]

Western support was, as Solzhenitsyn knew, a vital element in protecting him from Soviet retribution, and it continued at full force in 1970, when he was awarded the Nobel Prize for Literature. The official citation for the prize said simply, "For the ethical force with which he has pursued the indispensable traditions of Russian literature." In other words, it alluded to aesthetic and to moral/spiritual values, but not to political ones. The official Soviet reaction was predictable: it turned these terms upside down. *Izvestia* editorialized, "One can only regret that the Nobel committee has allowed itself to be drawn into an unseemly game, undertaken by no means in the interests of the development of spiritual values and literary traditions, but dictated by speculative political considerations."[37] Was the Nobel committee's choice politically motivated? If so (and the Swedish ambassador's shabby refusal to honor Solzhenitsyn with a public ceremony in Moscow belies the charge), *Izvestia* and the other Soviet periodicals which followed its lead should have blamed Khrushchev first of all, for he set in motion the political approach to Solzhenitsyn's writings.

Zhores Medvedev spoke for many Soviet dissidents in denying that the award was "determined by political factors."[38] Acknowledging the high praise for Solzhenitsyn all over the world, Labedz cast an interesting light on the issue: "If anything, *not* to have awarded the prize to Solzhenitsyn would have been a political decision arising from other than literary considerations."[39] Only later would it seem to some Westerners, such as Gore Vidal,[40] that the award was politically motivated. At the time, even French and Italian Communists praised the choice as non-partisan.[41]

BOTH *THE FIRST CIRCLE* AND *CANCER WARD* were published in the West in 1968, within weeks of each other. Praise for them was strong, though not unanimous. What is most noteworthy, in hindsight, is how tightly the reviewers' attention remained fixed on literary, rather than political, considerations, even though the slandering of Solzhenitsyn was now at its most intense in the Soviet press. Preferring *Cancer Ward* to *The First Circle*, Emile Capouya wrote, "In comparison with Solzhenitsyn's novel, the light wines and strong liquors of our own literature during the last quarter-century offer nothing in the way of nourishment for the spirit."[42] Patricia Blake, preferring "the supreme spareness" of *One Day*, found both novels in need of cutting, but concluded her review of *Cancer Ward* with "mixed and turbulent feelings. On the one hand I am thankful that I have had the opportunity to read a work that, in spite of its weaknesses, towers above the novels that glut our marketplace. On the other, I am sickened by the knowledge that it cannot be read in Russia. . . ."[43] Maurice Friedberg declared, "Aleksandr Solzhenitsyn is the greatest living Russian writer, and *The Cancer Ward* is his best work to date." Inadvertently, however, he tipped us off to what would happen later to Solzhenitsyn's Western reception when, denying the appropriateness of drawing a parallel between Solzhenitsyn and Dostoevsky, he said,

> Nothing in Solzhenitsyn's life and work suggests that he might follow in his predecessor's footsteps and ultimately become a champion of political reaction and submission to authority. For, in spite of his outward preoccupation with politics, Solzhenitsyn's basic concerns are really moral and ethical, though in a nonreligious sense. . . .[44]

The First Circle, which made its way onto best-seller lists, received some glowing accolades. Harrison Salisbury hailed it as "the greatest

Russian novel of the last half of the century."[45] Jeri Laber described it as "a distinguished work, thoroughly contemporary, authentically Russian, yet so profound in its vision and its implications that it transcends both its locale and the specificities of its subject matter." Revealingly, given her later criticisms, she added that Solzhenitsyn "is not a polemicist," calling him instead "the symbol and the embodiment of an undaunted creative spirit."[46] C. J. McNaspy, citing Yevgeny Yevtushenko's well-known opinion that "Solzhenitsyn is our only living classic," expressed uncertainty about the "only" but confidence about the "classic": "One puts down *The First Circle* with the unshakable assurance that here is something Tolstoy might have written, or Turgenev, or even, in one of his gentler moods, Dostoevsky, had they lived in the Stalinist era."[47] Deming Brown offered this assessment:

> With the appearance of *Cancer Ward* and *The First Circle* it becomes clear that Alexander Solzhenitsyn is the most powerful writer and most versatile stylist in Russia today. No longer can there be the slightest question about his literary stature or doubt of its permanence. We can be certain that his reputation as a man of letters will outlive the political prominence which his fearless battle for creative freedom has earned him. Solzhenitsyn is no meteor; he will not fade into obscurity.

Brown did touch upon a matter, however, which only a few years later was to be clarified, and then not to the benefit of Solzhenitsyn's Western reputation. Granting that "freedom is clearly for him a spiritual matter," Brown drew back from ascribing to the author a religious belief as the grounding for this commitment.

> Solzhenitsyn's solicitude for churches and his sympathetic portrayal of humble faith do not, however, warrant conclusions about the degree of his possible belief in Christianity. He admires the ethical values of Christianity and shares its spiritual concerns, but there is no discernible symbolism, no firm structure of Christian doctrine.[48]

The reception in Great Britain was even warmer than that in the United States. Julian Symons, in the *Sunday Times*, called *The First Circle* "a majestic work of genius," which described human behavior in extreme situations with such power that "the mass of contemporary fiction dealing with this theme look[s] trivial by comparison." Ronald

Hingley, in *The Spectator*, called it "arguably the greatest Russian novel of the twentieth century."[49]

Not all reviewers were enthusiastic about *The First Circle*. Pritchard Flynn, while acknowledging its author's status as "a Russian hero," contradicted Laber's praise of the novel's up-to-dateness: "For Solzhenitsyn, the watch stopped during Stalin's regime, and, consequently, his art is the art of the past."[50] Robert Garis judged *The First Circle* "mediocre" and the author of it and *Cancer Ward* a "non-novelist":

> . . . it was disconcerting to discover, when I read these long novels, that although Solzhenitsyn is beyond question an immensely honorable, movingly simple-hearted (and sometimes startlingly simple-minded) man, his specific talent for fiction is undistinguished, to say the least, and his style is what you wouldn't be surprised to find in a novel on the American best-seller list, where in fact *The First Circle* has been occupying a respectable position for seventeen weeks now, as I write.

Garis did end up—distinguishing between literary quality and human worth, as many commentators were later to do—with approval of the man: "If Solzhenitsyn were a good novelist he might be a great one; in any case, he is a human being grown up to full size." Garis also pointed out (as he saw it) Solzhenitsyn's "lack of interest in politics and his interest in a church-less and dogma-less religious contemplation," though he condescendingly considered these preferences part of "Solzhenitsyn's naively simple-minded view of life."[51]

That there was a minority opinion about Solzhenitsyn in the late 1960's, here represented by Garis, is befitting to a free press. What is most memorable, though, in retrospect, about the Western reception of Solzhenitsyn then is not even the general praise for him but the absence of politics as the primary prism through which to approach him. Literary criteria prevailed. The obvious temptation to approach him otherwise, given his beleaguered personal situation, was observed by many and was delineated by Harrison Salisbury in these words:

> The problem of presenting Solzhenitsyn to the American audience (as it was of Pasternak before him) is to distinguish between Solzhenitsyn the literary genius and Solzhenitsyn the center of politico-literary contro-

versy, the target of repression and censorship, hero of the fight against a return to Stalinism.[52]

The determined effort not to muddy the waters of literary criticism appears also in Earl Rovit's review.

> Solzhenitsyn has yet to make his way through and beyond the cliché that welcomes him to the West as an anti-Soviet Soviet. I think we shall come to recognize, however, that *The First Circle* and *Cancer Ward* are "political" only in a peripheral way (like Dostoevski's *The Possessed*) and I should not be surprised to find that we will have to reckon with the imaginative thrust of these novels as parts of a major artist's vision of the universe that all of us equally inhabit.[53]

As late as 1971, there was a widespread consensus in the West about Solzhenitsyn. The opening lines of an early Italian biographical study of him encapsulate it: "Solzhenitsyn is first a great writer and only second a literary sensation. His greatness is not due to the publicity he has received; on the contrary, there would hardly have been such worldwide interest in his fate if he had been a mediocrity."[54] Ideological considerations rarely entered into the discussion of Solzhenitsyn. Obviously, not all of his world view had yet been revealed; there was more, much more, to come. And when it came, it brought into play the ideological filter which has so distorted our understanding of the author. Not yet widely perceived were the political and religious commitments which many Western intellectuals would find uncongenial and sometimes even repugnant.

One pauses momentarily to wonder what his standing in literary circles would be today had nothing other than the works published in the 1960's come to light. Indeed, one can wonder if in that case these works themselves might not be held in higher regard than they are today, for the controversies of the 1970's seem to have cast a retrospective pall over these works, as well. For many, what once seemed pristine in its humanism now seems tarnished by unacceptably unfashionable views which, if the initial praise of the early works is to be trusted, were not inherent within the works themselves. In any case, 1972 rolled around, Solzhenitsyn continued to write and publish, and the tide which had been rising in his favor began to recede, and with an apparent inexorableness from which it has not yet returned.

IN 1972 SOLZHENITSYN REVEALED that he was a religious believer, a Christian, a Russian Orthodox. His political heterodoxies became known only in 1974, and they hit like a bombshell. For persons committed to the primacy of politics, the 1974 revelations were the devastating ones. However, the 1972 revelations had a chilling effect, with a kind of foreboding of more bad news to come.

Actually, there were signs aplenty in the early-published works that Solzhenitsyn was both favorably disposed toward religion and unfavorably disposed toward Western liberalism. As to the former, the climactic role given to the sympathetically depicted character of Alyosha the Baptist in *One Day* was one such clue. More revealing was the coming to an affirmation of belief in God by Gleb Nerzhin, the author's *alter ego* in *The First Circle*. As to the latter, there was the unflattering portrayal of Eleanor Roosevelt as a soft-headed liberal do-gooder in *The First Circle*. And that novel ends with the grimly ironic passage about the progressive French newspaper correspondent who sees in the Moscow streets many vans with the word *meat* written on their sides in four languages, vans actually transporting political prisoners to hard-labor camps, and who naively concludes, in the novel's last words, that "the provisioning of the capital is excellent."[55]

If the shape of Solzhenitsyn's world view remained generally unnoticed as late as 1971, as a point of fact some did discern it. The most important example is Alexander Schmemann. His essay "On Solzhenitsyn," cited in the preceding chapter,[56] appeared before news came that Solzhenitsyn had publicly taken communion in a Russian Orthodox Church and before he published his open "Lenten Letter" to Patriarch Pimen; his prose-poem prayer, which begins, "How easy to live with You, O Lord, / How easy to believe in You"; and *August 1914*, his most overtly Christian novel.

August 1914 first appeared in 1971 in the original Russian from an émigré publishing house in Paris. Its American publication was accompanied with the fanfare of a June 23, 1972, *Life* magazine cover story by translator Michael Glenny and a major excerpt. This was an index of the strength of consensus in favor of Solzhenitsyn, now also a Nobel Prize winner, and this time marks the high-water mark of his reputation in the West. An air of expectancy greeted the new novel. It shot onto the best-seller lists. Michael Scammell is certainly correct, however, that "the reviews of the novel were decidedly mixed" and that its appearance "disrupted the unanimity of opinion that had enveloped his earlier works." Similarly, he is fair in summarizing, "The overall response, in short, was one of respectful bewilderment."[57] Solzhenitsyn himself was later to acknowledge, "It is . . . from the appearance of *August 1914* that we must date the schism among my readers, the steady loss of supporters, with more leaving me than remained behind."[58] His reference is specifically to Soviet readers, who would now perceive that he was not only anti-Stalinist but also anti-Leninist. But something of the same defection occurred among his Western critics.

This defection was not entirely the result of the ideological resistance to which Solzhenitsyn called attention. Some sympathetic readers found this "archive novel" satisfying; but others, perhaps a majority, of them expressed misgivings about its aesthetic quality. Even apart from extra-literary considerations, the publication of *August 1914* caused a shadow to fall across Solzhenitsyn's literary reputation which lingers to this day.

It is necessary to clarify Solzhenitsyn's position in 1971, particularly as he saw it. For years following the legal publication of *One Day in the Life of Ivan Denisovich*, he had sought to have other works of his legally published in the Soviet Union. The official campaign of slander against him became so intense in the late 1960's, culminating in the vilification greeting his receipt of the Nobel Prize, that all hope had vanished for future publication at home. The secretiveness of his life was wearing on him: "For how many years can I go on like this?" It was time to go public—for instance, no longer to keep covert his Christian faith, which some were already discerning from his published works anyway. As he later put it, "In my first works I was concealing my features from the police censorship—but, by the same token, from the public at large. With each subsequent step I inevitably revealed more and more of myself: the time had come to speak more precisely, to go even deeper."[59]

With *August 1914* he was sending forth the first part of what he had always planned, from his teen-aged years, would be his *magnum opus*: a novelistic treatment of the events leading up to and culminating in what he had all along considered the most important event in modern world history, the Bolshevik Revolution. Historical fiction would lack the immediacy of his earlier novels with their contemporary settings, but it was a necessary contribution if the truth of the history of his people was to be preserved for future generations. He knew, especially because of his criticisms of Lenin, that he was running the risk of "los[ing] my contemporaries in the hope of winning posterity."[60] But this risk was an inescapable part of fulfilling his mission of truth-telling.

According to Zhores Medvedev, the response of Soviet readers to *August 1914* was generally favorable. It made, he said, "a very deep impression on me," though not the "emotionally exhilarating" one of the novels of contemporary setting. After cataloguing the somewhat mixed responses of other readers, he concludes, "*August 1914* was unconditionally acknowledged as an outstanding work and an indication that the author's talent was reaching to still greater heights."[61] Tvardovsky, too, was enthusiastic about the novel.[62]

Among Russians abroad, Alexander Schmemann wrote, ". . . several days have passed since I closed that remarkable book, so permeated with light, sadness, joy, anger, love—and still I have the same sensation in my soul of a feast, a celebration, and I have difficulty returning to mundane, earthly affairs." About this most Russian and most Christian of Solzhenitsyn's novels, Schmemann made two particularly telling points. One is that Solzhenitsyn, however obvious and deep his love of his country, was demythologizing the "myth of Russia," to which both Dostoevsky and Tolstoy had, in their differing ways, been committed. "It is precisely against this *myth* (that Russia had a peculiar, sanctified destiny, that she was governed by a unique spirit, that her natives were endowed with an unmatched and generally undefined spiritual perception) that Solzhenitsyn rebels in his novel. He exposes it as false and ruinous. . . ." Western critics generally missed this point; in fact, some of them turned it exactly inside out. The other is the delineating of the centrality of Christianity in the novel:

> Thus in the last analysis Solzhenitsyn "liberates" even religion from the petty human idolatry which has encrusted it, . . . from everything essentially pseudo-religious and pseudo-Christian in it. Perhaps this is most important, since nothing has so obscured the visage of God in this world, or so hinders men from seeing Him, as all these "human, all too human"

political, social, racial or ethnic reductions of religion. Purifying religion, Solzhenitsyn sets it again at the center of all.[63]

Nikita Struve, another Russian abroad, wrote with similar appreciation for *August 1914*. Like Schmemann, he noted that the "perception of the world" in this novel is "unquestionably Christian." Citing Schmemann on Solzhenitsyn's attitude toward Russia, he concurred "that Russia has been both great and petty, holy and sinful, and also that she must be formed in the image of the free and wilful men who will recreate her." And he offered as partial motivation for the debate over the novel "a reluctance to acknowledge that which is superior; we fear that a phenomenon of a higher order will degrade us, and, therefore, something unquestionably low and sinful within us struggles against the recognition of such phenomena."[64] Another Slav, Milovan Djilas, the well-known Yugoslavian dissident, expressed his view that in *August 1914* Solzhenitsyn "is returning Russia its soul," and that "[b]y returning Russia to herself, by rejecting ideological Russia, Solzhenitsyn is returning her to the human community."[65]

The Western response to *August 1914* was considerably less welcoming. A few highly favorable reviews did appear, but disappointment was the dominant note. Many reviews expressed ambivalence, but these usually were weighted toward the side of disapproval. Reviewers seemed put off by the novel's thoroughgoing Russianness and its overt religiosity, which distanced it from them. Though most endeavored to stick to literary considerations, matters of conflicting world views often intruded. One would expect that great caution would be used in reviewing a book which was to be the first part of a much longer whole, but only sometimes, and too seldom, was this the case. Too infrequently, whatever the particular issue at hand, do we come upon such concessions as this, by Pearl Bell: ". . . one owes this extraordinary man the homage of patience. . . . And it may be that in the volumes about the War yet to come, we will learn something of its meaning for Solzhenitsyn that *August 1914* by itself fails to yield."[66]

When reviewers stuck to literary considerations, the most frequently featured element was the relationship between Solzhenitsyn and Tolstoy. The result of these speculations was a tangle of confusion. This topic need not detain us. Suffice it to say that, the closer the reviewers perceived the linkage between Solzhenitsyn and Tolstoy to be, the more they got the novel wrong and also were inclined to dislike it. Nevertheless, such reviewers were making an honorable effort to locate Solzhenitsyn's proper place in the Russian literary tradition. At this stage, the politicizing of the Western discussion of Solzhenitsyn was only beginning.

Among the most favorable reviews was one in a religious periodical, by Alfred P. Klausler, who rhapsodized, "*August 1914*, eagerly awaited ever since news of its existence filtered out of Russia, meets all expectations and indeed surpasses them. . . . The truth is that once you pick it up and begin reading, you won't lay it down."[67] The truth is that very few others said so.

Simon Karlinsky's highly laudatory front-page review in the *New York Times Book Review* was one of the earliest, but it did not set the tone for those to follow, despite the authority of the reviewer and the prestige of the medium. Karlinsky considered Solzhenitsyn's position as the foremost living Russian writer "self-evident" and "unassailable on any imaginable literary grounds." Of *August 1914* he says, "Thematically and stylistically the book constitutes an entirely new departure for Solzhenitsyn; and it is, if anything, even more remarkable than his other work." He notes in passing, without personal reaction, that "Solzhenitsyn's religious concerns, which were perceptible but muted in his other books, come out in the open in this novel." He praises the author's "stylistic complexity" and "verbal inventiveness," lamenting that English translations obscure his innovative language. Karlinsky's most astounding sentence is this: " 'August 1914' is sure to be the most accessible of Solzhenitsyn's works for non-Russian readers."[68] His reasoning is that totalitarian Stalinist Russia is even more remote from our experience than is pre-revolutionary Russia.

Even reviewers who seemed not put off by the novel's Russianness and religiosity could not share Karlinsky's praise for it. In Victor Erlich's view, it "lacks the firmness of outline, the sureness of touch, in a word, the authority of *One Day in the Life of Ivan Denisovich* or *The First Circle*. The prose is not infrequently contrived and unwieldy. The account of the East Prussian campaign is overdocumented." Erlich does allow, "Though *August 1914* is a seriously flawed work, at its best it is as moving and vivid as any of Solzhenitsyn's previous creations."[69] Similarly, Naomi Bliven could grant that "Solzhenitsyn has an awesome ability to realize his characters concisely when he wants to."[70] And in a rather lukewarm review, which noncommittally takes note of the religion and nationalism in the novel, Philip Rahv finds Solzhenitsyn in some ways superior, as well as in other ways inferior, to Tolstoy.[71] Reviews such as these have about them a sense of balance and even-handedness, and when not favorable, were also not prejudicial.

Many other reviews were in a different key, and in some of them we begin to see an extra-literary animus developing. Gore Vidal, for instance, dismissively asserted, "At the book's core there is nothing beyond the author's crypto-Christianity. . . ." Rating *August 1914* below Herman Wouk's *Winds of War* and its author as unworthy of the Nobel Prize, he could still manage to grant that "we must honor if not the art the author," which honoring took the following supercilious form: "To give the noble engineer his due he is good at describing how things work, and it is plain that nature destined him to write manuals of artillery or instructions on how to take apart a threshing machine."[72] Other negative reviewers stopped short of Vidal's demeanor of caustic condescension. William H. Pritchard found it "hard to imagine how the multitude of pages to come can redeem large swatches of the book to hand," and he declared that "Solzhenitsyn is a monotonous writer with little variation in the tone used to treat all subjects." Like Vidal, he still found the man "admirable."[73]

Philip Toynbee, signatory to an aforementioned 1969 letter in Solzhenitsyn's defense, found the comparison to Tolstoy "disastrous for Solzhenitsyn" and *August 1914* to have "moments of tired mystical jingoism." Whereas it was common to criticize the new novel by setting it in contrast to the successful earlier novels, Toynbee expressed a low view of Solzhenitsyn's literary works in general. Generalized disapproval of Solzhenitsyn's literary art was absent prior to 1972, though soon thereafter it was to become frequent. Parceling out some of the blame to the Soviet system for "the failure of this talented man to find and express a vision of his own" hardly softened Toynbee's basic indictment. Nor did his ranking Solzhenitsyn with Jules Romains and Roger Martin du Gard and *August 1914* below Romain Rolland's *Jean-Christophe*, then calling this estimate "not negligible praise," disguise the damning with faint praise.[74]

It is particularly instructive to listen to Jeri Laber's voice in the chorus of disapproval. Her review of *August 1914* carries no hint that four years earlier she had bestowed unqualified praise upon *The First Circle*. Characterization seemed strong then, weak now. She had made no mention of religion in the early review; now she does not seem pleased by the "spiritual attitudes" expressed in "this overtly religious novel." Laber retains respect for the man's personal qualities, just no longer for his literature: "I cannot question Solzhenitsyn's exceptional courage and sincerity. . . . Yet the pedantic and highly moralistic tone of this book, its constant repetition of his overly simplified beliefs, become tiresome." Give her two more years, and her opinion will decline yet further. She herself offers this anticipatory note: "It may be that Solzhenitsyn will move on to polemics and abandon the novel altogether. This would accord with his creed and with the public role he has assumed."[75]

It was left to Mary McCarthy, in her satisfyingly plainspoken review, to explain the root problem between the author of *August 1914* and his Western commentators: namely, the conflicting political perspectives. She says openly what others only hint at obliquely.

> To be fair to the book will not be easy for many readers, particularly those who like an author to conform to their own notions of political good manners. Solzhenitsyn himself, to say it straight out, is rude and unfair in his novel to a whole category of society: the "liberals" and "advanced circles" of 1914, those who opposed the war and patriotic sentiments, who yearned, they thought, for revolution, despised religion, authority, tradition, anything respected and handed down. He has it in for those people, just as he would have it in for you and me, if he could overhear us talking.

The *inter nos* linkage of "you and me" bespeaks a deliciously unguarded assumption that all of her readers join her in a sense of belonging to the elite "advanced circles" who locate themselves on the Left. It is important to alert them, us, that "[t]his novel is *not* the work of a liberal imagination."[76]

McCarthy is not quite right when she claims that Solzhenitsyn's single yardstick for measuring his character is, "What is their attitude to military service?" For here she has selected an issue which preoccupies her, not him. Nonetheless, she is exactly right when, after a bit of discussion, she says, "None of this can sit very well with American liberals, who have consistently sought to dissuade young men from sharing in the Vietnamese tragedy." She is also right not to read this novel (as some readers did) as a mere period piece:

> It is hard to read this volume without an eye nervously straying to current events and one's own responsibility in them. The temptation to do so has been put there by Solzhenitsyn himself, who clearly intends his reader to draw inferences from what he describes and apply the lesson to present-day life.

McCarthy draws her inference from Solzhenitsyn's bitingly satirical depiction of Ensign Lenartovich, a young revolutionary characterized by his "very apartness from the others, his quality of onlooker, his coldness and self-satisfaction, his indifference to the colors, his irreligion." This "despicable" figure is "the only so-called revolutionary we really get to know"—the only one, that is, for "advanced people" to identify with. And so she applies the lesson: "It is as if his book had been designed to offend 'advanced people' wherever they are to be found— . . . all those who wish . . . to be ahead of their time rather than behind it or in the middle of it."[77]

Michael Scammell, Solzhenitsyn's biographer, has called Solzhenitsyn "a born outsider," one who always stood "apart from the main body of intelligentsia," one "who was fundamentally a lone wolf and not disposed to run with the pack." His comment about the McCarthy review is quite revealing, especially in its concluding phrase: "Mary McCarthy, in a determinedly sympathetic review, pointed out that Solzhenitsyn's novel seemed almost deliberately designed to offend the sensibilities of Western liberals—in other words, the sort of people most likely to be reviewing it."[78] George Steiner, too, took note of Solzhenitsyn's apartness from Western liberalism: "His notion of man and the state is, by liberal and rational standards, archaic and menacing. . . . The Western adoption of Solzhenitsyn as a symbol of freedom, of man's opposition to absolute rule, is an ironic muddle."[79]

It is surprising how little attention Solzhenitsyn's *Nobel Lecture* received when it was published in 1972, especially given the turmoil among his Western erstwhile sympathizers caused by the roughly simultaneous appearance of *August 1914*. Edward Weeks called the speech "[t]he most eloquent response in the long history of the Prizes."[80] Raymond Rosenthal, who reviewed it and the new novel together, took quite a different view. Sometimes with tongue in cheek, he imagines how anachronistic Solzhenitsyn's spiritual utterances in the speech will seem to many Western readers.

> This man not only defies the Soviet overlords but also has no compunction about trampling on *our* most treasured feelings of cultural dereliction, our inalienable modernist heritage of dislocation and despair. But what can we expect of a semi-barbarian Russian, who has, moreover, been subjected to material hardships of the worst description; he was bound to seek refuge in some pipe dream. Though we must admit that, like his forebears, Gogol, Dostoevsky and Tolstoy, he somehow manages to combine the most precise and practical realism with the most absurd "private" opinions concerning the spiritual life and its meaning for us.

Rosenthal promises to "try to overlook this essentially racial peculiarity," since "Americans, by and large, like the critics who mold their opinions and tastes, are too down to earth, too materialistic, too reasonable to be led astray by such maunderings." After another quotation from the lecture, he pauses, "I know, I know—it gets worse and worse." Mentioning "medieval rubbish," he continues, "There is a great deal more in Solzhenitsyn's lecture that would be sure to repel or horrify most up-to-date citizens of our artistic commonwealth, but simple decency and the obligation of maintaining ties with our Russian brothers . . . can only suggest that we draw a veil of compassion over his other extravagances."[81]

Rosenthal's review concludes with a challenge to Western intellectuals, to Mary McCarthy's "you and me":

> The chronic malady of every literary community is parochialism, an inability to entertain ideas that don't "fit in." The generally ham-fisted reception of Solzhenitsyn's novel, with its unaccustomed juxtapositions and ironies, its truly revolutionary perspectives . . . could be a salutary warning, if it were pondered in all its aspects and connections. Why should Solzhenitsyn be freer in his thought than so many of our leading literary and cultural lights?[82]

Indubitably, *August 1914* marks the turn in the Western reception of Solzhenitsyn. It established doubts about him which prepared the way for the yet more negative judgments which were to greet other works of his over the next few years. My own assessment is that, of all the offenses which Solzhenitsyn committed in this novel, the most egregious was the overt manifestation of his Christian faith. One who believed such "medieval rubbish" could be fully expected to misunderstand the modern world. What does Jerusalem have to do with Athens? Or with New York? Kathryn Feuer, seconding Simon Karlinsky, would soon write, "Solzhenitsyn's deep religious faith and intense patriotism have been universally noted. These fundamentals of his creed were apparent in *The First Circle* and *Cancer Ward*; their consummate importance became clear, however, in *August 1914*. . . ."[83] She has it almost right. For too many, Solzhenitsyn's world view was not in the least apparent until *August 1914*; and, as soon as it was apparent, it was like an alarm bell going off. And so we had "the *de facto* situation that other works of Solzhenitsyn are acknowledged as masterpieces and only *August 1914* is singled out for public exasperation and, indeed, scorn."[84]

Writing about Solzhenitsyn, Czeslaw Milosz put this question: "Why is it that a major Christian writer has appeared in Russia where the Christians have been oppressed for decades, while in the West, where there is complete freedom of religious practice, literature is nearly synonymous with agnosticism and moral relativism?"[85] This book does not attempt to answer that question. But that question certainly does frame the conflict between Solzhenitsyn and the Western intelligentsia.

4

Western Critics (II)
From 1974 to 1977

IN EARLY 1974, Aleksandr Solzhenitsyn was front-page news around the world. The key episode was his arrest on February 12, 1974, and his forcible expulsion from his homeland the next day. The immediate cause of this episode was the KGB's discovery of a manuscript copy of his massive indictment of the Soviet system, *The Gulag Archipelago*. For more than a decade, the world had watched the unfolding struggle between an independent citizen and a repressive regime—a struggle which Solzhenitsyn himself was later to recount in his book of memoirs, *The Oak and Calf*. The title comes from a Russian proverb in which a tender calf, oblivious to the odds against him, keeps butting his head against a massive oak tree trying to knock it down. Now the plot line was coming to a climax, and the world watched more intently than ever. For the first time since the case of Leon Trotsky in 1929, the Soviet Union was sending into exile one of its famous public persons.

For some time, rumors had circulated within the Soviet Union that Solzhenitsyn had written a large work about the Soviet concentration-camp system. In late 1973, KGB officers brought in for interrogation a Leningrad woman, Elizaveta Voronyanskaya, who had once worked as an amanuensis for Solzhenitsyn, and after five days and five nights of non-stop interrogation and torture, she finally cracked and told them where she had hidden a copy of the manuscript. Shortly after her release she was found dead. It looked like a case of suicide, but Solzhenitsyn believes it likely that, even then, the KGB murdered her.[1]

Before the KGB procured its copy of *The Gulag Archipelago*, Solzhenitsyn had secretly transmitted the work to Western publishers, with strict orders that it not be published until he gave the word to proceed. Because it names persons still living, his original intention had been not to publish it until well after he and they were dead. He was dismayed that Voronyanskaya had not followed his instructions to destroy her copy, precisely so that it would not fall into the KGB's hands, though we can see the heroism of her motivation to preserve her copy lest all others be lost. Solzhenitsyn knew how easy it would be to quote snippets out of context to make him look anti-Russian, pro-Nazi, or whatever. Therefore, in self-defense, his hand forced by the KGB, he gave the order for the Western presses to roll.

When Solzhenitsyn was arrested—for the second time, the first being in 1945—he was charged with treason and stripped of his citizenship. The next day, February 13, 1974, he was put on an airplane. He did not know his destination, or even if he would still be on the plane when it landed, until he saw the airport sign reading "Frankfurt-am-Main." He came, he said, "as naked as Adam," dressed in his "KGB clothes." His only personal possessions were a wristwatch and a small cross. He came without his wife and children. He came to a hero's welcome. He was the lead story on television news programs and the banner headline in newspapers.

Daily stories followed. Would his family be allowed to join him? Would his archives be sent to him? Where would he settle? He was initially hosted by German author Heinrich Böll. Leaders of Western governments published declarations of praise. Soviet dissidents wrote statements of protest on his behalf. He traveled to Norway in search of a home. He settled in Zurich, Switzerland. His family and manuscripts came West. He quickly tired of what he considered excessive intrusions by the press and complained when journalists wrote things that he said were untrue. Editorialists showered him with respect and admiration. The Soviet press maligned him mercilessly, but in the West only Communist Party spokesmen saw merit in this vilification. Only gradually did the newsworthiness of his personal drama subside.

As soon as he arrived in the West, Solzhenitsyn announced that he

fully expected to return home someday. In the meantime, it was revealed, he had given a parting word to his countrymen. Dated the day of
his arrest, his statement was entitled "Live Not by Lies." Western
newspapers duly published it a few days thereafter. It calls upon Soviet
citizens to assert their spiritual liberation simply by refusing to participate in the system's official lies. Were enough individuals to exercise
this passive resistance, the whole system would crumble. "If there are
thousands of us, they will not be able to do anything with us. If there are
tens of thousands of us, then we would not even recognize our country."[2] This clarion call, so far from a call for political revolution, was for
Solzhenitsyn the most important thing that he could say to his countrymen as he departed from them. It was also the first piece of his to be
printed in the public Soviet press during his time in the West. Some
editor must have considered it as pertinent in 1989 as the author thought
it was in 1974.

When Solzhenitsyn was shipped into exile, he became, in the words
of the *London Times*, "the man who is for the moment the most famous
person in the western world."[3] Cries of outrage against the Soviet
government's action were abundant, and mounds of telegrams and
letters in his support piled up for him. Nevertheless, the chorus of
approval was not universal.

The weightiest dissonant voice was that of Henry Kissinger, the U. S.
Secretary of State, whose reaction to Solzhenitsyn's expulsion was
emphatically tepid. He expressed the obligatory regret about the affair,
but the amorality of his posture of *realpolitik* was transparent when he
observed further:

> We do not know enough about the circumstances of the departure of Mr.
> Solzhenitsyn and the only problem that we have seen here is the extent to
> which our human, moral and critical concern for Mr. Solzhenitsyn and
> people of similar convictions would affect the day-to-day conduct of our
> foreign policy.

When pressed at his news conference, Kissinger allowed that Solzhenitsyn would be welcome to settle in the United States. (Imagine the
reaction had he said otherwise.) But he immediately added, "Our
constant view has been that the necessity for détente does not reflect
approbation of the Soviet domestic structure."[4]

Kissinger's mealy-mouthed response drew sharp rebukes. Senator Henry M. Jackson, Democrat from Washington state, charged that it "posed a false choice . . . between avoiding nuclear war and keeping faith with traditional values of human decency and individual liberty."[5] But President Nixon hewed to the Kissinger line. Shortly thereafter, American labor leader George Meany invited Solzhenitsyn to tour the United States under the auspices of the AFL-CIO, an offer which Solzhenitsyn received with gratitude but declined for the time being. Meanwhile, the administration devoted its energies to scuttling attempts in the Senate, led by Jesse Helms of North Carolina but with the co-sponsorship of twenty-four senators spanning the political spectrum, to bestow upon Solzhenitsyn honorary U.S. citizenship. Twice the senators tried, and twice the administration stymied them.

In the summer of 1975, Solzhenitsyn did accept the AFL-CIO invitation, and he came to the United States to deliver two speeches to the labor organization. He also spoke briefly in the Senate Office Building to some members of the Senate and the House of Representatives. Presumably, by then Kissinger had had time to learn "the circumstances of the departure of Mr. Solzhenitsyn." He recommended that Solzhenitsyn not be accorded honorary citizenship and also that the President, by then Gerald Ford, "not receive Solzhenitsyn" at the White House. In Kissinger's view, the social nicety of a courtesy call was not worth the risk of offending the Kremlin. Also in Kissinger's view (and from what sources did he get it?), "Solzhenitsyn is a notable writer, but his political views are an embarrassment even to his fellow dissidents."[6] In his turn, President Ford, like President Nixon before him, embraced Kissinger's view—in his own way. He called Solzhenitsyn "a goddam horse's ass." The President speculated that the author "wanted to visit the White House primarily to publicize his books and drum up lecture dates."[7]

Ford's snub of Solzhenitsyn met with uniform disapproval. Of five hundred letters and telegrams to the White House, not one was favorable. Columnist Anthony Lewis summed up the general mood: "The decision not to invite Aleksandr Solzhenitsyn to the White House has been deplored by now from all points of the ideological compass. For sheer political ineptitude it was in a special class. . . . Men will remember and read Aleksandr Solzhenitsyn when Gerald Ford is a footnote to history. . . ."[8] There was also political fallout. In the 1976 campaign for the Republican nomination for the presidency, Ronald Reagan proposed a plank to the convention entitled "Morality in Foreign Policy," which said in part, "We recognize and commend that great beacon of human courage and morality, Alexander Solzhenitsyn, for his compelling message that we must face the world with no illusions about the nature of tyranny."9

A mere five days after Solzhenitsyn's exile, William Safire published an odd column in which he seemed to wish to be on both sides of the fence at the same time. It opens, "I am the first on my block to feel misgivings about Alexander Solzhenitsyn." It moves on to predict, correctly, that the huge consensus in Solzhenitsyn's favor at the moment will quickly enough come apart: soon enough "the flip-flopping will begin." (Yet this column is nothing if not flip-flopping.) One theme in the article is the effort to cut Solzhenitsyn down to size. His Nobel speech is "not in the same league with William Faulkner's." And "the adversary of our adversary is not always our ally." The other theme in this essay suggests that "the Schweitzerization of Solzhenitsyn" will not last. "Then some against-the-grain profilists may report him to be crabbier, more messianic and less beatific than is customarily associated with sainthood, and today's intellectual inspiration may become tomorrow's former hero, the old champ who turns into a bore."10 So Safire at least serves the useful purpose of indicating the trendiness of the adulation of Solzhenitsyn at the time of his exile, an adulation based very little on knowledge of the man and his ideas.

Despite the general condemnation of the Soviet leaders, *Time* magazine observed that "the worldwide response was largely one of relief." The same article describes the decision as "a shrewdly calculated maneuver to rid themselves of their most eloquent critic while defusing the explosion of protest in the West."11 A week later, *Time* observed that "Solzhenitsyn's deportation created scarcely a dent in East-West relations," and it characterized official reactions:

Diplomats in most major European capitals generally agreed that the Soviets acted with a degree of restraint in exiling Solzhenitsyn rather than liquidating him. . . . One measure of détente, argued a high-ranking State Department official, is "that Solzhenitsyn is now speaking to the Western press and is not in Siberia or in prison."12

Robert Kaiser concurred in this sanguine appraisal: "Western opinion might accept exile as the least of the possible evils that could follow from Solzhenitsyn's arrest."[13]

This attitude is quite naive. Solzhenitsyn had written that exile abroad was "the equivalent of execution by shooting."[14] Later, he expressed his main fear: "that off Russian ground I am doomed to lose my feel for the Russian language."[15] And some insightful analyses did appear. An editorial in the *London Times* observed, "Of course a labor camp would have been worse in every obvious sense, and for that perhaps we should be duly grateful but it could have been less final, less spiritually damaging to Solzhenitsyn. . . ." The reason offered for this attitude was also fitting: "Yet Solzhenitsyn himself is about as far as one could imagine from the salon intellectual dabbling in foreign ideas. He draws his entire spiritual strength from the Russian soil."[16] Unlike most Western commentators, James J. Kilpatrick kept in mind the author's goal of changing his homeland and therefore commented more astutely than most: "If Solzhenitsyn had been executed or imprisoned the prospect might be different, but the Kremlin masters are brutal, not stupid. Exiles, even brilliant exiles, get to be tedious old men. Banishment was better."[17]

One tries to imagine what would have been the effects of other courses of action. Had Solzhenitsyn been sent to prison or internal exile, he would have been a hero to future generations and a rallying point for any budding movement of civic non-cooperation. Also, he probably would have found a way to keep writing. Had he been killed, however accidental it may have been made to look, he would have been a martyr to generations of Russians and an even more powerful rallying point. Had the government done nothing, the calf would have won and the oak would have lost. No, exile was the best way out for the government. Besides, he is a prickly fellow; let him be a burr under the saddle of the West. One Soviet leader reportedly "remarked to the effect that now he will be out of our hair and you Westerners will soon find him a bore, a nuisance and a neurotic, just as we did."[18] And even today we have no way of knowing to what extent his literary art might have been adversely affected by his exile. So fearful was he of living away from his homeland that he did not go to Stockholm in 1970 to receive his Nobel Prize. Exiling Solzhenitsyn had a placating effect on Western diplomats, who desperately wanted the process of so-called détente to continue undisrupted. It sentenced the author to a condition akin to spiritual death. The Soviet leaders won all the way around.

THE GENERAL MOOD of admiration and even adulation which enveloped Solzhenitsyn when he first came West quickly dissipated among the intellectuals of the West. Very shortly after the date of his exile, two works by Solzhenitsyn appeared in print almost simultaneously. One the critics knew was coming: *The Gulag Archipelago*. The other one, *Letter to the Soviet Leaders*, they did not.

On September 5, 1973, Solzhenitsyn sent a letter privately to the Kremlin leaders. He received no reply. Once in exile, he released it to the public; it appeared in Russian just days after his banishment. On March 3, 1974, the *London Times* carried an English translation of it, and it appeared in book form shortly thereafter. Thus, as soon as Solzhenitsyn arrived in the West, commentators had not only the dramatic events but also both *The Gulag Archipelago* and the *Letter to the Soviet Leaders* to take into account. All this was quite a bit to digest.

As John Dunlop has remarked, "The real watershed for liberals . . . was probably Solzhenitsyn's 'Letter to the Soviet Leaders.' " Dunlop cites a response by Harry Schwartz as typical:

> For over a decade now Western liberals and conservatives had debated uneasily about which camp could legitimately claim Aleksandr Solzhenitsyn as its own. . . . Now all doubt has been resolved. . . . In the strict sense of the word, he is a reactionary. . . . No one who reads this letter attentively can doubt that if Solzhenitsyn had been an American citizen in 1972 he would have voted for Richard Nixon against George McGovern. . . .[19]

One could, on this basis, have observed how much in tune with the American electorate Solzhenitsyn was. Rather, the moral generally drawn was how anti-Western he was. Of course, the great problem with Schwartz's analysis was that it sought to locate Solzhenitsyn within the spectrum of American political opinion. Though not all commentators were as explicit as Schwartz on this point, this beclouding approach, which annoyed Solzhenitsyn,[20] was indeed widespread.

Schwartz was at least correct that American conservatives did not react to the letter with the hostility that marked liberal reactions. William F. Buckley, Jr., considered it "an act of audacity unequaled in recorded history," found it "sublime in its impact," and remarked that it conveyed "a great vision to Soviet leaders, if only they would turn their attention inward." His piece concluded, "But his great epistle to the Russian leaders—an instant classic—will survive them all: and may yet be critical in ensuring the survival of the country he loves so deeply."[21]

Although few reviews appearing in the West were as generous as Buckley's column, some were at least evenhanded. One such is by Abraham Brumberg. He scores William Safire for writing in response to the letter "a piece [entitled "Aleks, Baby"[22]] distinguished as much by vulgarity as by ignorance," and he says about Western responses in general, "But disagreements are one thing, and primitive condemnations (or facile comparisons) another." In Brumberg's own view, the letter, "though in many respects curious and disturbing, is immensely powerful and entirely consistent with the author's previous writings." And he immediately adds, "Indeed, for all its faults (which Solzhenitsyn notes in his introduction, he is ready to correct if confronted with 'cogent and constructive criticism'), it may ultimately be regarded as one of the most important documents to come from the pen of a contemporary Russian writer." Although Brumberg finds that "Solzhenitsyn's practical suggestions are often oddly and hopelessly impractical," about the letter's analysis he concedes, "Yet stripped of their apocalyptic overtones and read simply as social criticism, Solzhenitsyn's angry words make sense." Moreover, Solzhenitsyn's ideas "have nothing in common with the xenophobia, anti-Semitism and philistine provincialism that characterize the thinking of many Soviet patriots today." If his isolation inhibits his appreciation of our electoral process, "A careful reading of Solzhenitsyn's *Letter* . . . makes it clear that he is not in principle opposed to democracy." According to Brumberg, Solzhenitsyn's widely touted anti-Western posture derives largely from "a reaction to the rampant cynicism and hypocrisy that he perceives in contemporary Western societies," and he remarks shrewdly that, similarly, "Alexander Herzen, the most Western-minded of all the 19th-century Russian writers, was revolted by many of Western Europe's democratic institutions."[23]

The review of the *Letter* by Richard and Judith Mills is a considerable cut above most—and for a very simple reason: they accept without prejudice the centrality of religion for Solzhenitsyn's world view; and so they discuss, as few have done, his indebtedness to Father Alexander Schmemann's explanation of his perspective. Also, they avoid the most common errors in analyzing the *Letter*, and they see what is wrong with many other reviews of it. For instance, they state, "The dissidents' criticisms of Soviet reality were easy for Westerners to accept when they coincided with those made in the West." Though to their taste nationalists and Slavophiles (and here they include Solzhenitsyn) have "anachronistic ways of perceiving things," they candidly acknowledge, "How one reacts to the *Letter* very much depends upon who one is." Apropos of the shocked reactions of some reviewers, the Millses assert, "Some of these ideas should come as no surprise to Western readers. They have been present in Solzhenitsyn's writings. . . . But only partially noticed, or even sometimes totally ignored, were the adumbrations of a positive program that emerges in the *Letter*." When Solzhenitsyn advocates the abandonment of Russian imperial designs, whether inside or outside Soviet borders, the Millses properly distinguish between him and both the Soviet leaders and some nationalists, "who, quite unlike Solzhenitsyn's nationalism of ethnic retrenchment, are partisans of empire." Finally, though they consider him a proponent of authoritarianism for Russia, they grant him this much: "Solzhenitsyn has asked a very old question in the history of political thought—what is the best form of government? His answer is that no one form is best *in practice* because governments must grow out of the character-people being governed."[24]

Jeri Laber's "The Real Solzhenitsyn" can serve as a *locus classicus* of the liberal animus against Solzhenitsyn spurred by the publication of the *Letter to the Soviet Leaders*. Discerning at the start what she calls "the authentically reactionary nature of Solzhenitsyn's political statements," she continues,

> Those who *have* remarked upon it have done so with surprise. Many Western admirers of his fight against despotism had considered Solzhenitsyn an advocate of liberal values and had, until the publication of the *Open Letter*, refused to acknowledge what should have been evident from a careful reading of his fiction and his earlier political pronounce-

ments. Steeped in a mysticism distinctively Russian, shaped by circumstances peculiarly Soviet, Solzhenitsyn has evolved a unique, eccentric viewpoint.[25]

When Laber says that readers of Solzhenitsyn's earlier works should not have been surprised by this letter's offenses against liberalism, since they were evident all along, she convicts herself out of her own mouth. As we saw in the preceding chapter, she had high praise for *The First Circle* and its author. Nowhere in her review of *August 1914*, in this essay, or in a contemporaneous piece which we shall examine next does she acknowledge that she once praised Solzhenitsyn. In fact, one letter-writer in response to this essay declares, "In contrast to Mrs. Laber, I regard *The First Circle* as a great novel. . . ."[26] How was he to know?

Laber's animus encompasses Solzhenitsyn's art, his world view, and (most strenuously) his person. About his art, Laber now asserts, "His work, for the most part, is didactic, as he intends it to be, and it is often dull and ponderous." She takes unseemly pleasure in suggesting that "Solzhenitsyn is probably one of the least read of best-selling novelists," and she continues in a vein which brazenly magnifies her unacknowledged self-condemnation:

Despite the inflated praise he has received from Western reviewers, whose admiration for Solzhenitsyn's courage is often mistakenly expressed as esteem for his works, many Western readers appear to find his novels heavy-handed, humorless, and monotonous. Solzhenitsyn's characters lack dimension: his heroes are all passive. . . . The political and philosophical theories for which the novels serve as vehicles are oversimplified and irritatingly presented with a repetitious, self-indulgent verbosity.[27]

Only *One Day in the Life of Ivan Denisovich* gets a small escape clause from this general denunciation; not *The First Circle*!

As for his world view, Laber seems most eager to show persons on the Left that Solzhenitsyn is not one of them: "Reactionary, authoritarian, chauvinistic—hardly adjectives that sit comfortably with the typical image of a freedom-fighter and Nobel Prize winner." It displeases her that "Solzhenitsyn blames not Stalin but Marxism itself for the system that destroyed millions of his countrymen. . . ." In short, Solzhenitsyn is excoriated for not taking the Western liberals' benign view of Marxist ideology. And what would he have instead of Marxism? "Definitely *not* Western democracy." Instead, she espies "his belief in authoritarianism" and his "chauvinistic dream for the Russia of the future."[28]

Laber is equally misguided concerning Solzhenitsyn's moral vision, starting with his "view of human nature": "Like the characters in his novels, people for him are essentially good or bad." His embrace of religion is seen only as the move of an "authentic reactionary," which merits belittling commentary: "While in prison he had become a very religious man. He saw the ordeals that he had survived as trials devised by God to strengthen his moral character." Some people, and not only religious believers, might find a certain nobility here. Not Laber. She sees him "evidently preparing for martyrdom." Soon we come upon this snide comment: "And the unwavering self-assurance with which he has pursued his own goal demonstrates Solzhenitsyn's personal identification with 'the righteous'—a very select company." Believers, who do understand the category "the righteous," might look here for some reference to divine grace, as would be befitting. They will not find it in Laber. Instead, they will find only an attribution of egotism: Solzhenitsyn believes himself qualified "for membership in the spiritual elite."[29]

Commentary published four letters of reply. The one by Donald W. Treadgold was particularly incisive. He declared Laber's essay

> to be gravely mistaken in its content and to represent a series of misconceptions that may be current in various quarters for various reasons, not least because we have trained a generation of Soviet specialists who are strong on their understanding of the political side and weak on the side of culture, especially religion. . . .

In particular, he commented, "In our time Christian writers cannot expect a reception based on an understanding of their position."[30]

Laber was little chastened by these critical letters. She does grant a few qualifiers, but her overall reaction is pugnacious: "Rather than making me feel that I have gone too far, their letters lead me to believe that I have not gone far enough, not only in explaining *why* I have used these adjectives ['reactionary, authoritarian, and chauvinistic'] but in pointing out why I find the views that they characterize potentially dangerous." To Norman Gelman, "the only correspondent who agrees with me about something," she does mention, belatedly, that she had praised *The First Circle*.[31]

It was specifically in response to Laber's "The Real Solzhenitsyn" that Kathryn Feuer wrote,

> Solzhenitsyn's patriotism, his Christianity, his refusal to summon the Russian population to take up their pitchforks against their armed government, his unwillingness to demand nothing less than immediate parliamentary democracy from rulers who have waded to power through corpses, all this has dismayed many Western liberals, as have his trenchant criticisms of their double standard by which Soviet mass atrocities are regarded as less scandalous than democracies' misdemeanors or authoritarian governments' individual atrocities.[32]

Jeri Laber's second article from this time, startlingly entitled "The Selling of Solzhenitsyn," reiterates and reinforces points she had already made. Referring to his "misleadingly 'liberal' image," she asserts that "he is not the 'liberal' we would like him to be." Though she says that this fact "should not really matter," it seems to matter a great deal to her, for she keeps making the same point: "Solzhenitsyn's beliefs are, in fact, quite alien to Western liberal thought. He condemns Marxism not as a democrat but as an elitist, deriding Western democracy and scorning its 'decadence.' " The main burden of this article is to debunk the heroic image we have of Solzhenitsyn "[a]s a media creature." Here Laber verges on alleging conspiracy:

> As if by tacit consent, the press and the public have been satisfied not to probe the established image of Solzhenitsyn. The absence of detailed information about Solzhenitsyn's life has facilitated this; it has been encouraged by Solzhenitsyn's own use of the media for his urgent purposes; and it has been welcomed by a public that longs for authentic heroes.

If the press and the public must shoulder their share of the blame, the lion's share falls to Solzhenitsyn himself. He is to be faulted for the apparent inconsistency of combining "his own eccentric reticence" about his private life with efforts "to use the Western press to publicize his writings and his views."[33] In short, if we knew "the real Solzhenitsyn," rather than the image he is "selling," we would not find him so heroic.

In the summer of 1974, Timothy Foote observed, "The going literary view . . . is that Solzhenitsyn's fame depends on politics more than art, that Solzhenitsyn is a great man, but not a great writer."[34] Yet at this very time, the media consensus that he is a great man was breaking up. Attempts to blacken his personal reputation had been underway, and viciously, in the Soviet media throughout the late sixties. I suggest only a parallel and not direct influence when I observe that in 1974, with Laber as the most forthright example, a loosely similar effort to undermine Solzhenitsyn's stature as an admirable figure was commencing.

Jeri Laber was far from alone in her hostile response to the *Letter to the Soviet Leaders*. Nan Robertson, in the *New York Times*, piles up her own list of adjectives: "messianic, patriotic, utopian and religious in tone; anti-democratic, anti-Western." The utopianism refers in particular to his ecological concerns, where Robertson is careful to make her distinctions: "Mr. Solzhenitsyn reveals himself as not just an environmentalist in the current mode, but a utopian in the grand Russian tradition." In the *current* mode? Solzhenitsyn, she says, wants to "go back to the electric automobile." *Back*? He is out of step and isolated: "a seared soul, a burning mind, an old-fashioned idealist, a classic Russian patriot—and alone."[35]

Robertson also brought to light that, from the initial version of the *Letter* to the published version, Solzhenitsyn had "deleted and softened some denunciations of Western democracy."[36] Her cataloguing of details is designed to imply that Solzhenitsyn exercised self-censorship in order to curry favor in the West. The obvious rejoinder is that the second version was sent to a different readership, and good writers are always aware of their audience. Moreover, the plain fact is that every single point deleted—the criticism of Daniel Ellsberg, the West's inability to deal with terrorists, every single point—appeared in other speeches and interviews over the next few years. Indeed, it is very odd to suggest that this supremely plainspoken man is guilty of pulling his punches. The more common (and legitimate) complaint has been that he is sometimes blunt to the point of tactlessness.

Anthony Astrachan added his voice to the chorus of disapproval of the *Letter*. Writing for the *Christian Science Monitor* News Service, he says that Solzhenitsyn "is no liberal" and notes his "contempt for the Western world." He charges that Solzhenitsyn's "nationalism verges on chauvinism and racism though it never falls into the abyss." If he is not chauvinist or racist, why bring up these odious labels at all? Astrachan does grant that Solzhenitsyn favors "giving up Russian hegemony over

Eastern Europe and most of the non-Russian parts of the Soviet Union."[37] One might hope for some small word of approval here, but none is forthcoming. In fact, Western responses to the *Letter* paid almost no attention to Solzhenitsyn's advice to the Soviet leaders to set the captive nations free.

Another voice in the negative chorus is that of Jonathan Yardley, of Knight Newspapers. His column opens, "It is time to come to grips with Alexander I. Solzhenitsyn. For more than a decade, the Russian author has accepted his image as a modern saint uncomplainingly." As with Laber, so with Yardley, in his attempt "to separate the man from the myth," most of the blame for the alleged Western misperception accrues to Solzhenitsyn himself.

> He is adroit at self-promotion, and has skillfully used the western press both to enhance his "image" and to advance his own purposes. There is no evidence that he is offended or embarrassed by those who would portray him as the Joan of Arc of the Russian intelligentsia.

We read, predictably, that "he is neither a 'liberal' or a 'democrat.'" We read also that he is "a not-very-thinly disguised Czarist."[38] If just a little bit disguised, how and where?

Shortly after Western reviews of the *Letter to the Soviet Leaders* began to appear, Solzhenitsyn granted an interview to the Associated Press to express his reaction to them. He objected to what he called "primitive and even mistaken interpretations" of his *Letter*. Noting that the press described his views as "nationalism," "utopianism," and "a call to return to the past," he asserted, "in this way the press is capable of introducing incomprehension between distant parts of the planet rather than internal understanding." Also, he called for direct contact between the peoples of the USSR and the USA, since "mutual understanding between the peoples of my country and the United States is . . . very difficult to establish from afar using the superficial and often insufficiently thought out judgments of the daily press."[39]

THE FIRST VOLUME OF *The Gulag Archipelago* was published by the Russian-language YMCA Press in Paris on December 29, 1973. That day the *New York Times* carried the first installment of a three-part excerpt from it. The whole work had been in virtually complete form by 1968; Solzhenitsyn had begun researching it in 1958 and writing it in 1964. The first volume was published in English translation shortly after Solzhenitsyn's exile. At his insistence it was initially published in inexpensive paperback as well as hard cover. Its sales were sensational; more than three million copies of the first volume have been purchased in the United States, most of them early.

Its initial reception by Western reviewers, unlike that of the roughly contemporaneous *Letter to the Soviet Leaders*, was marked by considerable warmth and approval. *Time* magazine commented, "*Gulag* struck its early readers as both a literary masterpiece and an unparalleled indictment of the Soviet regime."[40] On the other hand, some reviews were noticeably cool, with praise which seemed more obligatory than heartfelt and with quibbles about points of factual accuracy. One wonders what dampening effect carried over from the negative reviews of *August 1914* and *Letter to the Soviet Leaders*. However strange it may seem, the publication of *Gulag* does not mark a decisive moment in the story of Western media reactions to Solzhenitsyn; with some exceptions, notably in France, it did little to rehabilitate the image of Solzhenitsyn among intellectuals.

It seems to have taken any hard edge off of Western responses to *The Gulag Archipelago* that Roy Medvedev, a fellow dissident but a Leninist, praised the book. His review reached the West even before Solzhenitsyn was exiled; and Robert Kaiser, in the *Washington Post*, called it "a rave review."[41] *Ramparts*, a New Left magazine, published excerpts from it.[42] Medvedev said, "I cannot accept certain of Solzhenitsyn's assessments or conclusions. But it must be said emphatically that all the basic facts in his book . . . are completely authentic." Medvedev's sharpest disagreement is about Lenin and his legacy, but it results in no disrespect: ". . . the general result of Lenin's work, I am convinced, is positive. Solzhenitsyn thinks otherwise. That is his right." Although he finds no appeal in the religious path that Solzhenitsyn has chosen, Medvedev says merely, "Having passed all of the cruel trials that are described with such merciless truth in *Gulag Archipelago*, Solzhenitsyn lost his faith in Marxism. Solzhenitsyn has betrayed or sold out no one. Today he is an opponent of Marxism, and he does not hide that."[43]

George Kennan's review is masterful, at times luminous. He is aware that "[t]he book has its faults," which led some reviewers to cavil and quibble, but he comments, "Considering the circumstances under which it must have been written, the only occasion for surprise is that it does not have more of them." Accepting the book on its own terms as moral and not political, he declares, "The supreme value of the work lies in its exemplary quality—its quality as an example of ruthless and fearless honesty in the exploration of the weaknesses in one's own personal behavior and in one's own society." Recognizing that "[i]t will shake the whole structure of Soviet power as heretofore known," he predicts, in words that now sound prophetic,

> It is too large for the craw of the Soviet propaganda machine. It will stick there, with increasing discomfort, until it has done its work.
> And what is this work, as Solzhenitsyn perceives it? It is, surely, to restore the integrity of the Russian conscience; to compel the Soviet regime to come to terms, at long last, with its own history . . . to identify the basic flaws in the system that permitted it to happen; and then to set about . . . to eradicate those flaws. . . .[44]

Likewise, Harrison Salisbury eschews the political prism in his review of *The Gulag Archipelago*. Recognizing Solzhenitsyn's sense of "a mission to seek the truth and to right wrongs," Salisbury explains that, because of imprisonment, "Solzhenitsyn's sense of mission became fixed upon awakening the Russian people to the inhumanity which the Soviet regime had wrought." In his role as critic of society, Solzhenitsyn is squarely in the line of Pushkin, Dostoevsky, Turgenev, Tolstoy, and Gorky, says Salisbury; and he adds that in Russia "the intelligentsia are well aware that Solzhenitsyn is a figure in the mainstream of Russian history and culture." Salisbury concludes his review with this ringing peroration:

> Against the powerful state stands a single man. . . . The odds against Solzhenitsyn seem tremendous. Yet I know of no Russian writer who would not trade his soul for Solzhenitsyn's mantle, who does not know that one hundred years from now all the world (including the Russian world) will bow to his name when most others have been forgotten. . . . I think the fear within the Russian leadership at Solzhenitsyn's voice is justified. . . . He will be heard.[45]

Robert Conquest's review was similarly warm. He hailed *The Gulag Archipelago* as "a truly exceptional work: For in it literature transcends history, without distorting it." This review valuably demonstrates how much the works of others, including Conquest himself, corroborate what Solzhenitsyn says. Unlike many other Sovietologists, Conquest is sympathetic to Solzhenitsyn's total break with "the myth of a constructive and humane Lenin." Also, he seconds Solzhenitsyn's contrast between the brutality of the commissars and that of the czars: "And, in peacetime, at the height of the terror, a *minimum* of just under a million were executed in two years—that is, a rate about *fifty thousand times* as great as that of sixty years of czardom back to Nicholas I!"[46] Bringing this factual information to public attention no more makes Conquest an apologist for the czars than it does Solzhenitsyn.

There was, however, another register in the Western reviews of *The Gulag Archipelago*. It was not one of denunciation. Rather, it was one of lukewarm praise, often seeming forced and perfunctory, followed by a focusing on alleged errors of historical analysis. And the least forgivable error (though Roy Medvedev did not find it a major distraction from his praise of the book) was Solzhenitsyn's straight-line linkage of Lenin and Stalin.

Thus, Joshua Rubenstein said, "Solzhenitsyn's uncompromising hatred of the Soviet regime occasionally leaves him purblind or indifferent to several historical judgments generally accepted in the West." There is not a flicker of a suggestion that perhaps the received opinions of Western scholars should be modified. Among Solzhenitsyn's "inadequate historical judgments," Rubenstein features the relationship between Lenin and Stalin: "Neither Lenin nor Bukharin, of course, were democrats; they both believed in dictatorship. Still, it is historically inaccurate for Solzhenitsyn to claim that Stalin merely inherited a political program from Lenin and then carried it to its logical conclusion." (Why do many Western critics consider it much more excusable for Lenin than for Solzhenitsyn to be deemed no democrat?) Viewing Solzhenitsyn through political lenses inevitably gets him wrong on moral matters, too. Thus, we read that, unlike Dostoevsky, "Solzhenitsyn discourages a belief that the prisoners' spiritual awakening might reflect the possibilities of change in the society at-large"—and, further, that "Solzhenitsyn is not the first Russian to mistrust the moral attitude of his fellow citizens."[47] Solzhenitsyn has devoted his life to nurturing a movement of moral and spiritual renewal among the Russian people; but, with vision befogged by political differences, Rubenstein misses this biggest of points.

There is a similar majoring in minor points in Stephen Cohen's review. While granting that Solzhenitsyn's "reconstruction" of historical information about the Gulag system is "a heroic accomplishment under Soviet conditions," Cohen is quick to point out, "Not all of Solzhenitsyn's information about larger political affairs can be taken at face-value." He does concede, "These are minor points, though, and do not diminish their truthfulness of Solzhenitsyn's account." What most displeases him is what he considers Solzhenitsyn's erroneous political analysis of the Soviet experience: "Leaving aside the fact that Soviet 'ideology' has undergone radical changes over the years, and that Solzhenitsyn essentially equates Marxism with Stalinism, his general explanation . . . is one-dimensional and selective in its historical evidence." In addition, Cohen takes Solzhenitsyn to task for the "one-sidedness" of his view of Lenin: "Most Western historians would at least agree that Lenin's legacy was ambiguous." As he moves toward his conclusion, Cohen wants his readers to be sure to understand that "Solzhenitsyn's outlook does not reflect the whole, or perhaps even a major part, of dissident thinking in the Soviet Union today," and he duly mentions Sakharov and Roy Medvedev.[48] The problem with this review lies less in Cohen's disagreement with Solzhenitsyn's perspective on Soviet politics than in the selection of concerns to highlight as the ones central to *Gulag*. He simply has not caught the spirit of Solzhenitsyn's fundamentally moral vision.

Similarly soft in its praise but firm in its criticism is Priscilla Macmillan's review. In her view, *The Gulag Archipelago* "is not a literary masterpiece. Solzhenitsyn's moralism, his strong sense of 'ought,' gets in his way as an imaginative artist." (A strong "ought" characterizes Dostoevsky, Tolstoy, and much of the Russian literary tradition.) "Nor," Macmillan continues, "is the book an historical masterpiece— as some critics claim. Solzhenitsyn is only diminished as an historian when he suggests, for example, that the Soviet penal system sprang more or less entirely from the head of Lenin, with flourishes added on by Stalin." She thinks that the 1891 account of Tsarist penal colonies written by George Kennan (forebear of the policymaker whose review of *Gulag* is cited above) "simply dwarfs Solzhenitsyn in the precision of its reporting, and the meticulous fairness of its judgments." Macmillan's view of Russian history emphasizes that "as Kennan reminds us . . . key abuses of the Soviet era have their origins in Tsarist times." Stalin outdid his predecessors, "[b]ut the historical precedent, and a frightful one it was, went back to the Tsars."[49] Kennan the reviewer did refer to his forebear's book, but his emphasis is quite different from Macmillan's. Says he, ". . . what Solzhenitsyn is here describing is a phenomenon not only much worse (Kennan would have found this hard to believe) in degree of inhumanity but also greater in scale, by a factor of several hundred times, than the comparable phenomenon that presented itself to Kennan's view."[50]

George Steiner's review also emphasizes the negative. "Moral genius cannot be separated from intelligence, from the power to inform judgment through a constant, life-giving sense of discrimination. At key points in 'The Gulag Archipelago,' this intelligence is lacking." Steiner particularly objects to Solzhenitsyn's recurring use of "they" for the perpetrators of brutality and "we" for the victims; he seems unaware that this is universal usage in the Soviet Union, not an invention by Solzhenitsyn. "There is a terrible truth" in this diagnosis by Solzhenitsyn, but "there is, as well, a drastic oversimplification." Steiner observes, also, "Khrushchev's thesis, which has become the current Soviet orthodoxy, was that the abuses of justice under Stalinism were the direct consequence of the personality of the dictator. . . . 'The Gulag Archipelago' utterly rejects this version of history."[51] In emphasizing the linkages from Lenin through Stalin to Khrushchev and his successors, Solzhenitsyn is out of step with both Soviet orthodoxy and revisionist Western Sovietology. And Steiner is not alone among Western intellectuals in preferring Khrushchev's historical analysis to Solzhenitsyn's.

IN 1975 AND 1976, Solzhenitsyn gave speeches and interviews in the United States and Great Britain, which certainly did not contribute to a refurbishing of his image among the West's cultural elite. Also around this time, the rest of *The Gulag Archipelago* was published in English, the second volume in 1975 and the third in 1978. These served as reminders that Solzhenitsyn was not only, or primarily, a polemicist, but that he was a historical chronicler and literary interpreter of the Soviet experience.

Although the second half of the decade of the 1970's produced many disparaging articles about Solzhenitsyn, the reviews of the *Gulag* volumes themselves remained largely appreciative. The reviews of Volume II by Leonard Schapiro in the *New York Review of Books*, by Lionel Abel in *Commentary*, and by Patricia Blake in the *New York Times Book Review* are good examples.[52] In particular, Blake drew attention to the corrective available in this volume to the solidifying consensus against Solzhenitsyn. As she was aware, "Uneasiness among many of his admirers grew into dismay as he offered instruction, judgments and proposals intended to reverse the course of East-West relations." However, " 'Gulag II' comes to us now as a reminder of Solzhenitsyn's immutable achievements." She was especially at pains to point out that, "[a]lthough it has become the fashion to dismiss 'Gulag' as 'nothing new,' this is, in fact, the first time that the entire range of the calamity has been recounted—and by a great *Russian* writer."[53]

The third volume of *The Gulag Archipelago* also received largely favorable reviews—from such reviewers as Adam Ulam, Patricia Blake, Hilton Kramer, Robert Conquest, and even (for the most part) Alfred Kazin.[54] Abraham Brumberg's review, however, was a kind of defection. He makes some effort to bring the evenhandedness evident in his review of the *Letter to the Soviet Leaders* to his review of this volume, but the balance now tips toward the negative. "It would be as inexcusable to ignore its flaws as to underrate its searing achievements." In particular, he raises questions about Solzhenitsyn's character. "Where, one sometimes wonders, is Solzhenitsyn's charity and compassion—the two qualities he prizes so highly? And what explains his venomous and often fatuous polemical attacks on Western 'liberals'?" His answer, already used by others to denigrate the person of the author, is that "in some essential respects he is very much a creature of the system he so passionately loathes."[55]

Brumberg's review elicited three rejoinders, which had no chastening effect on him, as his reply to them shows. Delba Winthrop explained, "Solzhenitsyn faults Western liberals not so much for their liberalism as for their failure adequately to defend liberty in fact and principle. . . ."[56] Charles H. Fairbanks, Jr., of Yale University, exclaimed, "I was astonished to see Abraham Brumberg in his review of *The Gulag Archipelago*, Volume III, joining the campaign that has been going on for two or three years to discredit, or perhaps to tame, Solzhenitsyn." Fairbanks concludes,

> Like many Americans, I do not know exactly what to think of Solzhenitsyn, and some of the things he has said were not what I most wanted to hear. But that seems all the more reason to consider them thoughtfully. Mr. Brumberg's review, on the other hand, is not only thoughtless but a call for thoughtlessness.[57]

The essays, speeches, and interviews which Solzhenitsyn delivered from 1974 to 1976 only confirmed the worst fears of those in the West who had been distressed by the *Letter to the Soviet Leaders*. These include his three essays in *From Under the Rubble* (1974), his 1974 interview for American television by Walter Cronkite, three speeches in the United States in the summer of 1975, and an interview and speech for the British Broadcasting Corporation in March of 1976. Invitations to speak to Western audiences were invitations to speak about his view of the West, and he complied.

Robert Conquest devotes his essay "Solzhenitsyn in the British Media" to precisely these three years. On the very day that Solzhenitsyn arrived in the West, *The Guardian* greeted him by noting "a new bitterness" in his voice: "More and more he has appeared to be a lonely, cussed, and at times arrogant man." The next day, Stanley Reynolds asserted in the same newspaper that passages of his *Nobel Lecture* "sound very much like moral rearmament propaganda" and declared him "not a liberal." The day thereafter, *The Times Literary Supplement* cautioned, "There is nothing of a western democratic programme, of western enlightenment about Solzhenitsyn's position." A few weeks later, in the *Sunday Times*, Alan Brien asked rhetorically if Solzhenitsyn was "a crank" and called the *Letter to the Soviet Leaders* a "collection of inflammatory half-truths." In Conquest's judgment, an editorial in *The Observer* "summed up the tone of such attacks admirably":

> An affinity has been growing up between some Western journalists and those intellectuals in Moscow and Warsaw who, while proclaiming themselves liberals and not men of the regime, speak debunkingly of the leading Soviet dissidents. Their line on Solzhenitsyn is identical.

He is a brave man and no doubt admirable, but . . . and then they make the fact that he has become a Christian imply that he is also an apologist for the Orthodox church. . . . [H]is plea that Western intellectuals should take as much interest in the repressive acts of the Soviet regime as in those of non-Communist dictatorships is twisted to suggest that he actually sympathizes with the latter; his nostalgia for Russian history is represented as a soft spot for the Tsar, and so on.

Too seldom was Solzhenitsyn greeted with the respectful disagreement of Francis Hope in *The New Statesman*:

I deeply disagree with much of what I can discern of Solzhenitsyn's political views. . . . But . . . I must pay attention to what he says. Even when I have made allowance for . . . the religious beliefs which I do not share, for the rhetorical exaggerations and the unreal aspirations . . . I am left with something which cannot be absorbed even into my own privileged view of the world.[58]

British reports on Solzhenitsyn's 1975 visit to the United States hit a new low in Simon Winchester's reporting for *The Guardian*. Winchester claimed astonishment that certain people have "expressed hurt belief that some observers had actually had the temerity to query the hysterical author's mental stability."[59] Expressions such as this brought forth a defense by Bernard Levin, who, along with Malcolm Muggeridge, was the most ardent British admirer of Solzhenitsyn; it was entitled "Solzhenitsyn Among the Pygmies."[60]

In March 1976, the BBC carried a television interview and a radio talk by Solzhenitsyn. About the television performance Robert Conquest observed, ". . . those whom he now made his antagonists had a disproportionate influence in the media, and their animus now lay in wait for him." And it is true that most of the press coverage was hostile. The *Daily Mirror* even entitled a column "Solzhenitwit." Letters to editors told a different story, however. One D. Bernard Hadley wrote to *The Times*:

How small our national leaders look before the towering figure of Solzhenitsyn. How petty our internal problems seem in the face of the fundamental questions which he poses about the very survival of our way of life.

I was moved by Solzhenitsyn in his interview on BBC 1's *Panorama* as I have never been moved by any politician or philosopher living.[61]

Bernard Levin said that he had received "a flood of letters, the theme of which, all the time, has been: 'Thank God somebody has said this, somebody has expressed what *we* are feeling, rather than these unrepresentative people who command so much of the public voices in this country.' " He cited one particular letter, which he called "absolutely representative":

Solzhenitsyn spoke on *Panorama* and somehow the world of communication had been changed. The power of the little men, our pundits, evaporated. No use their complaining about Solzhenitsyn's pessimism or ignorance, or lack of subtle understanding of our nuances: we saw the measure of the man, and we silently and almost unconsciously compared it with the others, and the clear superiority of the one over the many was as obvious as the difference between day and night.[62]

Also in 1976, *Atlas World Press Review* took note of "The Solzhenitsyn Controversy" by carrying three pieces under that rubric. Bernard Levin, while not a religious believer, saw Solzhenitsyn as "a man in a state of grace." Levin's contribution states his overarching view of the author's significance:

What can we do about the presence in our midst of such men as Alexander Solzhenitsyn? Well, first what *do* we do? We turn away in embarrassment—an embarrassment that rises to act as a protection against the pain of admitting both that he is right in his analysis of evil, and that his very existence is a reproach to our society embedded as it is in the granite of his faith. I do not believe (though presumably he does) that faith has to be a religious faith to be effective; but what is wrong with the West—and one can sense in his condemnation of us that it is this which excites his anger and contempt, more even than the strategic, political, and moral retreat in which the West is engaged—is that we do not even have the courage of our secular convictions, we do not seem to care enough about our liberty to be willing to consider that it is under assault and to think about ways of sustaining it, indeed to consider that it *ought* to be sustained.[63]

Edward Crankshaw, while finding Solzhenitsyn "unerring in matters of the spirit," recited a litany of familiar criticisms. Solzhenitsyn does not "really like the West . . . does not like our basic ways"; "he is not democratic by nature"; he "thinks far too much in terms of Marxist ideology as the key to Russian actions."[64]

The judgment of Octavio Paz, Mexican poet and diplomat, fell between those of Levin and Crankshaw; it was mixed but respectful. For instance, while disagreeing with Solzhenitsyn about Christianity, he grants that "Solzhenitsyn's Christianity is neither dogmatic nor inquisitorial." And Paz objects to the simple rejections of Solzhenitsyn.

> To be sure, his logic often doesn't convince me and his intellectual style is alien to my habits of mind, my esthetic tastes, and even my moral convictions. . . . However, Solzhenitsyn's direct and simple gaze penetrates the present and unmasks what is hidden. . . . There is a prophetic element in his writings that I don't find in any other of my contemporaries.[65]

Solzhenitsyn's three speeches in the United States in 1975, two for the AFL-CIO and one to Congress, were greeted in the press mostly with resistance. Norman Cousins, who was an interviewer on a "Meet the Press" appearance by Solzhenitsyn while he was in America, "resent[ed] his reference . . . to Franklin D. Roosevelt and Winston Churchill as 'cowardly' " for truckling to Stalin. Like many others, Cousins preferred the pre-exile Solzhenitsyn: "In the Soviet Union his dissent was majestic, but it is the fact of that dissent even more than the substance of it that gives him his claim on history." He concluded on a note by now wearisomely familiar: "Solzhenitsyn's problem is . . . that he is anachronistic. . . ."[66]

The November/December 1975 issue of *Society* reprinted the two AFL-CIO speeches under the title "Détente and Democracy." Following them were seven reactions to the speeches.[67] Only the essay by Irving Louis Horowitz was not predominantly negative.[68]

Richard Lowenthal grants that "Solzhenitsyn is a great writer and one of the outstanding moral personalities of our time," then expresses his "shock at finding myself in almost total disagreement with Solzhenitsyn's views on the past, present and future of Western relations with the Soviet Union." He elaborates:

> But I have read his Washington speech with feelings mixed of fascina-
> tion, amazement and shock: fascination at the nearly seemless [*sic*]
> consistency of his vision of world affairs, amazement at its utter disac-
> cord with the facts of recent international history and shock at the radical
> moral wrongness of the position he has now taken on questions upon
> which the survival of mankind may depend.[69]

The essay then discusses strategic considerations primarily, with Lowenthal holding out for the necessity of the *realpolitik* approach in the
quest for détente.

A common thread running through these responses in *Society* is the
notion of the moral equivalence between the USSR and the USA, an
analytical framework with considerable currency in the 1970's. Thus,
Melvin Gurtov accuses Solzhenitsyn of "fueling another anti-
Communist crusade," and he notes with displeasure that "he has cast
the Union of Soviet Socialist Republics as the consistent villain in
international politics. . . . As for the United States, he seems unaware of
the American share of responsibility for bringing on the cold war
between 1945 and 1947. . . ."[70] Similarly, Amitai Etzioni laments that
Solzhenitsyn, while personally courageous, "is nonetheless so wrong-
headed in his counsel to the United States." After all, "the Soviet Union
is presently not a genocidal sinner"; furthermore, "If nations were to be
barred from sitting down at the international bargaining table or participating in the world community on the basis of their past sins against
democracy and human rights, then the United States would also be
prohibited from taking a seat."[71]

Lynn Turgeon emphasizes a point made by other contributors to this
symposium: that "repression today is far less than it was under Stalin."
For example, as for the fate of the Estonian, Latvian, and Lithuanian
peoples, Turgeon finds it "difficult . . . to muster up any great sympathy
for their 'plight.' . . . It is no exaggeration to say that these talented
peoples have never enjoyed comparable well-being—thanks primarily
to their peaceful employment operations under the Soviet nuclear umbrella."[72] Similarly easygoing toward the Communists, Norman Birnbaum scores Solzhenitsyn's "Manichean world view" and "the
antihistorical quality of [his] position": "His prescriptions for an end to
the Soviet regime take us back to a Russian ideology remote from

liberalism. Indeed, many of the abhorrent features of the Soviet regime stem from its historical continuity with the czarist state."[73]

In summary, these responses criticize Solzhenitsyn for telling the West to be strong. Shortly, in response to his commencement address at Harvard University, Solzhenitsyn was to be criticized for telling the West that it is weak. Whichever of these notes he sounded, it did not sit well with Western opinion-shapers.

In 1976, Hedrick Smith, who had served as Moscow correspondent for his newspaper, the *New York Times*, published a highly readable and very popular book entitled *The Russians*. His view of Solzhenitsyn serves as a neat summary of the received opinion established among Western intellectuals by the mid-seventies.

> The West has fallen into belated disenchantment with Aleksandr Solzhenitsyn. . . . People were disconcerted that the heroic dissident who had documented the terrors of a police state should also scorn democracy. It became a nuisance that he was such a moral absolutist, so obsessed with his holy mission to purge Mother Russia of Stalinism and Marxism that he would not stay the volcanic flow of his works when foreigners were sated. It was a shock that when his own manifesto appeared, it offered not a model of an open, urban, scientific society joining the modern world but a mystic vision of a future-past. . . . Westerners, quick to focus on dissent from the left in their own image, too easily disposed to ignore the Russian right, found his prescription awkwardly archaic.

How easily Smith makes synonyms of "Westerners" and "the left." No wonder he describes the *Letter to the Soviet Leaders* as "the most stridently anti-Communist statement by a major Russian figure since the Revolutionary period" and its author as "a religious fundamentalist."[74]

The distance between Solzhenitsyn's world view and that which Western intellectuals could find within the pale of acceptability was perceptible to some by 1972 and clear to most by 1974. Between 1974 and 1976, a consensus view disparaging Solzhenitsyn—in his politics, in his art, in his person—had been fleshed out. When he spoke at Harvard in 1978, he provided the conclusive piece of evidence to confirm that his world view was anathema to the Western intelligentsia.

5

Western Critics (III)
From 1978

SOLZHENITSYN AND HIS FAMILY MOVED from Zurich, Switzerland, to Cavendish, Vermont, in the summer of 1976. Immediate benefits of the move were a quiet place to live and access to the rich library holdings in the United States. Hardly had the family settled in, however, when newspaper articles appeared featuring prominently the fence surrounding the fifty-acre property and the television camera trained on the gate. The tenor of these articles was to the effect that Solzhenitsyn somehow felt a need to be fenced in and that he had an inordinate concern about security. The article by Charles Leroux, of the *Chicago Tribune*, carried the headline "Solzhenitsyn Makes Freedom a Prison"; that by William Claiborne, of the *Washington Post*, was entitled "Solzhenitsyn's Barbed-Wire Freedom."[1] As Solzhenitsyn was soon to explain at a Cavendish town meeting, the chain-link fence was designed to keep out snowmobilers and hunters and also to discourage Soviet agents from harassing him.[2] Michael Scammell notes that "death threats had already been slipped under his gate."[3] Later, for a *Vermont Life* feature article, Mrs. Solzhenitsyn was to add journalists to this list of unwanted intruders.[4]

The *Vermont Life* article conveys well the pleasant social intercourse that prevails between the Solzhenitsyns and the other residents in and around Cavendish. The three sons have ridden yellow schoolbuses to American public schools, the family stops at the general store and post office in town, and they worship at a Russian Orthodox church twenty miles away in Claremont, New Hampshire. Invited guests, including some locals, frequent the home, and Russian-speakers gather occasionally for church services in the chapel that Solzhenitsyn included when he had his library building constructed adjacent to the house. Yet even today many think that there is something odd about the way the Solzhenitsyn family lives in America, and that sense of estrangement seems to emanate from those early articles by the likes of Leroux and Claiborne. I think that such articles, whatever their motivations, have done more damage to Solzhenitsyn's reputation among non-intellectuals than everything else written about him put together.

My personal experience at the Solzhenitsyn home was exactly the same as that reported by Bernard Pivot, a French television interviewer:

> Upon returning to Paris, the one question we were being asked everywhere was: Is it true that Solzhenitsyn has built for himself a gulag? Some people have spread the story that Solzhenitsyn's estate is closed off with barbed wire, that he has built a long, mysterious tunnel under his house and that he relishes living in a sinister atmosphere in his beleaguered camp.
>
> I have seen the enclosure with my own eyes. The fence is plain, common wiring. The tunnel is a mere extension of the cellar by some 10 yards to allow Solzhenitsyn to rejoin the [library building] in which he works on days when there is too much snow to move around. He does have a dog. . . . The reason is that one day a photographer stole onto the premises and, hidden behind the trees, kept shooting pictures for hours of the writer and his family.

Pivot also corrects the record about the barbed wire: "Pending construction of a gate, a builder's aide had the unfortunate idea of closing the roadway with a length of barbed wire. Photographers promptly took snapshots of the enclosure and the photographs appeared around the world."[5]

Still, there remained an aura about Solzhenitsyn. That he had curtailed his public pronouncements upon moving to Vermont and apparently was living reclusively made him all that much more appealing a target for invitations to speak. On June 8, 1978, after a silence of two years, he appeared at Harvard University to deliver the commencement address. He gave exactly two congratulatory sentences typical of this most forgettable of genres, then launched into a discourse to this Western audience about the condition of the West as he saw it. It would contain "[a] measure of bitter truth," he promised at the outset, "but I offer it as a friend, not as an adversary."[6] Not many of those who publicly commented upon the speech considered what he said friendly. Seldom, if ever, has a commencement speech met with such wide and clamorous attention. Commentators who seldom had a good word to say about America were driven to defend their country against the perceived attacks of this outsider. The most common approach among reviewers was to open with a concession that Solzhenitsyn is a great man, then to move to a rejection of one or more of his points.

A good number of commentators took issue with Solzhenitsyn's complaints about certain cultural epiphenomena: commercial advertising, TV stupor, intolerable popular music, the ready availability of pornography, excessive litigiousness, passivity in the face of such overt criminality as terrorism. (Strangely, few remarked on his criticism of the West's history of colonizing other peoples.) Many more of them disputed his criticisms of current political practices in the West, here frequently charging him with being anti-democratic. Most of them wrestled with the awkward subject of religion which Solzhenitsyn had thrust upon them. It was with considerable discomfort, it seemed, that they felt forced to defend that secular humanism which was for them an article of faith in the modern American gospel. The net effect was to show world views in conflict—exactly what Solzhenitsyn was trying to show. The two particular points which most immediately exercised the commentators were the stinging rebukes of the loss of will power and decline of courage among the intelligentsia and the hasty and superficial judgments by the press.

To appreciate the enormity of the offense given by these charges, one must try to recreate in the mind's eye the scene on that day. Ten thousand celebrants representing America's best and brightest gathered for the august occasion of commencement at Harvard. That the university could land such a famous yet reclusive personage as the speaker was a coup. Yet this man came to this citadel of enlightened thought to denounce secular humanism. At this nursery of the powerful and the influential, he asserted, with no tempering qualifiers, that "a decline in courage is particularly noticeable among the ruling and intellectual elites" of the West. At the most highly reputed university in America, he took the occasion to say that he had "received letters from highly intelligent persons—maybe a teacher in a faraway small college who could do much for the renewal and salvation of his country, but the country cannot hear him because the media will not provide him with a forum." In a substantial section on the press, he charged, "Hastiness and superficiality—these are the psychic diseases of the twentieth century and more than anywhere else this is manifested in the press." He even pointed out "a common trend of preferences within the Western press as a whole (the spirit of the time), generally accepted patterns of judgment."[7]

One could say that the press rushed out to prove him right in this estimate. Amid the welter of opinions expressed about the address, there was an identifiable predominant perspective. At its core lay a flat rejection of his use of religion as the primary category by which to analyze our times and our history. Some time later there appeared a book entitled *Solzhenitsyn at Harvard*, comprising the address itself, twelve early responses, and six later reflections. As its very organization suggests—and some of its inclusions illustrate—there was *prima facie* cogency to Solzhenitsyn's accusation that the Western press is guilty of making "hasty, immature, superficial, and misleading judgments."[8] That the book appeared at all indicates a certain cultural preference of the sponsoring organization, the Ethics and Public Policy Center of Washington, D.C. In his introduction, Ronald Berman sizes up the situation correctly: "A good deal of the criticism of 'A World Split Apart' assumes that the authority of the speech was weakened by a religious view of human nature."[9] So it is not surprising that, for all its showing the range of reactions to the speech, the book presents a more even balance between negative and positive assessments than was true in the press at large—that is, that positive assessments, though still in the minority in this book, were featured disproportionately. Also, on balance, the later reflections found more of worth in the speech than did the impulsive early responses.

In retrospect, we might well ask, Did Solzhenitsyn know his audience? Did he realize what egregious umbrage his listeners would take at his speech? The answer is, Not entirely. He was aware of the pointed contrast between his own world view and what he perceived to be the prevailing opinion of his audience. But he misgauged the extent to which the free and democratic West was open to sharp criticism. He had anticipated that a university committed, even by its motto (to which he calls attention), to the pursuit of truth would, having invited him to speak, respectfully ponder his words. A university committed to giving all points of view a hearing could surely accommodate his. Logically, this should be especially true for moral relativists.

One of the more jejune comments on the address came from First Lady Rosalynn Carter. Declaring herself "not a Pollyanna," she told the National Press Club in good Chamber-of-Commerce style, "Alexander Solzhenitsyn says he can feel the pressure of evil across our land. Well, I do not sense that pressure of evil at all."[10] Columnist Carl Rowan was even more obtuse. According to him, Solzhenitsyn "left many Americans . . . wondering if he is 'an agent of influence' of the Soviet Union." After all, Solzhenitsyn attacked Western materialism, and so did Khrushchev! Rowan records his own considered judgment: "I don't really think that the Kremlin planted Solzhenitsyn here as 'an agent of influence,' but the Soviets surely cannot be displeased by that strange speech this former Soviet prisoner made at Harvard."[11] Rowan need not have worried about Americans. After the *Boston Globe* published a broadside against Solzhenitsyn by columnist Mike Barnicle, it received one hundred letters from readers, six in agreement with Barnicle and ninety-four in disagreement.[12]

The editorial about the speech in the *New York Times* is entitled "The Obsession of Solzhenitsyn." The opening paragraph is primarily devoted to the obligatory praise of Solzhenitsyn's personal nobility, but it concludes, "Mr. Solzhenitsyn's world view seems to us far more dangerous than the easygoing spirit which he finds so exasperating." The subsequent six paragraphs are decidedly confrontational. The paper pitches its tent with "the men of the Enlightenment, trusting in the rationality of humankind," and thus it warns against one who "believes himself to be in possession of The Truth and so sees error wherever he looks." This jaundiced diction at least aligns correctly the terms of the debate. At stake are competing world views. But then the editorial descends into a hysteria of its own making by charging that Solzhenitsyn is "calling up a holy war."[13] The *Washington Post* editorial is in the same vein. Its structure is the same, though this time with only one opening sentence devoted to acknowledging "Solzhenitsyn's personal credentials." Emphasizing the speaker's "gross misunderstanding of Western society," the editorial concludes that "he is summoning Americans to a crusade. . . . He speaks for boundless cold war."[14]

The usually unflappable *New York Times* columnist James Reston said that the address "sounded like wanderings of a mind split apart." It does not help, of course, that he misses that most fundamental of Solzhenitsyn's distinctions, between *Soviet* and *Russian*; thus, where Solzhenitsyn said "our country," Reston places in brackets "the Soviet Union," rather than "Russia." In that light, we can understand his silly conclusion about this anti-Communist: "But at least he was allowed to say all these things. On commencement day at Moscow University, if they have one, the 'spiritual superiority' of the Soviet Union probably wouldn't have allowed it."[15]

Arthur Schlesinger, Jr., shared Reston's failure to distinguish between *Soviet* and *Russian*: "Even today the Soviet Union, he assures us, provides a healthier moral environment than the United States." Schlesinger's way of dismissing Solzhenitsyn is to consign him to the (apparently properly) "forgotten tradition of apocalyptic prophecy," which allows Schlesinger (after some awkward tiptoeing around the charge of American capitulation in Vietnam) to conclude smugly on the note of "the irrelevance of his grand vision to a democratic and libertarian society."[16]

Mary McGrory, too, sprang to America's defense:

> . . . nothing Solzhenitsyn said went so much against the grain as his negative view of our society. The unspoken expectation was that after three years in our midst, he would have to say we are superior, that our way is not only better, but best. . . . It is hard for us to face the fact that the giant does not love us. . . .

So how should we react? Not with thought, but with an *ad hominem* approach: "Maybe we would be better off if we stopped grappling with the politics and even the morality of what Solzhenitsyn said at Harvard and look at it in a different way—as the personal statement of a conservative, religious, and terribly homesick Russian."[17]

The eight responses solicited by *Time* from "members of 'the ruling groups and the intellectual elite' that Solzhenitsyn was scolding"[18] were, on balance, somewhat gentler on Solzhenitsyn than was true of the total mass of commentary on the commencement address. There was, however, that rather surprising patriotic note of defending America from perceived attack. Barbara Tuchman found it "useful to hear his strictures; they make us think." She concluded, "I would rather live in America than anywhere else I could think of—and so, evidently, would Solzhenitsyn."[19] (His choice of a place of residence was worth deeper reflection than it received.) Archibald MacLeish, too, brought his patriotism out into the open. "If Solzhenitsyn had talked to us . . . [h]e would have learned that we have not lost our will as a people—that it is precisely our will as a people which makes us true believers in that human spirit for which he means to speak."[20] Daniel Boorstin, also, was happy to be an American. "We are lucky to be able to provide Solzhenitsyn a platform for his dyspeptic comments on us," even though "he says very little about us. He has missed the point." Trying in return not to miss the point about Solzhenitsyn, Boorstin analyzes, "Solzhenitsyn's own experience seduces him to hope that the cure for evil totalitarianism . . . may be a good totalitarianism. . . ."[21]

Three of the eight responses in *Time* strongly affirmed Solzhenitsyn. Father Theodore Hesburgh accepted the speaker's "highly unfashionable and unpopular truths" about "the moral mediocrity of the times."[22] George Meany noted approvingly "how violently Solzhenitsyn provoked the knee-jerk minds of the day, immersed as they were in an unhealthy mixture of post-Viet Nam guilt and a fashionable anti-anti-Communism."[23] Sidney Hook expressed agreement with Solzhenitsyn's "moral and political values" and "many of his political judgments as well."[24] Hook was rare among secular humanists for embracing more of Solzhenitsyn than he rejected.

George Will's review is positive, also. He counters the editorials of the *Washington Post* and of the *New York Times*, "whose spacious skepticism extends to all values except its own." Of Solzhenitsyn's views, he states:

> His ideas about the nature of man and the essential political problem are broadly congruent with the ideas of Cicero and other ancients, and those of Augustine, Aquinas, Richard Hooker, Pascal, Thomas More, Burke, Hegel and others.

Compared to the long and broad intellectual tradition in which Solzhenitsyn's view are rooted, the tradition of modernity, or liberalism, is short and thin.

Will places Solzhenitsyn in another line of worthies, as well: "De Tocqueville, Henry Adams, Irving Babbitt, Paul Elmer More, Peter Viereck and others constitute a submerged but continuous tradition that shares Solzhenitsyn's anxiety about American premises and the culture they produce."[25]

Charles Kesler, like Will a conservative, also preferred Solzhenitsyn over his critics. About the latter he observes, "When Solzhenitsyn declared that the contemporary West could not serve as a proper model for his country, he touched the love-it-or-leave-it nerve of many Americans." And Kesler carefully clarifies, "Solzhenitsyn's opposition to modernity should not be identified as an opposition to the West. He is, in many ways, the greatest living representative of the West, an avatar of the West's most ancient and honorable principles." As his title, "Up from Modernity," suggests, a rejection of modernity does not necessarily entail a desire to return to the past; it could mean, as the ending of the Harvard speech specifies, a movement toward a new and different future.[26]

The six later reflections upon the speech in the collection *Solzhenitsyn at Harvard* represent something of the range of the early reviews; but they are, in contrast, more nuanced and thoughtful. The least sympathetic of these essays is the one by William H. McNeill, who found the speech "an Orthodox Christian's caricature of our society." Though he grants validity to some of Solzhenitsyn's criticisms of the West, his basic antagonism is clear: ". . . on a practical level I see in Solzhenitsyn's speech only incoherence and confusion. Like some lapsed Catholics who as fanatical anti-clericals reproduce in reverse the dogmatism of the faith they reject, Solzhenitsyn carries with him the impress of the Communism he repudiates. . . ."[27]

Ronald Berman offers this thesis: "The most important single thing that can be said of 'A World Split Apart' is that it is *a reading of the West through Western eyes*." He astutely observes that Solzhenitsyn shares "the doubt expressed by Conrad about the effects of civilization when defined by purely political ideals."[28] Berman's view resonates here with those of Will and Kesler. Too seldom have Solzhenitsyn's critics noted his indebtedness to the Great Tradition of the West.

Of all the analyses of the Harvard address, the one that captured best its spirit and meaning is the essay by Michael Novak which concludes *Solzhenitsyn at Harvard*. Novak calls Solzhenitsyn's speech "the most important religious document of our time," and he gets its motivation exactly right: "Solzhenitsyn was saved by faith in the power of simple truth. His was not solely a salvation for his soul through faith in Jesus Christ; it was also a ray of light for the entire race of men. He kept his eye upon the need to tell the truth, come what may." Solzhenitsyn's awareness of a loss of will and courage in the West leads him to "a profound investigation into the soul and intellectual roots of the West." And here "[h]e offers two diagnoses of the malady's origin, one centering on the institutions of Western society (notably the law and the press), the other on the vision of man fashioned at the very beginning of the modern era." Novak, a Roman Catholic, finds this analysis "classically Catholic." I, a Protestant in the Reformed tradition, find it altogether consonant with my theological framework. So we would best say that it is classically, or generically, Christian. At the same time, Novak makes a discrimination which should have pleased Sidney Hook: "Solzhenitsyn is not, I think, impugning the heroism of spirit possible to the individual atheist or agnostic. He cannot be doing so from a religious point of view, in any case, for as he well recognizes, faith is a gift; without it, before it, a man must do his utmost alone." Nevertheless, in Novak's mind, "The positive antipathy to religion common among the enlightened remains . . . a fundamental weakness in our culture."[29]

Novak finds in the speech "a stunning observation," and it has to do with the relativism which pervades modern thinking:

There is one major difference . . . between a society that is anthropocentric and a society that is theocentric. That difference is that in a society whose moral roots lie solely in individual conscience, a certain diffidence inexorably results: You have your moral convictions, I have mine, who can tell who is right? Directly there follows . . . a loss of will, of moral certainty, of direction. The Soviets have their system, we have ours, everything depends on your point of view, and so on—it is all, culturally speaking, devastatingly familiar.

Novak brings up another point which is stunning by its general absence from criticisms of the Harvard address:

> It is fascinating indeed, to note that our nationally syndicated columnists, cultural leaders, and editorialists frequently castigate the American public in terms harsher than those used by Solzhenitsyn. They call our people too rich, soft, flabby, greedy, selfish, gluttonous, decadent, self-preoccupied, narrow, racist, imperialist, militarist, corrupt.[30]

Of all the charges against Solzhenitsyn's commencement address at Harvard, the most common one was that he does not understand the West. There is indeed something to this criticism, as we shall see in Chapter Six. Nevertheless, it would have been helpful, first, if those who levied the charge had understood better just what Solzhenitsyn was accusing the West of. Moreover, if the furor over this speech provides any gauge, he certainly understood his Western critics better than they understood him.

IN THE SPRING 1980 ISSUE of *Foreign Affairs*, Solzhenitsyn published a long essay entitled "Misconceptions About Russia Are a Threat to America." This was soon published in book form as *The Mortal Danger*. The Summer and Fall 1980 issues of *Foreign Affairs* carried six letters of response. A second edition of the book includes the six letters plus Solzhenitsyn's reply to them.

This essay was Solzhenitsyn's one foray into the world of discourse of American scholarship about Russian history, and it did his reputation no good. Solzhenitsyn declared that, among Western policy advisers and political leaders, two mistakes are

> especially common. One is the failure to understand the radical hostility of communism to mankind as a whole. . . . The other and equally prevalent mistake is to assume an indissoluble link between the universal disease of communism and the country where it first seized control—Russia.

The second fallacy is the focus of the essay. Solzhenitsyn is especially outraged by the Western habit of using *Russian* and *Soviet* as synonyms: ". . . these concepts are not only opposites, but are *inimical*. 'Russia' is to the Soviet Union as a man is to the disease afflicting him." He follows quickly with the charge that "American historical scholarship . . . often unwittingly adopts the Procrustean framework provided by official Soviet historiography. . . ."[31] It seems that the scholars did not find this opinion, or the argumentation that followed, endearing. Five of the six letters were strongly negative.

Adam B. Ulam, in his review of *The Mortal Danger*, provides an excellent framework within which to understand this contretemps. This essentially sympathetic review opens, "It is with a mixed feeling of admiration and exasperation that one puts aside Solzhenitsyn's little book. As in most of his polemical writings, he is so often right, but occasionally, and infuriatingly, wrong-headed." Among the "certain idiosyncrasies of his which must sadden and irritate his most fervent admirers," Ulam stipulates "the occasional intemperance and peremptoriness of his historical judgments." Nevertheless, Ulam concludes, "But such inconsistencies and irascibility should not be allowed to obscure the inherent common sense and urgency of Solzhenitsyn's message. It is a justifiable anger and impatience which explain his irascibility."[32]

It is fair enough for Ulam to call attention to the problematic nature of Solzhenitsyn's style of argumentation. Other sympathetic commentators have lamented it, as well. James Pontuso takes note of Solzhentitsyn's "disturbing habit of overstating his case."[33] David Remnick chimes in, "He lacks the modernist leveler of irony. Instead he can be chillingly sarcastic. Rarely does he show much more than disdain in political argument." Too infrequently does his debating style leave room for conceding a point. Thus, he "creates some of his own problems with his pitch of voice. . . ."[34] Here the problem is mostly his. On the other hand, it is not the case that Solzhenitsyn is altogether unaware of this problem. He knows that "all generalizations overstate their case."[35] He admits, "It's never harder to speak than when you have too much to say."[36] Remnick notes, "Solzhenitsyn is also disturbing to our modern sense of decorum because he is immodest in an unmodern way. He is convinced that what he says matters greatly."[37] Well, maybe it does. Here the problem is mostly ours.

If Solzhenitsyn sometimes overstates, too often his detractors not only overstate but flagrantly misstate. His tactlessness has unfortunately served as static obscuring his message. This failing, however, belongs to the realm of manners, not of morals. And Ulam is right to concede that the recurring obtuseness of his critics gives Solzhenitsyn some grounds for his righteous indignation.

Of the five negative letters on *The Mortal Danger*, the one by Silvio J. Treves was, by the correspondent's own admission, not "a rebuttal in any sense of the word," but rather "merely the angry, off-the-cuff reaction of a reader who had sincerely hoped that the Harvard speech was enough abuse for us to swallow from this most unappreciative visitor." Treves considers *The Mortal Danger* "a disparaging and abusive tirade against the American people" by "a not universally welcome guest." Though it is easy enough to dismiss this America-love-it-or-leave-it outburst, Treves does raise openly the issue of Solzhenitsyn's perceived "bad manners."[38]

The two most substantive rebukes of Solzhenitsyn were by prominent historians: Alexander Dallin of Stanford University and Robert C. Tucker of Princeton University. Complaining about Solzhenitsyn's "characteristic hyperbole," Dallin discerns "misconceptions . . . inaccuracies and exaggerations" in the article. Challenging what he considers "an uncritical defense of 'old Russia,' " Dallin finds, among other current realities to praise, that "the Soviet standard of living has gone up at a rather impressive rate" and that "public education has made significant strides." Very surprisingly (and unfairly), he criticizes "Mr. Solzhenitsyn's single-minded belief in the efficacy of armed force in combating the Soviet Union."[39]

One passage by Dallin deserves special attention for its highlighting of the rhetorical difficulties engulfing the debate about this article:

> He has—it pains me to say—a lot to learn about the morals of public denunciation in our society. I yield to no one in my fundamental disagreement with the political views of Richard Pipes. But I will defend him as an honest and dedicated scholar, well informed in the areas of his genuine expertise.[40]

The background is that Solzhenitsyn had severely criticized Pipes for his 1974 book *Russia Under the Old Regime*, because of "his derisive and openly hostile description of Russian history and the Russian people." In Solzhenitsyn's view, "Pipes shows a complete disregard for

the spiritual life of the Russian people and its view of the world—
Christianity."[41] The fact is that, when apportioning blame for the
current Soviet situation between Marxist ideology and the Russian soul,
some American reviewers of Pipes's book had sided more with Solzhenitsyn than with Pipes.[42] Dallin charges Solzhenitsyn with a breach
of morals. But, surely, Solzhenitsyn is here guilty of a breach of
manners, at most. The substance does not offend Dallin; only the
manner of expression does. Were harsh criticisms always to be equated
with a breach of morals, Dallin's criticism of Solzhenitsyn would qual-
ify, as well. In any case, Solzhenitsyn's rhetorical strategies have sometimes affected his Western reception adversely.

The longest reply came from Robert C. Tucker, the only respondent
criticized by name in *The Mortal Danger*. It is similar in mood to
Dallin's. Tucker mentions Solzhenitsyn's "acrimonious and disdainful
tone," promises not "to reply in kind," then writes a long letter bristling
with disdain. He writes in the conviction that "Mr. Solzhenitsyn's basic
view of communism [is] unsound," and he replies to criticisms of
himself. His vehement denial of Solzhenitsyn's direct linkage of Lenin
and Stalin leads him to disparage *The Gulag Archipelago* in terms
harsher than anything which it met upon initial publication (though
Tucker's view of it has consanguinity with Stephen Cohen's):

> *The Gulag Archipelago* does a disservice to historical understanding by
> compressing the factual material into the author's simplistic, straight-
> line scheme of Soviet development, a scheme that treats all the horrors of
> the Stalin era as the logical and necessary unfolding of what was embry-
> onic in Lenin's communism from the start. From this standpoint, there
> *was* no distinct Stalin era, and the very word "Stalinism" is taboo.[43]

One charge by Solzhenitsyn was resisted by both Tucker and Ulam.
Examining this issue clarifies how misunderstandings arise between
Solzhenitsyn and his critics. Here is the offending sentence: "It is
sufficient to recall that until the most recent times the very existence of
the Gulag Archipelago, its inhuman cruelty, its scope, its duration, and
the sheer volume of death it generated, were not acknowledged by
Western scholarship."[44] Ulam, in citing this passage, omits the words
"its scope, its duration, and the sheer volume of death it generated."[45]

But are not these exactly the elements to which Solzhenitsyn is referring? Without them the Gulag Archipelago would not be what in fact it is. In other words, he need not be saying that no Western scholar has ever made reference of any sort to the Soviet system of concentration camps, but that the fullness of their horror, including their establishment by Lenin and not Stalin, never became a standard part of the story of the Soviet Union as told by Western historians. Tucker's rebuttal of the offending sentence lists Western books about the Gulag, starting with David J. Dallin and Boris I. Nicolaevsky's *Forced Labor in Soviet Russia* (1947). Tucker says that he has read the full text of *The Gulag Archipelago*.[46] These authors are named on page 595 of Volume I. Whatever Solzhenitsyn meant in *The Mortal Danger*, he did not mean that they did not write their book. In any case, however the fault is to be parceled out, the misunderstanding between Solzhenitsyn and his critics arose.

The only letter of response supportive of Solzhenitsyn was by John R. Dunlap, a college English teacher; it appeared in the Fall 1980 issue of *Foreign Affairs* and took to task the two letters in the Summer 1980 issue, those by Tucker and Treves.

> The responses were both so energetically hostile as to send me back to Mr. Solzhenitsyn's article, which I read carefully a second time. I think I now understand Mr. Solzhenitsyn's recurrent use of the term "astonishment" when he relates his perceptions of the West. There's no better word for it: after rereading Mr. Solzhenitsyn's article, I was astonished by the responses of Professor Tucker and of Mr. Treves.

Dunlap knows "educated people who allow that they don't read Mr. Solzhenitsyn 'on principle'—by which I gather they mean on the strength of their preferred faith in the hostile articles and reviews directed against Mr. Solzhenitsyn by so many Western intellectuals." Dunlap describes Tucker as devoting "six full pages, in small type, to a rambling rebuttal aimed at less than two full pages of Mr. Solzhenitsyn's thirty-seven-page long article," and he judges that Tucker "scores a few interesting debater's points" but avoids Solzhenitsyn's central concern. As to Treves's charge of bad manners, Dunlap remarks, "Surely the West, and especially America, is no stranger to trenchant criticism; but

I don't recall a Marxist ever coming under such fire or contempt from the intellectual community as Mr. Solzhenitsyn has encountered in the West."[47]

Solzhenitsyn's response to the critics of *The Mortal Danger* is his most sustained statement about the hostility with which Western critics greeted his polemical utterances. Unrepentant but distressed, he asserts, ". . . it is painful to hear flimsy and irresponsible judgments pronounced with a scholarly air. . . ." He elaborates on his dismay thus:

> A good indicator of the viability of any system is its receptiveness to criticism. I had always assumed that the American system desires criticism and even appreciates it. This belief was shaken after my Harvard address. . . . I had no intention of "lecturing" anyone; I wished to share the experience of living under communist rule. Nothing could be simpler for me than to keep my peace and leave the concern for America's future to Mr. Treves and those who share his views.

If, as he believes, the key problem is "a misunderstanding of the nature of communism: a failure to acknowledge it as the quintessence of dynamic and implacable evil," the most troubling thing is to find an opposing unshakable consensus among the elite intellectuals:

> It is clear that Robert C. Tucker's essay reflects not only his personal opinions but the established views of a milieu which exerts a formative influence upon U.S. policy. . . . (It is symptomatic that Professor Dallin concurs with the essential arguments of Professor Tucker.)[48]

Solzhenitsyn is greatly saddened that always "the same old thinking persists." It is highly revealing to read what he considers the chief culprit here: "There are no new ideas, and it would be strange were any to arise amid the smug secularism which cannot see beyond itself." To interject the word *secularism* into a political discussion must seem odd to those for whom politics constitutes a self-contained realm of discourse not amenable to religious reflection. The conclusion of Solzhenitsyn's response to critics of *The Mortal Danger* expresses his despair of being heeded by America's established intellectuals:

> I might just as well not have hurried to present all these arguments. It is becoming increasingly clear that no essay of mine, nor ten such essays,

nor ten individuals such as I, are capable of transmitting to the West the experience gained through blood and suffering, or even of disturbing the euphoria and complacency that dominate American political science.[49]

It is in fact the case that, following the exchange over *The Mortal Danger*, for the most part Solzhenitsyn fell silent. When he visited Japan, Taiwan, and Great Britain in 1982 and 1983, he obliged his hosts by giving speeches. However, these were little noted by the American press. It is especially disappointing that so few readers know of his Templeton Address of 1983, for it is the most succinct statement of the religious underpinnings of his world view.

BY THE LATE 1970's and into the 1980's, the negative consensus about Solzhenitsyn was so well-established that critics routinely attributed to him theses and positions which he nowhere proposed. These were often presented by bald assertion and without argumentation or development, as if by now all agreed they were self-evident. Our purpose here is served by looking at just a few examples from established critics: Olga Carlisle (and, behind her, Alexander Yanov), George Feifer, and Michael Scammell. All three knew Solzhenitsyn personally, and all three experienced personal conflict with him. All three, also, found his world view and theirs to be mutually incompatible. Yet all three presumed to be able to read his mind.

Olga Carlisle, granddaughter of the famous Russian author Leonid Andreyev, had played a major role in the efforts to get some of Solzhenitsyn's works published in the West. She tells the sad story of their falling out in *Solzhenitsyn and the Secret Circle*.[50] Though it is impossible to determine to what extent her later antagonism toward Solzhenitsyn is rooted in personal misunderstandings, it is clear that the religious cast of his dissidence was not to her sophisticated taste.

In her essay on the Harvard address, she says that "he was scornful of our free press." The implication is that it is the freedom *per se* which he scorns, though obviously his scorn is directed toward the press's irresponsibility—its irresponsible use of its freedom. Yet she elaborates as follows:

It did not occur to him that he owed his own opportunity to speak out on that day to generations of Americans who shaped and preserved those liberties Russia has never had, the secular liberties formulated in the eighteenth century, particularly freedom of speech and of the press.

It did not occur to him? The indulgence in mind-reading displayed here is extended in her next paragraph; she "knows" who his real, invisible audience was on that day at Harvard: "He was really speaking to the Soviet leaders and to the Russian people. He wanted them to know he had not been seduced by the false values of the West." Carlisle then assigns Solzhenitsyn to the appropriate political category: he belongs to the "new Russian right." He desires "a benevolently autocratic, religious state." Since this "new dissenting right" is anti-Semitic, presumably he is, too, though she coyly avoids saying so outright. Instead, she says, "Should a new right ever come into its own in the Soviet Union, Solzhenitsyn . . . might well return home in triumph."[51]

In her book, Carlisle gives her before-and-after view of Solzhenitsyn. It is a classic case of one who discovers belatedly that he is not the liberal she would like him to be. She notes, "The flood of favorable reviews of *The First Circle* and *Cancer Ward* expressed the same passionate admiration we had been feeling for their prodigious author for a long time." She uses the adjective *breathtaking* to describe "the literary mastery" of *The Gulag Archipelago*. However, when a visitor reports that Solzhenitsyn is "a deeply religious man," she and her husband are bemused: "Our silence asked the question in both our minds. We had had indications that the Orthodox Church was of importance to Solzhenitsyn, but we were surprised that his religious nature was one of [the visitor's] stronger impressions of him." The fact of her bringing up this point indicates how distancing she felt this matter of religion to be. So she puzzles over the fact that Solzhenitsyn had chosen two persons of socialist background, herself and Swiss lawyer Fritz Heeb, to help him.[52]

When Carlisle wrote to Solzhenitsyn to withdraw from the work of getting *The Gulag Archipelago* translated into English and published in the West, he asked her to reconsider—or else to burn her copy of the work, including the translation in progress. Her evaluation, which contains an astounding false analogy, is that he is

> an authoritarian figure who thought nothing of attacking those who had helped him, none more virulently than those in the West. Their contribu-

tions must be ceremoniously burned. All trace incinerated, just as, in *Gulag One*, the tons of seized documents are burned in the Lubyanka furnaces to rain as fine ash on the prisoners.[53]

Carlisle readily reveals the yawning gulf between her outlook and Solzhenitsyn's. Joining a march to protest the war in Vietnam, she reflects, "At this moment, the march and Solzhenitsyn's mission seemed to me a part of a single, proud enterprise. . . . I had no notion that Alexander Solzhenitsyn might view our steps along the freezing avenues of the American capital as a craven retreat from a just war, as a sign of the moral weakness of the West." She reports the similar disillusionment with Solzhenitsyn on the part of Daniel Ellsberg, a personal friend of hers. After Ellsberg released the Pentagon papers, he was "shaken" by Solzhenitsyn's "singling me out as a traitor to my country in time of war," for he had felt a certain moral equivalence between the zeks in *The First Circle* and himself as an employee of the Rand Corporation. So he asks, "On what grounds was Solzhenitsyn condemning me? I had tried to emulate him. Of course I had acted in far less dangerous conditions. Nor do I mean to compare the Soviet regime with ours. And yet. . . ."[54]

The obvious inference to be drawn is that Carlisle and Ellsberg had gotten Solzhenitsyn wrong in the first place. Yet Carlisle's imagination can extend no further than to speculate about some enormous change in the character of Solzhenitsyn.

And as always when I searched for the truth about Solzhenitsyn, the same enigma reappeared: Was he the author of *One Day* and of *The First Circle*, the man I had met in 1967, or had his sensibilities undergone some radical mutation, the effect of great personal trials, political pressures, and also of fame, of ambition, of power?[55]

A year later, Carlisle wrote another essay entitled "Reviving Myths of Holy Russia," in which she again linked Solzhenitsyn with those extreme nationalists who advocate Great Russian chauvinism, messianism, anti-Semitism. She now identifies the source for her label "new Russian right": Alexander Yanov, long a Soviet journalist and, in emigration, author of *The Russian New Right*.[56] John Dunlop has described this article by Carlisle as "poorly researched and replete with factual errors and uninformed assertions." In particular, Dunlop says, "Carlisle's view of Russian nationalism is, in short, a caricatured one, in which its most 'liberal' representatives, such as Solzhenitsyn and Osipov, are depicted as virtual Nazis."[57] Following Yanov's lead, Carlisle finds the whole "broad spectrum of nationalistic ideas . . . cause for alarm": "The prospect that these deeply held, atavistic beliefs might affect Russia's direction . . . must give us pause."[58] In Dunlop's opinion, "Olga Carlisle's diatribe" is "[a]n example of what happens when Ianov's ideas percolate downward."[59]

Although Carlisle does not say so, Yanov and Solzhenitsyn are sworn foes.[60] Yanov devotes fully one-seventh of *The Russian New Right* to arguing directly against Solzhenitsyn.[61] Placing the greatest distance possible between them, Yanov calls Solzhenitsyn a monarchist; and, lumping all manifestations of Russian patriotism and nationalism together, he also calls him "a New Right party propagandist."[62] A similar indiscriminacy marks Yanov's writings throughout. It is symptomatic how much more resonance many Western critics find with Yanov than with Solzhenitsyn.[63]

OF ALL THE DIATRIBES against Solzhenitsyn, the most vicious one was George Feifer's "The Dark Side of Solzhenitsyn." Feifer concedes, more than most Western detractors, Solzhenitsyn's greatness as a literary artist, and he worrisomely acknowledges both how valid are Solzhenitsyn's indictments and how deeply appealing many Russians find Solzhenitsyn's religious vision and political program. Therefore, he is reduced to taking the tack of blackening the character of the man: "The infection lies not so much in his ideas as in his temperament." As preparation for showing the "feet of clay," Feifer presents a litany of Solzhenitsyn's offenses against enlightened opinion: "[h]is antipathy to Western democracy," his "profound mistrust of the institutions vital to a free society," the "marching toward his anachronistic Russia of the future." But his emphasis is on character defects: his "moralistic, painfully simplistic solutions to social problems," his "zealous missionary mentality," his "personal despotism," "his bullying weaker people," his "moral absolutism," his "posture of moral superiority," his "quasi-religious ideology."[64] Although other Western critics did not always restrain themselves from indulging in personal attacks on

Solzhenitsyn, their emphasis was, by and large, on the incorrectness of his ideas. With Feifer the balance tips the other way. The erroneous thinking being by now presumably well-established and obvious to all, he can move on to concentrate on the personal deficiencies.

The "dark side" of Solzhenitsyn is so dark that *side* is too tame a metaphor, for the darkness goes to the depths of his character. Feifer asserts, "The stern preacher of the Christian ethic instinctively, and calculatingly, uses slander, intimidation, and rage in his own dealings with people who displease him, with or without cause." Here Feifer draws partly upon personal experience, for Solzhenitsyn has expressed his strong disapproval of the early biography of him written by Feifer and David Burg. Solzhenitsyn was not the only one to find the Burg-and-Feifer biography deficient, especially for its lack of documentation and its heavy reliance on the prejudicial reportage of Solzhenitsyn's first wife, herself the author of a screed against her former husband on which Western commentators saw the obvious fingerprints of the KGB. Feifer is disingenuous in not bringing up the resultant animosity between him and Solzhenitsyn. Choosing instead to present himself as a neutral observer and a reporter of others' personal conflicts with Solzhenitsyn, he refers to "dozens of Russian and Western laymen [who] also served the man who is convinced he is serving God." And of these, calling up the authority of numbers, he declares,

> With few exceptions, they began in awe and finished in bewildered or bitter disappointment. . . . [M]any who believed that nothing was more important than his message of Soviet brutality now feel more strongly that his ruthless manipulation of people and his liberties with the norms of civilized conduct have revealed him as a menace.[65]

What Feifer leaves totally out of account here is that the wedge driving apart the author and his erstwhile supporters was their eventual discernment of the unbridgeable chasm between their world views.

About his own motivation Feifer is guilelessly forthcoming. Perversely but logically, he sees Solzhenitsyn's literary virtuosity as precisely what makes him dangerous. Had Solzhenitsyn stuck to his last and not made pronouncements about politics, he would not be the "menace" that he has become.

> What does it matter why a writer produces such epochal books or by
> what route he reached their terrible truths? . . . The personal motives
> behind such an accomplishment should play no part in its evaluation.
>   But they do matter when an artist offers political wisdom together with
> his literature.[66]

In brief, politics really matters. For the politically engaged commenta-
tor, anything, including character and motives, is fair game for criticism. Eccentricity and crankiness are luxuries to be permitted to
literary figures but not to political figures. In this Feifer essay we see in
microcosm the whole history of the response to Solzhenitsyn by Western intellectuals. Only apart from his polemical writings could he be
tolerantly indulged without the bother of refutation. When politics
surfaces, dispassionateness vanishes.

Undermining Solzhenitsyn's authority becomes all the more urgent if
there is a prospect that people will actually heed him. Although many
Western critics have tried to describe Solzhenitsyn as an isolated
thinker, Feifer knows better.

> Imagine life and liberty under a Solzhenitsyn state. (This is not so
> farfetched as it may sound. The dissolution of belief in Communism and
> its replacement by the caste system's corruption and cynicism make
> Soviet rule inherently unstable; the leviathan may live another 100 years
> or collapse overnight. Solzhenitsyn's conviction that the Motherland will
> welcome him home has more foundation than Lenin's hope to return in
> 1916.)[67]

Feifer's *ad hominem* attacks in this article stand in sharp contrast to
the portrayal of Solzhenitsyn's character in the Burg-and-Feifer biography. There we are told, ". . . his disposition is essentially gentle and has
mellowed distinctly with his advance in age—'easygoing,' 'genial,'
'even-tempered,' and 'kind' are the adjectives most often used by those
who know him well. . . ." We read of "his natural modesty" and of his
"instinctive gregariousness and unfeigned curiosity in others' interests
and opinions." We learn also, "Apart from compassion, Solzhenitsyn's
consideration for people in personal matters is mentioned as often as his
sense of urgency about time." When we are shown the other "side," it
seems not to be very dark: he is "the prickly, uncompromising artist
with the saintly ideals and somewhat monkish asceticism."[68]

*   *   *

THE SPIRIT OF FEIFER LIVES on in Michael Scammell's thousand-page-long biography of Solzhenitsyn. This fat volume has done incalculable damage to Solzhenitsyn's reputation—and most of all because it is thoroughly wrong about what matters most to Solzhenitsyn: his Christian faith. Published in 1984, it serves as a kind of culmination and compendium of the received opinion about Solzhenitsyn as established by secular Western intellectuals. It sits on library shelves as the primary single repository of information about Solzhenitsyn. Every student interested in the author will be directed to it. Yet those who consult it will have no way of knowing how far from definitive and authoritative it is. The book does contain much valuable information, but it is also peppered with gratuitous conjectures about Solzhenitsyn's motives, which consistently cast him in a negative light. Almost invariably, Scammell subtly reduces each of Solzhenitsyn's actions to mediocrity and, out of all possible explanations, chooses the most banal and base one. He consistently sides with Solzhenitsyn's ill-wishers. Reading this book is like walking through a minefield unawares.

Though reluctant to have his biography written during his lifetime, Solzhenitsyn eventually submitted to Scammell's requests for help and in 1977 granted him a week's time at the family home in Vermont. During this time Scammell was allowed to interview the author every day and also had daily access to the author's wife, a ready source of information. Afterwards, and beyond their agreement, Scammell sent lists of further questions, which Solzhenitsyn answered, albeit in brief form, until 1979. At that point, with Scammell's deadline for finishing the work receding seemingly endlessly into the future, Solzhenitsyn stopped replying. The deterioration in the relationship between the two men frames a hidden agenda in the book, as both of them came to realize the irreconcilability of their divergent world views, a point which it would have been fair of Scammell to make overt. The judgment of Veronika Stein, a cousin of Solzhenitsyn's first wife, is that, in the biography's opening pages, we have "a less than honest portrayal of Scammell's own relationship with Solzhenitsyn."[69]

Some index of this book's pattern of misleading accounts of situations, unfounded innuendoes, and prejudicial interpretations can be garnered from a perusal of the sources cited in the endnotes. The chief source is Solzhenitsyn's first wife, Natalya Reshetovskaya; by my count, there are 211 citations of her. Fifty-four of these are to seven letters which she sent to Scammell when she knew that he was writing this biography. The remaining 157 notes refer to her book *Sanya*. By contrast, only 134 notes are drawn from Scammell's extensive tape-recorded interviews with Solzhenitsyn himself. (There are of course citations from Solzhenitsyn's works.) Scammell's use of Solzhenitsyn's taped testimony is largely limited to the author's ancestry and his life up to 1955. After that, for the public years and the controversies swirling about Solzhenitsyn, Scammell's primary extra-literary source is the embittered ex-wife. Solzhenitsyn's second wife is cited only eight times. And Irene (Irina) Alberti, a long-time adviser and deeply trusted confidante of the Solzhenitsyns who was present on the premises during Scammell's visit, is cited only once. (Scammell refers to her as a secretary, but for years she has been the editor of *Russian Thought*, published in Paris and the primary Russian weekly for émigrés.)

Although neither party in the messy divorce was blameless, Scammell's unduly long lingering over it assigns the major portion of fault to Solzhenitsyn. At almost every point, he simply accepts at face value Reshetovskaya's explanations of the dynamics at work between the estranged pair. Others saw things differently. These include Galina Vishnevskaya, a famous opera soprano and the wife of cellist and conductor Mstislav Rostropovich (Solzhenitsyn was living with them during the time of the divorce), and Veronika Stein.[70] Many will read Scammell's version; few will know of Vishnevskaya's and Stein's correctives.

Scammell's preface suggests that the reader of this biography can expect a balanced portrayal of Solzhenitsyn. With ostensible evenhandedness, he calls Solzhenitsyn "a man with substantial faults, as well as with some towering virtues." Yet what a different sense of the balance would have been struck had the phrasing read, "a man of towering virtues, as well as with some substantial faults." And no one who reads the last quarter of the book will find anything of virtue left intact. As the book progresses, Scammell increasingly offers gratuitous harsh comments: "Only with the passage of many years did the vengeful, Old Testament side of Solzhenitsyn gain ascendancy over his Christian humility." Later, we read, "Solzhenitsyn was not above lending God a helping hand if there was a risk of His being late for His appointed time. . . ." This offensive comment is utterly out of harmony with Solzhenitsyn's statements about the Almighty, as is Scammell's travestying remark about "his eminently practical attitude to religion—God was there to help him accomplish things."[71]

By the late part of the book, the vitriol flows freely. Now Scammell speaks of "Solzhenitsyn's camouflage as a man of left-wing leanings," thus implying that the author was duplicitous and dishonest, instead of admitting that left-wingers had simply miscalculated in imagining Solzhenitsyn to be one of their own. With a niggling spirit, Scammell spends a full page imperiously berating Solzhenitsyn for not hiring a secretary to answer the mountain of letters which came to him in Zurich. Eventually, Scammell's Solzhenitsyn becomes "an anachronism" and "a tragic personal failure."[72]

Running throughout the book is an impugning of Solzhenitsyn's motives based on unsubstantiated mind-reading. Scammell finds "a hint of rivalry in Solzhenitsyn's feelings toward Sakharov," for instance. The later part of the book is dotted with such wordings as "there can be little doubt that" and "Solzhenitsyn must have felt." For example, he "must have felt frustrated" and "[h]e must have seen and felt himself to be a prophet crying in the wilderness." Scammell's mind-reading ability extends to "most Americans." Most Americans "resented" Solzhenitsyn's criticism of Henry Kissinger, we are told; and "most Americans" were "perhaps relieved that the proposal to grant Solzhenitsyn honorary citizenship had been allowed to lapse by Congress."[73]

Scammell's bias extends beyond the person of Solzhenitsyn to his works. For the key points of his portrait of Lenin, Solzhenitsyn has "no evidence at all." Does Solzhenitsyn say that 66 million died in the Gulag? (The figure, despite Scammell, is not of Solzhenitsyn's own calculating.) This figure is too high; it is incorrect. Scammell's most scathing comments are reserved for Solzhenitsyn's polemical essays. They are "silly." This journalist dismisses them as "journalism" and finds in them "crudity and coarseness." Of the speech given to the AFL-CIO in Washington, Scammell says, "On the face of it, it was another triumph," one greeted by "spontaneous applause." But the real estimate? "It was a dismal failure, worse than anything he had done before." A subsequent speech in California is derided as "Solzhenitsyn at his demagogic worst again." The polemical pieces "always" had "the same dismal results." Solzhenitsyn's "addiction" to this genre "was slowly killing not him but his reputation." Then again, what else should we expect from a "vehement ecclesiastical maximalist blinded by his utopian vision"?[74]

Scammell does his own charting of the West's "public response" to Solzhenitsyn. His categories are the familiar political ones. About one small episode during the mid-1970's, he analyzes, "Once again there was a split between the Left and liberals, on one side, and his conservative supporters on the other." At least, Scammell acknowledges that Solzhenitsyn had tried to deflect him from using these categories:

> I was obliged to take an interest in [politics] owing to the appalling circumstances of our life. But I would much prefer not to. . . . Whenever I am attacked, my opponents always insist on regarding me in political terms, . . . completely missing the point that this is not my framework, not my task, and not my dimension. I cannot be regarded in political terms.

And Scammell's comment? "There was an element of disingenuousness in these protestations. . . ."[75]

Of all of Scammell's misrepresentations of Solzhenitsyn, the one that most outraged family friend Irene Alberti is the statement that "there is no evidence that he was anything other than delighted by the decision to send him abroad. . . ."[76] Alberti calls this "a particularly revolting lie . . . with the insinuation that he voluntarily accepted the exile solution as opposed to a term in prison." She vehemently rejects the insinuation: "This is so completely false—and besides there is the implicit and explicit charge that Solzhenitsyn lied in his *Oak and the Calf* when recounting the story of his expulsion. It is simply anti-history, a distortion of fact in the Soviet way—based on *what*? On nothing."[77]

In my view, Scammell's greatest transgression is his analysis of Solzhenitsyn's religious position. Although Solzhenitsyn has been clear about his move from Marx to Jesus while in prison, this turning point is glossed over. What Scammell handles most poorly is what is central to a correct understanding of Solzhenitsyn: his Christian faith. (But what should we expect from one who thinks that "Know thyself" is a "biblical injunction"?) Although Scammell perforce makes passing references to Solzhenitsyn's religious views, he saves his summary judgment for the climactic position of the closing pages. Here he casts the most hapless judgment imaginable: that Solzhenitsyn is "a deist."[78]

Thus, for instance, Scammell can find "nothing mystical or intimate" about the prayer that Solzhenitsyn had published. Yet his very next sentence, summarizing the prayer however snidely, touches upon the obvious themes of Solzhenitsyn's faith in God and his confidence that God would direct him in the affairs of his life. Solzhenitsyn's personal relationship with God is at a far remove from what the Deists of the eighteenth century felt for the Great Clockmaker. Scammell adds, "Nor did he seem attracted to the mysteries of the church ritual." But he seems to say so because Natalya Reshetovskaya told him that Solzhenitsyn did not kiss the hands of Orthodox priests, and Scammell listens when she speaks. It is no wonder that Scammell finds it "rather surprising, therefore, that he should have come to the idea of building a church" in his homeland with the proceeds from his royalties, especially since he "does not understand mysticism or the life of the church." Nonetheless, Scammell persists: "Religion for him, it seems, is not an essential part of his being, but a contingent tool and even a weapon. The sentimental picture of him as a pious man of God is false. Solzhenitsyn certainly believes in God, though it is not always clear whether it is a Christian God. . . ."[79]

About Scammell's book, and particularly its heavy reliance on the highly prejudicial testimony of Natalya Reshetovskaya, Irene Alberti registers this bitter judgment: "The story is too disgusting for words. A man like Solzhenitsyn, who has suffered as he has and done for mankind what he has done and which is truly unique, really does not deserve this treatment."[80]

Scammell, in response to the critical letter by Veronika Stein, has written, ". . . no one who has read my book could possibly accuse me of unfairness. . . ."[81] Yet, in response to a trenchant negative review, he concedes, "I accept that my treatment of Solzhenitsyn's religious faith is sketchy and unsatisfactory. I was aware of it at the time of writing. . . ."[82] Solzhenitsyn's religious faith is the bedrock of his whole world view, and no responsible biographer of him could take Scammell's cavalier attitude toward it. Scammell speculates freely about Solzhenitsyn's motives, but about this most fundamental of motive forces he confesses his ineptitude.

IN 1989 SOLZHENITSYN BROKE a long silence to give an interview to David Aikman of *Time*, in which he said, "It is quite extraordinary the extent to which I have been lied about. . . . Some people distort things consciously, others just don't take the trouble to check their sources. It is remarkable, and it makes me ashamed of journalists." When asked, "How do you account for the violent feelings about your views?" Solzhenitsyn answered:

> In Europe the response to me is very varied. But in the Soviet Union and the U.S., it's like an assembly line: all opinions about me are exactly the same. In the Soviet Union I can understand it. . . . But in the U.S. fashion is very important. If the winds of fashion are blowing in one direction, everybody writes one way and with perfect unanimity. It is perfectly extraordinary.
>
> Then there was the Harvard speech. . . . Maybe democracy likes and wants criticism, but the press certainly does not. The press got very indignant, and from that point on, I became the personal enemy, as it were, of the American press. . . .[83]

Fashion is the word that John Bayley, too, used in 1989 to sum up Western criticism of Solzhenitsyn: "It has become the fashion to write off Solzhenitsyn as a has-been, an old fuddy-duddy, still lamenting in voluminous pages at longer and longer intervals the disappearance of Holy Russia. . . ."[84] The demise of the Soviet Union is an event momentous enough to change this fashion. The appearance of Solzhenitsyn's forward-looking *Rebuilding Russia* in 1990 should make such a change inevitable. It sufficed to cause reviewer David Remnick to observe, "Solzhenitsyn remains one of the most poorly understood, intimidating personalities of our time."[85]

But intellectual fashions die hard. In the fall of 1991—after Solzhenitsyn's 1989 interview in *Time*, after the *New York Times* published excerpts from and commentary on *Rebuilding Russia*, after various reviews of the new essay appeared—Shlomo Avineri published an op-ed piece in the *New York Times* entitled "Where's Solzhenitsyn?" It opens, "Soviet Communism has collapsed. . . . But Russia's most renowned writer, Aleksandr I. Solzhenitsyn, has remained strangely silent." Calling upon the writer to "speak up," it concludes, "Because if he chooses to keep silent at such a moment, his silence, too, will speak out loud and clear." In between, Avineri speculates on the reasons for Solzhenitsyn's supposed silence:

Or does Mr. Solzhenitsyn, for all his anti-Communism, feel uneasy about the shape of things emerging in post-Communist Russia? Is he disturbed that the 1991 revolution has been launched in the name of democracy, individual freedom and a call for a free market economy— all ideas as anathema to him as Communism? . . . Is he deeply disappointed to see that Russia's new leaders look to the West as a model rather than to the old Czarist Russia he so admires?

Avineri casts the perfect judgment (except for the tentative opening word) on his own piece: "Maybe all this is unfair."[86]

The prevailing view of Solzhenitsyn in the West is so firmly implanted that it will not easily be uprooted. Essays promulgating it continue to appear.[87] Nevertheless, it remains, in its main features, firmly wrong. It must be cut down branch by branch. The following three chapters, examining in turn Solzhenitsyn's views on the West, on democracy, and on nationalism, will seek to remove three of its main branches.

6

On the West

> I am not a critic of the West. . . . [F]or nearly all our lives we worshipped the West—note the word "worshipped." We did not admire it, we worshipped it. I am not a critic of the West.

Thus spoke Solzhenitsyn, and that much is true. But, to get the whole truth, we must read on:

> I am a critic of the weakness of the West. I am a critic of a fact which we can't comprehend: how one can lose one's spiritual strength, one's will power, and possessing freedom, not value it, not be willing to make sacrifices for it.[1]

That in a nutshell is Solzhenitsyn's view of the West. It is essential that we understand both parts of it. The received opinion is that Solzhenitsyn is anti-Western. But to take this view is to seize upon only one half of his equation. Indeed, it would be much more accurate to call Solzhenitsyn pro-Western than anti-Western. He wants the West to be strong. In his view, the means to that end is for the West to reattach itself to its spiritual moorings. In brief, Solzhenitsyn wants the West to be more the West. Ambivalence creeps in only as he sees that the idol which he once worshipped has feet of clay.

126

This chapter and the two to follow take up issues which, to judge from the reception accorded Solzhenitsyn, are high on the agenda of Western critics. They are not unimportant issues to him; yet, in the overall scheme of his vision, they are less important to him than they are to his critics. Because they matter to him, to get them straight is an intrinsically valuable thing to do. Because misperception of them is an impediment to a proper understanding of Solzhenitsyn's vision as a whole, to get them straight is also a necessary thing to do.

It is worth remembering how it happened that Solzhenitsyn made most of his comments about the West. Lionized in the West upon his exile, he was invited to give speeches and interviews. Because his audiences were Western, he addressed Western issues. Candor compelled him to make incisive critiques. When his utterances were met with massive and hostile rebuffs, he was clearly surprised. He had expected the free West to be more hospitable to criticism than it proved to be. The reactions could hardly have caused him to think that the West was in better shape than he had thought; more likely, they confirmed all his worst fears. Yet he always made clear his friendly intentions. To the AFL-CIO he said, "I have come . . . as a friend of the United States. . . ." Then he explained, "There is [a] Russian proverb: 'The yes-man is your enemy, but your friend will argue with you.' It is precisely because my speech is prompted by friendship, that I have come to tell you: 'My friends, I'm not going to give you sugary words.' "[2] Solzhenitsyn's repeated remarks about friendship passed with little notice.

The allegation that Solzhenitsyn is anti-Western is particularly ironic in light of events in 1967. The Writers' Union placed as a virtual condition of publication of *Cancer Ward* that he make an anti-Western statement. It was precisely his refusal to condemn the West that kept him from his coveted goal of being published in his homeland.[3] The irony is compounded by the fact that most of his criticisms of things Western were not novel with him, but were common fare in the Western press itself.

Solzhenitsyn's expressions of praise for the West were not polite niceties; they were extensive and lavish. He called the West "not only the stronghold of the spirit but also the depository of wisdom." Along with the heartfelt praise, he was also specific about what caused him and his generation to come to have doubts about the West:

In the fifties, after the end of the war, we literally worshipped the West. We looked upon the West as being the sun of freedom, a fortress of the spirit, our hope, our ally. We all thought that it would be difficult to liberate ourselves, but that the West would help us to rise from slavery. Gradually, . . . this faith began to waver and to fade. . . . We realized with bewilderment that the West was not showing that firmness and that interest in freedom in *our* country as well; it was as if the West was separating its freedom from our fate.[4]

Solzhenitsyn expressed special affection, among Western nations, for the United States.

The United States has long shown itself to be the most magnanimous, the most generous country in the world. Wherever there is a flood, an earthquake, a fire, a natural disaster, an epidemic, who is the first to help? The United States. Who helps the most and unselfishly? The United States.[5]

Seeing America for himself confirmed his belief in "the soundness, the healthiness of the roots, of the great-spirited, powerful American nation—with the insistent honesty of its youth, and its alert moral sense."[6] In particular, his travels through many of the states convinced him that "the American heartland is healthy, strong, and broad in its outlook." And he concedes, "In your wide-open spaces even I get a little infected, the dangers seem somehow unreal. On this continent it is hard to believe all the things which are happening in the world." His praise for America, however, is not indiscriminate. To audiences in Washington and New York, he expressed his awareness that those two cities "do not reflect your country as a whole with its tremendous diversity and possibilities."[7]

It galls Solzhenitsyn that generous America was treated so shabbily by the recipients of its help. "The Americans had never begged for their loans to be repaid, never made political conditions. . . . What then happened to America? . . . The most fashionable thing for politicians in the Third World to do and even in Europe was to attack America." The Russian view of America, he says, is quite different: "In spite of all the newspaper lies . . . there is an internal sympathy on the part of the Russian people for the American people. Although people are very ungrateful to America there is paradoxically the fact that your activity is very highly esteemed in Russia."[8] Nor is this receptive attitude new; though that fact is now forgotten, the friendship goes back to the founding of the American nation.[9] Today, however, this kindly disposition is not unalloyed. "America evokes a mixture of admiration and compassion. . . ." Even here some credit redounds to the United States: "But these qualities—strength, generosity, and magnanimity—are usually combined in a man and even in a whole country with trustfulness. And this has done you a disservice several times." So he urges, "I would like to call upon America to be more careful with its trust. . . ."[10]

For his analysis of the West, Solzhenitsyn claims only amateur status. (The word *amateur*, with its etymological link to *lover*, is exact.) To the British he admitted that he was "not all that well acquainted with the internal affairs of your country. . . ."[11] About the West as a whole, he conceded freely, "I'm not an expert on the West—I've only been observing it from the inside for two years." He immediately explained his dilemma and his resolution of it: "I can either hold my peace or speak out, but I've chosen, once and for all, to tell what I believe to be the truth." And what was that truth which was so important as to compel him to break his silence? "Here it is: the Western world is nearing a moment of decision. In the years to come, it will be gambling with the civilisation that created it. I don't think it quite realises this." Therefore, as he understood it, "Without having meant to, I'm playing a dual role. I'm telling the story of Russia, but at the same time I'm telling the West what its own story could be. Well, the living have always detested harbingers of the future."[12] With the world's future at stake, it is no wonder that sometimes he felt that he bore a "responsibility almost too massive for the shoulders of a single human being."[13]

Understanding Solzhenitsyn's pure-hearted motivation in speaking to the West helps considerably in understanding why he spoke as he did. Although his information was incomplete, it was not negligible, and it certainly was sufficient to see the perils lurking ahead. Met, like Cassandra, with disbelief, he pressed his case even more insistently whenever Western groups asked him to speak. Given this situation, it is easy enough to understand how he came to overstate on some points, how he overreached what he had enough information to declare with such certainty as he conveyed.

The demise of Soviet Communism demonstrates that some of his

fears for the West were excessive. It demonstrates even more conclusively that his understanding of the Soviet scene, especially of the
relationship between the captive peoples and the ruling Communist
Party, was accurate and foresighted. Though Solzhenitsyn sometimes
errs, one should not exaggerate his errors. The movement of history
supports his analysis of the modern world much more than it undercuts
it. Furthermore, though Bernard Levin is surely correct that Solzhenitsyn "underestimated the reserves of moral strength" in the West,
Robert Conquest is equally correct to bring up this mitigating factor:

> But, paradoxically, if he has made our position out to be even worse than
> it really is, this would be due to his having unavoidably gained most of
> his impressions from the Press, especially the liberal Press. Indeed, it is
> surprising that he doesn't go a good deal further in a diagnosis of extreme
> decadence, if he has relied on most of our self-appointed leaders of
> opinion. [14]

A large part of the difficulty in understanding correctly Solzhenitsyn's view of the West is that he uses the term *the West* in two different
ways. This practice is so familiar that it is easy to lose sight of the
distinction entailed in it. One usage refers to the historical heritage; this
one envisions the West as a spiritual/cultural entity. The other usage
refers to the contemporary geopolitical alignment between East and
West; this one envisions the West as a political entity. These two usages
do not refer to mutually exclusive entities, but neither are they identical
entities. For history moves on, and changes have occurred in the West.
The West of the present is different in important ways from the West of
the past.

In general, it is the West of the past which elicits Solzhenitsyn's deep
sympathy. In this sense, he is pro-Western. In the West of the present,
he sees the heritage still alive, but now marked by corrosions and
corruptions which weaken it. In this sense, he is ambivalent toward the
West. One can catch some sense of the direction of his thought from this
recent statement:

> In Western civilizations—which used to be called Western-Christian but
> now might better be called Western-Pagan—along with the development

of intellectual life and science, there has been a loss of the serious moral basis of society. During these 300 years of Western civilization, there has been a sweeping away of duties and an expansion of rights. . . . We must avail ourselves of rights and duties in equal measure.[15]

In place of "the high-minded view of the world which the West has lost," Western society has substituted "that sleek god of affluence . . . as the goal of life."[16]

By sliding away from the Christian foundation of its culture, the West diminishes its resources to engage in the climactic struggle of the modern world: "a global battle between world communism and world humanity."[17] As mankind comes to this "nodal point of all human history," the real nature of the conflict is better understood in Communist countries than in the free West. Thus, Solzhenitsyn asserts, ". . . we have already won the main victory over communism—we have stood out for sixty years and not been infected by it."[18] Meanwhile, the West appeases and accommodates Communist rulers. Two major, but contradictory, historical movements are at work at the same time. The irony here has to do with timing: ". . . our movement of opposition and spiritual revival, like any spiritual process, is slow. But your capitulations, like all political processes, can move very quickly." Solzhenitsyn's warnings to the West are designed to bring these two movements into harmony. "If we can at least slow down that process of concession, if not stop it altogether, and make it possible for the process of liberation to continue in the Communist countries, then ultimately these two processes will yield us our future."[19]

Solzhenitsyn has hopes that his warnings will be heeded. Asked if the West is doomed, he replies, "No, not doomed, but by and large, the scales are tilted to the bad. . . . Can forces emerge in the West to awaken and restore it to health? I still hope so. If not I would not be issuing warnings."[20] His hopefulness is bolstered by his confidence that many common people appreciate him. He notes, for instance, "The Harvard speech rewarded me with an outpouring of favorable responses from the American public at large. . . ."[21]

In contrast, Solzhenitsyn meets with stiff resistance among the elite groups of Western society. In a sense, he deserves their opposition, for they are specifically the targets of his criticisms. Whenever he is described as anti-Western, he is objecting to attitudes that he believes characterize not the West as a whole but its elites. It is among these groups that he observes the greatest departures from the West's traditional spiritual moorings. He takes aim at four separate categories of the elite: the press, the intelligentsia, governmental leaders, and (to a lesser extent) leaders of big business. We shall examine in turn what Solzhenitsyn says about each of these four.

SOLZHENITSYN'S POSITION on the Western press is clear, consistent, and uncomplicated. He supports the freedom of the press (by which he explicitly means "all the media"[22]), and he thinks that the press should be responsible in handling its freedom. As early as his 1974 interview with Walter Cronkite, he asserted, "Not only do I not criticize the system of freedom of the press, on the contrary I consider it one of the great good things of the western way of life." His earlier call for glasnost in the Soviet press, which antagonized Soviet officialdom, is of a piece with this commitment, and he has never reneged on this position of principle. Moreover, Solzhenitsyn has expressed gratitude to the Western press for its role in protecting Sakharov and himself by publicizing their plight. It was particularly valuable in August and September of 1973, when these dissidents were hardest pressed. "It was then that, in alliance with the western press, we won an important battle."[23] One of the most puzzling criticisms of Solzhenitsyn is that he used the Western press. At most, he was guilty of wishing to preserve some realm of his and his family's privacy from the tabloid-style gossip columns. In the public discussion of his views, there was never anything devious about his dealings with the press.

Solzhenitsyn's overarching criticism of the Western press is that it is irresponsible. The first thing that he means here, the point which he reiterates most insistently, is that it does not exercise proper self-restraint. This position could be construed (as it was) as a limitation on liberty. Solzhenitsyn would consider it an avoidance of license. He believes that "every profession must put some restraints on itself," because "[e]very quality, every good quality, if they aren't restrained in some way, become vices." (The translation of this interview contains several grammatical solecisms.) Carrying a good thing too far—this constitutes a veritable definition of vice, as distinguished from virtue (in this case, license as opposed to liberty). Members of the press themselves bear the responsibility to draw the line, day by day, between vice and virtue, license and liberty. "Externally, the press must be absolutely free, as it is with you, but internally everyone must know where to draw the line."[24]

If this is censorship, it is not censorship by government, which Solzhenitsyn knows about all too well from personal experience. It is, rather, self-censorship, the need for which the press itself freely discusses. And when Solzhenitsyn complains about the "shameless intrusion into the privacy of well-known people according to the slogan 'Everyone is entitled to know everything,' " he strikes a chord familiar among the populace. The prurient tastes of tabloid journalism have become, if anything, more common in the Western press since the time of Solzhenitsyn's strictures. It is precisely in this context that we are to understand the notion in his next sentence of "the forfeited right of people *not to know*, not to have their divine souls stuffed with gossip, nonsense, vain talk."[25] Only if taken out of its context could this striking phrasing be construed as an attack on the press's freedom *per se*.

Solzhenitsyn's own treatment by the Western press doubtless intensified his disdain for its practices. Two years prior to the Harvard address, BBC interviewer Michael Charlton asked him if he accepted such Western criticisms of him as that he was "in some respects an impassioned critic" of the West and that he was "asking for a return to something in Russia that is plainly impossible, a return to a patriarchal kind of Russia, a return to Orthodoxy." He replied in part, "You have just enumerated several propositions and practically all of them are not true." He placed the blame for these misperceptions squarely on "the weak sense of responsibility of the press," adding, "Mediocre journalists simply make headlines of their conclusions, which suddenly become generally accepted." To the charge of patriarchalism, he replied particularly acidly, "It is quite easy to imagine that some journalist writing mostly about women's fashions thought up this headline, and so the story gets around that I am calling for a patriarchal way of life."[26] As for Solzhenitsyn's unwillingness to ingratiate himself with the press, one might question his prudence but not his integrity.

If the main manifestation of the press's irresponsibility is its lack of self-restraint, three others can be enumerated. Here is one of them:

Hastiness and superficiality—these are the psychic diseases of the twentieth century and more than anywhere else this is manifested in the press. In-depth analysis of a problem is anathema to the press; it is contrary to its nature. The press merely picks out sensational formulas.

Another—and this one Solzhenitsyn says surprised him—is "a common trend of preferences within the Western press as a whole (the spirit of the time), generally accepted patterns of judgment, and maybe common corporate interests, the sum effect being not competition but unification."[27] These complaints are hardly novel.

There is one more aspect of Solzhenitsyn's charge against the press of irresponsibility. This one, however, stems not from too little but from too much self-restraint by the press. In his view, the press inhibits itself unduly in reporting about life under Communism. ". . . I insist that if the press has such freedom in the West then it must carry the same kind of freedom when it gets into the East." He finds it "strange" and "extraordinary" that, with "one or two remarkable exceptions," "when this western press gets to Moscow or to eastern Europe, or even to China," it "changes completely":

> Here there's nothing sacred for them. They go at presidents, military, ministries and so forth, but there, if some miserable Bulgarian policemen tells them not to photograph a church, they stop. Or the Red Guards . . . in China. If they hang up some kind of leaflet and a correspondent comes up to read it and some wretched little Red Guard tells him not to read it, the correspondent turns and walks away. Why do they do that? Why such a difference?[28]

When the press reacted strongly to his criticisms of it, Solzhenitsyn was surprised. A sense of widespread public support for his position, however, kept him from being dismayed:

> For that reason I was not perturbed by the outburst of reproaches that an angry press rained down upon me. I had not expected it to be so unreceptive to criticism: I was called a fanatic, a man possessed, a mind split apart, a cynic, a vindictive warmonger; I was even simply told to "get out of the country." . . .

And he mentioned a particular case. "Richard Pipes brought up the 'freedom of speech which so annoys Solzhenitsyn.' In fact, it was stated plainly enough for all who can read that I had in mind not freedom of speech, but only the irresponsible and amoral abuse of this freedom."[29]

Intellectuals are another of the constituent groups comprising the Western elite. Sometimes Solzhenitsyn lumps these groups together because of a perceived symbiotic relationship among them. When at Harvard he pointed to a "decline of courage" as perhaps "the most striking feature that an outside observer notices in the West today," he added that it was "particularly noticeable among the ruling and intellectual elites." But sometimes Solzhenitsyn singles out intellectuals for specific disapprobation. About the Vietnam war he charges, "The American intelligentsia lost its nerve. . . ." He has intellectuals in mind when, with wording sure to antagonize, he scolds, "Western thinking has become conservative: the world situation must stay as it is at any cost; there must be no changes. This debilitating dream of a status quo is the symptom of a society that has ceased to develop."[30]

Solzhenitsyn is particularly astounded by the blind spot of Western intellectuals concerning the nature of Communism. They suffer from "a failure to acknowledge it as the quintessence of dynamic and implacable evil."[31] Among Soviet citizens Marxism has become such a "joke" and "object of contempt" that "[n]o serious person . . . , not even university and high school students, can talk about Marxism without a smile or a sneer."[32] But among Western intellectuals there is such "great sympathy for socialism and communism" that "[t]o be a Marxist in an American university today is an honor, and there are many university departments that are Marxist through and through."[33]

According to Solzhenitsyn, two philosophical factors contribute to this blind spot. One is the moral relativism regnant among intellectuals, which views evil as "an unscientific concept, almost a four-letter word, for instead of 'good' and 'evil' there exist only a multiplicity of opinions, each one as valid as the next."[34] The other is that "the intellectual West's sympathy for the Soviet system is also conditioned by the common source of their ideological origins: materialism and atheism. A movement openly connected with religion always alarms, if it does not scare them."[35] Both factors have to do not with political positions *per se* but with clashing world views. It is understandable that some persons of the anti-Communist Left would be rankled by such broad brushstrokes. The question is whether, as generalizations, such statements have any truth value. Perhaps the real offense was in interjecting such categorical moral terms into the ongoing discussion of political positions.

Because of their symbiotic relationship, Solzhenitsyn implicated the West's ruling elite along with its intellectual elite in the charge of a decline in courage. Referring to "the established views of a milieu," he remarked that "whether Democrats or Republicans are in power, and regardless of who is in the White House, the leading experts and advisers are drawn from these same circles."[36] The symbiosis remained in effect even when intellectuals challenged and demonized certain political leaders. For the transgressions lay precisely in departures from the elites' established views; and thus the attacks, as essentially family fights, are the exceptions that prove the rule. John Dunlop has said that in the 1970's Solzhenitsyn "exerted an influence on the political life of America which has perhaps been unequalled by any other foreigner in the two hundred year history of the United States." This may be true. For example, at the 1976 convention of the Republican Party, the forces of insurgent candidate Ronald Reagan overrode the objections of the supporters of President Ford to place into the party platform a "Solzhenitsyn plank" about foreign policy which mentioned the author by name. One may speculate how much Ford's snub of Solzhenitsyn by not inviting him to the White House cost the President with the voters.[37] On the other hand, Solzhenitsyn's views made little imprint on the political establishment.

In Solzhenitsyn's view, the major issue facing the West's political and diplomatic elite was its relationship with Communist-ruled nations, especially its superpower opposite number, the Soviet Union. The prevailing policy was détente, an effort to decrease tensions so as to ensure peaceful coexistence in a world made exceedingly dangerous because of nuclear weaponry at the ready. Because Solzhenitsyn was highly critical of proponents of détente, it would be easy to assume that he opposed the policy *per se*. His own words say otherwise: "Is détente needed or not? Not only is it needed, it is as necessary as air. It is the only way of saving the earth. . . ." But honest détente demands two partners committed to the same goal, not mere indulgence in the rhetoric of détente. Such honesty, he said, was not the case. "The Cold War—the war of hatred—is still going on, but only on the Communist side." Yes, détente is necessary, but détente with open hands!" Otherwise, "Détente becomes self-deception. . . ."[38]

Moreover, détente as practiced by Western diplomats was of no help to the Soviet citizenry. According to Solzhenitsyn, "The whole existence of our slaveowners from beginning to end relies on Western economic assistance." Because "[t]he Soviet economy has an extremely low level of efficiency" and "cannot deal with every problem at once," any food or other assistance helps not the people but the rulers: ". . . indirectly you are helping their military preparations. You are helping the Soviet police state." How grating it must have been for Solzhenitsyn to read Western assessments about the rising standard of living in the Soviet Union. Nor did détente improve the conditions for intellectual and spiritual life in the Soviet Union. On BBC television Solzhenitsyn declared, "You Westerners simply cannot grasp Soviet propaganda. Today you remain British imperialists who wish to strangle the whole earth." Persecution of dissidents continued unabated, though Western "journalists have bowed to the spirit of Helsinki" and stopped reporting it. So he says, "What seems to you to be a milder atmosphere, a milder climate, is for us the strengthening of totalitarianism."[39]

One unhappy effect of détente which particularly exercised Solzhenitsyn was the inhibition placed on foreign broadcasting supported by Western governments. The Russian section of the Voice of America "serves American interests poorly, in fact frequently does them great disservice." Indeed, it "seems to go out of its way to repel the thoughtful Russian listener from any understanding of America, to alienate his sympathies, and even to shock and distress him." Its programs, "instead of bolstering the anti-communist spirit of these potential allies of the U.S.A.," are "filled with trite and inconsequential drivel." After citing examples of material not permitted, he concludes, ". . . at times the Voice of America dances to the tune called by the communist regime or indeed becomes indistinguishable from a Moscow radio station." The same indictment applies in general to the venerable BBC.[40]

Of all the representatives of the West's ruling elite, the one who raised Solzhenitsyn's ire the most was Henry Kissinger. Solzhenitsyn referred to him as "[y]our short-sighted politician who signed the hasty Vietnam capitulation."[41] In late 1975, Solzhenitsyn published an article in the *New York Times* lamenting the dismissal of Secretary of Defense James Schlesinger and suggesting that Secretary of State Kissinger influenced President Ford to make that decision. Solzhenitsyn excoriated Kissinger for "his policy of unending concessions," and he called him "*least of all a diplomat.*" To pave the way for his appeasements, "Mr. Kissinger endlessly deafens us with the threat '. . . but otherwise, nuclear war,' " with the result was that "his opponents are always *winning* and he is always *yielding*." To take the main case in point, "The celebrated Vietnam agreement, the worst diplomatic defeat for the West in 30 years, hypocritically and very conveniently for the aggressor prepared the way for the quiet surrender of three countries in Indochina." Where Kissinger's style of diplomacy was headed was, to Solzhenitsyn, clear: "The very process of surrender of world positions has the character of an avalanche. At every successive stage it becomes more difficult to hold out and one must yield more and more." Thus, Solzhenitsyn concluded with a contrast which appears often in his writings: that the opposite of peace is not war but violence; and one should "not consider Cambodian genocide and Vietnamese prison camps as the attainment of *peace.*"[42]

In addition to criticizing the Western elites of the press, the intelligentsia, and the rulers, Solzhenitsyn criticized the elite of Western business. With certain big-business leaders in mind, he spoke accusingly of "the alliance between our Communist leaders and your capitalists." Starting with Armand Hammer, friend of Lenin, he told of the "continuous and steady support by the businessmen of the West for the Soviet Communist leaders." Citing a recent episode involving criminological technology, he declared, "And if today the Soviet Union has powerful military and police forces . . . —forces which are used to crush our movement for freedom in the Soviet Union—we have Western capital to thank for this as well." Herein he was not criticizing free-market enterprise *per se*, any more than he was challenging the concept of a free press by pointing out the press's irresponsibility. Rather, he was demonstrating the evils that arise when persons violate the principles governing the moral universe: "This is something which is almost incomprehensible to the human mind: a burning greed for profit that goes beyond all reason, all self-control, all conscience, only to get money."[43]

IN THE 1990'S, it takes considerable exertion of memory and imagination to reconstruct mentally the mood of the West, and of America in particular, during the middle and late 1970's. The great episode of the time had been the war in Vietnam, and it wreaked severe havoc with the American psyche. America's self-doubts were pervasive, and they would not soon go away. Jimmy Carter, during his presidency, would continue to acknowledge and to bemoan the malaise of spirit in the nation. Even at the time of the 1991 war in Kuwait and Iraq, the experience of Vietnam provided the touchstone for judgment, as President George Bush announced that the United States had finally purged itself of the "Vietnam syndrome."

It was in this perfervid period of American history that Solzhenitsyn moved to the United States. Almost at once, he took up sides. He used public platforms provided by his hosts to criticize the elites of his host nation and their allies. Many heard or read such statements of his as this: "But, in fact, members of the U. S. antiwar movement became accomplices in the betrayal of Far Eastern nations, in the genocide and the suffering today imposed on thirty million people there."[44] It is not surprising, especially in this situation, that the accused took up self-defensive positions and lashed back at their accuser. The ensuing antagonism was exacerbated by the approval of his words in some quarters of the West.

We can perhaps see more clearly now than we could at that time how deeply the anxieties about that war affected Solzhenitsyn's reception in the West. Indeed, it would seem fitting to talk about the "Vietnamization" of his reputation. Had Solzhenitsyn come to the United States at a less discontented time in the nation's history, his reception would have been different. And of course he would not have felt constrained to say some of the things that he said. It has taken many years for Americans to utter the word *defeat* in describing the debacle of Vietnam. Today more and more Americans can acknowledge that his plainspoken judgments had at least a certain plausibility. As historical interpretations go, they fall within the range of the legitimate and defensible. And now the demise of Soviet Communism will take its (large) part in the ongoing process of reinterpreting the Vietnam war.

In any case, the impeccability of his motivations for his pronouncements is easier to accept now. When Solzhenitsyn left the Soviet Union, he told his countrymen not to live by lies. When he arrived in the West, he said the same thing to Westerners. He himself has always sought to tell the truth:

I think the first universal rule, with you as with us, is not to accept lies. To speak the truth is to ensure the rebirth of liberty—regardless of pressure, interests and fashions. . . . And if some people shrug their shoulders, repeat it again. Those who shrug their shoulders at the story of a tragedy on this scale are wittingly, or unwittingly, abetting the executioners.[45]

To tell the truth in the pursuit of liberty is a noble motive. It does not, however, guarantee that everything that one says will turn out to be accurate. Fallibility dogs even the noblest intentions. In his friendly desire to warn the West about the dangers confronting it, Solzhenitsyn sought for specificity to buttress his general position. It is in the specifics that his predictive blunders can be seen at their most pointed. But the course of history makes his general assessment of Western weakness look too bleak, too.

In early 1976 Solzhenitsyn said about his two years in the West, "During these two years the West has become weaker in relation to the East. . . . Moscow now takes infinitely less note of the West." Therefore, he continued, "I wouldn't be surprised at the sudden and imminent fall of the West. . . . The West is on the verge of a collapse created by its own hands." About these two years, he said reproachfully, ". . . terrible things have happened. The West has given up not only four, five, or six countries; the West has given up all its world positions."[46] This apocalyptic note was not new with him in 1976; it continued and intensified the note struck in the 1974 interview with Walter Cronkite: ". . . never before has the superiority of the Soviet Union and the Warsaw Pact over the countries of NATO been so great as it is at the moment," and ". . . never before has the President of the United States been in such a weak position. . . ."[47]

Within this general framework, Solzhenitsyn got down to specifics. For instance, "Portugal has, in effect, fallen out of NATO already. I don't wish to be a prophet of doom but these events are irreversible. Very shortly Portugal will be considered a member of the Warsaw Pact." Needless to say, the internal political conflict in Portugal at that time did not have the dire results that Solzhenitsyn predicted. He was less wide of the mark about Angola, which, as he observed, could provide a coveted location in the Atlantic Ocean for Soviet naval power. But enough years have now passed to bring a waning of Marxist power there, too. He said, in addition, "In 1975 alone four countries were broken off. Four—three in Indochina plus India. . . ."[48] About the three in Indochina we can understand. But India? It would take a historian to remind most of us of what internal affairs there so exercised him then. There is more: "Italy and France are still free, but they have already allowed themselves to be corroded by powerful communist parties."[49] In a statement to the French newspaper *Le Monde*, Solzhenitsyn provided a kind of compendium of his geopolitical outlook in the 1970's. In his view, the West had

> abandoned to an implacable enemy whole territories and populations: China . . . , North Korea, Cuba, North Vietnam, today South Vietnam, today Cambodia. Laos is being lost; Thailand, South Korea, and Israel are in danger; Portugal is throwing herself irretrievably into the abyss; Finland and Austria are resigned to their fate, powerless to defend themselves and unable, on the evidence, to expect help from outside. There is no room to list all the little countries of Africa and the Middle East that have become puppets of Communism, and all the others, even in Europe, that hasten to grovel on their knees in order to survive. And the UN has become a podium from which to ridicule the West—a measure of the brutal collapse of Western power.[50]

What was it that caused Solzhenitsyn to make such apocalyptic predictions? Exactly what? The answer comes in one word: *Vietnam*. In the long struggle between Communist power and the Free World known as the Cold War, the conflict in Vietnam seemed to him (and of course to many others, too, at the time) the decisive turning point, after which the West would find no reprieve from the debilitating consequences of its ignominious defeat. As he put it, "Today the longest and most visible battle of this war, Vietnam, is ending tragically, with the assassination of thousands, the subjugation of millions more, the creation of immense concentration camps."[51] To Americans specifically, he said, "Your country has just recently passed through the extended ordeal of Vietnam, which exhausted and divided your society. I can say with certainty that this ordeal was the least of a long chain of similar trials which awaits you in the near future."[52]

In Solzhenitsyn's reaction to the Vietnam war, there is a great and painful irony. The very event which caused the elites of the West to be unable to penetrate to the core of his moral vision also somewhat beclouded his political, specifically geopolitical, vision. For on no other subject did he make as many specific misjudgments as on the relative weakness of the West. If his reception in the West suffered, as I have suggested, from a kind of "Vietnamization" among his critics, he, too, suffered a degree of "Vietnamization" in his own thinking. Some of his prophecies simply did not come to pass, and the main reason is that he allowed the Vietnam war to loom too large in his thinking. But who did not?

This is not to say that Solzhenitsyn was wrong about where to draw the main battle lines in the struggle between Communist power and the Free World. On the contrary, the disappearance of the Soviet Union demonstrates that he understood the nature of Communism much better than did his detractors. Rather, it is to say that, although he knew much about the West, he did not appreciate adequately just those reserves of civic virtue in the West which he was trying to promote. The irony here is compounded by his having taken as more representative than they were those very elites which he castigated.

In his piece for *Le Monde* in 1975, Solzhenitsyn provided a heuristic device useful for understanding his view of world history over the prior thirty years. He calls this period the Third World War, and he says that it "has ended in defeat." He traces it from its start:

> The Third World War began at the end of the Second, in 1945 at Yalta, thanks to the shaky pens of Roosevelt and Churchill, who celebrated the victory by handing out concessions: Estonia, Latvia, Lithuania, Moldavia, Mongolia, millions of Soviet citizens forcibly handed over to face death or the camps; and soon Yugoslavia, Albania, Poland, Bulgaria, Rumania, Czechoslovakia, Hungary, East Germany were abandoned to unrestrained violence.

This "unbroken descent toward enfeeblement and decadence" proceeded apace and came to include the capitulation of additional countries and the imperilment of others. The process culminated with Vietnam. Thus, he concluded his *Le Monde* piece, "It is too late to worry about how to avoid the Third World War. But we must have the courage and clear-headedness to stop the Fourth. To stop it, not grovel on our knees."[53]

What has transpired in world history since the 1970's is what Solzhenitsyn would then call the Fourth World War. Because he fell silent in the early 1980's, we do not have from him the kind of sustained analysis that he provided for the so-called Third World War. Recent events make obvious, however, that, if the balance of power had tilted the Soviets' way by the 1970's, things went badly for them thereafter. Nor did Solzhenitsyn discount that such a favorable turn of events might transpire, or else he would not have said what he did in the 1970's. Familiar usage labels everything from 1945 to 1991 as the Cold War, which, as we now say, the West finally won. Solzhenitsyn divided this period into two parts. The first, he declared, was disastrous for the Free World. The second, he was ready and eager to allow, could be different. He was not announcing the end of history.

Despite his general silence in the 1980's, we can discern what Solzhenitsyn thought were some of the historical forces that would continue to be at work in the period of his so-called Fourth World War. He was always keenly aware of the inner rot of Communist-run societies. Communism would one day pass away. The only question was when. Sooner or later? Also, he was aware, much more than most Westerners, of the profound alienation from Communism felt by those who lived under it. These people yearning to be free were natural allies of the Free World.

To speed the fall of Communism, all that was needed, to go in tandem with the internal resistance of the oppressed, was external resistance from the Free World. Would a new Western resolve to withstand Communism be forthcoming? It had to be gratifying to Solzhenitsyn to hear President Ronald Reagan's anti-Communist rhetoric, to perceive his words and deeds in behalf of Western strength. That other Western leaders in the 1980's joined the President of the United States in demonstrating firmness toward the Soviet Union also had to please him. Reagan's description of the Soviet Union as an evil empire, words out of keeping with the spirit of accommodation of the 1970's and seeming to his critics to reify goodness in the West, must have struck Solzhenitsyn as an invocation of the moral language which he himself always employed. We know that Solzhenitsyn valued Reagan.[54] We do not know details of his estimation of the President. In any case, it is easy enough to see that the so-called Fourth World War concluded just as Solzhenitsyn wished that it would, with the death of the Soviet Union. The major glory for this outcome need not be attributed to Reagan and the other Western leaders. It would be praise enough to say that they did no harm (though one could make the case that they did help somewhat). It is an open question whether we should say that the West won the Cold War. It is a settled matter that the Soviet Union lost it.

We are aided in understanding Solzhenitsyn's analysis of the Fourth World War by retracing his steps of analysis, in reverse order, through its three predecessors. Solzhenitsyn had said, "The Third World War attacks the West at its most vulnerable point: the side of human nature willing to make any concession for the sake of material well-being."[55] When BBC interviewer Michael Charlton brought up Bertrand Russell's famous dictum, "Better Red than dead," Solzhenitsyn immediately countered this "terrible statement" with a question: "Why did he not say it would be better to be brown [Nazi] than dead?" Solzhenitsyn's own stance was, "Better to be dead than a scoundrel." As he explained, "In this horrible expression of Bertrand Russell's there is an absence of all moral criteria."[56]

It was not always so, he reminded a British radio audience. At the time of the Second World War, "Britain assumed a moral stance against Hitler, and it was this that inspired her to one of the most heroic acts of resistance in her history." He then added this generalization, as apposite to the Fourth World War as to the Second: "A moral stance, even in politics, always safeguards our spirit; sometimes, as we can see, it even protects our very existence. A moral stance can suddenly turn out to be more farsighted than any calculated pragmatism."[57]

Solzhenitsyn also drew lessons for our time from the First World War and the subsequent Bolshevik Revolution. Here he engages in a risky argument by analogy. He views the "liberal statesmen" who engineered the revolution of February 1917 as "a collection of spineless mediocrities" who "brought [Russia] to a state of complete collapse within six months." The West needs to learn the lesson in the analogy:

> The way in which our Russian liberals and socialists gave way to the Communists has been repeated on a worldwide scale since those days. The only difference is that the process has been spread out over several decades. The same process of self-weakening and capitulation is being repeated on a massive scale.[58]

And so today, following its untrustworthy elites, "The entire Western world is presently being swept toward socialism. . . ."[59]

Solzhenitsyn seeks to draw lessons from all three of the world wars of the twentieth century. His analysis includes episodes of vice and episodes of virtue. The picture is mixed, variegated, though admittedly he thought that the times when he was uttering his warnings were very dark. The motivation to sound the alarm is not difficult to discern. Solzhenitsyn's concern was for the future. He was not indulging in a rehash of the past out of a dilettantish taste for historical inquiry. He hoped to make a difference in future behavior.

Solzhenitsyn's analysis of the twentieth century is open to challenge at various points. What is not open to challenge is that at every point Solzhenitsyn allies himself with the interests of the West. And for the simple reason that the West is the main proponent in the modern world for human freedom, which is always his passion. The West is the Free World, and Solzhenitsyn wishes for the whole world to be free.

IN HIS SEARCH TO UNDERSTAND his times, Solzhenitsyn does not limit himself to an analysis of the twentieth century. His historical inquiry takes him back two centuries, and it takes him beyond the range of political history and into the more fundamental arena of intellectual history. He rivets his attention on the Enlightenment, which originated in eighteenth-century France but the effects of which rayed out to encompass the entire Western world. It is here, in the Enlightenment, that he locates the source of the ideas which have riven the modern world and which have infected both political East and political West. In terms of the history of ideas, the Enlightenment is his great enemy. Solzhenitsyn focuses on what he considers its central theme, namely, secularization. It dismisses God as an agent in the drama of human life. He is keenly aware of such Enlightenment ideas as the doctrines of progress and of human perfectibility, as well as the post-Enlightenment political ideologies which they spawned. He keeps his eye trained on what for him is the central issue: the usurpation by Man of the role of supreme moral arbiter formerly reserved for God.

Solzhenitsyn gave fullest articulation of his analysis of intellectual history to his Harvard audience. After presenting his exposition of the ills plaguing the modern West, he devoted the climactic section of his address to his historical analysis of the factors underlying those ills.

This closing movement of the speech has three parts. The first of these is a succinct articulation of the fundamental cause of today's troubles:

> . . . the mistake must be at the root, at the very foundation of thought in modern times. I refer to the prevailing Western view of the world which was born in the Renaissance and has found political expression since the Age of Enlightenment. It became the basis for political and social doctrine and could be called rationalistic humanism or humanistic autonomy: the proclaimed and practiced autonomy of man from any higher force above him. It could also be called anthropocentricity, with man seen as the center of all.

Solzhenitsyn understood the historical reaction against the Middle Ages, with its "intolerable despotic repression of man's physical nature in favor of the spiritual one." Nevertheless, the reaction had carried the West to the opposite extreme. "The humanistic way of thinking . . . did not admit the existence of intrinsic evil in man, nor did it seek any task higher than the attainment of happiness on earth. It started modern Western civilization on the dangerous trend of worshipping man and his material needs."[60]

The issue had been engaged. It was one of world view. Solzhenitsyn's task was to explain his religious world view to an audience presumed to be, for the most part, secular. To do so, he sought common ground between himself and America's Founding Fathers. However much or little they were influenced by Enlightenment thinking, they had not severed the tie to religion, and so "all individual human rights were granted on the ground that man is God's creature. That is, freedom was given to the individual conditionally, in the assumption of his constant religious responsibility." However boldly human rights were proclaimed, they were still perceived to be limited by duties. "Subsequently, however," as the influence of Enlightenment thinking deepened, "all such limitations were eroded everywhere in the West; a total emancipation occurred from the moral heritage of Christian centuries with their great reserves of mercy and sacrifice." And then Solzhenitsyn made a statement which baffled some of his auditors: "The West has finally achieved the rights of man, *and even to excess*, but man's sense of responsibility to God and society has grown dimmer and dimmer" (emphasis added).[61] But he was merely invoking the familiar traditional distinction between liberty and license.

The next move in the speech, if the responses are to be trusted, made matters between him and his audience only worse. In a brief section entitled "An Unexpected Kinship," Solzhenitsyn notes that the elites of both political East and political West are under the sway of this same Enlightenment thinking. And so, even knowing for potential for offense, he says,

> It is no accident that all of communism's rhetorical vows revolve around Man (with a capital *M*) and his earthly happiness. At first glance it seems an ugly parallel: common traits in the thinking and way of life of today's West and today's East? But such is the logic of materialistic development.

In the speech entitled *A World Split Apart*, he asserts that "the essence of the crisis" of the modern world is that "the split in the world is less terrifying than the similarity of the disease afflicting its main sections." If we limit our thinking to political formations, we emphasize the split; if, however, we think in terms of underlying world views, as Solzhenitsyn does, we emphasize the similarity. Moreover, as the Free World struggles against Communism, "Humanism which has lost its Christian heritage cannot prevail in this competition." As the lessons of twentieth-century history teach us, "Liberalism was inevitably pushed aside by radicalism, radicalism had to surrender to socialism, and socialism could not stand up to communism."[62] The sterner heirs of the Enlightenment win out over the softer heirs.

Solzhenitsyn's final move in the speech points toward the future; it is entitled "Before the Turn." He explicates the "disaster which is already very much with us," namely, "an autonomous, irreligious humanistic consciousness," in these terms:

> On the way from the Renaissance to our days we have enriched our experience, but we have lost the concept of a Supreme Complete Entity which used to restrain our passions and our irresponsibility. We have placed too much hope in politics and social reforms, only to find out that we were being deprived of our most precious possession: our spiritual life.

Considering it "retrogressive to hold on to the ossified formulas of the Enlightenment," Solzhenitsyn urges us to reconsider the most basic elements of our world view:

We cannot avoid reassessing the fundamental definitions of human life and human society. Is it true that man is above everything? Is there no Superior Spirit above him? Is it right that man's life and society's activities should be ruled by material expansion above all? Is it permissible to promote such expansion to the detriment of our integral spiritual life?[63]

It is the age-old question: Does God exist? If he does, that fact makes a difference in how we define ourselves and therefore in how we actually live, individually and corporately. If God exists, Enlightenment thinking has led us astray and into a dead end. Tell me what you think of the Enlightenment, and I will tell you what you think of Solzhenitsyn.

The final two paragraphs of the Harvard address received scanty attention from the commentators; yet they are where the whole speech heads. Although we must look to the past to get our bearings, the purpose of doing so is to prepare for the future. These paragraphs are future-oriented.

If the world has not approached its end, it has reached a major watershed in history, equal in importance to the turn from the Middle Ages to the Renaissance. It will demand from us a spiritual blaze; we shall have to rise to a new height of vision, to a new level of life, where our physical nature will not be cursed, as in the Middle Ages, but even more importantly, our spiritual being will not be trampled upon, as in the Modern Era.

This ascension is similar to climbing onto the next anthropological stage. No one on earth has way other way left but—upward.[64]

That Solzhenitsyn considered this passage of supreme importance, despite Western inattention to it, is apparent from a later reference of his to it: "The path that I do propose is set forth in the conclusion of my Harvard speech . . . : there is no other way left but—*upward*. I believe that the lavishly materialistic twentieth century has all too long kept us in a subhuman state—some of us through superabundance, others through hunger."[65]

Materialism is, from Solzhenitsyn's Christian viewpoint, a subhuman philosophy of life because it overemphasizes what humans have in common with animals: bodies. At the same time, Solzhenitsyn does not call for a return to the Middle Ages; for in that time, also, there was an imbalance—in the opposite direction, toward the spirit at the expense of the body. Once, when referring to the Enlightenment, he noted that "its materialistic excesses were explained away by the previous excesses of Catholicism." Solzhenitsyn's hope for the future is for a culture which fuses the best of the medieval era and the best of the modern era and avoids the excessive emphases of both. Since the modern era's excesses comprise the world now too much with us, it is against materialism that he concentrates his attention. Nonetheless, because of the criticisms leveled against him, it is essential to observe that he does not call us back to a univocal spirituality of the Middle Ages—or back to any other past, for that matter. As he once phrased it, ". . . apart from the half-witted, no normal person could ever propose a return to the past. . . ."[66]

Solzhenitsyn's thinking about the relative merits of the medieval era and the modern era can be sharpened by recourse to some musings by Professor Andozerskaya, a medieval historian in *August 1914*. She tells her students, ". . . don't mistake the branch for the tree. The Western Enlightenment is only one branch of Western culture, and by no means the most fruitful. It starts from the trunk, not from the root." When the students ask what is more important than it, she replies, "If you like, the spiritual life of the Middle Ages. Mankind has never experienced such an intense spiritual life, with the spiritual so far outweighing the material, either before or since." And she proceeds to praise "the religious transmutation of beauty in the Middle Ages and the Renaissance" and also "the mystical poetry of the Middle Ages."[67] Assuming for the moment that Solzhenitsyn agrees entirely with his character here, we can judge that, if he had to choose between the spiritual (that which links humans upward to God) and the physical (that which links humans downward to the animals), he would choose the spiritual. Anyone who believes in God would make the same choice. That is, however, a false dichotomy. Humans need not accept either the cursing of their physical nature or the trampling upon their spiritual being. We stand on the brink of a transition in history as important as was the Renaissance. As the medieval era passed, so now maybe the modern era is about to pass.

The conclusion of the Harvard address is not the only place where he has expressed his anticipation of an approaching watershed in history. Perhaps the most illuminating iteration of this expectation is the one which fuses political history and intellectual history.

In addition to the grave political situation in the world today, we are also witnessing the emergence of a crisis of unknown nature, one completely new, and entirely non-political. We are approaching a major turning point in world history, in the history of civilization. It has already been noted by specialists in various areas. I could compare it only with the turning from the Middle Ages to the modern era, a shift in our civilization. It is a juncture at which settled concepts suddenly become hazy, lose their precise contours, at which our familiar and commonly used words lose their meaning, become empty shells, and methods which have been reliable for many centuries no longer work. It's the sort of turning point where the hierarchy of values which we have venerated, and which we use to determine what is important to us and what causes our hearts to beat is starting to rock and may collapse.

These two crises, the political crisis of today's world and the oncoming spiritual crisis, are occurring at the same time. It is our generation that will have to confront them.[68]

Solzhenitsyn is both predicting and trying to foster the arrival of this watershed moment.

Is SOLZHENITSYN LIKELY to be proven right? We have seen the political crisis come to a head. Despite his fears, Western civilization has negotiated a dangerous curve without slipping down the precipice. What about the non-political crisis, the one of unknown nature? Are we seeing a revival of spirituality? Certainly, we are seeing it in post-Soviet Russia. Are we seeing a loss of faith in Enlightenment ideals? Are there those "specialists in various areas" whose analysis of our times might support Solzhenitsyn's contention that we are approaching the end of the era which we have called modern? Here, too, we find evidence for an answer in the affirmative.

In a densely argued philosophical disquisition on moral theory, *After Virtue*, Alasdair MacIntyre describes the failure of the Enlightenment "project" (as he calls it). Its "secularisation of morality," he says, ultimately produces incoherence. All the various endeavors of nineteenth- and twentieth-century moral philosophers have failed "to rescue the autonomous moral agent from the predicament in which the failure of the Enlightenment project of providing him with a secular, rational justification for his moral allegiances had left him." This "breakdown

. . . provides the historical background against which the predicaments of our own culture can become intelligible." MacIntyre identifies both Marxism and liberal individualism as inheritances of the Enlightenment, which intellectual movement gives formative shape to "the *ethos* of the distinctively modern and modernising world." And he declares that "nothing less than a rejection of a large part of that ethos will provide us with a rationally and morally defensible standpoint from which to judge and to act. . . ."[69]

By the end of his book, we find MacIntyre reaching for a communitarian basis for virtue, a way lying between collectivism and individualism. His conclusion startlingly echoes the conclusion of Solzhenitsyn's Harvard address, as both writers imagine that we are on the brink of a major turning point in our history. MacIntyre gently, tentatively draws a parallel between "our own age in Europe and North America and the epoch in which the Roman empire declined into the Dark Ages." The people of that time, he says, became engaged in "the construction of new forms of community within which the moral life could be sustained so that both morality and civility might survive the coming ages of barbarism and darkness." He completes his historical analogy as follows:

> If my account of our moral condition is correct, we ought also to conclude that for some time now we too have reached a turning point. What matters at this stage is the construction of local forms of community within which civility and the intellectual and moral life can be sustained through the new dark ages which are already upon us. And if the tradition of the virtues was able to survive the horrors of the last dark ages, we are not entirely without grounds for hope. This time however the barbarians are not waiting beyond the frontiers; they have already been governing us for quite some time. And it is our lack of consciousness of this that constitutes part of our predicament.[70]

One should not press the parallels between MacIntyre and Solzhenitsyn too far. What they are saying is similar, not identical. But MacIntyre does serve as one example of those specialists to whom Solzhenitsyn made general reference. Both locate in the Enlightenment the source of the troubles of the modern world. Both are critical of the notion of human autonomy in morals. Both eschew collectivism and individualism, preferring communitarianism. And both imagine that we are at a watershed moment in which history is passing beyond the era to which the Enlightenment gave normative shape. These similarities are all the more striking for the very different contexts of analysis of the two. However lightly one may wish to press the parallels between them, what is patent is that Solzhenitsyn is not alone in his criticism of the Enlightenment. Nor is MacIntyre the only other interpreter who is supportive of this critical posture.

One need not share the moral concerns of Solzhenitsyn and MacIntyre to sense that we are at the end of an age. Just to mention the academically fashionable term *postmodernism* is to make the point. Persons who use this term to describe themselves clearly illustrate in their thinking that settled concepts have become hazy and lost their precise contours and that words have lost their meaning. The sense that we are at a civilizational turning point is much in the air today.

This mood affects academic historians, among others. Christopher Lasch, writing in 1991 specifically about American politics, takes as his underlying premise for *The True and Only Heaven* that "old political ideologies have exhausted their capacity either to explain events or to inspire men and women to constructive action. . . ." A man of the Left himself, he asks, "Who would have predicted, twenty-five years ago, that as the twentieth century approached its end, it would be the left that was everywhere in retreat?" About "the dominant tradition deriving from the Enlightenment," he observes, "Everywhere we see signs of this growing disaffection with liberalism. . . ." He remarks that "the Enlightenment . . . gave rise to the dangerous fantasy that man could remodel both the natural world and human nature itself." Also, Lasch takes note of the gap between the Enlightenment's modern American heirs and the American populace at large: "Their confidence in being on the winning side of history made progressive people unbearably smug and superior, but they felt isolated and beleaguered in their country. . . ." He even refers to "the left's fear of America."[71]

Given the "exhaustion of the progressive tradition," Lasch, too, senses that we are at a historical turning point. America needs some new idea to reinspirit its politics. Referring to political Left and Right, he declares, "Neither side wants to admit that our society has taken a wrong turn, lost its way, and needs to recover a sense of purpose and direction." Since "neither fascism nor socialism represents the wave of the future," America must look inward: "None of this means that the future will be safe for democracy, only that the danger to democracy comes less from totalitarianism or collectivist movements abroad than from the erosion of its psychological, cultural, and spiritual foundations from within." And so Lasch calls for a new populism. He is drawn to "small-scale production and political decentralization." And he sees in a new populism the potential to generate "a distinctive kind of politics and . . . a distinctive tradition of moral speculation drawn from everyday experience (as well as from the heightened experience of spiritual fervor). . . ."[72] Is it possible that, in the unexpected happenings of the 1992 American presidential campaign, we are already seeing signs of prescience on Lasch's part in his call for a new and non-ideological populism?

In Lasch, as in MacIntyre, one sees significant areas of consanguinity with Solzhenitsyn. Both Lasch and Solzhenitsyn sense that, in the liberalism of the Western elites, the historical motive force of the Enlightenment has reached a point of diminishing returns. The doctrine of progress no longer satisfies. Neither does political ideology. Small-scale production and political decentralization are themes common to them both. So is the need for a renewed sense of spirituality, even though Lasch does not share Solzhenitsyn's religious orientation. Lasch, too, is one of those "specialists" whose analysis has its resonances with Solzhenitsyn's.

Historian John Lukacs expresses his own version of ennui about being at the end of an era. In his disturbing book, *The Passing of the Modern Age*, he traces the transitions from Antiquity to the Middle Ages and from the Middle Ages to the Modern Age. Then he asks, "What will the third transition be? A second Dark Ages? A second Renaissance? A mixture of both? I cannot tell. But I can tell this: the term 'Modern Age' no longer fits; it is no longer real." Remarking that "the fatal encumbrances" of our modern thought "are embedded in the materialist philosophies of human nature whose origins go back for more than one hundred, even two hundred years," he concludes with only the slimmest of hopes: that our consciousness of the past, of times when civilization was healthier than it is now, will eventually bring civilization out from "beneath the waves of a new barbarism."[73] Lukacs seems, by disposition, unable to share in the hopefulness which always invigorates Solzhenitsyn.

MacIntyre, Lasch, and Lukacs are but three interpreters of the modern world who serve to confirm major elements of Solzhenitsyn's interpretation. Although their illustrative value is limited, since they and Solzhenitsyn are not writing out of the same intellectual contexts, the accumulation of enough interpreters of similar mood would move beyond the level of illustration. There are other such interpreters. Some of them have acknowledged indebtedness to Solzhenitsyn. We shall consider this group in Chapter Thirteen.

The late Leonard Schapiro forthrightly conceded the excesses and exaggerations of Solzhenitsyn's judgments about the West. Yet he also insisted that Solzhenitsyn's "message is of vital relevance to our age. . . . Clearly the time has not yet come to assess the importance and influence of a man who, I venture to predict, is destined to rank as one of the most remarkable human beings of this generation. . . ."[74] Were he still alive today, perhaps Schapiro would say that the time for that assessment has now come. That assessment should result in the West's embracing Solzhenitsyn as its friend.

7

On Democracy

THE MOST WIDESPREAD SPECIFIC CRITICISM directed toward Solzhenitsyn is that he is anti-democratic. Within his supposed anti-Western posture, no single theme has so exercised his critics as his supposed antagonism toward democracy. Yet one looks in vain for a single statement by Solzhenitsyn in opposition to democracy *per se*.

Of course, Solzhenitsyn has made comments critical of democracy. Otherwise, the charge of anti-democracy would never have been leveled. These criticisms, however, have always been directed toward certain practices of democracy, not toward democracy in principle. Such criticisms are common fare among virtually all democrats. Nor are any of Solzhenitsyn's criticisms novel or unique. He zeroes in on problems already familiar to proponents and practitioners of democracy.

Two concerns motivate Solzhenitsyn to examine Western democracies. One is that he is always trying to imagine whether and how democracy might work in Russia's future—and, if so, in which of its forms. The other is simply that he cares about the West. It is in regard to this second concern that his view of democracy constitutes a subpoint under his view of the West. However, because of the enormous confusion that it generated, this one merits chapter-length treatment.

That Solzhenitsyn is positively a proponent of democracy became unarguably clear in 1990, with the publication of *Rebuilding Russia*. There were earlier signs that he favored democracy. However, when he was addressing the Western audiences, presumably already committed to democracy, he judged that they needed to hear not an explanation of the virtues of democracy but a warning about its potential and actual perversions. He may have been well-advised to make clear the extent of his common ground with Western democrats, but this is a question more of rhetorical strategy than of political commitment.

In any case, in 1990 a new situation confronted him. Russia was moving beyond Communism. As a patriot he felt compelled to interrupt yet again his main mission of writing historical novels, this time to give practical political advice to his people. When he did so, he recommended democracy as the preferred form of government. *Rebuilding Russia* presents Solzhenitsyn's most sustained discussion of democracy, both the theory and the practice of it. We shall follow the flow of that argument in Chapter Twelve. This chapter features his prior statements on the subject, for they are the ones which were interpreted as substantiating an anti-democratic posture on his part. This chapter will argue that he is not anti-democratic. Chapter Twelve will demonstrate that he is pro-democratic.

Solzhenitsyn might fairly be called a reluctant democrat. He is a classic case of one who, as in Winston Churchill's famous dictum, believes that democracy is the worst form of government, except for all the others. This least-of-all-evils approach is at the furthest remove from the utopian impulse. Solzhenitsyn is a reluctant democrat in exactly the way that Churchill is. Most democrats are. Or at least it is common to pay lip-service to the Churchillian apothegm. Solzhenitsyn really believes it.

It is generally considered acceptable for self-avowed democrats to specify criticisms of certain practices of a given democracy. Objections arise, however, when one who is not known beforehand to be a democrat criticizes anything about democracy, even practices so glaringly flawed that all can see the problem. This is essentially a matter of social etiquette; yet it has played a part in Solzhenitsyn's reception in the West. Since we now know that he is a self-avowed Russian democrat, the question arises whether he underwent a change of heart regarding democracy between the 1970's and 1990. The evidence suggests rather strongly that he did not. Or, if he did, it was not a change from anti-democracy to pro-democracy but only from uncertainty about democracy to certainty—and, even then, only in regard to the Russian setting. He always denied the allegations that he is anti-democratic in principle.

The note of uncertainty was sounded in 1980, when he said, "As concerns the theoretical question whether Russia should choose or reject authoritarianism in the future, I have no final opinion, and have not offered any. My criticism of certain aspects of democracy is well known."[1] A decade later he did offer his "final opinion." In 1980 he was speaking about Russia only. About the United States he had said to Walter Cronkite in 1974,

> You know, it's not right to say that I haven't noticed the good sides of American democracy. I've noticed a lot of good sides to American democracy, but when we're talking together, publicly, I think we just can't go on endlessly praising each other and paying each other compliments. Normally one criticizes.[2]

In a press conference of the same year, he declared, "I am not against democracy as such, and not against democracy in Russia, but I am in favour of a sound democracy, and I want us in Russia to move toward it smoothly, cautiously, and slowly."[3] These citations suggest that, when Solzhenitsyn first arrived in the West, he had sympathy for American democracy and entertained the prospect that democracy might be good for a free Russia. Indeed, if anything, a half decade in the West caused him to have some doubts about this latter! At no time, however, did he suggest that democracy as such was a bad thing for America and other Western countries.

These citations suffice to provide a context within which to consider the criticisms which Solzhenitsyn leveled against certain Western practices of democracy. As we proceed, we shall discover other intimations that he has always tended toward favoring democracy. In other words, continuity, rather than discontinuity, is the hallmark of Solzhenitsyn's thinking about democracy, as it is about other subjects, as well.

The most striking thing about Solzhenitsyn's comments on democracy is simply their sparseness. We find a reference here and a reference there, generally in passages where something else is the major topic under consideration. As he said in 1980, when he was winding down his involvement in polemics, "I have never attempted to analyze this whole question [of democracy] in theoretical terms, no do I intend to do so now, for I am neither a political scientist nor a politician. I am simply an artist who is distressed by the painfully clear events and crises of today."[4]

Therefore, those searching to identify Solzhenitsyn's view of democracy have had to extrapolate from very limited evidence. They have had to pick up on apparent hints and intimations in order to construct an overarching interpretation. There has been much reading between the lines, instead of reading the lines themselves, for the simple reason that there are not many lines to read on the subject. Thus, we encounter more assertion than argument. It is noteworthy how few quotations from Solzhenitsyn are offered to buttress ·the interpretations of his detractors. This method of extrapolation, always risky, is particularly likely to yield bad fruit when the interpreter is operating out of a world view at odds with that of the author under scrutiny.

Given Solzhenitsyn's disavowal of expert status on political theory, we best approach his thinking about democracy without recourse to technical definitions. He means by the term simply that governmental leaders are chosen by the people whom they govern and are answerable to them. There are broader usages of the term, as in referring to mass culture as the democratization of culture. There are narrower usages, as well, as in assuming a conjunction between democracy and a two-party or multi-party system of electoral politics. Though Solzhenitsyn does comment on party politics, as we shall see, it is helpful at this point to stick to the plain, common-sense usage of the term.

Democracy is, in this usage, one political option among others. The others pertinent to this discussion are totalitarianism, monarchy, theocracy, and authoritarianism. The only one which crosses Solzhenitsyn's mind as possibly viable for Russia is authoritarianism. His comments about it, especially in *Letter to the Soviet Leaders*, are the main source of the anti-democratic charge against him. For the other options, though he has been charged with holding each one of them, he has denied all such charges.

The label of totalitarian is so patently false as to be unworthy of consideration. Everything in Solzhenitsyn's life and writings bespeaks his militant opposition to totalitarianism. It is an interesting question why the attribution of monarchism ever arose, for nothing in his writing gives support for it. It is pure speculation, a classic example of hasty and superficial judgment. Apparently sensing something alien in his outlook and noticing his love of old Russia, certain commentators put two and two together and got nine. In response to the charge that he favors a return to tsarism, he asserts, ". . . nowhere have I written anything of the sort. Nowhere have I written that monarchy is an ideal system."[5] (Despite all, President Gorbachev said on television that in *Rebuilding Russia* Solzhenitsyn came out in favor of monarchy!)[6] Solzhenitsyn is equally emphatic in denying the allegation that he is a theocrat: ". . . I have been repeatedly charged with being an advocate of a theocratic state, a system in which the government would be under the direct control of religious leaders. This is a flagrant misrepresentation; I have never said or written anything of the sort."[7] Indeed, absent direct evidence, theocracy is a strange thing with which to charge anyone in the late twentieth century.

Though it must be conceded that even some critics generally friendly toward Solzhenitsyn have considered him anti-democratic, I am not alone in defending him from the charge. Of "his supposed hostility to democracy," Robert Conquest asserts, "This is, of course, a complete misrepresentation of Solzhenitsyn's position."[8] Sidney Hook concurs: "I, for one, believe that despite some ambiguous expressions, Solzhenitsyn, like his great compatriot Andrei Sakharov, can be counted on the side of democracy."[9]

Moreover, one must guard against conflating the moods of the 1970's and the 1990's. Today, with the collapse of the Soviet Union, there seems to be a sort of inevitability about the triumph of democracy, and we can read about the end of history's struggles over conflicting political systems. It did not seem so in the time of the Vietnam war. Then Solzhenitsyn said, "You have a feeling that the democracies can survive, but you aren't certain. The democracies are islands lost in the immense river of history. The water never stops rising. Some of the simplest laws of history militate against democratic societies, but this evidence doesn't stare you in the face."[10] Leonard Schapiro understood:

> . . . I think many of us are beginning to fear (as of course the ancient world knew only too well) that mass democracy contains within itself the seeds of its own destruction and presents a threat to freedom and to the

individual. Hence the constant message of Solzhenitsyn is for the need for the rule of law above all.

As for Solzhenitsyn's view of democracy itself, Schapiro observed, "Nor does he believe . . . that democracy for its own sake is the be all and end all of human existence. What Solzhenitsyn is primarily concerned with is freedom. Democracy may or may not ensure freedom. . . ."[11]

Here Schapiro lights upon the most important point of all regarding Solzhenitsyn's view of democracy. Solzhenitsyn's passion is for freedom, not democracy. Some set up heuristically the opposition of Communism and capitalism. Some set up the opposition of Communism and democracy. Not Solzhenitsyn. For him the opposite of Communism is freedom.[12] If democracy can further the prospects for freedom, well and good. It can and should serve this purpose. It can serve as a hedge against incursions into the sacred precincts of a person's liberty. This is not to say that freedom is its own end; this is not the view of freedom as *telos*. That position is part of the Enlightenment heritage. It is to say, rather, that freedom has ontic status, for it is part and parcel of the image of God which we human beings bear.

In 1985 Norman Podhoretz published a searching article entitled "The Terrible Question of Aleksandr Solzhenitsyn." It evoked a flood of letters to the editor. Podhoretz said, "I cannot remember writing anything that has provoked so wide a range of conflicting responses" as this article.[13] Anything but a mean-spirited detractor of Solzhenitsyn, Podhoretz penned some marvelous words of praise for him. But he also wrote of "the anti-democratic Slavophilia of [Solzhenitsyn's] message to the Russian people." And he took note of "a number of staunch anti-Communists who oppose him not because he is a 'cold warrior' but because he espouses a species of Russian nationalism that is explicitly anti-democratic and (so they claim) implicitly anti-Semitic."[14] Though Podhoretz exonerated Solzhenitsyn from the charge of anti-Semitism, he joined the consensus that Solzhenitsyn is explicitly anti-democratic.

I was one of those many letter-writers who responded to this essay. My letter contained five assertions about Solzhenitsyn's view of democracy:

1. He never urges the states of the West to abandon democracy.
2. He speaks freely of the faults of modern Western democracies, but his criticisms are always of the faults and not of democracy *per se*.
3. He fears the social upheaval which he expects would be the likely result if democracy were suddenly to be introduced into the political life of the Russians, who in their thousand-year history have known democracy (and then only abortively) for six months. [I should have said eight months.]
4. He imagines that, as a substitute for the totalitarianism of the Soviet Union, authoritarianism might be preferable to democracy *at the present moment*.
5. Most important, he has not declared, ever, a theoretical preference for authoritarianism over democracy.

My letter concluded, ". . . I am convinced that the received opinion that he is explicitly anti-democratic is quite wrong."[15]

In his reply, Podhoretz was unpersuaded: ". . . [Ericson's] five assertions, with all of which I agree, are perfectly compatible with what can be legitimately described as an anti-democratic position." At least, he dropped the adverb *explicitly*. To call Solzhenitsyn anti-democratic requires extrapolation, since there is no direct statement in his writings to that effect. Podhoretz continues, "At the same time, however, it is the kind of anti-democratic position with which I, as a virtual idolator of democracy, . . . can live."[16] The religious diction here is noteworthy. Not all idolators of democracy seem to have been as generously inclined toward Solzhenitsyn as Podhoretz was. In any case, a problem of logic persists. The most that one who agrees with my five assertions could logically say is that Solzhenitsyn is not pro-democratic, or is neutral about democracy, not that he is anti-democratic.

One thing that this exchange highlights is the need to distinguish carefully between the two different settings concerning which Solzhenitsyn discusses democracy: the West of the 1970's and the Russia of tomorrow. Exactly in the failure to observe this distinction lies the genesis of the charge that Solzhenitsyn is anti-democratic. Podhoretz is willing to generalize from what he perceives to be Solzhenitsyn's anti-democratic posture in regard to the Russian context and thus to find Solzhenitsyn anti-democratic in principle. This is an unsafe tack to take.

Though Solzhenitsyn says much about the West in general, he says much less about democracy in general or about Western democracy in particular. For example, in the three speeches and two interviews gathered into the volume *Warning to the West*, there is only one comment about democracy.[17]

Similarly, one might expect that, if Solzhenitsyn were anti-democratic, this plainspoken man would have made his position clear in his much-publicized commencement address at Harvard—and certainly so if this political issue were as important to him as it is to his critics. Indeed, many critics of the speech did repeatedly and insistently find it anti-democratic. The responses to this speech are what crystallized his reputation as an anti-democrat. Yet the fact is that only five mentions of democracy appear in the speech, and in no way do they add up to a documenting of the charge. If one coolly examines the speech to see how many of the West's problems Solzhenitsyn blames on its democracy, the answer is—startlingly—none. Of the five references to democracy, two are in mere passing, two are of middling importance, and one is of major importance.

Of middling importance is the assertion, "Thus mediocrity triumphs under the guise of democratic constraints." Democrats concede a certain validity to the charge and sometimes make it themselves. Often they do so in regard to the quality of political candidates for high office. And this is precisely the context in which Solzhenitsyn does so. Also of middling importance is the observation that "in the twentieth century Western democracy has not won any major war by itself."[18] One may challenge Solzhenitsyn's judgment that the West was strong enough to defeat Hitler without Stalin's aid. But his argument here points only to a tactical error and says nothing against the democratic nature of the West.

The major mention of democracy in the speech comes late. And, as the climax offers historical reasons for the decline of the West, so this reference to democracy is set in historical (and moral) terms.

> And yet in early democracies, as in American democracy at the time of its birth, all individual human rights were granted on the ground that man is God's creature. That is, freedom was given to the individual conditionally, in the assumption of his constant religious reponsibility.[19]

This is anything but an anti-democratic statement. Indeed, it is in praise of a kind of democracy which contributes to liberty and not to license—albeit, lamentably, to be found not in the present but in the past. It is highly significant that this Christian writer locates the origin of American democracy in the religious impulse. Only secularists could be displeased, and then on grounds that have to do with religion rather than politics. Solzhenitsyn laments the weakness of the modern West, but never does he attribute the cause of it to democracy. To secularism, atheism, materialism—yes. But not to democracy.

IN THE LIGHT OF the preceding citation, it is disconcerting to read Michael Novak's analysis of Solzhenitsyn's view of democracy. Precisely because Novak understands so much of Solzhenitsyn so well, his statements on this subject merit our attention. On the relationship between Christianity and democracy, a topic on which Novak is an unsurpassed expert, he declares, "I do not think Solzhenitsyn understands that connection well at all." And why? Because "Solzhenitsyn believes that democracy is an invention of the Enlightenment. In this he is profoundly wrong, wrong above all about the very texts he holds most dear: the Gospels." Thus, Novak goes so far as to say, "Solzhenitsyn often seems to wish to reject modernity, 'Western ideas'—above all, *democracy* and all its works and pomps."[20]

As regards Solzhenitsyn and democracy, Novak is not wrong about democracy; he is wrong about Solzhenitsyn. Indeed, Novak and Solzhenitsyn have remarkable congruence in their views of democracy. Solzhenitsyn is as careful as Novak to dissociate the origins of democracy from the Enlightenment project. Solzhenitsyn locates the origins of American democracy not in the secular impulse of the Enlightenment but in the historically antecedent religious impulse, which still beat strong in eighteenth-century America. The two agree on the essential character of the Enlightenment.

It is common enough to base one's case for democracy on an optimistic view of human nature, such as that generated by the Enlightenment. If human beings are not innately good, how can they be entrusted with the final say in governance? It is just this assumption that Novak rejects. He imagines a "[r]epublic of sinners." He declares,

> By a kind of practical alchemy, democracy attempts to turn even self-interest into mutual service to all. Democracy accepts the Jewish and Christian vision of human fallibility, bestiality, will-to-power, world, flesh, and devil. It takes human beings as they are and tries . . . to hold the rickety human enterprise on a course of liberty and justice for all.[21]

This statement, though jarring to some democrats, is consonant with Solzhenitsyn's thinking. He knows that "a nation can no more live without sin than can an individual."[22] A democracy of sinners—this is exactly what Solzhenitsyn favors. For instance, he understands, as many modern Americans do not, why the Founding Fathers established the electoral college. Though both Novak and Solzhenitsyn understand the risks of the democratic gamble, Novak seems to see a tighter and more organic connection between democracy and freedom than Solzhenitsyn does; he seems less concerned than Solzhenitsyn that democracy could go far astray. Nonetheless, the differences between Novak and Solzhenitsyn concerning democracy are differences of degree only, not of kind.

Novak is simply wrong to assert about Solzhenitsyn, "He sometimes seems to desire a world of soul alone. . . . If this were a world of angels, Solzhenitsyn's vision would create a City of Light. Its rulers would be saints, its people willing followers, its constitution the very laws of God." Surely, Solzhenitsyn, with all his anti-Enlightenment sentiments, is immune to the charge of utopianism—including Novak's variant of angelism (a term, incidentally, used by some literary critics to describe the fictive worlds of literary works far different from the kind of Christian realism found in Solzhenitsyn's works). Novak is wrong to say, "Democracy may be too imperfect for Solzhenitsyn, but only if humankind is too imperfect for him. . . . Democracy is a sort of non-prophet organization. It is better cut to sinners than to saints." Novak may think of Solzhenitsyn as a prophet, but Solzhenitsyn thinks of himself as first of all a sinner sharing the common human lot, as is abundantly clear from his many confessions of missing the mark in *The Gulag Archipelago* and *The Oak and the Calf*. On the other hand, Novak could virtually be quoting Solzhenitsyn when he declares, "Democracy by no means ensures virtue, though without virtue it cannot survive." And no one knows better than Solzhenitsyn this truth: "The human heart is endlessly mixed. 'In God we trust'—in nobody else."[23]

It is symptomatic that Novak quotes virtually none of Solzhenitsyn's own words on the subject. There are such words for us to quote. For example, Solzhenitsyn declares,

> Democratic society in the last two centuries has gone through a very, very striking and powerful development. What we used to call a democratic society a few centuries ago is not at all the same as that which we call a democratic society today. Two hundred years ago, when democratic society was being created in certain countries, there was still a clear conception of the Almighty, of God. And the very idea of equality was taken in fact from religion, from religious concepts; in other words, that all men are equal as the children of God. . . . And thus, democracy comes into its own, has a full meaning up to the point at which men start to forget God. In the last two hundred years we have really turned away from God, and democracy has lost its higher centre.[24]

The concept of equality is a necessary assumption for democracy's power-sharing, but it does not begin with the Enlightenment. Prior to that time, the West's traditional religious outlook provided a firm basis for believing in equality. Solzhenitsyn believes (as others before him have put it) that all men are *created* equal. Take away the link between creature and Creator, and one must locate a different basis upon which to establish the concept of equality. Keep that link, and, since all have sinned, one arrives at a democracy of sinners. This is exactly our metaphysical condition before God. It would be in perfect keeping with this metaphysical democracy to propose a political democracy. A democracy of sinners is thoroughly congruent with the least-of-all-evils approach of Churchill's apothegm. Indeed, if the line by Churchill does not square with any of the varieties of democracy, it is a conception of democracy based on the Enlightenment doctrine of human perfectibility.

As Solzhenitsyn uses religious categories to justify democracy, so he uses them to validate human freedom itself. In his view, freedom belongs to the highest level of human concern, and it is more important than democracy, which serves to realize and support it. Nevertheless, he treats freedom in the same terms of historical analysis that he uses concerning democracy:

> . . . you have forgotten the meaning of liberty. When Europe grasped it in the 18th century or thereabouts, it was a sacred concept stemming

directly from the old religious world which it both denied and perpetuated. . . . Its function was to render possible the emergence of values. Liberty pointed the way to virtue and heroism. That is what you have forgotten. Time has eroded your conception of liberty. You have retained the word and manufactured a new conception: the petty liberty that is only a caricature of the great, a liberty devoid of obligation and responsibility which leads, at best, to the enjoyment of material possessions. Nobody is prepared to die for that. [25]

This parallel treatment of freedom and democracy does not add up to an argument that democracy is the only political formation which can foster freedom. It does suggest, however, that freedom and democracy comport well together. Solzhenitsyn does not suggest that sort of fittingness between freedom and authoritarianism; rather, he sees authoritarianism as preferable only to totalitarianism. Furthermore, the parallel treatment suggests that, in regard to both freedom and democracy, moderns are living off the accrued moral capital inherited from their forebears; in regard to both, they have gone soft and effete.

The preceding quotation suggests one other aspect of the relationship between democracy and freedom. Democracy will have justification only if one's understanding of freedom is virtuous and ennobling. If one says that democracy is *for* freedom, one must then say what freedom is *for*. The issue must be engaged at the fundamental level of world view.

The concept of freedom cannot be grasped correctly without an appreciation of the vital objectives of our earthly existence. I am an advocate of the view that the aim of life for each of us is not to take boundless pleasure in material goods, but to take our departure from the world as better persons than we arrived at it, better than our inherited instincts would have made us; that is, to travel over the span of life on one path or another of spiritual improvement. (It is only the sum of such progressions that can be called the spiritual progress of humanity.)

If, however, one changes the meaning of freedom, one also ineluctably changes the character of democracy. This is what Solzhenitsyn believes the modern West has done. "Regrettably, in recent decades our very idea of freedom has been diminished and grown shallow in comparison with previous ages; it has been relegated almost exclusively to freedom from outside pressure, to freedom from state coercion—to freedom understood only on the juridical level, and no higher."[26] Democracy, along with freedom, becomes a hollow shell of its former self.

One gauge of the distance between Solzhenitsyn and most modern democrats is to imagine how unlikely it is that a candidate for political office today would speak about freedom in rhetoric akin to Solzhenitsyn's: "Genuinely human freedom is *inner* freedom, given to us by God: freedom to decide upon our own acts, as well as moral responsibility for them. . . . That which was called in an age-old, and now quaint, word—*honor*."[27] One's rhetoric about freedom is an index of one's view of the nature and ends of the democracy ostensibly designed to foster it. The rhetoric of Western political campaigns is largely bound up with material concerns. Most citizens would be befuddled to hear a candidate invoke the concept of a democracy of sinners.

WHEN SOLZHENITSYN TOLD Walter Cronkite that he saw "the good sides" of America's democracy, he proceeded to say, "But in general terms, it seems to me that now the governments of the major democracies are in great danger. Democracy itself is in great danger."[28] Manifestly implicit in this statement of warning is a concern not to undermine but to edify the world's democracies. This concern underlies all of Solzhenitsyn's criticisms of the democracies.

Also observable in this warning is the fact that most of Solzhenitsyn's criticisms of the democracies have to do directly with the geopolitical struggle between the Free World and the Communist bloc, with only occasional intrusions into internal affairs of Western countries. One of his geopolitical themes is that the advanced democracies employ a double standard in judging weaker, and also more exposed, members of the Western alliance. In his only statement about democracy in *Warning to the West*, Solzhenitsyn says,

> We are told: "We should not protect those who do not have a full democracy." This is the most remarkable argument of all. This is the leitmotif I hear in your newspapers and in the speeches of some of your political leaders. Who in the world, when on the front line of defense against totalitarianism, has ever been able to sustain a full democracy? You, the united democracies of the world, were not able to sustain it.

America, England, France, Canada, Australia together did not sustain it. At the first threat of Hitlerism, you stretched out your hands to Stalin. You call that sustaining democracy? Hardly.[29]

Thus, the advanced democracies stand accused of hypocrisy in their treatment of weaker members of their alliance. Not only so, but they are imprudent and foolish, as well.

The foolhardiness of such a posture was particularly evident to Solzhenitsyn in a time when Third-World countries seemed to be rejecting alliance with the Western democracies, when the Communist bloc seemed to be thriving in the global competition, when Vietnam was teetering on the brink—when, in short, Western democracy seemed (and not only to Solzhenitsyn) to be in retreat and in need of all the allies it could muster. The theme of the folly of this democratic purism is a recurring one with Solzhenitsyn. In Taiwan he expressed his solidarity with his hosts in these words:

It seems to be fashionable in the West to demand from all who stand in the forefront of defense, under machine-gun fire, to demand the widest democracy, and not just simple, but absolute democracy, bordering on total dissoluteness, on state treason, on the right to destroy their own state and country—such freedom as Western countries tolerate. Such is the price the West demands from each menaced country. . . ."[30]

This demand makes of democracy a shibboleth. It does not, in his mind, necessarily contribute to the long-term cause of freedom in imperiled countries or to the solidifying and expanding of the Free World.

In Great Britain Solzhenitsyn pointed out to interviewer Bernard Levin not only the folly but also yet another kind of hypocrisy in the West's management of the Cold War:

Now when you hear an SOS signal you must ask: "Who are you, do you have a democracy?" All right, if they're a democracy, let's go and save them. If it's a communist SOS then we really *must* save them because we must avoid any unpleasantness. But if it is an undemocratic Western regime, they can go to the bottom and sink! This is madness.

He uses El Salvador as an illustration:

In Salvador the elections took place under machinegun fire and indeed, yes, the voters were mown down by machinegun fire. The American Congress and American public opinion shout "there isn't enough democracy—start talks with the bandits, let's have more and more elections under machinegun fire." And those are the sorts of examples which really make me think of the West as a madhouse.[31]

To demand elections even when they might destabilize an ally is to reify democracy. It is to accord to voting a status on the primary level of significance in human life. This is what Solzhenitsyn refuses to do.

To make matters worse, there is, in Solzhenitsyn's view, a gaping discrepancy between applying democratic purism to friends and *realpolitik* to foes. About efforts of Western powers to play off China against the Soviet Union, Solzhenitsyn says, "I hardly dare ask where that leaves the principles of democracy. Where is the vaunted respect for the freedom of all nations?"[32] But that is a rebuke which implies a linkage between democracy and freedom. Democracies *should* foster freedom. The rebuke comes when they do not. The odd double standard for friends and foes is another indication that the trappings of democratic form are valued above freedom itself.

That Solzhenitsyn is not antagonistic toward all aspects of Western democratic life, but only toward certain ones, is clear from the Levin interview. Solzhenitsyn speaks approvingly of the American President of that time, Ronald Reagan, whom the voters elected by a wide margin, and disapprovingly of the elite press, which seeks to shape and to purvey public opinion. Turning aside Levin's invitation to offer Reagan advice, he replies, "I don't think Reagan's problem is a lack of understanding, but he has to struggle against the blindness and shortsightedness of public opinion."[33] The point here is not to judge whether Solzhenitsyn is right or wrong in his political preferences. It is, rather, to buttress the case that his own words do not support the charge that he is anti-democratic; the hints are not in that direction. He does disapprove of what he considers to be folly and hypocrisy in some contemporary democratic practices.

One aspect of democratic practice about which Solzhenitsyn expresses serious reservations is the division of the populace into political parties. Some may consider this an unassailable principle of political organization. Solzhenitsyn questions it.

> Do we not discern in the multiparty parliamentary system yet another idol, but this time one to which the whole world bows down? "Partia" means a *part*. Every party known to history has always defended the interests of this one *part* against—whom? Against the rest of the people.

The choice of the word *idol* here is intriguing, especially with Podhoretz's use of *idolator* in mind. There is something of the contrarian in Solzhenitsyn. If "the whole world" favors something, his first impulse is to resist it, at least long enough to inspect it thoroughly. It is also pertinent here to bring to mind Solzhenitsyn's Soviet experience, with its domination of every aspect of life by a political party (with omnipresent billboards announcing, "The will of the Party is the will of the People"). But common sense also suggests that there is nothing sacrosanct about political parties, as witness the nonpartisan elections in many American cities and counties. The party system of politics gives rise to such problems as these:

> . . . the leader of the opposition (except perhaps in England) will never praise the government for any good it does—that would undermine the interests of the opposition; and the prime minister will never publicly and honestly admit his mistakes—that would undermine the position of the ruling party. If in an electoral campaign dishonest methods can be used secretly—why should they not be? . . . As a result of all this a society in which political parties are active never rises in the moral scale.[34]

Thus, Solzhenitsyn asks whether the Russians can "advance toward a dimly glimpsed goal: can we not, we wonder, rise above the two-party or multiparty parliamentary system? Are there no *extraparty* or strictly *nonparty* paths of national development?" This question does not close the door on democracy, though neither does it close the door on authoritarianism. It does, however, suggest that, if Russia is to have a democracy, it will not be based upon "our traditional passive imitation of the West."[35]

Some Russians, Solzhenitsyn concedes, consider the "multiparty parliamentary system" to be "the only true embodiment of freedom." For him, though, it has "dangerous, perhaps mortal defects," such as are on display "when superpowers are rocked by party struggles with no ethical basis[,] when a tiny party can hold the balance between two big ones and over an extended period determine the fate of its own and even neighboring peoples. . . ." As Russians look westward for a political model, Solzhenitsyn urges caution and tries to put them on their guard:

> The Western democracies today are in a state of political crisis and spiritual confusion. Today, more than at any time in the past century, it ill becomes us to see our country's *only* way out in the Western parliamentary system. Especially since Russia's readiness for such a system, which was very doubtful in 1917, can only have declined still further in the half century since.

Beyond that, he reminds his fellows that "in the long history of mankind there have not been so very many democratic republics, yet people lived for centuries without them and were not always worse off."[36]

IN HIS SEARCH for a usable past, Solzhenitsyn's attention naturally turns not to Western but to Russian history. The authoritarianism observable in it demands not thoughtless dismissal but evenhanded judgment. There are some things to be said in favor of it.

> Russia too existed for many centuries under various forms of authoritarian rule, Russia too preserved itself and its health, did not experience episodes of self-destruction like those of the twentieth century, and for ten centuries millions of our peasant forebears died feeling that their lives had not been too unbearable. If such systems have functioned for centuries on end in many states, we are entitled to believe that, provided certain limits are not exceeded, they too can offer people a tolerable life, as much as any democratic republic can.[37]

But there is another side. Observing the virtues of authoritarianism does not constitute a brief in favor of the system. At best, its fruits were not unbearable but tolerable. Along with the merits, there are demerits, too:

> Together with their virtues of stability, continuity, immunity from political ague, there are, needless to say, great dangers and defects in authoritarian systems of government: danger of arbitrary decisions and the difficulty of correcting them, the danger of sliding into tyranny.[38]

These are the weighed words of a true student of the subject—of a searcher, not of an ideologue. Missing here is any sense of a utopian yearning for some past authoritarianism.

In fact, concerning authoritarianism Solzhenitsyn sets up a contrast familiar to us from his parallel treatment of democracy and freedom: the contrast between past and present—to the advantage, again, of the past. "The autocrats of earlier, religious ages . . . felt themselves responsible before God and their own consciences. The autocrats of our own time are dangerous precisely because it is difficult to find higher values which would bind them." In other words, past manifestations of authoritarianism were at least better than present manifestations of it. Modern examples of authoritarianism are truly fearsome ones. But the reason has to do with the neglect of the moral sphere of our lives; it does not have to do with authoritarianism *per se*. Thus, about the Soviet Union he says,

> The state system which exists in our country is terrible not because it is undemocratic, authoritarian, based on physical constraint—a man can live in such conditions without harm to his spiritual essence.
>
> Our present system is unique in world history, because over and above its physical and economic constraints, it demands of us total surrender of our souls. . . .[39]

The implicit contrast here is between what is commonly meant by authoritarianism and totalitarianism, a contrast which not all Sovietologists embrace but which is very meaningful to Solzhenitsyn.

The consequence of all this searching exposition is a broaching of the next step in the unfolding political history of the Russian people. Here it is to be noted both how pragmatic and how tentative his approach is.

> If Russia for centuries was used to living under autocratic systems and suffered total collapse under the democratic system which lasted eight months in 1917, perhaps—I am only asking, not making an assertion— perhaps we should recognize that the evolution of our country from one form of authoritarianism to another would be the most natural, the smoothest, the least painful path of development for it to follow?

He remarks that "we have never been shown any realistic path of transition from our present system to a democratic republic *of the*

Western type" (emphasis added). That being the case, he speculates that "the first-mentioned transition seems more feasible in that it requires a smaller expenditure of energy by the people."[40]

These reflections are not those of a person ideologically committed to authoritarianism. Neither modern authoritarianism nor modern democracy holds intrinsic allure for Solzhenitsyn. The urgent political task is not to impose any particular new political arrangement but simply to get rid of the old one: Soviet totalitarianism. Solzhenitsyn's twin fears of anarchy and revolution are such that he is open to whatever will work to move Russia out of totalitarianism without falling into either of these two extremes. The gradualism implicit in a move from totalitarianism to authoritarianism might, he says at this time, be the preferable route. If so, however, it is to be seen as a transitional stage. In the early 1970's, the situation is such that Solzhenitsyn is not even trying to contemplate what the best long-term political arrangement might be. His least-of-evils approach is fixed here solely on the first stage beyond Communism. Only in this context does he express an openness to authoritarianism, and then only in regard to Russia—and only in a tentative and questioning way, at that.

As Solzhenitsyn searches Russian history for a political model for the future, authoritarianism is not the only approach to governance that he finds. There is also a democratic strain of thought and practice. It entails representation but not voting or parties. Here is a passage which partially describes it:

> According to another traditional Russian concept, the truth cannot be determined by voting, since the majority does not necessarily have any deeper insight into the truth. (And what we know of mass psychology would suggest that the reverse is often true.) When representatives of the entire country gathered for important decisions (the so-called Assemblies of the Land), there was no voting. Truth was sought by a lengthy process of mutual persuasion, and it was determined when final accord was reached.[41]

The goal here is clearly to achieve the popular will. In the process, it is necessary to avoid the potential tyranny of the majority, which has been considered at length by Western political theorists. But perhaps the main thing for our purposes is that it describes an experience familiar to citizens of democracies. In neighborhood organizations, civic clubs, church councils, and other groups, people gather to discuss and to decide. The discussion continues until a consensus is reached. The will of the people gathered in the group has been made known. They may then take a vote, which is usually unanimous or nearly so. But the real decision-making has been done through the discussion. The vote is a formality. Yet the participants sense that they have fulfilled the requirements of democracy. This is the kind of democratic process that has precedent in Russian history. It is with this experience as background that Solzhenitsyn develops his own program in *Rebuilding Russia*.

Finally, here is another passage to consider:

> First, I know of no evidence that "democracy" . . . is the natural state of most of mankind. It seems rather to be a form of government . . . which evolved in the Eighteenth and Nineteenth Centuries in northwestern Europe . . . and which was then carried into other parts of the world, including North America, where peoples from that northwestern European area settled. . . .
>
> Second, I know of no reason to suppose that the attempt to develop and employ democratic institutions would necessarily be the best course for many of these peoples. . . . Time and time again, authoritarian regimes have been able to introduce reforms and to improve the lot of masses of people, where more diffuse forms of political authority had failed. . . . Particularly in a society accustomed to brutal or authoritarian rule, it is hard for anyone to govern, however lofty his original intentions, by methods strikingly different than those to which people have become accustomed by long experience and tradition.[42]

The author of these words is not Solzhenitsyn; it is George F. Kennan, one of America's foremost career diplomats. Kennan gives greater latitude about form of government than Solzhenitsyn does. Kennan's credentials as a democrat are in good order, and these ruminations do not call them into doubt. Solzhenitsyn's less extreme reflections have resulted in the allegation that he is anti-democratic. That allegation is without foundation.

8

On Nationalism

AS THE RECEIVED OPINION HAS it that Solzhenitsyn is anti-Western and anti-democratic, so it is equally settled that he is a nationalist. Indeed, the ascription of this label seems so obvious and is so widespread that some may wonder at the temerity of anyone who would challenge it. Here are words that Solzhenitsyn wrote: ". . . the Russian people is the noblest in the world. . . ." Ask a Sovietologist if these words fairly summarize Solzhenitsyn's attitude, and the answer will likely be yes. But he wrote them only to deny them! He takes his stand against a whole constellation of ideas, including the notion that "blood alone determines whether one is Russian or non-Russian," which he gathers under the rubric of "the Russian idea."[1] The very position that is routinely attributed to him he is at pains to reject.

The charge against Solzhenitsyn that he is a Russian nationalist—and it is indeed usually formulated as an accusation, rather than a neutral description—has come from many quarters. Every time he has taken notice of it, he has replied with a disavowal. For instance, on BBC television he remarked,

> . . . take the word "nationalist'—it has become almost meaningless. It is used constantly. Everyone flings it around, but what is a "nationalist"? If someone suggests that his country should have a large army, conquer the countries which surround it, should go on expanding its empire, that sort of person is a nationalist. But if, on the contrary, I suggest that my

175

country should free all the peoples it has conquered, should disband the army, should stop all aggressive actions—who am I? A nationalist! If you love England, what are you? A nationalist! And when are you not a nationalist? When you *hate* England, then you are not a nationalist.[2]

In a 1989 interview, David Aikman asked Solzhenitsyn directly, "Are you a Russian nationalist, and what does that mean to you?" Solzhenitsyn observed what commonly happens when commentators misrepresent his views: "No one ever gives any quotes." His answer was clear and unqualified:

The same is true for the charge that I am a nationalist. I am a patriot. I love my motherland. I want my country, which is sick, which for 70 years has been destroyed, and is on the very edge of death, I want it to come back to life. But this doesn't make me a nationalist. I don't want to limit anyone else. Every country has its own patriots who are concerned with its fate.[3]

As usual, Solzhenitsyn cares about precision of diction. The word *nationalist* must be defined with exactness. Loose usage blurs significant distinctions. This concern is not a mere semantic quibble. Solzhenitsyn is well aware that this word generally carries a pejorative coloration and is used as a club against one's presumed ideological opponent. Using this label has obscured, not clarified, Solzhenitsyn's view of Russia. This chapter is devoted to explaining how he views his nation and what his own posture toward it is. After examining his position in some detail, we shall consider competing positions, thus placing him in the national context. We shall also see how his view of Russia, as well as Russian nationalism in general, has been mediated to the West by Western commentators. Finally, we shall take note of the Russian intellectual antecedents of his attitude. The subject of Russian nationalism is a thicket; we must cut our way through it patiently and methodically.

SOLZHENITSYN'S ATTITUDE TOWARD his country can be stated as simply as this: he loves it. Or, slightly expanded, this: he loves Russia, and therefore he feels sorry for Russia because of its much suffering; and yet he has hope for Russia, hope that it can heal itself of its many and deep hurts. And the one word which encompasses these aspects and summarizes this attitude is *patriotism*. Solzhenitsyn is a Russian patriot. But here is his problem: "The simple love of one's mother country, an inborn feeling of patriotism, is today branded 'Russian nationalism.' "[4]

To distinguish between patriotism and nationalism should not be a difficult thing for citizens of Western countries to do. Many Americans, for instance, would readily identify themselves as patriots, but they would not feel the fit right if someone were to call them nationalists. At a minimum, the connotations of the two words are different. To one sedulous about word choice, the denotations are different, too. We should not run roughshod over, but instead take with utmost seriousness, the distinction which Solzhenitsyn painstakingly insists upon.

Solzhenitsyn has given a straightforward definition of patriotism: "As we understand it patriotism means unqualified and unwavering love for the nation, which implies not uncritical eagerness to serve, not support for unjust claims, but frank assessment of its vices and sins, and penitence for them." This definition is a far cry from that encapsulated in the popular phrase, "My country, right or wrong." Indeed, its last long subordinate clause sounds not like the so-called "super-patriot" but like one who is critical of the "super-patriot." This sense is reinforced by his very next sentence: "We ought to get used to the idea that no people is eternally great or eternally noble . . . ; that the greatness of a people is to be sought not in the blare of trumpets . . . but in the level of its *inner* development, in its breadth of soul. . . ."[5]

Solzhenitsyn's patriotism has its origins in what Stephen Carter has called "a subtle and original view of nations" ("which," he adds, "has been widely misunderstood").[6] The most succinct statement of this view is in the *Nobel Lecture*: "Nations are the wealth of humanity, its generalized personalities. The least among them has its own special colors, and harbors within itself a special aspect of God's design."[7] For this view of nations Solzhenitsyn finds biblical sanction; the account of Pentecost is evidence of divine approval of the variety of nationalities: ". . . by descending upon the apostles with many tongues the Holy Ghost confirmed the diversity of the nations of mankind, as they have existed since that time."[8] The divine validation is why Solzhenitsyn can say that, unlike political parties, nations "are very vital formations, susceptible to all moral feelings."[9] The divine validation is also why

Solzhenitsyn can speak in praise of individuality but not of individualism—and now of nationality but not of nationalism. As individuals are equal before God, so are nations. "Indeed, it seems inconceivable that in our sordid age any people on earth would have the gall to deem itself 'chosen.' "[10] Carter explains perceptively,

> He argues that nations have separate characters; each one is an individual, providing richness and variety in much the same way as individual people impart different colours, contributions, to human society. . . . Like the individual, a nation . . . has a personality of its own which is mutable, changing. Like a person, a nation may sometimes do good and sometimes evil things.[11]

This is why Solzhenitsyn can call for repentance and self-limitation in the life of nations.

In support of his view of nationhood, Solzhenitsyn cites "the high moral argument" of Vadim Borisov, a collaborator with him on *From Under the Rubble*,

> who reminds us about the nation-as-personality within the hierarchy of the Christian cosmos; that it is not history which creates nations, but nations which create history throughout their long lives, at times in light, at times in darkness, while seeking to express their personality to the fullest extent. The suppression of this personality is a most grievous sin.[12]

Nations function within the same moral universe and under the same divinely generated moral principles that persons do. They belong to the cosmos established by God.

Solzhenitsyn imagines that the passage from the *Nobel Lecture* cited above "was received with universal approval: a general obeisance pleasing to everyone." I doubt it. The religious rhetoric of it would be alien to the secular mind. Be that as it may, he says what he does here to launch into a statement about Russian nationhood in particular:

> But as soon as I drew the conclusion that it applies to the Russian people *too*, that the Russian people *also* has a right to national consciousness, to a national rebirth in the wake of the most excruciating spiritual illness, this was furiously labeled great power nationalism. . . . Russians are not supposed to be able to love their own people without hating others.[13]

As we shall see, he has cause to say that "there is a long tradition of speaking ill of national Russia."[14]

In the opening pages of *August 1914*, Sanya Lazhenitsyn, the character apparently based on the author's father, says, twice, "I feel sorry for Russia."[15] In 1967, Solzhenitsyn said, "For my entire life, I have had the soil of my homeland under my feet; only *its* pain do I hear, only about *it* do I write."[16] He, too, feels sorry for Russia. He thinks that "the Russian impulse toward national consciousness today is the defensive cry of a drowning people."[17] He says, "No country in the twentieth century has suffered like ours, which within its own border has destroyed as many as seventy million people over and above those lost in the world wars—no one in modern history has experienced such destruction."[18] Of all the persons whom Communism has brutalized, it "has always been most ruthless of all in its treatment of Christians and advocates of national rebirth." Of all the peoples suppressed by the Soviets, the Russians have suffered most of all. "Each of the republics was exploited without mercy, but the ultimate degree of exploitation was reached in the R.S.F.S.R., and today the most poverty-stricken rural areas of the U.S.S.R. are the Russian villages. The same is true of Russian provincial towns."[19]

It is therefore bitterly ironic that among Western academics there has developed "the false cliché according to which the Russians are the 'ruling nationality' of the U.S.S.R." For, according to Solzhenitsyn, "in the U.S.S.R. there simply was no 'ruling nationality': the communist internationalists never had need of one." As he puts it, ". . . just because a rapist addresses his victim in her own language, this does not make it any less of a rape."[20]

Solzhenitsyn's one entry into the discussion among American historians of Russia, *The Mortal Danger*, was designed to counteract the fallacy of "assum[ing] an indissoluble link between the universal disease of communism and the country where it first seized control—Russia." It astounds Solzhenitsyn that even scholars would carelessly equate the concepts *Russian* and *Soviet*, for "these concepts are not only opposites, but are *inimical*. 'Russia' is to the Soviet Union as a man is to the disease afflicting him."[21] Indeed, wherever it appears, "Communism can implement its 'ideals' only by destroying the core and foundation of a nation's life," for "Communism is inimical and destructive of *every* national entity."[22] Solzhenitsyn makes only this much of a concession: "Does the fact that communism is an international phenomenon rule out the possibility of any national peculiarities or local variants? Not really, since communism has to operate in a real world, among actual people. . . ."[23] That is to say, whatever Russian traits may appear in the Soviet system are tangential, secondary; they are not the driving motive force. Nevertheless, it is toward Russian national consciousness that "Western public opinion is being encouraged to respond with fear and even hatred."[24]

Solzhenitsyn casts a very stern judgment upon Western scholars who interpret this relationship fallaciously: "The West often sees an explanation for the phenomenon of 20th century Communism in some supposed defects of the Russian nation. This is ultimately a racist view. (How then can China be explained? Viet Nam? Cuba? Ethiopia? . . .)" Their analysis gets the case exactly backwards. "They insist that the enemy to be opposed is any manifestation of the Russian national consciousness, when, in reality, it is the only force that is realistically capable of weakening Soviet Communism from within."[25] Today many interpreters grant the force of what met with great resistance when Solzhenitsyn articulated it more than a decade ago. The future of Russia belongs not to the Communists but to the Russian patriots who cultivate the national consciousness. Some Western experts, however, continue to resist the possibility that this national rebirth can prove to be a healthy phenomenon.

For all of Solzhenitsyn's charting of the calamities that have befallen the Russian people in the twentieth century, never does he descend into personal or national self-pity. Solzhenitsyn urges the Russians to solve their own problems and not to look to others for their salvation. Furthermore, and flatly at odds with his reputation as a Jeremiah figure, he always retains hope that the Russians have the inner resources needed for this herculean task. He rejects the "tendentious generalization about 'perennial Russian slavery' and 'Asiatic tradition,' "[26] and he expresses his abiding faith thus:

> I believe in our people at all levels—wherever they may be. It cannot be that the 1,100-year existence of our people will not, in some as yet unknown form, overcome the sixty-five-year frenzied sway of the Communists. Our strain is the stronger, and we must overcome them and shake them off.[27]

If this faith once seemed misplaced, it does not seem so now, after the collapse of the Soviet Union. Nor does he now seem excessively sanguine in this assessment:

> You Westerners have a false idea of Russia. You think we're a handful of dissidents in an ocean of resigned or purblind people, but I tell you that 80% of Russians have a pretty fair idea of the nature and merits of the Soviet regime. They think as I do. They've chosen to obey, that's all, but they live like émigrés of the heart.[28]

Now that we have traced the main lines of Solzhenitsyn's portrait of and identification with the Russian nation, we can ask this question: What is it about nationalism that causes Solzhenitsyn to be so insistent that the term does not apply to his position? A glance at Kenneth Minogue's seminal study, entitled simply *Nationalism*, starts us toward the answer. Minogue calls nationalism "the foremost ideology of the modern world." He traces the origins of this ideology to the period of the Enlightenment, especially to Johann Gottfried von Herder and other eighteenth- and nineteenth-century German thinkers. Herder's central concept was the *Volk*, and Minogue notes that "Herder regarded the common human nature shared by all men as a trivial abstraction." For our purposes, it is crucial to understand that "nationalism grew up in the world at just the moment when a religious view of reality was losing its grip on the minds of European men. As religion declined, so political ideologies, especially nationalism, advanced." Equally important for our purposes is this observation by Minogue:

> The point we have had to emphasize about modern nationalism is that the politics comes first, and the national culture is constructed later. We have found nationalism without nations, aspirations substituted for reality. Instead of a dog beginning to wag its political tail, we find political tails trying to wag dogs.[29]

It should be apparent how alien all of this is to Solzhenitsyn. He is an inveterate foe of the Enlightenment. His world view is religious; the fundamental human reality is our shared human nature. For him, politics is secondary, not primary. Everything in Minogue's exposition of nationalism in general is at odds with Solzhenitsyn's conception of a moral universe established by God.

* * *

WHEN WE TURN our attention directly to the subject of Russian nationalism today, we find that, in Solzhenitsyn's understanding, it has two essential ingredients, both of which he finds objectionable. They are imperialism and chauvinism. We shall treat these two points in order.

That Russian nationalism includes the imperialistic impulse is a historical conjunction which Solzhenitsyn takes for granted. And he is resolutely opposed to it. To a Japanese audience he declares, "As a Russian writer, I have already stated repeatedly that the goals of the true Russia are not compatible with military occupation or interference in the affairs of other countries."[30] To American scholars he says, "I acknowledge with sorrow and shame that my country participated along with the rest of Europe in the subjugation of weaker nations. . . ." (At the same time, however, he also remarks upon an anti-Russian predisposition among these scholars: "Territorial aggrandizement is likewise proclaimed a primordial Russian trait, even though England had seized a good deal more territory and France did not lag far behind.")[31]

As Solzhenitsyn carefully specifies that advocates of the revival of Russian national consciousness find the idea of empire "repulsive,"[32] so he is equally adamant that this budding patriotism is not to be equated with chauvinism. He regards Western critics' broad-brush use of the label *Russian chauvinism* as "just a phantom to scare the gullible." He derides "the West's glib and garrulous informants" who prejudicially use this label to identify what they consider to be "the supreme threat to contemporary mankind, a menace greater by far than the well-fed dragon of communism."[33]

It follows that Solzhenitsyn is also caustic in rejecting the charge, which also comes from the West, that renewed Russian patriotism is to be equated with Russian messianism. He calls this accusation "a bizarre fabrication," and he impatiently dismisses it: "As for 'historical Russian messianism,' this is contrived nonsense: it has been several centuries since any section of the government or intelligentsia influential in the spiritual life of the country has suffered from the disease of messianism."[34] Alexander Schmemann knows about this chauvinistic and messianic "*myth of Russia*," and he distances Solzhenitsyn from it: "It is precisely against this *myth* (that Russia had a peculiar, sanctified destiny, that she was governed by a unique spirit, that her natives were endowed with an unmatched and generally undefined spiritual perception) that Solzhenitsyn rebels. . . ."[35]

Solzhenitsyn's rejection of the hoary myth of Russia exonerates him from the allegation that he holds some sort of mystical view of the Russian people. The common bonds connecting all Russians are, in his view, nothing so ethereal as to deserve this undefined epithet. The term *mystical* might apply if Solzhenitsyn gave vent to praise of Russian blood, but he does not. In his view, "Nationality is determined not by one's origins alone, but also by the direction of one's loyalties and affections."[36] It is not well enough known in the West how very multiethnic and multi-racial the population of contemporary Russia is. Perhaps only the United States has a more ethnically and racially mixed population than Russia. Solzhenitsyn's attitude is at the furthest possible remove from Hitlerian thinking about racial purity and racial or ethnic supremacy. Therefore, as regards the revival of Russian national consciousness which he promotes, he laments that in the West "contrived and disingenuous attempts have been made to link that revival with the government's calculated encouragement of anti-Semitism."[37]

When Solzhenitsyn is not writing in the polemical mode, we can catch him unawares, as it were, in his attitude toward persons different from him. And here we find him as good as his word. For instance, in *The Gulag Archipelago* we come upon this passage: "I found the Estonians and Lithuanians particularly congenial. . . . They had harmed no one, lived a quiet, orderly life, and a more moral life than ours. . . ." There is no Great Russian chauvinism here. Similarly, this Russian Orthodox man, for all of Orthodoxy's historic claims to exclusivism, has high praise for the Baptists in the Gulag: ". . . their faith was firm, pure, and ardent. . . . They were all honest, free from anger, hardworking, quick to help others, devoted to Christ."[38] In *One Day in the Life of Ivan Denisovich*, the author embodies his religious ideal in Alyoshka the Baptist.[39]

Imperialism and chauvinism are rooted in national pride. Solzhenitsyn's message to Russia is rooted, instead, in national humility. He calls Russia to repentance and self-limitation, in that order. Everything in the Soviet experience militates against such a penitential attitude. "In the twentieth century the blessed dews of repentance could no longer soften the parched Russian soil, baked hard by doctrines of hate. In the past sixty years we have not merely lost the gift of repentance in our public life but have ridiculed it." Nevertheless, it is to just this attitude that Solzhenitsyn calls his fellow countrymen, and he even has hopes that they will embrace it:

> It is, however, only fitting that a Russian author, writing for Russia, should turn to the question of Russia's need to repent. This article is written with faith in the natural proclivity of Russians to repent, in our ability even as things are now to find the penitential impulse in ourselves and set the whole world an example.[40]

If Russia is to be a model to the world of anything in particular, let it be of repentance.

Once the nation repents, "*self-limitation* comes into its own as the most natural principle to live by." For a nation to adopt such a policy would be most unusual, perhaps even unprecedented: "But so far as I know, no state has ever carried through a deliberate policy of self-limitation or set itself such a task in general form. . . ."[41] It would be an odd definition of nationalism that would encompass the repentance and self-limitation that Solzhenitsyn commends to Russia.

Russia is not the only country which would benefit from embracing repentance and self-limitation. Speaking to the Japanese, of whom he is noticeably fond and respectful, he calls attention to their need of them, too:

> I am amazed that . . . there should today be those among you who would evade responsibility for the recent past and prettify it for the benefit of the younger generation. I am certain that neither moral growth nor progress toward self-limitation in the future is possible unless past errors and transgressions are admitted and repented. Your vast expansion in the 1930s and during the Second World War was an outburst of overweening pride and has to be acknowledged as such, not simply glossed over. It was a grave mistake, an act of blindness. . . .

But Russia and Japan are only two nations. Solzhenitsyn tells his Japanese audience, "I regard self-limitation as the supreme principle for every individual and nation."[42] Nations, as well as individuals, are moral agents functioning within the moral universe. Obviously, our world would be unrecognizably different if all nations practiced self-limitation.

Russian national consciousness is, after more than a millennium of inheritance, deeply religious. All the official Soviet campaigns of atheistic propaganda and required academic courses in atheism have failed to drive religious consciousness out of the Russian people. (Nor is Russia the only country in which national and religious identities merge; Poland and Israel are just two others which come readily to mind.) Roy Medvedev disputes this point. He recognizes that the main difference between Solzhenitsyn and himself is on religion. "But," he counters, "for the overwhelming majority of the Soviet people, the truth is no longer and can never be religion. And the youth of the twentieth century are hardly likely to find guidance in faith in God."[43] Yet Solzhenitsyn has only to point to Stalin's efforts to appeal to Russian patriotism for support during World War II. Stalin's first move was to ease the restrictions on churches. Despite the severe repression of the pre-war years, says Solzhenitsyn,

> The Russian people had remained deeply religious, just as they had remained Russian. All at once, Christianity restarted of its own accord. Religious faith has continued to gain ground in spite of persecution. Are you aware that in the district of Riazan, which I used to know well, 70% of children are baptised?[44]

As John Dunlop notes, "All the major dissenting nationalist spokesmen—Solzhenitsyn, Shafarevich, Osipov, Ogurtsov, Vagin, Borodin, Ogorodnikov, Shimanov—are professed Orthodox believers; indeed, religion occupies a, if not the, central place in their world views."[45]

In Solzhenitsyn's judgment, "The significance of the current spiritual processes in Russia is seriously misrepresented to the West." This is what so agitates him about fellow anti-Communist Richard Pipes, Harvard historian and national policy adviser. Solzhenitsyn takes Pipes's book *Russia Under the Old Regime* "as typical of a long series of pronouncements that distort the image of Russia," and precisely because "Pipes shows a complete disregard for the spiritual life of the Russian people and its view of the world—Christianity."[46]

*   *   *

AS CAREFUL AS SOLZHENITSYN IS not to invoke the term *nationalism* to describe his position, the fact remains that most commentators, including those favorably disposed toward Solzhenitsyn and kindred spirits, regularly use it in discussing his view of the Russian nation. Although this attribution does not comport well with the project of coming to terms with a primarily spiritual writer, it need not becloud the issues at stake if care is taken to make proper distinctions. And so, for the balance of the chapter, I shall grudgingly submit to the common usage.

Such care, however, is not usually taken. Indeed, sloppy and indiscriminate usage is probably another reason why Solzhenitsyn himself avoids the term. Often *nationalism* is used in the same disparaging and pejorative manner as are *racism, sexism, ageism, speciesism*. Seldom does the result resemble subtle analysis. Here is a thoroughly typical sentence about the prospects for a post-Communist Russia: "The bad news is that Marxist-Leninist ideology will be replaced by Russian nationalism."[47] The common assumption underlying this and many similar statements is that nationalism and democracy are inimical and that the future of Russia belongs to one or the other. The great problem with the taxonomy which divides the field into opposing camps of nationalists and democrats is that it treats today's Russian nationalism as if it were a monolithic entity. Since the nationalists include extremists who are openly anti-Semitic, such as Pamyat, all persons described by Western critics as nationalists get tarred with the same brush. Guilt by association becomes the critics' *modus operandi*. In Solzhenitsyn's case, despite his espousal of democracy, he continues to be counted in the nationalist camp because of his patriotic call for a renewal of Russian national spirit. Yet his case should call into question the adequacy of the familiar taxonomy.

Some Western critics do attempt to draw distinctions among those whom they label Russian nationalists. Too often, however, these attempts are perfunctory. Typical in this respect is Bill Keller's 1990 essay "Yearning for an Iron Hand":

> While much of the Soviet bloc seems to be lunging toward Western freedoms, the Russian nationalists—or Russian patriots, as they prefer to be called—deplore the chaos of Western-style democracy and the materialism of Western markets. They pine for a romanticized, patriarchal Russia.

Although he exculpates Solzhenitsyn and Sakharov (and Gorbachev!), Keller deprives Solzhenitsyn of his treasured distinction between nationalism and patriotism. Furthermore, we recognize how frequently Solzhenitsyn has been charged with the viewpoint that Keller is here castigating. In midcourse, Keller allows that there are some voices of moderation, such as Alla Latynina. She is among those "trying to find a liberal alternative to the Russian patriotic movement." Not an alternative *within* but an alternative *to*, says Keller. For he emphasizes the specter of extreme nationalism as if it were likely to prevail, and most of the time he deletes the adjective *extreme*. He deploys the Solzhenitsyn-style phrase "the Russian patriotic movement" to designate those very extremists whose positions are at odds with Solzhenitsyn's. Thus, we read, "Self-pity is the life-juice of Russian patriotism. In their self-pity, the Russian nationalists look for culprits and they usually find the scapegoats of history: the Jews." Keller concludes his essay, "But given how late the West recognized the political strength of the National Socialists in the 1930's Germany or the Islamic Fundamentalists in 1970's Iran, it would be foolish to write off the Russian nationalists."[48]

In short, Russian nationalism becomes a bogeyman, not a term of analysis. Its use keeps the West from distinguishing its friends from its enemies. Nicolai Petro puts it this way:

> Acknowledging the dark side of the Russian national revival, one must at the same time avoid blurring some important distinctions, a mistake that would be as serious as confusing the conservatism of a William Buckley or a George Will with the reactionary racism of the Ku Klux Klan. Indeed, the failure to distinguish between chauvinism and patriotism feeds the counter-accusation of "Russophobia."[49]

Nowhere is a critic's blurring of distinctions among those labeled Russian nationalists more clearly on display than in the writings of Alexander Yanov, formerly a Soviet journalist and now in emigration in the West. Solzhenitsyn has accused Yanov of being "extremely hostile to everything Russian" and has specified, "In his books, for instance, you will find no hint that the Russian people might have some sort of religion or that this might have some significance in its history and its aspirations. And these are the lips that interpret Russia over here!"[50]

Yanov's version of Russian history features "piling one bloody dictatorship on top of another. To look for a validation of 'enlightened' authoritarianism in this terrible history is to look for a philosopher's stone." Actually, he does mention Russian religiosity, but only to belittle it as a dangerous anachronism. And he blithely trumpets his ignorance about religion ("my hopeless ignorance in questions of the hierarchy of the cosmos").[51]

Yanov is fixated upon the threat of the rise of "Russian Nazism,"[52] and he singlemindedly ferrets out and lashes any phenomena which in his mind might contribute to this rise. His one-term-covers-all label for these phenomena is the Russian New Right (the title of one of his books), and in the Gorbachev era he speaks darkly of "the Russian New Right's plan to topple the regime of reform and introduce a regime of dictatorship by the year 2000." In Yanov's vocabulary, an exact synonym for *Russian New Right* is *Russian nationalism*, the "main traits" of which are "its militant anti-Westernism, rendering it similar to the ideology of the Ayatollah Khomeini; its dogmatism and intolerance, bringing it closer to contemporary Soviet Marxism; its extremism and explosive potential."[53] Yanov asserts that at its "deepest roots lies a threefold struggle against communism, democracy, and Jewry."[54]

Therefore, Yanov urges the West to unite with "the constructive forces of the USSR" in order "to prevent the triumph of the New Right."[55] The final words of his 1987 book are a call to the West "to clear the way for the idea of a world safe for diversity" by coming to the aid of the beleaguered President Gorbachev: ". . . it is not Gorbachev who should ask the West to support his bold effort to prevent a garrison state in Moscow, it is the West who should guide him into this—for all of us to survive in the nuclear age."[56] Better Soviet Communism (preferably some reformist variety) than Russian nationalism (of any variety). I do not credit Yanov with being directly influential on the Bush administration when I observe simply that American foreign policy was supportive of Gorbachev to the very end of his stay in office.

No person comes in for more of Yanov's attention than Solzhenitsyn. Yanov professes to have been an admirer of the earlier Solzhenitsyn. However, he says with ostensible sadness, "The tragic aspect of the phenomenon of Solzhenitsyn is that he has turned up in the ranks of the Right."[57] Indeed, Yanov's Solzhenitsyn has become "a New Right party propagandist," whose "current truth" is that "there cannot be a

Russia without an Orthodox monarchy."[58] He also stands accused of "a reactionary utopianism." ("Utopianism has been another result of this combination of a passion for political prophecy with political infantilism.")[59] Solzhenitsyn's ubiquitous attention to inner freedom is turned by Yanov into "a justification of 'outward unfreedom.' " Thus, we are to understand that Solzhenitsyn gradually became more and more pro-authoritarian, more and more anti-democratic.[60] (On this model, we would expect from *Rebuilding Russia* something quite different, of course, from what we get.)

Yanov also tars Solzhenitsyn with the brush of anti-Semitism. Here the lack of clear evidence taxes Yanov's ingenuity. He avoids laying out a readily quoted accusation, working instead by way of innuendo and circumlocution—the intent of which is crystal clear, however. For example, he gratuitously takes note of "Solzhenitsyn's credentials as an Aryan." He says that *Lenin in Zurich* "represents the quintessence of the contemporary Russian Idea" because in it Parvus, a Jew, is depicted as the evil genius behind Lenin and the Bolshevik Revolution: ". . . this character is himself Satan (the Jew Antichrist. . .)." In *August 1914* it is a Jew who kills Solzhenitsyn's hero, Stolypin. So Yanov asks, "What is it that keeps 'accumulating' in Solzhenitsyn's 'brain? or craw? or tooth?' that makes him incapable of resisting the demonic temptation to identify the Jew with Satan?"[61]

Yanov's depiction of Solzhenitsyn is a gross caricature. Yanov gives us not a Solzhenitsyn recognizable from his writings but a misshapen lump. Alas, his mission of damaging Solzhenitsyn's reputation has not been without some effect. Yanov frequently turns up in footnotes of Western scholars, and his thesis that any and all forms of Russian nationalism ineluctably drive toward anti-democratic extremes and will ultimately be swallowed up by a new Russian fascism is accorded respect.

On the principle that every action causes an opposite and equal reaction, we might very well expect some extreme form of nationalism to come to the fore in post-Communist Russia. Such a prospect is all the more possible in a time of such wrenching social upheaval as the former denizens of the Soviet state are now experiencing. As a vice is sometimes described as a virtue carried to an extreme, so Russian nationalism could take a nasty turn. Therefore, the whole world has every reason to rejoice that such a prestigious personage as Solzhenitsyn speaks in favor of moderation and against extremism.

It is very painful, then, to observe how many Western critics lump Solzhenitsyn with those very extremists from whom he carefully distances himself. And it is particularly ironic when, as sometimes has happened, the critics who disallow discriminations among Russian nationalists have developed great adroitness at drawing fine distinctions among various national Communisms around the world and even among various representatives of Soviet Communism. Furthermore, in a time of refined multicultural sensitivities, it is jarring to happen upon general slurs against a whole people. No service is rendered by promoting the stereotype of the longsuffering Russian with the slave mentality. Solzhenitsyn may sometimes be too quick to detect slights against the Russians among Western critics. Yet there is an undeniable strain of skepticism that the Russians will be capable of handling their newfound freedom. It would be in order for such skeptics at least to express gratitude for the tonic of Solzhenitsyn's common-sensical advice to his fellow countrymen.

As IS TO BE EXPECTED of a newly free people, there is in Russia today a maelstrom of competing political positions. Within this mix Russian nationalism in all its variants looms very large, indeed can fairly be described as the majority view. Contemporary Russian nationalism is already a byzantine subject, and it is becoming more so all the time, as different groups emerge, as some of them split into factions, as alliances among them shift kaleidoscopically. As crucial as this complex subject is for any serious student of Russia, few in the West have a satisfactory grasp of it. It is far beyond the scope of this study to plumb its labyrinthine depths. Still, it is an inescapable duty to get some sense of the leading tendencies of current political thinking in Russia, and especially of nationalistic thinking, if one is to locate correctly Solzhenitsyn's place in this mix. What follows is intended only to be sufficient to achieve that end. If it is necessarily somewhat schematic, it is written with uninformed Western readers particularly in mind.

To begin, we can revert to the familiar taxonomy of dissidence: the neo-Leninism represented by Roy Medvedev, the democratic socialism (or social democracy) represented by Sakharov, and the nationalism (or movement of national rebirth, as he would prefer) represented by Solzhenitsyn. Of these three, the position with least popular appeal is neo-

Leninism. Indeed, one reason why Gorbachev experienced dwindling popular support and ultimately proved ineffectual is that he never could make a clean break from this position. (Roy Medvedev's allegiance he gained and kept, however.)

The social-democratic position represented by Sakharov might also be called liberal democratic. Though it has greater appeal than does Medvedev's neo-Leninism, it, too, is today a minority position. It has greatest appeal among persons whose world view is secular, not religious. Its main error, according to John Dunlop, at least as far as gathering a following is concerned, is its "generally undiscriminating application of Western liberal solutions to indigenously Russian problems."[62] When Western scholars divide the Russian political field today between democrats and nationalists, this is the position they have in mind as the democratic option.

That there is a certain family resemblance between the neo-Leninists and the social democrats can be seen by referring to the nineteenth-century division of Russian thought into Westernizers and Slavophiles. Both of these current positions can fairly be called neo-Westernizer. Both also retain some claim on socialism. If neo-Slavophilism can be imputed to Solzhenitsyn and like-minded nationalists, it is on this side of the ledger of Russian intellectual history that the great energy and popular following now is. What Dunlop said more than a decade ago is even more true now:

> As [Roy] Medvedev and other *zapadniki* [neo-Westernizers]—whether of the Marxist, socialist or liberal variety—are beginning to realize but fear to admit, the 19th century shoe is now on the other foot, and a revived Slavophilism is carrying the ideological field against a Westernism irretrievably compromised by the experience of the past sixty years.[63]

If there is some limited usefulness in employing the Westernizer/Slavophile contrast, there is virtually none in employing the left/right contrast. Yet this least helpful device of classification is the one most commonly used in the Western media. Where, for example, would one place Stalinists and neo-Stalinists? It would be bizarre to place hard-line Communists on the right of the political spectrum, where hard-line anti-Communists also are to be located. Yet just that was routine practice in the Western media leading up to and during the time of the failed coup of August 1991. The importation of familiar Western categories into the Russian scene confuses more than it clarifies, and it reveals both the limited knowledge and the biases of the users. The terms *left* and *right* can be, and regularly are, used to discuss the Russian political scene, but not if (as in much popular Western commentary) they are thought to mean the same things that they mean in the Western political scene. Even so, this superficial and confusing usage has the virtue of suggesting a family resemblance between the extremes on the left-right continuum, as this heuristic line bends around so that its ends touch each other. (In Russia both extremes, for instance, favor continuing imperial designs and incline toward anti-Semitism.) Therefore, we should not be surprised if a strange alliance of far left and far right were to develop; and something of that sort has indeed occurred. Extremisms attract.

Nor does the democrat/nationalist contrast hold up under scrutiny. Some nationalists are democratic in orientation, and others are not. John Dunlop describes Solzhenitsyn and kindred spirits as liberal nationalists in order to distinguish them from others to whom the label of *nationalist* attaches. He makes this distinction, too: "The liberal nationalists are distinguished from Western-style liberals by their often fervent attachment to Russian Orthodoxy and to Russian traditions, and especially by their pronounced abhorrence of Marxist-Leninist ideology."[64] Yet both liberal nationalists and Western-style liberals have given rise to democratic political parties. As Vladislav Krasnov explains, the Russian Christian-Democratic Movement (RCDM), with Father Gleb Yakunin as one of its founding and leading figures, "openly proclaims 'consistent anti-Communism, Christian spirituality, and enlightened patriotism' as its main tenets." But there is also the Democratic Party of Russia (DPR): "Just as anti-Communist as the RDCM, the DPR stresses neither Christianity nor patriotism." Both called for the restoration of the old Russian flag, the tricolor, which "stands for political pluralism and national unity across ideological and ethnic lines." Krasnov notes, "While the RDCM was clearly inspired by Aleksandr Solzhenitsyn's call for a national and spiritual rebirth, the DPR bases its ideology on Andrei Sakharov's defense of human rights."[65] There is considerable shared ground among the heirs of

Solzhenitsyn and of Sakharov, and it is a promising sign whenever they make common cause.

The party of Father Yakunin is not the only Christian democratic party to have been formed recently. The Christian Democratic Union of Russia is another one. At its founding conference, leader Aleksandr Ogorodnikov declared, "We have to offer society a Christian solution to its painful problems." This party's platform calls for "a parliamentary democracy, a multi-party system, separation of the legislative, executive and judicial branches, and free elections." Basic freedoms—"of speech, of the press, of assembly, of religious pilgrimage, of emigration, and of choice of a place to live"—are to be guaranteed. In addition, as Dunlop reports, "The Communist Party is to lose its privileged position, and all ideologies—'except those that call for violence or religious or national enmity, or attempt to justify them'—are to be allowed to compete freely."[66] The period just prior to the demise of the Soviet Union "witness[ed] a tumultuous formation of parties," including "numerous splits and schisms." Yet, as Dunlop remarks, "the 'democrats' all agree on two critical points: they hate communism, and they are firmly convinced that power must be taken away from the Communist Party."[67]

It is noteworthy how consonant with and perhaps even partially indebted to Solzhenitsyn's thinking is all this Christian-democratic ferment. But shall we call it democratic or nationalist? Obviously, it partakes of both impulses. To set them in opposition is not a very helpful way to approach today's political realities in Russia. Dunlop hopes for "the emergence of two powerful movements, unions, or parties." One would be "social democratic in orientation" and would include such known personages as Eduard Shevardnadze, Aleksandr Yakovlev, and Aleksandr Rutskoi. The other would be "some kind of strong right-centrist conservative party, movement, or union" similar in spirit to "the Christian Democrat-Free Democrat alliance in present-day Germany" (the leading personages of this group being, symptomatically, not much known in the West, though now in contact with Germany's Christian Democratic Union). About this latter group, Dunlop states, "It strikes me that Russian right-centrists could perhaps benefit greatly from the return to Russia of . . . Solzhenitsyn," whose program allies him with this coalition.[68]

Nicolai Petro observes these same two groupings, though he invents his own terms for them. (Of the making of heuristic devices there is no end.) He loosely aligns the social democrats as *radicals* and the Christian democrats as *restorationists*. Petro sees a new consensus emerging between these two groups, one which "should be appealing to the West," since (to mention just a few points) "[b]oth radicals and restorationists share a belief in the rule of law, in a national revival based on Russian patriotic sentiment, and in an educational system resting not on ideological slogans but on a critical understanding of Russian and foreign history." According to Petro, both

> radicals and restorationists are consciously striving to build bridges, to wed the best elements of Western universalism and Russian particularism. . . . Their efforts embody Dostoyevsky's insistence that to "become a true Russian" means "to become a brother of all men, a *universal* man."[69]

To consolidate the ground covered thus far, let us note that John Dunlop, perhaps the West's leading authority on Russian nationalism, places Solzhenitsyn in a right-centrist political grouping overall but also describes him as a liberal nationalist. In other words, Dunlop locates other nationalists to the right of Solzhenitsyn. Where Yanov lumps all nationalists together, with the very logic of nationalism driving them ineluctably to the rightward extreme, Dunlop makes careful discriminations.

Because of the appeal of nationalist thinking among the Russian intelligentsia, Dunlop has claimed, "No task is more urgent and necessary for Western analysts of the Soviet Union than to distinguish between the various tendencies of contemporary Russian nationalism."[70] In 1985 he predicted, "Russian nationalism . . . has the most realistic chance to succeed Marxism-Leninism as the ruling ideology of the Soviet Union." And he described the gamut as running from "a Christian variety in the Solzhenitsyn mold to a version of neofascism."[71] As early as 1975, Dunlop was saying, "The real struggle of ideas in contemporary Russia may . . . be taking place between liberal nationalists, such as Solzhenitsyn, and the less liberal."[72] If indeed the tide of Russian nationalism continues to rise, as is the case so far, then which variant will prevail is a vital issue for the whole world. For the outcome of this rivalry will probably determine not only what kind of internal order will emerge but how Russia will relate to its neighbors and all the nations of the world.

THE VARIETIES OF RUSSIAN NATIONALISTS have been classified by various scholars.[73] For the sake of clarity, we shall retain John Dunlop as our guide for this topic. In his terms,

> Unquestionably, the two most significant tendencies in present-day Russian nationalism are (1) what Solzhenitsyn has named the "Russian national and religious renaissance" whose adherents I shall call *vozrozhdentsy* (from the Russian word for "renaissance"), and (2) the tendency usually termed National Bolshevism.

Dunlop places Solzhenitsyn not only among the *vozrozhdentsy* but on their "left wing." The *vozrozhdentsy* "hold that God and the Orthodox faith are higher than the nation,"[74] whereas the "National Bolsheviks lean toward a quasi-deification of the Russian people," suspect a "Jewish-Masonic-Plutocratic conspiracy," and feel "extreme hostility toward the West."[75] Though these two categories are not water-tight compartments but tendencies, the principal differences between them are rooted

> in their attitude toward Russian Orthodoxy and in their willingness to achieve at least a temporary *modus vivendi* with Marxism-Leninism. . . . Other differences center on the question of military-industrial and urban growth . . . and on the wisdom of conducting an expansionist foreign policy.[76]

Of Solzhenitsyn and company Dunlop says,

> Most *vozrozhdentsy* would agree on the following: the need to jettison Marxism-Leninism as the state ideology; the need for economic and administrative decentralization; the necessity of building up the church, family, and school (without, however, reestablishing the Russian church); decollectivization of agriculture and the introduction of a mixed economy; an emphasis on internal development; and withdrawal from involvement in the affairs of other nations.

As for that "more elusive tendency of thought and sentiment" called National Bolshevism, a term coined as early as 1921, it "advocate[s] a rapprochement between the Bolshevik Revolution and the Russian state, to be achieved through a squeezing out of the 'internationalist' elements of the revolution." Furthermore, Dunlop observes,

> The similarities between National Bolshevism and fascism are striking: a strong impulse toward deification of the nation; the desire for a strong state, the *stato totalitario*; a powerful leadership impulse . . . ; a belief in the necessity of an elite; a cult of discipline, particularly of the youth; heroic vitalism; an acceptance of military and industrial might . . . ; and a celebration of the glories of the past.[77]

It is worth remarking that fascism is a modern excrescence of nationalism, which itself is a post-Enlightenment phenomenon. By contrast, Solzhenitsyn and company adhere to a form of nationalism which depends on traditional props.

Dunlop has recently reported that the National Bolsheviks—with their platform of continuing the command economy, supporting dictatorship, retaining the inner empire, and opposing minority nationalisms—suffered a "humiliating rejection by RSFSR voters during the elections in March, 1990."[78] What he said some years ago still holds: nationalists whose thinking is compatible with Solzhenitsyn's "would appear to have the advantage of numbers."[79]

We have touched upon the strange alliance, as noted by various analysts, between extremists of both left and right. It is important enough to merit a bit more attention. Both extremes manifest reactionary and fascist proclivities. The National Bolsheviks are the most prominent grouping among what Dunlop calls the conservative nationalists. Although some conservative nationalists are religious, the National Bolsheviks are not. On the other side of the alliance are what he calls the neo-Stalinists. Both groups opposed President Yeltsin and other democratic reformers. When asked how this apparently odd alliance could be, "[o]ne conservative nationalist put it simply: 'Better the communists than the democrats.' " And some important commitments do conjoin these strange bedfellows. Both groups are hostile to the West, reject the idea of a market economy, and incline toward anti-Semitism, even to "a belief that the Russophobic West is in fact controlled by anti-

Russian and anti-Soviet Jews."[80] Also, both groups "are unable to envisage a future Russia without an empire."[81] Finally, and most importantly, neither group abjures Marxist ideology. Writing on the eve of the failed coup of August 1991, Dunlop remarked that this "alliance continues to enjoy strong support from such critical Soviet institutions as the KGB, the military, the military-industrial complex, and the Russian Communist Party."[82] Happily, things look brighter now.

Roman Szporluk brings an intriguing angle of vision (and another heuristic device) to our discussion when he says that there are now two basic responses to the question "What is Russia?" They are those of the "empire-savers" and the "nation-builders." The nation-builders "think of Russia as something very different from the USSR." They are concerned with how "ethnic communities 'construct' and 'reconstruct' themselves," and this concern extends to the rights of ethnic minorities.[83] There is no question that Solzhenitsyn is to be numbered among the nation-builders.

The empire-savers, explains Szporluk, "may include extreme right-wingers and no less extreme left-wingers." Here again is that strange alliance. However, according to Szporluk, the empire-savers also include some who "seem to favor Western, liberal-democratic, and constitutional institutions for the Soviet Union." And it is indisputably true that some of the best-known advocates of democratic reform, starting with Gorbachev and his supporters, refused to call simultaneously for an abandonment of at least the inner empire. Even President Bush, as in his speech at Kiev, was hoping that the center would hold the empire together, at least for the time being. For Szporluk the key test is geographical. Where does one wish to set the borders? And so he says, "Whether empire-savers are fascist or liberal, extremist or moderate, atheist or Orthodox, their 'geography' is the same—it is an imperial geography, and their Russia is co-extensive with the empire."[84]

Solzhenitsyn has such stature today that nationalists of various stripes are trying to claim him as their own. Because of this widespread approval, it is possible that his influence can be a moderating force upon some nationalists who nowadays are tending toward extremism, especially those of a religious cast of mind. Again, Dunlop seems to get the nuances right: "Deeply admired by both liberal and conservative nationalists, and tolerated for tactical reasons by National Bolsheviks,

Solzhenitsyn is undoubtedly the sole individual who could potentially unify the entire Russian nationalist tendency."[85]

Such a beneficent effect is, however, far from a sure thing, even among fellow religionists. The case of Igor Shafarevich, the prominent mathematician who was a major collaborator with Solzhenitsyn in *From Under the Rubble*, is not encouraging. He has become a leading spokesman for conservative Russian nationalism and speaks darkly of the threat of Russophobia. He openly expresses fears that Russia will be balkanized into spheres of interest by the United States, Germany, Japan, and China. When *Rebuilding Russia* first appeared, he wrote a lengthy "corrective" to it. "While Shafarevich did cite Solzhenitsyn's name once approvingly, it is clear that he is in deep disagreement with many of his former ally's present positions." In Dunlop's summary judgment, "Shafarevich's retrograde program demonstrates how far he and Solzhenitsyn have diverged in their views since the appearance of *From Under the Rubble* in 1974."[86]

Furthermore, it is most unlikely that Solzhenitsyn's influence will deflect National Bolsheviks from the position that they have staked out. In the very passage where he was defining patriotism and distinguishing it from nationalism, he identified the National Bolsheviks as the adherents of "the Russian idea" which he was rejecting.[87] They are the ones infected by chauvinism and messianism and committed to an ethnocentric, as opposed to (Solzhenitsyn's) polycentric, nationalism.[88] The West knows of Solzhenitsyn's stern objection to what he considers the anti-Russian bias of some. What it should also know, but for the most part does not, is his equally stern objection to those on the other side, the proponents of the myth of Russia. The West needs to know of his centrism.

Two years before the Soviet Union died, Alla Latynina, a self-proclaimed centrist, called for a political realignment. She perceived two coalitions then in place. One, clustering around Gorbachev, was comprised of "neo-Leninist" reformers within the Communist Party and of social democrats and Western-style liberals (generally speaking, the lines represented by Roy Medvedev and Andrei Sakharov). The other was comprised of conservative nationalists and of "neo-Stalinists" within the Communist Party (the strange alliance previously discussed). Her goal was to coax some social democrats and Western-style liberals, on the one hand, and some conservative nationalists, on the other, into joining with liberal nationalists and centrists like herself in "a 'centrist' coalition based on a repudiation of the official ideology and on a commitment to parliamentary democracy and a state based on law." As Dunlop notes, "If Latynina's views seem close to those of Solzhenitsyn, it is not a comparison that would displease her." Latynina cites approvingly a recent major study of Solzhenitsyn (strongly recommended to all readers of Russian) by Dora Shturman, an émigré critic now living in Israel, which argues at length that he is "a religious moralist, a liberal in the classic sense of the word, and a convinced centrist in politics."[89]

WITHIN THE SPECTRUM of Russian nationalism, the group which has received probably the most attention in the Western press is Pamyat (Memory—not to be confused with Memorial, a group dedicated to commemorating Stalin's victims). Even so, as Geoffrey Hosking remarks, ". . . we are poorly informed about Pamyat'. We know next to nothing about its numbers, its membership or its organisations."[90] In fact, because of factionalism, it is not any longer just one group. Anti-Semitism is its best-known plank. The West has exaggerated the importance of Pamyat. I discuss it now for two reasons. First, because it is known of, omitting it would leave a lacuna. Second, because it is known for anti-Semitism, it comes into play when Solzhenitsyn is charged, as he has been, with anti-Semitism.

Michael Confino's recent article on Solzhenitsyn gives us a typical Western rendering of Pamyat and of Solzhenitsyn's ostensible relationship to it. Confino asserts that we must take Solzhenitsyn seriously, but the first reason to do so is that "various right-wing groups in Russia, including Pamiat and other anti-semitic nationalists, repeatedly use Solzhenitsyn's name and moral authority to boost their political propaganda." About Solzhenitsyn's insistence that he is a patriot, not a nationalist, Confino remarks, "This is also the stand now adopted by groups on the extreme right in Russia. . . ." He concedes that "Solzhenitsyn can do nothing to prevent black-shirted thugs from opposing, like him, Western-style democracy and materialism," then declares, "But the crux of the matter is that he has done nothing yet to dissociate

himself from these movements." Chief among Solzhenitsyn's objectionable positions "which may lead to, and breed, deplorable and even
dangerous feelings and actions" is his "religious fundamentalism."[91]

This is a classic case of assigning guilt by association. It culminates
in Confino's final words: ". . . is it not the Russian moral leaders'
greatest duty and responsibility—matters which Solzhenitsyn claims he
understands well—to refrain, today more than ever, from giving encouragement and comfort to the forces, old and new, which threaten the
freedom and dignity of man?" It is bad enough to give a faulty analysis
of Solzhenitsyn's views. It is worse to attribute to Solzhenitsyn some of
the blame for views in sharp contradistinction to his. At a minimum,
one would expect a clear exposition of the views of the extremists which
Solzhenitsyn is allegedly fostering. Yet Confino says only that Pamyat's
"political orientation, proto-fascism, anti-semitism and use of violence
need no elaboration here."[92] But of course they do—unless Confino is
willing to settle for using the fear of a bogeyman to attack Solzhenitysn.
As Hosking has noted, we do not know much about Pamyat.

It was Confino's misfortune that *Rebuilding Russia* appeared after his
article was submitted but before it was published. Confino mentions a
couple of its "main new ideas" in a footnote. He omits entirely any
reference to its long discourse on democracy, even though he had
described Solzhenitsyn as anti-democratic. Then he says, "These new
points do not in the least affect the main themes and treatment of the
present article."[93] In fact, *Rebuilding Russia* contradicts point after
point of Confino's article, indeed undermines its whole thrust. Certainly, the positions enunciated in Solzhenitsyn's essay are in marked
contrast to those espoused by Pamyat.

Pamyat's platform is sketched best by the indefatigable John Dunlop,
who sought out Pamyat leader Dmitrii Vasiliev for conversation. The
main planks are three: absolute monarchy, re-establishment of the Russian Orthodox Church, and "nationality" (a vague point which says that
the people "should have a consultative role in the running of the
Russian state. . . . There should be only a minimal apparatus separating
the tsar and the people"). Pamyat also favors a free-market economy and
the right to own land. "The centerpiece of Vasil'ev's 'negative' program
is his fervent belief in the existence of a Zionist-Masonic conspiracy. He
repeatedly stressed that he is an anti-Zionist, not an anti-Semite. . . ."
In addition, reports Dunlop, "Vasil'ev said that he detested Adolf Hitler

for his hatred of Christianity and for his racial theories, but he expressed warm sympathy for the 'idea' of fascism."[94] It is Dunlop's judgment that the "lurid programme" of Pamyat "is of interest only to limited elements of the Russian lumpen intelligentsia and working class" and that its following is small.[95]

A number of commentators have raised the issue of the coziness between the KGB and Pamyat. As Nicolai Petro reports, "Elena Bonner, wife of the late Andrei Sakharov, noted that the Leningrad KGB was protecting and promoting Pamyat."[96] Krasnov considers it "quite possible . . . that the KGB has infiltrated Pamyat's leadership and feeds it the anti-Semitic line in order to discredit Russian nationalism among Soviet intellectuals and the Western public." Moreover, one should not ignore the longstanding official anti-Zionism of the Soviet Union; Krasnov, for one, locates Soviet, rather than pre-revolutionary Russian, sources for the kind of anti-Zionism and anti-Semitism purveyed by Pamyat.[97] And, in regard to the "revival in Russian national awareness," Solzhenitsyn himself has noted that "contrived and disingenuous attempts have been made to link that revival with the government's calculated encouragement of anti-Semitism."[98] The almost invisible hand of the KGB may even be at work in sowing discord among adherents of Pamyat, thus heightening confusion among nationalist-minded patriots. Dunlop is inclined to accept "Vasiliev's contention that 'Pamyat'-II' was created by the regime to weaken and discredit" him and his followers. Another splinter group which uses the name of Pamyat "is extremely hostile to Christianity," and its leader "calls Jesus Christ the first leader of a Masonic lodge," a statement which Vasiliev, as an Orthodox Christian, finds abhorrent.[99]

The interjection of the subject of Pamyat into the discussion about Solzhenitsyn has usually had the effect of obfuscation. Far from fusing and confusing the two, we should be emphasizing how far apart they are. Indeed, as Krasnov puts it, "The best antidote to Pamyat-like extremism can be found in the moderate mainstream of the Russite movement" of which Solzhenitsyn is the pre-eminent representative.[100]

WE COME NOW to the charge that Solzhenitsyn is an anti-Semite. Some in the West have leveled it; many more have rejected it. The strangest part of this story is that in the Soviet Union there have been attempts, quite possibly with the connivance of the KGB, to smear him in just the opposite way: as a lover of the Jews or even as a Jew himself. Zhores Medvedev tells the story of the late sixties about a lecture in a Moscow publishing house in which Solzhenitsyn was continually referred to as "Solzhenitser." When an auditor sent forward a note to correct the mispronunciation, the lecturer replied, "No, it's not a mistake. The person known to you as Solzhenitsyn is really Solzhenitser and he's a Jew."[101] This was not an isolated incident.[102]

Then there is the bizarre 1971 open letter from one Ivan Samolvin, who accused Solzhenitsyn of having too many favorably depicted Jews among the characters in his novels and who asked why Solzhenitsyn's works were picked up by major newspapers and publishing houses, owned as they are by capitalist Jews. "You even call Christ a Jew though even I, a Christian only by virtue of baptism and ignorant of theology, know that nationality has nothing to do with God." Further, "Judging by everything, Solzhenitsyn, you like bourgeois-Jewish democracy." Samolvin delivers this final blow: "I do not know for sure who you are—a Russian or a Jew. Perhaps you are a proselyte. . . . Proselytes are usually more cruel than real Jews. Perhaps you are a Russian who is pressed by his environment, by a Jewish wife."[103]

In the West the judgment that Solzhenitsyn is anti-Semitic is not nearly so common as the judgments that he is anti-Western or anti-democratic or a chauvinistic Great Russian nationalist. However, it is important to note that those who do consider him anti-Semitic generally consider him to hold one or more—usually all three—of these other positions. It is also important to note that some who find him guilty on one or more of these counts absolve him of the charge of anti-Semitism.

Grounds for the allegation of Solzhenitsyn's anti-Semitism are hard to come by. For lack of clear evidence from his works, though they have been carefully combed for such evidence, the allegation, when it is made, is usually formulated tentatively. And so we typically find *suggestions* that he *might* be *implicitly* anti-Semitic. We find a tiptoeing up to the charge without ever quite making it. Although Solzhenitsyn has in fact denied that he is anti-Semitic, some have still asked why he has not done so, and others have said that he has not done so emphatically enough. This is the argument from silence, or negative evidence. When textual evidence is proposed at all, it usually has to do with a negative depiction of certain Jewish characters. The leading candidate here is

Dmitry Bogrov, the assassin of Stolypin (in *August 1914* and in historical fact), into whose villainous heart Solzhenitsyn probes as he does
with all his substantial characters. More commonly, accusers have
satisfied themselves that he holds other objectionable positions, especially chauvinistic nationalism, and conclude that the logic of his outlook compels him to be anti-Semitic as well.

In 1985 the *New York Times* carried a major article by Richard
Grenier entitled "Solzhenitsyn and Anti-Semitism: A New Debate."
The chief accuser in this piece is Richard Pipes, whose "impeccably
anti-Communist" credentials are noted. In Pipes's view,

> Every culture has its own brand of anti-Semitism. In Solzhenitsyn's case,
> it's not racial. It has nothing to do with blood. He's certainly not a racist;
> the question is fundamentally religious and cultural. He bears some
> resemblance to Dostoyevsky, who was a fervent Christian and patriot and
> a rabid anti-Semite. Solzhenitsyn is unquestionably in the grip of the
> Russian extreme right's view of the Revolution, which is that it was the
> doing of Jews.

Pipes is among those who find the depiction of Bogrov unacceptable,
since he believes that in real life Bogrov was not as much motivated by
his Jewishness as he is in Solzhenitsyn's novel. Mark Perakh, taking a
content-analysis approach, is cited as feeling that "a disproportionately
large number of unattractive Jews appear in his [Solzhenitsyn's]
work."[104]

Grenier's list of defenders of Solzhenitsyn from the charge of anti-
Semitism is impressive: Elie Wiesel, Mstislav Rostropovich, Adam
Ulam, Robert Conquest, Vladislav Krasnov, Lev Lossev [Loseff], Mikhail Agursky. Although Wiesel's exoneration of Solzhenitsyn is firm,
he does allow, "I am only disturbed by what seems to be an unconscious
insensitivity on his part to Jewish suffering." Conquest's vigorous defense includes this interesting point: ". . . unfortunately the charge falls
on the ears of many American Jews predisposed to believe it because
their notions of Orthodox Christianity and anti-Semitism in Eastern
Europe are out of date." In letters to Grenier, Solzhenitsyn himself
"denounced anti-Semitism, calling the charges against him 'base.' "
Solzhenitsyn's wife, whose half-Jewish ancestry Grenier finds a datum
significant enough to mention, called the charges "nonsensical" and
"absolutely absurd."[105]

Norman Podhoretz, too, judged Solzhenitsyn innocent, finding "no overt anti-Semitism" and observing that "the charge of anti-Semitism rests almost entirely on negative evidence." In a vein similar to that of Wiesel, he did add, ". . . while there is no clear sign of positive hostility toward Jews in Solzhenitsyn's books, neither is there much sympathy."[106] When one letter complained that "Mr. Podhoretz uses qualifiers . . . which dilute his defense of Solzhenitsyn to the point that it almost becomes an accusation,"[107] Podhoretz called attention to Solzhenitsyn's "consistently fervent support of Israel."[108] One's attitude toward Israel is a frequently used litmus test of one's attitude toward Jews. It is possible to be anti-Zionist without being anti-Semitic; this has been the announced position of Soviet officialdom. It is impossible to be anti-Semitic without being anti-Zionist. The printed reactions to Podhoretz's article roughly mirror the range conveyed in the Grenier article. Some charge Solzhenitsyn with anti-Semitism. More stop short of concurring but also stop short, on the other side, of laying the charge to rest altogether. Most defend Solzhenitsyn.

Andrei Sinyavsky, the noted Russian author now in exile, is an interesting example of one occupying the middle ground. When Olga Carlisle interviewed him about Solzhenitsyn, to question after question Sinyavsky answered with antagonism toward Solzhenitsyn. When, however, she asked flatly, "Do you think that Solzhenitsyn is anti-Semitic?" he replied, "Not particularly, psychologically speaking." Though he went on to speak of Russian resentments about the involvement of Jews in the Bolshevik Revolution, Sinyavsky offered nothing to substantiate Solzhenitsyn's alleged anti-Semitism.[109] Readers could be pardoned if they concluded that Sinyavsky was hinting that where there is smoke, there may just possibly be fire. And this interview (along with the letters discussing Podhoretz's article) is footnoted by Confino to support his opinion that "with regard to his [Solzhenitsyn's] alleged anti-Semitism (explicit, implicit or potential), opinions differ and the issue is still open."[110]

In 1991, David Remnick observed that "despite years of rumors and innuendoes from his critics, no one has yet made a cogent, sustained textual case that Solzhenitsyn is himself an anti-Semite." It is true that Remnick adds, "One only wishes that Solzhenitsyn himself would put the matter to rest by taking a firm and public stand against anti-

Semitism instead of making a few passing remarks in interviews."[111] Although Solzhenitsyn's Western friends might well wish this, they would actually be asking him to write according to their agenda and not his own. And there would be some justice if he were to reply that he had already taken such a firm and public stand. When David Aikman raised the issue in a 1989 interview, particularly in regard to the character of Bogrov in *August 1914*, Solzhenitsyn, typically, defined the term ("a prejudiced and unjust attitude toward the Jewish nation as a whole") and called its application to *August 1914* "an unscrupulous technique." But then he added this intriguing remark: "In writing a book one cannot always ask, How will this be interpreted? You have to think, What actually happened? My duty was to describe things as they happened." In other words, he writes according to his own agenda of historical truth-telling, not according to the dictates of tender Western sensitivities. Also, he observed, "The word anti-Semitism is often used thoughtlessly and carelessly, and its actual meaning becomes soft and squishy."[112] One might well say that it is not Solzhenitsyn's stand which lacks firmness. In any case, the burden of proof is upon the accusers.

Of all the defenders of Solzhenitsyn from the charge of anti-Semitism, none has been more eloquent or insistent than Leonard Schapiro. He states flatly that "the charge is not borne out by the evidence," and he calls it a "slanderous and totally untrue allegation."[113] Schapiro makes the kinds of distinctions which too seldom mark Western commentary, starting with the incorrectness of identifying nationalism with anti-Semitism. And he brings up a point which is generally passed over in silence: that Solzhenitsyn "has been subjected to violent attacks by right-wing extremists on the grounds of his alleged friendship for Jews."[114] This latter citation comes from the journal *Soviet Jewish Affairs*, and it is to be noted that the preponderance of the considerable argument about Solzhenitsyn in that journal defends him from the charge of anti-Semitism.[115]

In summary, the evidence is overwhelming that the charge against Solzhenitsyn of anti-Semitism is fallacious. Most critics, including many Jews and many who get Solzhenitsyn wrong on other issues, join in this exoneration. Those who construe from other points to find him guilty are generally wrong on those other points, as well.

*   *   *

IT REMAINS in this chapter to give a sketch of some of the intellectual antecedents of Solzhenitsyn's commitment to a renewal of the Russian national spirit. Working our way backward in time, we shall begin with the revolutionary organization known by its Russian acronym as VSKhSON and the *samizdat* journal *Veche*. Their leading figures— Igor Ogurtsov (born in 1937) and Vladimir Osipov (born in 1939), respectively—are both still alive. The activities of theirs which we shall consider predate Solzhenitsyn's exile. Next, we shall observe the significance for Solzhenitsyn of the *Vekhi* group, comprised of Russian intellectuals of the early twentieth century. Finally, we shall examine the extent of influence and kinship of nineteenth-century Slavophilism. What unites these antecedents is their conjoining of Russian national awareness and Christian, specifically Russian Orthodox, belief.

John Dunlop devoted his 1976 book *The New Russian Revolutionaries* to telling the story of VSKhSON, the All-Russian Social-Christian Union for the Liberation of the People, also sometimes known informally as the Berdyaev Circle in Leningrad. Established by Ogurtsov in 1964 and never exceeding twenty-eight members (with thirty others having candidacy-for-membership status), this group set as its goal to rescue Russia from Communism by means of a coup d'état. Thus, it was a truly revolutionary group, and in this respect it was at odds with Solzhenitsyn. The group existed underground for three years, coming to an end in 1967 with the arrest of all members.

Shortly before the arrests, a copy of the program of VSKhSON was sent West, and Dunlop has reprinted it in an appendix to his book. The program was implacably opposed to the militant atheism and determinism of Marxism-Leninism. It considered Soviet totalitarianism to be worse than fascism because of its doctrine of global revolution. In short, it condemned Bolshevism as immoral, inhumane, and anti-national. On the positive side, in its philosophy of "Christian *personalism*," it began with "the inestimable worth of the individual human being." Then it developed a social blueprint for the nation, intended to be "a sweeping substitute for the philosophy, economics and politics of Marxism-Leninism" and featuring political and economic decentralization.[116]

The intricate details of this program need not detain us here. What is essential for our purposes is to see that the program of VSKhSON was "an interesting attempt at a pathbreaking type of liberal Russian nationalism," and one in fact which "anticipated the programmatic efforts of

Solzhenitsyn and his friends a decade later."[117] Indeed, Dunlop asserts that the program of VSKhSON "is far more detailed and specific in both its negative critique and positive proposals than is Solzhenitsyn's *Letter*." Though its "flaws . . . pale before its immense significance," Dunlop does consider to be a flaw "its uncritically positive opinion of the West and, in general, the whole non-Communist world."[118]

Vladimir Osipov admired Igor Ogurtsov, calling him "one of the noblest and most courageous Soviet dissidents."[119] However, he took as his work not Ogurtsov's revolutionary activism but the editing of a journal, *Veche* (*Assembly*). It appeared in ten issues from 1971 to 1974—in *samizdat*, of course—and was then suppressed. Osipov has spent a total of fifteen years in the Gulag. Dunlop considers *Veche* "the most important of nationalist forums," and he asserts that its significance "can scarcely be exaggerated."[120] The journal allowed for a range of nationalist opinion to be expressed, and not all of it is compatible with Solzhenitsyn's thinking (or with Osipov's, for that matter). What *Veche* does demonstrate is that, well before Gorbachev's campaign of glasnost, percolating beneath the surface of officially sanctioned thought, nationally minded Russians were busy imagining alternative futures for their country. "Of one thing there can be little doubt, *Veche*'s interests meshed with those of a not inconsiderable reading public." Just two months before Solzhenitsyn was exiled, he received an open letter of birthday greetings from seven former political prisoners; they included Osipov and a former member of VSKhSON.[121] Others were developing ideas similar to Solzhenitsyn's, and they were happy to acknowledge his importance to them.

Of the importance of *Vekhi* to Solzhenitsyn there is no doubt. In his own words, "*Vekhi* today still seems to us to have been a vision of the future."[122] *Vekhi* (*Landmarks*, or *Signposts*) was a collection of essays published in 1909, seeking to turn Russia away from the siren song of Marxism and related post-Enlightenment ideologies. In general, the authors had once embraced such views but had come to reject them in favor of spiritual, usually explicitly religious, belief. As Max Hayward, in his introduction to *From Under the Rubble*, summarizes their position,

> The main attack was against the narrowness of outlook and sectarianism that had led the majority of Russian intellectuals to seek solutions in an

uncritical adaptation of the West European enlightenment in its nineteenth-century forms of positivism, atheist materialism, "scientific socialism" and so on. The authors called for a return to traditional spiritual values—which for most of them meant those enshrined in Christian teaching—as a necessary condition for a regeneration of the country's intellectual, cultural and social life.[123]

The contributors to *From Under the Rubble* took *Vekhi* as their direct guide and sought to update it. As their predecessors sought to spare Russia from going under the rubble, so they now called upon Russia to come out from under it. As the *Vekhi* authors desired to avoid what we now can see as the Soviet parenthesis in the flow of Russian history, so their self-proclaimed heirs hoped to help put in place the final punctuation mark on that disruptive era. Members of both groups had made their individual journeys from socialist ideological commitments to spiritual belief and thinking, and in both cases they sought to mobilize other intellectuals on behalf of their cause. Solzhenitsyn thought that such a renaissance among Russian intellectuals was already underway, with the authors of *From Under the Rubble* in the vanguard: "And I am entirely in accord with those who want to see, who want to believe that they can already see the *nucleus of an intelligentsia*, which is our hope for spiritual renewal."[124] Leadership from intellectuals would be a crucial ingredient in this renaissance, and those who stood athwart its development by being locked into old thinking he derisively labeled smatterers. (Donald Treadgold suggests *dilettantes* as a synonym, though "it may lack the element of moral opprobrium present in the original.")[125]

Leonard Schapiro writes most illuminatingly about the *Vekhi* group. Their main burden was that "the radical intelligentsia . . . had borrowed the empty shell of atheistic socialism from the West, without its important Christian substratum or heritage of law, order and social morality." Schapiro's placement of *Vekhi* within the context of Russian intellectual history is very helpful:

> If one had to attempt a rough summary of the position of *Vekhi*, one could say that they stood midway between the Slavophils and the Westerners. They accepted the Slavophil veneration of Russian national tradition, while rejecting their romantic idealisation of innate Russian virtues as a substitute for the more usual civic virtues. They accepted the Westerners'

desire to learn from the countries of the West, while rejecting their atheism, their socialism and their utilitarianism.[126]

Schapiro is clear, also, about Solzhenitsyn's direct indebtedness to *Vekhi*: " . . . the central theme of *Vekhi*—that solutions to man's problems do not lie in systems or in the elimination of enemies, but in the moral position of individuals—is the core of Solzhenitsyn's faith."[127] Or, in Richard Pipes's formulation, "the thesis" of *Vekhi* was that "the intellectual and moral improvement of man had to precede political and social reform."[128]

Donald Treadgold has studied carefully the relationship between *Vekhi* and *From Under the Rubble* (especially Solzhenitsyn's contributions). There are some differences between the two manifestoes, due in large part to their different time settings. More significant are the borrowings by Solzhenitsyn and company, especially this key one:

> . . . assertion of Russian national feeling was made not in opposition to Western themes but alongside and in tandem with them. Not universalism—which eliminates all categories between the individual and mankind itself—and not nationalism—which claims superiority for one's own nation, but Christian *agape* among all men, with due attention to their real and valid associations in family, fellow-workers, nation, and state; that is the message of *From Under the Rubble*, in which Solzhenitsyn plays the leading role.[129]

In short, in his general perspective Solzhenitsyn has company among his contemporaries, and he and they stand in an intellectual tradition.

Solzhenitsyn's indebtedness to nineteenth-century Slavophilism is real, but it is more ambiguous than his indebtedness to the *Vekhi* group. Complicating this picture further is the fact that the Slavophiles themselves were a rather heterogeneous grouping, and the Westernizers, their opposite number, were even more so. Moreover, these two strains of thought are tendencies, not water-tight compartments. As *Vekhi* itself demonstrates, it is possible to draw upon both of them at once. Nevertheless, most Western commentary which aligns Solzhenitsyn with the Slavophiles does so quite indiscriminately. The general intent seems to be to belittle him by tying him to an ostensibly outmoded and discredited line of nineteenth-century thought.

Richard Pipes, who knows of the diversity among the Slavophiles, asserts that "Solzhenitsyn's conservatism is Slavophile in character." Yet, when he draws distinctions, they are to the disadvantage of Solzhenitsyn. After all, "In its original form, as popularized in the 1840s and 1850s, Slavophilism contained strong liberal elements."[130] At least, we gain here the insight that Slavophilism is not altogether retrograde.

That it is retrograde remains, of course, the widespread understanding. As John Dunlop justifiably laments, "Part of the reason that Solzhenitsyn's views are distorted and, at times, caricatured in the press lies in the nearly total ignorance concerning neo-Slavophilism among many journalists reporting on the USSR."[131] The same point applies to Slavophilism *per se*. Treadgold elaborates:

> The facile juxtaposition of this group of men with the so-called Westerners, as if Slavophiles were mindlessly reactionary xenophobes as against the rationally progressive Westerners, became the mode in Western analyses of the two "circles" and in the consciousness of Russian intellectuals themselves.[132]

That juxtaposition is operative when critics make straight-line alignments between Sakharov and the Westernizers, on the one hand, and Solzhenitsyn and the Slavophiles, on the other, as if the two giants of contemporary dissent had nothing in common.

Of the traits of the Westernizing tendency we need say little, since the West presumably understands itself. For our purposes, it suffices to note, with Dimitry Pospielovsky, that "Russian Westernism, at least since the 1840s, has been predominantly secular, materialistic, positivistic, and ahistorical in the sense of rejecting culturally Russian continuity and values." That is, it is an authentic heir of Enlightenment thinking. Therefore, it was virtually inevitable that current thinkers of a religious cast of mind would turn not to this but to the counter tendency for inspiration. Intensifying this drive for today's generation is the simple fact of Marxism's Western origin. For Solzhenitsyn and company, Marxism is seen as

> a manifestation of the impasse of the materialistic-utilitarian school of thought, in the final analysis as an impasse of the liberal tradition of thought and social construction, albeit in its extreme (and hence, per-

haps, most logical) and utopian reduction. A person rejecting Marxism out of an existential experience of its application often also rejects liberalism, treating Marxism as a branch of the tree of liberalism, with its materialism, relativism, utilitarianism, and religion of progress.[133]

Nor need we be comprehensive in enumerating points of agreement and disagreement between Solzhenitsyn's thinking and Slavophilism in general. Dunlop uses "neo-Slavophilism" and "Russian national and religious renaissance" as synonyms.[134] The prefix *neo* is designed to indicate that not all positions of Slavophilism are to be held (for or) against its modern-day heirs—the ones, that is, whom he alternately calls liberal nationalists. In general, what both groups share is "a commitment to the Russian Orthodox Church and the belief that Russia's future development should not be a slavish imitation of the West."[135]

However, extreme nationalists, those whom Dunlop places to the right (and far right) of the liberal nationalists, have their claim on Slavophilism, too. Thus, V. Gorskii warns against Slavophile influence, particularly its messianism. Yet he paints all variants of the Russian national revival with the same brush when he says, "The true ground of Russian nationalism is religious messianism which is clearly analogous to ancient Hebrew messianism." Therefore, Solzhenitsyn argues particularly passionately against Gorskii in "Repentance and Self-Limitation in the Life of Nations." Gorskii ties the messianism among the Slavophiles to "the old tradition of the exclusiveness of Russian Orthodoxy." And he warns against the Slavophiles' "dangerous prejudice" of confusing a "return to the Church" with "*going to the people.*"[136]

But of course, as we have seen, the charge of messianism does not apply to Solzhenitsyn. Through Gleb Nerzhin of *The First Circle*, he rejects "going to the people." Nor, for that matter, does he adhere to the exclusiveness of Orthodoxy. Gorskii's warnings fit some Russian nationalists but not all, and not Solzhenitsyn. Indeed, Pospielovsky points to the "relative absence of messianism" among the neo-Slavophiles as one of the factors which "distinguishes them from their nineteenth-century forebears." He points also to another important factor: "Again except for the extremists, the neo-Slavophiles . . . generally have more faith in constitutional guarantees and the rule of law than did the original Slavophiles."[137]

About Solzhenitsyn's indebtedness to Slavophilism, we may say in summary that the aspects of it which nowadays are considered the most retrograde and reactionary are the very ones which he eschews. Moreover, the borrowings that indubitably do pertain are not of such a nature as to cause him to seal himself off from any and all ideas of Western origin. Treadgold summarizes exactly correctly:

> Solzhenitsyn is best understood as the chief figure in the contemporary generation of the continuing if sometimes interrupted effort to recover the Russian national tradition within a context of cosmopolitan reflection and acceptance of many aspects of Western culture.[138]

The development of a healthy Russian patriotism will not be an easy task. The pathway to national recovery is strewn with many obstacles. Solzhenitsyn himself provides an apt extended image which begins like this:

> A society so vicious and polluted . . . can only be cured and purified by passing through a spiritual filter. And this filter is a terrible one, with holes as fine as the eye of a needle, each big enough for only one person. And people may pass into the spiritual future only one at a time, by squeezing through.

Eventually, he says, as the image comes to its climax, "The filter will grow wider and easier for each subsequent particle—and the number of particles passing through it will increase all the time, so that on the far side these worthy individuals might reconstitute and re-create a worthy *people*. . . ."[139]

Amid the raucous chorus of Russian nationalists screaming out conflicting calls about the way out from under the rubble of Soviet Communism, Solzhenitsyn's is a sweet voice. It can rise in righteous indignation; there is much to be indignant about. But its message is one of moderation. The prospects for domestic tranquility and world peace will be well served if his ideas find broad acceptance in Russia. If we in the West correctly hear and heed him, we shall do no harm toward Russia, and we may even do some good.

9

"Letter to the Soviet Leaders"

NOTHING DAMAGED SOLZHENITSYN'S REPUTATION so much as his publication in the West of his *Letter to the Soviet Leaders*. The misinterpretations of this letter established in the West's popular imagination a false view of Solzhenitsyn, and persons who have read little or nothing of his work now regularly refer to him according to this stereotype—as if it were fact. Personally, I have sometimes (though only fleetingly) wished that he had never published this letter, for all the grief it occasioned.

Of all the misinterpretations of *Letter*, the most myopic, even ethnocentrically provincial, is the one that viewed it as an attack on the West in general and on Western liberals in particular. As if Solzhenitsyn thought to pen a note to the leaders of the Soviet Union in order to register with them his complaints about Western liberalism! It is one thing to say (as of course a good many have done) that he does not understand Russia, about which at least he is writing in this letter. It is quite another not to get right the subject matter with which he is dealing.

In the preceding three chapters, we examined thematic issues about which there has been great confusion. Now, in this chapter and Chapters Eleven and Twelve, we turn to a running commentary on two texts, *Letter to the Soviet Leaders* and *Rebuilding Russia*. I choose these for close reading because they present proposals for change in Russia. They deal with that enduring question, What is to be done? In the case of *Letter*, it is particularly revealing to read it closely some two decades now since it was written. For there is a prescience in it which surpassed the imaginative stretch of its initial critics. Had it been held for publication until now, its reception would have been quite different from what it actually was. *Rebuilding Russia*, which is in important ways an updating and elaboration of themes in *Letter*, was received much more respectfully (though less widely) than was its predecessor.

The heart of this chapter is an exposition of the letter itself. Before we launch into it, however, we must address some preliminary matters. These include the issues of genre and of audience. We must also take some note here of the reception of the letter, for it elicited from Solzhenitsyn further explanations clarifying his intent. Because the Western reception has already been described, most of the attention here will be directed to comments by intellectuals within the Soviet Union.

The first difficulty to be dispensed with in reading *Letter* is simply that of genre. Solzhenitsyn is here exercising the art of the pamphleteer. This is not an unknown art. Americans may wish to think of Thomas Paine as an apposite parallel. But Solzhenitsyn's previously published belletristic works did not prepare readers to expect him to turn adviser on practical affairs of state. A pamphlet is not, by its nature, a comprehensive and definitive statement of its author's position on matters of political theory and practice. We may well wish for something more complete from Solzhenitsyn (which it is not impossible that we shall eventually have); and at least now we have also the somewhat longer *Rebuilding Russia*, though it, too, is in genre a pamphlet. Nevertheless, we must judge *Letter* according to criteria appropriate to the confines of its genre, not as if it were something more or other than what it is.

As a pamphlet *Letter to the Soviet Leaders* is a supremely practical effort. It is born out of desperate circumstances. How to find some path down from the icy cliff of totalitarianism without plunging into the abyss of anarchy and civil war among the nations comprising the USSR? That is the motivating question. The essay has to do not with the long term but only with the first stage of a post-Soviet scenario. It is so thoroughly pragmatic that it even entails some compromise with principles. The clearest example of this spirit of compromise is in the huge concession that the Communists can retain power—for the time being.

Yet in the West we repeatedly heard the wrong-headed reading that the letter was utopian.

As a pamphlet *Letter* is also programmatic. It is too brief to be a full program. John Dunlop neatly calls it "proto-programmatic."[1] For instance, it does not take into account such important issues as political institutions and structures. They are for later, after the initial transition; and, suitably, *Rebuilding Russia* does take up such issues. Also, *Letter* contains considerable analysis, of the kind necessary to clear the decks for any programmatic advice.

The matter of audience is as important as the matter of genre if one is to approach *Letter* properly. The title specifies the audience: the Soviet leaders. The essay was not written with Western readers primarily in mind. Yet this obvious point was too seldom accorded due weight by Western commentators. It was not written as an open letter. Only after Solzhenitsyn received no reply from the addressees did he, several months later, let the rest of us see what he had said to them. Nor was he the first dissident to write a letter to the Soviet leaders. Sakharov, for one, had also done so, more than once. He, too, then informed the world of what he had written.

Between the time of the letter's initial composition—it is dated September 5, 1973—and its publication in early 1974, the KGB got hold of a copy of *The Gulag Archipelago*. During this tumultuous time, Solzhenitsyn fretted about how his drastically altered situation would affect the reception of *Letter*. He worried that its "conciliatory tone" (as he saw it) "might be taken to mean that I was giving way, that I was scared." So, on the eve of his exile, "I had to change its original tone; an appeal to reason would look like a confession of weakness now." In the result, he "paired" *Letter* with "Live Not by Lies," addressed to the citizenry and released the day before he was exiled. "[T]he leaders and the people, two sides of the whole, could be addressed simultaneously, government and people could recoil together from the same abominations."[2]

What is most striking in all this is that Solzhenitsyn had to have thought that there was a real chance that the Soviet leaders would give his letter some serious consideration. Sometimes he was of a mood to think that, though Communism could not hold power forever, it might last for a long time. But sometimes he imagined the possibility of an early moderating of it, of the beginning of a transition to the post-Communist society which must in any case someday come. In such a mood he sent his letter. Was the Soviet Union too strong to collapse soon? Everyone in the West, of whatever political stripe, thought so. Solzhenitsyn, ever the optimist, thought and hoped that it might be otherwise. And the calf butted his head against the oak.

Once in the West, Solzhenitsyn told us how the situation appeared to him back then:

> . . . two and three years ago . . . it was possible to believe that we inhabitants of the Soviet Union could sit down and consider our future. The Soviet leadership was experiencing so many difficulties, so many failures, that it had to seek some way out. . . .[3]

But what Solzhenitsyn hoped for was not to be. Not yet. As détente deepened into dogma and the West seemed to be weakening, the Soviet leaders (as Solzhenitsyn saw things) gained some respite from the tribulations confronting them.

Of Solzhenitsyn's various comments about *Letter* since his arrival in the West, one has to do directly with the matter of audience. And it is surprising.

> The main element in the "Letter to the Soviet Leaders" was not spelled out but implied: that I was actually appealing not to those leaders. I was trying to map out a path which could be taken by other leaders—not the current ones—who might suddenly come to replace them.

It was a time of stagnation. Brezhnev and his cronies were old. A generational changing of the guard might not be far off. And what might that next generation of leaders lead on to? As Solzhenitsyn explained, ". . . we have to think about the dangers of the transitional period which lies ahead of us."[4] This is exactly what he was doing in his letter of 1973.

Letter proposed that during the transitional period the Communists would stay in control but that they would replace totalitarianism with authoritarianism. This could be achieved by their abandoning various mandates of Marxist ideology. Writing shortly before Gorbachev's fall from power, Vladislav Krasnov shrewdly noted that what Solzhenitsyn pragmatically "envisioned as a transitional stage, a sort of authoritarian

Communism during which the Communist Party would remain in charge," is exactly what came to pass. "Whether Gorbachev intended it or not, this is the stage in which the country actually finds itself right now."[5] The logic of events drove Gorbachev along the path outlined in *Letter*, albeit against his will.

About the link between Solzhenitsyn and Gorbachev, Krasnov goes one step further. "Comparing the Letter with Gorbachev's own (or his ghostwriters') book *Perestroika: New Thinking for Our Country and the World*, it is hard to avoid the impression that the latter is but a watered-down version of the former. So striking are the similarities that one might even suspect plagiarism."[6] As intriguing as this suggestion is, there were of course sharp limits on any possible borrowings. With his steady drumbeat of invocations of Lenin as his model, Gorbachev always kept his proposals firmly within the confines of socialism. He could not follow Solzhenitsyn's most basic piece of advice and liberate himself from the authority of Marxist-Leninist ideology. Only as some of Solzhenitsyn's suggestions can be unnaturally squeezed into Gorbachev's classic neo-Leninist mold are parallels between the two to be glimpsed. Thus, Gorbachev sank in this contradiction: Everything must change, but nothing must change.

David Remnick, also, has noted parallels between Solzhenitsyn's letter and Gorbachev's reign. It is especially about *Letter*'s allowance of an authoritarian order that Remnick comments,

> Alien, even repulsive, notions for a Western readership accustomed to a liberal democracy. And yet there is a celebration among the same readership when Gorbachev, in effect, recommends the same thing, a "law-based state" that certainly shows every intention of retaining a degree of authoritarian leadership.

His elaboration in the next paragraph gets things just right.

> It is a wonderful irony of history that some of Solzhenitsyn's most scathing texts appear to have influenced the present Kremlin leaders. The emphasis on the ruined environment, the proposal to transfer land to the peasantry, the starvation of culture and spiritual life, the call for accurate histories and reevaluation of ideology, the need to shift attention from foreign adventures to the decay at home, all of it can be read now in Pravda and Izvestia.[7]

One can hope that the death of the Soviet Union will allow Westerners to read *Letter* afresh. Once upon a time, Olga Carlisle could ask with disbelief, "Could he really imagine now that the Soviet leaders would adopt the political alternative he proposed, a Russia without Marxist ideology?"[8] Once upon a time, Richard Lowenthal could answer with disbelief, "But Solzhenitsyn, for all the sincerity of his prophecy, is not a fool; he clearly does not expect such a radical transformation of the Soviet regime to come about by the struggle of his fellow dissidents in the foreseeable future."[9] And just here we see the main reason why this eminently pragmatic work was dismissed as utopian. What Solzhenitsyn was urging upon his country simply could not come to be, our critics told us. And what cannot come to be is by definition utopian; it is nowhere. An unbridgeable chasm separates utopia and reality. No one today, whatever one's opinion of Solzhenitsyn's prescriptions, will say that an unbridgeable chasm separates *Letter* from post-Soviet reality.

From the beginning, Solzhenitsyn was quite startled by the Western reception of *Letter to the Soviet Leaders*. He could scarcely believe what he was reading. As early as 1974, he told Walter Cronkite, "You see my letter to the leaders of the Soviet Union was really very incorrectly understood in the West. . . ." (This was directly in reply to Cronkite's summary of the presumably obvious: "In your letter to the Soviet leaders you favored an authoritarian system for the Soviet Union. . . .")[10] In *The Mortal Danger*, he said, "But the reaction of the Western and in particular the American press simply astonished me. My program was construed as conservative, retrograde, isolationist, and as a tremendous threat to the world!" He goes on to illustrate why he was astonished:

> Yet when I called for an immediate halt to all aggression, and to any thought of aggression, when I proposed that all those peoples who so wished should be free to secede, and that the Soviet Union should look to its domestic problems, this was interpreted as and even noisily proclaimed to be reactionary and dangerous isolationism.[11]

In *The Mortal Danger*, Solzhenitsyn also explained some of the mood and motivation underlying his letter. About his call to the leaders "to shake off the communist delirium and to minister to their own devastated country," he concedes, "The chances of success were naturally almost nil, but my aim was at least to pose the question loudly and publicly." If the Brezhnev generation would not pay heed, at least his agenda would have been set out for the next generation of leaders to do with as they pleased. In addition, he reinforces the sense of pragmatism governing the letter: ". . . I attempted to formulate the minimum national policy that could be implemented without wresting power from the incumbent communist rulers."[12]

Within the Soviet Union, *Letter* elicited a set of reactions somewhat different from those in the West, if only by being less one-sided. Above ground, from the leaders, there was of course no public response (and one can only wonder what discussions ensued behind Kremlin walls). But underground, in *samizdat* writings, there were responses, which are now public. These were mixed. Those who, along with Solzhenitsyn, hoped for a movement of spiritual renewal and a rebirth of Russian patriotism, found *Letter* inspiring. Mikhail Agurskii's response is illustrative:

> It appears quite obvious that the sole realistic alternative for those who would truly desire to revive Russian life in its fundamental form would be the acceptance (in its basic form, to be sure) of the humanistic program proposed by Solzhenitsyn in his *Letter to the Soviet Leaders*. Unfortunately, Western public opinion views this program as something of an extreme form of Russian nationalism. It does not understand that this is the only humanistic alternative in Russia to racism and neo-Nazism.[13]

Within the Soviet Union, friend and foe alike had to acknowledge, as Michael Meerson-Aksenov put it, that "Solzhenitsyn has had an enormous influence on the de-Stalinization of the consciousness of the intelligentsia." *Letter*, he adds "fell like a bomb—not on the Soviet leaders—but on the 'differently minded' intelligentsia."[14]

Prominent among these differently minded intellectuals are Andrei Sakharov, Roy Medvedev, and Lev Kopelev. All three resist Solzhenitsyn's vision of a movement of spiritual rebirth, and all three think that he makes too much of ideology as the villain. Yet Sakharov is a special case. Overall, where Medvedev and Kopelev reject, he objects only in part. Moreover, Solzhenitsyn replied to Sakharov's criticism, and therefore this stimulating debate is best described at the end of the chapter.

Lev Kopelev is the real-life prototype of the character Lev Rubin in *The First Circle*, whom Solzhenitsyn depicts affectionately yet critically, and the reader who knows Rubin's running debate with Gleb Nerzhin is well prepared for Kopelev's disagreement with Solzhenitsyn's letter. Though initially honoring the author and declaring the need for impartial analysis of his letter, Kopelev can find almost no redeeming qualities in it. His long, rambling response is often harsh and sarcastic in tone, sometimes reaching high dudgeon. But the nub of his resistance is ideological. Solzhenitsyn's "unmasking of ideology," according to this unreconstructed Marxist, "turns out to be a not too original hypnotic propagandistic approach." For the castigation of Marxist ideology "makes use of a demonic myth similar to the way the Nazis used the myth of 'World Jewry' and Stalinists and Maoists used the myth of 'world imperialism.' " Because of Solzhenitsyn's "naive political-economic fantasies," his letter's "critical judgments are far from past and present reality. Let us hope that its wishes, exhortations, and prophecies be no less distant from the reality of the future." Kopelev recognizes correctly that what lies at the root of the disagreement between Solzhenitsyn and himself is their conflicting views of the Enlightenment.[15]

Roy Medvedev finds Solzhenitsyn's *Letter* "a disappointing document," and he derides many of its proposals as "incongruous," even as "incompetent and utopian." He is representative of critics East and West in being scandalized by Solzhenitsyn's accommodating words about authoritarianism. He phrases his reaction thus: "In essence, Solzhenitsyn rejects not only the socialist perspective but even democracy for the U.S.S.R." And he imagines that "the overwhelming majority of Soviet citizens undoubtedly opts for the socialist path toward development of our society. . . ." They will not be lured by either Orthodoxy or capitalism. Yet he concedes that Solzhenitsyn's position also has a following: "That attitude, which appears in a maximally pointed, perhaps grotesque form, in Solzhenitsyn's letter, is peculiar to many people in our country." Like Kopelev, Roy Medvedev recognizes that the real issues dividing him and Solzhenitsyn are the underlying ones of world view—specifically, of Marxism and Christianity. *Contra* Solzhenitsyn, he asserts, "All the shortcomings and vices that exist in the Soviet Union cannot be blamed on Marxism-Leninism." He complains that "Solzhenitsyn treats Marxism as a faith," whereas it is in truth a science. And he adds, in wonderful words, that sciences "have the right to be imprecise and to err." Also *contra* Solzhenitsyn, he declares, "I am convinced that it is not Christianity which will stand at the basis of the moral and spiritual regeneration and development of the Russian people."[16]

INTERACTION WITH SOLZHENITSYN at the level of world views which both Kopelev and Roy Medvedev engaged in is helpful preparation for the exposition of *Letter* itself. For, although he endeavors to be as practical as possible in giving advice to the Soviet leaders, his advice manifestly emanates from his own world view, which is in opposition to theirs. If he cannot convert them from one world view to another, neither can he ignore or disguise the fundamental differences of outlook separating writer and intended readers.

After a brief, five-paragraph introduction, Solzhenitsyn divides *Letter to the Soviet Leaders* into seven parts. They are as follows:

1. The West on Its Knees
2. War with China
3. Civilization in an Impasse
4. The Russian Northeast
5. Internal, Not External, Development
6. Ideology
7. But How Can All This Be Managed?

We shall make our way through the letter section by section. The virtue of this approach is that we see how Solzhenitsyn unfolds his argument; we follow the linkages in his mind. The vice of it is that the sections are not altogether discrete units; sometimes themes loop back and forth through the letter, appearing in more than one place. Organization is not always a strong point in Solzhenitsyn. Everything is related to everything.

The introduction begins quite strikingly. "I do not entertain much hope that you will deign to examine ideas not formally solicited by you. . . ."[17] So Solzhenitsyn begins on a realistic note which acknowledges the power relationship pertaining to his writing to those readers, yet without forgoing that grim but tenacious hope which is his hallmark.

And he offers, as a reason for the leaders to read his letter, his independence of mind. He calls himself "a fellow countryman of a rare kind"; he is one of them and not one of them. He is

> one who does not stand on a ladder subordinate to your command, who can be neither dismissed from his post, nor demoted, nor promoted, nor rewarded by you, and from whom therefore you are almost certain to hear an opinion sincerely voiced, without any careerist calculations, such as you are unlikely to hear from even the finest experts in your bureaucracy. (p. 7)

Solzhenitsyn will not truckle nor flatter, even as he acknowledges their power.

In a later explanation of what he perceived to be the realistic limits on what he could propose in this letter, Solzhenitsyn remarked, ". . . it was plain that the very most one could hope for would be concessions on their side, certainly not capitulation: neither free general elections nor a complete (or even partial) change of leadership could be expected."[18] Keeping this limitation in mind helps us avoid the widespread error of reading the letter as a statement of Solzhenitsyn's political ideal. The reference to free elections, though impossible to propose to the then-current leadership, is a hint in the direction of the democratic option that he advocates in *Rebuilding Russia*.

Solzhenitsyn next addresses the issue of genre: ". . . I shall try to say what is most important in a short space. . ." (p. 7). *Letter* will not provide a full-blown program of reform, such as that enunciated by VSKhSON. A letter is too brief for that purpose. Implicit here also is the fact that the most important step is the first step. Although *Letter* occasionally glances into the distance, mostly it remains focused upon what can be done right away, and by the current leaders.

Solzhenitsyn then places another restriction upon the scope of his letter. Although his world view is a worldwide view, the letter will focus upon domestic concerns. As he puts it, "I wish all people well, and the closer they are to us and the more dependent upon us, the more fervent is my wish. But it is the fate of the Russian and Ukrainian peoples that preoccupies me above all. . ." (p. 7). They are also the ones, he says, who have suffered the most.

Solzhenitsyn supposes that the leaders will resonate with this domestic focus, "that you are not alien to your origins, to your fathers, grandfathers and great-grandfathers, to the expanses of your homeland; and that you are conscious of your nationality." Already he implies here what will become explicit later: that the grip of their internationalist ideology upon them is tenuous at best and that national spirit is a stronger motive even for them. He does allow that he might be misreading them: "If I am mistaken, there is no point in your reading the rest of this letter" (p. 8). But he does not really think so. In *The Oak and the Calf*, he said, "We cannot give up all hope of converting them: we would be less than men if we did. Surely they are not bereft of every last trace of humanity."[19]

The introduction ends with a specifying of the two "chief dangers facing our country in the next ten to thirty years." They are "war with China, and our destruction, together with Western civilization, in the crush and stench of a befouled earth" (p. 8). But who would have guessed, from the critics' emphasis on Solzhenitsyn's alleged hostility to the West and advocacy of authoritarianism, that the center of gravity in this letter lay with these two concerns?

THE FIRST OF THE SEVEN SECTIONS, "The West on Its Knees," is to be read as background for the sections that follow. It is ludicrous to imagine that Solzhenitsyn feels compelled to tell the Soviet leaders of his personal estimate of Western weakness just for the sake of the point itself. No, he is trying to deflect them from their all-consuming attention to issues of the Cold War. Any external threat will not come from the westward direction in which they are looking. And one reason—not the total reason but the one that his auditors are likely to appreciate—is that the global balance of power no longer clearly tips toward the West's side. Therefore, the Soviets now have the luxury of attending to needs which they had sacrificed in the name of the Cold War. This argument is all very far from supporting Solzhenitsyn's reputation as a Cold Warrior.

The first piece of evidence adduced about Western weakness is the Vietnam war. In the whole twentieth century, only now can we imagine what we are seeing: that the West's "rulers would resort to all manner of concessions simply to win the favor of the rulers of a future Russia." Only now is it possible

that even the mightiest transatlantic power, having emerged all-
victorious from two world wars as the leader and provider for all mankind, would suddenly lose to a tiny, distant Asiatic country, and show
internal dissension and spiritual weakness. (p. 9; see also p. 46)

It brings this erstwhile worshipper of the West no joy that "the
Western world, as a single, clearly united force, no longer counter-
balances the Soviet Union, indeed has almost ceased to exist" (p. 11).
But it should alleviate some of the Cold-War anxieties of the Soviet
leaders. If this characterization of Western weakness in 1973 is exaggerated, as I think it is, such were the effects of the Vietnam war on
his global thinking.

Soviet leaders, however, should find "little cause for self-
congratulation" in this situation, for the West's wounds are mostly self-
inflicted. Here Solzhenitsyn offers the Soviet leaders in capsule form
the same historical analysis that he presented to his Harvard and other
Western audiences:

The catastrophic weakening of the Western world and the whole of
Western civilization is . . . the result of a historical, psychological and
moral crisis affecting the entire culture and world outlook which were
conceived at the time of the Renaissance and attained the peak of their
expression with the eighteenth-century Enlightenment. (pp. 11–12)

Soviet diplomacy suffers from modernity's lack of moral vision, as
well. In fact, whatever successes it may wish to claim vis-à-vis the
West—and, in retrospect, it is truly remarkable that such a backward
country achieved the status of one of the world's two superpowers—
Soviet diplomacy has experienced "two astonishing failures." In its
history it has "bred two ferocious enemies, one for the last war and the
other for the next war—the German Wehrmacht and Mao Tse-tung's
China" (p. 12). As he heads toward the next section on war with China,
he specifies Soviet complicity in bringing Mao to power "in place of a
peaceable neighbor such as Chiang Kai-shek." It resulted from "an
exact adherence to the precepts of Marxism-Leninism," according to
which all "*national* considerations were completely lacking" (pp. 12–
13). As transition to the next section, he again expresses his aware-

ness that "I am talking to total realists"; so he will not "waste my breath" on appeals to idealism and morality (p. 13).

IN THE SECTION on "War with China," Solzhenitsyn does not give the background explanation for this threat which Western readers might need. His intended audience, he is sure, is well aware of the peril and is already thinking about it. So he takes that much for granted and focuses on how to avoid the war. "There must never be such a war. *This war must not happen, ever!*" (p. 16). This war, he predicts, will not be a nuclear war. With China's vast numerical superiority ranged along Russia's empty lands, the war is sure to be devastating to Russians. "After *this* war the Russian people will virtually cease to exist on this planet. And that alone will mean the war has been lost *utterly*," he tells the leaders—"along with your power, as you realize" (p. 15).

The worst of it is that this war would be waged over ideology. "To die in an *ideological* war! And mainly for a dead ideology! I think *even you* are not able to take such an awesome responsibility upon yourselves!" (p. 15). So Solzhenitsyn suggests that they do with the ideology what Stalin did in World War II. (This may be his only approving reference to Stalin.) "He wisely discarded it, all but ceased to mention it and unfurled instead the old Russian banner— sometimes, indeed, the standard of Orthodoxy—and we conquered!" (p. 17). If the Chinese leaders want the ideology, "Give them their ideology!" Let them "glory in it for a while." Let them also "shoulder the whole sackful of unfulfillable international obligations," including the support of terrorists and guerrillas and the "absurd economics (a million a day just to Cuba)" (p. 18).

Once on the subject of ideology, Solzhenitsyn cannot quickly let go of it. It is for him the chief villain, and he will devote the whole of the sixth section to it. Here he says,

Take an unbiased look: the murky whirlwind of *Progressive Ideology* swept in on us from the West at the end of the last century, and has tormented and ravaged our soul quite enough; and if it is now veering away farther east of its own accord, then let it veer away, don't try to stop it! (pp. 18–19)

He interpolates that he does not "wish for the spiritual destruction of

China," but "it is enough for the time being for us to worry about how to save *our own* people." And he unflinchingly tells the Soviet leaders that Communism's days are numbered. "I believe that our people will soon be cured of this disease, and the Chinese too, given time. . ." (p. 19). This faith that the end of Communism as a geopolitical force was not far off very few Western commentators could fathom; it seemed like a utopian's dream.

This section of *Letter* now seems the part most off the mark. Yet Solzhenitsyn was not alone in fearing war with China. On this subject he was most strongly influenced by Andrei Amalrik, author of the stunningly prophetic little book *Will the Soviet Union Survive Until 1984?* Solzhenitsyn refers to him by name when suggesting what war with China might entail: ". . . it will certainly last a minimum of ten to fifteen years—and, incidentally, will run almost exactly along the lines forecast by Amalrik, who was sent to his destruction for what he wrote instead of being invited to join the inner circle of our advisers" (p. 15). Amalrik, twenty years Solzhenitsyn's junior, spent time in the Gulag and died mysteriously in Spain in 1980 in an automobile crash while on his way to a conference on the Helsinki Accords. In that little book for which he is best remembered, he declared, ". . . I have no doubt that this great Eastern Slav empire . . . has entered the last decades of its existence." He was quite sure that Soviet Communism was too internally corrupt to reform itself. Though more in the Westernizing line than Solzhenitsyn, he, too, felt the need for an alternate belief system, one which he hoped would feature the value of the human personality; also, he lamented the loss of the Christian ethic among the Russian people. He predicted the de-Sovietization of Eastern Europe. Because of the combination of internal rot and external pressures, particularly from China, he prophesied that "the collapse of the regime will occur sometime between 1980 and 1985."[20] As wild-eyed as all this seemed in 1970 (though not to Solzhenitsyn), Amalrik was off by only a handful of years.

If this brief summary does not do justice to the due tentativeness of Amalrik's predictions, about war with China he was less hopeful than Solzhenitsyn that it could be avoided. And it is about China that both Amalrik and Solzhenitsyn have proven to be least accurate in their predictions. So far. Although a war between Russia and China seems now only a remote possibility, history could still write a bloody chapter along this unequally populated border.

SECTION THREE IS ENTITLED "Civilization in an Impasse," and it casts its geographical net widely enough to encompass the advanced countries in general. It is listed as the second danger, after war with China, and it is described as "the multiple impasse in which Western civilization (which Russia long ago chose the honor of joining) finds itself, but it is not so imminent; there are still two or three decades in reserve" (p. 19). The parenthesis is important. Although we frequently speak of Russia and the West in opposition, Solzhenitsyn is pleased to acknowledge that in broad cultural terms Russia is part of the West. It is of course in the choice of Christianity a millennium ago that Russia identified itself as part of the West.

The impasse is that the human race is close to ecological catastrophe. At the rate that humanity is currently consuming its nonrenewable resources, the earth cannot much longer sustain life as advanced societies have become accustomed to living it. Although some who do not share his world view will like this aspect of his thinking, Solzhenitsyn clearly sees his environmentalism as an integral part of the seamless web of his moral vision. We can discuss the ideas in this section according to three points: first, an analysis of the current impasse; second, an analysis of the historical roots of the crisis; third, a suggestion of a solution for the problem. This third point, while articulated in Section Three, carries over into and dominates Sections Four and Five, as well.

The current situation, "[i]f the available information is to be believed," is that "some of the earth's resources are rapidly running out." For instance, "there will be no more oil in twenty years, no more copper in nineteen, no more mercury in twelve; many other resources are nearly exhausted; and energy and fresh water are very limited" (p. 23). The exponential burgeoning of technological development is approaching the limits of the earth to sustain it. "All the unrestrained industrial growth has taken place not over thousands or hundreds of years (from Adam to 1945) but only over the last twenty-eight years (from 1945 onward)" (p. 22). Appealing to the leaders' pride in being the "first socialist country in the world," with the self-appointed role of setting an example to others, he asks, ". . . so why, then, have we been so dolefully unoriginal in technology, and why have we so unthinkingly, so blindly, copied Western civilization?" (p. 25).

Only with the Chernobyl disaster did the West become widely aware of the ecological depredations wreaked by the Soviets. Today no report of disaster is too horrible for us to believe. In Solzhenitsyn's summary, "We have squandered our resources foolishly without so much as a backward glance, sapped our soil, mutilated our vast expanses with idiotic 'inland seas' and contaminated belts of wasteland around our industrial centers. . ." (p. 26). In retrospect, it is bizarre and embarrassing that many Western commentators dismissed him as a romantic primitivist when he raised these issues in 1973.

For his analysis of the current crisis, Solzhenitsyn identifies two sources: the Teilhard de Chardin Society and the Club of Rome. He seems to have in mind particularly the much-discussed report to the Club of Rome entitled *The Limits to Growth*, published a year before *Letter*. Although this man trained in mathematics and physics summarizes its conclusions and refers to its computer calculations, he does not necessarily subscribe to everything in the report. For instance, it says that population growth is "[t]he greatest possible impediment to more equal distribution of the world's resources,"[21] whereas he mentions population only in passing and argues only for survival and not for equal distribution *per se*. He seeks to bring these Western insights to the attention of those ruling over his homeland. What matters most for him is to take the long view and to act now according to its dictates.

But how did the West, and Russia blindly following along, get into this mess? What is the historical cause? It is the doctrine of "*endless, infinite* progress dinned into our heads by the dreamers of the Enlightenment." What we learn from the Club of Rome is that "[s]ociety must cease to look upon 'progress' as something desirable. 'Eternal progress' is a nonsensical myth" (p. 21). The club's report "pointed ominously to the catastrophic destruction of mankind sometime between the years 2020 and 2070 *if it did not relinquish economic progress*" (p. 22). We read, "The fact remains: the earth's finite resources will not support an indefinite expansion of industrial civilization." These words are Christopher Lasch's; they could as easily have been Solzhenitsyn's. As could these: "The attempt to extend Western standards of living to the rest of the world will lead even more quickly to the exhaustion of nonrenewable resources, the irreversible pollution of the earth's atmosphere, and the destruction of the ecological system, in short, on which human life depends." And Lasch traces the problem to the same Enlightenment source: "The belated discovery that the earth's ecology will no longer sustain indefinite expansion of productive forces deals the final blow to the belief in progress."[22] Like Solzhenitsyn, Lasch features the economic and technological ramifications of the doctrine of progress.

What, then, is to be done? The path is obvious: renunciation. Renunciation not of technology *per se* but of the doctrine of progress which currently impels its development.

> Unless mankind renounces the notion of economic progress, the biosphere will become unfit for life even *during our lifetime*. And if mankind is to be *saved*, technology has to be adapted to a stable economy in the next twenty to thirty years, and to do that, the process must be started *now, immediately*. (p. 23)

The goal must be "a *zero-growth economy*, a stable economy. *Economic growth is not only unnecessary but ruinous*. We must set ourselves the aim not of *increasing* national resources, but merely of *conserving* them." Mankind must abandon "the gigantic scale of modern technology in industry, agriculture and urban development (the cities of today are cancerous tumors)." Technology will certainly be needed, but "[t]he chief aim of technology will now be to eradicate the lamentable results of previous technologies" (p. 22). As Solzhenitsyn put it in "Repentance and Self-Limitation," "We must go over from uninterrupted progress to a *stable economy*, with *nil growth* in territory, parameters, and tempo, developing only through improved technology (and even technical successes must be critically screened)."[23]

Although Solzhenitsyn's focus, given his audience, is on the nations in the Soviet Union, the same conservationist ethic applies elsewhere. Thus, he urged the Japanese to observe whaling restrictions, "out of love for the planet."[24] As for "[t]he 'Third World,' which has not yet started on the fatal path of Western civilization," he believes that it "can only be saved by 'small-scale technology,' which requires an increase, not a reduction, in manual labor, uses the simplest machinery and is based purely on local materials" (p. 22).

Whereas many readers will give general consent to Solzhenitsyn's assessment of the current situation, some will resist his laying the blame on the Enlightenment's doctrine of progress, and perhaps more will reject his remedy. Be that as it may, what matters is that his position be correctly understood. Solzhenitsyn took umbrage at his critics' distortions of it:

> . . . I was accused of propounding some kind of "way back"; one must think a man a fool to ascribe to him the desire to move against the flow of time. It was alleged that I am asking the future Russia "to renounce modern technology." Another fabrication: I had in fact called for "highly developed technology," albeit "on a small, non-gigantic scale."[25]

The themes of conservationism and environmentalism dominate Sections Four and Five, also. Section Four features (as it is entitled) "The Russian Northeast." As he thought about "the whole central zone of Siberia" in "Repentance and Self-Limitation," he observed that "there are hardly any open spaces like it left on the civilized earth." And he summarized his vision for the development of it:

> The Northeast could not be brought to life by camp watch-towers, the yells of armed guards and the barking of man-eating dogs. Only free people with a free understanding of our national mission can resurrect these great spaces, awaken them, heal them, beautify them with feats of engineering.[26]

In *August 1914* a wise engineer, Obodovsky, says, "Russia's center of gravity will shift to the Northeast. That's a prophecy. There's no avoiding it. Incidentally, Dostoevsky came to the same conclusion at the end of his life."[27] The fourth section of *Letter* expands upon the point.

"*The supreme asset* of all peoples is now *the earth*." There is "some extra hope" for Russia, because it is one of only "four fortunate countries still abundantly rich in untapped land even today." The others are Australia, Canada, and Brazil. Stolypin spoke "prophetically" when he said in 1908, "*The land is a guarantee of our strength in the future, the land is Russia*" (pp. 26–27). It is in "our vast northeastern spaces" that

> we can build *anew*: not the senseless, voracious civilization of "progress"—no; we can set up a *stable* economy without pain or delay

and settle people there for the first time according to the needs and principles of that economy. These spaces allow us to hope that we shall not destroy Russia in the general crisis of Western civilization. (p. 27)

What is preventing this internal development? Just one thing: ideology. Because of Marxist doctrine, "For half a century we have busied ourselves with world revolution, extending our influence over Eastern Europe and over other continents. . ." (p. 28). At home, that same doctrine attends to the wrong things: "the reform of agriculture according to ideological principles," "the annihilation of the landowning classes," "the eradication of Christian religion and morality," "the useless show of the space race" (pp. 28–29). The right course is clear:

> . . . *throw away the dead ideology* that threatens to destroy us militarily and economically, throw away all its fantastic alien global missions and concentrate on opening up . . . the Russian Northeast—the Northeast of the European part and the North of the Asian part, and the main Siberian massif. (p. 28)

Although admittedly "the difficulties are universal," what qualifies this approach as "moral" is that "our people" have "suffered more in the twentieth century . . . than any other people in the world." Add to the 66 million who statistician I. A. Kurganov estimates died in the Gulag[28] those who died in the two world wars; and, though official statistics are kept secret, we arrive at Dostoevsky's number: "a hundred million *are no more* (exactly *a hundred*, just as Dostoyevsky prophesied)" (p. 30). So the first task is "to put our own house in order before we busy ourselves with the cares of the entire planet"—though, "by a happy coincidence, the whole world can only gain by it" (p. 31).

Solzhenitsyn deals briefly with the "moral objection" that "our Northeast is not entirely Russia's, that a historical sin was committed in conquering it." He is attentive to the concerns of the indigenous peoples, and he spends more time on ethnic relationships in *Rebuilding Russia* than he does here. Here he merely notes briefly that "the people of the North number 128,000 in all," that already "we are now sustaining their way of life . . . as a matter of course," and that "they seek no separate destiny for themselves and would be unable to find one"

(p. 31). On the other hand, for whatever reasons, in that successor essay he does not pick up for elaboration the theme of developing the Northeast.

THE FIFTH SECTION, "Internal, Not External, Development," extends smoothly from the fourth, but its scope widens to include internal issues not directly related to opening up the frontier lands. John Dunlop correctly captures the mood of this section: "The Russia Solzhenitsyn envisages would draw into herself, not out of isolationism (which he rejects), but for a necessary period of healing."[29] Solzhenitsyn himself uses family imagery:

> A family which has suffered a great misfortune or disgrace tries to withdraw into itself for a time to get over its grief by itself. This is what the Russian people must do: spend most of its time alone with itself, without neighbors and guests. It must concentrate on its *inner* tasks: on healing its soul, educating its children, putting its own house in order.
>
> The healing of our souls! Nothing now is more important to us after all that we have lived through, after our long complicity in lies and even crimes.[30]

As for external relations with other nations, Solzhenitsyn declares, "The aims of a great empire and the moral health of the people are incompatible" (p. 41). Many Western critics read this as isolationism. Say that it were. Would not Russian isolationism be vastly preferable, for the sake of world peace, to Soviet imperialism? Nevertheless, Solzhenitsyn bristles, "I never proposed any kind of total isolationism . . . , nor did I call for Russia to sequester herself as if there were no one else on the globe."[31]

The first and most dramatic effect of heeding Solzhenitsyn's anti-imperialistic advice would be an immense reduction in Soviet military might. As he later said to his detractors, "If Soviet . . . troops cease taking over the world and would go home, whom would this endanger? Could someone explain this to me? I cannot understand to this day."[32] In reality, says Solzhenitsyn, "we have only *one-tenth* of the military obligations that we pretend to have, or rather that we intensively and assiduously created for ourselves. . . ." And that need is defensive only, and only in regard to one country: China. "*No one else on earth* threatens us, and no one is going to attack us" (p. 35). Only "military and diplomatic vanity" keeps the huge military machine intact, and the time has come "to exempt the youth of Russia from universal, compulsory military service, which exists neither in China, nor in the United States, nor in any other large country in the world" (p. 36).

Abandoning imperialistic interventionism would free up energy for internal development, where there is very much to do. For one thing, "we" could "give up the forced collective farms and leave just the voluntary ones" (pp. 33–34). The "blunder" here is scandalous:

> For centuries Russia *exported* grain, ten to twelve million tons a year just before the First World War, and here we are after fifty-five years of the new order and forty years of the much-vaunted collective-farm system, forced to *import* twenty million tons per year! It's shameful—it really is time we came to our senses! The village, for centuries the mainstay of Russia, has become its chief weakness! (p. 33)

Gone is the incentive to produce. "Everybody is trying to make more money for less work" (p. 34).

"But even more destructive is vodka" (p. 34). The state's interest in the revenues generated by vodka sales prevents it from doing anything more effective about this social problem than uttering decrees.

Education is another pressing problem. Currently, the school system is so bad that it "merely cheapens and squanders the childhood and hearts of our young people." It needs to attract "people of the highest caliber and with a real vocation" (p. 39). Yet teacher-training institutes have such low prestige that "grown men are ashamed to be schoolteachers," says this former schoolteacher (p. 40).

In addition, the state undermines the family. While touting "equality for women," the state pays such poor wages that a man cannot support his family, and wives are forced to work, whether they would otherwise choose to do so or not. Solzhenitsyn feels "shame and compassion" at the sight of women doing heavy labor. "Who would hesitate to abandon the financing of South American revolutionaries in order to free our women from this bondage?" (pp. 40–41). Similarly repulsive is the scene of "these innumerable drunks and hooligans who pester women" (p. 39).

One paragraph of this section came in for particular criticism as utopian. It is about cities. He tells the leaders, "The urban life which, by now, as much as half our population is doomed to live, is utterly unnatural—and you agree entirely, every one of you, for every evening with one accord you all escape from the city to your dachas in the country." He reminds them evocatively of the old towns—

> towns made for people, horses, dogs—and streetcars too; towns which were humane, friendly, cozy places, where the air was always clean. . . . There was a garden to almost every house and hardly a house more than two stories high—the pleasantest height for human habitation. (p. 37)

Though we cannot go back to the old towns, "[a]n economy on *non*gigantism with small-scale though highly developed technology will not only allow for but necessitate the building of *new* towns of the *old* type" (pp. 37–38). What can be thus retained is the human scale. So can streetcars: efficient mass transit. "And we can perfectly well set up road barriers at all the entrances and admit horses, and battery-powered electric motors, but not poisonous internal-combustion engines. . ." (p. 38). One should have in mind here the horrid pollution emitted by Soviet automobiles. Electric cars are a classic example of the kind of technological development that appeals to Solzhenitsyn. This paragraph seems today less eccentric than when it first appeared. In the West, too, we observe citizens voting with their feet to leave the crowded and polluted big cities. For the growing number concerned about environmental degradation, Solzhenitsyn's vision seems not only pleasant but positively realistic.

THERE IS, however, in the case of Russia, just one catch. It is ideology. Finding it at every turn the chief obstacle to a good future for Russia, Solzhenitsyn entitles the sixth section simply "Ideology." The Marxist ideology which the current Soviet leaders have inherited is "decrepit and hopelessly antiquated now." It offers only a "primitive, superficial economic theory." And its fundamental flaw, for which there is no compensating, is its "sheer ignorance of human nature" (p. 42). Solzhenitsyn's indictment is impassioned:

> Marxism is not only not accurate, is not only not a science, has not only failed to predict a *single event* in terms of figures, quantities, time-scales

or locations (something that electronic computers today do with laughable ease in the course of social forecasting, although never with the help of Marxism)—it absolutely astounds one by the economic and mechanistic crudity of its attempts to explain that most subtle of creatures, the human being, and that even more complex synthesis of millions of people, society.

Briefly glancing westward, he observes a great irony:

> Only the cupidity of some, the blindness of others and a craving for *faith* on the part of still others can serve to explain this grim jest of the twentieth century: how can such a discredited and bankrupt doctrine still have so many followers in the West! In *our* country are left the fewest of all! (p. 43)

Underlying this indictment of Marxism is Solzhenitsyn's vision of the moral universe. The key issue for him is always how one defines the nature of human beings. Though it may be unfashionable among our social historians to say so, belief-systems really matter. Ideas have consequences. As Geoffrey Hosking, for one, observes, this maxim is especially pertinent concerning the Communist Party of the Soviet Union, for its members validate their claim on power by professing a superior understanding of history. "Since this right to rule rests on ideology, it follows that totalitarianism is a system which attributes paramount importance to ideas."[33]

It is very interesting to observe which example, of all of those available to him, Solzhenitsyn selects to illustrate the utter ineptitude of Marxist analysis. "It was mistaken when it forecast that the proletariat would be endlessly oppressed and would never achieve anything in a bourgeois democracy—if only we could shower people with as much food, clothing and leisure as they have gained under capitalism!" (p. 42). At a minimum, this statement cannot be construed as opposing democracy and capitalism.

Domestically, Marxism goads the Soviet leaders into "hounding their most conscientious workers, innocent of all cheating and theft"—namely, religious believers. "[R]eligious persecution . . . is very important for Marxism, but senseless and self-defeating for pragmatic state leaders." As Sergius Bulgakov has explained (and Solzhenitsyn summarizes), "Ferocious hostility to religion is Marxism's most persistent feature" (p. 44). James Schall notes that in this passage Solzhenitsyn is using essentially the argument found in St. Augustine's *The City of God*: "that Christians are good, simple, hard-working, loyal citizens, the best support of the true state."[34] So Solzhenitsyn tries to raise the leaders' level of consciousness:

> For the believer his faith is *supremely* precious, more precious than the food he puts in his stomach. Have you ever paused to reflect on why it is that you deprive these millions of your finest subjects of their homeland? All this can do you as the leaders of the state nothing but harm, but you do it mechanically, automatically, because Marxism insists that you do it. (p. 44)

They would not do it if they cared more for their country than for their ideology.

But Solzhenitsyn had indicated that very few in the Soviet Union believe in Marxist ideology. Surely, this is an exaggeration? Novelist Vladimir Voinovich corroborates that "ideology, communist ideology, lies in ruins. . . . I, for one, do not know a single person in the Soviet Union who believes in it."[35] What about the leaders themselves? Do not they, too, know that everything is "lies, lies, lies," that "[e]verything is steeped in lies and *everybody knows it*—and says so openly in private conversation, and jokes and moans about it, but in their official speeches they go on hypocritically parroting what they are 'supposed to say'. . ."? Pointedly, Solzhenitsyn asks, then answers, ". . . do *you yourselves* really believe for one instant that these speeches are sincere? No, you stopped believing long ago, I am certain of it. And if you didn't, then you must have become totally insulated from the inner life of the country" (p. 47).

What would happen to the leaders if they were to throw off "this rubbishy Ideology of ours"? They would "quickly sense a huge relief," but their hold on power would be not one whit impaired. "In our country today *nothing constructive rests upon it*; it is a sham, cardboard, theatrical prop—take it away and nothing will collapse, nothing will even wobble" (p. 46).

Many of Solzhenitsyn's critics have thought that Solzhenitsyn has an unwarranted fixation about ideology. In 1987, as the campaign for glasnost was getting underway, seven prominent émigrés submitted an article to the *New York Times* which in substance supports Solzhenitsyn's "fixation." Welcoming glasnost but wondering how much it will amount to, they observe, "What Westerners fail to understand is that if the Soviet leaders were really intent on radical change, they would have to begin by discarding the ruling ideology." And they arrive at the same advice that Solzhenitsyn offers in *Letter*:

> Even a fool can see by now that if 70 years of doctrine have brought to ruin one of the richest countries on earth, the doctrine must be faulty. Mr. Gorbachev admits that no one in all those years succeeded in putting the country right. Perhaps, then, the time has come to reject the system itself.[36]

Or, in Solzhenitsyn's strong and colorful language:

> Cast off this cracked Ideology! . . . Let us all pull off and shake off from all of us this filthy sweaty shirt of Ideology which is now so stained with the blood of those 66 million that it prevents the living body of the nation from breathing. This Ideology bears the entire responsibility for all the blood that has been shed. (p. 48)

At the same time, Solzhenitsyn advocates only abandoning Marxism, not banning it. "I am certainly not proposing that you go to the opposite extreme and persecute or ban Marxism, or even argue against it (nobody will argue against it for very long, if only out of sheer apathy)." The method of totalitarianism is not his method. People are free to believe Marxism and even to advocate it, if they wish. "*All you have to do* is to deprive Marxism of its powerful state support and let it exist of itself and stand on its own feet. And let all who wish to do so make propaganda for it . . . —but outside working hours and *not on state salaries*" (p. 48). When an interviewer later asked him about this passage on "the possibility of free competition between Communist and other ideologies," Solzhenitsyn explained that it "was really an ironic passage": "I was simply joking." No one could seriously think that "in their free time after real work—and without pay, of course—the Party propagandists would propagate communism. . . . They are so concerned with Number One that—without payment—they wouldn't lift a finger, even for their own ideology."[37] In a Russian free marketplace of ideas, Marxism would fail utterly.

And what does Solzhenitsyn propose as a replacement to Marxism? Patriotism. The Soviet leaders will need its reserves should war with China come, as Stalin needed them in World War II. Their chatter of combining Marxism and patriotism is "but a meaningless absurdity." He reminds them, presumably to their embarrassment, that "Lenin in 1915 actually proclaimed: 'We are antipatriots.' And that was the honest truth." Indeed, he emphasizes, ". . . the whole of this letter that I am now putting before you is patriotism, *which means* rejection of Marxism" (p. 45). Patriotism, be it noted, not nationalism.

IN THE SEVENTH AND FINAL SECTION, "But How Can All This Be Managed?", we see Solzhenitsyn at his most thoroughly pragmatic. It is from this section that Western critics took greatest offense. And precisely for the pragmatism of it—or, better, for their not recognizing the pragmatic intent governing it. Yet the opening of the section makes this intent clear. "I have not forgotten for a moment that you are total realists," Solzhenitsyn tells the leaders. "You are realists par excellence, and you will not allow power to slip out of your hands." Thus, whatever he proposes must be something that does not directly challenge their hold on power. It is intriguing to note what in particular he knows they will not accommodate: ". . . you will not willingly tolerate a two-party or multiparty parliamentary system in our country, you will not tolerate *real* elections, at which people might not vote you in" (p. 49). Furthermore, ". . . one must admit that this will be within your power for a long time to come." Solzhenitsyn then appends, ominously, "A long time—but not forever" (p. 50).

The first thing that Solzhenitsyn disavows, in the name of realism, is revolution. He tells these adherents of the Marxist doctrine of revolution,

> . . . I have become an opponent of all revolutions and all armed convulsions, including future ones—both those you crave (*not* in our country) and those you fear (*in* our country). Intensive study has convinced me that bloody mass revolutions are always disastrous for the people in whose midst they occur. (p. 50)

Elsewhere, he says, "No, let us not wish either 'revolution' or 'counter-revolution' on our worst enemies."[38] Also, he gives the reason why he has "never advocated physical general revolution": it "would entail such destruction of our people's life as would not merit the victory obtained."[39] Even to rid Russia of the hated Communism, he will not recommend the "sudden upheaval of any hastily carried-out change of the present leadership." In any case, according to his expectation, it "would certainly lead to only a very dubious gain in the quality of the leadership" (p. 50). The fall of Soviet Communism has sometimes been called the Second Russian Revolution. By any definition that Solzhenitsyn would recognize, it was not a revolution.

Solzhenitsyn prefers gradual change. Which brings him to democracy. Which gets him into trouble with Western critics. For implementing democracy at one stroke would mean breaking radically from the status quo of 1973. Besides, democracy has its own set of problems. It is better not to rush into it unprepared. There must be a conjunction of what would work and what the Soviet leaders would accept.

Here is the passage which so upset Western critics:

In such a situation what is there left for *us* to do? Console ourselves by saying "Sour grapes." Argue in all sincerity that we are not adherents of that turbulent "democracy run riot" in which once every four years the politicians, and indeed the entire country, nearly kill themselves over an electoral campaign, trying to gratify the masses . . . ; in which a judge, flouting his obligatory independence in order to pander to the passions of society, acquits a man who, during an exhausting war, steals and publishes Defense Department documents. (p. 50)

Clearly, Solzhenitsyn does not like (presumably American) electioneering, and he does not approve of Daniel Ellsberg's actions. He mentions other problems of democracy, as well, such as the frustrating of the majority will by strikers and democracies' powerlessness to thwart terrorism. He doubts that coalition governments resulting from multi-party elections necessarily express the will of the majority. In short, he itemizes some problems in Western democracies to reassure the Soviet leaders that he is not advising them to adopt wholesale a foreign model which in any case they would not accept.

What matters is not the form of democracy but the substance of freedom. Solzhenitsyn continues, "Yes, of course: freedom is moral. But only if it keeps within certain bounds, beyond which it degenerates into complacency and licentiousness." It is democracy which can degenerate into these vices. But there is the other side: "And *order* is not immoral if it means a calm and stable system. But order, too, has its limits, beyond which it degenerates into arbitrariness and tyranny" (p. 51). Soviet totalitarianism exemplifies this kind of degeneration. Somewhere on the continuum from total freedom to total order, a proper balance must be struck.

Solzhenitsyn is on the verge of offering his recommendation for a change in governance. Before he does, he primes what he hopes is the leaders' readiness to hear it by mentioning one other reason why he will not be recommending immediate democracy. It comes from Russian history. "Here in Russia, for sheer lack of practice, democracy survived for only eight months—from February to October, 1917" (p. 51). Though even that turned out to be "merely a chaotic caricature of democracy," prospects are yet grimmer now. "Over the last half-century Russia's preparedness for democracy, for a multiparty parliamentary system, could only have diminished. I am inclined to think that its sudden reintroduction now would merely be a melancholy repetition of 1917" (p. 52).

If not democracy, what about authoritarianism? After all, "for a thousand years Russia lived with an authoritarian order—and at the beginning of the twentieth century both the physical and spiritual health of her people were still intact." But authoritarianism, too, has its pluses and minuses. On the positive side, "in those days an important condition was fulfilled: that authoritarian order possessed a strong moral foundation, embryonic and rudimentary though it was—not the ideology of universal violence, but Christian Orthodoxy. . . ." On the negative side,

> . . . the ancient, seven-centuries-old Orthodoxy of Sergei Radonezhsky and Nil Sorsky . . . was battered by Patriarch Nikon and bureaucratized by Peter the Great. From the end of the Moscow period and throughout the whole of the Petersburg period, once this moral principle was perverted and weakened, the authoritarian order . . . gradually went into a decline and eventually perished. (p. 52)

The reader need not know all the history being alluded to here in order to grasp that, in Solzhenitsyn's view, authoritarianism, too, can be either good or bad.

If it is "premature" to reintroduce democracy into Russia, should we, then, Solzhenitsyn asks tentatively, acknowledge "[t]hat for the foreseeable future, perhaps, whether we like it or not, whether we intend it or not, Russia is nevertheless destined to have an authoritarian order? Perhaps this is all that she is ripe for today?" (p. 53). This is clearly the language of compromise—one could say, even, the language of the politician practicing the art of the possible. It is far from being the "apologia for an authoritarian form of government"[40] that it was crudely called in the West. As Solzhenitsyn later explained, "The most I called for was a renunciation of communist ideology and of its most cruel consequences. . . . And the only path down from the icy cliff of totalitarianism that I could propose was the slow and smooth descent via an authoritarian system."[41] Concerning even this first step into Russia's post-Communist future, a qualification is necessary: "Everything depends upon *what sort* of authoritarian order lies in store for us in the future." Nonetheless, "It is not authoritarianism itself that is intolerable, but the ideological lies that are daily foisted upon us" (p. 53).

Were the Soviet leaders to heed Solzhenitsyn's advice, both the world and the nation would benefit. Their Communist Party could "renounce its unattainable and irrelevant missions of world domination, and instead fulfill its national missions and save us from war with China and from technological disaster" (pp. 54–55). It could "encourage the *inner*, the moral, the healthy development of the people" (p. 55). Moving from ideology-driven totalitarianism to merely power-driven authoritarianism could suffice to alter the rulers' posture toward the citizenry: "Let it be an authoritarian order, but one founded not on an inexhaustible 'class hatred' but on love of your fellow men—not of your immediate entourage but sincere love for your whole people." Without the ideology, the leaders could grant freedoms now curtailed. Religious freedom is the one that comes immediately to Solzhenitsyn's mind. The leaders could "allow competition on an equal and honorable basis—not for power, but for truth—between all ideological and moral currents, in particular between *all religions*" (p. 56). Religious youth organizations could be permitted, and believers could be granted "the right to instruct and educate children, and the right to free parish activity" (pp. 56–57).

Solzhenitsyn then interjects a parenthesis which, while seemingly clear enough, was miserably misunderstood: "(I myself see Christianity today as the only living spiritual force capable of undertaking the spiritual healing of Russia. But I request and propose no special privileges for it, simply that it should be treated fairly and not suppressed)" (p. 57). On the basis of this parenthesis—there is no other passage in *Letter* that pertains—he has been called a theocrat. He vehemently rejects the allegation:

> . . . I have been repeatedly charged with being an advocate of a theocratic state, a system in which the government would be under the direct control of religious leaders. This is a flagrant misrepresentation; I have never said or written anything of the sort. The day-to-day activity of governing in no sense belongs to the sphere of religion. What I do believe is that the state should not persecute religion, and that, furthermore, religion should make an appropriate contribution to the spiritual life of the nation. Such a situation obtains in Poland and Israel and no one condemns it; I cannot understand why the same thing should be forbidden to Russia. . . .[42]

Yet such charges, though refuted, stick in the popular Western mind.

The egregious error here arises from the failure to distinguish between the religion-and-society nexus and the church-and-state nexus. To fuse the two is to confuse Solzhenitsyn's meaning utterly. He desires religious freedom, yes, but "not for power." Moreover, he is talking in the parenthesis about Christianity generically, not about (for instance) Russian Orthodoxy. He proposes only fair treatment, no special privileges. He wishes for Christianity exactly the same status before the law that he wishes for Marxism—or any other belief. In addition, if atheists can bring themselves to grant religious freedom, other freedoms, such as "a free art and literature" (p. 57), will logically follow with a relative ease.

Solzhenitsyn concludes his letter on the same note with which he opened it, envelope-structure style. He acknowledges the prevailing power relationship and reiterates his intention of realism and pragmatism. He notes again "my original assumption that you are not alien to your fathers, your grandfathers and the expanses of Russia." His hope is that, in the end, their Russianness will win out over their Sovietness. He magnifies the principle of gradualism: "Of course, decisions like these are not made overnight. But now you still have the opportunity to make the transition calmly, over the next three years perhaps—or five, or even ten, allowing for the whole process" (p. 58). *Transition*, be it noted.

Yet the balance would not be quite right if Solzhenitsyn did not remind the leaders that their desired totalitarian control was not total, after all—that he, for one, was already independent of them.

> You will have noticed, of course, that this letter pursues no personal aims. I have long since outgrown your shell anyway and my writings will be published irrespective of any sanction or prohibition by you. All I had to say is now said. I, too, am fifty-five, and I think I have amply demonstrated that I set no store by material wealth and am prepared to sacrifice my life. To you such a vision of life is a rarity—but here it is for you to behold. (p. 59)

How long ago it all seems now when such a disclaimer of subservience was necessary. How greatly expanded now is the freedom for Russians to speak out freely. History may someday make it clearer than it is to us today how much *Letter to the Soviet Leaders* contributed to this enormous change.

IN THE LIGHT of this extended exposition of *Letter*, it is rather surprising to read some of the criticisms that Andrei Sakharov leveled against it. Sakharov's response was motivated "by my disagreement with certain fundamental tenets of Solzhenitsyn's letter."[43] Solzhenitsyn, for his part, complained that Sakharov had been "extremely careless in his interpretation of my point of view."[44] However, "By any standards this was a gentlemanly exchange."[45] As Vladimir Maximov, editor of *Kontinent*, explained, this "dialogue, not an argument," between Sakharov and Solzhenitsyn is notable for

> a total absence of that element of irreconcilability, bitterness, and anger that have accompanied the verbal battles of other inexperienced democrats and old-fashioned patriots. Quite simply, two great thinkers of modern Russia are examining, calmly and in depth, each in his own way, the problem of their people's and their country's future.[46]

It is important to establish this point because, as Leonard Schapiro has remarked, this debate has been "distorted and misrepresented by many who have commented on it," especially by making it out to be "a revival of the Slavophile-Westerner controversy." In Schapiro's view,

"... their shades of opinion are quite insignificant in the light of the great bond which unites these two moral giants in our age of moral pygmies."[47] In the early 1970's the two men had a number of meetings, at Solzhenitsyn's initiative.[48] Solzhenitsyn proposed Sakharov for the Nobel Peace Prize, which Sakharov eventually won. Despite occasional friction, the prevailing mood was one of mutual respect. Solzhenitsyn said, "I myself find much that I cannot support in Sakharov's concrete proposals for our country, but their *constructiveness* is indisputable. None of his proposals is a chimerical daydream. . . ."[49] Sakharov said, "There is no question that Solzhenitsyn is one of the outstanding writers and political commentators of our time" (p. 3). And he called *Letter* "an important political event, another major contribution to the free discussion of key problems," and its author "a tower of strength in the struggle for human dignity in our tragic world" (pp. 13–14).

In their shared desire to see the Soviet parenthesis of Russian history come to an end, one thing that united these two was their common commitment to gradualism. One of them said, "... to reorganize the state—that is unthinkable; there always must be some kind of continuity and some kind of gradualness, otherwise there would again be the terrible destruction through which we have passed several times and a total collapse." But which one? Sakharov, as it happens.[50] Solzhenitsyn, in turn, said, "... I thought that the way out was to seek the path of evolution, certainly not the path of *revolution*, not an explosion. On this, Sakharov and I agree. . . ."[51]

Still, there were the differences. Sakharov mentions a few general ones before engaging in his "analysis of Solzhenitsyn's positive program" (p. 8). One of them is the problem of China. He thinks that Solzhenitsyn overdramatizes it, though he concedes that he had expressed similar fears just a few years earlier (p. 7). Another is Solzhenitsyn's emphasis on ideology as the culprit. Here, too, he thinks that Solzhenitsyn exaggerates. Sakharov says, "I see present-day Soviet society as being marked rather by ideological indifference and the cynical use of ideology as a convenient façade. . ." (p. 6). But, in reality, this sounds more like Solzhenitsyn than unlike him. For Solzhenitsyn thinks that even the Soviet leaders themselves are personally indifferent to their proclaimed ideology.

A third general point of difference, in Sakharov's words, is this: "I also find it difficult to accept Solzhenitsyn's view of Marxism as a

'Western' and antireligious doctrine which distorted a healthy Russian line of development." It is not that Sakharov denies the Western origin of Marxism, and he certainly knows that it is anti-religious. But he asserts, "The very classification of ideas as Western or Russian is incomprehensible to me" (p. 6). This statement does not much advance the argument. Solzhenitsyn, too, embraces ideas which originated outside of Russia, starting with Christianity. As for that "healthy line of Russian development," Sakharov simply does not see as much of it as Solzhenitsyn does. But the difference here is one of degree, not of kind.

A fourth distinction which Sakharov draws has to do with the concept of progress. He says, "I find Solzhenitsyn's treatment of the problem of progress misleading" (p. 6). *Progress* is a good word for Sakharov, not a good word for Solzhenitsyn. It is also a word and a concept propagated by the Enlightenment. Ernest Gellner spoke accurately when he said that Sakharov "represents the *beau ideal* of the Enlightenment: morally firm, yet open in matters of belief."[52] Truly, only an heir of the Enlightenment could have said these words of Sakharov's: "Progress is a worldwide process. . . . Given universal scientific and democratic management of the economy and of the whole of social life . . . , this, I am quite convinced, is not a utopia but a vital necessity" (pp. 6–7).

When Sakharov proceeds to discuss Solzhenitsyn's "positive program," he enumerates ten points. He agrees with seven of them and disagrees with only three. Here are the seven points (renumbered) with which Sakharov agrees:

1. "The withdrawal of state support for Marxism as the official and compulsory ideology." (He calls this point "incontestable," adding only the reiterated mild qualifier that one should not "overestimate the role of the ideological factor in present-day Soviet society.")
2. "The withdrawal of support for revolutionaries, nationalists, and partisans all over the world, and the concentration of effort on internal problems."
3. "The cessation of guardianship over Eastern Europe, and the release of the national republics from forced incorporation in the U.S.S.R."
4. "An agrarian reform on the Polish model (my own wording)."
5. "Disarmament, as far as the Chinese threat allows."

6. "Democratic freedoms, toleration, the release of political prisoners."
7. "The strengthening of the family and child-rearing; freedom of religious education."

Of these last three points, he notes that they already "have appeared in documents of the democratic movement," then adds, "Their reiteration by an authoritative figure is welcome, and they are well argued in the letter" (pp. 8–9).

Here are the three points of Solzhenitsyn's letter with which Sakharov disagrees:

1. "The development of the northeast of the country not by innovative technology but by means already available. . . ."
2. "An end to the selling off of national resources, natural gas, timber, etc.; economic isolationism as a corollary of military, political, and ideological isolationism."
3. "The preservation of the party . . . ; the preservation of the basic authoritarian features of the system is seen as permissible, provided the rule of law is assured and freedom of conscience guaranteed" (pp. 8–9).

Sakharov then works backwards, since the first two of these three points are, he thinks, Solzhenitsyn's "central points."

Of the third and last point above, Sakharov will not brook Solzhenitsyn's compromise with the leaders which would allow them to retain power in an authoritarian mode for the time being. "I consider a democratic mode of development the only satisfactory one for any country" (p. 10). Although Sakharov casts this as an objection in principle, it could equally well be seen as an argument over means to an end. Surprisingly, Solzhenitsyn is the one with the more pragmatic and accommodating posture here.

As to the two "central points," Sakharov objects to what he considers Solzhenitsyn's isolationism and nationalism. He rejects "the notion that our country should be fenced off from the supposedly corrupting influence of the West. . . ." But this surely is to attribute more of isolationism to Solzhenitsyn than is there in *Letter*. And Sakharov sounds very much like Solzhenitsyn when he proceeds in the next sentence to say,

"The only form of isolationism which makes sense is for us to refrain from imposing our socialist messianism on other countries, to give up secret and open support for subversion in other continents, and to cease the export of lethal weapons" (p. 10). On "the question of decentralizing industry and organizing it communally," Sakharov thinks that "Solzhenitsyn and political commentators close to him greatly overestimate industrial gigantism as a cause of our contemporary problems." But surely Sakharov misconstrues when he talks of "Solzhenitsyn's dream of making do with the simplest technology, indeed virtually with manual labor" (p. 12). Solzhenitsyn has as much claim on the need for "innovative technology" as Sakharov does. Their difference is about size, whether on small scale or large.

As for nationalism, Sakharov concedes that Solzhenitsyn's version "is not aggressive, but mild and defensive in character, only aiming to save and revive one of the most long-suffering of nations." What troubles Sakharov here is not what Solzhenitsyn says but what others later might make of it. "History shows . . . that 'ideologists' are always milder than the practical politicians who follow in their footsteps" (p. 13). It is difficult to know how to respond to a demurrer of this kind. Should one resist proposing something virtuous for fear that others will make of it a vice by carrying it to unacceptable extremes? Sakharov knows to distinguish Solzhenitsyn from the extreme nationalists, but he does share in mild form the Western fear that Solzhenitsyn will give them unintended succor.

It is necessary to understand from just what position of his own Sakharov is generating his criticisms of Solzhenitsyn. Sakharov declares himself "quite convinced, unlike Solzhenitsyn, that there is no really important problem in the world today which can be solved at the national level." Instead, he insists that "a strategy for the development of human society on earth, if it is to be compatible with the continuation of the human species, can only be worked out and put into practice on a global scale" (p. 11). Though not at all a Marxist, Sakharov shares with Marxists an inheritance of Enlightenment thinking that results in common commitments to socialist economics and a globalist outlook. This overlapping explains in part why, though Sakharov is as resolutely opposed to Soviet repression as is Solzhenitsyn, he minimizes (by comparison) the damaging effects of Marxist ideology *per se*. In short, the differences between these two thinkers are rooted in their different world views. They can agree on many practical proposals for change, but they operate out of different mind-sets.

Sakharov is justly known for his theory of convergence between socialist East and democratic West. He spelled out his democratic-socialist vision in his memorandum "Progress, Coexistence, and Intellectual Freedom" of 1968,[53] written during the heady days of Alexander Dubcek's initiative to bring "socialism with a human face" to Czechoslovakia. With its call for a one-world government directed by the intellectual elite, it is much more utopian than anything Solzhenitsyn ever proposed. Indeed, Solzhenitsyn's proposals are markedly modest by contrast. Solzhenitsyn wrote the initial version of "As Breathing and Consciousness Return" in response to this memorandum, sending it privately to Sakharov. Events caused Sakharov to temper the doctrinaire optimism of this memorandum, and Solzhenitsyn took due note of this change of heart in the expanded, public version of his reply.[54] He referred to it again in his response to Sakharov's criticism of *Letter*:

> I am happy to note that the number of questions he and I are in agreement about today is incomparably greater than it was six years ago, when we became acquainted during the very months in which his memorandum made its appearance. (I should like to hope that in another six years the area of our agreement will double.) (p. 15)

Donald R. Kelley has written a book about the Solzhenitsyn-Sakharov dialogue, and it helps us fix in place the competing world views of the two men. In Kelley's analysis, Solzhenitsyn embraces a traditional moral order, while Sakharov adopts a rational-scientific world view. This contrast is serviceable as long as we see that Solzhenitsyn rejects not reason and science but rationalism and scientism. As Kelley, in his evenhanded way, carefully notes, Solzhenitsyn

> is not hostile to science and technology per se but rather to the uncritical extension of the intellectual frame of reference engendered by each into the realm of cultural and moral life. One might argue that his true enemy is "scientization" rather than science itself, that is, the assumption that the logic of science can be applied to all spheres of life to eliminate empathy, intuition, and revelation as sources of knowledge.[55]

Kelley writes well and at some length about the attitudes toward technology of these two thinkers, and he finds them mostly in agreement—more so than Sakharov acknowledges in his reply to *Letter*, I would add. Both of them fear that "technological imperatives . . . have acquired a self-sustaining and potentially deleterious dynamic of their own." Kelley notes the striking similarities between Solzhenitsyn's call for new cities of the old type and Sakharov's desire to create Preserve Territories demarcated from Work Territories—the chief difference being that Sakharov's preserves would be places to which workers could escape for brief reprieves and Solzhenitsyn's locales would be places of primary residence. The similarities extend even to the recommendation of developing battery-powered vehicles. Of Sakharov specifically, Kelley says, "He is no unstudied proponent of growth and progress for their sake alone, but rather a man who recognizes the dual potential for benefit and harm in virtually all modern technologies."[56]

It is not when Sakharov's rational-scientific world view fixes upon Russia's internal needs that Kelley emphasizes the differences between Sakharov and Solzhenitsyn. The differences come to the fore when Sakharov goes global. Just here is where the Enlightenment doctrine of progress comes into play. Even his call for Soviet leaders to abandon Marxism as the official ideology is motivated by his devotion to this doctrine, with its global imperative. For Sakharov, Marxism must go because it has become "an anti-progressive force" in the world; in practice, it "has been an obstacle to material and technical progress."[57]

For Sakharov, with his theory of convergence, progress has as its *telos* a unified world. To this end, according to Kelley, "Sakharov strongly implies that he sees the scientific and technical intelligentsia as the principal 'carriers' of the concept of 'progress' and as the primary movers in the process of rationalizing society." Though the "institutional structure" to which these "managerial and technocratic elements" would carry us is not stated, "Ultimately, Sakharov foresees the emergence of a vaguely defined world government." But this desired future can come into reality (in Sakharov's own words) "only under highly intelligent worldwide guidance."[58]

This vision is indeed quite different from, and much more grandiose than, Solzhenitsyn's desire for a healthy future Russia. If it seems, by comparison, utopian, that is precisely how Kelley describes it: "the ultimate 'converged' society as a social and technological utopia."[59] It could even be said to have a less democratic feel to it than what

Solzhenitsyn envisions, especially in *Rebuilding Russia*. In regard to the intelligentsia, it is not too much to say that Sakharov's deep attachment to elitism is at a further remove from the democratic impulse than is Solzhenitsyn's call for a sacrificial elite. Solzhenitsyn's intellectuals would guide by example; Sakharov's, through access to power.

The differences in world view between Sakharov and Solzhenitsyn are dramatic. Even a brief examination of them helps explain why Sakharov objected to certain points in *Letter*. Communicating across the divide separating world views is a difficult thing to do well. Sakharov did much better at it than did many other critics of *Letter*. Still, the conflict in world views did keep him from seeing at how many points his hopes for a post-Communist Russia were compatible with those of Solzhenitsyn. Were the future of Russia to be determined by persons within that band on the political spectrum running only from Sakharov to Solzhenitsyn, world fears could be much allayed. For their views, if and as given political expression, would cluster toward the center of the spectrum. As regards Solzhenitsyn's political centrism, we come upon its fullest articulation in *Rebuilding Russia*.

10

"Rebuilding Russia" (I)
An Overview

There is no escaping the fact that our country has cruelly forfeited the entire twentieth century: all our much-trumpeted achievements have turned out to be illusory. From a flourishing condition we have been hurled back to a state of semi-barbarity, and we sit amid the wreckage.[1]

Such was the devastation that Solzhenitsyn saw when he examined his homeland as it entered the last decade of the century. Far from demonstrating the fruits of progress, it displayed the ravages wrought by a barbarous wrecking crew, such as would daunt all but the most hopeful of human breasts. And, indeed, the overwhelming impression that the reader of *Rebuilding Russia* forms is one of utter ruination. This chapter and the next two are devoted to discussing that work. This chapter of overview will provide background information useful as preparation for a close reading of the text. The next two chapters will provide the running commentary itself.

More than a decade before Solzhenitsyn wrote this essay, an interviewer asked him how he saw Russia's future. He replied, "I see it in *recuperation*. Renounce all mad fantasies of foreign conquest and begin the peaceful, long, long, long period of *recuperation*." Recovery after illness, rebuilding amid rubble—these are the recurring metaphors that Solzhenitsyn uses to explain what is to be done to reverse the calamities

251

produced by three-quarters of a century of Communist experimentation. As he told his interviewer, "They are exhausting the country, misdirecting the people's efforts, each year clouding and spoiling millions of young souls. For every Communist year that passes we shall have to pay with several years of recuperation."[2]

Solzhenitsyn wrote *Rebuilding Russia* in July of 1990. It was the first work of his since the early 1960's to receive its initial publication inside the Soviet Union. It appeared in print on September 18, 1990, in two mass-circulation periodicals. One was *Komsomolskaya Pravda*, with a print run of 22 million copies. It is a rich irony that the house organ of the Young Communist League was publishing this supreme anti-Communist. The other was *Literaturnaya Gazeta*, with a print run of 4.5 million copies. A mere five years earlier, this journal had called Solzhenitsyn "that vile scum of a traitor."[3]

There is an important correlation between the timing of the publication of this essay and its primary intended audience. It is addressed not to the Soviet leaders but directly to the Russian people. Mikhail Gorbachev had been in power for five years; the failed coup of August 1991 had not yet occurred. Many promising changes had taken place, such as would allow the publication of this essay and also previously forbidden literary works by Solzhenitsyn and others. Yet, along with the notable expansion of freedom resulting from the campaign for glasnost, there was an ever-deepening sense of humiliation resulting from the realization that the policy of perestroika not only was worsening living conditions but held no hope of extrication from the morass. It was clear to most citizens that this regime was moribund, strangled by its own ideological commitments.

A new leadership would soon, of necessity, be coming to the fore. Perhaps this time, finally, the will of the people could make itself felt in public life. There was no point in addressing the current leaders, who were ineffectual and soon-passing. Besides, Solzhenitsyn's prescriptions were ones which could work only from the bottom up, not from the top down. And so he wrote to the citizenry at large. He sought to help rouse them from the lethargy of generations and to encourage them to lift themselves from their humiliation. He wrote to energize, to galvanize public opinion for the enormous task ahead of recuperation, of reconstruction. This man, born a year after the Bolshevik coup of 1917, had lived through the whole Soviet parenthesis in Russian history, and now he was living to see the end of it. After a long silence, he could now address the audience that mattered the most to him.

The title of this essay, *Kak nam obustroit' Rossiyu?*, is only partially rendered by the serviceably brief English-language translation, *Rebuilding Russia*. It keeps the imagery of construction amid the rubble, but it leaves out the magical word *we* (*nam*). Many variants could be offered to elucidate Solzhenitsyn's untranslatable idiom: how to reconstruct Russia, how to reconstitute Russia, how to revitalize Russia, how to make Russia livable, how Russia should be. It is a "how-to" book. But there is a play on words that should not be missed. As John Dunlop describes it, Solzhenitsyn "practices a form of lexical one-upmanship by employing the resonant phrase *obustroit' Rossiyu . . .* in place of Gorbachev's bland and pedestrian word *perestroika.*"[4] Vladislav Krasnov says that Solzhenitsyn's choice of verb

> suggests a task that is both less ambitious and more vital for the country than Gorbachev's "restructuring." Why should the Soviet system be "restructured" when it is obvious that it stands on a rotten foundation? The most one can do under the circumstances is take certain emergency measures ("obustroit' ") in order to protect people's lives from the debris of the collapsing Soviet state.[5]

Here we see highlighted the modesty of Solzhenitsyn's essay, its great distance from utopianism. David Remnick, too, explicates the play on words. Gorbachev's perestroika, he explains, means "the democratization and 'rebuilding' of socialism, a cleansing of the Stalinist 'deformations' of Leninism." Solzhenitsyn's verb, for which Remnick prefers the translation "reconstitute," carries connotations of "fix, fix up, refurbish, make comfortable, organize, or, even more loosely, revitalize." He takes note, as well, of the obvious substitution of "Russia" for the (not-yet-dead) "Soviet Union."[6]

Still, there is that word *we*. It is a precious word to Solzhenitsyn, for it conveys his cherished notion of human solidarity. Despite all Soviet efforts to deform the word so as to lose all individuality in an undiscriminating mass of collectivity, he calls it a "sweet" and "joyous" word. It says what prisoners especially needed to remember: that "you are not alone in the world!"[7] It is in the spirit of this sense of solidarity with his countrymen that Solzhenitsyn has earmarked the royalties from

Rebuilding Russia for victims of Chernobyl. So perhaps the best renderings of the essay's title will begin with "How shall we" or "How are we to" [reconstruct, reconstitute, revitalize, make livable]? Krasnov explains that, in political terms, the use of this pronoun "proclaims loud and clear that Solzhenitsyn and the viewpoint he represents can no longer be excluded from making decisions on the country's future."[8] Nor was the force of this pronoun lost on readers inside Russia. USSR People's Deputy Yuri Chernichenko, noting "the coincidence of views between writing Moscow and thinking Vermont," declared,

> I am grateful to Solzhenitsyn—touched and tearfully grateful, to the point of bowing down before him—for the pronouns "we," "ours," and "us" in his thoughts on our affairs. . . . Without Solzhenitsyn, Russian public thought is a square missing one side, or a tub without a bottom. Thank you for the "we."[9]

In genre, *Rebuilding Russia* is, like *Letter to the Soviet Leaders*, a political pamphlet. As such, it is not comprehensive in scope, as Solzhenitsyn knows. The relationship between the two pamphlets is primarily one of continuity. As Krasnov puts it, they are "pieces of the same cloth. Both are based on the same set of beliefs. . . ."[10] Not only does the underlying world view remain steadfastly in place, but events since the letter of 1973 serve to confirm the prescience of *Letter*. The transitional period of Communist authoritarianism which Solzhenitsyn foresaw as a probably necessary historical stage on the way out of Soviet totalitarianism had come into being, and already it seemed to be approaching its end. During that transition (the Gorbachev era), developments were, generally speaking, going Solzhenitsyn's way. Freedoms were increasing; religious persecution was declining; the Communist Party was in deepening disrepute; a spirit of national renewal was emerging. It was time (a bit past time, some afterwards said) for Solzhenitsyn to write again.

Though the emphasis should be on the continuity of vision from *Letter* to *Rebuilding Russia*, there are important differences between them, too. In content, these "are due not so much to the evolution of the author's views as to the historical changes that have occurred in the past seventeen years."[11] Thus, for example, the theme of war with China is featured in the letter but ignored here. Also, developing the Northeast no longer seems of high priority in Solzhenitsyn's mind. And, most importantly, the call to abandon Marxist ideology is itself abandoned, the motive power of that ideology being now obviously in eclipse. It is remarkable at how very many points passages from Solzhenitsyn's earlier works, both belletristic and publicistic, could serve as glosses on this text. At the same time, we come upon themes—and especially elaborations of themes—which are to be found nowhere before in his writing. Solzhenitsyn has had years to read and to reflect at leisure. In Dunlop's words, this "brochure represents the results of decades of research into and reflection about the reasons for the Bolshevik coup of 1917 and the ensuing terror and genocide"; and Dunlop finds its latter two-thirds "tightly argued and packed with information"—therefore "of compelling interest to political scientists and historians."[12] *Rebuilding Russia* is considerably more systematic than *Letter*.

Dunlop had called *Letter to the Soviet Leaders* "proto-programmatic."[13] *Rebuilding Russia* is less "proto" and more "pro-grammatic." Richard Pipes had voiced a widespread complaint that "Solzhenitsyn is far better at diagnosing ills than at providing remedies."[14] Whatever the legitimacy of this complaint in the past, with the publication of this essay it no longer applies.

Another complaint from the past which is inapplicable to this work is the one about Solzhenitsyn's alleged shrillness of tone—that is, his bad manners. Here it is important to keep in mind who is the primary intended audience of this pamphlet: the Russian people. Toward Western intellectuals and Soviet leaders he can be caustic, impatient, irritated. But, when it comes to the Russian people, he wants them to be— and believes them already in large part actually to be—on his side. Toward them his tone is calmer, less embattled. And toward the Ukrainians he assumes a tone of supplication which it would be unbefitting to adopt toward his intellectual and political opposite numbers. Only occasional flashes of the old peremptoriness intrude, and they are not directed toward the citizenry. As the subtitle, "Reflections and Tentative Proposals," suggests, when writing to his fellows, he conveys his ideas with due, and disarming, modesty and tentativeness.

Both before and after the publication of *Rebuilding Russia*, there has been considerable speculation about Solzhenitsyn's long silence about public affairs. His wife, Natalia Dimitrievna, has now explained to David Remnick that her husband was "determined that his literary work return to Russia without the interference of politics." Thus, *Time* interviewer David Aikman was required to agree not to ask any detailed questions about Gorbachev or the current reforms. Only after his literary works, starting with *The Gulag Archipelago*, were published in the Soviet Union would Solzhenitsyn make his political return. Exactly that is what *Rebuilding Russia* is. And only after his citizenship was restored and his treason charge was dropped could he return home in the flesh. As Remnick reports, Ivan Silayev, the Russian prime minister, published an open letter in *Komsomolskaya Pravda* pleading with Solzhenitsyn to return. In Silayev's words, "Your coming to Russia is, in my view, one of those moves that our homeland needs as much as air." In Remnick's view, "For the first time since the early 1960s Solzhenitsyn was in nearly complete command of the situation."[15] We now know that he was at work preparing for his political return—and presumably also for his personal return. We know, also, why, in accordance with his self-perception as a literary writer first of all, he felt that he could not speak out on public affairs in the vein of this essay sooner than he did.

In May 1992, Natalia Solzhenitsyn and three of her four sons flew to Moscow to do house-hunting. When President Yeltsin visited the United States in June 1992, one of his first acts was to telephone Solzhenitsyn to invite him personally to return to Russia. Solzhenitsyn's homecoming was nearing.

MY PURPOSE in this chapter and the next two is, first, to make clear just what Solzhenitsyn is saying in *Rebuilding Russia* and, second, to argue that he is being realistic and pragmatic. Knowing that history is a tapestry uniting past and future, he looks to past experience (Russia's, first of all) for usable models. Knowing that no sane person can think of returning to the past, he draws upon those models which can be adapted for use in the future. Solzhenitsyn does not sit hatching vain empires of perfection. But Russia is not some other planet. Solzhenitsyn, viewing Russia as part of Western civilization, has read widely in Western classics, and he draws freely from them and also from Western social experience. This is nowhere more true than in regard to republican democracy as America's Founding Fathers conceived of it.

More than once before, Solzhenitsyn had said that the healing of Russia would take 150 to 200 years. In *Rebuilding Russia* he sets no such timetable. This absence may be taken as a sign of hope. The emphasis is not on the note of national self-pity for all the long and difficult work ahead but on the need to get started. Though it takes less time to destroy than to rebuild, we Russians can do good things and can begin to do them right now, he tells his fellows. Stalin exterminated in the Gulag millions of the best citizens, and millions more died in the war; other independent-minded people have been lost to emigration. Russia suffers severely from diminished human capital. But the remaining ones must and can take up the burden of liberty. Many today doubt that the Russians are up to the task. Solzhenitsyn does not. Well before the Soviet Union collapsed, he was saying, "I believe in our people at all levels. . . ."[16] Reason to believe is significantly greater now than it was then.

Solzhenitsyn is also a voice of moderation. He is beholden to no party and rides no ideological hobby-horse. In a time of severe economic dislocations and political searching, Russian public life will need all the voices of moderation it can get. This is especially so when the state that has collapsed is one that was ideologically driven. Extremists lurk. The rightward drift of such important figures as mathematician Igor Shafarevich and village writer Valentin Rasputin demonstrates all the more how valuable, even perhaps indispensable, the moderating influence of Solzhenitsyn is.

One must ask, of course—it is the obvious and inescapable question—how influential *Rebuilding Russia* is likely to prove to be. Few today will deny that Solzhenitsyn's earlier writings, especially *The Gulag Archipelago*, played a significant role in delegitimizing the Communist regime. Only the future will tell what impact this new essay will have, though some (not many) have already dismissed it as an irrelevancy. On the largest of all issues at the time of the essay's composition, Solzhenitsyn's call has already been answered: the Soviet Union must go, and a new Russia must be born. Writing in late 1991, John Dunlop asked if current policy reflects the views of Solzhenitsyn, and he gave his own answer that "significant steps have been taken in the direction Solzhenitsyn has recommended over the years."[17] As of this writing, the Yeltsin regime is pursuing a course not out of harmony with Solzhenitsyn's proposals, and Solzhenitsyn has now indicated that he "earnestly support[s] the reforms and the policy of the president."[18] The door remains open for a favorable hearing of and response to what he recommends—if not in every detail, at least in some details and certainly in general spirit. And Solzhenitsyn himself does not conceive of the essay as a package which must be embraced or rejected *in toto*. It is true that in a few cases decisions made seem already to have superseded what Solzhenitsyn advises. Ukrainian independence is the most striking example. But even these may not be the final word but elements of an ongoing development. Nor do they cut to the heart of his vision in this essay. The moderate course charted by Russia to date comports well with Solzhenitsyn's moderate vision.

Although *Rebuilding Russia* is the work of one man, it would be a serious error to view its ideas as idiosyncratic and without popular support. The ideas that Solzhenitsyn articulates are in the air these days, and probably every aspect of his program (though not necessarily all of them taken together) finds many supporters in the new Russia. We have already had occasion to refer to the detailed political program of VSKhSON as one precursor of Solzhenitsyn's thinking. Another programmatic essay in tune with Solzhenitsyn is Vladimir Maximov's "Reflections on Democracy" of 1979.[19] Western readers have only to pick up Geoffrey Hosking's *The Awakening of the Soviet Union* to see how consonant with Solzhenitsyn's vision is the Russian social landscape as depicted therein. To cite just one small example, Hosking says of the Russian people, "But they *have* survived, battered, bruised and intimidated though they may be. . . . I believe, in fact, that the Russian people have demonstrated an extraordinary capacity to improvise humane and functioning grass roots institutions in extremely adverse circumstances."[20] As we anticipate an avalanche of books about the new Russia, we can confidently expect that many of them will display, whether or not by design, a similar consonance with Solzhenitsyn's vision.

In 1974 Solzhenitsyn told Walter Cronkite that he believed that he would return to Russia. Asked when, he said that his works would have to precede him—which meant, in short, that "[t]he system must be changed." Then he added, "At that time I could be useful."[21] What did he mean? We find a hint toward clarification in his statements to the press in September 1991, when the treason charges until then still outstanding against him were dropped, thus removing the last obstacle to his move back home. The series of historical novels, for which he depended on American library resources, would soon be finished. Upon his return to Russia, he explained, "I will immediately become immersed in other concerns that I have in common with everyone."[22]

The suggestion here is that, once in Russia, Solzhenitsyn will consider it his duty to become involved in the public life of the nation. The major literary project which had for decades comprised his main mission in life he would call finished, albeit in a form somewhat less expansive than he had initially intended (though few will consider it too short!). It is a reasonable conjecture, then, that, with whatever years are left to him, his life in Russia will be different from his life in Vermont, where he stuck to his novel-writing and kept distractions to a minimum. In his old age he is likely to become a public figure, though probably even he does not know exactly what will be the shape of this elder-statesman career. If this conjecture proves true, *Rebuilding Russia* will be looked back upon as the bridge to his new role, perhaps the firstfruits of his late-in-life publicistic endeavors.

Similarly, one can only speculate about what his homecoming reception will be. One doubting Thomas, Russian journalist Sergei Panasenko, is quoted as saying that the ideas of "the Vermont wise man," when applied to "our insane days, do not work and will not work." But he also predicts, "His coming back will probably cause on the one hand an unprecedented wave of almost religious worship and that of fierce criticism on the other."[23] Here is an estimate in a somewhat different key, rendered a year before the treason charges were dropped. Calling Solzhenitsyn "that mighty fortress of integrity . . . who could yet play a massive part in the new Russia, were he to return," Xan Smiley observes,

> He is now acknowledged throughout the Soviet Union as a literary and moral colossus, the symbol of a Russia that need not be fed on lies and half-truths. . . . Above all, the Soviet people thirst for a figure like Czechoslovakia's Václav Havel, whose prime purpose is the uncompromising telling of the truth.[24]

And Lawrence Uzzell predicts, "But if he does return, his homecoming will energize the moderate Russian Right in much the same way that Andrei Sakharov inspired the moderate Left. He will be a mass-media 'star' in a culture that lionizes men of letters."[25] The homecoming invitation from Yeltsin raises the possibility of a warm official embrace.

WHILE WE MAY only speculate on future events, we are not left to speculation about how *Rebuilding Russia* has been initially received, both in the West and in Russia. About the essay's reception in the West, the first thing to say is that it was relatively sparse. Apparently, for many outlets of Western opinion, Solzhenitsyn's thought is so resolutely out of fashion that nothing he says will jar them to consider him afresh. The second thing to say is that the reception was quite mixed. The picture of Solzhenitsyn's thinking which emerges in *Rebuilding Russia* is strikingly at odds with the received opinion of his thinking. Either he changed his mind radically, or the received opinion is faulty. In either case, attention is called for. *Time* magazine said, "The article may also liberate him from his reputation as an advocate of authoritarianism."[26] Yes, but only if the essay is read before it is commented on. Some of the remarks ostensibly about the essay are nothing more than regurgitations of received opinion which flatly contradict plain words in the essay itself.

Michael Ignatieff, writing for the London Observer Service, helps us understand why this intellectual shoddiness intruded into the Western reception of *Rebuilding Russia*. Noting that Solzhenitsyn "leaves no one indifferent," he remarks, "The intense dislike Solzhenitsyn always stirs up makes it increasingly difficult for him to be heard. But," he adds, common-sensically enough, "look at what Solzhenitsyn is saying. . . ." Ignatieff then shows that he has looked:

> He should not be dismissed as a reactionary simply because he seeks prerevolutionary models, or because he doubts that Western examples can be imported wholesale. . . . In the Soviet context, it appears that he has made an astute and somewhat unexpected marriage of themes that have appeared in both the Russian nationalist Right and the democratic Left: fusing the language of Russian national pride with the language of de-colonization and democracy.

Ignatieff encourages appreciation of Solzhenitsyn: "The Russian national debate is finely poised between reactionary chauvinism and the democrats. We have reason to support anyone who wants to revive the Russian belief in themselves and in their lost democratic traditions."[27] Or as Robert Legvold put it, "The essay's real merit is in Solzhenitsyn's touching and didactic exploration of democracy's essence and pitfalls, presented like a gift to innocent Russian compatriots."[28]

As for looking before commenting, *The Economist* of London looked just long enough to comment, "Much of the article looks like plain nonsense. Full of musings about the nature of the Russian soul, it calls for a new state to be based on the system of village councils that existed in the nineteenth century and gives a warning about the dangers of capitalism."[29] Margaret Shapiro, writing from Moscow in 1991, acknowledged, "Solzhenitsyn stirred up a political storm here a year ago when he wrote what may turn out to be a prophetic treatise on the future of the Soviet Union." As for evaluation, however, with Gorbachev's attribution of tsarism to Solzhenitsyn ringing in her ears, she chose to ascribe to the author "slightly monarchist leanings"—a condition akin, one might say, to being a little bit pregnant. To fill out the picture, Shapiro brings in Vitaly Korotich, who "once referred to the writer as a potential 'Soviet Khomeini.' "[30] *Commersant* correspondent Maxim Sokolov also found "Solzhenitsyn's monarchism" the keystone for interpreting an essay devoted in substantial part to explicating democratic theory.[31]

There are some signs, but not many, that the *New York Times* editorialist read *Rebuilding Russia* before writing about it. Using Gorbaphilia as a gauge by which to find Solzhenitsyn wanting, the editorial asserts, "Mr. Solzhenitsyn is impatient with parliaments and elections, and urges instead a paternal autocracy rooted in Orthodox religion and Russian nationalism." Though the essay advocates democracy, not autocracy, and makes decentralization its governing political principle, the editorial proceeds, "And in belittling democracy, Mr. Solzhenitsyn seems to ignore the dangers of unchecked, rapacious power so memorably exposed in his books." There is a piece of advice for Russian readers: "No longer reviled and ostracized, Mr. Solzhenitsyn can be more fairly viewed by Russians for what he is: a prophet whose angry eloquence exceeds his political sense." Using a device by now familiar, the editorial sets Sakharov against Solzhenitsyn: "But Sakharov deplores the writer's peremptory judgments, his anti-Western bias and lack of tolerance." It is a minor inconvenience that Sakharov was dead when *Rebuilding Russia* appeared. A sixteen-year-old quotation by Sakharov prepares for the conclusion: "But in the ongoing debate between Westernizers and Slavophiles, the scientist continued to grow and learn while the author forever plows the same field."[32]

The *New York Times* news story about Solzhenitsyn's ("acid-tinged") essay, though sharing the Gorbaphiliac perspective, was a bit better. It mentioned Solzhenitsyn's commitment to democracy and free enterprise, albeit only in a subordinate grammatical construction. "But the Nobel laureate's major point was that, amid a future of democracy and free enterprise, the Soviet Union must be disbanded and the Slavic nation resurrected. . . ." Actually, the essay's balance is just the reverse; all else stands if the call for a union of Slavic peoples into one state goes unheeded. Though the article predicted that "[h]is message is certain to give comfort and fresh energy to various nationalist movements," it did concede, if contradictorily, that "the writer also condemned the mindless ethnic and nationalist fervor that lead to violence." We read, also, "His spirit of dismissal of the union approached sneering."[33] One should not sneer at Father Lenin's legacy? The excerpts accompanying the article included not one from Solzhenitsyn's long discourse on democracy.

The more substantial reviews of *Rebuilding Russia* tell an interesting story. There are many fewer of them than there were reviews of *Letter to the Soviet Leaders*, but some of them are quite favorable. The major exception is Michael Scammell's review.

Scammell's opening paragraph says of Solzhenitsyn, "As for glasnost, he had nothing to say, although some comments suggested that, if anything, he felt that glasnost had gone too far." Which comments? The next sentence says, "In general there was little in Solzhenitsyn's criticisms of the present system that does not appear daily in the Soviet press already. . . ."[34] The implication is that Solzhenitsyn lacks freshness. One could as easily have suggested that Solzhenitsyn is not an eccentric but that others think as he does—not to mention that others are now saying openly what Solzhenitsyn said openly long ago. Solzhenitsyn's sin here is that he does not give Gorbachev sufficient credit.

Scammell notes that there are parallels and differences between *Letter* and *Rebuilding Russia*. He reminds us of his view of *Letter* as retrograde, mentioning again, for instance, Solzhenitsyn's "Old Testament certitude" and his supposed "unwavering belief in the spiritual superiority of the Russian people." He emphasizes continuity over discontinuity, but with his own spin: "The latest document . . . demonstrates that Solzhenitsyn's vision, though changing in many details, has not varied as much as some had expected in response to the radical changes of the last five years."[35] Scammell's method is to generalize forward from his reading of *Letter* and thus to make *Rebuilding Russia* conform to that already established view. Another approach would have been to read *Rebuilding Russia* with fresh eyes and to allow it to challenge points which it contradicts in that already established view.

Whenever he summarizes a position of Solzhenitsyn's that readers might find praiseworthy, Scammell is quick to add a qualifier. Thus, "He comes out in favor of some forms of privatization, but the restrictions he proposes cripple them." What restrictions? That farmers cultivate the land granted them? "On land, he supports the right of farmers to possession of their plots for life, and even, grudgingly, their right to pass property on to their heirs."[36] Grudgingly? Not so.

On democracy Scammell goes beyond adding a qualifier to getting Solzhenitsyn's position wrong.

> Part two consists of a dense disquisition on the nature of democracy . . .
> designed to show not only that representative democracy in all its known
> forms is a highly flawed form of government and incapable of eradicating
> injustices, but that it also fails to reflect the true will of the people, and is
> therefore unsuitable for Russia.

From this summary what reader would guess that Solzhenitsyn flatly says that Russia will need democracy very much? Democracy is incapable of eradicating injustices? Say, rather, it is not always successful at eradicating injustices. Democracy fails to reflect the true will of the people? Say, rather, that it sometimes fails, even that it often fails, not simply that it fails. Democracy is unsuitable for Russia? On the basis of earlier evidence, Scammell has established to his own satisfaction that Solzhenitsyn favors authoritarianism. The hope expressed in *Time* that this new evidence would liberate Solzhenitsyn from his reputation as authoritarian in politics is not fulfilled in the case of Scammell. Is Solzhenitsyn a democrat? He is "a patriarchal populist"! In addition— and because he derides those sloppy-thinking intellectuals whom he calls "smatterers"—he "loathes the middle and professional classes."[37]

How to pigeonhole Solzhenitsyn? "His vision is stuck in the nineteenth century. . . . Unfortunately, such myopia almost certainly will undermine his reputation. . . ." Thus, the new essay deserves this concluding judgment:

> Had Solzhenitsyn stuck to what he knows and understands best, it is safe to say that the significance and impact of his words would have been greater. He could have acted (and might still act) as a moral force to his nation. . . . Instead he has virtually ignored this aspect of his responsibilities and has gone even further than he did in 1973 with a detailed political and economic program that is likely to be ignored, if not laughed out of court.[38]

Pipes scolds Solzhenitsyn for only diagnosing ills and not providing remedies. Scammell scolds him for providing remedies.

Conor O'Clery, whose remarks appear as a sidebar to Scammell's review, knows that Russian readers are not laughing *Rebuilding Russia* out of court. But he finds his own way to dismiss it: "The essay caused a flurry of excitement, but in the end it was something of a one-day wonder." This judgment appeared in actual print two months and a day after the essay appeared. The initial round of responses was not yet in. Would it be fair to call this (borrowing from Solzhenitsyn's Harvard address) a hasty judgment by the press? O'Clery does acknowledge that "the essay laid to rest some of the worst fears of the reformers that right-wing 'patriots' would find their manifesto in Solzhenitsyn's letter." However, though the pamphlet eschews Russian expansionism, he tells us that "[t]he letter has crystallized in people's minds as a call for a greater Russia." He, too, contrasts Solzhenitsyn and Sakharov to Sakharov's advantage—and in part because Sakharov stayed at home. And he agrees with *Commersant*'s Maxim Sokolov: "Today Solzhenitsyn the political figure has been eclipsed."[39]

Scammell's viewpoint does find support from John Gray. "Needless to say," he glibly says, "Solzhenitsyn is not what you might call a convinced democrat. Or even half-convinced. The second half of the book is essentially an elaborate prescription for avoiding democracy." When Solzhenitsyn returns home, "as he has threatened," citizens will be grateful for his revelations about their past. "But it is to be profoundly hoped that his homeland does not turn to him for guidance to the future."[40]

When we turn to Senator Daniel Patrick Moynihan's review of *Rebuilding Russia* in the *New York Times Book Review*, we enter quite a different register. Moynihan entitles his review "Two Cheers for Solzhenitsyn," which is at least one and a half more than the *Times* had heretofore given the author of this essay. And he gives credit where credit is due: "Well, the Soviet Union has broken up. No one anticipated it more than Aleksandr Solzhenitsyn." Indeed, it is odd to come upon recent comments about Solzhenitsyn which neglect any link between his witness and the Soviet breakup. About the prickliest of post-Soviet problems, how the various nationalities might get on with one another, Moynihan scans Solzhenitsyn's analysis and hopeful suggestions and judges that "the evidence is with Mr. Solzhenitsyn, who is, after all, scarcely a man given to avoiding unpleasant facts." Taking note of Solzhenitsyn's much study, Moynihan thinks that he "has understood the major 20th-century thinkers very well. . . ." About Solzhenitsyn on democracy, Moynihan says,

> He is mostly for democracy. Two Cheers, as E. M. Forster would say. For Mr. Solzhenitsyn, democracy works well in small units, where the voters know the candidates personally and exercise "self-restraint." He cites Switzerland as his ideal, along with "citizens' assemblies" in the United States (clearly thinking of the New England town meeting).

If in the Harvard address Solzhenitsyn "seemed at times contemptuous of American democracy," Moynihan is, on the basis of this new evidence, willing to let bygones be bygones: "But that was then."[41]

In fact, Moynihan is the one reviewer who points out this crucial nexus: that Solzhenitsyn and the American Founding Fathers are kindred spirits. As regards democracy, the Fathers deserve two cheers, too. Moynihan phrases it this way:

> In "Rebuilding Russia" he comes across as a thoroughly practical man, even something of an 18th-century man. As you might say, Jefferson. Or Madison, who wrote of the "fugitive and turbulent existence" of ancient republics, and might find the Russian tough-mindedness of this essay refreshing.

When Solzhenitsyn observes that for some in our time democracy has become "almost a cult," Moynihan concurs. And he expands upon the parallels between Solzhenitsyn's thinking and that of the founders of the American democracy:

> Mr. Solzhenitsyn would build a democracy from the ground up, beginning with small regions . . . and on the whole he would build slowly. He has no enthusiasm for the secret ballot, which was in fact an unthinkable notion when the United States got started. (Good-government types— "goo-goos"—imported it from Australia to thwart dear old Tammany Hall.) He would have a lot of indirect representation. Well, so did the Framers of the American Constitution: the Senate was to be chosen by the state legislatures, and was until 1914; and, as best one can tell, they assumed the choice of President would more or less automatically end up in the House of Representatives.

In general, those who value what early American democracy was both trying to achieve and trying to avoid will like Solzhenitsyn's proposals for democracy in the new Russia. Moynihan's warmth of response shows itself again in his conclusion: "And so, great joy to him and to his people—to *all* those peoples."[42]

David Remnick's substantial review is similar to Moynihan's in understanding and evaluation. Remnick is particularly good at clarifying points over which other commentators have stumbled. For instance,

> Solzhenitsyn continues to have serious questions about the nature and fairness of particular democratic mechanisms in Europe and the United States. There is nothing new there. But there is little sign of his flirtation with even the most benign sort of authoritarianism.

Remnick values Solzhenitsyn's "fascinating argument . . . for the radical decentralization of political power, for the primacy of the local." Of Solzhenitsyn's stern dismissiveness toward Gorbachev's stabs at reform, he comments, "While that judgment seemed almost incredibly harsh when it was published in September, the brutal crackdown in Lithuania and Gorbachev's disdain for the democratically elected parliament there give it the painful ring of truth."[43]

Shortly after *Rebuilding Russia* was first published in the Soviet Union, Radio Liberty's *Report on the USSR* carried "The Solzhenitsyn Debate," a sheaf of articles discussing the pamphlet and especially its Soviet reception. The authors focus primarily on Solzhenitsyn's proposed rearrangement of the republics, with all going their separate ways except for the unification in one state of Russia, Ukraine, Belarus, and the Russified northern part of Kazakhstan.

Roman Solchanyk, calling Solzhenitsyn "arguably the most respected contemporary Russian writer and thinker," focuses upon "the decidedly negative reaction in Ukraine to Solzhenitsyn's essay."[44] So, for the most part, does Kathleen Mihalisko. Recognizing that "Solzhenitsyn regards Ukraine as the burning issue," she finds in the new essay a "hardening" of his views on Ukrainian independence over those expressed in *The Gulag Archipelago*.[45] Bess Brown focuses upon the reception in Kazakhstan, where the essay "caused immediate outrage." Six thousand people rallied for three days in the capital city of Alma-Ata, burned copies of the two periodicals which carried the essay, and "displayed banners denouncing Solzhenitsyn."[46] The Kazakhs evidently do not view Solzhenitsyn as passé. Ann Sheehy covers this and other reactions. Noting that Solzhenitsyn's "view that the Soviet Union cannot exist much longer in its present form can be seen as realistic," she observes, "The publication of the brochure . . . has justly been described as a political event in the life of the country, and Solzhenitsyn's suggestions for a future Russian Union are likely to feature prominently in the nationwide debate for some time to come."[47]

Vera Tolz says, "As regards general ideas and broad conclusions, the pamphlet contains little that is new. . . ." Yet she proceeds to mention important points which longtime readers of Solzhenitsyn's Western critics would be unlikely to know from them. These points include Solzhenitsyn's advocacy of "a market economy, the distribution of land as private property among peasants, and the encouragement of all sorts of individual initiatives." Tolz describes the care with which Grigorii Pomerants, an old foe of Solzhenitsyn, read the new essay: "with two pencils in hand, marking those thoughts he favored in red and those he found unacceptable in blue." Tolz herself favors the blue pencil. She thinks, "The most serious shortcoming in the economic chapters . . . is that he does not try to explain how such an economic system—combining all the advantages but excluding all the excesses of a market economy—is to be achieved." She is also critical of what she considers to be

Solzhenitsyn's loyalty to one single line of prerevolutionary Russian intellectual thought and his almost complete disregard of the lessons of

Russian history since October, 1917. These lessons show that attempts to create utopian societies in which people's natures are expected to change and the law plays a secondary role result in serious violations of human rights.[48]

As INTERESTING AS these Western reactions are, the reactions within the Soviet Union are more interesting. Understanding of the essay was keener, and appreciation was greater; and, as befits observers who are also participants, there was often an earnest passionateness about the responses. A good number of them, taking what we might call the red-pencil/blue-pencil approach, demonstrate just the kind of independence of thought that Solzhenitsyn seeks to encourage and to participate in with his fellows. All told, *Komsomolskaya Pravda* received 1,070 letters about the essay within a month of its appearance.[49] In Vladislav Krasnov's overview, "It is quite natural that virtually all moderate Russites welcomed Solzhenitsyn's pamphlet enthusiastically. . . . What *is* surprising is the fact that . . . the pamphlet proved its power to appeal across ideological and political divisions (with the exception of die-hard Communists)."[50] Mikhail Gorbachev was among the displeased. He found Solzhenitsyn's views "alien" and "far removed from reality": "He is completely in the past—Russia's past, and the tsarist monarchy."[51]

Alexander Verkhovsky is melancholy about the prospects of Solzhenitsyn's getting a fair hearing. "The extreme politicization of Soviet society makes it likely that only those already in agreement with the Nobel laureate will pay him much attention." In particular, he is pessimistic about the role of the press: "Moreover, the public's grasp these days of any new idea depends largely on its exposure in the press, and the most important commentators will not only slide past Solzhenitsyn's political views but also make little attempt to assess his enormous moral influence on Russian readers."[52]

Alexander Dobrynin is more optimistic. "No longer a supplicant attempting to attract the attention of mighty rulers, Solzhenitsyn has returned in full glory by publishing his essay. . . ." Dobrynin shrewdly remarks that the essay "is least of all a program to be approved or rejected on the spot. Rather, it is more an occasion, so rare in these times, to consider carefully our circumstances and the tomorrow that will be born from them." What he calls "the most controversial idea in the essay" is also the most important: "Everything is not yet lost, and Russia can be rebuilt because the tradition of Russian life, though badly mangled, remains unbroken. What Russia needs is a caring gardener who can clear away the deadwood and nurture the fragile shoots struggling to survive." Dobrynin accords *Rebuilding Russia* an importance beyond that generally imagined in the West:

> The only sure thing at this juncture is the importance of the living words addressed by Solzhenitsyn to his countrymen, though not everything that he wrote will strike a chord in Russia. By no means! As his homeland lies in ruins, he is honor-bound to say things too bitter to be swallowed easily. Yet Solzhenitsyn has returned, and some sixth sense . . . hints that his words will count for more than all the hasty political and economic reforms taken together.[53]

The Current Digest of the Soviet Press pulled together a sampling of responses to *Rebuilding Russia*. It begins with Aleksandr Afanasyev, who recounts receiving telephone calls from friends asking him if he had heard that Solzhenitsyn had come out in favor of monarchy. When he asked where they had gotten that idea, they explained that Gorbachev had just said so on television. Afanasyev comments, ". . . I understood just how myth-making mechanisms function in our society. . . ." As for his own view, Afanasyev allows that Solzhenitsyn may be mistaken about some things. "He is a major influence on many generations and a great writer, but he is not a demigod, and therefore his article does not and cannot make any claims to 'definitiveness.' " Nevertheless, his appreciation is evident as he defends Solzhenitsyn's drawing upon the past "for reflections on the future" and as he judges, "Despite its extremes and the harshness of some of its judgments, it seems to me that this work is in its own way carefully considered and remarkably balanced."[54]

Literary critic Igor Vinogradov takes to task Mikhail Gorbachev, as well as two hostile Ukrainian commentators, Boris Oleinik and Yuri Shcherbak, who seconded Gorbachev's appraisal of the essay.[55] For Vinogradov, the question always is, "What does Solzhenitsyn actually say, and what is he calling for?" So he challenges Gorbachev and company: "Now really, from which lines in Solzhenitsyn's work does it follow that the author advocates Russia's return to the past, to a monarchy?" Vinogradov is disappointed that not all democrats see that Solzhenitsyn's proposals "have a very clearly expressed *liberal democratic* orientation. . . . How can anyone ignore the powerful spiritual support that Solzhenitsyn's voice can lend, and is lending, precisely to our nascent *democracy*. . . ?" His own approach is that of a free man:

> There are quite a few . . . points that make me want to enter into debate with Solzhenitsyn, sometimes very serious debate; and in defending him from the invective that was delivered from the country's highest rostrum, I certainly am not trying to protect him from any and all criticism whatsoever, no matter how highly I respect his every word and how authoritative that word is for me.[56]

The estimable Father Gleb Yakunin declares, "I am extremely glad that after many years of absence, A. I. Solzhenitsyn has at last begun speaking with his fellow countrymen." Yakunin had "literally condemned him in my soul for his long silence." It pleases him immensely that "Aleksandr Isayevich will no longer be able to remain silent." For he has long believed that Solzhenitsyn's "voice was very badly needed . . . and that in the current situation he was simply essential to the intelligentsia, which regards his name with reverent respect." At the same time, this leader of the Christian Democratic Movement and member of the RSFSR Supreme Soviet is no mindless camp follower: "While I accept a great deal of what Solzhenitsyn proposes, there are some things I cannot agree with."[57]

Galina Starovoitova, a USSR People's Deputy, observing that "Solzhenitsyn's penetrating voice has reached us rather faintly in recent years," expresses pleasure to learn "that throughout all this time that he has lived as a recluse in Vermont, his thoughts have been of us, of Russia." She adds, "Across all that distance, his feel for many things is correct." She likes "his view concerning the development of the provinces," but she wonders why Russia should "be in a hurry" to separate from the other republics. She says also, "Aleksandr Isayevich speaks out as a determined opponent of direct elections. But our people today are politically mature enough to see that three- or four-level elections are an infringement of rights."[58]

The *Current Digest* sampling includes two decidedly negative responses. Vladimir Ovchinsky, an officer in the Ministry of Internal Affairs, declares, "I am no admirer of A. I. Solzhenitsyn's works, and what's more, I do not accept his anticommunist views. But I respect the writer for his objectivity in assessing the situation, and for the alarm that can be felt in his thoughts on Russia's future." (He refers here particularly to warnings about the potential dangers of a market economy.) Kazakh writer Abdizhamil Nupreisov expresses surprise and hurt by Solzhenitsyn's apparent callousness toward Kazakhs. He wants Kazakhstan for the Kazakhs and is against ceding any part of it to Russia.[59]

Both John Dunlop and Vladislav Krasnov have catalogued Russian responses to *Rebuilding Russia*. Their accounts include writers cited above, plus others. Both of them mention Boris Yeltsin's reaction. He had the text photocopied so that all RSFSR deputies could read it "very carefully." In Yeltsin's view, it contained "a lot of interesting thoughts," and he was particularly "intrigued by the idea of a union of the three Slavic republics." Dunlop comments, "Thus, El'tsin's basically positive opinion of Solzhenitsyn's brochure contrasted graphically with Gorbachev's dismissive attitude toward it."[60] Krasnov, though, noting that Yeltsin "stopped short of unequivocally endorsing any of Solzhenitsyn's ideas," passes this judgment: "One has the impression that El'tsin's attitude toward Solzhenitsyn depends on political rather than moral considerations." (If so, it seems that the politically prudent thing to do is to praise Solzhenitsyn.) Krasnov observes, also, that Yeltsin has not yet answered Solzhenitsyn's call for ex-Communists to express penitence for their prior activities.[61] It can be added now that, when Yeltsin phoned Solzhenitsyn in June 1992, a Yeltsin spokesman reported, "In the words of the president, one could feel undertones of repentance."[62]

Both Dunlop and Krasnov take note of the response by Yuri Karyakin, a democrat who "vigorously defended Solzhenitsyn"[63] from the criticisms of Gorbachev and the Ukrainian writers Oleinik and Shcherbak. Karyakin sounds notes similar to those of Vinogradov, and he mentions various particulars on which he agrees with Solzhenitsyn. Without mentioning Gorbachev by name, he asserts:

Of course, one does not have to agree with Solzhenitsyn in everything, and yesterday such disagreements surfaced. But it seems to me that we should be careful not to proceed too quickly here. . . . For example, on the question of monarchism, there are simply no grounds for claiming Solzhenitsyn is a monarchist. He has more than once refuted such a charge. So let us read and reread the text more calmly [Gorbachev had declared that he had read the brochure twice], let us think and reflect on it more calmly.[64]

A. Surazhsky, too, cares about accurate reading. "Who hasn't heard that Solzhenitsyn is a monarchist, a chauvinist, and, of course, an anti-Semite?" In the actual text, however,

> Not only does Solzhenitsyn not make a reference of any kind to the possibility of restoring the monarchy, but he concretely discusses various forms of state organization that exclude monarchy. Not only does he not proclaim any chauvinistic ideas, but, on the contrary, he sharply attacks the imperial psychology. . . . Finally, Solzhenitsyn does not once mention, either directly or indirectly, those fashionable topics that boil down to one thing: "the Jews organized the revolution and destroyed Russia." He says not one word about "Russophobia."

Surazhsky also remarks the substantial compatibility between Solzhenitsyn's and Sakharov's programmatic views.[65]

Mikhail Sokolov, also, saw consanguinity of outlook in Solzhenitsyn and Sakharov. Future Russia, he speculated, might arrive at "a compromise between Westerners and Slavophiles." If so, "the first step towards it would have been made by Solzhenitsyn."[66] Similarly, novelist Viacheslav Kondratiev thought that *Rebuilding Russia* might be (in Krasnov's summarizing words) "a last chance for preventing the ship of state from sinking." Given the exasperating tendency of intellectuals to split into warring factions, Kondratiev hoped that the essay would become a focal point for "the consolidation of all progressive forces."[67]

In Krasnov's opinion, Alla Latynina "gave the most penetrating assessment of the impact of Solzhenitsyn's pamphlet on the debate about Russia's future." Of the *New York Times* editorial, which she heard on the Voice of America, she says that it consists of falsehoods and inaccuracies, and she suggests that the newspaper itself is guilty of intolerance and bigotry. Both Gorbachev's "clichés" and the *Times*'s "hurried response" stem from the same source: "superficial [play at] democracy, the herd instinct, passion for platitudes, and a religious faith in progress, against which none dare to stand!"[68] Latynina, too, scolds

Oleinik and Shcherbak for careless reading. And she corrects Starovoitova: Solzhenitsyn does not advocate the separation of Russia "in one hour"; rather, he recommends that specialists prepare the "divorce" over a long period of time. Finally, Latynina says that Russian intellectuals have been asking the wrong questions about Solzhenitsyn. "We were agitated by the question: with whom will Solzhenitsyn turn out to be [in alliance]?" The right question is,

> Who is able to evaluate and accept Solzhenitsyn's program, in which political and spiritual radicalism are combined with a firm emphasis on tradition and in which a series of bold reforms push us rapidly into the future, across a bridge that unites us with our thousand-year history (only taking us around the obdurate and ill-fated past seventy years)?[69]

One more commentary worth noting is that of Ukrainian nationalist spokesman Svyatoslav Karavansky, who detailed his objections to Solzhenitsyn's views on Ukraine. To this one Solzhenitsyn replied, conciliatorily. Contrasting Karavansky's "soft voice" to the shrill attacks of unnamed others, he emphasized that the central question is "the movement of hearts" in Ukraine. "If the hearts of Ukrainians desire separation today, then there is nothing to argue about. That movement of hearts is sufficient, and that is precisely what I said in my article. And it was about that that I wrote in *The Gulag Archipelago*." However, it is not clear that all residents and all districts of Ukraine agree. Furthermore, at a time when Western Ukrainians "are knocking down monuments of Lenin," why do they "call so passionately for the Ukraine to have precisely those Leninist borders that were granted to her by grandfather Lenin?"[70]

BEFORE WE TURN to the text itself of *Rebuilding Russia*, there is one final matter to explain. *August 1914* contains a long section about the political thinking of Pyotr Stolypin which anticipates *Rebuilding Russia*. Solzhenitsyn ardently admires Stolypin, Prime Minister of Russia from 1905 to 1911, and he sets him in contrast to Lenin: Stolypin the reformer *versus* Lenin the revolutionary. According to Krasnov, the Gorbachev leadership showed itself "worried about the growing attractiveness of Stolypin's reforms as an example of successful *perestroika*."[71] Stolypin was much on Solzhenitsyn's mind in the years leading up to the writing of *Rebuilding Russia*, as we know from interviews in 1987 and 1989. Solzhenitsyn described Stolypin as "a real liberal," a man hated by both extreme right and extreme left. "His idea was to liberate the peasants from economic dependency, then they would become citizens. First, you'd have to make the citizen, then civic consciousness would be born too."[72] In Solzhenitsyn's view, "Stolypin was, without doubt, the major political figure of Russian 20th century history." However, the abortive attempt at democracy in February 1917 actually "abolished all his reforms and went back to square one."[73]

Solzhenitsyn takes Stolypin as his inspiration. (He kept Stolypin's picture above his writing desk.) He sees himself as standing in Stolypin's line and his pamphlet as resuscitating and updating Stolypin's thinking so as, this time, to build a democratic Russia free of the errors of the woebegone experiment of February 1917. We need not detain ourselves with a scrutiny of the Stolypin section of *August 1914*, since all of its essentials (and more) are in the pamphlet. The novel's section does, of course, remind us of the long period of germination of the pamphlet's ideas. And we do read in the novel this very intriguing sentence: "It would be more discreet of us to postpone our pronouncement on the correct relation between parliamentary procedure and the individual will of the responsible statesman until the beginning of the twenty-first century."[74] In significant measure, *Rebuilding Russia* is that pronouncement.

11

"Rebuilding Russia" (II)
First Priorities

BECAUSE OF THE TIMELINESS of *Rebuilding Russia*, two chapters of exposition are devoted to it. The subtitle, "Reflections and Tentative Proposals," indicates that the pamphlet will contain both problems and solutions, analysis and advice. "Reflections" is oriented to the past but also takes in the present; "Proposals" points toward the future, appropriately taking a posture of tentativeness. The word *tentative* signals Solzhenitsyn's desire to enter into dialogue, not to present prescriptions peremptorily. The pamphlet is organized into two roughly equal parts of fourteen brief chapters apiece. The parts are entitled "First Priorities" and "Looking Ahead." That is, the first part is about short-term matters, and the second is about long-term matters.

The essay's memorable opening words are about history and its movement:

> Time has finally run out for communism.
> But its concrete edifice has not yet crumbled.
> And we must take care not to be crushed beneath its rubble instead of gaining liberty.[1]

Solzhenitsyn is writing a year before Soviet power expires in the aftermath of the failed coup of August 1991. He has no doubt what the turbulent times portend: Communism in Russia and the other Soviet republics is in its death throes, and his cherished dream of a free Russia is not far off. The Gorbachev regime, however, belongs not to the dawn of the new day but to the last hours of the old night. The "concrete edifice" still stands, if not for much longer. The transition about to begin will be a dangerous time.

THE FIRST CHAPTER, "At the End of Our Endurance," summarizes quickly the squalid and treacherous current state of affairs culminating "seventy years in labored pursuit of a purblind and malignant Marxist-Leninist utopia" (p. 3). A third of the population has been lost. The cities are "befouled" and the countryside "plundered." Family life has been brutalized. Health care and housing are in shambles (p. 4).

Faced with a plethora of urgent issues begging for immediate attention, Solzhenitsyn cannot get out of this first brief chapter without bringing up the nationalities question, to which he devotes the next four chapters, also. He evidently sees this as the first problem to be addressed once Communism falls, the problem which could dash all hopes for a sensible process of reconstruction before it ever got underway. His first words on this topic should surprise many of his critics: "Human beings are so constituted that we can put up with such ruination and madness even when they last a lifetime, but God forbid that anyone should dare to offend or slight our *nationality*!" He is warning against nationalistic chauvinism. Now that Communism is departing, the people must be careful not to rush to the other extreme. "Such is man: nothing has the capacity to convince us that our hunger, our poverty, our early deaths, the degeneration of our children—that any of these misfortunes can take precedence over national pride" (p. 5). The extreme nationalists who had hoped for aid and comfort from Solzhenitsyn will not get it. It is as if he can hardly wait to distance himself from them. The route pursued in this essay will be a centrist one between the extremes of Communism on the one hand and chauvinistic nationalism on the other.

The concluding lines of the opening chapter put the question which is discussed in the following chapters and which, indeed, dominates the first half of the essay. "How will the problem of the nationalities be approached? And within what geographical boundaries shall we heal our afflictions or die? And only thereafter shall we turn to the healing process itself" (p. 5). Geography is no small matter in a multi-national empire, especially in one where traditional boundaries have been capriciously redrawn, where whole nationalities have been removed to locations far from their ancestral lands, where members of the most populous nationality (the Russians) have been scattered hither and yon across the vast landscape. Only if the grave complications of geographical boundaries inherited from the Communists can be peaceably resolved to the general (albeit probably not full) satisfaction of all peoples will each people experience the inner freedom needed to rebuild its society and to re-establish its culture.

A number of commentators have considered this "macro" concern the main feature of the essay. It is not. The heart of Solzhenitsyn's advice lies in applying the principle of decentralization. Social problems are best addressed at the "micro," or local, level. But there will be no peace to attend to local matters until the "macro" issues settle down. The separation and realignment of the nations encompassed in the old Soviet Union take priority only chronologically. First things first, but not first things most important.

CHAPTER TWO IS entitled, simply, "What is Russia?" The word "has become soiled and tattered through careless use" (p. 5). Russia is certainly not to be equated by the world with "the monster-like U.S.S.R." once "lunging for chunks of Asia and Africa." Inside the boundaries of the old empire, it is even more crucial to answer this question properly. "What exactly *is* Russia? Today, now? And—more important—tomorrow? Who, today, considers himself part of the future Russia? And where do Russians themselves see the boundaries of their land?" The inheritance from the Communists is such that "one can no longer see the way back to the peaceful coexistence of nationalities, that almost drowsy non-perception of distinctions that had virtually been achieved—with some lamentable exceptions—in the final decades of prerevolutionary Russia." The only practicable resolution to "the all-pervading ethnic bitterness" is "a decisive parting of the ways for those who should separate" (p. 6).

Thus, Solzhenitsyn offers the first proposal of the essay, the one on the "macro" level:

In many of the republics at the periphery, centrifugal forces have built up such momentum that they could not be stopped without violence and bloodshed—*nor should they be checked at such cost.* The way things are moving in our country, the "Soviet Socialist Union" will break up *whatever* we do: we have no real choice, there is nothing to ponder, and it remains only to bestir ourselves in order to forestall greater misfortunes and to assure that the separation proceeds without needless human suffering and only in those cases where it is truly unavoidable. (p. 7)

It is not theoretical principle but concrete historical reality which provides the main motive force for Solzhenitsyn's call for separation. However, neither is there any theoretical principle, once the centripetal imperative of Marxism-Leninism is gone, for holding the empire together. At the time of Solzhenitsyn's writing, this point had not yet registered upon a good many high government officials in the West. Even so, the divisions should go no further than the minimum required to satisfy ethnic strivings for self-determination. The desire to separate is not a sacrosanct principle overriding all other concerns. In a land of more than a hundred different nationalities, utter fragmentation is an evil to be avoided, too. In short, Solzhenitsyn here again shows himself to be both a realist and a moderate.

For Solzhenitsyn, what this means in the "macro" picture is that, of the fifteen republics in the Soviet Union, "eleven will be *separated off unequivocally and irreversibly*" (p. 7) from his Russian homeland. These are the three republics in the Baltic area, the three in Transcaucasia, Moldavia ("if it feels drawn to Romania"), and four of the five republics of Central Asia. Kazakhstan is a special case. Kazakhs comprise less than half of its population, the northern half of it is inhabited largely by Russians, and "in any case Kazakhstan was considered an Autonomous Republic within the R.S.F.S.R. until 1936, when it was promoted to Union Republic status." As for the Kazakhs' "longstanding ancestral domains along a large arc of lands in the south," where the population remains predominantly Kazakh, "if it should prove to be their wish to separate within such boundaries, I say Godspeed" (p. 8). This is the part of the pamphlet that evoked violent reaction among some leading Kazakh intellectuals and government officials.

After subtracting these eleven and a half republics, we are left with

Russia, Ukraine, Byelorussia (now Belarus), and the Russified part of Kazakhstan—

> an entity that might be called Rus, as it was designated in olden times (the word "Russian" had for centuries embraced Little Russians [Ukrainians], Great Russians, and Belorussians), or else "Russia," a name used since the eighteenth century, or—for an accurate reflection of the new circumstances—the "Russian [*Rossiiskii*] Union." (p. 9)

The majority people of this vast remaining territory have common ethnic roots and a common cultural heritage, starting with religion. There is no compelling reason why the very real centrifugal pressures must pull them apart.

Some have suggested that Solzhenitsyn might have enhanced the prospects for Ukrainian and Byelorussian compliance in this projected union had he used the word *Slavic* for it, and possibly they are correct. However, these peoples are Eastern Slavs only; West Slavs and South Slavs would in no one's mind be appropriate candidates for this union. Also, *Rus* is the ancient root word; it has the weight of history on its side, and its use would neatly capture the desired tie between past and future. Moreover, it is very important to observe that, of the two words translated into English as *Russian*, Solzhenitsyn uses *Rossiiskii*, not *Russkii*. The latter refers to ethnicity and would suggest the supremacy of ethnic Russians in the new union. The former encompasses all persons of whatever ethnic derivation (not just Slavs) who consider Russia their homeland.

In fact, in the remaining Russian Union there would still be a hundred different nationalities and ethnic groups. So there would remain "the task of consolidating a fruitful commonwealth of nations, affirming the integrity of each culture and the preservation of each language" (p. 9). The Commonwealth of Independent States is almost universally assumed to be a holding operation. From its inception the real power lay not with it but with the separate republics. However, even in the much-reduced territory which would comprise the Russian Union, the principle of a commonwealth would have to be in force if the majority population were not to be given excessive power over the remaining minorities. Solzhenitsyn then turns to addressing directly each of these constituent groups—the Great Russians, the Ukrainians and Byelorussians, and the smaller nationalities and ethnic groups—in a chapter apiece.

CHAPTER THREE IS "A Word to the Great Russians." This constituent group is the largest one by far, and it is the one which needs to be shorn of any dreams of imperial grandeur. Thus, this chapter is Solzhenitsyn's most pointed and sustained anti-expansionist, anti-imperialist argument. And the first reason he offers is this: "*We don't have the strength* for the peripheries either economically or morally. *We don't have the strength* for sustaining an empire. . . ." Lest one think that weakness is the only reason, however, he adds immediately, ". . . and it is just as well" (p. 10).

Solzhenitsyn has long called for a revival of Russian patriotism. Now he sees it developing. It is, however, in too large measure taking a turn which distresses him: "I note with alarm that the awakening Russian national self-awareness has to a large extent been unable to free itself of great-power thinking and of imperial delusions, that it has taken over from the communists the fraudulent and contrived notion of 'Soviet patriotism.' . . ." Whom does he have in mind here? Extreme nationalists, to be sure. But the National Bolsheviks in particular. Those who took pride in the "Soviet superpower" status trumpeted during "the reign of the dull-witted Brezhnev." Those who took pride in "the 'superpower' status that brought shame upon us, presenting us to the whole world as a brutal, insatiable, and unbridled aggressor." Behind this false and inglorious façade, the fact is that "our knees were beginning to shake and weakness was bringing us to the verge of collapse" (p. 10).

Solzhenitsyn offers Japan as a model of a one-time superpower "able to find a way to be reconciled with its situation, renouncing its sense of international mission and the pursuit of tempting political ventures." In the result, Japan flourishes. So may Russia. Its options are stark. "The time has come for an uncompromising *choice* between an empire of which we ourselves are the primary victims and the spiritual and physical salvation of our own people." As things stand, "Holding on to a great empire means to contribute to the extinction of our own people." By the "seeming sacrifice" of forgoing empire, "Russia will in fact free itself for a precious *inner* development" (p. 11). And who nowadays gives an affirmative answer to this historical question: "Did Russia lose out through the separation of Poland and Finland?" (p. 12). No matter how one assesses the accuracy of Solzhenitsyn's grim analysis of Russia's straitened circumstances (though who today doubts it?), his advice to the Russians would, if followed, contribute greatly to world peace. One must be mightily attached to the status quo not to welcome the abandonment by the new Russia of the old Soviet imperial designs. Solzhenitsyn's position is not only not Russian messianism *redivivus* but its exact opposite.

As much as Solzhenitsyn loves Russia, he knows when a virtue, by being carried to extremes, turns into a vice. So he rebukes the chauvinists: "We must stop reciting like parrots: 'We are proud to be Russian.' " The times call for national humility and self-limitation. Not only Soviet imperialism but even the past glories of pre-revolutionary Russia must not be pursued: "No longer can we be so presumptuous in our plans for the future as to dream of restoring the might and eminence of the former Russia." How different all of this is from what Solzhenitsyn's critics have led us to expect of him. Far from "taking pride," he tells his fellows, "We must, rather, grasp the reality of the acute and debilitating illness that is affecting our people, and pray to God that He grant us recovery, along with the wisdom to achieve it" (p. 13).

CHAPTER FOUR IS "A Word to the Ukrainians and the Belorussians." It opens on a (little-known) personal note: "I am well-nigh half Ukrainian by birth, and I grew up to the sound of Ukrainian speech." Also, he spent the greater part of his front-line military service in Byelorussia. "Thus, I am addressing both nations not as an outsider but *as one of their own*." The division of "our people" into three branches was a historical accident caused by the Mongol invasion and Polish colonization. It is "a recently invented falsehood" that the Ukrainian people existed separately from the ninth century and has its own non-Russian language. Rather, "We all sprang from precious Kiev, . . . from which we received the light of Christianity" (p. 14). All historical argument urges the reunification of the three branches of the Eastern Slavs. Ukrainian émigrés who blame Communist depredations on the Russians do a disservice. "As common victims . . . , have we not been bonded by this common bloody suffering?" (p. 16).

Solzhenitsyn's effort to establish a common bond between the Russians on the one side and the Ukrainians and Byelorussians on the other is obviously in preparation of his call for these nations to join together in a new union. He is alternately stern and supplicating. He is stern in finding "lunatic vehemence in statements such as: 'Let communism live so long as the Muscovites perish.'" Yet the fierce anti-Russian sentiment among some Ukrainians also causes him to be supplicating, as in the rhetorical question, "How can we fail to share the pain and anguish over the mortal torments that befell the Ukraine in the Soviet period?" Still, even that enormous suffering does not "justify the ambition to lop the Ukraine off from a living organism" (p. 17).

Ukrainian nationalists advocate self-determination for Ukraine. So does Solzhenitsyn. But the situation is very complex. The two populations, Ukrainian and Russian, are "thoroughly intermingled." In Ukraine, especially in the eastern parts, "there are entire regions where Russians predominate," and therefore "many individuals would be hard put to choose between the two nationalities." Many are, like himself, "of mixed origin, and there are plenty of mixed marriages (marriages which have indeed never been viewed as 'mixed')" (p. 17). So he pleads with the Ukrainians,

> Brothers! We have no need of this cruel partition. The very idea comes from the darkening of minds brought on by the communist years. Together we have borne the suffering of the Soviet period, together we have tumbled into this pit, and together, too, we shall find our way out.

Let there be "[n]o forced Russification." But, given the mixed population, let there be "no forced Ukrainization either." Let fairness prevail. "There must be an untrammeled development of parallel cultures and school instruction in either language, according to the parents' choice" (p. 18).

Solzhenitsyn has long known how difficult it will be to persuade the Ukrainians to join in a union with Russians. In *The Gulag Archipelago* he stated, "But from friendly contact with Ukrainians in the camps over a long period I have learned how sore they feel. Our generation cannot avoid paying for the mistakes of generations before it." Given the "white heat" of Ukrainian resentment, he said even then, ". . . it is up to us to show sense. We must leave the decision to the Ukrainians themselves. . . ." However, his prediction about Ukrainian separation was not sanguine: "They will soon find that not all problems are solved by secession."[2]

In 1990 Solzhenitsyn is still recommending that the residents of Ukraine decide for themselves. He softens his tone by leaving out his dismal prediction. However, as if to underline the difficulty of arriving at a nationwide consensus, he proposes that residents make their decision district by district.

> Of course, if the Ukrainian people should *genuinely wish* to separate, no one would dare to restrain them by force. But the area is very heterogeneous indeed, and only the *local* population can determine the fate of a particular locality, while every ethnic minority created by this process in a given district must count upon the same kind of forbearance toward itself. (p. 18)

One follows the point here. There are eleven million Russians in Ukraine, and in some districts, including areas where the Soviets arbitrarily redrew boundary lines, they constitute the majority. Evenhanded application of the principle of self-determination should spare them the tyranny of a Ukrainian separatist majority. Yet this specific proposal has the potential to dismember Ukraine. And it is easy enough to understand why it infuriated Ukrainians passionate for their own independence. In no other case does Solzhenitsyn float a proposal with such light regard for (what many would consider) territorial integrity.

In the penultimate paragraph of this chapter, Solzhenitsyn finally gets around to the Byelorussians, and then only briefly. "All the above holds fully for Belorussia as well, except that the passions of separatist extremism have never been stirred up in that land." In the final paragraph he says, "And finally let us bow our heads before the Ukraine and Belorussia in recognition of the Chernobyl disaster. It was brought about by the careerists and fools generated by the Soviet system, and we must help set things right to the extent that we are able to do so" (p. 19). Earmarking the income from *Rebuilding Russia* for the victims of Chernobyl typifies Solzhenitsyn's commitment to the Russian Union.

In July of 1990, even as Solzhenitsyn was composing this essay, Ukraine declared its sovereignty. In December of 1991, Ukraine voted for independence. Even regions with majority Russian populations voted in favor of it, albeit sometimes by relatively narrow margins. So it might seem that Solzhenitsyn's call for a district-by-district vote has been met. A number of commentators think that the vote for Ukrainian independence renders moot his recommendation of the Russian Union. Time may prove them correct, but it is not yet necessarily so. As the Commonwealth of Independent States seems to be a temporary arrangement, so the bolt by Ukraine may prove to be transitional. Nothing prevents a later union—Solzhenitsyn would say reunion—of the currently separate Eastern Slavic peoples. Today there is, as a loose analogy, the centripetal movement of the European Community, bringing together nations with much less in common historically than is the case among the Eastern Slavs. Were such a union yet to occur, the Ukrainians and Byelorussians would enter with heads unbowed, as free and equal partners with the Russians.

However the "macro" picture develops, one thing is clear: Solzhenitsyn is keenly aware that Ukrainian-Russian relations are the key ingredient to a peaceful post-Soviet future. Certain open hostilities among nationalities, starting with the Armenian-Azerbaijani strife over the tinderbox enclave of Nagorno-Karabakh, are inevitable. But will the Ukrainians and the Russians get along? They must do so, by whatever means will work best. Each has resources that the other needs. Each also has the potential for considerable power. At the moment, the tide is not running in Solzhenitsyn's preferred direction. At the same time, it must be remembered that he never disallowed separate development of the Slavic nationalities. In fact, he required that they exercise self-determination. His plea for political union is not, despite what many commentators have said, the linchpin of his essay. Everything else that Solzhenitsyn advises about the moral, social, economic, and political development of Russia pertains equally well if the geography of Russia ends up being more limited than he prefers. To resolve the issue of geography is merely to set the stage upon which the action is to unfold.

CHAPTER FIVE IS "A Word to the Smaller Nationalities and Ethnic Groups." Here the focus shifts to Russia proper, within which are sixteen Autonomous Republics and more than a hundred ethnic groupings. Thus, the Russian "state will inevitably remain a multicultural one, despite the fact that this is not a goal we wish to pursue." Realities are what they are. When they are fraught with the peril of ethnic rivalries and dissension, they must be coped with as amicably as possible, to the mutual benefit of majority and minority populations. For minority groups whose territories have an external border, "if they should wish to separate, no impediment can be placed in their way." For those without that geographical endowment, "there would seem to be virtually no choice, because it is simply impractical for one state to exist when it is surrounded on all sides by a second one." Then there is "the added difficulty that in some Autonomous Republics the indigenous population constitutes a minority" (p. 19). In all of these cases, Solzhenitsyn advises, "But on the condition that all their unique national characteristics—culture, religion, and economic structure—are preserved, it may make sense for them to remain in the union" (pp. 19–20). The *may* signals again Solzhenitsyn's tentativeness, as well as his tender concern for self-determination for all peoples, even small ones. Just to mention the need for trade and also the "great burden . . . of supporting a plethora of governmental agencies, diplomatic missions, and armies" is enough to suggest that "[i]t is not the large Russian Union that needs to have the smaller peripheral nations joined to itself; it is, rather, they who may have the greater need to join up. Should they wish to be with us, more credit to them." To guarantee these small groups access to power, Solzhenitsyn is willing to borrow from the "deliberately deceptive and mendacious Soviet system" the concept of the Council of Nationalities, as well as the present hierarchical structure of governmental units according to size and scope: in descending order, Union Republics, Autonomous Republics, Autonomous Oblasts, and National Okrugs (p. 20).

Solzhenitsyn has thought long about Russia's ethnic minorities. Some two decades ago, he said, ". . . my heart sinks at the thought of our age-old sin in oppressing and destroying the indigenous peoples." Though the "faint sprinkling of them on the Siberian continent" is insufficient warrant to keep all other people out, "we must show a tender fraternal concern for the natives, help them in their daily lives, educate them, and . . . not forcibly impose our ways on them."[3] (Americans, Canadians, and others might here ponder their treatment of their own indigenous peoples.) Sounding a theme expressed in the *Nobel Lecture*,[4] Solzhenitsyn here says, "Every people, even the very smallest, represents a unique facet of God's design." This religious outlook issues in protection for minorities. "As Vladimir Solovyov has written, paraphrasing the Christian commandment: 'You must love all other people as you love your own' " (p. 21). In a century "warped by a politics that has liberated itself from all moral criteria," Solzhenitsyn concludes this chapter, "It is high time to seek loftier forms of statehood, based not only on self-interest but also on compassion" (p. 22). Chauvinistic nationalists do not talk this way.

CHAPTER SIX IS entitled "The Process of Separation." On the requirement that the non-Slavic republics go their own ways, Solzhenitsyn is firm. If they hesitate, the Russian Union will need to take the initiative and "proclaim *our* separation from them." There are no two ways about it; the old Soviet empire must be broken up. "The parting of the ways is long overdue, the process is irreversible, and the situation will only keep exploding in unpredictable places. It is plain to all that we cannot live together." The requisite commonalty of culture is simply absent. The need for separation being established, he now attends to the process of it, which will be "painful and costly," and the more so in a poverty-stricken time (p. 22). Actual separation, this confirmed gradualist says, "will not be accomplished by any quick declaration. Any abrupt unilateral action would result in injury to countless human lives and in mutual economic ruin" (pp. 22–23). The Portuguese flight from Angola is an example to be avoided. After the declaration of separation, "panels of experts representing all concerned parties must begin deliberations." Given "the irresponsibly haphazard way in which the Soviet demarcation of borders was carried out," one of the first tasks for the experts will be to draw "more accurate lines . . . in order to reflect the actual population patterns." But even "[t]his sorting process might well take several years" (p. 23).

Solzhenitsyn is well aware of the dislocation which separation will entail for millions. Almost a fifth of all Russians, some 25 million, live in other Soviet republics, and many non-Russians live in Russia and not in their native republics. His plan does not require that they all relocate; but those who do will need "substantial assistance," and the experts should not leave these individuals to fend for themselves (p. 23). "And every newly formed state must provide explicit guarantees of minority rights" (p. 24). This is all far removed from the Serbian approach to the disintegration of Yugoslavia.

Also complex will be "the problem of devising a painless method of partitioning the national economies or the establishment of trade links and industrial cooperation on an independent basis." At least then, as this process of separation unfolds, each new nation will "come to recognize its genuine problems, rather than that chronic 'nationality problem' which has chafed our necks to the point where it has distorted all our feelings and our sense of reality" (p. 24). None of this will come easily, as the case of Georgia illustrates. No sooner did Georgia gain its yearned-for independence, Solzhenitsyn scolds, than it turned to persecuting its internal minorities. The magnitude of the nationalities problem may be difficult for many Westerners to grasp, but any Soviet citizen knows that there can be no peace until it is ameliorated.

CHAPTER SEVEN IS entitled "Urgent Measures for the Russian Union." Communist tyranny has brought such poverty and despair "that many of us are ready to give up, and it seems that the intercession of heaven alone can save us." Solzhenitsyn, congenitally the optimist, counsels hope, not despair. "But miracles do not descend upon those who make no effort on their own behalf." If heaven helps those who help themselves, the Russians must be up and doing. He believes that they will "find the strength to prevail." The one-horse-shay-like collapse of the Soviet Union means that "[w]e may have been granted no time for reflecting upon the best-suited paths of development, no time to put together a reasoned program, and we may have no choice other than racing around frantically, plugging leaks. . . ." And, indeed, this sounds like the Yeltsin regime in action. "Yet we must preserve presence of mind and the wisdom of circumspection in our choice of initial measures" (p. 25). Just this calm may be what Solzhenitsyn himself is contributing to with this essay.

Pointing out the right direction in a time when "[a]ll things cry out for help" is of course not a one-man job. "I cannot presume to enumerate all these steps by myself; this must be done by a council drawing on the clearest practical minds and the best available energies" (pp. 25-26). In addition to the familiar litany of social ills, from lack of housing to dire poverty of the elderly and the handicapped to "the radioactive blotches from Chernobyl and elsewhere," there is now, with Solzhenitsyn's plan, the additional cost of resettling Russians who will be moving back in from the other republics. "Wherever shall we find the money?" (p. 26).

Solzhenitsyn lists six sources. First are the "tens of billions each year" which now go to propping up Communist regimes around the world: Cuba, Vietnam, Ethiopia, Angola, North Korea. "He who cuts off *all this* at one fell stroke will deserve to be called a patriot and a true statesman." Second are the hundreds of billions annually which go into producing offensive weapons. Third, the preferential supplying of Eastern Europe must end. "We rejoice for the countries of Eastern Europe, may they thrive in freedom, but let them pay for everything at world prices." Fourth, investing in "industries that do not show signs of recovery" must stop. Fifth, "the unimaginably huge assets of the Communist Party" (p. 27) should be expropriated. "Of course, there is no way to get back all that has been wasted, scattered, and plundered, but let them at least return what is left: the buildings, resorts, special farms, and publishing houses." Sixth, "the whole army of appointive bureaucrats, that parasitic multimillion-strong governing apparatus which inhibits all living forces in the nation—with their high salaries, various benefits, and special stores—we shall feed no more!" (p. 28). Eighty percent of the bloated bureaucracy can be eliminated in the new society. Although these sources of revenue do not suffice to cope with the whole economic mess left by the Communists, we do see Solzhenitsyn thinking in practical terms about details.

This sharp change of course is exactly what was not occurring under the then-current (Gorbachev) regime, and Solzhenitsyn draws attention to the contrast. In words offensive to Gorbaphiles, he says,

> And what have five or six years of the much-heralded "perestroika" been used for? For some pathetic reshuffling within the Central Committee. For the slapping together of an ugly and artificial electoral system designed to allow the Party to continue clinging to power. For the promulgation of flawed, confusing, and indecisive laws. (p. 28)

A free society should not ban but tolerate the Communist Party. However, "it must remove itself completely from all involvement in the economy and affairs of state; it must cease controlling us. . . ." About a year later, these words began to become reality. Solzhenitsyn adds, "One would prefer to see this happen without the Party's being squeezed out or ejected by force, but rather as a result of its own public repentance. . . ." It is the great wonder of the age that Soviet Communism was shouldered aside with so very little bloodshed. So far, however, there has been precious little public repentance, precious little "acknowledgment by the Party that it has led the country into an abyss by a long series of crimes, cruelties, and absurdities, and that it does not know the way out" (p. 29). Instead, and unsurprisingly, one sees Party members clinging to remnants of their power, especially in the hinterlands, and gumming up efforts to develop institutions befitting a free society.

If the Communist Party must be allowed continued existence in the new order, "the concrete monolith of the KGB" must not. "The assertion that they are particularly needed now for international intelligence-gathering is but a transparent stratagem; it is obvious that the reverse is true" (p. 29). Its record is of "bloodstained villainy," and it "can no longer have either justification or right to exist" (p. 30).

"LAND" is the simple title of Chapter Eight. In the moral universe, "Land embodies moral as well as economic values for human beings," and Solzhenitsyn writes with enthusiasm about the earth and its "miraculous and blessed property of bearing fruit." In his view, "A weakening desire to work the land is a great danger to the national character," and he frets that "the peasant sensibility has been trod underfoot and expunged so thoroughly that it may be too late, far too late, for it to be revived" (p. 30). Reinvigorating a sense of attachment to the land would be a good thing to do. How can it be done?

Personal leasing of land would, in comparison to the prevailing system of collective farming, be "unquestionably a step in the direction of improving our agriculture" (p. 31). However, the leasing allowed by the land reforms of the self-styled reformist regime "is largely an exercise in deceit and mockery," for it places lessees "in suffocating dependency to the collective farm or state farm authorities, who can ignore the law at will" (p. 30). As the then-current system also demonstrates by default, "a piece of land does not by itself mean freedom for the peasant: he also needs a free market, access to transportation, financial credit, technical repair facilities, and construction materials." To be viable, leasing should be "from a local self-governing body," and it also "should be for life, with the unrestricted right to pass the parcel of land to one's heirs" (p. 31). Solzhenitsyn goes into careful and protective detail here: ". . . dispossession must not occur due to illness in the lessee's family, but only in cases of negligent land use; and the lessee must have the right to give up his holdings, in which case he should be reimbursed for any investment he has made. . ." (pp. 31–32).

There is a better way than land leasing: private ownership. For one thing, people have a "justified distrust of the authorities," whatever the size of the governmental unit. More important, however, private ownership of land, in comparison to which "the leasing option will not be economically competitive," is that system

> which guarantees the long-term improvement of the plot rather than its depletion, and which alone can ensure that our agriculture will not continue to lag behind the West. When we anticipate and demand initiative in all spheres of life, how can we prohibit it with respect to land? To deny private ownership of land to the village is to finish it off forever. (p. 32)

Despite his enthusiasm for private ownership, Solzhenitsyn insists that it "must be introduced cautiously" (p. 32). With "nothing left of our eradicated peasantry," land for sale might be grabbed up by "the anonymous speculators of our 'shadow economy' " or by foreigners (pp. 32–33). Or " 'joint-stock companies,' 'organizations,' and 'cooperatives' could well buy up huge tracts of land in order to lease them out on their own. Such purchases must clearly be prohibited." Soviet citizens have had enough of gargantuanism. Solzhenitsyn is on the side of the little people. Given the deformed economy in the imminent period of transition, Russia must be careful to avoid making irreversible mistakes concerning land ownership. One other complication, albeit mentioned only in a parenthesis, is "the imminent overpopulation of our planet, and obviously of our country as well" (p. 33). Here he touches upon a theme of the Club of Rome which in *Letter* he passed over.

Solzhenitsyn concludes this chapter with some details regarding land ownership. Multi-year repayment and preferential tax treatment can enhance personal purchasing power. In a given area, size of lot may be appropriately limited. "The fact that tiny private plots have fed the country under the vaunted collective farm system demonstrates that our people can work miracles along these lines. . ." (p. 33). Small plots for growing vegetables can be distributed for free to workers, including "city dwellers who seek relief from their cooped-up existence," with farmers receiving an extra portion of equal size at no extra cost. "There should be enough land for everybody" (p. 34).

CHAPTER NINE IS on "The Economy" in general. Its central burden is to advocate a market economy, starting with private property. Solzhenitsyn readily acknowledges, "I have no special expertise in economics, and I have no wish to venture definite proposals here" (p. 35). Details will have to be worked out by professional economists ("who," he notes wryly, "admittedly, disagree strongly among themselves") (p. 36). Indeed, he writes much less about economics than about politics. But he is sure that he has more to offer than "the clamorous perestroika," which in six years "has yet to have any healing effect on either agriculture or industry" and which is "a delay that represents years in the people's life given up to pointless suffering" (p. 35). Whereas Gorbachev harks back to Lenin and his New Economic Policy for inspiration, Solzhenitsyn here invokes Stolypin, his hero in *August 1914*. Solzhenitsyn sees an independent citizenry as the key to a healthy economy, and he accords a priority to economics over politics: ". . . social structure precedes any political program and is a more fundamental entity." He adds immediately, "But there can be no independent citizen without private property" (p. 34).

Solzhenitsyn's commitment to private property and free enterprise took some readers of *Rebuilding Russia* by surprise. It is, however, a long-held position of his. In "Repentance and Self-Limitation in the Life of Nations," he said, "The fundamental concepts of private property and private economic initiative are part of man's nature, and necessary for his personal freedom and his sense of normal well-being." That is to say, a free-market economy is not just one option among others which societies are free to choose or to reject according to taste. It is, rather, the economic system which comports with the nature of free human beings who inhabit the moral universe. At the same time,

Solzhenitsyn is well aware that this inherently virtuous economic system can, by an ideological manipulation which would carry it to extremes, turn vicious. In the same "Repentance" essay, he immediately adds that the aforementioned fundamental concepts

> would be beneficial to society *if only* . . . if only the carriers of these ideas on the very threshold of development had *limited themselves*, and not allowed the size of their property and thrust of their avarice to become a social evil, which provoked so much justifiable anger, not tried to purchase power and subjugate the press. It was as a reply to the shamelessness of unlimited money-grubbing that socialism in all its forms developed.[5]

In the result, the practice of free-market economics is as mixed as human nature itself, and "the defects of capitalism represent the basic flaws of human nature."[6]

A sense of balance and moderation permeates this chapter, as later it does the chapters propounding democracy. Solzhenitsyn's first task here is to persuade his Sovietized fellows of the falsity of the propaganda that "one must fear private property and avoid hired labor as though they were the work of the devil: that represents a major victory of ideology over our human essence." Pointedly, this resident of the United States explains, "Our entire view of Western economy has been likewise inculcated in a form that is a caricature of reality" (p. 34). Western workers do not comprise an exploited class. Not only need private property not be feared, but "[t]he truth is that ownership of modest amounts of property which does not oppress others must be seen as an integral component of personality, and as a factor contributing to its stability" (pp. 34–35). Similarly (as is often, though not always, true in the West, he implies), "conscientiously performed, fairly compensated hired labor is a form of mutual assistance and a source of goodwill among people" (p. 35).

The difficulty of getting from the present "ideologically regulated economic system," with its "parasitic bureaucracy," to a system of free enterprise must not be underestimated. Anticipating the dislocations to come, Solzhenitsyn advises that "we must take every measure to soften the blow that will be dealt to millions of unprepared and unadapted people by the transition to a market economy." This is the concept of a safety net, in today's familiar American rhetoric. Funding for this purpose will come from the "billions upon billions that are being squandered in ways enumerated earlier" (p. 35).

Although Solzhenitsyn is here focusing on the need for a safety net during the economic transition period, an interesting passage in *Cancer Ward* suggests that social welfare will always be part of the government's budget. Dr. Oreshchenkov, a favorite of the author, advocates private health care because it improves quality. Patients should pay for their "primary treatment." So-called free health care will result in "depersonalized treatment," in which doctor and patient do not know each other. However, "After a patient has been directed to enter hospital or undergo treatment that involves complicated apparatus, then it's only fair it should be free."[7]

In "the overall picture," Solzhenitsyn's commitment to a market economy is emphatic and unequivocal: "healthy private initiative must be given wide latitude." Most especially, "small enterprises of every type must be encouraged and protected, since they are what will ensure the most rapid flowering of every locality." At the same time, many large issues must be resolved, and there are limits to every good thing. For example, it remains an open question how many and which assets of the state should be privatized. It is clearer to Solzhenitsyn that there must be "firm legal limits to the unchecked concentration of capital" and that monopolies must be disallowed. Just one of their faults is that they contain no brake on planned obsolescence (p. 36). (It is difficult to mount a moral defense of planned obsolescence. Among the details in this pamphlet surprising by their minuteness, and for some their seeming quaintness, is the effort to resuscitate "the healthy notion of *repair*.") The "psychological plague of inflation" must be avoided. Antitrust laws and progressive taxation will mitigate against "[e]xcessive growth in any sector of the economy." Banks are necessary, of course; "but they must not be permitted to become usurious growths and the hidden masters of all life" (p. 37).

Solzhenitsyn is particularly wary of "foreign capitalists," and there is little here to give comfort to multi-national corporations. He considers it "a dangerous idea to attempt to salvage by means of foreign capital what has been destroyed by our internal disarray" (p. 37). Short-term benefit should not be pursued at the long-term cost of becoming an economic colony. Therefore, "Western capital must not be lured in on terms that are advantageous to it but humiliating to us, in come-and-rule-over-us style." On the other hand, he would not forbid foreign investment. It is to be permitted—but "on the strict condition that the economic stimulation it introduces will be exceeded neither by the profits exported nor by the damage to the natural environment." Such conditions are likely to spur Russian industry to become competitive in the world marketplace (p. 38).

This chapter closes on the note of hope. There is the Japanese model of a people who recovered from disaster. With the removal of state control and the achieving of fair wages, "the quality of work will improve at once, and skilled craftsmen will come to light everywhere" (p. 38). Russians must unlearn old lessons and learn new ones. One of these latter is to "learn to respect healthy, honest, and intelligent private commerce," for "such commerce stimulates and unifies society, and it is one of the very first things we need" (p. 39).

THE TENTH CHAPTER IS entitled "The Provinces." Here we see in operation Solzhenitsyn's dedication to the principle of decentralization. In fact, Solzhenitsyn goes so far as to say, "The key to the viability of the country and the vitality of its cultures lies in liberating the provinces from the pressure of the capitals" (p. 39), though these "unhealthy" and "overburdened" giants need normalcy, too. Rather than locating great power in the four capitals—Moscow, Petrograd, Kiev, and Minsk—Solzhenitsyn urges the emergence of "perhaps forty centers of vitality and illumination," loci of economic activity, culture, education, library resources, and publishing enterprises. Thus, for example, education of roughly equal quality will be available throughout the country. The dispersion of power will enhance the diversity of the nation by giving free play to "unique local features" (p. 40). It will also speed up the process of rebuilding Russia, since people will be able to see right around them the fruits of their labors. In short, "the road back to health must begin at the grass roots" (p. 41). Let localism prevail.

THE ELEVENTH CHAPTER IS entitled "Family and School." Solzhenitsyn views the family as the basic building block of society, and his devotion to the traditional—his word is *normal*—family is manifest. Of all of society's mediating structures—that is, structures mediating between individuals and the nation as a whole—the family, by virtue of being closest to the individual, is the most important one. And the school is the next most important one. These are the two agencies directly affecting how children are reared and what kinds of adults they will turn out to be. Solzhenitsyn's concern in this chapter is for the fabric of daily life, and his goal is to improve its texture.

Of all of the social ills deforming normal family life, the first one Solzhenitsyn singles out for attention is the "disastrous plight of women." It is, he says, "common knowledge and a regular topic of conversation that evokes no arguments, since everything is clear" (p. 41). It is an issue about which the West should already be reasonably well informed—as, for instance, through the chapter "Women: Liberated but Not Emancipated" in Hedrick Smith's popular book *The Russians*.[8] A recent, and compelling, presentation is Francine du Plessix Gray's *Soviet Women*.[9] Because "the family has a fundamental role in the salvation of our future," Solzhenitsyn would like for mothers to have the option of staying at home to rear the children, an option which by implication he clearly hopes many of them will exercise. To do so will be possible, of course, only when men are paid salaries adequate to support the family. And, given the expected high unemployment rate during the period of transition to a market economy, "some families will be glad that at least the woman will have kept her job" (p. 42). Solzhenitsyn's traditionalist attitude toward the family is part and parcel of his general traditionalism, and it is also another instance of his passionate opposition to centralism.

The schools, too, need immediate and sustained attention. Solzhenitsyn judges Soviet education an abysmal failure, and the more so the farther from the capitals. His desire is that educational revitalization begin at the lowest grades. Humanities curricula and textbooks are especially in need of "fundamental revision if not outright rejection." And he takes the time to say, lest others ignore it, that "the drumming-in of atheism must be stopped immediately" (p. 43).

As a former schoolteacher himself, Solzhenitsyn zeroes in on the treatment of teachers. They need lighter teaching loads and better pay, especially so as to attract and retain male teachers. But specific reforms such as these would be merely aspects of raising the general level of respect due teachers: ". . . schoolteachers are supposed to be the cream of the nation, they are people with a calling, to whom we entrust our future." Therefore, their needs must be addressed even before those of the pupils are. And their first need is for good training. "All changes and all efforts to salvage true knowledge must begin with revamping the curricula at the teachers' colleges" (p. 43). In attending first to these institutions of higher learning, rather than to prestigious universities, Solzhenitsyn shows both his pragmatism and his anti-elitism.

Years ago, Solzhenitsyn declared, "*The school*—that is the key to the future of Russia!" Its problems, he added, "cannot be solved in one generation." The task is huge, and it will demand great resources. "The whole public educational system must be created anew, and not with rejects but with the people's best forces. It will cost billions—and we should take them from our vainglorious and unnecessary foreign expenditures."[10] As he has thought about this problem over the years, he has arrived at the conclusion that tuition-charging private schools would be part of the solution. Their curricula should, however, be supervised by the local educational authorities (pp. 43–44).

Dysfunctional families and ineffectual schools leave a vacuum in the rearing of young people which is more and more being filled by popular culture, particularly the high-prestige imports from the West. Is Solzhenitsyn about to show himself anti-Western, as some critics claim that he is? Not at all, as the context makes clear. He introduces his lament about the importation of the tawdriest aspects of Western culture with this sardonic sentence:

> The Iron Curtain of yesterday gave our country superb protection against all the positive features of the West: against the West's civil liberties, its respect for the individual, its freedom of personal activity, its high level of general welfare, it spontaneous charitable movements.

In all these aspects Solzhenitsyn would happily see Russia follow the Western model. For Russia to find its own path of national development never means, for Solzhenitsyn, to reject out of hand everything Western in origin. On balance, *Rebuilding Russia* has many more kind than unkind words about the West. Not the West itself but Western decadence can and should be resisted. He continues, "But the Iron Curtain did not reach all the way to the bottom, permitting the continuous seepage of liquid manure. . . . And today's television obligingly distributes these streams of filth throughout the land" (p. 44). Though he expects some to consider his objections "a sign of hopeless conservatism," he cites approvingly similar alarms being sounded in Israel: "The Hebrew cultural revolution did not take place in order to make our country capitulate to American cultural imperialism and its byproducts . . . Western intellectual trash" (pp. 44–45).

The knee-jerk Western response is that one must take the bitter with the sweet—such is the nature of a free society. And the received Western opinion of Solzhenitsyn might anticipate that a proposal for censorship would be forthcoming. There is nothing of the sort. Rather, albeit only by implication (including the placement of this topic in this chapter), Solzhenitsyn sees the family and the school as the agents best positioned to resist the noxious sludge of decadent pop culture. The government can play a positive role in culture by providing subsistence funding for libraries, reading rooms, and museums (not for sports, though, "even in the hope of gaining world fame") (p. 45). Soviet citizens have had more than their fair share of experience with government as the self-appointed agent for the moral guidance of the youth.

CHAPTER TWELVE GETS AROUND to politics—finally, some might say. The chapter title is telling: "Is the System of Government Really the Central Issue?" Answer: no. Not at the start of the process of rebuilding the nation. Solzhenitsyn is well aware, from the "passionate discussions about the kind of government system that would suit us," that many consider this "the key to everything" (pp. 45–46). That is what "our luckless fathers and grandfathers" thought in February 1917. Solzhenitsyn, who has spent many years studying the nineteen-teens, is not among those excited by the obvious parallels between that time and this. There will soon be "[a] decisive change in regime," yes. But it "calls for thoughtfulness and a sense of reponsibility." As he cautions, "There is no guarantee whatever that the new leaders now coming to the fore will immediately prove to be far-sighted and sober-minded" (p. 46).

The "cannibalistic period" of Soviet rule has acclimated Russians to strong central authority. There is now a danger of overreaction, and "it behooves us not to make rash moves toward chaos. For, as 1917 has taught us, anarchy is the ultimate peril." This gradualist declares, "Unless one craves revolution, a state must possess the qualities of continuity and stability." Therefore, he approves of the statute, instated at Gorbachev's initiative, creating a potentially strong presidency, which "will prove useful for many years to come" (p. 47). This is not a decentralizer's ideal. It is a pragmatic compromise with reality, roughly analogous to the allowance in *Letter* that those leaders could hold authoritarian power during a stage of transition out of ideologically driven totalitarianism. Only, of course, now the situation is advanced to the point where the strong president will not be a Communist, and the power will be somewhat less than that suggested by the term *authoritarian*. Still, "Some elements of the current structure will have to serve for the time being, for the simple reason that they already exist" (p. 48).

"For the time being" is the key phrase. "It goes without saying that we shall gradually reshape the entire state organism." Moreover, this "process should start at the local level with grass-roots issues." A strong central authority can serve as an umbrella under which we "patiently and persistently expand the rights of local communities." Reshaping political institutions will be gradual; it will also be from the bottom up, not from the top down. Besides, first things first. There are other, more pressing, needs; and "it is simply not feasible for us to attempt to resolve issues of government structure at the same time as we address problems relating to land, food, housing, private property, finances, and the army" (p. 48). That is how devastated Russia is.

"With time, we shall of course adopt some particular type of political structure. . . ." But wise choices demand a leisure not at the moment available, and "in view of our total inexperience in such matters, our choice may not be a felicitous one at first" (p. 48). Solzhenitsyn has often said, and repeats here, that "the structure of the state is secondary to the spirit of human relations" (p. 49). Unless and until the people have internalized a democratic culture, the top-down imposition of democratic forms would be an ineffectual mechanical crudity. However, it is of overriding importance to recognize that he takes with utmost seriousness the issue of establishing political institutions serviceable for the long haul. In no way does he treat this issue dismissively or cavalierly. Indeed, the second half of this essay is devoted almost entirely to grappling with it. That is how important he considers it.

Whatever structures are finally established, "We must resolutely seek our own path here." Solzhenitsyn counters those who think that, without "any quest or reflection on our part," the new Russia can simply and quickly import "the way it is done in the West." For starters, "in the West it is done in, oh, so many different ways, with every country following its own tradition" (p. 48). Russia should, imitating Western countries this far, proceed accordingly; it should look to its own traditions for guidance.

IN THE FINAL TWO CHAPTERS of the first half of *Rebuilding Russia*— "Taking Our Own Measure" (Chapter Thirteen) and "Self-Limitation" (Chapter Fourteen)—Solzhenitsyn reverts to general themes of his overall moral vision and applies them to current public life. These two chapters thus provide a closing framework within which to understand the more particularized issues treated in the pamphlet's first half. What, in the final analysis, determines the strength or weakness of a society? "The purity of social relations," "the level of its spiritual life," "a nation's spiritual energies"—such intangibles count for more than any achievements in industry, economics, politics (pp. 49-50). In Solzhenitsyn's image, "a tree with a rotten core cannot stand." Apart from morality, "the freedom to be unscrupulous" is the freedom that will prevail. "And that is why the destruction of our souls over three-quarters of a century is the most terrifying thing of all" (p. 50).

The cause of social purification would be greatly boosted if "the corrupt ruling class—the multimillion-strong appointed bureaucracy [*nomenklatura*]" would repent. Germany put its villainous officials on trial in courts of law, but Russia will probably not subject its "state criminals" to even "a public moral trial" (pp. 50–51). Nor have the "glorious forces of glasnost and perestroika" improved the moral climate. "Of every four troubadours of today's glasnost, three are former toadies of Brezhnevism, and who among them has uttered a word of *personal* repentance instead of cursing the faceless 'period of stagnation'?" The "smatterers," also, with their "hypocrisy and weather-vane mentality: should we not expect repentance from any of them, and must we really drag along these festering moral sores into our future?" (p. 51). In such a fetid moral atmosphere, it is no wonder that we see a "pervasive animosity of our people toward one another" and also an "upsurge of criminal behavior among those whose access to all honest paths of development has been blocked throughout their young lives." In West Germany repentance preceded the economic boom. "But in our country no one has even begun to repent." The "same old plump and heavy clusters of lies" prevail under glasnost. It is all "a recipe for warped development" (p. 52).

When one looks to the church for moral leadership—Solzhenitsyn says, in terms reminiscent of his open letter to Patriarch Pimen—one finds that, "alas, even today, when everything in the country has begun to move, the stirrings of courage have had little impact on the Orthodox hierarchy" (pp. 52–53). Only "at the most humble levels, with the activity of rank-and-file clergymen," do we see the church breaking free of its subservience to the state and restoring "a living bond with the people" (p. 53). Then again, this is a microcosm of the bottom-up, grass-roots movement of revitalization which Solzhenitsyn advocates in all spheres of life. Solzhenitsyn spends only a page discussing the church. Father Gleb Yakunin wished for more, even for the naming of delinquent Orthodox hierarchs.[11]

THE MAIN THEME OF Chapter Thirteen is repentance; the main theme of Chapter Fourteen is self-limitation. The chapters are, taken together, an updating of the themes of "Repentance and Self-Limitation in the Life of Nations." The last chapter of the essay's first half juxtaposes self-limitation to what is "currently the most fashionable and most eagerly repeated slogan among us": namely, "human rights" (p. 53). Solzhenitsyn is obviously not opposed to human rights; they are, he says without irony, "a fine thing." But the educated people of the capital cities, who talk so much about them, have a jaundiced and self-serving—one might even say, provincial—view of them. They think in terms of the standard freedoms of speech, press, public assembly, emigration. But what about human rights "as they are seen by the ordinary people: the right to live and work in the same place where there is something to buy" (p. 54)— that is, for now, in the capitals? Capital-dwellers tend to ignore the elementary human rights of those who reside elsewhere.

In the good society there will be a balance between rights and duties, not a quest after "unlimited rights." All citizens must "make sure that our rights do not expand at the expense of the rights of others," and "each of us must rein himself in." Self-limitation means living "by the principle that we are always duty-bound to defer to the sense of moral justice" (p. 54). The population explosion makes "voluntary self-limitation" all the more urgent. "Our duty must always exceed the freedom we have been granted." Living by this principle is more than a utilitarian gesture. Even an animal possesses "the freedom to seize and gorge oneself." It is precisely self-limitation which allows the human being to rise above the bestial level and to find "a sense of balance and tranquillity in his soul" (p. 55).

Achieving inner harmony will not be easy. The constant bombardment from the omnipresent media may do as much harm as good. It is natural enough that, "after our long period of enforced ignorance, . . . we avidly want to learn the truth about what happened to us" (p. 55). But there can be an information overload. Thus, this question arises: "How can we protect the *right* of our ears to silence, and the right of our eyes to inner vision?" Russia needs "to find a steady way out of its era of misfortunes," and this task will be "harder than shaking off the Tartar Yoke: the very backbone of the nation was not shattered at that time, and the people's Christian faith was not undermined." The whole of Part One of *Rebuilding Russia* turns out, in Solzhenitsyn's concluding words—and here he borrows from the title of an eighteenth-century work—to be *A Plan for Saving the People*. Is this eccentric? he asks. He answers that it "reflects the essence of state wisdom" (p. 56).

12

"Rebuilding Russia" (III)
Looking Ahead

PART TWO OF *REBUILDING RUSSIA*, as its title, "Looking Ahead," indicates, takes the long view. After Russia has weathered the turbulent transition from enslavement to freedom, problems will remain. And the main one, in Solzhenitsyn's mind, one so important that it is best left until after "our current 'time of troubles,' "[1] is political restructuring. What sort of government should the new Russia have? It is a crucial question, one to which the right answer must be found, down to fine details. The second half of the essay is given over to Solzhenitsyn's answer to this question.

Although Russia should not rush to final judgment on this matter, Solzhenitsyn explains in the two prefatory paragraphs why he is presenting his position now. For one thing, "considerations of age" may prevent him from participating in the later discussions. Also, to avoid the error of setting out irretrievably on a wrong path early, "it behooves us to give advance thought to the shape of our future arrangement" (p. 59). One useful contribution that Solzhenitsyn sees himself in a position to make is "to focus on the precise meaning of some terms" (p. 60). Of these the most important one is *democracy*. Solzhenitsyn will argue in favor of it consistently and at length. But there is democracy and there is democracy. Even the Soviets claimed this word for their totalitarianism.

302

The term is very elastic, and many conflicting proposals can pass under its colors. When Russia embraces democracy, it should be clear what it understands the term to mean for itself. The most impressive thing about the second half of *Rebuilding Russia* is simply how long and hard Solzhenitsyn has thought about democracy.

As in Part One, so in Part Two there are fourteen chapters. The first, entitled "Concerning the Forms of Government," opens with references to Spengler, Montesquieu, and Jeremiah; and it is quite striking how often Solzhenitsyn cites Western sources, particularly traditional ones, in his discussion of democracy. He agrees with Spengler that "there is no definitive 'best' form of government which needs to be borrowed from one great culture for use in another." He agrees with Montesquieu that "there exists a particular form of government appropriate to every physical size of state" (p. 60). The people's first need from government is "to have a stable order." However, about Christian socialist George Fedotov's call for a strong executive answerable to the legislature only at considerable intervals, Solzhenitsyn says, "That seems pretty extreme" (p. 61). There will be nothing extreme in Solzhenitsyn's proposals.

The key to the "plan" that Solzhenitsyn is about to set forth is "building the institutions of freedom from the bottom up while temporarily preserving the existing formal features of the central authority." This process will take years, during which "there will be time for substantial discussion of sound principles of state-building." Any proposals presented today, including his own, can be in the nature of "only temporary pronouncements." The final result, if such a thing can ever be arrived at, "will be the product of successive approximations and trials" (p. 61). From the start, and throughout, Solzhenitsyn's stance is one of modesty.

Plato and Aristotle listed three types of states: monarchy, aristocracy, and polity ("we now term this democracy"). They also noted the perversions to which each was particularly susceptible: "respectively, tyranny, oligarchy, and mob rule." It is definitely not Solzhenitsyn's view that one of these types is inherently good and the others inherently bad. "Each of the three basic forms of rule can be beneficial if directed toward the public good, and all three become perverted when they serve private interests." At the outset Solzhenitsyn makes his choice known: "the whole flow of modern history will unquestionably predispose us to choose democracy" (p. 62). It is important to understand that Solzhenitsyn's argument is historical, not theoretical. But is there then an implication that in the abstract Solzhenitsyn would prefer one of the other two basic forms? Not at all. To ask of Solzhenitsyn what he would prefer in the abstract is to ask the wrong question, for human beings and human society never operate in the abstract.

Why, then, does Solzhenitsyn not choose monarchy? It has, after all, a long tradition in Russian history, and monarchist sentiment is indubitably on rise in Russia (and elsewhere in Eastern Europe) today.[2] So his rejecting monarchy is not a mere filling out of a taxonomy. He never explicitly explains this rejection. But his mention of the flow of modern history suggests that he views monarchy as belonging to the past. If so, this is an illustration of his reiterated point that only a fool could wish to return to the past. It would be possible, of course, to argue for a constitutional monarchy with a democratic government and a royal figurehead, as Richard Brookhiser in all earnestness proposed for the new Russia.[3] Solzhenitsyn does not choose this option, either.

As for aristocracy, or "the rule of the best or for the best purpose" (p. 62), this is the type of governance which comports best with the term *authoritarianism*. Against the grain of all the attributions by his critics, Solzhenitsyn does not propose this form, either. Again, he does not specify why not.

At the same time, his embrace of democracy is not that of an enthusiast. He does not number himself among those who indulge in "an elevation of democracy from a particular state structure into a sort of universal principle of human existence, almost a cult" (p. 63). Rather, he chooses democracy "as a means, not as an end in itself" (pp. 62–63). He agrees with contemporary philosopher Karl Popper that "one chooses democracy, not because it abounds in virtues, but only in order to avoid tyranny. We choose it in full awareness of its faults and with the intention of seeking ways to overcome them" (p. 63).

HE WILL TRY to "clarify the meaning of this term" in Chapter Two, "What Democracy Is and What It Is Not." This is the first of six consecutive chapters in which Solzhenitsyn describes the difficulties and limitations inherent in democracy. These are in the nature of concessions, and he follows the sound rhetorical principle of getting the concessions out of the way before presenting the thesis. In the eighth chapter, or the first chapter of the second half of Part Two, he will then proceed to his thesis that, despite all these qualifications, Russia will nevertheless need democracy.

In the mere two pages that make up the second chapter, Solzhenitsyn cites eight authorities, five Western and three Russian. First, he cites Tocqueville to indicate that liberty and democracy are not coterminous. Indeed, Tocqueville, who favored liberty ardently but democracy not at all, goes far beyond Solzhenitsyn by casting liberty and democracy as "polar opposites." John Stuart Mill is cited to warn against "the tyranny of the majority" in an "unlimited democracy" (p. 63). George Fedotov saw atheistic materialism as distorting democracy. Austrian Joseph Schumpeter "referred to democracy as the surrogate faith of intellectuals deprived of religion, cautioning against any view of democracy outside the context of time and place." Sergei Levitsky distinguished between "the *essence* of democracy," individual freedom and a government of laws, and "its secondary, non-mandatory features," the parliamentary system and universal suffrage. Here Solzhenitsyn pauses to observe, "Respect for the individual represents a broader principle than democracy. . . ." Whatever form of democracy becomes established, it must ensure this principle "without fail" (p. 64).

Always, balance is needed. Even this principle of individual rights "must not be exalted to the point of eclipsing the rights of society." Solzhenitsyn cites approvingly Pope John Paul II's granting of priority to national security, "because without the integrity of the larger structure the life of individuals will crumble as well" (p. 64). Also eliciting Solzhenitsyn's approval is President Ronald Reagan's observation at Moscow University in 1988 that "[d]emocracy is less a system of government than a means of *limiting* government, preventing it from interfering in the development of the true sources of human values that are found only in family and faith" (pp. 64–65). Democracy is "a supremely fashionable word" for Russians today, even though they may not have grappled with exactly what it is and is not. In this chapter Solzhenitsyn is preparing his Russian readers for his leading them through a consideration of elements generally considered to be democracy's component parts. In order to approach the subject responsibly, they should keep in mind the remark by Vasili Maklakov, uttered after "the bitter experience" of 1917: "In order to function, democracy needs a certain level of political discipline among the populace" (p. 65).

CHAPTER THREE IS entitled "Universal and Equal Suffrage, Direct Elections, Secret Ballots." It is a profound irony that these elements of democracy, constituting "the pattern that the contemporary world looks upon almost as if it were an indisputable law of nature," were introduced to modern Russians by Stalin! (p. 65). France did not introduce universal and equal suffrage until more than a half century after its great revolution. England did not get around to it until after 1918. Dostoevsky opposed it. Solzhenitsyn comments, "At any rate, it is not Newton's Law, and it is permissible to have doubts about its alleged merits." Raising doubts about universal and equal suffrage, not rejecting it outright, is Solzhenitsyn's main burden here. If Russia is to adopt it, let it do so thoughtfully—aware, for instance, that this form of suffrage "represents the triumph of bare quantity over substance and quality" and that the assumption underlying it is that the nation "is not a living organism but a mere mechanical conglomeration of disparate individuals" (pp. 66–67). Is there not, perhaps, a better way?

"Nor does secret voting represent something to be admired in and of itself. It facilitates insincerity or is an unfortunate necessity born of fear" (p. 67). Readers scandalized by this questioning of what for many must by now seem a cherished right in a democracy would do well to recall that it is not a right guaranteed in the United States Constitution. As Senator Moynihan intimated in his review of *Rebuilding Russia*, the secret ballot was imported from Australia, and it was adopted by most states only around 1890, after a full century of democratic experience in America. That it entered because of electoral abuses is, of course, something that Solzhenitsyn might do well to keep in mind. At any rate, he is quite brief about this subject.

Solzhenitsyn is less brief about the subject of direct elections. He is thinking here about national elections primarily, and he is definitely uneasy with an electoral system that "results in voters not knowing their deputies." Such a situation, instead of enhancing the prospects of determining the popular will, "benefits the smoothest talkers as well as individuals with strong behind-the-scenes support." He would like to find a way of "depriving the [political] parties of the ability to impose their own candidates from the center" (p. 67). He will return to this subject when he presents his own electoral program.

CHAPTER FOUR IS about "Electoral Procedures." Solzhenitsyn lists three competing systems: proportional representation, plurality voting, and voting requiring an absolute majority. All three have their flaws (which he details in three pages of smaller-than-normal print). Though the "aim of universal suffrage is to permit the Popular Will to be manifested," one must wonder if such a thing even exists. For "it is remarkable that different systems of counting votes will produce different or even diametrically opposed readings of this Popular Will" (p. 68). This is an awkward subject for all democrats, but Solzhenitsyn does not dodge it.

Descending into the small print, Solzhenitsyn spends two-thirds of it trying to demolish the case for proportional representation. Its primary vice is that it gives inordinate power to political parties. Voters choose among slates of candidates drawn up by the parties. Seats are allocated on a proportional basis to parties, not individuals. It is no wonder to Solzhenitsyn that all the political parties of 1917, Lenin and his Bolsheviks included, favored this system of voting. Among this system's drawbacks are that it "leads to a multiplicity of parliamentary factions and a dissipation of energy on petty squabbles" and that it "can tempt parties to improve their status by forming coalitions that cynically disregard their platforms for the sake of gaining votes and taking control of the government" (p. 70).

A year after this pamphlet was published, Poland gave a clear demonstration to other post-Communist countries of the perils of proportional representation. With sixty-nine parties competing, twenty-eight won seats in the 460-seat Sejm (the lower house of the parliament). No party received as much as fourteen percent of the vote. With no party gaining more than sixty-two seats, it took a coalition of several parties to form a government. The Friends of Beer Party won eighteen seats.

The plurality voting system is also a flawed vessel for carrying the Popular Will. In this model the "unnatural compromises" between parties comes in pre-election alliances. In close votes the party or bloc slightly ahead wins an inordinate number of seats, and it is possible to win forty-nine percent of the votes but no seats in parliament. It is even possible (as has happened three times in France, Solzhenitsyn notes) that, with an uneven distribution of electoral districts, winners can gain fewer total votes than losers. "On the other hand," he adds, "this system provides for a stable government" (p. 71).

The absolute majority electoral system, "which is being introduced in our country (and which permits run-off elections)," also militates against smaller parties but allows bargaining for votes between rounds of voting. The two-party system of the United States is hard on independent candidates because of the powerful organization and financial leverage of the major parties. In this system it is difficult for social dissatisfaction to find an outlet. When it does, it takes the negative form of "ejecting the party in power . . . , even when there is no certainty about the plans of those who will replace it" (p. 71).

However one looks at it, voting is problematical, and the more so the larger the populace. Certainly, it "does not represent a quest for truth," and anyway the majority is not always right. (Here Solzhenitsyn cites Exodus 23:2.) Nationwide campaigns can become "so frivolous and shrill that, given the frequent bias of the media, a large proportion of the voters can turn away in disgust." Television can display a candidate's "appearance" and "public demeanor" but not "his abilities as a statesman." Such campaigns "invariably entail the degradation of political thought" (p. 72). One can understand why "Tocqueville concluded that democracy denotes the reign of mediocrity" (though Solzhenitsyn, never actually adopting Tocqueville's position, notes that extraordinary circumstances can bring forth strong personalities) (p. 73).

Whatever one may conclude about the program which Solzhenitsyn will present, it is impossible to deny the cogency of his criticisms. Indeed, there is not a single one with which inhabitants of democracies are not already familiar and which they do not voice themselves. It is one thing to be already located in a given democratic system. It is easier then to rationalize its vices and to find them a bearable burden to endure for the sake of the greater virtues that the system offers. It is another thing to be standing at the dawn of a new day in the history of one's nation. The intelligent thing to do in that case is to learn as much as one can about the deficiencies and limitations of others' systems and to devise a new system, suitable to one's nation, which avoids as many of them as humanly possible.

CHAPTER FIVE IS on "Representing the People." The goal of a democracy is to elect legislators who function in a way truly representative of the people. At one extreme, Athenian democracy, by virtue of its small size, could reject, "as a form of oligarchy," the indirection of representation. At the other extreme, the French Estates-General subsumed deputies into the collective body which ostensibly manifested the will of the people, thus cutting them off from their voters. A truly representative democracy must find a middle way between these two extremes. This the four State Dumas, or representative assemblies, of pre-revolutionary Russia failed to do, since they "represented only certain narrow strata in a few cities" (p. 73).

Solzhenitsyn identifies several factors that work to thwart the project of expressing the popular will through elected deputies. An obvious one is that deputies have no sufficient stimulus "to rise above their *future* electoral interests and above party machinations." Instead, they have strong motivation to take actions "having immediate appeal to the voters, even though the long view might suggest that these actions will bring them harm" (p. 74). In a parliamentary system (such as Great Britain's), the legislature too readily becomes subordinate to the executive. Moreover, "the special demands of an election campaign require human qualities that have nothing in common with the qualities essential for leadership of a state" (p. 75). Then, there is the odd phenomenon that modern democracies produce a class of "professional politicians" who make "a lifelong career" of representation, "and there is little point in speaking about 'the will of the people' in this context" (pp. 75–76). Furthermore, one is struck by "the preponderance of jurists and lawyers in most parliaments; one might designate it a 'jurocracy' " (p. 76).

CHAPTER SIX IS entitled "How It Can Turn Out," and it argues that democracy can turn out badly. For one thing, contemporary democracies have proven not immune from producing "ponderous bureaucracies." For another, often the vote designed to locate the popular will turns out to be very light, thus "making the whole exercise rather meaningless" (p. 76). When achieving electoral victory requires bringing into coalition "a tiny and insignificant party," that small group "will then in effect decide the fate of the country or its general course." Also, modern democracy has proven "adept at deflecting popular protest and depriving it of any powerful outlet" (p. 77). Additional problems are "the aristocracy of money" and (under the Soviets) the development of a "shadow economy" (p. 78). In short, "Democracy, like other systems, is not immune to injustice, and dishonest individuals know how to evade responsibility." Even in Switzerland, the world's oldest functioning democracy and one which Solzhenitsyn unabashedly admires, citizens worry that, through the influence of pressure groups, decisions are being made "behind the scenes" and "without public scrutiny" (p. 77).

The chapter ends on a familiar moral note.

> European democracy was originally imbued with a sense of Christian responsibility and self-discipline, but these spiritual principles have been gradually losing their force. Spiritual independence is being pressured on all side by the dictatorship of self-satisfied vulgarity, of the latest fads, and of group interests. (pp. 78–79)

Solzhenitsyn has made this point elsewhere. Here it serves as a harbinger of things to come in his positive program. But he knows from what precincts to expect resistance: "It is also depressing to note that the intellectual pseudo-elite . . . ridicules the absolute nature of the concepts of good and evil, masking its indifference toward them by appeal to the 'pluralism' of ideas and actions" (p. 78). Although Russia must press forward to democracy, the last line of the chapter concedes, "We embark on democracy at a time when it is not at its healthiest" (p. 79).

Chapter Seven is entitled "Political Parties." Although today we have "become incapable of imagining political life without parties," it is just that act of imagination to which Solzhenitsyn beckons us in this chapter. "The word 'party' implies *part*." So it is worth asking "whom a party opposes" (p. 79). And the answer "must evidently be all the rest of the people" (pp. 79–80). By their nature, party goals, pre-eminently re-election, eclipse the national interest. Nor do party goals necessarily jibe with voters' interests. And it is risible to think that competition between parties is "even remotely concerned with the search for truth." "Party rivalry distorts the national will" and "necessarily involves the suppression of individuality": "An individual will have views, while a party offers an ideology" (p. 80). Therefore, Solzhenitsyn counsels, "No fundamental decisions affecting the state should be sought out along party paths, or handed over to the parties for resolution" (p. 81).

This is not to say that political parties are to be banned. Like any associations and unions, they "can exist freely, propounding any views and issuing publications at their own expense." However, they must be registered; secret organizations are to be disallowed. Also, they may not interfere in the workplace, the service sector, or the schools. (Here Solzhenitsyn is obviously thinking of the *modus operandi* of the old Communist Party.) They are permitted to nominate and campaign for candidates, "but without drawing up party tickets: the vote must be for specific individuals, not parties" (p. 81). To put teeth into his non-party plan, Solzhenitsyn would require that anyone elected "suspend any party membership for the duration of his term in office, assuming personal responsibility for his acts before his constituents" (pp. 81–82). There would be no such thing as a "ruling party" (p. 82).

For many readers this non-party plan may sound so out of keeping with how modern democracies actually operate as to seem unrealistic and impracticable. How did Solzhenitsyn ever dream up such a scheme? To persons knowledgeable about the founding of the American republic, however, it will have the ring of the familiar. The initial democratic design of the United States did not call for the vehicle of political parties. Some of the most illustrious Founding Fathers abhorred the prospect that parties might develop. In 1787, as the Constitution of the United States was being crafted, James Madison in *The Federalist* cautioned explicitly against "the violence of faction." He defined faction as "a number of citizens, whether amounting to a majority or minority of the whole, who are united and actuated by some common impulse of passion, or of interest, adverse to the rights of other citizens, or to the permanent and aggregate interests of the community."[4] Solzhenitsyn's view is so close to Madison's here that one cannot rule out direct indebtedness. The most famous warning against the establishment of political parties came from George Washington in his revered "Farewell Address" of 1796. With great emphasis Washington declared, "Let me now . . . warn you in the most solemn manner against the baneful effects of the Spirit of Party, generally." In his not inconsiderable elaboration of the point, he stated, "The alternate domination of one faction over another, . . . which in different ages and countries has perpetrated the most horrid enormities, is itself a frightful despotism." Party spirit "serves always to distract the Public Councils and enfeeble the Public administration," and thus it is "the interest and the duty of a wise People to discourage and restrain it."[5]

Solzhenitsyn's advice to reject the party system of politics is not the only point on which his ideas are akin to those of the American Founding Fathers, as we shall see. That this is so should not be surprising. He has often spoken with open admiration about early American democracy, particularly because he discovers there a recognition that human beings are morally responsible before God to order a good society. Post-Enlightenment ideologies have led societies away from this fundamental condition of the moral universe. Sometimes Solzhenitsyn's criticisms of democracy refer directly to the modern American experience, and this is to be expected from one who has spent many years living in the United States. Clearly, Solzhenitsyn believes that Russia today can learn more about a wholesome democracy from early America than from contemporary America. It would be a curious provincialism of present-mindedness—or, perhaps, a zealotry for the doctrine of progress—to hold that every single deviation in American democracy from its original pattern marks an unquestionable improvement.

CHAPTER EIGHT, "THE DEMOCRACY OF SMALL AREAS," BEGINS the second half of Part Two of the essay. Its opening two sentences are as important as any in the whole essay. "The critical comments about contemporary democracy expressed above are not meant to suggest that the future Russian Union will have no need for democracy. *It will need it very much*" (p. 82). These sentences are the pivot of Part Two and thus clarify its structure. Seven chapters have been devoted to criticisms of—be it noted—*contemporary* democracy, not democracy *per se*.

Despite them all, the future Russia still will need democracy—and very much, not by a close call. (And Russia will need it whether or not Ukraine and Belarus join in the new union.) Now seven chapters will be devoted to Solzhenitsyn's positive democratic program.

In 1980 Solzhenitsyn had said, "As concerns the theoretical question whether Russia should choose or reject authoritarianism in the future, I have no final opinion, and have not offered any."[6] A decade later, he does come to a final opinion, though it turns out to be historically rooted and not theoretically conceived. Russia will need not authoritarianism but democracy. What caused him to abandon his agnosticism? For this historical thinker, it can only have been historical developments. The decline and imminent collapse of Soviet power was developing in such a way that one could now realistically imagine Russia to be approaching readiness for democracy. Whatever the intentions, the authoritarianism of the Gorbachev era had done its transitional work. Solzhenitsyn is not changing his mind about the flaws in modern practices of democracy. But there must be a way to develop a democracy which would minimize those readily perceptible flaws and at the same time be suitable to the Russian social realities. The second half of Part Two is devoted to Solzhenitsyn's sketch of what he thinks that way is.

That way must, as the chapter title suggests, start "from the bottom up." The new Russian democracy must also be built "gradually, patiently, and in a way designed to last rather than being proclaimed thunderously from above in its full-fledged form." Solzhenitsyn would rein in those democratic enthusiasts who are trumpeting grandiose and quick-fix schemes. As for the "failings" that he has methodically exposed, they "would rarely apply to democracies of small areas," up to the size of a county (p. 82). And why not? Because voters have personal knowledge of the candidates "both in terms of their effectiveness in practical matters and in terms of their moral qualities" (pp. 82–83). Local voters will not be deceived by "phony reputations," "empty rhetoric," or "party sponsorship" (p. 83).

Thus commences Solzenitsyn's exposition of the theme of decentralization, which for the balance of the essay winds it way as a unifying thread to which cling all details of his program. His localism in politics is of a piece with his emphasis on the primacy of the individual. There must truly be citizens before there can be a civic culture. Solzhenitsyn seeks to bring political power as close to the individual as possible.

Many nation-builders might be inclined to start with the "macro" picture; the attention of Western commentators has certainly gravitated toward it. Solzhenitsyn's way is just the opposite. The impersonalism of mass society is ever his dread foe. And have not Soviet citizens, of all people, had their fill and more of centralism?

The primacy of the local cannot, for Solzhenitsyn, be overstated. "Without properly constituted local self-government, there can be no stable or prosperous life, and the very concept of civic freedom loses all meaning." Nothing done at the top can compensate for insufficiency at the local level. For only here is democracy *"unmediated."*[7] Ancient Athens had such direct democracy. So still do the town-hall meetings in localities of the United States. Solzhenitsyn's favorite example is what he observed first-hand in Switzerland. He recalls fondly how he watched citizens standing closely packed on the town square deciding issues by an open show of raised hands. They readily re-elected the head of the canton government, then immediately voted down three of his bills. "We trust you, the voters seemed to be saying, to govern us, but without those proposals" (p. 84).

Not only could this kind of democracy of small areas work in Russia, but Russians have in fact practiced various forms of it over the centuries, Solzhenitsyn cites several examples: the peasant council [*mir*], the *veche* assemblies, Cossack self-government, the *zemstvo*. Unfortunately, the *zemstvo* structure was replaced by *soviets*, or collectives, which became subservient to the Communist Party, thus did not function as independent governing bodies, and now are thoroughly discredited. Rather than trying to redeem them, as some suggest, Solzhenitsyn urges that a new *zemstvo* system replace them. Even this vestige of Communism, though, should be replaced only gradually (p. 86).

Geoffrey Hosking's chapter on "Communities and Ideals in Russian Society" describes just the sort of ability at and experience in grassroots self-governance upon which Solzhenitsyn seeks to base a home-grown Russian democracy.[8] In the concluding paragraph of this eighth chapter, Solzhenitsyn says that, based on his many years of studying pre-revolutionary Russian history, he will draw for the succeeding details of his program from "the legacy of our best statesmen and theoreticians, combining it with my own attempt at elaboration." It is obvious, he notes, that "the experience of the past cannot simply be transplanted to the mutilated land of today." It is equally obvious to him that "without reference to this background our recovery is unlikely to proceed in a healthy manner." He will, he explains, use some old terms and concepts, though only "in order to avoid inventing new ones," not because they are sacrosanct. Some of them may survive; others of them "will no doubt be replaced in common usage" (p. 86).

ONE OF THE OLD TERMS, "The Zemstvo," is the title of Chapter Nine. Elected representatives served as legislators in the *zemstvo* system of the nineteenth century. They had administrative staffs for such local needs as education, health care, veterinary service, insurance, roads, establishment of food reserves for emergency. The word itself "connotes land, country, or people, as distinct from the central government."[9] As Vladislav Krasnov remarks, Solzhenitsyn recognizes "the *zemstvo*'s affinity with American townhall meetings and the self-governance of Swiss cantons."[10] He sees a revivifying of this traditional Russian political conception as the way to democratize government in the new Russia.

There are to be four levels of the *zemstvo*. The *local zemstvo* would serve a mid-sized town, a district in a large city, a settlement, or a group of villages. The *uyezd zemstvo* would serve a large city or a *rayon* (district). The *oblast zemstvo* would serve an *oblast* (region, or province) or an Autonomous Republic. The *all-Russian* (or *all-Union*) *zemstvo* would serve the whole nation. That is to say, the same principles of self-government would apply at all levels, from local up to national. Solzhenitsyn advises that this system be introduced "step by step, starting from the bottom." Indeed, he pays as much attention to the step-by-step timing, or process, of establishing this system as he does to the four-level organization itself. Local self-governance will allow many to develop political skills, and "God preserve us from political wheelers and dealers" (p. 87).

Voting in local elections will be for specific individuals only, not for representatives of parties. Normally, voters will be choosing among candidates well known to them. Campaigns should be "short and modest affairs, involving nothing beyond a factual statement on each candidate's program, biography, and views." (Westerners might think of similar elections in such non-governmental settings as professional societies, corporations, neighborhood associations, churches.) These elections should not be funded by the state. Funding and many other procedural details should be decided locally, and it is all right with Solzhenitsyn if they "differ substantially from region to region" (p. 87). Let the principle of decentralization prevail.

However, certain requirements should be established nationwide. Here Solzhenitsyn specifies age and residency requirements. He very tentatively suggests a minimum voting age of twenty, singling out as a troublesome factor the unstable upbringing of today's adolescents, and would allow localities or districts to set a higher minimum age than the national floor. The minimum age for candidates would be "perhaps thirty, or twenty-eight." Because it is important that voters and elected officials "have roots in a given locality," he suggests a residency requirement for voters of three years and for candidates of five years— "or, perhaps, the three preceding years plus five years at an earlier time" (p. 88). The repeated use of *perhaps* is just one signal of Solzhenitsyn's modest tentativeness; the detail provided is a signal of his ongoing practicality, even of the striving for concreteness which comes naturally to a novelist.

Localities would decide upon the number of legislators to be elected. These legislators would choose and supervise administrative officials; in rural districts and small settlements, a single individual might serve the administrative purpose. At the *uyezd* level, the administrators might consist of members elected to the assembly, or they might be specialists appointed by that body. At both levels, the newly elected officials would assume the functions currently belonging to local and district soviets, which would then be abolished.

Solzhenitsyn carefully specifies how the transition from the soviet to the *zemstvo* system might proceed. Local officials will be elected "by direct vote only." Representative democracy can work at its purest in small areas. Depending on "the size of the territory and the voters' familiarity with the candidates," the voting procedure at the *uyezd* level might call for two-stage elections. Local *zemstvos* would replace local soviets immediately. At the halfway point of the first ("two-year?") term, "with members now familiar with one another," these locally elected officials would then elect from among themselves members to serve in the *uyezd zemstvo*, at which time the regional soviets and their administrative apparatus would go out of business. Democracy would be introduced at the two lowest levels. "Given our lack of political skills, the local and *uyezd zemstvo* organizations will serve as training ground as they perform the day-to-day tasks of governing our localities" (p. 89). In the gradualist design, "the process will begin shaping and bringing to the fore individuals with the potential for more challenging levels of service." Solzhenitsyn concludes this chapter by announcing himself "impressed" by the recent endeavors of the "miners' strike committees as well as by the 'unions of workers' which have displayed exceptional levels of awareness and organization" (p. 90). There is some reason to be hopeful about the prospects for instituting democracy in the new Russia.

BEFORE WE PROCEED to the essay's tenth chapter, we should pause to consider contextual material which enriches our understanding of Solzhenitsyn's political thinking. Solzhenitsyn has thought long and hard about how to get the best persons into positions of responsibility. It is a common concern among students of representative government. Solzhenitsyn's proposal is to have tiered elections. The whole populace would elect directly their local officials. Those representatives would then be entrusted to select the best members among them for service at the next higher (*uyezd*) level, and so on through the layers of government on up to the national legislature. This tiered approach may seem foreign to the practice of modern democracies, but it is not as foreign as it may at first seem. In addition, this approach has a long history in democratic thought as one option for political organization.

We shall pursue these two points; but, before we do, we must ask why Solzhenitsyn would propose this tiered pattern of elections. What is he trying to avoid, and what is he trying to achieve? He is trying to avoid all those vices and abuses that occupied his attention in the first half of Part Two of this essay. His observation of democracy in action has made him keenly aware of some of the problems in modern democracies, especially of the gap between theory and practice. These have caused him to be a cautious and even reluctant democrat in the Churchillian vein. The practice of democracy always entails a gamble. The dark side of human nature ever works to corrupt democracy from its theoretical pristineness. Solzhenitsyn is trying to locate a democratic option which will minimize the risks inherent in any actual practice of democracy. He is trying to put hedges along the pathway of the new Russian democracy that will serve, insofar as any theoretical construct can, to keep it from being sidetracked into swamps of corruption.

What he is trying positively to achieve is twofold. First, he is trying to discover a democratic structure which has roots in indigenous Russian historical experience; hence the *zemstvo* system. Second, he is trying to construct a democratic edifice established on his bedrock moral vision that human nature is an endless mixture of good and evil. It will be a democracy made to order for sinners. It will emphatically not be a democracy rooted in a philosophical view of human nature as perfectible. He knows of no better place to locate ultimate sovereignty than in the people; thus, he is a democrat. But he knows, also, that the people are not always wise, not always undeceived. The odds that they will make wise choices as voters are enhanced when they know the candidates personally. This localism is also a hedge against their being deceived by the blandishments of candidates for office.

If Solzhenitsyn's plan is to be questioned on the grounds that it places limits on democracy, the answer is that all functioning democracies do the same, though the nature and extent of the limits vary from one democracy to another. The very principle of representation is a limitation upon democratic practice. Only if all citizens had a direct and equal say in all decisions would there be a full participatory democracy, and this is beyond the managing of all but the very smallest of units. Nevertheless, it is to be conceded that Solzhenitsyn's limits allow a somewhat narrower range for direct participation in governance than do most of the systems practiced in the West. This is a difference of degree only, not of kind. And it is definitely related to the fundamental understanding of human nature out of which his plan emerges.

Let us return to the assertion that the tiered system of elections is not a novelty with Solzhenitsyn but has a long history in democratic thought. Our purposes can be served by looking at a case in point. A particularly apposite one for this discussion is to be found in the political writings of the great English poet John Milton. In 1660, as the cause of the English Commonwealth, which Milton had long served as Latin Secretary of State, seemed to be running out of steam, as the English people hankered after a return to the stable authority of monarchism, Milton wrote a treatise entitled *The Ready and Easy Way To*

Establish a Free Commonwealth. It was a rearguard effort to fend off the restoration of the royal family to the throne, and it failed.

To attain the stability of state for which the people were clamoring and yet to retain the sovereignty of a free people, Milton proposed that the power of governance be delegated to "a general council of ablest men, chosen by the people to consult of public affairs from time to time for the common good." His hope was that this general council, "being well chosen, should be perpetual," itself filling gaps in its ranks as they occurred. (The Achilles' heel of this proposal is that Milton provides no mechanism for ensuring that, just this once, the people would choose wisely, whereas presumably they would not do so in succeeding elections.) Anticipating various objections to this proposal, Milton offered, as a second choice, that there be ongoing elections of council members on a rotating basis, a third of them at a time, their terms of office therefore overlapping.[11] (To get slightly ahead of our story, this is exactly what happens today in the elections for the Senate of the United States.)

Milton had grown wary of entrusting all electoral power to the masses. They were the very ones, after all, who were now willing to forgo self-governance and to return to the one-person rule of monarchism, with all its potential for capricious exercise of power. So he proposed a tiered system of electing national officials. His proposed structure was

> . . . to well qualify and refine elections, not committing all to the noise and shouting of a rude multitude, but permitting only those of them who are rightly qualified to nominate as many as they will; and out of that number others of a better breeding to choose a less number more judiciously, till after a third or fourth sifting and refining of exactest choice, they only be left chosen who are the due number and seem by most voices the worthiest.

Milton's siftings are quite similar, albeit not identical, to Solzhenitsyn's tiers. Also similar is the moral concern to find a way "[t]o make the people fittest to choose, and the chosen fittest to govern." To be capable of responsible self-government will require his contemporary Englishmen to mend our corrupt and faulty education, to teach the people faith, not without virtue, temperance, modest, sobriety, parsimony, justice; not to admire wealth or honor; to hate turbulence and ambition; to place every one his private welfare and happiness in the public peace, liberty, and safety.[12]

Even more apposite than Milton as a parallel to Solzhenitsyn is the early American experiment in republican democracy. There are many signs that Solzhenitsyn has carefully studied the Constitution of the United States and American political history, and it seems likely that several of his particular proposals draw directly from the American model. He is aware that the attitude of the Founding Fathers toward democracy was to be not entirely trusting of it and to hedge it about with limits. For example, in the bicameral legislature, members of one house were to be elected directly by the people, district by district across the nation. Members of the other house, however, were to represent not people but states. So the United States Senate has two members per state, regardless of the states' population. Furthermore, only in 1913, with the Seventeenth Amendment, did the U. S. Constitution allow the people to vote for senators. Until then, they were chosen by the state legislatures. This is a tiered system of representation quite similar to that proposed by Solzhenitsyn.

Parenthetically, other Western democracies have tiered representation, as well. For instance, the upper house of the German legislature, the Bundesrat, is selected along the lines of the pre-1913 U. S. Senate. Each state's representatives vote as a bloc, and the chamber can veto bills dealing with states' interests. Also, members of the less powerful French Senate are chosen indirectly by an electoral college composed of locally elected officials.

The President of the United States was and is to be chosen by the Electoral College, not by the direct vote of the people. Although the current practice is a mere vestige of the original design, the 1992 election season reminded voters how crucial this entity can be. Article Two of the Constitution says that the electors of each state, equal in number to their congressional delegation, shall vote by ballot for two persons, at least one of whom is not an inhabitant of their state. If only one person receives a majority of these votes, he has been elected President. If more than one receives a majority, the House of Representatives shall select the President by majority vote. If no one receives a majority, the House of Representatives shall choose from among the five highest vote-getters. In the House vote each state delegation shall have one vote. The Vice President shall be the person with the second highest vote total. (The Twelfth Amendment of 1804 reduced the number of presidential finalists for House consideration from five to three and established that the Vice President would be chosen from candidates standing specifically for that office.) In this system the odds are high that the selection of the President will end up in the hands of the House delegations. Again, the tiered system of elections is present, and with more tiers than pertain to the election of senators. The people are yet further removed from the power of choice in the case of the President than in the case of the senators.

Nor were these all the limits that the Founding Fathers placed upon democracy. Here are a few additional examples. There were age and residency requirements for voters and candidates, plus other limitations of suffrage. The President was granted the power of veto, which could be overridden only by two-thirds of both houses of Congress, one of which already was not popularly elected. Judges were to be appointed, not elected. Indeed, of the three branches of government, only a part of one of them, the House of Representatives, was to be chosen in accordance with our currently prevailing notions of what constitutes real democracy. One recalls the schoolbook maxim that the United States is a republic, not a democracy.

One sees how similar in spirit are Solzhenitsyn and America's Founding Fathers on the matter of implementing the principles of democracy. Both he and they accept the principle that sovereignty rests with the people. But both also accord greater power to some people—namely, those elected close to home—than to others. When Solzhenitsyn differs from them, as we shall see, he embraces more of the democratic principle than they do and accords greater power than they do to the people as a whole. Nevertheless, as with his eschewal of parties, so with his embrace of tiers, Solzhenitsyn has more in common with America's original approach to democracy than with its current approach. In general, whatever one thinks of the Founding Fathers' attitude toward democracy, one should think of Solzhenitsyn's.

*   *   *

RETURNING TO THE TEXT after this excursus, we come to Chapter Ten, "Stages in the Transfer of Power." Since "direct elections of representatives to a central legislature could not be a productive exercise" in a country of Russia's size and physical conditions, Solzhenitsyn proposes "three- or four-tier elections." Whereas a direct national election would involve "far-off and poorly known individuals with a recognition factor founded solely on the election campaign," the tiered system would at each level involve "long years of knowledge and trust" of the candidates (p. 90).

After this brief introductory defense of the tiered system, Solzhenitsyn devotes the bulk of this chapter to the stages by which the higher levels of the *zemstvo* system are to be added. He is painfully aware that the old apparatchiks are still honeycombed through the power structure of the old soviets, but even here he chooses the path of gradualism. Such is his fear of a violent upheaval which could usher in either revolution or anarchy. After one or even two terms of office in local and *uyezd* assemblies, members will be sufficiently seasoned to serve on the *oblast* level. These deputies will be selected by the members of the regional *uyezd* assemblies, plus the assembly of the main city in the region. And they will be selected "from their own, now thoroughly familiar, ranks" (p. 90). At this time, the remaining *uyezd* assemblymen will stand for re-election. In other words, the *oblast zemstvo* will come into being at least one term later than the *uyezd zemstvo*. *Oblast* assemblymen will convene at set intervals, between which they will reside in their home districts. One sees here Solzhenitsyn's desire for citizen legislators, not for full-time professional politicians. In a parenthesis Solzhenitsyn would allow, for the sake of stability, an across-the-board extension of the terms of office (akin to one of Milton's ideas).

For the sake of continuity in the stage of transition, Solzhenitsyn borrows an idea from Dmitri Shipov, a leader in the pre-revolutionary *zemstvo* movement, which would allow an assembly "to co-opt into its ranks (by full consensus, rather than a vote) prominent and urgently needed local figures, not exceeding one-fifth of its membership." This procedure will allow "successful members of the present-day *soviets* (including the Supreme Soviet) to be smoothly integrated into the new power structure" (p. 91). One might have anticipated from this fervent anti-Communist a firmer line demarcating free future from tyrannical past, but good sense calls not for revenge but for continuity and stability.

After the *oblast* assemblies have functioned for one electoral term, they would choose the (presumably) best of their number to serve in "the Union Chamber (replacing the Soviet of the Union) of the All-Zemstvo Assembly, which would replace the Supreme Soviet." That would also be the time for the *oblast*-level assemblymen to stand for re-election by the *uyezd* assemblies. The Union Chamber would be one of two chambers in the All-Zemstvo Assembly, the other being, as at present, the Soviet (now to be Chamber) of Nationalities. Solzhenitsyn is willing to borrow whole this second chamber of the current Soviet structure, as long as it is provided that "each nationality would decide for itself the manner of filling the seats allocated to it, whether by general election or by appointment based on merit, as well as the length of term involved" (p. 92). Here this Great Russian takes great care to protect the rights of the minority nationalities in the new system of self-governance.

The transition to this new national organization might take four to six years. In the meantime, some way must be found to reform the current Soviet of the Union, since it is currently "constituted according to an ill-defined and hybrid principle" in which the Communist Party and other organizations appoint some members and others are elected territorially. And the current Congress of People's Deputies not only adds to the "cumbersome structure" but causes "needless complexity and duplication in legislative work" (pp. 92–93). The final result should be an All-Zemstvo Assembly in which delegates "have gained considerable know-how in the course of their work" at lower levels, are "well-tested," and combine "*oblast*-level experience . . . with a national perspective." To ensure that they not lose touch with the grass roots, national legislators, also, should be required to reside for part of each year in their home district. "(Such a rule also exists in the United States)" (p. 93).

"A COMBINED SYSTEM OF GOVERNMENT" IS the subject of Chapter Eleven. "What is meant here is a rational way for the centralized bureaucracy to collaborate with grass-roots public activity" (p. 93). Muscovite Russia had this sort of partnership, but it was undermined in the late stages of tsarist rule. Solzhenitsyn would see it restored. The problem lies with the centralized bureaucracy, which "by its very nature tries to restrict the sphere of society's self-management." Thereby it "weakens the people's habit of self-reliance." A proper balance needs to be established. "In healthy times, the public hungers for activity, and the broadest possible opportunities should be made available for this urge," whether in local self-government or in associations and unions (p. 94). This "combined system," or "working partnership," is what Dmitri Shipov termed "the *state-zemstvo system.*" Whereas in preceding chapters Solzhenitsyn had been hedging against placing excessive power in the hands of the people, here he is working to ensure that they do not have too little power. In regard to the central government, he is obviously much more wary of the bureaucrats than of the legislators. And "the cooperation of the public is an indispensable help in controlling the central bureaucracy and ensuring that its officials will perform honest and efficient service" (p. 95).

During the transition to a new structure of governance, the old bureaucrats may retain too much power. However, "the grass-roots social forces are slowly gathering strength, acquiring experience, and shaping the leaders of tomorrow." So, although "the present-day bureaucracy, with its habit of unchecked power, will do all it can to cling to its rights," the coming of economic independence from the bureaucracy means that "a sharp reduction of these rights is imminent." Furthermore, and in hopeful conclusion to this chapter, "the constructive forces that are already coming to light in today's freshly elected, transitional *soviets* will help the movement toward an ever-broader social independence" (p. 95).

CHAPTER TWELVE IS entitled "Concerning the Central Authorities." The first issue that Solzhenitsyn addresses in it is the need for "a strong presidency." Here, it is clear, he agrees with Gorbachev. "However, all the prerogatives of the head of state together with the manner of dealing with potential conflicts must be rigorously stipulated by law. . . ." Here, it seems, he disagrees with Gorbachev, at least with some of Gorbachev's actions. His primary concern is with the procedure of electing the President. "He will acquire genuine legitimacy only after being elected by national vote to a term of five or perhaps seven years." Here he abandons the principle of tiers, or of indirection, on a crucial item for which the Founding Fathers of the United States retained and even emphasized it. Presidential candidates must be native-born and must meet a residency requirement of seven or ten years. Given a non-party organization of political life, candidates would be nominated by the All-Zemstvo Assembly, and there would be several of them. "The Assembly would subject these candidates to a thorough review and would then issue public statements of equal length on each, stating the basis for its findings, together with a summary of any dissenting views." This approach should ward off the unhappy prospect that the national presidential election will "become an occasion for wasting the energies of the nation on a vehement and slanted campaign lasting weeks or months where the paramount goal is smearing one's opponent." The winner would have to receive an absolute majority of the popular vote, which might necessitate two rounds of voting. "It would probably be wise to follow the American model in establishing the office of Vice-President," with each presidential aspirant choosing his running mate (p. 96). This is one point on which Solzhenitsyn prefers modern American practice to the Founders' design. Solzhenitsyn's proposal for presidential elections more nearly approaches pure democracy than does the practice of the United States. There would be more candidates. Mainly, there would be direct popular vote. In the United States it remains quite possible for a minority of voters to produce a majority in the Electoral College.

As with impeachment of a President in the United States, so in Solzhenitsyn's scheme, it is possible to remove from office a President "discharging his duties unsatisfactorily." The All-Zemstvo Assembly would publish a statement about the unsatisfactory performance and then submit it to a popular vote. In other words, only the people, not their delegates, could turn the President out of office. On the other hand, if two-thirds of each chambers of the Assembly concurs, "there would seem to be no reason not to extend his tenure for another term without a new national election" (p. 97). If the President dies in office in the second half of his term, the Vice President assumes the post; if the President dies during the first half of his term, a new national election is held. On these details, judged strictly by the standard of democratic theory, sometimes Solzhenitsyn's plan exceeds American practice, and sometimes it falls short. What is most noteworthy is how similar the two are.

As with the Cabinet in the United States, the President will appoint a

Council of Ministers, who will report both to him and to the legislators, but "they will not be removable by the legislature." Solzhenitsyn likes Pyotr Stolypin's idea of establishing "a two- or three-year academy for those aspiring to top government posts" (p. 97). Ministers must be "so highly qualified" to lead that nation that they do not slip "into a bureaucratic mode of thinking." Administrative appointment "must not be viewed as a reward or special privilege." In a democracy, "every kind of authority is by definition indebted to the people," and every appointee must be dedicated to "the present task of rebuilding and making up for all that has been destroyed" (p. 98).

"There are not many ways in which we can emulate Switzerland, given that country's size and the history of its formation as a union of independent cantons" (p. 98). But one idea that Russia can borrow is that of a petition. If it receives the requisite number of citizens' signatures, the legislature must review it. If the signatures reach a higher floor, "in the millions," then "a plebiscite on the question becomes mandatory." This chapter on the central government concludes, "Apart from such plebiscites and the infrequent presidential elections, no other national elections would be necessary" (p. 99). Solzhenitsyn's concern for order and stability is manifest. Still, in his new Russia there would be more by way of national election than there is in the United States, where no national plebiscite is possible and where, technically, because of the Electoral-College mode of choosing the President, there is no such thing as a national election.

Chapter Thirteen is entitled "A Consultative Body." It carries a proposal designed not for the present moment but only for the distant future, when, however, it might be of great importance. It calls for the creation of a third parliamentary chamber, the main purpose of which would be to serve as an additional hedge against the potential tyranny of the majority. This body would consist of "representatives of social strata and various professions, or, one might say, 'estates.' " This would be a second way of cutting up the pie of the citizenry, one which would draw upon those informal affiliations which arise naturally among the mediating structures of society. It would recognize that "[t]he two most natural conditions promoting interaction and cooperation among people are a shared territory and a common occupation or type of activity."

This proposal would seek to avoid a "[c]omplete and faceless equality" and would acknowledge the principle that "[a] society lives precisely by virtue of its differentiation" (p. 101).

This third chamber would be "a supreme moral entity endowed with an advisory role." It would not normally "resort to voting but would instead present in-depth arguments and counterarguments offered by the most respected authorities upon whom the state could draw." Solzhenitsyn finds in the Assembly of the Land of Muscovite Russia "a reliable model" for this proposed third chamber, and he notes that "[t]here is no recorded instance of the Tsar acting contrary to the Assembly's judgment" (p. 100).

Solzhenitsyn's purpose here is to create an institutional embodiment of the venerable Russian principle of *sobornost*. This concept refers to the spirit of community, or conciliarity; it stands in opposition to radical individualism. In Solzhenitsyn's words, "*Sobornost* is a system of trust which is based on the assumption that moral unity is both possible and achievable" (p. 101). Alexis Klimoff, who translated and annotated *Rebuilding Russia*, adds, "The concept of *sobornost* refers to the kind of spirit that prompts freely offered agreement. It has been defined as expressing 'unity in multiplicity' " (p. 113). It would not be impossible for public life to demonstrate this moral unity apart from creating this third chamber. However, the purpose would be aided if there were "an assembly of highly respected individuals of lofty moral character, wisdom, and rich experience," a body which would "reflect the national conscience" (p. 101). And using the principle of estates would provide a clear method of choosing such persons. One belongs to an estate automatically, simply by virtue of one's profession. An estate is thus different from a trade union, in which membership is optional and which is organized on the principle of mutual self-interest. "And no one is better equipped to offer advice about a specific project than a representative of the specialty in question" (p. 102). An instance of thinking in terms of the potential beneficent influence of such estates appears in *August 1914*, when engineer Obodovsky ruminates about the Engineers' Union. Though he does not conceive of it as taking a direct part in government, he does imagine that it "could become one of the leading forces in Russia. More important and more productive than any political party."[13] It is very interesting to note that, in the Congress of People's Deputies of 1989, only two-thirds of the delegates were elected by territorial constituencies. One-third of the seats were reserved for "public organizations." These were not informal associations but established Communist organizations. Yet it was precisely as a representative of one of these, the Academy of Sciences, that Andrei Sakharov gained his seat in the Congress.[14] At any rate, there is here some small precedent for a parliamentary presence of persons other than those elected according to territory.

As is his wont in this essay, Solzhenitsyn proceeds to provide the bare bones of details about this long-range proposal. Each estate would determine how to elect or to appoint those "experienced and respected individuals who could be trusted to express the general views of the group." The size of this third chamber, or Duma, would be no larger than 200-250 delegates. If the number of estates turns out to be greater than that, some smaller estates would band together to select one delegate. If more than half of the Duma concurs in an "opinion, judgment, or request for information," it will be published. The addressee of the statement could be the President, the Council of Ministers, either chamber of the Assembly, or the Supreme Court. (Solzhenitsyn nowhere else refers to the Court, but it is obvious that he assumes that there will be one, in accordance with the principle of the separation of powers; and we are reminded again that this is a pamphlet, not a comprehensive program.) The addressee "will be obligated to respond positively or to publish the reasons for non-compliance within a two-week period" (p. 103). Only in exceptional cases involving military secrets will the exchange take place behind closed doors. This Duma will also be able to nominate candidates for the presidency. There are two situations in which, were the Duma's judgment to be unanimous, its normally consultative role would rise to the level of authoritative policy-making. In one case, it can "interdict any law or any action by a government institution or agency, and . . . mandate changes or corrections." In the other case, it can "veto any candidacy for the office of President" (p. 104).

Although the huge task of instituting all levels of the *zemstvo* system of self-governance must take precedence over the proposal for a third parliamentary chamber, the moral purpose to be served by this proposal is manifest. For Solzhenitsyn, morality is always a more fundamental concern than politics, or even of law *per se*. In relation to politics, he thinks that this projected Duma "will have a direct moral and intellectual impact on all facets of government, whereas the potential for improving society by exclusively political means is not very great." In relation to the law, he says, "Laws designate the minimum moral standards below which an individual represents a danger to society" (p. 104). After citing four Russian authorities in support of his view of the primacy of morality, he concludes this chapter thus: "Moral principles must take priority over legal ones. And justice means conformity to moral law beyond any purely legal compliance" (p. 105). Government, too, must function within the moral universe and be subservient to its laws.

THE FINAL CHAPTER OF *REBUILDING RUSSIA*, "Let Us Search," is an engagingly modest conclusion. Solzhenitsyn lists areas that he has left untouched: the army, the militia, the courts, the trade unions, most legislative and economic issues. "My purpose was simply to offer a number of proposals, none of which lay claim to finality, so as to prepare the ground for discussion." As he acknowledges, "Building a rational and just state order is a task of surpassing difficulty. . . ." That is why he advocates the gradualism of "successive approximations and small, cautious steps." Even "the thriving lands of the West" have not been entirely successful in this task. Having in mind the newly en-livened democrats who would recommend a wholesale importation of a Western pattern, he advises viewing the West "with eyes clear of rapture." In any case, the task "will be infinitely more difficult and painful for us, starting as we do with a country in catastrophic ruin and a population deprived of the habits and skills of a viable society" (p. 105).

Solzhenitsyn offers this pamphlet as a "plan for future action," but he readily concedes that it is "impossibly difficult to design a *balanced* plan" (p. 105, emphasis added). Indeed, even of his own carefully wrought plan, he declares that "there is every likelihood that it will contain more errors than virtues and that it will be unable to keep pace with the actual unfolding of events" (pp. 105–06). On the other hand, and implying his sense of patriotic responsibility, he adds that "it would also be wrong not to make the effort." This essay, he says in his final sentence, draws upon the reflections of many Russian thinkers of the past (presumably even beyond those named), not to suggest a return to the past but to orient Russian reflection about the future: ". . . my hope is that bringing their thoughts together here will contribute to a vigorous new growth" (p. 106).

IN SUMMARY, this concluding brief chapter highlights matters which we have observed throughout this running commentary on *Rebuilding Russia*. Solzhenitsyn's call for ongoing discussion bespeaks one for whom the democratic temper is congenial and naturally fitting, not forced. His modesty and tentativeness are so marked as to be almost palpable. This essay is the product of a man thoroughly grounded in history and its lessons. It is the offering of a selfless patriot.

This essay belies the West's received opinion of Solzhenitsyn. One who credits the received opinion would expect something far different from what *Rebuilding Russia* presents. The discrepancy is flagrant, startling. Authoritarian, highhanded, anti-democratic, reactionary, chauvinistic, messianic, utopian, extremist, intemperate—where are all these traits of personality and outlook widely imputed to Solzhenitsyn? Wherever they are, they are not here in the text.

13

Conclusion
Influence

THE BURDEN OF THIS BOOK has been, in large part, to correct misperceptions of Solzhenitsyn. Much of what has been written in it thus far could be brought together under the heading "Those Who Do Not Understand." This has been a necessary part of the task of reassessment, because the misunderstandings have been so many, so severe, and so widespread. Nevertheless, throughout the three decades since Solzhenitsyn made his dramatic appearance on the world stage, his writings have drawn a host of deeply appreciative and sympathetic readers. Many persons view their times and the human condition in general differently because they have read Solzhenitsyn. The thesis of this book is that Solzhenitsyn's ideas are highly significant and powerfully relevant for the modern world, and many they are who can give existential witness to the truth of it. Them we may call "Those Who Understand." This chapter will be devoted to them.

These beneficiaries of Solzhenitsyn's life and work are located throughout the world. Despite whatever filters have been interjected between them as readers and Solzhenitsyn as writer, they have perceived in his works profound insights into the modern world and lasting sustenance for their souls. They may not always be sure just what to make of what others have written about him; but they know that there is much in his words to be treasured, and they will gladly tell of his value to them. I have come upon many such people. Sometimes I meet them after my talks about Solzhenitsyn at book clubs, civic groups, churches, college and university campuses. For the most part, they are people who do not write books, who do not make the news, who seem to affect only a small number of others in the daily rounds of their ordinary lives. Yet they think, they vote, and they care about their world. In my personal, unscientific estimate, these readers whom Solzhenitsyn has affected for good outnumber his cultured despisers. Who can know for sure? They are there, at any rate; and a meditation upon Solzhenitsyn's influence cannot leave them entirely out of account.

Most persons who know of Solzhenitsyn are aware of the intensity of his sense of mission about his life as an author. The audience which he has always had in mind as his primary audience is that comprising future generations of Russian readers. About these we can of course say nothing. Only time, much time, will tell whether his life has its intended effect. And just here we come upon the great but unavoidable shortcoming of this chapter. It seeks to recount a story which has not yet been told in the event. Of the consequences of Solzhenitsyn's actions as a writer, we can see so far only the firstfruits. The man, after all, still lives. And we cannot know but what some surprises from his pen may yet be in store for us. His impending return to his homeland makes even more uncertain what will be the shape of the final chapter of his own life story.

On the other hand, it is very widely recognized today, even if sometimes a bit grudgingly, that Solzhenitsyn has had a profound influence on the modern world. There is broad agreement that no single book contributed so directly and forcefully to the collapse of the Soviet Union as *The Gulag Archipelago*, even that its delegitimizing of Communist power in the eyes of its surreptitious Soviet readers was of crucial importance. That this connection is widely remarked suggests how readily it comports with the evidence available. In other words, we may say that within his lifetime we are observing the success of a cause to which he devoted great energies, that the post-Soviet future for which he yearned has now already arrived. This is an influence of world-historical proportions.

Acknowledging that Solzhenitsyn's analysis of the past has affected the shape of the present should open us to the possibility that his influence will extend into the shaping of the future. Recent events have enhanced his credibility, not diminished it. Those who dismissed him as passé seem themselves to have been left behind. In Russia in particular, the path into the future marked out by Solzhenitsyn is so far, in broad terms, being followed. Thus, as speculations about the future go, the weight of the evidence to date lies on the side of anticipating that his stock will continue to rise and that his influence will expand. And Western readers should keep in mind that he has things to say about their lives, too, about the condition of modern humanity as a whole.

Given the open-ended nature of the story of Solzhenitsyn's influence, this chapter will not be a comprehensive recitation. It will have the effect, rather, of a series of snapshots. Each section of the chapter can be considered a synecdoche, in which the part stands for a whole which is larger than the part but is of the same consistency throughout. But even a selective sampling of Solzhenitsyn's influence conveys a very interesting picture. Solzhenitsyn has proven useful to other people in quite a variety of ways. We shall start with a little story of a zek in the Gulag who drew from her reading of *The Gulag Archipelago* some helpful hints from a wily camp veteran about how to cope with her straitened circumstances. Next, we shall move to the most obvious sphere of Solzhenitsyn's influence, namely, the appropriations of his moral and political insights by other Russians his age and younger. His line of dissenting thought has grown, and it now bids fair to become (again, in broad terms) the prevailing outlook in his country. We shall consider, also, the relationship between Solzhenitsyn and the revival of religious spirit in today's Russia. Citizens of the Soviet satellite countries in Eastern and Central Europe also have learned some lessons from Solzhenitsyn; Václav Havel will serve as our case in point. Then, there is Solzhenitsyn's impact upon Western readers. We shall restrict our scope here to book-writing intellectuals. We shall look at the "New Philosophers" of France, where Solzhenitsyn's influence upon a nation's intellectual life has been generally acknowledged. Also, we shall describe a book by an American scholar who takes Solzhenitsyn as one of his major guides in analyzing where in the modern world we are and where we might be heading. The organization of this chapter can be described as a series of concentric circles. Like a stone dropped in a pond, Solzhenitsyn's influence is seen first in the Gulag itself, then in Russia as a whole, then in the larger Communist bloc of nations, then rippling out through the whole world.

*   *   *

HERE IS a snapshot of Irina Ratushinskaya, born in 1954, a second-grader when *One Day in the Life of Ivan Denisovich* appeared. By the time she was imprisoned at age twenty-eight for writing her poetry, she had read her Solzhenitsyn, and so she knew not to eat the proffered herring before embarking on her journey to the Gulag camp.

> Eating the herring is inadvisable, because it makes you terribly thirsty, and there will be nothing to drink. Thank you, Alexander Solzhenitsyn, for your priceless counsels! Who can say whether Igor and I would have had the presence of mind to burn all the letters and addresses while the KGB hammered on our doors, had we not read your works? Or would I have been able to summon sufficient control not to bat an eyelid when they stripped me naked in prison? Without you, would I have grasped that cardinal principle for all prisoners of conscience: "Never believe them, never fear them, never ask them for anything"? Thanks to you, even such trivia as the business with the herring is known to me in advance.

As for being forced to stand naked before a male prison guard, "I was prepared for much worse things than that, thanks to having read Solzhenitsyn's *Gulag Archipelago*." Thus was zek wisdom passed from one generation of political prisoners to the next. Retushinskaya, in turn, passed it along to other zeks, sharers of a dreadful pilgrimage and eager listeners. "Yes, all this tallies with what Solzhenitsyn has written. I try to quote him as closely as I can from memory. The carriage is enthralled: what else has he written? Impossible to retell the whole *Gulag Archipelago*, of course, but I recount as much as I can."[1]

It may at first seem strange to imagine Gulag denizens knowing *The Gulag Archipelago*. But a moment's thought makes it obvious that in time they would. And further reflection upon the work would bring to mind many passages that it would be especially valuable for fellow members of the nation of zeks to know. Indeed, these persons, who belong to the innermost of the concentric circles of this chapter, would naturally be the best readers of all for Solzhenitsyn's history of the Soviet concentration camps. They would find many occasions when they could apply immediately and directly what they had learned. Their knowledge of his work would be the surest way to undermine not only the legitimacy but also the smooth functioning of the whole dehumanizing camp system. As the preceding citations from Ratushinskaya's first book of memoirs, *Grey Is the Color of Hope*, indicate, she drew from Solzhenitsyn her whole orientation to camp life and how to survive it. The camps could damage her, could impair her health perhaps irreparably. But she had learned how to resist and to endure. There was never any question about her having her spirit broken. To the contrary, she grew spiritually during her four-plus years in the camps. Much of this was owing to the influence of Solzhenitsyn, to whom she pays tribute with alacrity and fulsomeness.

Many voices from the zek chorus have corroborated Solzhenitsyn's reports of camp life: Varlam Shalamov, Yevgenia Ginsburg, Anatoli Marchenko, Alexander Dolgun, Solzhenitsyn's friends Lev Kopelev and Dmitri Panin. Among this chorus Irina Ratushinskaya has unsurpassed skill as a miniaturist. Within Solzhenitsyn's panoramic view of the Gulag, she fills in the details of one otherwise-unknown little corner of the camp system. As she tells of the meager life of the handful of women prisoners who dwell together in the Small Zone (for political prisoners), she offers a story self-consciously congruent, down to the last detail, with Solzhenitsyn's sweeping account. How he said life was in camp is exactly how she found it. What he said to do about it is exactly what worked for her. In the camps, she says, we can be "human beings in the full sense of the word"; we can "retain our human dignity." She explains, "Yes, we are behind barbed wire, they have stripped us of everything they could, they have torn us away from our friends and families, but unless we acknowledge this as their right, we remain free."[2] We have read those sentiments before; so has she.

Ratushinskaya could get her bearings for Gulag life from Solzhenitsyn because beforehand she drew from him her fundamental inspiration about how to live in that larger Gulag called the Soviet Union. *In the Beginning*, her second volume of memoirs, traces her life up to her imprisonment. She tells how the atheist instruction struck her as a third-grader. "Why do grown-ups spend so much time talking about something that doesn't exist? You can't help feeling suspicious." So this little contrarian decides to take God's side. "Yet one can't help feeling sorry for God: He's going to be left completely alone and friendless when all the believers die. He's all by Himself, and everybody's ranged against Him. . . ." She starts talking to Him. "There is no feeling of remoteness, no sense that He is God, an exalted being, and I am just one of His lesser creations, nor do I address Him with the kind of politeness demanded by adults. The questions I fire at Him are demanding and unceremonious." The childhood friend whom she was to marry, Igor Geraschenko, had also come to God on his own. As a student of science, he learned the second law of thermodynamics and concluded that God must exist: "there had to be a beginning of some kind for our world. . . . An impulse and meaning." Of them and their contemporaries, Ratushinskaya says, "Later, this same generation was to turn to God, to the consternation of the Soviet authorities."[3]

In the Beginning tells Irina Ratushinskaya's story, but the name of Solzhenitsyn is peppered through the account. A conversation between Irina and Igor begins with a question from her to him:

> "Have you read Solzhenitsyn's *Living Without Lies*?"
> "Yes, of course, it's going around in *samizdat*. There were some fine people in that generation, though, weren't there?"
> "And what will we do, once we are all married with children, and the children ask us: 'Why were you cowards?' "
> "We won't be cowards!"
> "In that case, sooner or later they'll be after our heads."
> "There's got to be some other way."
> "So? Let's find it, then!"
> "We'll just have a different set of values."[4]

When Irina and Igor reach adulthood, they become involved in dissident activism, and directly because of the set of values provided by their Christian faith. Igor and a friend print and circulate in *samizdat* copies of Solzhenitsyn's works, notably *The Gulag Archipelago*. They become aware of the underground Russian Social Fund for Aid to Political Prisoners and Their Families, which Solzhenitsyn had established with royalties from *Gulag*. They commit themselves to following his example.

> You fulfilled the paternal duty of the older generation: you called upon us to live without lies, and we could never again retreat into servile indifference. Although you were not there in the flesh, we argued with you over your now-famous letter to the Soviet leadership; we did not agree blindly with everything you said, but after reading your *Gulag Archipelago* we were afraid, and we understood, and everything became clear:

if need be, we, too, would pass through that infernal circle, and would not commit any of the errors against which you warned us. Maybe we would make other errors: if so, and we survived, we should also write about them as honestly as you did, and they would serve as a warning to the next generation of young people in our unfortunate, beloved and shamed country.[5]

Many years later Irina and Igor met "an American professor who began to tell us that Russians are slaves by nature, that such is their mentality. We didn't bother to argue with him, just exchanged a resigned smile: he wasn't worth the argument." But we know from what source Ratushinskaya learned the rudiments of her moral vision, "that the division between those who are free, and those who are not, lies in the heart, it is not determined by geographical boundaries."[6] She was released from the Gulag on the eve of the Gorbachev-Reagan summit conference at Reykjavik, Iceland, and sent West for medical treatment. The Geraschenkos, after a sojourn in the United States, now live and work in England.

ARE THE GERASCHENKOS an isolated case? How many other such persons roughly of their vintage are there who have learned their lessons from Solzhenitsyn? Vladislav Krasnov's book *Russia Beyond Communism* suggests that, in various ways and to varying degrees, others have taken their bearings from Solzhenitsyn, as well. We have had numerous occasions in this study to cite this volume in support of various points of argument. Here we return to the book in its own right and attend to its own thesis.

Krasnov reports that the idea for his book germinated in the early years of Gorbachev's rule. His original plan was to provide a critical evaluation of the various alternative visions of the future of Russia which were then appearing in the Soviet press. However, "by the end of 1987 I became convinced that no such evaluation was needed, because the Russian national alternative already had clearly shown the greatest vitality." The *partiots* (his neologism) were declining in influence, and the patriots were gaining the ascendancy in the political and cultural debates. Krasnov methodically summarizes and analyzes the views of many of these debaters, some of whom have already been mentioned in this study. Among them there is much intellectual ferment, much argument and disagreement—just the sorts of stirrings one would expect from thoughtful people coming newly to freedom of public expression. Some of Krasnov's essayists are consciously indebted to Solzhenitsyn; others are not. But the general tendency of the discussion is clear: "from ideological to spiritual, from 'internationalist' to national, from formal to non-formal, from rigid to spontaneous, from Marxism-Leninism to no 'isms' at all, from *Partia* to *Patria*, from things Communist to things Russian."[7] The triumph of this tendency is now so universally recognized that there is a welcome quality of datedness to Krasnov's survey; already it serves largely the purpose of historical documentation of a period of transition.

Lying behind this tendency, as its primary source, Krasnov points to Solzhenitsyn's publicistic efforts, especially his pre-exilic essays addressing the Soviet reality. These, he says, "have anticipated, urged, and prepared the way for the spiritual and intellectual catharsis that has now gripped the country." And the most significant and influential of these has been *Letter to the Soviet Leaders*. Well before Gorbachev fell from power, Krasnov intuited that, whatever Gorbachev's intentions, "the policy of glasnost would inevitably lead to a *de facto* abolition of the Marxist-Leninist ideological monopoly, the key demand of Solzhenitsyn's *Letter*." Moreover, although not all Soviet intellectuals were ready to accept Solzhenitsyn as their beacon, Krasnov concluded, "The country [Gorbachev] rules seems to be irrevocably drifting toward Solzhenitsyn's path."[8]

THE WRITERS SURVEYED by Krasnov demonstrate that current discussions about Russia's future cannot take place without recourse to Solzhenitsyn's thinking. But these commentators, whether agreeing or disagreeing with Solzhenitsyn, are not the first to feel that magnetic pull of his ideas. That honor is to be accorded to his collaborators on *From Under the Rubble*. That collection of essays, now some two decades old, fell out of print for lack of sales. Nevertheless, much of what is now transpiring in Russia was forecast in that volume. Solzhenitsyn's collaborators were younger than he, some by a full generation. They are his immediate heirs. These essays merit much more extended pondering than can be provided by the brief sampling offered here.

Vadim Borisov, who today serves as Solzhenitsyn's literary agent in Russia, is representative of these essayists in his use of Solzhenitsyn's rhetoric of "Russian national rebirth." The key to this rebirth is spiritual; we Russians, says Borisov need to "discover *in ourselves* the source of some power to lead our ravaged consciousness back to a single spiritual center." He specifically rejects "the present enthusiasm for social experiment." Forgetting God, we feel now "the fatal blows the twentieth century has dealt to our faith in man *as such*." Yet even in the early 1970's he thought that the end of an era might be coming into view: "But present developments offer a glimmer of hope that an end to peremptory Marxist decisions and predeterminations of Russia's fate may now be near and that henceforward her crippled soul and body may *themselves* begin to seek ways back to health."[9]

A major source of inspiration for Borisov is the American Founding Fathers. Solzhenitsyn looked their way, too. This will seem odd to Westerners who think of Russia as alien, maybe Asiatic, only peripherally Western. Yet it was those Fathers who "first propounded the 'eternal rights of man and the citizen.' " And they did so because they "postulated that *every* human being bears the form and likeness of God; he *therefore* has an *absolute* value, and consequently also the *right* to be respected by his fellows." Needless to say, not all modern Americans view their Founding Fathers this way, nor do all American schoolchildren learn this view of them. As Borisov puts it, "Humanism has forgotten what the human personality is." For him, it is precisely Christianity that "gave birth to the very concept of the human personality" upon which the West established its institutions; "*personality* in its original sense is a specifically Christian concept."[10]

Attributing absolute value to the individual does not make Borisov an individualist. Far from it. Basic Christian teaching says otherwise. According to Borisov, "Having assumed the *perfect* nature of man in the Incarnation, Christ *forever* confirmed the natural unity of mankind, once enshrined in the person of the first man, 'Old Adam.' " He elaborates, "In other words, Christianity introduced to the world the concept of the *plurality of personalities of a single mankind*." Like Solzhenitsyn, Borisov finds in the events of Pentecost the sanction for the concept of a national personality. In language akin to that in the *Nobel Lecture*, Borisov explains,

The nation is a level in the hierarchy of the Christian cosmos, a part of God's immutable purpose. Nations are not created by a people's history. Rather, the nation's personality realizes itself through that history or, to put it another way, the people in their history fulfill God's design for them.

If this notion strikes the reader as puzzling, what it leads Borisov to is quite comprehensible. "A necessary precondition of the people's existence and development," he says, "is *historical memory*. If this is destroyed, the people's self-awareness suffers pathological distortion. . . ." Communism has been at work for decades trying to distort and even to erase the historical memory of his Russian people. It is precisely the passion to tell the truth of history that drove Solzhenitsyn to spend the best years of his life writing historical novels, not to mention *The Gulag Archipelago*. He mainly writes to Russians about Russia, but not because Russia, or any nation, is a self-contained entity—any more than an individual is a self-contained entity. Rather, he writes within the framework here articulated by Borisov: the framework of "an awareness of the individual's metaphysical relationship with the corporate self of the people, and *through it* with the corporate self of mankind." Borisov consciously articulates what he understands to be the Christian world view, and that is why for him the key question is always the "question about human nature."[11]

Christian theorizing by Borisov and the other contributors about the nature of man, the transformation of the world, and Russian religious renewal are all well and good. But is anyone listening? What are the prospects that the ideas in *From Under the Rubble* will gain a following in Russia? The necessarily pseudonymous A. B. thinks that he espies an audience in the making.

Mysteriously and unsuspected by the busy multitude, Christian consciousness, once almost defunct, is stealing back. In the last few years Christianity's word has suddenly and miraculously evoked a response in the hearts of many whose whole education, way of life and fashionable ideas about "alienation" and the historical pessimism of contemporary art would seem to have cut them off from it irrevocably. It is as if a door had opened while nobody was looking.

Clearly, A. B. is not referring to the babushkas, those little old ladies who have kept showing up at church, generation after generation, through the Soviet period—always a new generation of them. He is talking about intellectuals like himself. It is about these that he asks, "Why is this rebirth taking place in our country, where Christianity is attacked particularly systematically and with great brutality, while the rest of the world suffers a general decline in faith and religious feeling?" His answer features that staple theme of the great literary tradition of Russia: growth through suffering. About Russia under Communism, he says,

We have passed through such bottomless pits, . . . we have experienced such utter exhaustion of human resources that we have learned to see the "one essential" that cannot be taken away from man, and we have learned not to look to human resources for succor. In glorious destitution, in utter defenselessness in the face of suffering, our hearts have been kindled by an inner spiritual warmth and have opened to new, unexpected impulses. [12]

Not only does A. B. detect "the return of Christian consciousness"; he senses, also, "the presentiment of change." These two factors, taken together, "mark the special responsibilities of our time." Speaking for his compatriots in this volume, he asserts, "We are profoundly convinced that Christianity alone possesses enough motive force gradually to inspire and transform our world." Others have done Christian theorizing; without contradicting them at all, A. B. takes things a step further: "Christianity is more than a system of views, it is a way of life." In the Christian way of life, man will find true freedom. "Freedom is man's formula, but he will never find it so long as he seeks it in parties and ideologies. . . ." He elaborates in terms familiar to religious believers but perhaps incomprehensible to others. "This freedom is not man's 'natural' inheritance, but rather the aim of his life and a 'supernatural' gift. 'Servitude to sin' is how Christianity defines the normal condition of man's soul and it summons man to free himself from this servitude." [13]

In his closing paragraphs, A. B. brings up a contrast of particular interest to Western readers.

But we are confused. In the search for a solution our eyes habitually turn toward the West. There they have "progress" and "democracy." But in the West the most sensitive people are trying, with similar alarm and hope, to learn something from us. They assume, probably not unreasonably, that our harsh and oppressed life has taught us something that might be able to counteract the artificiality and soullessness of their own world—something that they have lost in all their worldly bustle.[14]

Solzhenitsyn has repeatedly wondered aloud if it is possible for one people to learn from the experience of another people, and specifically if the twentieth-century experience of the Russians can serve as an example of what others should not let happen to them. Is it also possible that, if the world is indeed at a watershed moment in history, the Russians can serve as the heralds and exemplars of how a new religious consciousness can take hold among a whole people? Westerners, accustomed to being world leaders, may be reluctant to contemplate this possibility, and the more so the lower their view of religion.

We do not know how the collaboration on *From Under the Rubble* came about. It is clear that Solzhenitsyn was the leading spirit, *primus inter pares*. He was the editor of the volume, not only a contributor. How much did he influence the thinking of these younger men, and how much did they come to their understandings separately? Ultimately, it does not matter that we cannot answer these questions. What does matter is to recognize that Solzhenitsyn is not alone in his thinking. It is useful to think of him and his collaborators as a vanguard group in the spiritual renaissance of Russia in the late twentieth century. Some of them are even clearer and more precise than he on theological and biblical matters, and thus they fill in details of the Christian vision which all of them hold in common. Two decades ago, the Soviet Union seemed to almost everyone to be a permanent fixture on the world scene. This small band saw the future differently. These men imagined themselves to be on the eve of a momentous change in their country and thus in the world as a whole. In some significant measure, what they were describing then looks like what we are seeing now. Let us give credit where credit is due.

GIVING DUE CREDIT to Solzhenitsyn is what is happening in Russia today. We have noted the appreciation expressed for *Rebuilding Russia*.

When the first parts of *The Gulag Archipelago* were being published in 1989 in the literary journal *Novy Mir*, editor Sergei Zalygin wrote that Solzhenitsyn "is simply essential for us today—we must know him and hear him, and we have no moral or intellectual right not to know him and hear him." However much or little one agrees with Solzhenitsyn, Zalygin proceeds, ". . . now, when we are settling accounts with our past, we can be sure that he resisted it. . . . This fact obliges us to think about many things."[15]

Viktor Astafyev, himself an author of some note, asserted in an interview, "I believe that the number one writer in the world now is Solzhenitsyn. . . ." This "greatest writer of our time" is also, for Astafyev, "a hero of the spirit." In his view, *The Gulag Archipelago* is "a verdict of 'guilty' "—and not only "against a cruel time and against violence" but "against us, too. Through our forbearance, we indulged violence." Clearly implicit here is that note of repentance which Solzhenitsyn urges upon his fellows as the first step toward spiritual recuperation. When the interviewer brought up hostile remarks about Solzhenitsyn by another writer, Astafyev replied,

> In the first place, he is an old man, but, although he was cut down by the camp, he is still strong in spirit. He is not consumed with vanity. Not like us weak people. In the second place, he is a believer. . . . Believers are always focused, always self-contained, and they bear in mind God and their work.

Here Astafyev gets right the main thing about Solzhenitsyn, his Christian faith. Whatever influence Solzhenitsyn is having and will have upon Russia, this is the central factor. All of his thoughts ray out from it. And Astafyev, with vivid imagery, is happy to acknowledge that Solzhenitsyn has influence: "The presence in the world of Aleksandr Isayevich, his work and his honor[,] has been like a lodestar—but this word has been overused. He has not been like a star but like the moon, shedding light on us. So that we wouldn't run into dark corners or stumble over logs." Therefore, he says, "If Aleksandr Isayevich comes back home, I will be very glad. I will bow to the ground before him, happy that this happened in my lifetime."[16]

*   *   *

ABOUT THE RELIGIOUS REVIVAL in Russia for which Solzhenitsyn has been calling, the one thing we can say for sure is that it is happening. John Meyendorff, an American theologian of Russian Orthodoxy, describes it as "very spectacular."[17] As more and more fragments of evidence surface, we shall doubtless have systematic accounts of it soon enough. The question here is whether Solzhenitsyn had any influence upon it. It is always difficult to prove influence. The only decisive evidence is the recipient's testimony. For the rest, one looks for consanguinity of outlook. This is allowable particularly when the source is well known and the viewpoint diverges from the norm. Solzhenitsyn called for religious revival, and now it is occurring. This could be, in terms of logic, a case of the *post hoc ergo propter hoc* fallacy. Or there could be some causal connection. It could be that Solzhenitsyn helped prepare the soil for the sprouting of this new religious devotion. Of course, no one would claim that he alone is the source for this renewal. No single person could be entirely responsible for a large social movement such as this, let alone a person half a world away and to whose words the general populace has had restricted access. Nor is he, in any generally understood sense of the term, a leader of a religious movement. At the same time, it is equally unlikely that there is no relationship between him and this phenomenon.

As the Soviet Union neared its end, Geoffrey Hosking observed, "Spiritually, the Soviet Union today is in an extraordinarily labile state. A secular Utopia has finally and completely collapsed, leaving many bewildered and bereft of hope or belief." He specifically uses religion as a category by which to address its denouement:

> Communism has never been a religion in the full sense of the word, but it has adopted many of the outward appurtenances of one. When its conviction fades, therefore, as it certainly has in the Soviet Union, it is natural that many of its adherents should seek a genuine religion to put in its place.[18]

Kent Hill, a close student of religion in Russia, sees a link between Solzhenitsyn and the current religious revival. Writing, like Hosking, just before the Soviet Union died, he calls the Soviet publication of *The Gulag Archipelago* "[p]erhaps the most dramatic sign of *glasnost*," and he comments on its impact:

It is hard to overestimate the historical and political significance of the publication of *Gulag* in the Soviet Union. In symbolic terms, it represents something like the removal of the Berlin Wall. It means that the old ideology with its totalitarian control of information is a thing of the past. It means new opportunities for religious perspectives to help inform and shape the future of what has been the Soviet Union.

His conviction that there is a link between Solzhenitsyn and the religious revival causes this normally cautious scholar to speculate, "One hundred years from now historians may well write that the person who best epitomizes the victory of the Russian religious spirit over Soviet communism is Alexander Solzhenitsyn."[19]

The Western press has paid some (but quite insufficient) attention to the new outburst of religious consciousness in Russia. We can read that more than forty percent of Soviet citizens retain a religious identity, also that, whereas there were 48,000 Russian Orthodox churches before the Communist era, there are now only 6,800.[20] Then again, we read that one-third of the citizens consider themselves believers and that from 1985 to 1990 some 5,500 parishes (4,100 of them Russian Orthodox) were established or reactivated, for an increase of almost fifty percent.[21] And we realize at once that there are discrepancies, sometimes wide ones, in the figures being reported. Oddly, the person who places the percentage of believers the highest, at seventy percent, is Konstantin Kharchev, at the time Chairman of the Soviet government's Council for Religious Affairs![22] There is much that we do not know about the details of the religious scene in Russia today.

We do know that in 1988 the New Testament appeared in serialized form in a periodical; David Powell says that it is the first time since the Bolshevik Revolution that a state publishing house made religious materials available. Also in 1988 the government approved the importation of one million Bibles. In 1989 churches and even some schools were granted permission to give religious instruction. In March 1990 three hundred clergymen were selected as "people's deputies" in legislative bodies.[23] We know that in 1990 the Soviet parliament passed a new Law on Freedom of Conscience, by a vote of 341 to 2, by which were legalized property rights for religious groups, the public practice of pastoral and religiously motivated charitable work, the opening up of seminary training, religious education of children.[24] We know that there is much restoration and refurbishing of church buildings, that church bells now ring again, that religious services now occur in cathedrals within the Kremlin walls, that religion is featured in Russian news telecasts more than it is in American counterparts, that secret believers are coming out of the closet, that atheism is in retreat. About this last, Powell says, "Finally given a chance to read the Old and New Testaments, many atheists and agnostics experienced a genuine spiritual awakening." And he cites one such, age thirty, who wrote, "I simply understood that I never was and never will be an atheist."[25]

Kent Hill's 1991 book, *The Soviet Union on the Brink*, is a repository of information about the state of religion under Gorbachev. It is worth consulting for its statistics and vignettes. It gives examples of the wave of repentance sweeping through the land, catching up even former persecutors of believers (though not high officials). This book is an updating of his 1989 book *The Puzzle of the Soviet Church*.[26] Yet, by limiting the scope of its speculations mostly to what Gorbachev might do by way of reforms affecting religion, this updated version, too, became somewhat outdated almost as soon as it appeared. Typical of Hill's caution is this statement: "Although we ought not to declare a full-fledged religious revival in the USSR, the signs of response by the Soviet people to the gospel are unmistakable."[27] Both politically and religiously, Russia keeps moving rapidly past the bounds of Western reports on it.

Here is an open-ended report which captures some of the pace of change:

> But Russia is a nation in search of spiritual rebirth as well as economic renewal and political reform. Sanctuaries where once only aged *babushkas* prayed are now filled with the faithful of all ages. Priests race from baptisms to bless homes and even state office buildings. They give church weddings to couples married years earlier at state wedding palaces. *Pravda*, long the mouthpiece of the Communist Party, is now publishing the Bible because it is good business.

And here is what, in all this religious ferment, strikes the reporter (or the magazine) as worthy of the large type at the head of the article: "The Orthodox Church is reviving. But will it be the repressive tool of a new nationalism?"[28] Why not think first of the spiritual thirst being slaked? If we believed in the primacy of the person, our thoughts might run in that direction. When we see all news, even religious revival, through the prism of politics, we think in terms of institutions and social forces. And so, in the name of the big picture, we miss the big story.

The most significant event granting room for this spiritual movement to flourish publicly was the government-approved celebration of the millennium of the Russian Orthodox Church in 1988. Many religious dignitaries from foreign countries traveled to Moscow to join in the festivities; Soviet television provided ample coverage. At the time, Father Gleb Yakunin wondered, "Is the great celebration to be only a lament for the historical past or the symbol and the archetype of a great new baptism?"[29]

Earlier in that same year, an academic conference was held in California to discuss religion in the Soviet Union. A major theme of the conference was "the growing importance of Christian culture to the process of *perestroika*." In that vein, "The consensus of the conference participants was that any alternative to socialism would probably draw from the national and religious heritages suppressed by the regime." But it was not yet clear how much public celebration of the church's millennium the authorities would permit. By the time the conference papers were ready for publication, the collection's editor, Nicolai Petro, stated, "In retrospect, the unprecedented amount of media coverage given to the clergy during this national celebration marks a turning point in official attitudes toward religion."[30] In his own essay, Petro refers to "Solzhenitsyn's popularity among today's intellectual elite"— and in large part because they recognize that "a main theme of Solzhenitsyn's writings has been the need to buttress democratic institutions with religious and patriotic commitments."[31] Alexander Ogorodnikov, reared a Communist but in adulthood a Christian political activist in the Soviet Union, had sent the conference a letter, saying in part, ". . . we believe that the time has come for a new self-determination by the church. Those spiritual processes which have been growing in peoples' hearts and in the grassroots communities have come to fruition. The harvest is ready to be reaped."[32] The events of the millennial year merely reinforced what Ogorodnikov already understood to be the case. We now know the answer to Yakunin's question.

Unfortunately, we must accord only limited credit to Mikhail

Gorbachev for allowing this religious festival. In a speech in late 1986, he was calling for " 'a decisive and uncompromising struggle' with religion and for an improvement in the quality of work done promoting atheism."[33] The next year the grand improviser was authorizing the big public celebration of the Russian Orthodox millennium. Given his waning popularity, he could not afford to antagonize yet further all those religious believers. This is a classic example of Gorbachev's instrumental view of freedom. The goal of the believers themselves, of course, was quite different: religious freedom for its own sake. As happened so often with Gorbachev, what he helped achieve was not what he aimed to achieve. Konstantin Kharchev, the Gorbachev administration official charged with overseeing religious activity, explained what the regime was up against: ". . . whether we like it or not, religion . . . is driving in like a train on a track. And since power belongs completely to us, I think we are capable of pointing this track in whatever direction is in our interest."[34] He was half right.

Kharchev gave a speech in early 1988 which was secretly recorded. He conceded that thirty percent of infants are christened and that a million religious funeral services are conducted per year, and he expressed his opinion that "funeral services are the most accurate indicator of religiosity." He explained to his presumably sympathetic auditors,

> We, the Party, have fallen into the trap of our own anti-church policy of prohibitions and persecutions; we drove a wedge between the priest and believers, yet this did not increase the believers' trust in local government bodies, and the Party and the state are increasingly losing control over believers.

It was of course his position that "the choice and appointment of priests is a Party matter" and that "[t]he most important task at the moment is to exercise effective control of the church through Party policy." But the evidence drove him to this melancholy generalization: "We are faced with an amazing phenomenon: despite all our efforts, the church has survived, and not only survived, but entered into a process of renewal." Most exasperatingly, believers band together to teach their children religion: "I can understand your indignation. I too am opposed to the teaching of religious instruction in schools. But what can we do?" His concluding note sinks toward hopelessness: "We are faced with

numerous problems, comrades. We have become accustomed to thinking that there's nobody but old women in the churches, but if you go into
a church nowadays you'll see hale and hearty people of our own age and
lots of young people."[35] Kharchev lost his office in 1989 for holding
attitudes too liberal toward believers.

In 1992 President Boris Yeltsin, after an extended period of frequent
church attendance, formally returned to the Russian Orthodox Church,
into which he had been baptized as an infant. He made it clear that he
had become "a believing Christian" and was "acquiring a different
world outlook." At the same time, he did not deny that, in light of the
religious revival, his conversion served a political purpose, as well. He
simply saw no conflict between the private and the public aspects of this
move. In his words, "I serve the Lord and the people."[36] Though there
is no clear reason to doubt the genuineness of his religious affirmation,
those who might be inclined to do so would still have to acknowledge
the powerful public pressure being exerted by the revival of religion in
Russia today. Most Western media did not consider Yeltsin's conversion
newsworthy enough to mention.

In his magisterial cultural history of Russia, *The Icon and the Axe*,
first published in 1966, James Billington concludes by speculating
about the future. "One cannot wishfully expect automatic evolution
toward democracy in the USSR," he says. "But Russia may well
develop new social and artistic forms presently unforeseen by either
East or West which will answer the restive demand of its people for
human freedom and spiritual renewal." He continues, "None can say
that rebirth will occur, none can be sure even that there is any sense to
be found in the history of a culture in which aspiration has so often
outreached accomplishment and anguish impaired achievement." Wist-
fully he muses, "Life out of death, freedom out of tyranny—irony,
paradox, perhaps too much to hope for." Yet, counseling patience, he
strikes a note of hope: "Impatient onlookers who have come to expect
immediate delivery of packaged products may have to rediscover the
processes of 'ripening as fruit ripens, growing as grass grows.' " And
he ends with hope-laden imagery of plants reaching full flower, of ships
finally reaching the destination of the other shore.[37] The fulfillment of
this hope is now much closer at hand than it was when Billington wrote
his book. It may not be too much to say, simply, that it has arrived.

* * * *

THE HISTORIC YEAR of 1991, when Communism relinquished control over the republics of the Soviet Union, was preceded by a similarly historic year, 1989, when the shackles fell from the Soviet satellite countries of Eastern and Central Europe. Solzhenitsyn's voice was heard by these peoples, too. Exactly how to sort out the extent of his influence upon them is for someone else to say in the future. That his writings helped them understand the nature of Communism is self-evident. The moral and political direction in which Solzhenitsyn pointed his fellow Russians has considerable congruence with the path that these nations have marked out for themselves. It is probably no accident that Poland, where religious faith remained least subjugated, led the way. More directly to the point, some writers in these countries have sounded themes strikingly similar to his; and, at a minimum, we can observe substantial consanguinity of outlook between them and him.

The most interesting of these is Václav Havel, the playwright who in late 1989 became the first non-Communist President of Czechoslovakia in forty years. Today he is widely respected as a practicing politician (whether in or out of office) but probably even more as a moral authority through his essays. If anything, Western commentators accord him deeper sympathy and appreciation nowadays than they do Solzhenitsyn. Yet the concord between Havel and Solzhenitsyn is very great. As independent thinkers their viewpoints are not of course identical. Nor is it helpful to think of Havel as a disciple of Solzhenitsyn. Nevertheless, their views overlap much more than they diverge, and the more so the closer we get to the hearts of their respective visions. On central matters they are in agreement. Moreover, Havel cites Solzhenitsyn on occasion. The nature of these citations does not suggest that Havel could have come up with certain of his ideas only because Solzhenitsyn first articulated them. It suggests, rather, that Havel found Solzhenitsyn's vision to comport well with his own. That is, what Solzhenitsyn said about the condition of the modern world turned out really to be its condition; Havel saw it, too. And he was glad to acknowledge this kinship of understanding. The following exposition of Havel's outlook is necessarily too brief to do justice to the subtlety of his thinking. It suffices only to show its kinship with and, by Havel's own testimony, a certain influence of Solzhenitsyn's outlook.

The first and most important thing to say about the kinship between these two writers is that they share the same language of moral discourse. Thus, Havel writes, in language reminiscent of Solzhenitsyn, "The worst thing is that we are living in a decayed moral environment. We have become morally ill, because we have become accustomed to saying one thing and thinking another. . . ."[38] So the first task facing a people who would be free is not political but pre-political. Political programs can come into effectual play only after people have attended to moral matters.[39] "Notions such as love, friendship, compassion, humility, and forgiveness have lost their depth and dimension."[40] Moral qualities such as these are what a subject people most need to revive.

As with Solzhenitsyn, so with Havel, the chief villain is ideology. Havel describes it as "a specious way of relating to the world. It offers human beings the illusion of an identity, of dignity, and of morality, while making it easier for them to *part* with them." Ideology has as its "primary excusatory function . . . to provide people . . . with the illusion that the system is in harmony with the human order and the order of the universe."[41] But the system which ideology imposes upon people is itself "built on lies." Havel elaborates, "Because the regime is captive to its own lies, it must falsify everything. It falsifies the past. It falsifies the present, and it falsifies the future. It falsifies statistics." Therefore, to get along, individuals "*must live within a lie*. They need not accept the lie. It is enough for them to have accepted their life with it and in it."[42] So Havel calls upon his people to live not in the lie but in the truth. And one is inescapably reminded of Solzhenitsyn's essay "Live Not by Lies."

Where are we to locate "this line of conflict" between living in the lie and living in the truth? Havel says that "this line runs *de facto* through each person, for everyone in his or her own way is both a victim and a supporter of the system." Again Solzhenitsyn leaps to mind; he wrote repeatedly that the line dividing good and evil cuts through the heart of every human being. Havel, too, sees that the task of transforming the nation must begin with "the transformation of human beings." The so-called dissidents of the Communist world "do not shy away from the idea of violent political overthrow because the idea seems too radical, but on the contrary, because it does not seem radical enough. For them, the problem lies far too deep to be settled through mere systemic changes."[43]

In no way is Havel here advocating the self-contained attention to the soul which we might label individualism. The "proper point of departure" for living within the truth is "concern for others."[44] Perhaps no theme looms larger in Havel's writings than the theme of responsibility. It is that "which makes one a person and forms the basis of one's identity." Human responsibility is "that fundamental point from which all identity grows and by which it stands or falls; it is the foundation, the root, the center of gravity, the constructional principle or axis of identity. . . ." In short, he asserts as his guiding principle, "I am responsible for the state of the world."[45] This is the same move from responsibility for the self to responsibility for the community that Solzhenitsyn makes.

There is more. In addition to human solidarity, there is

> a "higher" responsibility, which grows out of a conscious or subconscious certainty that our death ends nothing, because everything is forever being recorded and evaluated somewhere else, somewhere "above us," in what I have called "the memory of Being," an integral aspect of the secret order of the cosmos, of nature, and of life, which believers call God and to whose judgment everything is liable.[46]

Havel's insistence that there is a transcendent realm of reality to which we are beholden—a theme to which he returns repeatedly—again puts us in mind of Solzhenitsyn and his understanding of the moral universe.

Whenever Havel refers directly to Solzhenitsyn, it is always on a major, not a subsidiary, point. For instance, he asks why Solzhenitsyn was driven out of his own country. It was not because Solzhenitsyn "represented a unit of real power" and might replace the Soviet leaders in the seat of government.

> Solzhenitsyn's expulsion was something else: a desperate attempt to plug up the dreadful wellspring of truth, a truth which might cause incalculable transformations in social consciousness, which in turn might one day produce political debacles unpredictable in their consequences. . . . But the moment someone breaks through in one place, when one person cries out, "The emperor is naked!"—when a single person breaks the rules of the game, thus exposing it as a game—everything suddenly appears in another light and the whole crust seems then to be made of a tissue on the point of tearing and disintegrating uncontrollably.[47]

The power of truth is the power of words. Havel ruminates on this subject in his luminous essay "Words on Words." He begins by citing the opening words of the Gospel of John: "In the beginning was the Word." Then he brings the subject down to earth. "If the Word of God is the source of God's entire creation then that part of God's creation which is the human race exists as such only thanks to another of God's miracles—the miracle of human speech." The effect of language cannot be overestimated: ". . . whether we are aware of it or not, and however we explain it, one thing would seem to be obvious: we have always believed in the power of words to change history. . . ." These understandings have particular significance for persons living under totalitarian regimes.

> Yes, I really do inhabit a system in which words are capable of shaking the entire structure of government, where words can prove mightier than ten military divisions, where Solzhenitsyn's words of truth were regarded as something so dangerous that it was necessary to bundle their author into an airplane and transport him. Yet, in the part of the world I inhabit the word Solidarity was capable of shaking an entire power bloc.

Typically, this line of thought, too, brings Havel to his central theme of human responsibility: "Responsibility for and toward words is a task which is intrinsically ethical." Then he adds, as would befit Solzhenitsyn also, "As such, however, it is situated beyond the horizon of the visible world, in that realm wherein dwells the Word that was in the beginning and is not the word of Man."[48]

As it turns out, Havel does not like Western journalists' usage of the label "dissidents." In explaining why he always places quotation marks around the word, he refers again to Solzhenitsyn and explicitly remarks his political influence. "Dissidents," says Havel,

> are ordinary people with ordinary cares, differing from the rest only in that they say aloud what the rest cannot say or are afraid to say. I have already mentioned Solzhenitsyn's political influence: it does not reside in some exclusive political power he possesses as an individual, but in the experience of those millions of Gulag victims which he simply amplified and communicated to millions of other people of good will.

When journalists "institutionalize a select category of well-known or prominent 'dissidents,' " the unwitting effect is "to deny the most intrinsic moral aspect of their activity. . . . It is truly a cruel paradox that the more some citizens stand up in defence of other citizens, the more they are labelled with a word that in effect separates them from those 'other citizens.' " It would be better to consider the "dissidents" as being "like the proverbial one-tenth of the iceberg visible above the water."[49]

As surprising as it may be to Westerners who praise Havel but denigrate Solzhenitsyn, Havel agrees with Solzhenitsyn's analysis of the "deep crisis of traditional democracy" today. Both observe in it a deficiency of undergirding moral vision.

> In his June 1978 Harvard lecture, Solzhenitsyn describes the illusory nature of freedoms not based on personal responsibility and the chronic inability of the traditional democracies, as a result, to oppose violence and totalitarianism. In a democracy, human beings may enjoy many personal freedoms and securities that are unknown to us, but in the end they do them no good, for they too are ultimately victims of the same automatism, and are incapable of defending their concerns about their own identity or preventing their superficialization or transcending concerns about their own personal survival to become proud and responsible members of the *polis*. . . .

Therefore, Havel, too, warns against a wholesale adoption by post-Communist countries of a Western political model.

> But to cling to the notion of traditional parliamentary democracy as one's political ideal and to succumb to the illusion that only this "tried and true" form is capable of guaranteeing human beings enduring dignity and an independent role in society would, in my opinion, be at the very least short-sighted.[50]

In a passage which does not mention Solzhenitsyn directly, Havel crystallizes exactly the kind of influence which Solzhenitsyn has had on many in the Soviet bloc, including Havel himself. Prophetic moral voices "help . . . to raise the confidence of citizens; they shatter the world of 'appearances' and unmask the real nature of power. They do not assume a messianic role; they are not a social 'avant-garde' or 'elite' that alone knows best. . . ." There is no "arrogant self-projection" in them. "Nor do they want to lead anyone. They leave it up to each individual to decide what he or she will or will not take from their experience and work." What they do provide is the "far broader influence" of "the indirect pressure felt from living within the truth: the pressure created by free thought, alternative values and 'alternative behaviour,' and by independent social self-realization."[51] Solzhenitsyn has never seen himself as the fountainhead of a new social or political movement. Were that the case, it would be easy to describe the exact parameters of his influence. It is a hazier and less precise matter to describe influence in matters of the human spirit. But such influence is none the less real; it is, indeed, the most powerful and enduring kind of influence. To be specific, Havel's essay "The Power of the Powerless" owes more of its inspiration to Solzhenitsyn than to anyone else; it would not have been the same apart from the background provided by Solzhenitsyn.

The influence of Solzhenitsyn upon Václav Havel is all the more noteworthy for Havel's being unable to embrace unreservedly the Christian faith which provides the context for Solzhenitsyn's moral vision. Havel has said that he is "certainly not a proper Christian and Catholic."[52] Yet he can speak easily of "my conviction that the Lord didn't send me to prison in vain."[53] Also, he believes in the immortality of the human soul.[54] When an interviewer asked him if he had converted to Catholicism, he opened his reply, "It depends on how we understand conversion." He had not become a practicing Catholic, and he was not ready to replace "an uncertain 'something' with a completely unambiguous personal God, and fully, inwardly, to accept Christ as the Son of God." Nevertheless, he explained, "There are some things that I have felt since childhood: that there is a great mystery above me which is the focus of all meaning and the highest moral authority. . . ." He considers himself a believer only in the sense that "all of this—life and the universe—is not just 'in and of itself.' " And he adds, "I can try to live in the spirit of Christian morality."[55] As Havel says about God, ". . . my relationship to him is so difficult to pin down. . . ."[56]

In short, Havel has no reservations about affirming a transcendent realm of reality which provides meaning to our earthly lives, but he brings himself up short of accepting, as Solzhenitsyn does accept, that a personal God is the source of this moral order. However, he certainly flirts with the idea of a personalness to this source, as when he says,

Whether God exists or not—as Christians understand it—I do not and cannot know: I don't even know if that word is an appropriate label for the call to responsibility I hear. I know only this: that Being (which is, after all, easier to posit than the being of God) . . . takes on, in the sphere of our inner experience . . . an expressly personal outline. . . . In other words: the Being of the universe . . . suddenly assumes a personal face and turns this, as it were, toward us.[57]

Moreover, as between "the Judeo-Christian way of thinking and biblical metaphysics" on the one hand and "the whole tradition of European philosophy that grew out of classical philosophy" on the other, Havel says without hesitation that the way of thinking nearer to his own is "the Judeo-Christian way, with its concreteness and its respect for the world of the senses. . . ." He says, also, "I admit to an affinity for Christian sentiment and I'm glad that it's recognizable. . . ."[58] Finally, as any faith in transcendence might have an impact on how we live responsibly, Christianity has much to recommend it. "Historical experience teaches us that any genuinely meaningful point of departure in an individual's life usually has an element of universality about it." As attracted as Havel is to the counter-cultural ideas of the 1960's, he thinks that the retreat of Westerners to an ashram in India "lacks that element of universality." By contrast, "Christianity is an example of an opposite way out: it is a point of departure for me here and now—but only because anyone, anywhere, at any time, may avail themselves of it."[59] We see, then, that, although Havel and Solzhenitsyn are not at one in their attitude toward Christianity, they are close allies by virtue of their common conviction that meaning in this life has its source in the transcendent sphere.

Given the compatibility of their world views, it should not surprise us that Havel and Solzhenitsyn have much in common in their practical suggestions about politics. The heart of Havel's "presidential program," he asserts, is "to bring spirituality, moral responsibility, humaneness, and humility into politics and, in that respect, to make clear that there is something higher above us, that our deeds do not disappear into the black hole of time but are recorded somewhere and judged. . . ."[60] Solzhenitsyn's programmatic proposals have the same tenor. On economics, Solzhenitsyn's advocacy of free enterprise emphasizes the principle of decentralization. Havel favors "an economic system based on the maximum possible plurality of many decentralized, structurally varied, and preferably small enterprises that respect the specific nature of different localities and different traditions and that resist the pressure of uniformity." On politics, Solzhenitsyn argues for a non-party path of democracy. Havel concurs. "It would seem to make more sense if, again, people rather than political parties were elected (that is, if people could be elected without party affiliation)." He agrees with Solzhenitsyn exactly when he says, "There should be no limit to the number of political parties, but they should, rather, be something like political clubs. . . ."[61] These agreements on economics and politics are not a case of Solzhenitsyn's influence; Havel wrote his words before *Rebuilding Russia* appeared. They are clearly a case of consanguinity of thinking.

No area of agreement between Havel and Solzhenitsyn is more important than their overarching analyses of the condition of the modern world. Solzhenitsyn thinks that we are approaching a watershed moment in history. Ideas which have their roots in the Renaissance and took on normative shape in the Enlightenment have now run out of steam, and we stand in need of a new paradigm. To read Havel on this vast and vital subject is almost to reread Solzhenitsyn. In Havel's words,

> The modern era has been dominated by the culminating belief . . . that the world—and Being as such—is a wholly knowable system governed by a finite number of universal laws that man can grasp and rationally direct for his own benefit. This era, beginning in the renaissance and developing from the Enlightenment to socialism . . . was characterized by rapid advances in rational cognitive thinking.

This is an "era of belief in automatic progress brokered by the scientific method."[62] At its core, this modern era is marked by "a great departure from God which has no parallel in history. As far as I know," Havel states, "we are living in the middle of the first atheistic civilization." It is Havel's judgment that "this arrogant anthropocentrism of modern man, who is convinced he can know everything and bring everything under his control, is somewhere in the background of the present crisis."[63]

For those who have eyes to see, there is one great sign of the turning point in history which humanity has reached.

The end of Communism is, first and foremost, a message to the human race. It is a message we have not yet fully deciphered and comprehended. In its deepest sense, the end of Communism has brought a major era in human history to an end. It has brought an end not just to the 19th and 20th centuries, but to the modern age as a whole.

The fall of Communism is "a signal that the era of arrogant, absolutist reason is drawing to a close and that it is high time to draw conclusions from that fact."[64]

Westerners can see readily enough that the death of Communism radically alters the landscape of formerly Communist lands. But what does that have to do with the West? Havel's understanding of the relationship between political East and political West is virtually the same as Solzhenitsyn's. Havel, too, sees Soviet totalitarianism as "an extreme manifestation . . . of a deep-seated problem that also finds expression in advanced Western society." Both East and West participate in "a trend toward impersonal power and rule by megamachines or colossi that escape human control." Whether these "juggernauts of impersonal power" are "large-scale enterprises" or "faceless governments," they "represent the greatest threat to our present-day world." And this all came about when "humanity declared itself to be the supreme ruler of the universe—at that moment, the world began to lose its human dimension."[65]

The Cold War has inevitably conditioned Westerners to emphasize the differences between East and West, to think about the modern world in terms of competing principles: democracy *versus* totalitarianism, capitalism *versus* socialism. Both Havel and Solzhenitsyn see things differently. In Havel's words, "The West and the East, though different in so many ways, are going through a single, common crisis."[66] For Havel, Communism "is only one aspect—a particularly drastic aspect and thus all the more revealing of its real origins—of this general inability of modern humanity to be the master of its own situation." Thus, we are faced with "the general failure of modern humanity." We are faced with a "planetary challenge to the position of human beings in the world." And, as compared with what Communism has wrought, Havel judges, "There is no real evidence that western democracy . . . can offer solutions that are any more profound."[67]

Havel is well aware that "people in the West in general tend not to

admit that humanity is in a state of crisis and that therefore their own humanity is in a state of crisis too."[68] Precisely because persons in the East have experienced the full brunt of the modern world's dehumanization, they are in a position to offer advice and guidance to persons in the West. As Havel phrases the point, "And do we not in fact stand (although in the external measure of civilization, we are far behind) as a kind of warning to the West, revealing to it its own latent tendencies?"[69] Here we are put in mind of the many times Solzhenitsyn asked if the experience of people in one part of the world could be absorbed by people in another part in time for them to escape the same fate.

But what exactly can the East teach the West? Havel approaches this large question from a number of angles. Those who have suffered under totalitarianism are in a position to teach those who have not that "the salvation of this human world lies nowhere else than in the human heart," that the "general breakdown of civilization" cannot be avoided "[w]ithout a global revolution in the sphere of human consciousness," that we must learn "how to put morality ahead of politics, science and economics."[70] The East can teach the West that man "must discover again, within himself, a deeper sense of responsibility toward the world, which means responsibility toward something higher than himself." Specifically, this discovery must entail "directing ourselves toward the moral and the spiritual, based on respect for some 'extramundane' authority—for the order of nature or the universe, for a moral order and its superpersonal origin."[71] The inclination of the West, as Havel knows, is to look for systemic answers, for "a system that will eliminate all the disastrous consequences of previous systems." But the answer must be "something different, something larger. Man's attitude to the world must be radically changed. We have to abandon the arrogant belief that the world is merely a puzzle to be solved. . . ." On the immanent level, "In a word, human uniqueness, human action and the human spirit must be rehabilitated." On the transcendent level, we must learn—or relearn—"humility in the face of the mysterious order of Being. . . ." Only then will we be able to develop a politics ready for "the task of finding a new, postmodern face."[72]

What saves these future-oriented speculations from mere apocalypticism is the note of hope which ever intrudes into Havel's discourses, just as it does into Solzhenitsyn's. "Hope," Havel declares, "is definitely not the same thing as optimism. It is not the conviction that something will turn out well, but the certainty that something makes sense, regardless of how it turns out." And it is precisely about this steadfast sort of hope that he says, ". . . the only true source of the breathtaking dimension of the human spirit and its efforts, is something we get, as it were, from 'elsewhere.' "[73]

SOLZHENITSYN'S INFLUENCE upon his contemporaries extends beyond the inhabitants of the Communist world. In the West, too, people have changed their minds because of him. It would be impressive enough if, as is arguably the case, because of him leaders of the Western nations had strengthened their resolve to resist the expansionism of Communism and thereby contributed to the decline of Soviet power.[74] It would be even more impressive if his influence upon Westerners were to include causing Communists and close allies of theirs to change their mind. It would be most impressive if this influence were so pervasive as to reorient the intellectual life of a whole large nation in the West. Yet exactly this has been claimed to be the case in France. In the home country of one of the largest and most powerful Communist parties in the West, Solzhenitsyn has had the effect of so undermining Communism that the trumpeted goal of Eurocommunism has been thoroughly discredited.

This French connection has been remarked by many. Lawrence Uzzell, for one, declares that Solzhenitsyn "may deserve more credit than anyone else for the collapse of French Marxism." Uzzell cites Solzhenityn's French biographer, Georges Nivat, as recalling that "his unforgettable television appearances made him an intimate of the French public. He won us over with his ardor, his deftness, his knowing Gulag smile."[75] Robert Conquest, for another, notes that in France we see a "particularly striking" instance of Solzhenitsyn's influence. The "*bien pensant*" intellectuals who had resisted the logical arguments of a Raymond Aron and the polemics of a Jean-François Revel faltered before Solzhenitsyn's witness. In Conquest's words,

> The sudden disintegration of this new Age of Faith, the swift dissipation of the tenacious miasmas which had hung over the French mind, have been truly astonishing. This has largely been the work of a group of

young philosophers whose starting point had been the great left-wing protest of May 1968, but who had meanwhile been subjected to the immense shock of Solzhenitsyn and the *Gulag Archipelago*: that and that alone, as they themselves make absolutely clear, produced their change of heart and mind. For this single achievement in one country alone, its testimony to truth would have justified itself.[76]

These are the young intellectuals who became known as the French "New Philosophers." Even H. Stuart Hughes, who from his leftist position writes disdainfully of them, must acknowledge Solzhenitsyn's impact upon them: "It was symptomatic of France's lingering cultural provincialism that only with the publication of *The Gulag Archipelago* in the early 1970s did its complacent intellectuals of the Left awaken from their dogmatic slumbers." Hughes's main complaint against the "New Philosophers" is that they "lumped together without discrimination all forms of socialist theory and practice as variants of Soviet-style Marxism." This move is, for Hughes, "at the very least . . . irresponsible exaggeration."[77] Hughes singles out, as the most significant of these "New Philosophers," André Glucksmann and Bernard-Henri Lévy. Our snapshot of this instance of Solzhenitsyn's influence will be limited to these two, especially to Lévy.

The phenomenon of the French "New Philosophers" was deemed important enough for American public television to devote a documentary program to it. The program was entitled "Solzhenitsyn's Children"—followed, after ellipsis dots, by the subtitle "Are Making a Lot of Noise in Paris." It is, the lead-in says, about "a bunch of turncoat writers. Former Communists and Maoists who have been reading a certain Soviet writer." The documentary credits Solzhenitsyn with initiating the French debate about Marxism. Its focus is upon the generation of May 1968, those students and other youths who engaged in street demonstrations and protests then but who later read Solzhenitsyn. Glucksmann and Lévy are singled out for special attention. Lévy it calls "the big star." Glucksmann it cites as asserting that Marxism is as bad as Nazism and that "[w]hat really turned us around is the resistance of the dissidents in the Soviet Union."[78]

Lévy's book *Barbarism with a Human Face*, the centerpiece of this snapshot of ours, is a vehement repudiation of the Leftism upon which the author was nurtured. Lévy says that Glucksmann was the first of their generation to arrive at the understandings which this book is devoted to explaining. And Lévy is forthright about his own sense of indebtedness to Solzhenitsyn:

> I have learned more from reading *The Gulag Archipelago* than from many erudite commentaries on totalitarian languages. I owe more to Solzhenitsyn than to most of the sociologists, historians, and philosophers who have been contemplating the fate of the West for the last thirty years. It is enigmatic that the publication of this work was enough to immediately shake our mental landscape and overturn our ideological guideposts.

Calling Solzhenitsyn "the Shakespeare of our time" and "our Dante as well," he finds that the main power of *The Gulag Archipelago* is that it "bodies forth the unimaginable, gives a name to the unnamable, and above all forces us *to believe* what we were satisfied with *knowing*." Reading Solzhenitsyn set in motion, for him and his peers, "a chain reaction, first of all with reference to Marxism. All Solzhenitsyn had to do was *to speak* and we awoke from a dogmatic sleep. All he had to do was *to appear*, and an all too long history finally came to an end. . . ." Lévy pauses to reflect, "Just think of the monumental deception we have lived with for almost fifty years." For him, "Solzhenitsyn has the virtue of *forcing us to look*. The strength of his text is that it forbids blindness."[79]

Lévy sees in Solzhenitsyn's testament not merely a description of the Soviet prison-camp system as some self-contained entity but an account of something which is representative of the spirit of the age and which therefore demands of him a total reassessment of his thinking about the modern world. It leads him, first of all, to renounce his cherished belief in socialism: ". . . the Gulag is not a blunder or an accident, nor a simple wound or aftereffect of Stalinism; but the necessary corollary of a socialism which can only actualize homogeneity by driving the forces of heterogeneity back to its fringes. . . ." Marxism is now to be seen as "the religion of our time," as the veritable "opium of the people." Furthermore, Lévy has come to concur in Solzhenitsyn's larger historical interpretation of drawing a straight line from the Enlightenment to modern socialism. Although, as he knows from personal experience, the Left "makes a virtue out of its attachment to the principles of the

Enlightenment," he now concludes, "If socialism is the sinister reality embodied in the Gulag, this is not because it has distorted, caricatured, or betrayed, but because it is faithful, *excessively* faithful, to the very idea of progress as it has been produced by the West." Therefore, Lévy explains, he has come to see the concept of progress "as a reactionary mechanism which is leading the world to catastrophe," even "as a uniform and linear progression toward evil." So, pugnaciously, he calls upon us readers to "proclaim ourselves *anti-progressive*."[80] Lévy's new understanding of the modern world drives him to search for a spiritual, even religious, interpretation of the human condition. His book *The Testament of God* conveys his ruminations on this theme.[81]

ALTHOUGH THE FRENCH "New Philosophers" constitute a particularly impressive example of Solzhenitsyn's influence upon intellectuals beyond the confines of the old Soviet bloc, they are not an isolated case. Intellectuals need not have been under the spell of Marxism to have had their world views affected by reading Solzhenitsyn. Others are now saying things about the modern world that they could not have said without being exposed to his vision. Nowadays, it is not uncommon to find Solzhenitsyn's name listed in the indices of books analyzing the modern era. His writing has become an essential piece of the mental furniture of many participants of the cultural conversation of our time. For the last of the concentric circles in this chapter on Solzhenitsyn's influence, we shall consider the case of David Walsh, a member of the political science faculty at Catholic University of America. Walsh has written a daring and provocative book, *After Ideology: Recovering the Spiritual Foundations of Freedom*, and Solzhenitsyn plays a major role in it.

Walsh's thesis is that "the epochal challenges presented by our historical moment" demand nothing less than "the decisive reorientation of our civilization." The prevailing currents of thought have reached their dead end. Walsh's book is primarily "a study of the existential search for order in soul and society by some of the most profound thinkers of the contemporary world."[82] Among nineteenth-century thinkers, Fyodor Dostoevsky and Friedrich Nietzsche were the great prophets of the coming impasse. Walsh's great twentieth-century interpreters of modernity are political philosopher Eric Voegelin and novelists Albert

Camus and Aleksandr Solzhenitsyn. These three, along with Dostoevsky, serve for Walsh as not only the great analysts of the modern world but also the four avatars of a postmodern order devoutly to be pursued. They understand both the questions framed by the malaise of modernity and the vein of human experience in which to look for answers.

Walsh's analysis of the modern world comports well with those of the scholars cited in the late pages of Chapter Six. However, Walsh stands apart from these others on two counts. One is simply the extent of his indebtedness to Solzhenitsyn. The other is the clarity of his articulation of a way out of the modern impasse into a restorative and humane postmodern reality. These two counts are closely related; for Solzhenitsyn, the only one of Walsh's avatars still living, is also perhaps the clearest herald of the new age now in its birth pangs.

What the Enlightenment offered, in Walsh's analysis, was "the promise of universal human progress." What the twentieth century presents experientially is "the reality of persistent human failure." These two are necessarily and intrinsically linked. And the thread which binds them together is ideology. This is the central inheritance of the Enlightenment. Underlying all ideological appropriations and manipulations is a severing of the tie between the immanent realm of human experience and the transcendent realm of a divinely created order for human life. Man thus becomes the measure of all things, the sole arbiter even of morality; man is autonomous. This is (to use a term that Walsh shares with Solzhenitsyn and Havel) anthropocentrism. It could be called "[t]he Faustian bargain, by which a vast new power is given to us at the cost of the soul that alone can provide the wisdom for its use." It could also be called the "Promethean drive," in which "[n]othing can be allowed to stand in the way of attaining human happiness, least of all humanity itself." Thus, it turns out that "the most 'twentieth century' of phenomena" is the concentration camp of the totalitarian state, the goal of which is "the final and irrevocable transformation of human nature itself."[83]

The failure of the modern project is now widely perceived. Its unintended consequences, seen nowhere so clearly as in the experience of Communism, have set in motion a counter-movement.

The spirit of arrogant self-assertion has engendered a quite opposite sense of the limitation of power, of the finiteness of human nature, and of humility before the mystery of the cosmos. An age of extravagant ideological constructions has given way to a profoundly skeptical realism that is suspicious of all utopian suggestions. Most surprising of all, the resolute insistence on the death of God as the first principle of human freedom has engendered a persistent resurgence of faith in God as the bedrock of human dignity.

What sets Walsh's avatars apart from many other interpreters of an absurd modern world is that "they have entered fully into the spirit of modernity and emerged on the other side with a vision of reality that has proved itself superior." This vision is grounded not in abstract systems of thought but in the personal experience of our dehumanizing century. And the content of that vision, as Walsh explicates it, is consonant with what I have called the moral universe.

> One recognizes this experiential source as the fount for all the ideas of truth, goodness and justice within the great spiritual traditions of human history, only now one has made them one's own by living them out. A new or a newly rediscovered force is unleashed into history and the possibility of a renewed civilizational order has at last erupted into the modern world. [84]

In Solzhenitsyn's own case, he entered the Gulag a committed Communist and emerged "a faithful, repentant Christian." To him belongs "the catharsis of the victim who rises to the spiritual height of victory over his oppressors." That is why he could thank God for prison. It was there that he became not merely an anti-Communist but, more fully and exactly, "an anti-ideologist." It was there that he came to understand that "[t]he ideological project, the transfiguration of human nature on a mass scale, is an impossible task." It was there that he reached the conclusion that "[t]he only freedom worth having is the inner freedom of soul to pursue what is good without qualification"—and thus "the firm conviction that it is in relation to this inner spiritual life that all else must be measured." [85]

Walsh is at pains to argue—and here he draws heavily from Voegelin—that modern secular humanism, including its manifestation in atheistic socialism, is inherently "quasi-religious" and has affinities with the Gnosticism of early Christian history. It implicitly seeks "the divinization of human nature." Secular humanists may be "antitheistic," but they are not "unreligious." Moreover, Walsh explains, ". . . the increasing consensus on the pseudoreligious character of modernity has clearly been building toward a critical point, where it can no longer be ignored." Yet "the conventional secular conception" does exactly that. "Debate occurs within well-defined parameters; anyone straying outside to question fundamental assumptions is conveniently ignored."[86] That of course tells also the story of Solzhenitsyn's cold reception among Western intellectuals.

As an anti-ideologist, Solzhenitsyn understands that "the only way of achieving the moral regeneration of society" is, in Walsh's words, "to acknowledge the necessity for personal conversion." This position remains anathema to ideologists, who "have persistently rejected the call to repentance and submission to the transcendent order of rightness as the means of renewal." They remain committed to "[a] magical belief in the power of revolutionary or external action to perfect the inner person." In reality, order in the soul comes prior to order in society. As Walsh explains, "This is why as a group the postmoderns are characterized by a remarkable flexibility with regard to political structures. It is one of the most distinctive features of a viewpoint purged of virtually all ideological inclinations."[87]

Walsh's discussion of Solzhenitsyn's relationship with liberalism is particularly valuable. For Solzhenitsyn, liberalism has this element "in common with Communism and all ideological forms: the lack of a moral and spiritual foundation." Walsh elaborates, "Where Communism explicitly disavows the reality of any objective moral order, liberalism merely disregards it by reducing it to the level of private subjective opinion. In the end it comes to the same thing." Walsh then offers this intriguing critical comment about his heroes:

> What seems to be largely absent from all four is a recognition that a spiritually grounded liberalism is the most appropriate expression of what they have in mind. While they do not explicitly embrace liberal democracy, I believe it can be shown that a rejuvenated liberalism is in fact what their prescriptions imply.

That is to say, spiritually regenerated individuals will not hold their moral vision as a private subjective opinion but will wish and need to give it social institutional expression. Religious experience will not remain self-contained but will issue in a world view. This is what Walsh means by philosophy; what he wants is a philosophic, not merely an experiential, Christianity. And "[i]t is interesting to note that the post-modern thinkers surmounted their own personal crises only through the elaboration of its wider civilizational significance." Giving their faith social expression should bring his avatars, Walsh avers, to "a position equivalent to that of classical liberalism: government is there to serve the individual and not the other way around."[88] In this discussion Walsh unknowingly anticipates *Rebuilding Russia*, which appeared only shortly after he had finished his book. What Walsh thinks is the direction in which Solzhenitsyn's thought should logically move is exactly the direction in which it does.

According to Walsh, "The anchoring of individual and political order in the movement toward transcendent reality is the most profound and most remarkable feature of postmodern political thought." The question then becomes how representative Walsh's four men will prove to be. "Has the crisis of modernity been surmounted? Or are we merely witnessing the resurgence of a private experience of faith?" This is, says Walsh, "the question on which the fate of the modern world depends." We must wait to see whether these four "represent the beginning of a renewed civilizational order or are merely an epiphenomenal blip within the long protracted process of spiritual exhaustion." Here Walsh is very hopeful, and for this reason: "The basis for the expectation of relevance is that the postmodern thinkers have discovered the truth of philosophy and Christianity *within* the modern world." Far from being "antiquarians or devotees of a long forgotten past," these "thoroughly modern" men have "lived out in their lives" the very "crises and sufferings that their age has undergone." If "we finally break free from the prevailing worldview," it will be not in a spirit of retreat into some imagined safe haven of pastness but by a transcending of the modern experience, with its lessons now learned.[89]

Walsh is hopeful—maybe too hopeful. He asserts, "Liberalism in our own time has finally revealed its loss of inner spiritual direction. . . ." It is true that some modern secular liberals acknowledge the bankruptcy of liberalism, and thus we now have the phenomenon known as postliberalism. Such persons would be inclined to agree with Walsh that "[t]he collapse of the liberal moral consensus and the recognition of its dehumanizing consequences has rendered the nature of the modern crisis with a clarity unrivaled since the Renaissance." Walsh is also aware of the direction from which to expect antagonism toward his viewpoint. Modernity "continues to retain a good deal of anti-Christian prejudice. Will not contemporary society merely perceive this as one more reactionary attempt to assert religious controls?" Nevertheless, Walsh is persuaded that today's intellectual enterprise has moved definitively beyond ideological encapsulations to an embrace of "the incarnate truth of experience," and he believes that "the necessity of recovering the pre-articulate sources of order is becoming so widely recognized that it might be regarded as the common premise of all serious theoretical reflection today."[90]

In support of his optimism, Walsh gives an impressive list of critics who have recognized that modern liberalism "cannot long continue on its theoretically flimsy foundations." He mentions Leo Strauss, Hannah Arendt, Michael Oakeshott, Reinhold Niebuhr, John Courtney Murray, Jacques Maritain, Yves Simon, John Hallowell, Peter Berger, Alasdair MacIntyre, George Parkin Grant. In Walsh's summary judgment, "A new awareness is beginning to dawn that the most profound social problems cannot be solved by political means. The influential books are the ones that call attention to this quandary of liberal democracy: its inability to form the inner order of the souls of its citizens."[91]

Is the modern world passing? Is a new order of civilization in the process of being born? Walsh thinks so. So does Solzhenitsyn. Walsh has learned some considerable part of what he knows from Solzhenitsyn. Walsh's understandings and insights are overwhelmingly compatible with what I have been saying throughout this book, and obviously I have devoted these pages to his book in order to confirm and to strengthen my own case. Nevertheless, the main reason for this exposition of the Walsh book has been to demonstrate that people are reading and heeding Solzhenitsyn. If many intellectuals have turned a deaf ear in his direction, he is not without influence upon his contemporaries. And his influence is being felt even in the world of scholarship.

As HUMANKIND APPROACHES the end of another century of history, this time also the end of a millennium, we are readily enough inclined to think in apocalyptic terms of an impending catastrophe. In fact, we expect to read much that is in this vein. The usual *fin-de-siècle* mood is redolent of weariness, exhaustion, and decay, of calamity just around the corner. In our time there is indeed plenty of evidence of troubles on every hand. The surprising thing, however, is that the tendency toward apocalypticism seems today quite muted. That some of the main lines of thought of the twentieth century have reached a state of exhaustion is obvious enough. But the prevailing mood in reaction to the passing of this century seems to be marked more by hope than by despair. The year 1991, which in the future will be paired with 1917 as a great turning-point year in human history, has engendered a surprisingly fleeting celebration. Nevertheless, it has certainly dulled the appeal of apocalypticism, and there is now a widespread sense that something better may be in store for humankind in the twenty-first century.

It is especially noteworthy that many these days ground their sense of hope in an anticipation that religion, so long maligned, is on the verge of making a comeback. Of course, one need not be directly influenced by Solzhenitsyn to share this expectation. Indeed, that many others view the unfolding of history in terms akin to his serves to reinforce the sense that his is just one voice, albeit a major one, in a large chorus—and thus to provide further validation of the wisdom of his insights. Here is how James Billington put the matter in his 1980 study of the historical development of the secular faith in political revolution:

> The present author is inclined to believe that the end may be approaching of the political religion which saw in revolution the sunrise of a perfect society. I am further disposed to wonder if this secular creed, which arose in Judaeo-Christian culture, might not ultimately prove to be only a stage in the continuing metamorphosis of older forms of faith and to speculate that the belief in secular revolution which has legitimized so much authoritarianism in the twentieth century, might dialectically pre-figure some rediscovery of religious evolution to revalidate democracy in the twenty-first.[92]

In a 1992 essay entitled "The Year 2000: Is It the End—Or Just the Beginning?" Henry Grunwald writes in similar terms. He notes that "the most persistent forecasts of doom have so far not come true." Taking note of the stubborn insistence of secular humanism "that morality need not be based on the supernatural," he comments, "But it gradually became clear that ethics without the sanction of some higher authority simply were not compelling"—and that therefore the "ultimate irony, or perhaps tragedy, is that secularism has not led to humanism." So he speculates that "we may be heading into an age when faith will again be taken seriously, and when it will again play a major part in our existence." If so, heralds of this movement of the human spirit are to be found in Eastern Europe and the former Soviet Union, where, "despite decades of officially imposed atheism, religion is once again a major force."[93]

It is within the context of such thinking about the movement of history that we shall find the ultimate significance of Solzhenitsyn. If history does indeed unfold along the lines anticipated by Billington and Grunwald and similarly minded observers, Solzhenitsyn will be seen to have played an important role. That his *Gulag Archipelago* has, in Robert Conquest's words, "had an almost unprecedented, worldwide impact on the minds of men"[94] cannot be gainsaid. Solzhenitsyn's injection of the word *Gulag* into the languages of the world as a shorthand term for the dehumanizing horrors of the twentieth century has left an indelible mark upon our thinking. His effect upon us, however, goes beyond the undermining of modern modes of thought and action. He, along with others, points the way toward a more hopeful and humane future. If someday his countrymen name streets and parks and schools after him, they will do so not only because of his critique of the modern world. They will do so because he has contributed mightily to the preservation and restoration of our humanity. Solzhenitsyn will leave the world better than he found it. Whether we know it now or not, whether we have read him or not, whether we revile him or honor him, he has affected our lives. And he has affected them for good.

Notes

CHAPTER ONE

1. Stephen F. Cohen, "Voices from the Gulag," *New York Times Book Review*, 4 May 1980, p. 1.
2. Solzhenitsyn, *The Gulag Archipelago*, I (New York: Harper & Row, 1973), p. 194.
3. Bernard Levin, "Time To Stand Up for Britain," Interview with Alexander Solzhenitsyn, *The Times* (London), 23 May 1983, p. 11.
4. Solzhenitsyn, *The Gulag Archipelago*, III (New York: Harper & Row, 1978), pp. x, 36.
5. Heilbroner, "The World After Communism," *Dissent*, 37 (Fall 1990), pp. 429–30.
6. Bulgakov, *The Master and Margarita* (New York: Harper & Row, 1967), p. 272.
7. Heilbroner, p. 430.
8. Howe, "Some Dissenting Comments," *Dissent*, 37 (Fall 1990), p. 434.
9. Rorty, "The Intellectuals at the End of Socialism," *Yale Review*, 80 (1992), pp. 1, 2, 3, 10.
10. Bill Keller, "Obscure Soviet Magazine Breaks the Ban on Solzhenitsyn's Work," *New York Times*, 20 Mar. 1989, p. 1.
11. Felicity Barringer, "Kremlin Keeping Solzhenitsyn on Blacklist," *New York Times*, 30 Nov. 1988, p. 1.
12. *Gulag*, III, p. 28.
13. Levin, p. 11.
14. Solzhenitsyn, *The Gulag Archipelago*, II (New York: Harper & Row, 1975), pp. 213–14.
15. Solzhenitsyn, *The Oak and the Calf* (New York: Harper & Row, 1979), p. 387.

16. *Oak*, pp. 95, 374, 426, 439.
17. Martin Malia, "The Hunt for the True October," *Commentary*, 92 (Oct. 1991), p. 27.
18. Moynihan, "Two Cheers for Solzhenitsyn," *New York Times Book Review*, 24 Nov. 1991, p. 9.
19. *Oak*, p. 389.
20. Bailey, *Galileo's Children* (New York: Little, Brown, 1990), p. 325.
21. Maxim Sokolov, "Solzhenitsyn's Second Letter to Soviet Leaders," *Commersant*, 1 Oct. 1990, p. 14.
22. Bailey, p. 325.
23. Malia, "The August Revolution," *New York Review of Books*, 26 Sept. 1991, p. 28.
24. Pontuso, *Solzhenitsyn's Political Thought* (Charlottesville: University Press of Virginia, 1990), pp. 197–198.
25. Solzhenitsyn, *The First Circle* (New York: Harper & Row, 1968), p. 415.
26. Malia, "Hunt," p. 27.
27. Hosking, *The Awakening of the Soviet Union*, enlarged ed. (Cambridge, MA: Harvard University Press, 1991), p. 143.
28. Abel, "On the Crimes of Lenin, Stalin, and Hitler," *Partisan Review*, 58 (1991), pp. 83, 84, 87.
29. Rorty, p. 10.
30. Pontuso, p. 214.
31. Hughes, *Sophisticated Rebels* (Cambridge, MA: Harvard University Press, 1988), p. 115.
32. Dunlop, "Solzhenitsyn's Reception in the United States," in *Solzhenitsyn in Exile: Critical Essays and Documentary Materials*, ed. John B. Dunlop, Richard S. Haugh, and Michael Nicholson (Stanford: Hoover Institution Press, 1985), p. 49.
33. Hughes, p. 115.
34. Feifer, "The Dark Side of Solzhenitsyn," *Harper's*, 260 (May 1980), p. 58.
35. Milosz, "Questions," in *Aleksandr Solzhenitsyn: Critical Essays and Documentary Materials*, ed. John B. Dunlop, Richard Haugh, and Alexis Klimoff, 2nd ed. (New York: Collier, 1975), p. 450.
36. Cohen, *Rethinking the Soviet Experience* (New York: Oxford University Press, 1985), pp. 91, 92.
37. David Aikman, "The Man Who Rules Russia," *Time*, 2 Sept. 1991, p. 55.
38. Levin, p. 11.
39. Dunlop, "The Almost-Rehabilitation and Re-Anathematization of Aleksandr Solzhenitsyn," Working paper, Hoover Institution, Stanford University, Feb. 1989, pp. 11, 22.

40. Dunlop, "Solzhenitsyn Begins To Emerge from the Political Void," *Report on the USSR*, 8 Sept. 1989, pp. 2, 4, 5.
41. Confino, "Solzhenitsyn, the West, and the New Russian Nationalism," *Journal of Contemporary History*, 26 (1991), p. 611.
42. Solzhenitsyn, "Three Key Moments in Modern Japanese History," *National Review*, 9 Dec. 1983, p. 1536.
43. Solzhenitsyn, *Nobel Lecture* (New York: Farrar, Straus and Giroux, 1972), p. 4.
44. Lukacs, *1945: Year Zero* (Garden City, NY: Doubleday, 1978), pp. 243–44.

CHAPTER TWO

1. Solzhenitsyn, *Warning to the West* (New York: Farrar, Straus and Giroux, 1976), pp. 58–59.
2. Solzhenitsyn, *The Oak and the Calf* (New York: Harper & Row, 1979) p. 298.
3. *Warning*, pp. 57–58.
4. *Oak*, p. 330.
5. Solzhenitsyn, "The Templeton Address," *National Review*, 22 July 1983, p. 873.
6. "Templeton," p. 874.
7. Solzhenitsyn, "Repentance and Self-Limitation in the Life of Nations," in *From Under the Rubble* (Boston: Little, Brown, 1975), p. 125.
8. Solzhenitsyn, *The First Circle* (New York: Harper & Row, 1968), p. 484.
9. Solzhenitsyn, *Letter to the Soviet Leaders* (New York: Harper & Row, 1974), p. 44n.
10. Bulgakov, *Karl Marx as a Religious Type* (Belmont, MA: Nordland, 1979), pp. 41, 62.
11. Neuhaus, *The Naked Public Square* (Grand Rapids: Eerdmans, 1984).
12. Appendix 12, *Oak*, p. 494.
13. Solzhenitsyn, *The Gulag Archipelago*, I (New York: Harper & Row, 1973), p. 562.
14. Solzhenitsyn, *Nobel Lecture* (New York: Farrar, Straus and Giroux, 1972), pp. 22, 23.
15. Solzhenitsyn, *The Gulag Archipelago*, II (New York: Harper & Row, 1975), p. 143.
16. "Letter from Solzhenitsyn to Three Students," in *Solzhenitsyn: A Documentary Record*, ed. Leopold Labedz (Baltimore: Penguin, 1972), p. 151.

17. Hook, "Solzhenitsyn and Secular Humanism," *The Humanist*, 38 (Nov./ Dec. 1978), p. 5.
18. Schmemann, "On Solzhenitsyn," in *Aleksandr Solzhenitsyn: Critical Essays and Documentary Materials*, ed. John B. Dunlop, Richard Haugh, and Alexis Klimoff, 2nd ed. (New York: Collier, 1975), pp. 39–40.
19. Schmemann, "On Solzhenitsyn," pp. 43–44.
20. Solzhenitsyn, *Cancer Ward* (New York: Bantam, 1969), p. 428.
21. *Aleksandr Solzhenitsyn: Critical Essays and Documentary Materials*, p. 44.
22. Aikman, "Russia's Prophet in Exile," Interview with Aleksandr Solzhenitsyn, *Time*, 24 July 1989, p. 59.
23. *Gulag*, I, p. 168.
24. *Gulag*, I, p. 168.
25. *Gulag*, III, p. 70.
26. Schmemann, "Reflections on *The Gulag Archipelago*," in *Aleksandr Solzhenitsyn: Critical Essays and Documentary Materials*, p. 525.
27. Carter, *The Politics of Solzhenitsyn* (New York: Holmes & Meier, 1977), pp. 62, 64.
28. Krasnov, *Solzhenitsyn and Dostoevsky* (Athens: University of Georgia Press, 1980), p. 6.
29. *Gulag*, II, p. 615–16.
30. Minogue, *Alien Powers* (New York: St. Martin's Press, 1985), p. 2.
31. *Nobel Lecture*, p. 6.
32. For an elaboration of this point, see Krasnov, pp. 173–97.
33. Solzhenitsyn, *The Gulag Archipelago*, abridged by Edward E. Ericson, Jr. (New York: Harper & Row, 1985), p. x.
34. *First Circle*, pp. 451–52.
35. *Gulag*, I, pp. 3, 183–84.
36. Solzhenitsyn, "As Breathing and Consciousness Return," in *From Under the Rubble*, pp. 24–25.
37. "Repentance," *Rubble*, pp. 105–06.
38. "Repentance," *Rubble*, p. 107.
39. "Repentance," *Rubble*, p. 113.
40. Solzhenitsyn, *August 1914* (New York: Farrar, Straus and Giroux, 1989), p. 347.
41. Carter, p. 72.
42. August 1914, p. 347. See also *Warning*, p. 45: "Law is our human attempt to embody in rules a part of that moral sphere which is above us."
43. *August 1914*, pp. 347–48.
44. *Nobel Lecture*, pp. 13, 14, 30, 32.

45. Appendix, *Cancer Ward*, pp. 554–55. Session of Soviet Writers' Secretariat, 22 Sept. 1967.
46. "Letter to the Fourth Congress of Soviet Writers," in *Cancer Ward*, p. ix.
47. *Oak*, p. 2.
48. *Nobel Lecture*, p. 27.
49. *Nobel Lecture*, pp. 4, 5, 21–22.
50. *Nobel Lecture*, pp. 15, 17, 18.
51. *Nobel Lecture*, pp. 5, 19, 28.
52. *Nobel Lecture*, pp. 33–34.

CHAPTER THREE

1. Stanley Reynolds, *The Guardian*, 14 Feb. 1974. Cited in Robert Conquest, "Solzhenitsyn in the British Media," in *Solzhenitsyn in Exile: Critical Essays and Documentary Materials*, ed. John B. Dunlop, Richard S. Haugh, and Michael Nicholson (Stanford: Hoover Institution Press, 1985), p. 5.
2. *Die Zeit*, 5 Dec. 1975. Cited in Birgit Meyer, "Solzhenitsyn in the West German Press since 1974," in *Solzhenitsyn in Exile*, p. 69.
3. Jeri Laber, "The Selling of Solzhenitsyn," *Columbia Journalism Review*, 13 (May/June 1974), p. 7.
4. "Solzhenitsyn Unbound," *National Review*, 19 July 1974, p. 797.
5. Cited in Giovanni Grazzini, *Solzhenitsyn* (New York: Dell, 1973), p. 91.
6. Cited in *Solzhenitsyn: A Documentary Record*, ed. Leopold Labedz (Baltimore: Penguin, 1972), pp. 63–64.
7. "Khrushchev's Secret Tapes," *Time*, 1 Oct. 1990, pp. 77–78.
8. Cited in Labedz, pp. 41, 42.
9. Cited in Labedz, p. 39.
10. Medvedev, *Ten Years After Ivan Denisovich* (New York: Vintage, 1974), p. 195.
11. Rothberg, *Aleksandr Solzhenitsyn: The Major Novels* (Ithaca, NY: Cornell University Press, 1971), p. x.
12. Grazzini, p. 94.
13. Fanger, "Solzhenitsyn: Art and Foreign Matter," in *Aleksandr Solzhenitsyn: Critical Essays and Documentary Materials*, ed. John B. Dunlop, Richard Haugh, and Alexis Klimoff, 2nd ed. (New York: Collier, 1975), pp. 158, 165.
14. Jacobson, "The Example of Solzhenitsyn," *Commentary*, 47 (May 1969), p. 82.

15. Erlich, "The Writer as Witness," in *Aleksandr Solzhenitsyn: Critical Essays and Documentary Materials*, p. 17.
16. Feuer, "Introduction," *Solzhenitsyn: A Collection of Critical Essays*, ed. Kathryn Feuer (Englewood Cliffs, NJ: Prentice-Hall, 1976), p. 1.
17. Reeve, "The House of the Living," *Kenyon Review*, 25 (Spring 1963), pp. 356–58, 360.
18. Labedz, pp. 18, 21.
19. Feuer, p. 15.
20. Howe, "Predicaments of Soviet Writing—I," *New Republic*, 11 May 1963, p. 19.
21. Howe, "Predicaments of Soviet Writing—II," *New Republic*, 18 May 1963, p. 20.
22. Howe, "Lukacs and Solzhenitsyn," in *Aleksandr Solzhenitsyn: Critical Essays and Documentary Materials*, p. 151.
23. Howe, "An Open Letter," *New Republic*, 3 May 1980, pp. 18–19.
24. Howe, "The Great War and Russian Memory," *New York Times Book Review*, 2 July 1989, pp. 1, 17–18.
25. Medvedev, p. 72.
26. Cited in Labedz, pp. 78–79.
27. Medvedev, p. 72.
28. Labedz, pp. 101–04.
29. Medvedev, pp. 64–67.
30. Labedz, pp. 16, 109, 112.
31. Labedz, pp. 138–50.
32. Appendix, *Cancer Ward* (New York: Bantam, 1969), pp. 554–55. Also in Labedz, p. 147.
33. Labedz, pp. 152–53.
34. Michael Scammell, *Solzhenitsyn* (New York: Norton, 1984), pp. 623–24.
35. Labedz, pp. 177, 183.
36. Labedz, pp. 223, 224.
37. Labedz, pp. 237, 241.
38. Medvedev, p. 134.
39. Labedz, p. 11.
40. Vidal, *Matters of Fact and Fiction* (New York: Random House, 1977), p. 19.
41. Labedz, pp. 238–39.
42. Capouya, "Solzhenitsyn: Optimist and Realist," *Nation*, 6 Jan. 1969, p. 20.
43. Blake, "A Diseased Body Politic," *New York Times Book Review*, 27 Oct. 1968, p. 50.

44. Friedberg, "Gallery of Comrades Embattled Abed," *Saturday Review*, 9 Nov. 1968, pp. 43–44.

45. Cited in Scammell, p. 642.

46. Laber, "Indictment of Soviet Terror," *New Republic*, 19 Oct. 1968, pp. 32–34.

47. McNaspy, Rev. of *The First Circle, America*, 5 Oct. 1968, p. 295.

48. Brown, "*Cancer Ward* and *The First Circle*," *Slavic Review*, 28 (June 1969), 304, 312–13.

49. Cited in Scammell, p. 643.

50. Flynn, "Stalin's Victory," *Newsweek*, 30 Sept. 1968, pp. 108–09.

51. Garis, "Fiction Chronicle," *Hudson Review*, 22 (Spring 1969), pp. 148–49, 154.

52. Salisbury, "The World as a Prison," *New York Times Book Review*, 15 Sept. 1968, p. 1.

53. Rovit, "In the Center Ring," *American Scholar*, 39 (Winter 1969–70), p. 166.

54. Grazzini, p. 5.

55. Solzhenitsyn, *The First Circle* (New York: Harper & Row, 1968), p. 674.

56. Schmemann, "On Solzhenitsyn," in *Aleksandr Solzhenitsyn: Critical Essays and Documentary Materials*, pp. 28–44. I myself had my first essay on Solzhenitsyn in initial draft when the 1972 revelations broke: "The Christian Humanism of Aleksandr Solzhenitsyn," *Reformed Journal*, 22 (Oct. 1972), pp. 6–10; (Nov. 1972), pp. 16–20.

57. Scammell, pp. 790–92.

58. Solzhenitsyn, *The Oak and the Calf* (New York: Harper & Row, 1979), p. 327.

59. *Oak*, pp. 326, 327.

60. *Oak*, p. 327.

61. Medvedev, pp. 156, 160.

62. Scammell, p. 673.

63. Schmemann, "A Lucid Love," in *Aleksandr Solzhenitsyn: Critical Essays and Documentary Materials*, pp. 382, 385, 392.

64. Struve, "The Debate over *August 1914*," in *Aleksandr Solzhenitsyn: Critical Essays and Documentary Materials*, pp. 393, 396, 406–07.

65. Djilas, "Indomitable Faith," in *Aleksandr Solzhenitsyn: Critical Essays and Documentary Materials*, p. 330.

66. Bell, "Solzhenitsyn Grappling with History," *New Leader*, 2 Oct. 1972, p. 17.

67. Klausler, "Tragic Chaos," *Christian Century*, 22 Nov. 1972, p. 1192.

68. Karlinsky, Rev. of *August 1914*, *New York Times Book Review*, 10 Sept. 1972, pp. 1, 48–49.

69. Erlich, "Solzhenitsyn's Quest," in *Aleksandr Solzhenitsyn: Critical Essays and Documentary Materials*, pp. 351–52.

70. Bliven, "Days That Shook the World," *New Yorker*, 14 Oct. 1972, p. 178.

71. Rahv, "In Dubious Battle," in *Aleksandr Solzhenitsyn: Critical Essays and Documentary Materials*, p. 357.

72. Vidal, pp. 19, 21.

73. Pritchard, "Long Novels and Short Stories," *Hudson Review*, 26 (Spring 1973), pp. 225, 227.

74. Toynbee, Rev. of *August 1914*, *Critic*, 31 (Nov.-Dec. 1972), pp. 67–68, 69.

75. Laber, "Muted Echo of a Masterpiece," *New Republic*, 7 Oct. 1972, pp. 29–30.

76. McCarthy, "The Tolstoy Connection," *Saturday Review*, 16 Sept. 1972, pp. 80, 88.

77. McCarthy, pp. 80–82.

78. Scammell, pp. 557, 559, 620, 792.

79. Steiner, "More Notes from Underground," *New Yorker*, 13 Oct. 1975, p. 169.

80. Weeks, "The Peripatetic Reviewer," *Atlantic*, 231 (Apr. 1973), p. 124.

81. Rosenthal, "Solzhenitsyn and the Defeated," *Nation*, 12 Feb. 1973, p. 213.

82. Rosenthal, p. 215.

83. Feuer, p. 2.

84. John Heidenry, "Solzhenitsyn, Neo-Tolstoyan," *Commonweal*, 23 Mar. 1973, p. 64.

85. Milosz, "Questions," in *Aleksandr Solzhenitsyn: Critical Essays and Documentary Materials*, p. 454.

CHAPTER FOUR

1. Solzhenitsyn, *The Oak and the Calf* (New York: Harper & Row, 1979), pp. 347, 530.

2. Solzhenitsyn, "Live Not by Lies," *Washington Post*, 18 Feb. 1974, p. A26.

3. "Solzhenitsyn Was Warned of Treason Charge," *The Times* (London), 15 Feb. 1974, p. 1.

4. "U. S. Says Exile Does Not Alter Détente," *Washington Post*, 14 Feb. 1974, p. A16.

5. Murray Marder, "Nixon Lauds Solzhenitsyn's 'Courage,' " *Washington Post*, 26 Feb. 1974, p. A1.

6. John B. Dunlop, "Solzhenitsyn's Reception in the United States," in

Solzhenitsyn in Exile: Critical Essays and Documentary Materials, ed. John B. Dunlop, Richard S. Haugh, and Michael Nicholson (Stanford: Hoover Institution Press, 1985), p. 28. Dunlop has provided the full transcript of the Kissinger memorandum, plus much other information about official Washington's response to Solzhenitsyn.

7. Ron Nessen, *It Sure Looks Different from the Inside* (Chicago: Playboy Press, 1978), p. 345.

8. Cited in Dunlop, p. 30.

9. Nessen, p. 229.

10. Safire, "Solzhenitsyn Without Tears," *New York Times*, 18 Feb. 1974, p. 25.

11. "Solzhenitsyn: An Artist Becomes an Exile," *Time*, 25 Feb. 1974, p. 35.

12. "The Unexpected Perils of Freedom," *Time*, 4 Mar. 1974, p. 32.

13. Kaiser, "Arrest Shows Soviet System Still the Same," *Washington Post*, 13 Feb. 1974, p. A30.

14. Solzhenitsyn, *The Gulag Archipelago*, I (New York: Harper & Row, 1973), p. 352.

15. *Oak*, p. 13.

16. "Everyone's Loss," *The Times* (London), 15 Feb. 1974, p. 15.

17. Kilpatrick, "Seven Men Went To Get Solzhenitsyn," *Minneapolis Star*, 19 Feb. 1974, p. 8A.

18. James V. Schall, "Solzhenitsyn's Letter," *Worldview*, 17 (July 1974), p. 26.

19. Dunlop, p. 42.

20. Donald W. Treadgold, "Solzhenitsyn's Literary Antecedents," in *Solzhenitsyn in Exile*, p. 262.

21. Buckley, "Solzhenitsyn's Modest Proposal," *National Review*, 29 Mar. 1974, p. 390.

22. Safire, "Aleks, Baby," *New York Times*, 11 Mar. 1974, p. 29.

23. Brumberg, "Understanding Solzhenitsyn," *New Leader*, 27 May 1974, pp. 10–13.

24. Mills and Mills, "Solzhenitsyn's Cry to the Soviet Leaders," *Commonweal*, 9 Aug. 1974, pp. 433–36.

25. Laber, "The Real Solzhenitsyn," *Commentary*, 57 (May 1974), p. 32.

26. Norman I. Gelman, Letter, *Commentary*, 58 (Sept. 1974), p. 16.

27. Laber, "Real," pp. 33–34.

28. Laber, "Real," pp. 34–35.

29. Laber, "Real," pp. 32–35.

30. Treadgold, Letter, *Commentary*, 58 (Sept. 1974), pp. 12, 14.

31. Laber, Letter, *Commentary*, 58 (Sept. 1974), pp. 16, 18.

32. Feuer, "Introduction," *Solzhenitsyn: A Collection of Critical Essays*, ed. Kathryn Feuer (Englewood Cliffs, NJ: Prentice-Hall, 1976), p. 5, n. 9.
33. Laber, "The Selling of Solzhenitsyn," *Columbia Journalism Review*, 13 (May/June 1974), pp. 4, 5–7.
34. Foote, "Towering Witness to Salvation," *Time*, 15 July 1974, p. 90.
35. Robertson, "A Russian Nationalist Looks to the Past," *New York Times*, 3 Mar. 1974, p. 26.
36. Robertson, "Letter Softened by Solzhenitsyn," *New York Times*, 5 Mar. 1974, p. 9.
37. Astrachan, "Solzhenitsyn 'Contemptuous' of the U. S.," *Des Moines Register*, 17 Mar. 1974, p. 1A.
38. Yardley, "Solzhenitsyn—A Dispassionate Look at a Modern 'Saint,' " *Des Moines Register*, 23 June 1974, p. 6A.
39. Roger Leddington, "Solzhenitsyn Re-Explains Letter," *Milwaukee Journal*, 1 Apr. 1974, p. 7.
40. "Solzhenitsyn's Bill of Indictment," *Time*, 7 Jan. 1974, p. 49.
41. Kaiser, "Dissident Praises 'Gulag,' " *Washington Post*, 7 Feb. 1974, p. A22.
42. Roy Medvedev, "Gulag Archipelago," *Ramparts*, 12 (June 1974), pp. 49–55.
43. Medvedev, "On Solzhenitsyn's *Gulag Archipelago*," in *Solzhenitsyn: A Collection of Critical Essays*, pp. 97, 106, 110.
44. Kennan, "Between Earth and Hell," *New York Review of Books*, 21 Mar. 1974, pp. 3, 4, 7.
45. Salisbury, "Why the Kremlin Fears Solzhenitsyn," *Atlantic*, 233 (Apr. 1974), pp. 42, 44, 46.
46. Conquest, "Evolution of an Exile," *Saturday Review/World*, 20 Apr. 1974, pp. 22–24.
47. Rubenstein, Rev. of *The Gulag Archipelago*, I, *New Republic*, 22 June 1974, p. 22.
48. Cohen, "The Other Great Holocaust of the Century," *New York Times Book Review*, 16 June 1974, pp. 1, 10, 12.
49. Macmillan, "A Cool Appraisal of 'Gulag,' " *Christian Science Monitor*, 24 July 1974, p. 11.
50. Kennan, p. 3.
51. Steiner, "The Forests of the Night," *New Yorker*, 5 Aug. 1974, pp. 78, 85, 86.
52. Leonard Schapiro, "Disturbing, Fanatical, and Heroic," *New York Review of Books*, 13 Nov. 1975, pp. 10–17; Lionel Abel, "A Poem We Need Today," *Commentary*, 61 (Mar. 1976), pp. 64–68; Patricia Blake, Rev. of

The Gulag Archipelago, II, *New York Times Book Review*, 26 Oct. 1975, pp. 1, 18, 20, 22.

53. Blake, p. 1.
54. Adam B. Ulam, "Defiance in the Gulag," *Saturday Review*, 24 June 1978, pp. 31–33; Patricia Blake, "Great Escapes from the Gulag," *Time*, 5 June 1978, pp. 91–92; Hilton Kramer, "The Soviet Terror Continued," *New York Times Book Review*, 18 June 1978, pp. 1, 28–29; Robert Conquest, "Books Considered," *New Republic*, 27 May 1978, pp. 25–27; Alfred Kazin, "The Fury of Solzhenitsyn," *Esquire*, 23 May 1978, pp. 73–74.
55. Brumberg, "Soviet Terror," *Commentary*, 67 (Feb. 1979), p. 88.
56. Winthrop, Letter, *Commentary*, 67 (June 1979), p. 24.
57. Fairbanks, Letter, *Commentary*, 67 (June 1979), p. 23.
58. Conquest, "Solzhenitsyn in the British Media," in *Solzhenitsyn in Exile*, pp. 4–6, 7.
59. Conquest, "Solzhenitsyn in the British Media," p. 14.
60. Levin, "Solzhenitsyn Among the Pygmies," *The Times* (London), 17 July 1975, p. 14.
61. Conquest, "Solzhenitsyn in the British Media," pp. 15, 18, 20.
62. Conquest, "Solzhenitsyn in the British Media," pp. 20–21.
63. Levin, "The Vision of a Prophet," *Atlas World Press Review*, 23 (May 1976), pp. 11–12.
64. Crankshaw, "Why the Prophet Is Wrong," *Atlas World Press Review*, 23 (May 1976), pp. 13–14.
65. Paz, "How History Will Judge," *Atlas World Press Review*, 23 (May 1976), p. 14.
66. Cousins, "Brief Encounter with A. Solzhenitsyn," *Saturday Review*, 23 Aug. 1975, pp. 4, 6.
67. This issue of *Society* was subsequently published in slightly augmented form, as a book: Aleksandr Solzhenitsyn, *Détente: Prospects for Democracy and Dictatorship* (New Brunswick, NJ: Transaction Books, 1980).
68. Horowitz, "An Amnesty International of One," *Society*, 13 (Nov./Dec. 1975), pp. 45–47.
69. Lowenthal, "The Prophet's Wrong Message," *Society*, 13 (Nov./Dec. 1975), p. 40.
70. Gurtov, "Return to the Cold War," *Society*, 13 (Nov./Dec. 1975), p. 37.
71. Etzioni, "Intervening in the Soviet Union," *Society*, 13 (Nov./Dec. 1975), pp. 39–40.
72. Turgeon, "In Defense of Détente," *Society*, 13 (Nov./Dec. 1975), pp. 38–39.

73. Birnbaum, "Solzhenitsyn as Pseudo-Moralist," *Society*, 13 (Nov./Dec. 1975), p. 44.
74. Smith, *The Russians* (New York: Quadrangle/New York Times Book Co., 1976), pp. 417, 425.

CHAPTER FIVE

1. Leroux, "Solzhenitsyn Makes Freedom a Prison," *Des Moines Register*, 17 Dec. 1976, pp. 1A, 12A; Claiborne, "Solzhenitsyn's Barbed-Wire Freedom," *Des Moines Register*, 28 Jan. 1977, p. 1B.
2. "Solzhenitsyn Speaks at Town Meeting in Vermont," *Des Moines Register*, 2 Mar. 1977, p. 12B.
3. Scammell, *Solzhenitsyn* (New York: Norton, 1984), p. 955.
4. Andrew Nemethy, "The Solzhenitsyns of Cavendish," *Vermont Life*, 38 (Autumn 1983), p. 25.
5. Pivot, "Solzhenitsyn at Work," *Boston Globe*, 24 Feb. 1984, p. 2.
6. Solzhenitsyn, *A World Split Apart* (New York: Harper & Row, 1978), p. 1.
7. *A World*, pp. 11, 27, 29.
8. *A World*, p. 25.
9. Berman, "Introduction," *Solzhenitsyn at Harvard*, ed. Ronald Berman (Washington: Ethics and Public Policy Center, 1980), p. xiv.
10. "Rosalynn Rejects Solzhenitsyn's Criticism," *Grand Rapids Press*, 21 June 1978, p. A4.
11. Rowan, "Solzhenitsyn: Agent of Soviet Influence?" *Grand Rapids Press*, 23 June 1978, p. A11.
12. "Solzhenitsyn: 'Con Man' or 'Worshipper of Man'?" *Boston Globe*, 19 June 1978, p. 13.
13. "The Obsession of Solzhenitsyn," in *Solzhenitsyn at Harvard*, pp. 23–24.
14. "Mr. Solzhenitsyn as Witness," in *Solzhenitsyn at Harvard*, pp. 25–26.
15. Reston, "A Russian at Harvard," in *Solzhenitsyn at Harvard*, pp. 36–38.
16. Schlesinger, "The Solzhenitsyn We Refuse To See," in *Solzhenitsyn at Harvard*, pp. 63–71.
17. McGrory, "Solzhenitsyn Doesn't Love Us," in *Solzhenitsyn at Harvard*, pp. 60–62.
18. "Is Solzhenitsyn Right?" *Time*, 26 June 1978, p. 18.
19. Tuchman, "America's Savonarola," *Time*, 26 June 1978, p. 22.

20. MacLeish, "Our Will Endures," *Time*, 26 June 1978, p. 21.
21. Boorstin, "The Courage To Doubt," *Time*, 26 June 1978, p. 21.
22. Hesburgh, "Unpopular Truths," *Time*, 26 June 1978, p. 18.
23. Meany, "No Voice More Eloquent," *Time*, 26 June 1978, p. 21.
24. Hook, "Above All, Freedom," *Time*, 26 June 1978, p. 22.
25. Will, "Solzhenitsyn's Critics," in *Solzhenitsyn at Harvard*, pp. 33–35.
26. Kesler, "Up from Modernity," in *Solzhenitsyn at Harvard*, pp. 48–56.
27. McNeill, "The Decline of the West," in *Solzhenitsyn at Harvard*, pp. 123–29.
28. Berman, "Through Western Eyes," in *Solzhenitsyn at Harvard*, pp. 75–83.
29. Novak, "On God and Man," in *Solzhenitsyn at Harvard*, pp. 131–32, 134, 139.
30. Novak, pp. 134, 136.
31. Solzhenitsyn, *The Mortal Danger*, 2nd ed. (New York: Harper & Row, 1986), pp. 1–2, 3, 7.
32. Ulam, "To the Brink," *National Review*, 14 Nov. 1980, pp. 1402–03.
33. Pontuso, *Solzhenitsyn's Political Thought* (Charlottesville: University Press of Virginia, 1990), p. 189.
34. Remnick, "Native Son," *New York Review of Books*, 14 Feb. 1991, p. 7.
35. Solzhenitsyn, *The Gulag Archipelago*, II (New York: Harper & Row, 1975), p. 261.
36. Solzhenitsyn, *The Gulag Archipelago*, III (New York: Harper & Row, 1978), p. 497.
37. Remnick, p. 7.
38. Treves, Letter, in *Mortal*, pp. 86–87.
39. Dallin, Letter, in *Mortal*, pp. 96–98, 102–03.
40. Dallin, p. 103.
41. *Mortal*, pp. 10–11.
42. See reviews by Donald W. Treadgold, *Slavic Review*, 23 (1975), pp. 812–14; Dorothy Atkinson, *American Historical Review*, 81 (1976), pp. 423–24; Nicholas V. Riasanovsky, *Russian Review*, 35 (1976), pp. 103–04; and Vladislav G. Krasnov's "Richard Pipes's Foreign Strategy: Anti-Soviet or Anti-Russian?" with a response by Pipes, *Russian Review*, 38 (Apr. 1979), pp. 180–97. See also John B. Dunlop, *The Faces of Contemporary Russian Nationalism* (Princeton: Princeton University Press, 1983, pp. 282–85.
43. Tucker, Letter, in *Mortal*, pp. 75, 84.
44. *Mortal*, pp. 7–8.

48. Solzhenitsyn, "The Courage To See," in *Mortal*, pp. 105–06, 111.

49. "The Courage To See," pp. 125, 130.

50. Carlisle, *Solzhenitsyn and the Secret Circle* (New York: Holt, Rinehart and Winston, 1978).

51. Carlisle, "Solzhenitsyn's Invisible Audience," *Newsweek*, 24 July 1978, p. 13.

52. Carlisle, *Secret Circle*, pp. 117, 128, 148, 161.

53. Carlisle, *Secret Circle*, p. 179.

54. Carlisle, *Secret Circle*, pp. 144, 208–09.

55. Carlisle, *Secret Circle*, p. 210. Readers may find Solzhenitsyn's comment on Olga Carlisle, as well as on "[t]he selfless Western people who aided me in substantial ways in my struggle," who "are all modestly silent to this day," in a long note on page 320 of *The Oak and the Calf* (New York: Harper & Row, 1979). This note prompted the Carlisles to sue Solzhenitsyn for two million dollars. The judge threw the case out of court (Scammell, *Solzhenitsyn*, p. 986).

56. Carlisle, "Reviving Myths of Holy Russia," *New York Times Magazine*, 16 Sept. 1979, pp. 48, 50, 65.

57. Dunlop, pp. 281–82.

58. Carlisle, "Reviving," p. 66.

59. Dunlop, p. 281.

60. For Solzhenitsyn's view of Yanov as once "an obscure Communist journalist" and still "extremely hostile to everything Russian," see Janis Sapiets' 1979 BBC interview of Solzhenitsyn, in Aleksandr I. Solzhenitsyn, *East and West* (New York: Harper & Row, 1980), pp. 169–70.

61. Yanov, *The Russian New Right* (Berkeley: Institute of International Studies, University of California, 1978), pp. 85–112.

62. Yanov, *The Russian Challenge and the Year 2000* (New York: Basil Blackwell, 1987), pp. 203, 206.

63. See, *e.g.*, Stephen F. Cohen, "A Left Right," *New York Times Book Review*, 7 Jan. 1979, pp. 9, 24, 26, 28.

64. Feifer, "The Dark Side of Solzhenitsyn," *Harper's*, 260 (May 1980), pp. 50–51, 54, 56–58. For Robert Conquest's judgment of Feifer's trustworthiness and veracity, see "Solzhenitsyn in the British Media," in *Solzhenitsyn in Exile: Critical Essays and Documentary Materials*, ed. John B. Dunlop, Richard S. Haugh, and Michael Nicholson (Stanford: Hoover Institution Press, 1985), pp. 10, 13.

65. Feifer, pp. 50, 51, 54.

66. Feifer, p. 55.

67. Feifer, pp. 57–58.

68. David Burg and George Feifer, *Solzhenitsyn* (New York: Stein and Day, 1972), pp. 4–5, 8, 9, 11.

69. Stein, Letter, *Commentary*, 79 (June 1985), p. 7.

70. See Galina Vishnevskaya, *Galina* (New York: Harcourt Brace Jovanovich, 1984), pp. 414–19; and Stein's Letter, *Commentary*, 79 (June 1985), pp. 6–7, to which Scammell replied in *Commentary*, 80 (Aug. 1985), p. 19.

71. Scammell, *Solzhenitsyn*, pp. 18, 394, 529, 609, 627, 641.

72. Scammell, *Solzhenitsyn*, pp. 848–49, 879–80, 928, 929.

73. Scammell, *Solzhenitsyn*, pp. 639–40, 933–34, 938.

74. Scammell, *Solzhenitsyn*, pp. 913, 923, 934, 944, 954, 982.

75. Scammell, *Solzhenitsyn*, pp. 940, 981.

76. Scammell, *Solzhenitsyn*, p. 845.

77. Alberti, Letter to Edward E. Ericson, Jr., 7 Nov. 1984.

78. Scammell, *Solzhenitsyn*, pp. 304, 992.

79. Scammell, *Solzhenitsyn*, pp. 641, 992.

80. Alberti, Letter to Edward E. Ericson, Jr., 7 Nov. 1984.

81. Scammell, Letter, *Commentary*, 80 (Aug. 1985), p. 19.

82. Scammell, Letter, *Problems of Communism*, 35 (July-Aug. 1986), p. 101.

83. Aikman, "Russia's Prophet in Exile," Interview with Aleksandr Solzhenitsyn, *Time*, 24 July 1989, p. 60.

84. Bayley, "God and the Devil," *New York Review of Books*, 21 Dec. 1989, p. 11.

85. Remnick, pp. 6–7.

86. Avineri, "Where's Solzhenitsyn?" *New York Times*, 12 Sept. 1991, p. A25.

87. For a particularly vituperative example, see Tatyana Tolstaya, "The Grand Inquisitor," *New Republic*, 29 June 1992, pp. 29–36.

CHAPTER SIX

1. Solzhenitsyn, *Warning to the West* (New York: Farrar, Straus and Giroux, 1976), p. 106.

2. *Warning*, p. 22.

3. *Solzhenitsyn: A Documentary Record*, ed. Leopold Labedz (Baltimore: Penguin, 1972), pp. 138–39, 150.

4. *Warning*, pp. 104, 124.

5. *Warning*, p. 27.

6. "Solzhenitsyn Speaks," Booklet, Hoover Institution, Stanford University, 1976, p. 9.

7. *Warning*, pp. 80–81.
8. "The Alexander Solzhenitsyn Interview," *Congressional Record—Senate*, 27 June 1974, p. 21486.
9. Solzhenitsyn, *The Mortal Danger*, 2nd ed. (New York: Harper & Row, 1986), pp. 16–17.
10. *Warning*, p. 49.
11. *Warning*, p. 123.
12. Georges Suffert, "Solzhenitsyn in Zurich," Interview with Solzhenitsyn, *Encounter*, 46 (Apr. 1976), p. 13.
13. *Warning*, p. 92.
14. Conquest, "Solzhenitsyn in the British Media," in *Solzhenitsyn in Exile: Critical Essays and Documentary Materials*, ed. John B. Dunlop, Richard S. Haugh, and Michael Nicholson (Stanford: Hoover Institution Press, 1985), p. 22.
15. David Aikman, "Russia's Prophet in Exile," Interview with Aleksandr Solzhenitsyn, *Time*, 24 July 1989, p. 60.
16. *Mortal*, p. 70.
17. *Mortal*, p. 71.
18. Solzhenitsyn, *East and West* (New York: Harper & Row, 1980), pp. 176–77.
19. *Warning*, pp. 46, 48, 108.
20. *East and West*, pp. 174–75.
21. *Mortal*, p. 64.
22. Solzhenitsyn, *A World Split Apart* (New York: Harper & Row, 1978), p. 23.
23. *Congressional Record*, pp. 21484–85.
24. *Congressional Record*, p. 21484.
25. *A World*, p. 25.
26. *Warning*, pp. 105–06.
27. *A World*, p. 27.
28. *Congressional Record*, p. 21484.
29. *Mortal*, pp. 64–65.
30. *A World*, pp. 9, 11, 45.
31. *Mortal*, p. 111.
32. *Warning*, p. 47.
33. *East and West*, p. 171.
34. *Mortal*, p. 111.
35. *East and West*, p. 172.
36. *Mortal*, p. 111.
37. Dunlop, "Solzhenitsyn's Reception in the United States," in *Solzhenitsyn in Exile*, pp. 24, 35–36.

38. *Warning*, pp. 38, 87, 121.

39. *Warning*, pp. 84–85, 116–17.

40. *Mortal*, pp. 50–53.

41. *A World*, p. 41.

42. Solzhenitsyn, "Schlesinger and Kissinger," *New York Times*, 1 Dec. 1975, p. 31.

43. *Warning*, pp. 11–13.

44. *A World*, p. 41.

45. Suffert, p. 15.

46. *Warning*, pp. 105, 108, 114–15.

47. *Congressional Record*, p. 21486.

48. *Warning*, pp. 69, 75, 120.

49. *Mortal*, p. 46.

50. Solzhenitsyn, "The Third World War Has Ended," *National Review*, 20 June 1975, p. 652.

51. "Third World War," p. 652.

52. *Warning*, p. 94.

53. "Third World War," p. 652.

54. See, *e.g.*, John O'Sullivan, "Friends at Court," *National Review*, 27 May 1991, p. 4.

55. "Third World War," p. 652.

56. *Warning*, p. 119.

57. *Warning*, p. 134.

58. *East and West*, pp. 150–55.

59. "Solzhenitsyn Speaks," p. 6.

60. *A World*, pp. 47, 49.

61. *A World*, p. 51.

62. *A World*, pp. 53, 55, 57.

63. *A World*, pp. 57, 59.

64. *A World*, pp. 59, 61.

65. *Mortal*, p. 64.

66. *Warning*, pp. 106, 127.

67. Solzhenitsyn, *August 1914* (New York: Farrar, Straus and Giroux, 1989), pp. 788–90.

68. *Warning*, p. 79; see also pp. 145–46.

69. MacIntyre, *After Virtue* (Notre Dame: University of Notre Dame Press, 1981), pp. viii, 38, 57, 60, 65.

70. MacIntyre, pp. 244–45.

71. Lasch, *The True and Only Heaven* (New York: Norton, 1991), pp. 21–22, 36–37, 170–71, 446.

72. Lasch, pp. 23–24, 532.

73. Lukacs, *The Passing of the Modern Age* (New York: Harper & Row, 1970), pp. 14, 210, 216.
74. Schapiro, "Disturbing, Fanatical, and Heroic," *New York Review of Books*, 13 Nov. 1975, pp. 16–17.

CHAPTER SEVEN

1. Solzhenitsyn, *The Mortal Danger*, 2nd ed. (New York: Harper & Row, 1986), p. 59.
2. "The Alexander Solzhenitsyn Interview," *Congressional Record—Senate*, 27 June 1974, p. 21486.
3. Cited in Michael Scammell, *Solzhenitsyn* (New York: Norton, 1984), p. 900.
4. *Mortal*, p. 60.
5. David Aikman, "Russia's Prophet in Exile," Interview with Aleksandr Solzhenitsyn, *Time*, 24 July 1989, p. 60.
6. "Solzhenitsyn Essay Draws Varied Response," *Current Digest of the Soviet Press*, 42 (1990), p. 4.
7. *Mortal*, p. 63.
8. Conquest, "Solzhenitsyn in the British Media," in *Solzhenitsyn in Exile: Critical Essays and Documentary Materials*, ed. John B. Dunlop, Richard S. Haugh, and Michael Nicholson (Stanford: Hoover Institution Press, 1985), p. 11.
9. Hook, "On Western Freedom," in *Solzhenitsyn at Harvard*, ed. Ronald Berman (Washington: Ethics and Public Policy Center, 1980), p. 92.
10. Georges Suffert, "Solzhenitsyn in Zurich," Interview with Solzhenitsyn, *Encounter*, 46 (Apr. 1976), p. 13.
11. Schapiro, "Some Afterthoughts on Solzhenitsyn," *Russian Review*, 33 (Oct. 1974), p. 418.
12. See, *e.g.*, his speech to Free China: "Solzhenitsyn Speaks," *Southern Partisan*, 4 (Winter 1984), pp. 33–35.
13. *Commentary*, 79 (June 1985), p. 15.
14. Podhoretz, "The Terrible Question of Aleksandr Solzhenitsyn," *Commentary*, 79 (Feb. 1985), p. 24.
15. Edward E. Ericson, Jr., Letter, *Commentary*, 79 (June 1985), p. 8.
16. *Commentary*, 79 (June 1985), p. 16.
17. Solzhenitsyn, *Warning to the West* (New York: Farrar, Straus and Giroux, 1976), pp. 28–29.
18. Solzhenitsyn, *A World Split Apart* (New York: Harper & Row, 1978), pp. 19, 43.

19. *A World*, pp. 49–51.
20. Novak, "Democracy Takes Sin Seriously," in George F. Will and Michael Novak, *Solzhenitsyn and American Democracy* (Washington: Ethics and Public Policy Center, 1981), pp. 9–12.
21. Novak, p. 14. For a full account of Novak's view of democracy, see his *The Spirit of Democratic Capitalism* (New York: American Enterprise Institute/Simon & Schuster, 1982).
22. "Repentance and Self-Limitation in the Life of Nations," in *From Under the Rubble* (Boston: Little, Brown, 1975), p. 109.
23. Novak, pp. 11–12, 13, 14.
24. Bernard Levin, "Time To Stand Up for Britain," Interview with Alexander Solzhenitsyn, *The Times* (London), 23 May 1983, p. 11. Note that this interview comes later than Novak's essay.
25. Suffert, pp. 13–14.
26. "Solzhenitsyn Speaks," Booklet, Hoover Institution, Stanford University, 1976, pp. 7, 8.
27. "Solzhenitsyn Speaks," Booklet, Hoover Institution, p. 9.
28. *Congressional Record*, p. 21486.
29. *Warning*, pp. 28–29.
30. "Solzhenitsyn Speaks," *Southern Partisan*, 4 (Winter 1984), p. 34.
31. Levin, p. 11.
32. *Mortal*, p. 49.
33. Levin, p. 11.
34. Solzhenitsyn, "As Breathing and Consciousness Return," in *From Under the Rubble*, p. 19.
35. "Breathing," *Rubble*, pp. 19–20.
36. "Breathing," *Rubble*, pp. 22–23.
37. "Breathing," *Rubble*, p. 23.
38. "Breathing," *Rubble*, p. 23.
39. "Breathing," *Rubble*, pp. 23–24.
40. "Breathing," *Rubble*, p. 24.
41. *Mortal*, pp. 61–62.
42. George F. Kennan, "Is the World Ready for U. S.-Style Freedoms?" *Des Moines Register*, 7 Aug. 1977, pp. B1–B2. Excerpted from *The Cloud of Danger* (Boston: Little, Brown, 1977).

CHAPTER EIGHT

1. Solzhenitsyn, "Repentance and Self-Limitation in the Life of Nations," in *From Under the Rubble* (Boston: Little, Brown, 1974), pp. 119–20.
2. Solzhenitsyn, *Warning to the West* (New York: Farrar, Straus and Giroux, 1976), p. 107.
3. Aikman, "Russia's Prophet in Exile," Interview with Aleksandr Solzhenitsyn, *Time*, 24 July 1989, p. 60.
4. Solzhenitsyn, *The Mortal Danger*, 2nd ed. (New York: Harper & Row, 1986), p. 33.
5. "Repentance," *Rubble*, p. 120.
6. Carter, *The Politics of Solzhenitsyn* (New York: Holmes & Meier, 1977), p. 88.
7. Solzhenitsyn, *Nobel Lecture* (New York: Farrar, Straus and Giroux, 1972), p. 19.
8. Solzhenitsyn, "The Smatterers," in *From Under the Rubble*, p. 263.
9. "Repentance," *Rubble*, p. 109.
10. *Mortal*, p. 34.
11. Carter, pp. 88, 91.
12. Solzhenitsyn, "Sakharov and the Criticism of 'A Letter to the Soviet Leaders,' " *Kontinent* (Garden City, NY: Doubleday, 1976), p. 20.
13. "Sakharov and the Criticism," p. 20.
14. Solzhenitsyn, *East and West* (New York: Harper & Row, 1980), p. 171.
15. Solzhenitsyn, *August 1914* (New York: Farrar, Straus and Giroux, 1989), p. 11.
16. *Solzhenitsyn: A Documentary Record*, ed. Leopold Labedz (Baltimore: Penguin, 1972), p. 130.
17. "Sakharov and the Criticism," p. 20.
18. "Repentance," *Rubble*, p. 119.
19. *Mortal*, pp. 31, 34.
20. *Mortal*, p. 31.
21. *Mortal*, pp. 2–3.
22. "Solzhenitsyn on Communism," *Time*, 18 Feb. 1980, p. 49.
23. Solzhenitsyn, "The Courage To See," in *Mortal*, p. 120.
24. *Mortal*, p. 23.
25. "Solzhenitsyn on Communism," pp. 48–49.
26. "Solzhenitsyn Speaks," Booklet, Hoover Institution, Stanford University, 1976, p. 5.
27. *East and West*, p. 181.
28. Georges Suffert, "Solzhenitsyn in Zurich," Interview with Solzhenitsyn, *Encounter* 46, (Apr. 1976), p. 12.

29. Minogue, *Nationalism* (New York: Basic Books, 1967), pp. 8, 58, 146–47, 154.

30. Solzhenitsyn, "Three Key Moments in Modern Japanese History," *National Review*, 9 Dec. 1983, p. 1536.

31. *Mortal*, pp. 117–19.

32. "Solzhenitsyn on Communism," p. 49.

33. *Mortal*, p. 33.

34. *Mortal*, pp. 25, 33–34.

35. Schmemann, "A Lucid Love," in *Aleksandr Solzhenitsyn: Critical Essays and Documentary Materials*, ed. John B. Dunlop, Richard Haugh, and Alexis Klimoff, 2nd ed. (New York: Collier, 1975), p. 385.

36. *Mortal*, p. 4.

37. *Mortal*, p. 24.

38. Solzhenitsyn, *The Gulag Archipelago*, III (New York: Harper & Row, 1978), pp. 43, 108.

39. Solzhenitsyn, *One Day in the Life of Ivan Denisovich* (New York: Bantam, 1963), pp. 28, 49, 120, 195–202.

40. "Repentance," *Rubble*, pp. 114–16.

41. "Repentance," *Rubble*, p. 135.

42. "Three Key Moments," pp. 1536–37.

43. Roy Medvedev, "On Solzhenitsyn's *Gulag Archipelago*," in *Solzhenitsyn: A Collection of Critical Essays*, ed. Kathryn Feuer (Englewood Cliffs, NJ: Prentice-Hall, 1976), p. 109.

44. Suffert, p. 12.

45. Dunlop, *The Faces of Contemporary Russian Nationalism* (Princeton: Princeton University Press, 1983), p. 167.

46. *Mortal*, pp. 10, 23.

47. Bruce D. Porter, "The Coming Resurgence of Russia," *National Interest*, no. 23 (Spring 1991), p. 16.

48. Keller, "Yearning for an Iron Hand," *New York Times Magazine*, 28 Jan. 1990, pp. 19, 48, 50.

49. Petro, "Toward a New Russian Federation," *Wilson Quarterly*, 14 (Summer 1990), pp. 117–18.

50. *East and West*, pp. 169–70.

51. Yanov, *The Russian Challenge and the Year 2000* (New York: Basil Blackwell, 1987), pp. 175, 177.

52. Yanov, *Détente After Brezhnev* (Berkeley: Institute of International Studies, University of California, 1977), p. 44.

53. Yanov, *Russian Challenge*, p. 268.

54. Yanov, *The Russian New Right* (Berkeley: Institute of International Studies, University of California, 1978), p. 38. For the sake of full disclosure, I inform the reader that Yanov and I have tangled in print before. I reviewed this book negatively; he accused me of anti-Semitism. See *New Oxford Review*, 46 (Dec. 1979), pp. 8–10; 47 (Apr. 1980), pp. 4, 6.

55. Yanov, *Russian New Right*, p. 161.

56. Yanov, *Russian Challenge*, p. 291.

57. Yanov, *Russian New Right*, p. 85.

58. Yanov, *Russian Challenge*, pp. 194, 203.

59. Yanov, *Russian New Right*, p. 87.

60. Yanov, *Russian Challenge*, pp. 169–73.

61. Yanov, *Russian Challenge*, pp. 186, 213, 223–24.

62. Dunlop, *The New Russian Revolutionaries* (Belmont, MA: Nordland, 1976), p. 166.

63. Dunlop, *New Russian Revolutionaries*, p. 225.

64. Dunlop, "The Russian Orthodox Church and Nationalism After 1988," *Religion in Communist Lands*, 18 (Winter 1990), p. 300.

65. Krasnov, *Russia Beyond Communism* (Boulder: Westview Press, 1991), pp. 338–39.

66. Dunlop, "Christian Democratic Party Founded in Moscow," *Report on the USSR*, 13 Oct. 1989, p. 1.

67. Dunlop, "Russian Christian Democrats Outline Their Views," *Report on the USSR*, 21 Sept. 1990, p. 19.

68. Dunlop, "Russia and the Republics," *Report on the USSR*, 11 Oct. 1991, p. 8.

69. Petro, pp. 118–22.

70. Dunlop, *Faces*, p. 242.

71. Dunlop, *New Russian Nationalism* (New York: Praeger, 1985), pp. 9, 38.

72. Dunlop, "Solzhenitsyn in Exile," *Survey*, 21 (1975), p. 144.

73. See *e.g.*, Dimitry Pospielovsky, "The Neo-Slavophile Trend and Its Relation to the Contemporary Religious Revival in the USSR," in *Religion and Nationalism in Soviet and East European Politics*, ed. Pedro Ramet (Durham: Duke Press Policy Studies, 1984), pp. 41–58.

74. Dunlop, *Faces*, pp. 242–43, 278.

75. Dunlop, *New Russian Nationalism*, pp. 91–92.

76. Dunlop, *Faces*, p. 264.

77. Dunlop, *New Russian Nationalism*, pp. 88–89.

78. Dunlop, "New National Bolshevik Organization Formed," *Report on the USSR*, 14 Sept. 1990, p. 7.

79. Dunlop, *Faces*, p. 265.
80. Dunlop, "Russia's Surprising Reactionary Alliance," *Orbis*, 35 (Summer 1991), pp. 424–25.
81. Dunlop, "Solzhenitsyn Calls for the Dismemberment of the Soviet Union," *Report on the USSR*, 5 Oct. 1990), p. 9.
82. Dunlop, "Russia's Surprising Reactionary Alliance," p. 426.
83. Szporluk, "Dilemmas of Russian Nationalism," *Problems of Communism*, 38 (July-Aug. 1989), pp. 17, 20.
84. Szporluk, pp. 17–18.
85. Dunlop, "Russian Nationalism Today," *Nationality Papers*, 19 (Fall 1991), pp. 162–63.
86. Dunlop, "Russian Reactions to Solzhenitsyn's Brochure," *Report on the USSR*, 14 Dec. 1990, p. 7.
87. "Repentance," *Rubble*, pp. 119–20.
88. Dunlop, *Faces*, p. 140.
89. Dunlop, "Alla Latynina: A Self-Proclaimed Centrist Calls for Political Realignment," *Report on the USSR*, 23 June 1989, pp. 8, 10. See also Dora Shturman, *Gorodu i miru: O publitsistike A. I. Solzhenitsyna* (New York: C.A.S.E./Third Wave, 1988).
90. Hosking, *The Awakening of the Soviet Union*, enlarged ed. (Cambridge, MA: Harvard University Press, 1991), p. 112.
91. Confino, "Solzhenitsyn, the West, and the New Russian Nationalism," *Journal of Contemporary History*, 26 (1991), pp. 611, 630–31.
92. Confino, p. 632.
93. Confino, pp. 632–33.
94. Dunlop, "A Conversation with Dmitrii Vasil'ev, the Leader of 'Pamyat','" *Report on the USSR*, 15 Dec. 1989, pp. 13–15.
95. Dunlop, "Russian Orthodox Church and Nationalism After 1988," pp. 304–05.
96. Petro, p. 121.
97. Krasnov, pp. 27–28, 312.
98. *Mortal*, pp. 23–24.
99. Dunlop, "Conversation with Dmitrii Vasil'ev," pp. 12–13.
100. Krasnov, p. 238.
101. Zhores Medvedev, *Ten Years After Ivan Denisovich* (New York: Vintage Books, 1974), pp. 100–01.
102. See Michael Nicholson, "Solzhenitsyn: Effigies and Oddities," in *Solzhenitsyn in Exile: Critical Essays and Documentary Materials*, ed. John B. Dunlop, Richard S. Haugh, and Michael Nicholson (Stanford: Hoover Institution Press, 1985), pp. 120–21.

103. Samolvin, "A Letter to Solzhenitsyn," in *The Political, Social, and Religious Thought of Russian "Samizdat"—An Anthology*, ed. Michael Meerson-Aksenov and Boris Shragin (Belmont, MA: Nordland, 1977), pp. 420–22, 426–27, 435, 437.

104. Grenier, "Solzhenitsyn and Anti-Semitism," *New York Times*, 13 Nov. 1985, p. 24.

105. Grenier, p. 24.

106. Podhoretz, "The Terrible Question of Aleksandr Solzhenitsyn," *Commentary*, 79 (Feb. 1985), p. 24.

107. Alexis B. Bogolubov, Letter, *Commentary*, 79 (June 1985), p. 8.

108. *Commentary*, 79 (June 1985), p. 16.

109. "The Dangers of Solzhenitsyn's Nationalism: An Interview with Andrei Sinyavsky," *New York Review of Books*, 22 Nov. 1979, pp. 4–5.

110. Confino, p. 629.

111. Remnick, "Native Son," *New York Review of Books*, 14 Feb. 1991, p. 10.

112. Aikman, p. 58.

113. Schapiro, "Disturbing, Fanatical, and Heroic," *New York Review of Books*, 13 Nov. 1975, p. 16.

114. Schapiro, "Antisemitism in the Communist World," *Soviet Jewish Affairs*, 9 (1979), pp. 51–52.

115. See, *e.g.*, Simon Markish, "Jewish Images in Solzhenitsyn," *Soviet Jewish Affairs*, 7 (1977), pp. 79, 81; Dimitry Pospielovsky, "The Jewish Question in Russian Samizdat," *Soviet Jewish Affairs*, 8 (1978), pp. 4, 15.

116. Dunlop, *New Russian Revolutionaries*, pp. 169–81, 189.

117. Dunlop, *Faces*, p. 36.

118. Dunlop, *New Russian Revolutionaries*, pp. 166–67, 181.

119. Dunlop, *New Russian Revolutionaries*, p. 159.

120. Dunlop, *Faces*, pp. 45, 168.

121. Dunlop, *New Russian Revolutionaries*, pp. 206–07.

122. "Smatterers," *Rubble*, p. 229.

123. Hayward, "Introduction," *Rubble*, p. vi.

124. "Smatterers," *Rubble*, p. 268.

125. Treadgold, "Solzhenitsyn's Intellectual Antecedents," in *Solzhenitsyn in Exile*, p. 254.

126. Schapiro, "The *Vekhi* Group and the Mystique of Revolution," *Slavonic and East European Review*, 34 (Dec. 1955), p. 66.

127. Schapiro, "Disturbing, Fanatical, and Heroic," p. 10.

128. Pipes, "In the Russian Intellectual Tradition," in *Solzhenitsyn at Harvard*, ed. Ronald Berman (Washington: Ethics and Public Policy Center, 1980), p. 117.

129. Treadgold, p. 260.

130. Pipes, p. 117.
131. Dunlop, "Solzhenitsyn's Reception in the United States," in *Solzhenitsyn in Exile*, p. 49.
132. Treadgold, p. 247.
133. Pospielovsky, "Neo-Slavophile Trend," p. 43.
134. Dunlop, "Solzhenitsyn's Reception in the United States," p. 49.
135. Dunlop, *New Russian Revolutionaries*, p. 334.
136. Gorskii, "Russian Messianism and the New National Consciousness," in *The Political, Social and Religious Thought of Russian "Samizdat,"* pp. 356, 363, 367.
137. Pospielovsky, "Neo-Slavophile Trend," pp. 51, 57.
138. Treadgold, p. 243.
139. "Smatterers," *Rubble*, pp. 272, 274.

CHAPTER NINE

1. Dunlop, *The Faces of Contemporary Russian Nationalism* (Princeton: Princeton University Press, 1983), p. 44.
2. Solzhenitsyn, *The Oak and the Calf* (New York: Harper & Row, 1979), pp. 387, 402.
3. Solzhenitsyn, *Warning to the West* (New York: Farrar, Straus and Giroux, 1976), p. 108.
4. Solzhenitsyn, *East and West* (New York: Harper & Row, 1980), pp. 156, 178–79.
5. Krasnov, *Russia Beyond Communism* (Boulder: Westview Press, 1991), p. 7.
6. Krasnov, p. 38.
7. Remnick, "A Witness Before His Own People," *Manchester Guardian Weekly*, 6 Aug. 1989, p. 25.
8. Carlisle, *Solzhenitsyn and the Secret Circle* (New York: Holt, Rinehart and Winston, 1978), pp. 209–10.
9. Lowenthal, "The Prophet's Wrong Message," *Society*, 13 (Nov./Dec. 1975), pp. 42–43.
10. "The Alexander Solzhenitsyn Interview," *Congressional Record— Senate*, 27 June 1974, p. 21486.
11. Solzhenitsyn, *The Mortal Danger*, 2nd ed. (New York: Harper & Row, 1986), p. 57.
12. *Mortal*, p. 56.
13. Agurskii, "The Intensification of Neo-Nazi Dangers in the Soviet Union," in *The Political, Social and Religious Thought of Russian*

"Samizdat"—An Anthology, ed. Michael Meerson-Aksenov and Boris Shragin (Belmont, MA: Nordland, 1977), p. 418.

14. Meerson-Aksenov, "The Debate Over the Democratic Movement: Introduction," in *Political, Social and Religious Thought of Russian "Samizdat,"* pp. 230–31.

15. Kopelev, "The Lie Can Be Defeated Only by Truth," in *Political, Social and Religious Thought of Russian "Samizdat,"* pp. 302–05, 317–18, 336.

16. Medvedev, "What Awaits Us in the Future?" in *Political, Social and Religious Thought of Russian "Samizdat,"* pp. 76, 81, 84, 88–89.

17. Solzhenitsyn, *Letter to the Soviet Leaders* (New York: Harper & Row, 1974), p. 7. All further references to this work are cited in the text.

18. *Mortal*, p. 59.

19. *Oak*, p. 437.

20. Amalrik, *Will the Soviet Union Survive Until 1984?* (New York: Harper & Row, 1970), pp. 10–11, 29, 34, 37, 44–55, 61–62, 64–65.

21. Donella H. Meadows, Dennis L. Meadows, Jorgen Randers, and William W. Behrens III, *The Limits to Growth* (New York: Universe Books, 1972), p. 178. See pages 23–24 for the study's three main conclusions, all of which Solzhenitsyn echoes.

22. Lasch, *The True and Only Heaven* (New York: Norton, 1991), pp. 23, 529.

23. Solzhenitsyn, "Repentance and Self-Limitation in the Life of Nations," in *From Under the Rubble* (Boston: Little, Brown, 1975), p. 138.

24. Solzhenitsyn, "Three Key Moments in Modern Japanese History," *National Review*, 9 Dec. 1983, p. 1538.

25. *Mortal*, p. 64.

26. "Repentance," *Rubble*, pp. 141–42.

27. Solzhenitsyn, *August 1914* (New York: Farrar, Straus and Giroux, 1989), p. 508.

28. Solzhenitsyn cites Kurganov's figure also in *The Gulag Archipelago*, II (New York: Harper & Row, 1975), p. 10. This is not a figure of Solzhenitsyn's own calculating.

29. Dunlop, "Solzhenitsyn in Exile," *Survey*, 21 (1975), p. 138.

30. "Repentance," *Rubble*, p. 140.

31. *Mortal*, p. 58.

32. *Mortal*, p. 58.

33. Hosking, *The Awakening of the Soviet Union*, enlarged ed. (Cambridge, MA: Harvard University Press, 1991), p. 11.

34. Schall, "Solzhenitsyn's Letter," *Worldview*, 17 (July 1974), p. 27.

35. Cited in John B. Dunlop, *The New Russian Nationalism* (New York: Praeger, 1985), p. 36.

36. "Is 'Glasnost' a Game of Mirrors?" *New York Times*, 22 Mar. 1987, p. 27. The seven signatories are Vasily Aksyonov, Vladimir Bukovsky, Edward Kuznetsov, Yuri Lyubimov, Vladimir Maximov, Ernst Neizvestny, and Aleksandr Zinoviev.

37. *East and West*, p. 178.

38. Solzhenitsyn, "As Breathing and Consciousness Return," in *From Under the Rubble*, p. 13.

39. *East and West*, p. 177.

40. Michael Scammell, *Solzhenitsyn* (New York: Norton, 1984), p. 668.

41. *Mortal*, p. 59.

42. *Mortal*, pp. 63–64.

43. Sakharov, "On Alexander Solzhenitsyn's 'A Letter to the Soviet Leaders,' " *Kontinent* (Garden City, NY: Doubleday, 1976), p. 3. All further references to this work are cited in the text. This essay is available elsewhere, as well: *e.g.*, "In Answer to Solzhenitsyn," *New York Review of Books*, 13 June 1974, pp. 3–6.

44. Solzhenitsyn, "Sakharov and the Criticism of 'A Letter to the Soviet Leaders,' " *Kontinent* (Garden City, NY: Doubleday, 1976), p. 22. All further references to this work are cited in the text.

45. George Bailey, *Galileo's Children* (New York: Little, Brown, 1990), p. 330.

46. Maximov, Foreword to "The Solzhenitsyn/Sakharov Debate," *Kontinent* (Garden City, NY: Doubleday, 1976), p. 1.

47. Schapiro, "Some Afterthoughts on Solzhenitsyn," *Russian Review*, 33 (Oct. 1974), p. 420.

48. Scammell, p. 798.

49. *Oak*, p. 523.

50. *Sakharov Speaks* (New York: Vintage Books, 1974), p. 175.

51. *Warning*, p. 108.

52. Gellner, "A Reformer of the Modern World," *Times Literary Supplement* (London), 17–23 Aug. 1990, p. 863.

53. *Sakharov Speaks*, pp. 55–114. Also published separately (New York: Norton, 1968).

54. "Breathing," *Rubble*, p. 3.

55. Kelley, *The Solzhenitsyn-Sakharov Dialogue* (Westport, CT: Greenwood Press, 1982), p. 154.

56. Kelley, pp. 143–44, 155, 157.

57. Kelley, p. 125.

58. Kelley, pp. 125–26, 129, 141.

59. Kelley, p. 128.

CHAPTER TEN

1. Aleksandr Solzhenitsyn, *Rebuilding Russia* (New York: Farrar, Straus and Giroux, 1991), p. 45.
2. Solzhenitsyn, *East and West* (New York: Harper & Row, 1980), pp. 180–82.
3. "Tolling the Death Knell," *Time*, 1 Oct. 1990, p. 58.
4. Dunlop, "Solzhenitsyn Calls for the Dismemberment of the Soviet Union," *Report on the USSR*, 5 Oct. 1990, p. 10.
5. Krasnov, *Russia Beyond Communism* (Boulder: Westview Press, 1991), p. 46.
6. Remnick, "Native Son," *New York Review of Books*, 14 Feb. 1991, p. 7.
7. Solzhenitsyn, *The Gulag Archipelago*, I (New York: Harper & Row, 1973), pp. 183–84.
8. Krasnov, p. 46.
9. "Solzhenitsyn Essay Draws Varied Reponse," *Current Digest of the Soviet Press*, 42 (1990), pp. 6–7.
10. Krasnov, p. 44.
11. Krasnov, p. 44.
12. Dunlop, "Solzhenitsyn Calls," p. 10.
13. Dunlop, *The Faces of Contemporary Russian Nationalism* (Princeton: Princeton University Press, 1983), p. 44.
14. Pipes, "Solzhenitsyn and the Russian Intellectual Tradition," *Encounter*, 52 (June 1979), p. 56.
15. Remnick, p. 7.
16. *East and West*, p. 181.
17. Dunlop, "Russia and the Republics," *Report on the USSR*, 11 Oct. 1991, p. 9.
18. John-Thor Dahlburg, "Russia Wants Solzhenitsyn Back in Fold," *Los Angeles Times*, 16 June 1992, p. A6.
19. See Dunlop, *Faces*, pp. 248–49.
20. Hosking, *The Awakening of the Soviet Union*, enlarged ed. (Cambridge, MA: Harvard University Press, 1991), pp. 23–24.
21. "The Solzhenitsyn Interview," *Congressional Record—Senate*, 27 June 1974, p. 21484.
22. Cited in Andrew Rosenthal, "Soviets Drop Solzhenitsyn Treason Charges," *New York Times*, 18 Sept. 1991, p. A8.
23. Margaret Shapiro, "Soviets Drop Solzhenitsyn Treason Charges," *Washington Post*, 18 Sept. 1991, p. B2.
24. Smiley, "Beyond Gorbachev," *National Review*, 28 May 1990, p. 27.

25. Uzzell, "Solzhenitsyn the Centrist," *National Review*, 28 May 1990, p. 29.
26. "Tolling the Death Knell," p. 58.
27. Ignatieff, "An Uncommon Russian Nationalist Returns," *Minneapolis Star Tribune*, 28 Sept. 1990, p. 19A.
28. Legvold, "Recent Books," *Foreign Affairs*, 71 (Spring 1992), p. 206.
29. "The Union of the States," *Economist*, 22 Sept. 1990, pp. 53–54.
30. Shapiro, p. B2.
31. Sokolov, "Solzhenitsyn's Second Letter to Soviet Leaders," *Commersant*, 1 Oct. 1990, p. 14.
32. "Two Soviet Giants, in Dissent," *New York Times*, 29 Sept. 1990, p. 22.
33. Francis X. Clines, "Russia Gets Call by Solzhenitsyn for Slavic State," *New York Times*, 19 Sept. 1990, pp. A1, A4.
34. Scammell, "To the Finland Station?" *New Republic*, 19 Nov. 1990, p. 18.
35. Scammell, p. 20.
36. Scammell, p. 20.
37. Scammell, p. 20.
38. Scammell, pp. 22–23.
39. O'Clery, "Back in the USSR," *New Republic*, 19 Nov. 1990, pp. 22–23.
40. Gray, "Solzhenitsyn's Flawed Blueprint," *Toronto Globe and Mail*, 21 Mar. 1992, p. C20.
41. Moynihan, "Two Cheers for Solzhenitsyn," *New York Times Book Review*, 24 Nov. 1991, pp. 9, 11.
42. Moynihan, p. 11.
43. Remnick, pp. 7–8.
44. Solchanyk, "Solzhenitsyn and the Russian 'Ukrainian Complex,' " *Report on the USSR*, 5 Oct. 1990, pp. 20–22.
45. Mihalisko, "Solzhenitsyn's 'Russian Union,' " *Report on the USSR*, 5 Oct. 1990, pp. 17–19.
46. Brown, "Kazakhs Protest Against Solzhenitsyn's Proposal for 'A New Russia,' " *Report on the USSR*, 5 Oct. 1990, pp. 19–20.
47. Sheehy, "Solzhenitsyn's Concept of a Future 'Russian Union,' " *Report on the USSR*, 5 Oct. 1990, pp. 15–16.
48. Tolz, "Solzhenitsyn Proposes a Plan for the Reconstruction of Russia," *Report on the USSR*, 5 Oct. 1990, pp. 12–14.
49. John B. Dunlop, "Russian Reactions to Solzhenitsyn's Brochure," *Report on the USSR*, 14 Dec. 1990, p. 3.
50. Krasnov, pp. 64–65.
51. Dunlop, "Russian Reactions," p. 4.
52. Verkhovsky, "Russians May No Longer Play Follow the Leader," *Glasnost News & Review*, Jan.–Apr. 1991, p. 60.

53. Dobrynin, "Solzhenitsyn Prophets in the Soviet Crash of 1990," *Glasnost News & Review*, Jan.–Apr. 1991, pp. 58, 60.
54. "Solzhenitsyn Essay Draws," pp. 4–5.
55. Dunlop, "Russian Reactions," p. 4.
56. "Solzhenitsyn Essay Draws," pp. 5–6.
57. "Solzhenitsyn Essay Draws," p. 7.
58. "Solzhenitsyn Essay Draws," p. 7.
59. "Solzhenitsyn Essay Draws," pp. 7–8.
60. Dunlop, "Russian Reactions," p. 5.
61. Krasnov, p. 64.
62. Dahlburg, p. A6.
63. Krasnov, p. 58.
64. Dunlop, "Russian Reactions," p. 4. The bracketed words are Dunlop's.
65. Dunlop, "Russian Reactions," p. 5.
66. Dunlop, "Russian Reactions," p. 5.
67. Krasnov, p. 65.
68. Krasnov, pp. 59–60.
69. Dunlop, "Russian Reactions," pp. 6–7.
70. Dunlop, "Russian Reactions," pp. 7–8.
71. Krasnov, p. 250.
72. "A Conversation with Solzhenitsyn," *Los Angeles Times Book Review*, 13 Aug. 1989, p. 4. These are excerpts from a 1987 interview by Rudolf Augstein in the German magazine *Der Spiegel*.
73. David Aikman, "Russia's Prophet in Exile," Interview with Aleksandr Solzhenitsyn, *Time*, 24 July 1989, p. 58.
74. Solzhenitsyn, *August 1914* (New York: Farrar, Straus and Giroux, 1989), p. 591.

Chapter Eleven

1. Aleksandr Solzhenitsyn, *Rebuilding Russia* (New York: Farrar, Straus and Giroux, 1991), p. 3. All further references to this work are cited in the text.
2. Solzhenitsyn, *The Gulag Archipelago*, III (New York: Harper & Row, 1976), pp. 45–46.
3. Solzhenitsyn, "Repentance and Self-Limitation in the Life of Nations," in *From Under the Rubble* (Boston: Little, Brown, 1975), p. 129.
4. Solzhenitsyn, *Nobel Lecture* (New York: Farrar, Straus and Giroux, 1972), p. 19.
5. "Repentance," *Rubble*, p. 138.

6. Solzhenitsyn, "The Templeton Address," *National Review*, 22 July 1983, p. 875.
7. Solzhenitsyn, *Cancer Ward* (New York: Bantam, 1969), pp. 423–24.
8. Smith, *The Russians* (New York: Quadrangle/New York Times Book Co., 1976), pp. 124–46.
9. Gray, *Soviet Women* (New York: Doubleday, 1989).
10. "Repentance," *Rubble*, p. 140.
11. "Solzhenitsyn Essay Draws Varied Response," *Current Digest of the Soviet Press*, 42 (1990), p. 7.

CHAPTER TWELVE

1. Aleksandr Solzhenitsyn, *Rebuilding Russia* (New York: Farrar, Straus and Giroux, 1991), p. 59. All further references to this work are cited in the text.
2. John B. Dunlop, "Monarchist Sentiment in Present-Day Russia," *Report on the USSR*, 2 Aug. 1991, pp. 27–30.
3. Brookhiser, "Why Not Bring Back the Czars?" *Time*, 11 Nov. 1991, p. 102.
4. Alexander Hamilton, John Jay, and James Madison, *The Federalist* (Philadelphia: J. B. Lippincott, 1873), pp. 104, 105.
5. *The Writings of George Washington*, 35, ed. John C. Fitzpatrick (Washington: United States Government Printing Office, 1940), pp. 226–27.
6. Solzhenitsyn, *The Mortal Danger*, 2nd ed. (New York: Harper & Row, 1986), p. 59.
7. Alas, the text has *unmeditated*, a typographical error.
8. Hosking, *The Awakening of the Soviet Union*, enlarged ed. (Cambridge, MA: Harvard University Press, 1991), pp. 21–40.
9. Nicholas V. Riasanovsky, *A History of Russia*, 4th ed. (New York: Oxford University Press, 1984), p. 375.
10. Krasnov, *Russia Beyond Communism* (Boulder: Westview Press, 1991), p. 56.
11. *John Milton: Complete Poems and Major Prose*, ed. Merritt Y. Hughes (New York: Odyssey Press, 1957), pp. 888–89.
12. Milton, p. 891.
13. Solzhenitsyn, *August 1914* (New York: Farrar, Straus and Giroux, 1989), p. 807.
14. Hosking, pp. 164–65.

CHAPTER THIRTEEN

1. Ratushinskaya, *Grey Is the Color of Hope* (New York: Knopf, 1988), pp. 10, 30, 303.
2. Ratushinskaya, *Grey*, p. 40.
3. Ratushinskaya, *In the Beginning* (New York: Knopf, 1991), pp. 26–28, 121.
4. Ratushinskaya, *In the Beginning*, pp. 120–21.
5. Ratushinskaya, *In the Beginning*, pp. 134–35.
6. Ratushinskaya, *In the Beginning*, p. 158.
7. Krasnov, *Russia Beyond Communism* (Boulder: Westview Press, 1991), pp. 8, 9.
8. Krasnov, pp. 8, 9, 32.
9. Borisov, "Personality and National Awareness," in *From Under the Rubble* (Boston: Little, Brown, 1975), pp. 195, 197.
10. Borisov, pp. 200, 202, 203, 208.
11. Borisov, pp. 209, 210, 211, 212, 218.
12. A. B., "The Direction of Change," in *From Under the Rubble*, pp. 145–46.
13. A. B., pp. 146, 147.
14. A. B., p. 150.
15. "Solzhenitsyn's Works Return to the USSR," *Current Digest of the Soviet Press*, 20 Dec. 1989, p. 4.
16. "Solzhenitsyn's Works Return," pp. 5, 21.
17. George W. Cornell, "Religious Revival in Soviet Union Is Spectacular, Theologian Says," *Grand Rapids Press*, 7 Sept. 1991, p. B4.
18. Hosking, *The Awakening of the Soviet Union*, enlarged ed. (Cambridge, MA: Harvard University Press, 1991), pp. 122–23, 135.
19. Hill, *The Soviet Union on the Brink* (Portland, OR: Multnomah Press, 1991), pp. 208, 210.
20. Richard N. Ostling, "Will Bells Chime Again?" *Time*, 4 Apr. 1988, pp. 62–63.
21. David E. Powell, "The Revival of Religion," *Current History*, 90 (Oct. 1991), p. 328.
22. Mikhail Morgulis, *Return to the Red Planet* (Wheaton, IL: Victor Books, 1989), p. 149.
23. Powell, pp. 329–30.
24. Richard N. Ostling, "No Longer Godless Communism," *Time*, 15 Oct. 1990, p. 70.
25. Powell, pp. 329–30.

26. Hill, *The Puzzle of the Soviet Church* (Portland, OR: Multnomah Press, 1989).

27. Hill, *Soviet Union on the Brink*, p. 408.

28. Victoria Pope, "God and Man in Russia," *U. S. News & World Report*, 2 Mar. 1992, p. 54.

29. Ostling, "Will Bells," p. 65.

30. Petro, "Preface," *Christianity and Russian Culture in Soviet Society*, ed. Nicolai N. Petro (Boulder: Westview Press, 1990), pp. vii, viii, ix.

31. Petro, "Challenge of the 'Russian Idea,' " in *Christianity and Russian Culture in Soviet Society*, p. 226.

32. Cited in Philip Walters, "Religion in the Soviet Union," in *Christianity and Russian Culture in Soviet Society*, p. 15.

33. Cited in Kent R. Hill, "The Discipline of Discernment," *The Public Eye*, 2 (Summer 1988), p. 12.

34. Cited in Kenneth L. Woodward, "Can Glasnost and God Coexist?" *Newsweek*, 20 June 1988, p. 52.

35. Appendix to Morgulis, pp. 150–56.

36. Michael Parks, "Yeltsin Sheds Atheism, Gets Religion Again," *Los Angeles Times*, 15 June 1992, pp. A1, A6.

37. Billington, *The Icon and the Axe* (New York: Vintage Books, 1970), pp. 593–96.

38. "Havel's New Year's Address to the Nation," *Congressional Record—Extension of Remarks*, 24 Jan. 1990, p. E48.

39. Havel, "The Power of the Powerless," in Václav Havel *et al.*, *The Power of the Powerless* (Armonk, NY: M. E. Sharpe, 1985), pp. 66–68.

40. "Havel's New Year's Address," p. E48.

41. "Havel's New Year's Address," p. E48.

42. Havel, "Power," pp. 31, 35.

43. Havel, "Power," pp. 37, 61, 71.

44. Havel, "Power," p. 80.

45. Havel, *Letters to Olga* (New York: Henry Holt, 1989), pp. 122, 145, 305.

46. Havel, "Paradise Lost," *New York Review of Books*, 9 Apr. 1992, p. 6.

47. Havel, "Power," pp. 42–43.

48. Havel, "Words on Words," *New York Review of Books*, 18 Jan. 1990, p. 5.

49. Havel, "Power," pp. 60, 65.

50. Havel, "Power," pp. 91–92.

51. Havel, "Power," p. 82.

52. Havel, *Letters to Olga*, p. 101.

53. Havel, *Disturbing the Peace* (New York: Knopf, 1990), p. 159.

54. Havel, *Letters to Olga*, p. 140.

55. Havel, *Disturbing*, pp. 189, 190.

56. Havel, *Letters to Olga*, p. 101.

57. Havel, *Letters to Olga*, p. 346.

58. Havel, *Letters to Olga*, pp. 196, 269.

59. Havel, "Power," p. 81.

60. Havel, "The Future of Central Europe," *New York Review of Books*, 29 Mar. 1990, p. 19.

61. Havel, *Disturbing*, pp. 16–17.

62. Havel, "The End of the Modern Era," *New York Times*, 1 Mar. 1992, p. E15.

63. Havel, *Disturbing*, p. 11.

64. Havel, "The End," p. E15.

65. Havel, "The Regime Within," *Harper's*, 274 (June 1987), p. 27.

66. Havel, *Disturbing*, p. 10.

67. Havel, "Power," pp. 90–91.

68. Havel, *Disturbing*, p. 168.

69. Havel, "Power," pp. 38–39.

70. Havel, "Help the Soviet Union on Its Road to Democracy," *Vital Speeches*, 15 Mar. 1990, p. 330.

71. Havel, *Disturbing*, p. 11.

72. Havel, "The End," p. E15.

73. Havel, *Disturbing*, p. 181.

74. James F. Pontuso, *Solzhenitsyn's Political Thought* (Charlottesville: University Press of Virginia, 1990), pp. 197–98.

75. Uzzell, "Solzhenitsyn the Centrist," *National Review*, 28 May 1990, p. 29.

76. Conquest, *Tyrants and Typewriters* (Lexington, MA: Lexington Books, 1989), p. 42.

77. Hughes, *Sophisticated Rebels* (Cambridge, MA: Harvard University Press, 1988), pp. 20–21.

78. Michael Rubbo, *Solzhenitsyn's Children . . . Are Making a Lot of Noise in Paris* (Boston: WGBH Educational Foundation, 1979), pp. 1, 7, 18.

79. Lévy, *Barbarism with a Human Face* (New York: Harper & Row, 1979), pp. 153–56, 203.

80. Lévy, *Barbarism*, pp. 125–26, 130, 158, 168.

81. Lévy, *The Testament of God* (New York: Harper & Row, 1980).

82. Walsh, *After Ideology* (San Francisco: HarperSanFrancisco, 1990), pp. xi, xii.

83. Walsh, pp. 9, 10, 13, 15.

84. Walsh, pp. 44, 45.

85. Walsh, pp. 48, 74, 76, 82.

86. Walsh, pp. 92, 94, 103, 137.

87. Walsh, pp. 139, 228.
88. Walsh, pp. 229, 231, 245.
89. Walsh, pp. 233, 241, 242, 243.
90. Walsh, pp. 257, 258, 265, 266.
91. Walsh, p. 271.
92. Billington, *Fire in the Minds of Men* (New York: Basic Books, 1980), p. 14.
93. Grunwald, "The Year 2000," *Time*, 30 Mar. 1992, pp. 73, 75, 76.
94. Conquest, p. 41.

Works Cited

Abel, Lionel. "On the Crimes of Lenin, Stalin, and Hitler." *Partisan Review*, 58 (1991), pp. 78–87.

——. "A Poem We Need Today." *Commentary*, 61 (Mar. 1976), pp. 64–68.

Aikman, David. "The Man Who Rules Russia." *Time*, 2 Sept. 1991, pp. 54–55.

——. "Russia's Prophet in Exile," Interview with Aleksandr Solzhenitsyn. *Time*, 24 July 1989, pp. 57–60.

Aksyonov, Vasily, *et al.* "Is 'Glasnost' a Game of Mirrors?" *New York Times*, 22 Mar. 1987, p. 27.

Alberti, Irene (Irina). Letter to Edward E. Ericson, Jr. 7 Nov. 1984.

"The Alexander Solzhenitsyn Interview." *Congressional Record—Senate*, 27 June 1974, pp. 21483–86.

Amalrik, Andrei. *Will the Soviet Union Survive Until 1984?* New York: Harper & Row, 1970.

Astrachan, Anthony. "Solzhenitsyn 'Contemptuous' of the U. S." *Des Moines Register*, 17 Mar. 1974, pp. 1A, 3A.

Atkinson, Dorothy. Rev. of Richard Pipes, *Russia Under the Old Regime*. *American Historical Review*, 81 (1976), pp. 423–24.

Avineri, Shlomo. "Where's Solzhenitsyn?" *New York Times*, 12 Sept. 1991, p. A25.

Bailey, George. *Galileo's Children: Science, Sakharov, and the Power of the State*. New York: Little, Brown, 1990.

Barringer, Felicity. "Kremlin Keeping Solzhenitsyn on Blacklist." *New York Times*, 30 Nov. 1988, pp. 1, 8.

Bayley, John. "God and the Devil." *New York Review of Books*, 21 Dec. 1989, pp. 11–13.

Bell, Pearl K. "Solzhenitsyn Grappling with History." *New Leader*, 2 Oct. 1972, pp. 16–17.

Berman, Ronald, ed. *Solzhenitsyn at Harvard: The Address, Twelve Early Responses, and Six Later Reflections*. Washington: Ethics and Public Policy Center, 1980.

Billington, James H. *Fire in the Minds of Men: Origins of the Revolutionary Faith*. New York: Basic Books, 1980.

————. *The Icon and the Axe: An Interpretive History of Russian Culture*. New York: Vintage Books, 1970.

Birnbaum, Norman. "Solzhenitsyn as Pseudo-Moralist." *Society*, 13 (Nov./ Dec. 1975), pp. 44–45.

Blake, Patricia. "A Diseased Body Politic." *New York Times Book Review*, 27 Oct. 1968, pp. 2, 50.

————. "Great Escapes from the Gulag." *Time*, 5 June 1978, pp. 91–92.

————. Rev. of *The Gulag Archipelago*, II. *New York Times Book Review*, 26 Oct. 1975, pp. 1, 18, 20, 22.

Bliven, Naomi. "Days That Shook the World." *New Yorker*, 14 Oct. 1972, pp. 178–81.

Bogolubov, Alexis B. Letter. *Commentary*, 79 (June 1985), pp. 8–9.

Boorstin, Daniel J. "The Courage To Doubt." *Time*, 26 June 1978, p. 21.

Brookhiser, Richard. "Why Not Bring Back the Czars?" *Time*, 11 Nov. 1991, p. 102.

Brown, Bess. "Kazakhs Protest Against Solzhenitsyn's Proposal for 'A New Russia.' " *Report on the USSR*, 5 Oct. 1990, pp. 19–20.

Brown, Deming. "*Cancer Ward* and *The First Circle*." *Slavic Review*, 28 (June 1969), pp. 304–13.

Brumberg, Abraham. "Soviet Terror." *Commentary*, 67 (Feb. 1979), pp. 84–88.

————. "Understanding Solzhenitsyn." *New Leader*, 27 Mar. 1974, pp. 10–13.

Buckley, William F., Jr. "Solzhenitsyn's Modest Proposal." *National Review*, 29 Mar. 1974, p. 390.

Bulgakov, Mikhail. *The Master and Margarita*. New York: Harper & Row, 1967.

Bulgakov, Sergei. *Karl Marx as a Religious Type*. Belmont, MA: Nordland, 1979.

Burg, David, and George Feifer. *Solzhenitsyn*. New York: Stein and Day, 1972.

Capouya, Emile. "Solzhenitsyn: Optimist and Realist." *Nation*, 6 Jan. 1969, pp. 20–21.

Carlisle, Olga. "Reviving Myths of Holy Russia." *New York Times Magazine*, 16 Sept. 1979, pp. 48, 50, 57, 60, 64–65.

————. *Solzhenitsyn and the Secret Circle*. New York: Holt, Rinehart and Winston, 1978.

_____. "Solzhenitsyn's Invisible Audience." *Newsweek*, 24 July 1978, p. 13.

Carter, Stephen. *The Politics of Solzhenitsyn*. New York: Holmes & Meier, 1977.

Claiborne, William. "Solzhenitsyn's Barbed-Wire Freedom." *Des Moines Register*, 28 Jan. 1977, p. 1B.

Clines, Francis X. "Russia Gets Call by Solzhenitsyn for Slavic State." *New York Times*, 19 Sept. 1990, pp. A1, A4.

Cohen, Stephen F. "A Left Right." *New York Times Book Review*, 7 Jan. 1979, pp. 9, 24, 26, 28.

_____. "The Other Great Holocaust of the Century." *New York Times Book Review*, 16 June 1974, pp. 1, 10, 12, 14.

_____. *Rethinking the Soviet Experience: Politics and History since 1917*. New York: Oxford University Press, 1985.

_____. "Voices from the Gulag." *New York Times Book Review*, 4 May 1980, pp. 1, 36–38.

Confino, Michael. "Solzhenitsyn, the West, and the New Russian Nationalism." *Journal of Contemporary History*, 26 (1991), pp. 611–36.

Conquest, Robert. "Books Considered." *New Republic*, 27 May 1978, pp. 25–27.

_____. "Evolution of an Exile." *Saturday Review/World*, 20 Apr. 1974, pp. 22–24.

_____. *Tyrants and Typewriters: Communiqués from the Struggle for Truth*. Lexington, MA: Lexington Books, 1989.

"A Conversation with Solzhentitsyn." *Los Angeles Times Book Review*, 13 Aug. 1989, p. 4. Excerpted from a 1987 interview by Rudolf Augstein in *Der Spiegel*.

Cornell, George W. "Religious Revival in Soviet Union Is Spectacular, Theologian Says." *Grand Rapids Press*, 7 Sept. 1991, p. B4.

Cousins, Norman. "Brief Encounter with A. Solzhenitsyn." *Saturday Review*, 23 Aug. 1975, pp. 4–6.

Crankshaw, Edward. "Why the Prophet Is Wrong." *Atlas World Press Review*, 23 (May 1976), 12–14.

Dahlburg, John-Thor. "Russia Wants Solzhenitsyn Back in Fold." *Los Angeles Times*, 16 June 1992, p. A6.

"The Dangers of Solzhenitsyn's Nationalism: An Interview with Andrei Sinyavsky." *New York Review of Books*, 22 Nov. 1979, pp. 3–6.

Dobrynin, Alexander. "Solzhenitsyn Prophets in the Soviet Crash of 1990." *Glasnost News & Review*, Jan.–Apr. 1991, pp. 58–60.

Dunlop, John B. "Alla Latynina: A Self-Proclaimed Centrist Calls for Political Realignment." *Report on the USSR*, 23 June 1989, pp. 8–10.

————. "The Almost-Rehabilitation and Re-Anathematization of Aleksandr Solzhenitsyn." Working paper, Hoover Institution, Stanford University, Feb. 1989.

————. "Christian Democratic Party Founded in Moscow." *Report on the USSR*, 13 Oct. 1989, pp. 1–2.

————. "A Conversation with Dmitrii Vasil'ev, the Leader of 'Pamyat'.' " *Report on the USSR*, 15 Dec. 1989, pp. 12–16.

————. *The Faces of Contemporary Russian Nationalism*. Princeton: Princeton University Press, 1983.

————. "Monarchist Sentiment in Present-Day Russia." *Report on the USSR*, 2 Aug. 1991, pp. 27–30.

————. "New National Bolshevik Organization Formed." *Report on the USSR*, 14 Sept. 1990, pp. 7–9.

————. *The New Russian Nationalism*. New York: Praeger, 1985.

————. *The New Russian Revolutionaries*. Belmont, MA: Nordland, 1976.

————. "Russia and the Republics." *Report on the USSR*, 11 Oct. 1991, pp. 6–10.

————. "Russian Christian Democrats Outline Their Views." *Report on the USSR*, 21 Sept. 1990, pp. 19–21.

————. "Russian Nationalism Today: Organizations and Programs." *Nationality Papers*, 19 (Fall 1991), pp. 146–66.

————. "The Russian Orthodox Church and Nationalism After 1988." *Religion in Communist Lands*, 18 (Winter 1990), pp. 292–306.

————. "Russian Reactions to Solzhenitsyn's Brochure." *Report on the USSR*, 14 Dec. 1990, pp. 3–8.

————. "Russia's Surprising Reactionary Alliance." *Orbis*, 35 (Summer 1991), pp. 423–26.

————. "Solzhenitsyn Begins To Emerge from the Political Void." *Report on the USSR*, 8 Sept, 1989, pp. 1–6.

————. "Solzhenitsyn Calls for the Dismemberment of the Soviet Union." *Report on the USSR*, 5 Oct. 1990, pp. 9–12.

————. "Solzhenitsyn in Exile." *Survey*, 21 (1975), pp. 133–54.

Dunlop, John B., Richard Haugh, and Alexis Klimoff, eds. *Aleksandr Solzhenitsyn: Critical Essays and Documentary Materials*. 2nd ed. New York: Collier, 1975.

Dunlop, John B., Richard S. Haugh, and Michael Nicholson, eds. *Solzhenitsyn in Exile: Critical Essays and Documentary Materials*. Stanford: Hoover Institution Press, 1985.

Ericson, Edward E., Jr. "The Christian Humanism of Aleksandr Solzhenitsyn." *Reformed Journal*, 22 (Oct. 1972), pp. 6–10; (Nov. 1972), pp. 16–20.

————. Letter. *Commentary*, 79 (June 1985), p. 8.

_____. Letter. *New Oxford Review*, 47 (Apr. 1980), pp. 4, 6.

_____. "Should We Fear Solzhenitsyn?" *New Oxford Review*, p. 46 (Dec. 1979), pp. 8–10.

Etzioni, Amitai. "Intervening in the Soviet Union." *Society*, 13 (Nov./Dec. 1975), pp. 39–40.

"Everyone's Loss." *The Times* (London), 15 Feb. 1974, p. 15.

Fairbanks, Charles H., Jr. Letter. *Commentary*, 67 (June 1979), p. 23.

Feifer, George. "The Dark Side of Solzhenitsyn: In the Manner of His Enemies." *Harper's*, 260 (May 1980), pp. 51–58.

Feuer, Kathryn B., ed. *Solzhenitsyn: A Collection of Critical Essays*. Englewood Cliffs, NJ: Prentice-Hall, 1976.

Flynn, Pritchard. "Stalin's Victory." *Newsweek*, 30 Sept. 1968, pp. 108–09.

Foote, Timothy. "Towering Witness to Salvation." *Time*, 15 July 1974, pp. 90, 92, 94.

Friedberg, Maurice. "Gallery of Comrades Embattled Abed." *Saturday Review*, 9 Nov. 1968, pp. 42–44.

Garis, Robert. "Fiction Chronicle." *Hudson Review*, 22 (Spring 1969), pp. 148–64.

Gellner, Ernest. "A Reformer of the Modern World." *Times Literary Supplement* (London), 17–23 Aug. 1990, pp. 863–64.

Gelman, Norman I. Letter. *Commentary*, 58 (Sept. 1974), pp. 14, 16.

Gray, Francine du Plessix. *Soviet Women: Walking the Tightrope*. New York: Doubleday, 1989.

Gray, John. "Solzhenitsyn's Flawed Blueprint." *Toronto Globe and Mail*, 21 Mar. 1992, p. C20.

Grazzini, Giovanni. *Solzhenitsyn*. New York: Dell, 1973.

Grenier, Richard. "Solzhenitsyn and Anti-Semitism: A New Debate." *New York Times*, 13 Nov. 1985, p. 24.

Grunwald, Henry. "The Year 2000: Is It the End—Or Just the Beginning?" *Time*, 30 Mar. 1992, pp. 73–76.

Gurtov, Melvin. "Return to the Cold War." *Society*, 13 (Nov./Dec. 1975), pp. 37–38.

Hamilton, Alexander, John Jay, and James Madison. *The Federalist: A Commentary on the Constitution of the United States*. Philadelphia: J. B. Lippincott, 1873.

Havel, Václav. *Disturbing the Peace: A Conversation with Karel Hvízdala*. New York: Knopf, 1990.

_____. "The End of the Modern Era." *New York Times*, 1 Mar. 1992, p. E15.

_____. "The Future of Central Europe." *New York Review of Books*, 29 Mar. 1990, pp. 18–19.

_____. "Havel's New Year's Address to the Nation." *Congressional Record—Extension of Remarks*, 24 Jan. 1990, pp. E47-E49.

_____. "Help the Soviet Union on Its Road to Democracy: Consciousness Precedes Being." *Vital Speeches*, 15 Mar. 1990, pp. 327–30.

_____. *Letters to Olga: June 1979–September 1982*. New York: Henry Holt, 1989.

_____. "Paradise Lost." *New York Review of Books*, 9 Apr. 1992, pp. 6–8.

_____. "The Regime Within." *Harper's*, 274 (June 1987), pp. 25–27.

_____. "Words on Words." *New York Review of Books*, 19 Jan. 1990, pp. 5–8.

_____, et al. *The Power of the Powerless: Citizens Against the State in Central-Eastern Europe*. Armonk, NY: M. E. Sharpe, 1985.

Heidenry, John. "Solzhenitsyn, Neo-Tolstoyan." *Commonweal*, 23 Mar. 1973, pp. 64–66.

Heilbroner, Robert. "The World After Communism: A Discussion of the Current Political Situation." *Dissent*, 37 (Fall 1990), pp. 429–32.

Hesburgh, Theodore. "Unpopular Truths." *Time*, 26 June 1978, p. 18.

Hill, Kent. R. "The Discipline of Discernment: Liberation Theology Reconsidered." *Public Eye*, 2 (Summer 1988), pp. 10–18.

_____. *The Puzzle of the Soviet Church: An Inside Look at Christianity and Glasnost*. Portland, OR: Multnomah Press, 1989.

_____. *The Soviet Union on the Brink: An Inside Look at Christianity and Glasnost*. Portland, OR: Multnomah Press, 1991.

Hook, Sidney. "Above All, Freedom." *Time*, 26 June 1978, p. 22.

_____. "Solzhenitsyn and Secular Humanism: A Response." *The Humanist*, 38 (Nov./Dec. 1978), pp. 4–6.

Horowitz, Irving Louis. "An Amnesty International of One." *Society*, 13 (Nov./Dec. 1975), pp. 45–47.

Hosking, Geoffrey. *The Awakening of the Soviet Union*. Enlarged edition. Cambridge, MA: Harvard University Press, 1991.

Howe, Irving. "The Great War and Russian Memory." *New York Times Book Review*, 2 July 1989, pp. 1, 17–18.

_____. "An Open Letter." *New Republic*, 3 May 1980, pp. 18–19.

_____. "Predicaments of Soviet Writing—I." *New Republic*, 11 May 1963, pp. 19–21.

_____. "Predicaments of Soviet Writing—II." *New Republic*, 18 May 1963, pp. 19–22.

_____. "Some Dissenting Comments." *Dissent*, 37 (Fall 1990), pp. 432–35.

Hughes, H. Stuart. *Sophisticated Rebels: The Political Culture of European Dissent, 1968–1987*. Cambridge, MA: Harvard University Press, 1988.

Ignatieff, Michael. "An Uncommon Russian Nationalist Returns." *Minneapolis Star Tribune*, 28 Sept. 1990, p. 19A.

"Is Solzhenitsyn Right?" *Time*, 26 June 1978, p. 18.

Jacobson, Dan. "The Example of Solzhenitsyn." *Commentary*, 47 (May 1969), pp. 81–84.

Kaiser, Robert G. "Arrest Shows Soviet System Still the Same." *Washington Post*, 13 Feb. 1974, p. A30.

————. "Dissident Praises 'Gulag.' " *Washington Post*, 7 Feb. 1974, p. A22.

Karlinsky, Simon. Rev. of *August 1914*. *New York Times Book Review*, 10 Sept. 1972, pp. 1, 48–51.

Kazin, Alfred. "The Fury of Solzhenitsyn." *Esquire*, 23 May 1978, pp. 73–74.

Keller, Bill. "Obscure Soviet Magazine Breaks the Ban on Solzhenitsyn's Work." *New York Times*, 20 Mar. 1989, pp. 1, 4.

————. "Yearning for an Iron Hand." *New York Times Magazine*, 28 Jan. 1990, pp. 18–20, 46, 48, 50.

Kelley, Donald R. *The Solzhenitsyn-Sakharov Dialogue: Politics, Society, and the Future*. Westport, CT: Greenwood Press, 1982.

Kennan, George F. "Between Earth and Hell." *New York Review of Books*, 21 Mar. 1974, pp. 3–4, 7.

————. "Is the World Ready for U. S.-Style Freedoms?" *Des Moines Register*, 7 Aug. 1977, pp. B1–B2. Excerpted from *The Cloud of Danger*. Boston: Little, Brown, 1977.

"Khrushchev's Secret Tapes." *Time*, 1 Oct. 1990, pp. 68–78.

Kilpatrick, James J. "Seven Went To Get Solzhenitsyn." *Minneapolis Star*, Feb. 1974, p. 8A.

Klausler, Alfred P. "Tragic Chaos." *Christian Century*, 22 Nov. 1972, pp. 1192–93.

Kramer, Hilton. "The Soviet Terror Continued." *New York Times Book Review*, 18 June 1978, pp. 1, 28–29.

Krasnov, Vladislav G. "Richard Pipes's Foreign Strategy: Anti-Soviet or Anti-Russian?" *Russian Review*, 38 (Apr. 1979), pp. 180–91.

————. *Russia Beyond Communism: A Chronicle of National Rebirth*. Boulder: Westview Press, 1991.

————. *Solzhenitsyn and Dostoevsky: A Study in the Polyphonic Novel*. Athens: University of Georgia Press, 1980.

Laber, Jeri. "Indictment of Soviet Terror." *New Republic*, 19 Oct. 1968, pp. 32–34.

————. Letter. *Commentary*, 58 (Sept. 1974), pp. 16, 18.

————. "Muted Echo of a Masterpiece." *New Republic*, 7 Oct. 1972, pp. 27–30.

————. "The Real Solzhenitsyn." *Commentary*, 57 (May 1974), pp. 32–35.

————. "The Selling of Solzhenitsyn." *Columbia Journalism Review*, 13 (May/June 1974), pp. 4–7.

Labedz, Leopold, ed. *Solzhenitsyn: A Documentary Record*. Baltimore: Penguin, 1972.

Lasch, Christopher. *The True and Only Heaven: Progress and Its Critics*. New York: Norton, 1991.

Leddington, Roger. "Solzhenitsyn Re-Explains Letter." *Milwaukee Journal*, 1 Apr. 1974, p. 7.

Legvold, Robert. "Recent Books: The Soviet Union and Eastern Europe." *Foreign Affairs*, 71 (Spring 1992), pp. 205–08.

Leroux, Charles. "Solzhenitsyn Makes Freedom a Prison." *Des Moines Register*, 17 Dec. 1976, pp. 1A, 12A.

Levin, Bernard. "Solzhenitsyn Among the Pygmies." *The Times* (London), 17 July 1975, p. 14.

————. "Time To Stand Up for Britain," Interview with Alexander Solzhenitsyn. *The Times* (London), 23 May 1983, p. 11.

————. "The Vision of a Prophet." *Atlas World Press Review*, 23 (May 1976), pp. 11–12.

Lévy, Bernard-Henri. *Barbarism with a Human Face*. New York: Harper & Row, 1979.

————. *The Testament of God*. New York: Harper & Row, 1980.

Lowenthal, Richard. "The Prophet's Wrong Message." *Society*, 13 (Nov./Dec. 1975), pp. 40–44.

Lukacs, John. *1945: Year Zero*. Garden City, NY: Doubleday, 1978.

————. *The Passing of the Modern Age*. New York: Harper & Row, 1970.

MacIntyre, Alasdair. *After Virtue: A Study in Moral Theory*. Notre Dame: University of Notre Dame Press, 1981.

MacLeish, Archibald. "Our Will Endures." *Time*, 26 June 1978, p. 21.

Macmillan, Priscilla. "A Cool Appraisal of 'Gulag': 'In Keeping Silent About Evil We Are Implanting It.' " *Christian Science Monitor*, 24 July 1974, p. 11.

Malia, Martin. "The August Revolution." *New York Review of Books*, 26 Sept. 1991, pp. 22–28.

————. "The Hunt for the True October." *Commentary*, 92 (Oct. 1991), pp. 21–28.

Marder, Murray. "Nixon Lauds Solzhenitsyn's 'Courage.' " *Washington Post*, 26 Feb. 1974, pp. A1, A13.

Markish, Simon. "Jewish Images in Solzhenitsyn." *Soviet Jewish Affairs*, 7 (1977), pp. 69–81.

Maximov, Vladimir. Foreword to "The Solzhenitsyn/Sakharov Debate." *Kontinent*. Garden City, NY: Doubleday, 1976, pp. 1–2.

McCarthy, Mary. "The Tolstoy Connection." *Saturday Review*, 16 Sept. 1972, pp. 79–82, 88, 90–92, 96.

McNaspy, C. J. Rev. of *The First Circle. America*, 5 Oct. 1968, p. 295.

Meadows, Donella H., Dennis L. Meadows, Jorgen Randers, and William W. Behrens III. *The Limits to Growth: A Report to the Club of Rome's Project on the Predicament of Mankind*. New York: Universe Books, 1972.

Meany, George. "No Voice More Eloquent." *Time*, 26 June 1978, pp. 21–22.

Medvedev, Roy. "Gulag Archipelago." *Ramparts*, 12 (June 1974), pp. pp. 49–55.

Medvedev, Zhores A. *Ten Years After Ivan Denisovich*. New York: Vintage, 1974.

Meerson-Aksenov, Michael, and Boris Shragin, eds. *The Political, Social, and Religious Thought of Russian "Samizdat"—An Anthology*. Belmont, MA: Nordland, 1977.

Mihalisko, Kathleen. "Solzhenitsyn's 'Russian Union': Swimming Against the Tide." *Report on the USSR*, 5 Oct. 1990, pp. 17–19.

Mills, Richard M., and Judith M. Mills. "Solzhenitsyn's Cry to the Soviet Leaders." *Commonweal*, 9 Aug. 1974, pp. 433–36.

Milton, John. *John Milton: Complete Poems and Major Prose*. Ed. Merritt Y. Hughes. New York: Odyssey Press, 1957.

Minogue, Kenneth R. *Alien Powers: The Pure Theory of Ideology*. New York: St. Martin's Press, 1985.

———. *Nationalism*. New York: Basic Books, 1967.

Morgulis, Mikhail. *Return to the Red Planet*. Wheaton, IL: Victor Books, 1989.

Moynihan, Daniel Patrick. "Two Cheers for Solzhenitsyn." *New York Times Book Review*, 24 Nov. 1991, pp. 9, 11.

Nemethy, Andrew. "The Solzhenitsyns of Cavendish." *Vermont Life*, 38 (Autumn 1983), pp. 20–27.

Nessen, Ron. *It Sure Looks Different from the Inside*. Chicago: Playboy Press, 1978.

Neuhaus, Richard John. *The Naked Public Square: Religion and Democracy in America*. Grand Rapids: Eerdmans, 1984.

Novak, Michael. *The Spirit of Democratic Capitalism*. New York: American Enterprise Institute/Simon & Schuster, 1982.

O'Clery, Conor. "Back in the USSR." *New Republic*, 19 Nov. 1990, pp. 22–23.

Ostling, Richard N. "No Longer Godless Communism." *Time*, 15 Oct. 1990, pp. 70–71.

_____. "Will Bells Chime Again?" *Time*, 4 Apr. 1988, pp. 62–65.

O'Sullivan, John. "Friends at Court." *National Review*, 27 May 1991, p. 4.

Parks, Michael. "Yeltsin Sheds Atheism, Gets Religion Again." *Los Angeles Times*, 15 June 1992, pp. A1, A6.

Paz, Octavio. "How History Will Judge." *Atlas World Press Review*, 23 (May 1976), pp. 14–15.

Petro, Nicolai N., ed. *Christianity and Russian Culture in Soviet Society*. Boulder: Westview Press, 1990.

_____. "Toward a New Russian Federation." *Wilson Quarterly*, 14 (Summer 1990), pp. 114–22.

Pipes, Richard. "Reply to Vladislav G. Krasnov." *Russian Review*, 38 (Apr. 1979), pp. 192–97.

_____. "Solzhenitsyn and the Russian Intellectual Tradition: Some Critical Remarks." *Encounter*, 52 (June 1979), pp. 52–56.

Pivot, Bernard. "Solzhenitsyn at Work." *Boston Globe*, 24 Feb. 1984, p. 2.

Podhoretz, Norman. "The Terrible Question of Aleksandr Solzhenitsyn." *Commentary*, 79 (Feb. 1985), pp. 17–24.

Pontuso, James F. *Solzhenitsyn's Political Thought*. Charlottesville: University Press of Virginia, 1990.

Pope, Victoria. "God and Man in Russia." *U.S. News & World Report*, 2 Mar. 1992, pp. 54–59.

Porter, Bruce D. "The Coming Resurgence of Russia." *National Interest*, no. 23 (Spring 1991), pp. 14–23.

Pospielovsky, Dimitry. "The Jewish Question in Russian Samizdat." *Soviet Jewish Affairs*, 8 (1978), pp. 3–23.

_____. "The Neo-Slavophile Trend and Its Relation to the Contemporary Religious Revival in the USSR." In *Religion and Nationalism in Soviet and East European Politics*. Ed. Pedro Ramet. Durham: Duke Press Policy Studies, 1984, pp. 41–58.

Powell, David E. "The Revival of Religion." *Current History*, 90 (Oct. 1991), pp. 328–32.

Pritchard, William H. "Long Novels and Short Stories." *Hudson Review*, 26 (Spring 1973), pp. 225–40.

Ratushinskaya, Irina. *Grey Is the Color of Hope*. New York: Knopf, 1988.

_____. *In the Beginning*. New York: Knopf, 1991.

Reeve, Franklin D. "The House of the Living." *Kenyon Review*, 25 (Spring 1963), pp. 356–60.

Remnick, David. "Native Son." *New York Review of Books*, 14 Feb. 1991, pp. 6–10.

_____. "A Witness Before His Own People." *Manchester Guardian Weekly*, 6 Aug. 1989, p. 25.

Riasanovsky, Nicholas V. *A History of Russia*. 4th ed. New York: Oxford University Press, 1984.

_____. Rev. of Richard Pipes, *Russia Under the Old Regime*. *Russian Review*, 35 (1976), pp. 103–04.

Robertson, Nan. "Letter Softened by Solzhenitsyn." *New York Times*, 5 Mar. 1974, p. 9.

_____. "A Russian Nationalist Looks to the Past." *New York Times*, 3 Mar. 1974, p. 26.

Rorty, Richard. "The Intellectuals at the End of Socialism." *Yale Review*, 80 (1992), pp. 1–16.

"Rosalynn Rejects Solzhenitsyn's Criticism." *Grand Rapids Press*, 21 June 1978, p. A4.

Rosenthal, Andrew. "Soviets Drop Solzhenitsyn Treason Charges." *New York Times*, 18 Sept. 1991, p. A8.

Rosenthal, Raymond. "Solzhenitsyn and the Defeated." *Nation*, 12 Feb. 1973, pp. 213–15.

Rothberg, Abraham. *Aleksandr Solzhenitsyn: The Major Novels*. Ithaca, NY: Cornell University Presss, 1971.

Rovit, Earl. "In the Center Ring." *American Scholar*, 39 (Winter 1969–70), pp. 166–70.

Rowan, Carl. "Solzhenitsyn: Agent of Soviet Influence?" *Grand Rapids Press*, 23 June 1978, p. A11.

Rubbo, Michael. *Solzhenitsyn's Children . . . Are Making a Lot of Noise in Paris*. Boston: WGBH Educational Foundation, 1979.

Rubenstein, Joshua. Rev. of *The Gulag Archipelago*, I. *New Republic*, 22 June 1974, pp. 21–22.

Safire, William. "Aleks, Baby." *New York Times*, 11 Mar. 1974, p. 29.

_____. "Solzhenitsyn Without Tears." *New York Times*, 18 Feb. 1974, p. 25.

Sakharov, Andrei. "On Alexander Solzhenitsyn's 'A Letter to the Soviet Leaders.' " *Kontinent*. Garden City, NY: Doubleday, 1976, pp. 2–14. Also published as "In Answer to Solzhenitsyn." *New York Review of Books*, 13 June 1974, pp. 3–6.

_____. *Progress, Coexistence and Intellectual Freedom*. New York: Norton, 1968.

_____. *Sakharov Speaks*. New York: Vintage Books, 1974.

Salisbury, Harrison E. "The World as a Prison." *New York Times Book Review*, 15 Sept. 1968, pp. 1, 37–41.

_____. "Why the Kremlin Fears Solzhenitsyn: 'A Great Writer Is a Second Government.' " *Atlantic*, 233 (Apr. 1974), pp. 41–46.

Scammell, Michael. Letter. *Commentary*, 80 (Aug. 1985), pp. 19.

―――――. Letter. *Problems of Communism*, 35 (July-Aug. 1986), pp. 100–02.

―――――. *Solzhenitsyn: A Biography*. New York: Norton, 1984.

―――――. "To the Finland Station?" *New Republic*, 19 Nov. 1990, pp. 18–23.

Schall, James V. "Solzhenitsyn's Letter." *Worldview*, 17 (July 1974), pp. 26–29.

Schapiro, Leonard B. "Antisemitism in the Communist World." *Soviet Jewish Affairs*, 9 (1979), pp. 42–52.

―――――. "Disturbing, Fanatical, and Heroic." *New York Review of Books*, 13 Nov. 1975, pp. 10–17.

―――――. "Some Afterthoughts on Solzhenitsyn." *Russian Review*, 33 (Oct. 1974), pp. 416–21.

―――――. "The *Vekhi* Group and the Mystique of Revolution." *Slavonic and East European Review*, 34 (Dec. 1955), pp. 56–76.

Shapiro, Margaret. "Soviets Drop Solzhenitsyn Treason Charges." *Washington Post*, 18 Sept. 1991, pp. B1–B2.

Sheehy, Ann. "Solzhenitsyn's Concept of a Future 'Russian Union': The Nationalities Angle." *Report on the USSR*, 5 Oct. 1990, pp. 15–16.

Shturman, Dora. *Gorodu i miru: O publitsistike A. I. Solzhenitsyna*. New York: C.A.S.E./Third Wave, 1988.

Smiley, Xan. "Beyond Gorbachev." *National Review*, 28 May 1990, pp. 25–29.

Smith, Hedrick. *The Russians*. New York: Quadrangle/New York Times Book Co., 1976.

Sokolov, Maxim. "Solzhenitsyn's Second Letter to Soviet Leaders." *Commersant*, 1 Oct. 1990, p. 14.

Solchanyk, Roman. "Solzhenitsyn and the Russian 'Ukrainian Complex.' " *Report on the USSR*, 5 Oct. 1990, pp. 20–22.

Solzhenitsyn, Aleksandr I. *August 1914*. New York: Farrar, Straus and Giroux, 1989.

―――――. *Cancer Ward*. New York: Bantam, 1969.

―――――. *Détente: Prospects for Democracy and Dictatorship*. New Brunswick, NJ: Transaction Books, 1980.

―――――. *East and West*. New York: Harper & Row, 1980.

―――――. *The First Circle*. New York: Harper & Row, 1968.

―――――. *The Gulag Archipelago, 1918–1956: An Experiment in Literary Investigation*. 3 vols. New York: Harper & Row, 1973, 1975, 1978.

―――――. *The Gulag Archipelago*. Abridged by Edward E. Ericson, Jr. New York: Harper & Row, 1985.

―――――. *Letter to the Soviet Leaders*. New York: Harper & Row, 1974.

―――――. "Live Not by Lies." *Washington Post*, 18 Feb. 1974, p. A26.

_____. *The Mortal Danger: How Misconceptions About Russia Imperil America.* 2nd ed. New York: Harper & Row, 1986.

_____. *Nobel Lecture.* New York: Farrar, Straus and Giroux, 1972.

_____. *The Oak and the Calf.* New York: Harper & Row, 1979.

_____. *One Day in the Life of Ivan Denisovich.* New York: Bantam, 1963.

_____. *Rebuilding Russia: Reflections and Tentative Proposals.* New York: Farrar, Straus and Giroux, 1991.

_____. "Sakharov and the Criticism of 'A Letter to the Soviet Leaders.' " *Kontinent.* Garden City, NY: Doubleday, 1976, pp. 14–23.

_____. "Schlesinger and Kissinger." *New York Times*, 1 Dec. 1975, p. 31.

_____. "Solzhenitsyn on Communism." *Time*, 18 Feb. 1980, pp. 48–49.

_____. "Solzhenitsyn Speaks." Booklet, Hoover Institution, Stanford University, 1976.

_____. "Solzhenitsyn Speaks." *Southern Partisan*, 4 (Winter 1984), pp. 33–35.

_____. "The Templeton Address." *National Review*, 22 July 1983, pp. 873–76.

_____. "The Third World War Has Ended." *National Review*, 20 June 1975, p. 652.

_____. "Three Key Moments in Modern Japanese History." *National Review*, 9 Dec. 1983, pp. 1536–38, 1540, 1544, 1546.

_____. *Warning to the West.* New York: Farrar, Straus and Giroux, 1976.

_____. *A World Split Apart: Commencement Address Delivered at Harvard University, June 8, 1978.* New York: Harper & Row, 1978.

Solzhenitsyn, Aleksandr I., *et al. From Under the Rubble.* Boston: Little, Brown, 1975.

"Solzhenitsyn: An Artist Becomes an Exile." *Time*, 25 Feb. 1974, pp. 34–36, 39–40.

"Solzhenitsyn: 'Con Man' or 'Worshipper of Man'?" *Boston Globe*, 19 June 1978, p. 13.

"Solzhenitsyn Essay Draws Varied Response." *Current Digest of the Soviet Press*, 42 (1990), pp. 4–8, 19.

"Solzhenitsyn Speaks at Town Meeting in Vermont." *Des Moines Register*, 2 Mar. 1977, p. 12B.

"Solzhenitsyn Unbound." *National Review*, 19 July 1974, pp. 797–98.

"Solzhenitsyn Was Warned of Treason Charge." *The Times* (London), 15 Feb. 1974, p. 1.

"Solzhenitsyn's Bill of Indictment." *Time*, 7 Jan. 1974, pp. 49–50.

"Solzhenitsyn's Works Return to the USSR." *Current Digest of the Soviet Press*, 20 Dec. 1989, pp. 1–5, 21.

Stein, Veronika. Letter. *Commentary*, 79 (June 1985), pp. 6–7.

Steiner, George. "The Forests of the Night." *New Yorker*, 5 Aug. 1974, pp. 78, 81–87.

————. "More Notes from Underground." *New Yorker*, 13 Oct. 1975, pp. 169–76.

Suffert, Georges. "Solzhenitsyn in Zurich," Interview with Solzhenitsyn. *Encounter*, 46 (Apr. 1976), pp. 9–15.

Szporluk, Roman. "Dilemmas of Russian Nationalism." *Problems of Communism*, 38 (July-Aug. 1989), pp. 15–35.

"Tolling the Death Knell." *Time*, 1 Oct. 1990, p. 58.

Tolstaya, Tatyana. "The Grand Inquisitor." *New Republic*. 29 June 1992, pp. 29–36.

Tolz, Vera. "Solzhenitsyn Proposes a Plan for the Reconstruction of Russia." *Report on the USSR*, 5 Oct. 1990, pp. 12–14.

Toynbee, Philip. Rev. of *August 1914*. *Critic*, 31 (Nov.–Dec. 1972), pp. 67–69.

Treadgold, Donald W. Letter. *Commentary*, 58 (Sept. 1974), pp. 12, 14.

————. Rev. of Richard Pipes, *Russia Under the Old Regime*. *Slavic Review*, 23 (1975), pp. 812–14.

Tuchman, Barbara. "America's Savonarola." *Time*, 26 June 1978, p. 22.

Turgeon, Lynn. "In Defense of Détente." *Society*, 13 (Nov./Dec. 1975), pp. 38–39.

"Two Soviet Giants, in Dissent." *New York Times*, 29 Sept. 1990, p. 22.

Ulam, Adam B. "Defiance in the Gulag." *Saturday Review*, 24 June 1978, pp. 31–33.

————. "To the Brink." *National Review*, 14 Nov. 1980, pp. 1402–03.

"The Unexpected Perils of Freedom." *Time*, 4 Mar. 1974, pp. 31–32.

"The Union of the States." *Economist*, 22 Sept. 1990, pp. 53–55.

"U. S. Says Exile Does Not Alter Détente." *Washington Post*, 14 Feb. 1974, p. A16.

Uzzell, Lawrence A. "Solzhenitsyn the Centrist." *National Review*, 28 May 1990, pp. 28–29.

Verkhovsky, Alexander. "Russia May No Longer Play Follow the Leader." *Glasnost News & Review*, Jan.–Apr. 1991, pp. 60–61.

Vidal, Gore. *Matters of Fact and Fiction*. New York: Random House, 1977.

Vishnevskaya, Galina. *Galina: A Russian Story*. New York: Harcourt Brace Jovanovich, 1984.

Walsh, David. *After Ideology: Recovering the Spiritual Foundations of Freedom*. San Francisco: HarperSanFrancisco, 1990.

Washington, George. *The Writings of George Washington*. Ed. John C. Fitzpatrick. 39 vols. Washington: United States Government Printing Office, 1931–44.

Weeks, Edward. "The Peripatetic Reviewer." *Atlantic*, 231 (Apr. 1973), p. 124.

Will, George F., and Michael Novak. *Solzhenitsyn and American Democracy*. Washington: Ethics and Public Policy Center, 1981.

Winthrop, Delba. Letter. *Commentary*, 67 (June 1979), p. 24.

Woodward, Kenneth L. "Can Glasnost and God Coexist?" *Newsweek*, 20 June 1988, pp. 48–52.

Yanov, Alexander. *Détente After Brezhnev: The Domestic Roots of Soviet Foreign Policy*. Berkeley: Institute of International Studies, University of California, 1977.

_____. Letter. *New Oxford Review*, 47 (Apr. 1980), p. 4.

_____. *The Russian Challenge and the Year 2000*. New York: Basil Blackwell, 1987.

_____. *The Russian New Right: Right-Wing Ideologies in the Contemporary USSR*. Berkeley: Institute of International Studies, University of California, 1978.

Yardley, Jonathan. "Solzhenitsyn—A Dispassionate Look at a Modern 'Saint.' " *Des Moines Register*, 23 June 1974, p. 6A.

Index